"Are you okay?" she asked quietly.

Chace rounded the side of the counter.

"Chace," she said, still talking quietly, "did some-thing—?"

She stopped talking abruptly when it came clear to her that he wasn't going to stop coming at her. She took a step back. Too late. He was on her, he rounded her waist with an arm and twisted them so he was moving her backward toward the door she'd come out.

"What are you—?"

She stopped talking abruptly this time because he tightened his arm around her waist and yanked it up, yanking her into her body. His other hand drove into her silken hair at the back of her head. He slanted his head to the other side and slammed his mouth down on hers.

She made a noise of surprise, her body tense against his and he thrust his tongue between her lips. Without a choice, they opened, another noise of surprise filled his mouth but he ignored that one too, carried on with what he was doing and took her mouth.

He deepened an already deep kiss, needing it and she gave it to him. The tension flowed from her body, it melted into his, her hands slid up his chest, one curving around the back of his neck, fingers going into his hair. The other one slid around his shoulders and held on tight...

BREATHE

Also by Kristen Ashley

The Colorado Mountain Series

The Gamble
Sweet Dreams
Lady Luck
Jagged
Kaleidoscope

The Dream Man Series

Mystery Man
Wild Man
Law Man
Motorcycle Man

The Chaos Series

Own the Wind
Fire Inside
Walk Through Fire
Ride Steady

BREATHE

KRISTEN ASHLEY

FOREVER

NEW YORK   BOSTON

Forever
Hachette Book Group
1290 Avenue of the Americas
New York, NY 10104

www.HachetteBookGroup.com

Printed in the United States of America

Originally published as an ebook

First mass-market edition: August 2014
10 9 8 7 6 5 4 3

OPM

Forever is an imprint of Grand Central Publishing.
The Forever name and logo are trademarks of Hachette Book Group, Inc.

The Hachette Speakers Bureau provides a wide range of authors for speaking events. To find out more, go to www.hachettespeakersbureau.com or call (866) 376-6591.

The publisher is not responsible for websites (or their content) that are not owned by the publisher.

To Carly Phillips:
Thank you for remembering what it's like
and doing your bit to pave my way.
You. Are. Awesome.

Acknowledgments

When I needed to understand how a small-town library works, I did what I usually do. I phoned a friend. Or, in this instance, I emailed the fabulous Dixie Malone at Denver Public Library. Dixie has provided a lifeline often throughout the years of our friendship, and she didn't disappoint. She laid it all out for me and gave me little bits and pieces to make Faye's experience as a small-town librarian richer for my readers.

So, Miss Dix, you know I adore you. Now I adore you even more. I thought this was an impossible task but there it is.

And, as always and ever, thank you, Chas, for taking my back.

Author's Note

I've said it before and I'll say it again, I encourage you to find the music I mention in this book and listen to it while you read or later. Ella Mae Bowen's "Holding Out for a Hero," Dobie Gray's "Drift Away" and all the rest will put you in the mood and place you right in the action. And I hope that's a good place to be.

Thank you to KT for sending me the link to Ella Mae's awesome freaking song. And bonus, Angela Gray, my Pinklady reader/friend, turned out to be Ella Mae's auntie. Now seriously, how is that for the sisterhood binding tighter?

Rock on!

CHAPTER ONE

Never to Be His

"Talk to me."

Chace Keaton was whispering to no one, sitting alone in the very early morning February cold of Harker's Wood.

The place where his wife was shot to death.

Harker's Wood was an unusual spread of trees in the Colorado Mountains. Unusual because it wasn't simply conifer and aspen. For some reason that was likely akin to the reasons Old Man Harker did all the crazy shit he did, he had cleared that space seventy years ago and planted hundreds of shoots of twenty different varieties of trees. Trees that shouldn't take root in the Colorado Mountains. Trees that, by some miracle, not only took root but grew tall and remained strong.

It was late night. The snow was thick and deep. It was freezing cold. There were a few clouds but the full moon shone bright through the trees, gilding them silver.

Chace didn't see the trees or the moon. He didn't feel the cold seeping through his jeans that were resting on the snow-covered log which his ass was on.

He saw nothing.

He heard nothing.

He waited for the wood to talk.

It wasn't talking.

He'd been up there countless times since Misty was shot there. Her death was purposefully not investigated by strict, detailed police protocol.

Not by the Carnal Police Department.

Not then.

Not when it was infested.

Now it was no longer infested.

But that didn't mean Chace didn't come up there alone, without a tail, and instigate his own detailed examination of the area.

He found nothing.

And the wood never talked to him. Not back then. Not now.

Misty's blood had long since washed away or mingled with the dirt. Now that dirt was covered in snow.

But Chace saw in his mind's eye the footprints.

And, Christ, the knee prints.

Two sets. A man's, a woman's. Both of them walking up the well-tended trail to the wood. Only the man's walking back.

Misty was wearing high heels. She always wore high heels. Chace liked women in heels. That said, the ones his wife wore made her look like a whore.

He'd noted several times in the footprints that marked her enforced walk, after being beaten badly, probably at gunpoint, definitely scared out of her mind, where she'd stumbled. Other times where she'd fallen.

But he'd done her on her knees.

Chace closed his eyes.

Very few people knew that they'd found semen on her chin and in her stomach. He knew because he was a cop in that town and her husband.

And he knew that before she was shot to death, she'd been forced to her knees in order to give her killer a blowjob.

The bile rushed up his throat, and in the months since his wife had been beaten, violated and murdered, that had happened countless times too.

Kiss me, Chace.

Her voice came at him in a memory, brutalizing his brain as it had every day, so many fucking times a day, he couldn't count.

Her last words to him.

She'd been begging.

Kiss me, Chace.

He hadn't kissed her. They'd been married for years, and except the kiss he had to give her at their wedding, he hadn't kissed her once.

Not once.

Instead, he'd felt his lip curl, something he didn't hide from her, and he'd walked away.

As he swallowed the bile down, his eyes flew open when he heard someone approaching.

Then he heard a stumble and a female hiss the bizarre word, "Frak."

He came to his feet silently, instantly alert, and his gaze swung to the trail where the noise was coming from. His hand went to the gun in the holster clipped to the side of his belt. It was his service weapon. He wasn't on duty but he always wore it. His mountain town of Carnal, Colorado, might have recently emerged out from under a small-town tyrant's thumb but that didn't mean it was safe.

He blinked when she came into view, her head down, the top of her hair covered in a knit cap the color he couldn't tell in the moonlight. Her eyes were to her feet as she stomped through the snow to get to the clearing.

As if sensing him, her head shot up and when she saw him, she stopped so abruptly, her body rocked.

Chace stared at her.

He knew her.

Jesus fucking Christ. What the fuck?

He said not one word. It was fucking two in the fucking

morning in the freezing cold in the middle of nowhere that just happened to be the scene of an ugly, bloody murder. And she was there. He didn't know what to say because he didn't know whether to be pissed or seriously fucking pissed.

She said not one word either. Then again, she was known for being quiet and not just because it was an occupational hazard, seeing as she was the town's librarian.

Surprisingly, she broke their stare but she did it mumbling, "Uh…"

At that sound, Chace decided to be seriously fucking pissed.

"What the fuck?" he asked.

"Um…uh, Detective Keaton," she replied, then said not another word but her eyes were locked to him. Her long, sleek hair flowing out from under her cap was a midnight shadow against her light, puffy vest and the scarf wound around her neck. Her face was pale in the moonlight.

And, fuck him, he liked her voice. He'd heard it before, not often but he'd heard it. And he'd liked it the other times too. Quiet, melodious, like a fucking song.

Yeah, he liked it. A fuck of a lot.

Just not right then even if it was the first time she'd uttered his name. Or one of his names. The name he'd prefer she say was his first and he'd like to hear her say it when she was on her back, her rounded body under his, his cock inside her and he'd just made her come.

Something he'd never have.

This reminded him he was seriously fucking pissed.

So he repeated, "What the fuck?"

"I…uh—"

"Spit it out, Miz Goodknight. What the fuck are you doin' in Harker's Wood at the scene of a murder at two in the fucking morning?"

"Well, uh…" Her head tipped to the side and her eyes remained on him. "What are *you* doing here?"

"My wife was murdered here," he replied instantly, tersely and with obvious anger and immediately wished he didn't. This was because he watched her face flinch at the same time she took a step back.

It took her a moment to call it up but she did. She straightened her spine and whispered, "I'm sorry," he watched her swallow, "I'm so sorry about Misty, Detective Keaton."

"No one's sorry about Misty," he returned.

For some reason he was unable to stop himself from being an asshole, and he watched as she scrunched her nose, another flinch. This one cute.

Really cute.

Fuck him.

But he was right. No one in town was sorry his wife was dead. Not even, if he dug down deep, Chace. He wouldn't have wanted that for her, not that. Not even if they just filled her with holes rather than beating her and debasing her before they did it.

That didn't mean he didn't want her way the fuck out of his life. In another state. Fuck, in another fucking *country*.

He did want that.

He'd even prayed for it, that was how much he wanted it.

And now she was very, very much out of his life.

"That isn't true." Her whispered words came at him and he focused on her again. "I mean, you know, she wasn't, uh . . . Miss Popularity, but what was done to her—"

Chace cut her off, "Let's get to why you're here, Miz Goodknight."

He saw her moon-shadowed teeth bite her bottom lip and she looked around. He'd been a cop for a while. Because of this, he knew she was buying time to come up with a plausible lie.

So he prompted impatiently, "Miz Goodknight."

She looked back at him and said in her quiet, appealing voice, "Faye."

"What?"

He heard her clear her throat and she said, louder this time, "Faye. My name is Faye."

"I know that," he informed her, his tone no less short, maybe even more so.

"Well, you can, uh…you know, call me that," she invited.

"Great," he bit off. "Now you wanna answer my question?"

"No, actually, uh…not really," she replied, and Chace stared.

He did this because he was surprised.

She was pretty, fuck, unbelievably pretty. Thick, straight, long, dark auburn hair with natural red highlights. Hair that shined so much it fucking gleamed. A body she didn't show off by any stretch of the imagination but that didn't mean a man couldn't see she had curves in all the right places and hers were attractively ample. She wasn't tall, she wasn't short. Tall enough she could wear heels and he'd still have to bend his neck to take her mouth. And she had a pretty mouth with full lips that were so pink it looked like they would taste like bubblegum. She also had high, rounded, extraordinary cheekbones that gave testimony to a fact everyone in town knew, she had Native American blood in her ancestry.

And her eyes. Clear light blue. Absolute. Not gray blue. *Blue*. He'd never seen a blue so perfect, so pure, so beautiful and sure as fuck not the color of someone's eyes.

But she was quiet. She was shy. It wasn't like she was a hermit or invisible. She went to work. She had lunch at the diner. She went to the grocery store, post office, the Italian place, La-La Land for her coffees. She had friends. She had a huge-ass family and she was close to them.

But everyone knew she lived in a book. She didn't date.

She didn't go to Bubba's bar and tie one on. Chace saw her in La-La Land drinking a coffee and eating one of Shambles's cakes, her nose in a book or her hand wrapped around one of those eReaders. Chace saw her at the diner, same pose. Christ, more than once in his years in that town, he'd seen her wandering down a grocery store aisle, walking out of the post office, out of the library, her head bent, eyes trained to a book.

Him catching her for whatever reason she was in Harker's Wood at two in the morning, he would not expect she'd have the courage to do anything but answer his questions. Maybe haltingly. But she'd do it.

He would never expect she'd refuse.

"I'm afraid that answer's unacceptable, Miz Goodknight," he informed her.

"Faye," she corrected quietly.

"Whatever the fuck," he clipped. "Now, again, what are you doing here?"

For several long moments she studied him before she took half a step toward him but stopped abruptly and asked softly, "Do you come here a lot?"

"Not sure that's your business," he answered.

"But you are sure it's your business to know why I come here?" she returned, not testy or sharp, just careful.

"It's a crime scene, Miz Goodknight."

"Faye."

He leaned in and bit out a curt, "Faye," and again wished he didn't because her nose scrunched again. Another flinch. The cute kind. He buried his reaction to learning that the town's pretty, curvy, probably virgin librarian, who he once marked as the woman he wanted to make his before his life turned to shit, could be cute. Then he pressed on, "This is a crime scene."

"The tape's down," she reminded him. "It's been down months."

"It's still a crime scene."

She took another step and again her spine went straight. "Mr. Harker gave this wood to the town of Carnal ten years ago, Detective Keaton. It's a park. Public property. I have every right to be here."

There it was. The backbone again, and even having seen it before, he was still surprised.

"Town ordinance states all parks close to the public at ten o'clock unless they're a campsite," Chace shot back and through the moonlight, he watched her press her lips together.

Then she unpressed them and whispered, "Oh."

And that one syllable was melodious and cute too, fuck him.

She went on, "I didn't know that."

"Now you do."

"Maybe I should be leaving," she suggested.

"No maybe about it, Miz Goodknight," he returned.

"Faye," she whispered, her eyes locked to his.

Chace didn't reply.

Faye Goodknight didn't leave.

Instead, she took two more steps toward him before she stopped only three feet away.

When she did, she asked softly, "Are you okay?"

He should have lied and said yes. Or maybe not answered and reminded her she was leaving.

He didn't do either of these.

"Miz Goodknight, it's two in the morning and I'm in the cold in the wood where my wife was murdered. Do you think I'm okay?"

Instantly, still soft, she replied, "No."

He remembered himself then he reminded her, "You were leaving."

She didn't leave. She took another step forward, tipped her ear toward her shoulder but jutted her face slightly toward him and peered up at him, examining his features.

This, too, was cute.

While he was dealing with that, her soft voice came at him. "Did you love her?"

"You know the answer to that," he returned immediately, and she did. Everyone did. Chace Keaton made it abundantly clear how he felt about his wife and not only just to his wife.

She righted her head on her shoulders and advised, "Maybe you should talk to someone about, uh . . . what you're feeling."

"You volunteering for that?" Chace asked, and his tone was cutting.

She didn't even blink before she offered, "If you like."

"No offense, *Faye*, but the person I pick to lay the fucked-up shit in my head on is not gonna be a woman who breathes and eats and works but lives in a fantasy world. You can't handle your own life, which is a good life, far's I can see, without escaping. No fuckin' way you can handle the shit I got in my head."

It was an asshole remark but it worked. Her shoulders slumped slightly and she took a step back.

"I'm just trying to be nice," she pointed out the obvious.

"What would be nice is if you'd haul your ass back up the trail and leave me be."

She didn't move. Not for long moments.

Then she leaned slightly into him and said gently, "I don't think you should be left be. I think you're dealing with something heavy, you're obviously doing it alone." She threw a mitten-covered hand out to indicate the area. "You need to unload it, Chace."

Christ.

Fuck.

Christ.

That voice, quiet, gentle, so fucking sweet saying his name, her eyes soft on him.

Fuck.

Better than he could have imagined.

Better than he ever could have dreamed.

And not his.

Never to be his.

Which meant finally hearing her say his name was torture.

"All right," he started, "I've been trying to be nice—"

Her head jerked and she cut him off, her tone surprised, and again, Christ, fucking cute, "You have?"

"Yeah," he fired back. "I have and you'll know I have when I say, Miz Goodknight, I do not want your concern. I don't want your listening ear. I don't want your company. What I want is for you to walk your fat ass up the trail and leave me the fuck alone."

He watched her body lock and her pale face in the moonlight become even paler.

This lasted less than half a second before she turned on her boot and ran from the clearing. She did it so fast, he could see the midnight shadow of her long hair streaming behind her even after she'd left the clearing and hit the trail.

Chace Keaton's eyes didn't leave the trail for a long while after she'd disappeared.

Kiss me, Chace.

He heard it in his head and he closed his eyes.

You need to unload it, Chace.

That time he heard Faye and his eyes shot open.

Just what he did not need.

Another demon.

"Fuck," he growled, his eyes moving through the clearing, seeing nothing, hearing nothing.

Nothing there.

It wasn't talking.

Fuck.

As he had, night after night, Chace Keaton strode through the clearing to the trail and went home.

*   *   *

Two days later...

"Would it kill you to come to dinner?"

Chace watched over the counter as Shambles made his coffee. He felt the muscle jump in his cheek as he held the phone to his ear thinking, yes. It would kill him to go to dinner at his mother and father's house.

Or, more to the point, it would drive him to murder if he had to breathe his father's air.

"Ma," he said into the phone, "like I told you, I'm busy."

"But I thought you said they were hiring new officers and things were getting back to normal," she replied.

"They are but it isn't normal. Things are busy. Very busy. When they cleaned house, we lost practically everyone. Those new officers have to be trained and after what went down and the time it lasted, the citizens of Carnal aren't gonna adjust in a few months to a force they can trust. They got a problem, they still call each other rather than the police department. Then, when that goes south, and it usually goes south, we have to clean up the mess. No way I could make dinner this week."

"How about next week?" she pushed as Shambles poured frothed milk from the little stainless steel pitcher into his drink.

"How about the weekend after next, I come to Aspen and take you out to dinner?" Chace suggested.

Her voice was disappointed when she replied, "But you

know your father always goes to that golf tournament in Florida the third weekend in February."

He absolutely did.

He also absolutely knew his father was not attending a golf tournament in Florida but doing something else that could, conceivably, require sporting equipment but its uses were not something his mother could comprehend.

Unfortunately, Chace could. He just tried not to.

Shambles turned, smiling at him and shoving the white lid on top of his coffee.

Chace jerked up his chin to Shambles but said into his phone, "Is Dad's attendance required at our dinner?"

"Chace, you never see your father," she replied quietly.

"And, Ma, you know that's by design," Chace returned just as quietly, pulling out his wallet, flipping it open and yanking out a bill. He handed it to Shambles, Shambles set his coffee on the counter and turned to the cash register as Chace kept talking. "Now, are we on the weekend after next?"

She ignored his question and whispered, "I wish you two would heal this breach."

That was not going to happen.

Ever.

And this was because he and his father did not have a breach that could heal. It used to be just a breach, years ago when Chace just wanted out of the house that he grew up in and out from under his father's thumb.

Now it was not a breach. It was a chasm he sure as fuck wasn't going to cross and if his father tried, Chace would shoot him.

"Ma—"

"I'm worried about you, what with Misty gone. I mean, who's taking care of you?"

His mother didn't know this, she wasn't Misty's biggest fan either, though she tried to hide it just as Chace tried to hide from his mother the fact that he hated his wife, but Misty never took care of him.

She tried that for a while, after she finally figured out that he was not going to fall head over heels in love with her because she was great at giving head. This was mainly since he wouldn't allow her to touch him and didn't sleep in the same bed with her.

Once she realized that her usual tricks were not going to win his heart, she'd branched out. And her branching out came in the form of her trying to be a good wife. She was a decent housekeeper, a decent cook. All this went to shit when he eventually refused to eat her food, left the house more often than not before she got out of bed, came home late and never commented on her loving care or how she kept their home. Finally, she started to get nervous and fucked everything up.

He'd been hard on her and, at the time, felt she'd deserved it. She had trapped him into marriage after having whacked, sick-fuck sex with his father, doing this while conspiring with a dirty cop to tape it. Then she'd blackmailed his dad and forced Chace into servitude not only to his father and his cronies, all of whom were under a local man's thumb, but also to a crew of dirty cops that were so dirty, they were made of pure filth.

Yeah, he thought she deserved that.

Now she was dead and how she got dead, he had that and his treatment of her for their very long, very unhappy, five-year marriage living as demons in his head too.

"I'm thirty-five, Ma. I can take care of myself," he told his mother while accepting change from Shambles and tossing a dollar in the tip bowl.

"But I worry about you." She was back to whispering, this time sad and concerned and, because he loved his mother, it killed.

He knew she worried. He was an only child. She could have no more. She was lucky to have him and she felt that acutely. She was also flighty, sensitive and nervous by nature. Therefore, she'd smothered him growing up, terrified the very air had it out for him.

Her tactics for raising her son clashed violently with her husband's.

Valerie Keaton was all about protection, love and care.

Trane Keaton was all about making his son *a man*.

This was not conducive to a loving, secure, understanding, supportive home.

Therefore, as he'd promised himself starting at around age eight, the minute Chace could get out, he did. He worked at it, hard, and he got it.

And he never went back.

"Don't worry," he assured her quietly. "I'm fine. Just busy." He replaced his wallet, grabbed his drink and gave Shambles another chin lift. He got one of the undeniably talented but definitely a full-blown hippie proprietor of the coffee shop's goofy grins in return and went on, "Though, I'd be better, my mother let me take her out to dinner the weekend after next."

He turned to the door just as it opened, the bell over it ringing and, her eyes to her eReader, Faye Goodknight wandered in.

Fuck.

Chace stopped dead.

"Okay, Chace, honey, I'd like that," his mother said in his ear.

"Good," he muttered into the phone.

At his voice sounding, Faye's head came up, her eyes hit him, she stopped moving and she gave it to him. The expression he couldn't fully see in the moonlight but he definitely saw in the daylight in La-La Land Coffee.

Her eyes instantly turned pained, her face paled, her full, pink lips parted.

And taking in that pain etched into her features hurt like a bitch.

She was wearing a wool overcoat, the design of it somehow cinched it at her tiny waist, which had the effect of throwing her curves into visible relief. It had a shawl collar around the neck and the coat was cream, its color highlighting the dark auburn of her hair. A light blue knit cap was pulled down to her ears, and, with the color of the coat, this accentuated her hair, displaying far more prominently an alluring feature that couldn't be missed. She had on dark brown leather low-heeled boots, and he knew she was wearing a dress or skirt under that coat because that was what she normally wore but also because all he could see on her legs up to the hem of her coat were the boots.

Her makeup, as he noted it normally was, was subtle. There simply to highlight her natural prettiness, not falsify it.

Her wounded, crystal blue eyes were wide.

"Do you want me to make a reservation at Reynaldo's?" his mother asked.

"Yeah, Ma," he answered. "That'd be good. Now I gotta go."

This time, hearing his voice sound took Faye out of her freeze and she didn't hesitate to turn right around and hurry out the door.

"But, Chace—" his mother began.

Instinctively and definitely stupidly, Chace moved swiftly to the door. "Something just came up, Ma. Really, gotta go."

He heard his mother sigh then, "Okay, honey. See you weekend after next."

"Weekend after next. Love you, Ma, 'bye."

He heard her good-bye but vaguely. He was out the door and moving quickly down the sidewalk behind a quickly moving Faye Goodknight.

And he had no idea why.

Except he still felt the pain of seeing the hurt he'd given her stamped in her features, and he had to do something about it.

He closed on her and called, "Miz Goodknight."

She hastened her step.

Chace went faster.

"Miz Goodknight."

She started run-walking.

His long strides no match for her, Chace easily caught up to her, wrapped his fingers around her bicep and halted her, turning her to him at the same time he turned his body into her and said softly, "Faye."

Her beautiful, injured eyes lifted to him, wounding him as sure as if she'd shoved a knife in his gut.

But her shoulders straightened. She was calling up the backbone.

"Good morning, Detective Keaton," she greeted, voice not cold but her usual quiet and now, unlike that night in Harker's Wood, definitely distant.

He kept his hand on her as he murmured distractedly, "Chace."

He said no more mostly because he had no fucking clue what to say.

She didn't speak.

This carried on awhile.

Then she spoke. "As you're detaining me," she slightly moved the arm he was holding, likely to point out he was still holding it and she didn't want that, "is there something I can help you with?"

"Yeah, actually," he replied, "I'd like to apologize for the other night."

"Apology accepted," she stated instantly. Then, again slightly shifting her arm in his hold, making her point that she wanted him to let her go, she finished, "Now you have a nice day."

He didn't let her go.

He also didn't know why he did it, he just did. And what he did was use his hand on her arm to pull her closer until they were inches apart.

That got him much the same look she gave him at La-La Land Coffee but without the pain. Her pretty pink lips parted, her beautiful blue eyes got wide and her flawless pale skin got paler.

Without the pain and with only inches between them, that look was fucking spectacular.

He also noticed she wasn't breathing.

Therefore, he bent his head toward hers and whispered, "Breathe, Faye."

Her breath left her in a soft whoosh.

That was cute, the look on her face still magnificent, the effect of both together with her proximity was just plain hot.

Jesus.

Making matters worse, she smelled good.

No, not good.

Fucking amazing.

Christ, he wanted to kiss her. Ached to do it.

"Is there more?" she whispered, and he blinked, his eyes shifting from their attention to her mouth to hers.

"You were right," he whispered back. "I'm workin' through some shit."

"I can imagine," she replied, swinging her body back a few inches, coolness washing through her features. No, not cold. Again distant.

"Doesn't make it okay to be a dick," he carried on.

"This is true," she agreed.

"What I said was not nice and it was not acceptable."

"I think I got that you felt that way when you apologized, Detective Keaton."

He pulled her back the inches she'd shifted away at the same time he curled his body closer to hers, locked his eyes with her blue ones and whispered, "Chace."

He watched her swallow, the coolness left her features, a flash of nervousness and uncertainty went through her eyes, but she didn't reply.

"I'd really like to know, Faye, that you accept my apology," he told her quietly.

"I already said I did." Her sweet, quiet voice came back at him instantly.

"Right, then what I'd like to know is that you mean it."

She held his eyes and he not only sensed but saw her breath escalating.

Cute and hot.

Fuck him.

Fuck *him*.

Then she whispered, "I mean it."

"You mean it what?" Chace returned immediately, going for it. Shit, even so much as *needing* it.

Her head gave a slight jerk as she blinked and that was also unbelievably cute.

"I mean it what um... *what*?" she whispered.

He pulled her closer using her arm at the same time he lifted his other hand with the coffee cup, touched it to her waist and whispered back, "You mean it, *Chace*."

Then, Christ, *Christ*, he watched the tip of her pink tongue move out to wet the fullness of her bottom lip. Her little, even white teeth sunk into that lip, and that was off-the-charts cute and so fucking hot, he felt it in his dick.

She let her lip go and she whispered, "I mean it, Chace."

He felt that in his dick too.

Jesus, what the fuck was he doing?

Abruptly, he let her go and stepped away. He regretted it immediately for she wasn't ready for it and visibly teetered without his hold on her, his body close. She steadied herself but he didn't like to see her teeter. However, he did like the knowledge that she was as absorbed in him as he was in her.

That didn't mean he shouldn't shut it down. He should.

And he did.

"Thank you, Faye," he said, his voice more formal. Not cold. Like hers, distant.

She blinked.

Then she pulled in breath.

Then she said, strangely, "Lexie."

"What?" he asked.

"Lexie," she repeated, leaned in almost the instant she leaned right back and then she squared her shoulders again and said in a firmer tone, "I bet Lexie Walker would be a good listener and I know she likes you. I've seen you two have lunch together at the diner and you make her laugh. I mean, everyone makes Lexie laugh. She's a laugher. But you do too. You should talk to her. She'd help."

And without another word, she turned and moved quickly down the sidewalk.

Everything that was Chace Keaton urged him to follow her. To ask her to dinner. To get to know her. To find the right time to taste her mouth. To find the right time to taste her body. To take the time to teach her how to pleasure his. To lay his burden on her.

Everything that Chace Keaton had done, seen and heard for near on a decade stopped him.

So he turned in the opposite direction and walked to his truck.

CHAPTER TWO

Bubblemint

"This is good."

"This is *not* good."

"I think it's good."

"It is definitely not good."

I was standing behind the checkout desk in the library and in front of me were Lexie Walker, Krystal Briggs and Lauren Jackson.

Lexie was married to Ty Walker. She was a beautiful brunette and her husband was a gorgeous half–African American, half-white man who'd recently made national news when it was uncovered he was framed and went to prison for a murder he did not commit.

Krystal Briggs was a petite, buxom woman who today (but it could be different tomorrow) had a mass of golden, honeyed locks akin to Farrah Fawcett's hair in *Charlie's Angels*. She was married to Jonas "Bubba" Briggs, who had for years partied hearty, and he did this without her while she worked at their bar called Bubba's. She'd kicked him out and then about a year and a half later, for some reason, she married him. I didn't get that and in the past few months, as Lexie introduced me to her posse, Krystal hadn't shared. Then again, Krystal kind of scared me so I didn't ask. What I did notice was that Bubba wasn't partying hearty anymore and instead seemed pretty devoted. So I guessed things were going all right.

Lauren Jackson was married to Tatum Jackson who I'd had a crush on for forever (or, until Chace Keaton moved to town). Growing up, anytime I saw him, my heart would skip a beat. This was because he was the most handsome man I'd ever seen (until Chace Keaton moved to town). He was a little rough around the edges but he made it beyond attractive. He was also a nice man, well liked if a little messed up, seeing as his on-again, off-again girlfriend was more than a little crazy. Now he was with Laurie and he was no longer messed up. Of course, this was after his on-again, off-again girlfriend was murdered by a serial killer and Laurie was almost murdered by the same guy. But now for Tate, and for Laurie, everything seemed cool.

Thinking all this, it brought to mind my dad's comment after Misty Keaton was killed, which was, "Used to be, Carnal was quiet. Sure, the bikers could make a ruckus and did. But no one got dead. Maybe stuck with a knife but not dead. Now seems everyone's gettin' dead or almost dead or doin' time for a crime they didn't commit. Quiet, small-town life ain't all it used to be."

This was, unfortunately, true.

Lexie was the first one who spoke after I told them what happened with Chace Keaton in Harker's Wood and on the sidewalk the day before. Krystal was the second and fourth comment. Laurie was third.

I watched Lexie turn to Krystal and ask, "How is it not good?"

"Uh...hello?" Krystal asked back sarcastically. "Did you not hear Faye? That boy is *fucked up*."

"Yes, so, he needs someone to help him get unfucked up," Lexie shot back.

"Is 'unfucked' a word?" Laurie asked me.

As usual when these girls were around, I didn't get the chance to say much since they were talking all the time, but

I did get the chance to get a shrug in to Laurie but just barely before Krystal spoke.

"Well, I had to unfuck one and, I'll remind you, so did you *and* Laurie," Krystal jerked a thumb at Lauren, "and it wasn't much fun."

"Mine was fun," Laurie whispered to me.

"Mine was too," Lexie did not whisper to Krystal. "Mostly because of all the fucking we did while I was unfucking him." She looked at me, grinning. "And other parts. But the fucking was a highlight." Then she muttered, "Still is."

Krystal turned and rolled her eyes at me before saying, "The pain, it fades. Trust me, it is *not* fun."

I could feel my cheeks burning and knew they were bright red at all this talk about fucking and, well, unfucking (whatever that was).

This was because I was a virgin, though recently I'd been spending some time with these women as they came into the library with relative frequency. Krystal, especially, rarely held any punches (as in, never), I wasn't used to talk about "fucking."

Incidentally, being a virgin was by choice.

Kind of.

First, as a starry-eyed adolescent, I'd made it my mission to give it away only after I found the right guy (not that, at the time, I actually knew what "giving it away" meant).

This was because I'd read romance novels since I was thirteen. Therefore, I decided, just like the heroines in my books, I would only give something that precious to a man who deserved it. The perfect man. The one who would sweep me off my feet, make my heart race, fire my blood and be happy to dance with me all night. The one who was smart, strong, handsome, good. The one who was larger than life. The one who would look after me. The one who would hold me close all night long.

Then, thirteen years ago, Chace Keaton showed up in town, in uniform, thick dark blond hair, intense dark blue eyes, handsome white smile, tall, straight, lean body, and I fell in love.

I know it sounds crazy but I did it. And I did it because I knew he was all that I needed him to be. A man like that could sweep me off my feet. He was strong, handsome and a cop so he had to be good. He was so beautiful, in uniform or out of it, wearing his jeans and western belt buckle and cowboy boots. Coming from Aspen money (big money, if rumor was true) but leaving all that to be his own man. A good man. A brave man. An officer of the law. He seemed larger than life.

I was sixteen but I knew he could make my heart race, fire my blood because I didn't even know him and I was young but he already did.

And I never let go of that feeling.

Even when he married Misty, the town slut who no one liked all that much.

I was shocked and, I'll admit, hurt when he did it. It wasn't nice to think but she *was* the town slut and she didn't suit him, she didn't fit him, it didn't make sense. Especially since everyone in the whole town knew she lied about Ty Walker's alibi. That made her a slut *and* a liar, and not the little white lie kind of liar but the huge, earth-shattering, life-altering, vicious, nasty kind of liar.

It didn't make sense, Misty and Chace. Chace was a good guy. A straight arrow. Well liked. Trusted. And in our town on the police force at that time, this was practically an unknown commodity.

But I didn't let go of the feeling I had deep down inside that Chace was the one because everyone in town was talking about how she trapped him. And Chace himself never acted like he was happy to be wed in holy matrimony to the town slut (and liar). He wasn't nice to her and he wasn't faithful to her and he was obvious about both.

I didn't know how she could trap him. I mean, I knew they'd been together if not together-together in a girlfriend/boyfriend way. Then again, as the town slut, everyone had been "together" with Misty. So, I thought at first he got her pregnant. But then she never had a baby.

Although I didn't like them together (as in, *really*), either "together" or together in the married way, it didn't faze me. Everyone knew the hero in any good romance had to have his fair share of experience. If he didn't, how was he going to be a good teacher, showing his lady love how to give him pleasure at the same time giving her more than she'd ever dreamed? So I didn't mind that Chace played the field, including with Misty.

But putting his ring on her finger? Then cheating on her openly?

No.

It never made sense.

And truth be told, I didn't like it much. It didn't say nice things about him at all.

For some reason, though, I never gave up hope. For some reason, even removed, I felt whatever was between them wasn't *right*. I knew just looking at him he wasn't happy. And after a while, I saw the same thing in Misty and by the end, for Misty, it was even worse.

It wasn't like they were married. It was like they were enemies legally bound together. This made Chace go about his life as if he wasn't married. And it wore Misty down. It was strange, it was sad and, in the end, it was tragic.

There was more talk after she died. Speculation that she was wound up in all the goings-on at the police station with dirty cops and corruption. Especially since it was found out to be true what everyone already knew, that she lied about

Ty Walker's alibi. So folks figured that Chace somehow got caught up in all that and Misty somehow got Chace out of the deal. But no one really knew the true story.

After Misty died and all that stuff at the station was brought out in the open, Lexie came to the library with the obvious intent to be my friend (for some reason). But even though I knew she knew Chace, like, for real, spending actual time in his presence instead of just seeing him around, she'd never shared. She just counseled me, frequently, to have a go at Chace, telling me she was certain he was into me.

As often as she informed me of this, he never gave any indication of it. In fact, after his wife was murdered, it was the first time he showed that he might care about her. It was clear it disturbed him, not a little, a lot. Of course, anyone being murdered would, even a wife you didn't much like who may have trapped you into marriage. And now I knew this to be true since now I knew he hung out in the dead of night in the cold at the spot where she was killed.

Seven months had passed and he wasn't shaking it off. And he was also hanging out at Harker's Wood in the middle of the night. So maybe everyone was wrong about Misty and Chace. Maybe, out there in the crazy world where things were messed up and not nice, a world, Chace was right, I didn't spend a lot of time in for a reason, they had something. Something it couldn't be denied was twisted. But it clearly was something.

So, in the end, I'd spent so much time admiring Chace from afar, and living in my books, time just got away from me. And now I was twenty-nine years old and still a virgin.

And also, I'd finally spoken words directly to the man I fell in love with at sixteen and I'd done it twice.

The first time he was not nice. And he was definitely no hero.

The second time, well, the second time, I didn't get. I'd heard the term "mixed messages" and now I understood it.

Boy, did I ever.

"What were you doin' up there in Harker's Wood anyway?" Krystal asked, taking me from my thoughts, and I blinked before I focused on her.

It then occurred to me, belatedly, that I probably shouldn't have told them that part.

"Oh God," Lexie whispered, leaning toward me over the counter, "are you stalking him?"

Oh no. Now I had to lie.

I didn't like lying. I also didn't like cursing, which Chace, I was surprised to discover, did with great frequency. I further didn't like any kind of cheating, the on tests kind, the in life kind or the in relationships kind, the latter something else Chace did with openness and, again, great frequency.

At least he wasn't in on all that dirty stuff at the station but instead had put himself in grave danger to uncover the corruption and sweep it free from the Carnal Police Department. That bit, I decided, forgave some of his other obvious sins.

"Are you?" Laurie asked, also leaning toward me. "Stalking him, that is?"

I wasn't. I had no idea he was out there. I was out there for something else. Something I'd gone out there several times to do. Something I couldn't share.

So I had to lie.

"Actually, Harker's Wood is kind of my place," I told them. "I go out there a lot. Always did."

Lie!

Lexie's brows drew together and her head twitched. "Really?"

"Uh...yeah," I replied.

Another lie.

"At two in the morning?" Krystal asked, and my eyes moved to her. Her arms were crossed on her large bosoms and her brows were drawn together too. Though hers were a bit scarier.

"Sometimes. If I can't sleep," I answered.

"You can't sleep?" Laurie queried quietly, and I bit my lip because this wasn't true either. I slept like a baby. Dropped off, usually with a book in my hand, and was out until the alarm clock went.

I stopped biting my lip and whispered another lie, "Yeah."

There it was. One lie led to another then another and another and then you were drowning in them.

"I had trouble sleeping all my life," Laurie told me then grinned. "Tate fixed that."

"I bet," Krystal muttered.

"And I bet Chace would find ways to keep you from driving up the mountain to Harker's Wood in the middle of the night if you had trouble sleeping," Lexie put in.

I didn't want to think about that.

No, that wasn't strictly true. I didn't want to think about that now, when I was at work. I wanted to think about it later, when I usually did. When I was in bed with the vibrator that it took me three months to psych myself up to buy on the Internet. Something I used often, considering I was a twenty-nine-year-old virgin with a thirteen-year crush on a man who, until a few of nights ago, I didn't think knew I existed.

Needless to say, Chace factored largely when my time was occupied with this activity.

"I think, now that the ice is broken, you need to give him a sign," Lexie went on.

"She needs to back off, let that boy sort his shit and, if he's salvaged something that makes him worth her while, *then* she can give him a sign," Krystal advised.

"Life is too short and too precious to wait for that, Krys," Laurie added in a quiet voice.

Krystal gave her a look that said she was right and Krystal found that annoying.

I had, in getting to know her, learned that Krystal found a lot annoying.

"I . . ." I started then finished softly, "wouldn't know how."

"Kiss him," Lexie suggested instantly. I blinked, my body locked but I felt my face heat again at the very idea.

"*Are you nuts?*" Krystal hissed, now leaning in close to Lexie.

"No," Lexie replied. "Nothing says 'I like you' like your tongue in their mouth."

One thing could be said for that, it was inarguably true.

"So, did that work for you? Did you kiss Ty and then everything was hearts and flowers?" Krystal asked, leaning back and again crossing her arms on her chest.

"Actually, no," Lexie returned. "I didn't. But things were hearts and flowers when I wanted to do it, had an overwhelming urge to do it and I didn't do it. And it was exactly the time I *should* have done it. Then things went bad and it would be days before I got another shot. Or, I should say, I did eventually kiss him and it didn't work out *then* things went bad and days after that Ty took his shot and that, well," she looked at me and grinned, "that worked out *great*."

As far as I could tell, it certainly did. I saw Lexie a lot because she came around to the library and sometimes sat with me in the diner when we were having lunch. I didn't see Ty very much but when I did and he was with his wife, it was clear they were close. Very close. Happy, loving close.

It also helped to know this seeing as she was currently six months pregnant.

"Not to put a damper on your enthusiasm, honey," Laurie entered the conversation at this point, eyes on Lexie, "but I'm uncertain with what Faye told us so far that going for that kind of gusto at this juncture is the right advice."

Lexie held Lauren's eyes as she spoke then her gaze swung to me. "Kiss him."

Krystal threw her hands in the air at the same time she threw her honeyed locks back as she stared up at the ceiling with easy-to-read exasperation.

Laurie gave me a grin.

As for me, I was not ever, *ever* going to kiss Chace Keaton.

Not until he kissed me.

If that should ever (please God!) happen.

Lexie kept speaking as that thought gave me a pleasant shiver.

"Now, I'm a girl and you're a girl, we're all girls." She lifted a hand and did a twirl to indicate Krystal and Laurie. "And it's my sworn duty as a girl not to lead you down the wrong path, *especially* in matters of the heart. But I'll tell you again what I've been telling you now for months. Chace Keaton is *into you*. Not just into you. Into you in a hungry-heart, longing, soul-destroying-if-you-can't-have-it, put-your-life-on-the-line-to-get-it kind of into you."

My heart skipped a beat at these words but she was not done.

"I know. I felt that for Ty and I still do. He feels it for me and I've been seeing it in his eyes since the beginning. At first, I didn't get it. You need to get it faster than I did. Learn from me. I see it in Chace when he looks at you. He's got issues. You help him deal and give him a little somethin' somethin' while you do, trust me, this is a tried and tested method and it works. I've done it and Laurie's done it. Now it's your turn. And, if he's fucked up, which he is, the shit that has gone down, he can't help but be it's going to have to be *you* who puts yourself out there."

She took in a breath, leaned across the counter to me and grabbed my hand before she finished.

"And I swear, honey, I would not lead you wrong."

Again, no way I was ever going to kiss Chace Keaton until he kissed me.

But something else she said captured my attention.

"What's gone down?" I asked softly and, as she'd been doing for months when this subject was broached, she leaned back, let me go and closed down.

This time, after what Chace said to me in the wood, the fact that he was at the wood at all, the way he was yesterday morning, the mixed messages that he was giving me, making me want to run at the same time I wanted to wrap my arms around him and absorb his pain, for the first time I pushed it.

"You can't expect me to put myself out there if I don't know what I'm dealing with," I informed her.

"That right there is a good point," Krystal backed me.

"And what she's dealing with is Chace's to share," Lexie returned.

Krystal disagreed. "You gotta give the girl something."

"She has it," Lexie retorted. "His wife was murdered. He didn't like her much but still, he's a good man and no one deserves that. And that's coming from me, a woman who intimately knows that Misty Keaton was the worst kind of bitch there is. And he's been working alongside scum for years. That shit will mark a man." Her eyes came to me. "And that has marked Chace. Help him heal his wounds then get past the scars. Don't delay, honey. Neither of you are getting any younger and I promise you, you do, you'll regret it for the rest of your life. That lost time, if you take your time. Or if you never do it at all, the loss of something beautiful you never had that was something you yourself let slip through your fingers."

It must be said, she made a case for throwing myself at Chace Keaton.

Still, I was never going to do it.

Nevertheless, I was forced to lie again just so we could stop talking about this.

"I'll think about it."

Lexie smiled huge.

Krystal closed her eyes.

Laurie made an "eek!" face that she quickly hid when my eyes hit her and she gave me a reassuring grin.

They left shortly after and when they did, they left me with visions of throwing myself in Chace Keaton's arms and kissing him.

This did not make it easy to focus on the work I had to do.

But I still saw him when he came in.

Sandy blond hair but this was at a guess seeing as it was dirty. Not dirty, *greasy*. It wasn't a day or two of missing the shampoo bottle. It was a whole lot more.

His clothes weren't any cleaner. And they hung on him. This was not hard to do considering he was skin and bones.

His pallor was marked too. It was February in the Colorado Mountains therefore cold and there was always snow on the ground. Even so, the sun shone regularly so the cold gave you rosy cheeks but the sun still could kiss your skin if you spent any amount of time outside. And most of the citizens of Carnal had been there awhile. The cold and snow didn't stop them from doing much, inside or out.

My guess was, he was nine, maybe ten and I figured it was a good guess. The Carnal Library was the only one in the county. This meant folks from Gnaw Bone and Chantelle came there even if it was a ways away. Also, the schools of Carnal, Gnaw Bone and Chantelle took field trips to my library so I'd seen a lot of kids. And, last, my sister had kids. And one was nearly nine, about that boy's size, his height but my nephew was a lot better fed.

He'd been coming in for a few months, once or twice a week.

And more than twice, I'd seen bruises. Once, around his jaw. Once on his cheekbone. Once around both wrists.

He always slunk in, eyes to the ground, shoulders hunched, thin, beaten-up coat way not warm enough for this weather hanging on him, obviously trying to be invisible.

And he stole books. One or two each time he came, whatever he could shove in his coat and take away.

I hadn't made a big deal of this because, with regularity, books not checked out were in the return bin in the morning and I'd put one and one together and made the two that he wasn't stealing them, he was borrowing them. Just not the normal way. And I'd tried to approach him on several occasions to tell him all he needed to do was apply for a library card. But the instant I got near, he shuffled away, darted between rows of books and eventually raced out.

The first time this happened, I thought he wouldn't come back. But he did.

This meant he liked his books like I liked mine. And clearly he didn't have the money to get them at a shop. So he got them the only way he could.

I didn't get why he didn't get a library card but at the same time I did.

Something was not right with that boy.

And today it was less right. I knew this because, even though he ducked his face away and headed straight to the short flight of stairs that led up to the fiction section, I saw he had bruising on his cheekbone *and* around his swollen eye.

This made me forget about Chace Keaton.

It also made me forget about the decision I made some time ago that I'd let him borrow as he felt he had to do it. He returned the books, it was no skin off my nose. And clearly they gave him something he needed enough to brave stealing them (essentially) and going out into a world filled with people that scared the heck out of him. I knew this because I was a librarian, I was a woman, I was five foot six and I was no threat and still, he ran away from me. Sure he was stealing my books (essentially) but also, he was not.

But seeing that black eye, I was reminded of something my dad said.

"A wrong is just wrong no matter who's doin' it or who it's done to. You know someone's doin' wrong and even if it has not one thing to do with you, you do what you can to right that wrong. You don't, you're no kind of person or, at least, no kind of person I'd wanna know."

These were words Dad lived by.

This was also a philosophy that meant him living in Carnal with what had been going on for as long as it had been going on had made his life a living hell.

He'd lodged formal complaints (twelve of them) against the Carnal Police Department. He'd also encouraged others to do the same, blatantly and with intent, even going so far as to go to their house and have a chat (or chats, plural, if need be) if he heard something not right had gone down. He'd also visited Mick Shaughnessy, the head honcho of the police force in Gnaw Bone and a buddy of my dad's, about how he could intervene and he did this more than once (in fact, five times that I knew). He'd further told Arnold Fuller, the dirty cop ringleader, the police captain then the chief of police, and now a dead man (literally), exactly what he thought of him on more than one occasion both publicly and privately.

As well as all this, even though everyone agreed, Dad was one of few who speculated openly and widely (in other words, to all who would listen, including Mick Shaughnessy) about the fact that Ty Walker was extradited to stand trial and then went down for a crime my father was certain (and he was right) Ty didn't commit.

And last, my dad had been pulled over and had more tickets than any other citizen in town and once had been arrested for drunk and disorderly when he was neither. And all this happened because he did all of the above.

Every single ticket, as well as the arrest, he fought loudly, boisterously but not always successfully.

But he never gave up.

And I knew, looking at that boy, wrong was being done to him. I also knew, with his eye swollen shut, I had to stop doing the little I was doing, letting him get away with stealing books (essentially), and I had to start doing something more.

I searched the immediate area, noted no patrons were close to approaching the checkout desk, and I skirted it to move out into the library. Cautiously and quietly, I moved up the steps then, like a super-sleuth, feeling more than a little idiotic, I rounded the shelves and stopped. Hiding my body, I peeked just my head around the side to check the aisle to see if he was there.

I found him three rows in.

I pulled my head back, pressed my back into the side of the shelf and took a deep breath.

Then I peeked just my head around again and called softly, "Please don't run. You aren't in trouble."

He was squatting to the bottom shelf, a book in his hand, and his head snapped around and up.

It was then I saw the full extent of damage to his face.

Not only a black eye, swollen shut, and a bruised cheekbone but a swollen, painful-looking nose and a gash on his lip that glistened, not because it had been treated with ointment but because it was gaping and exposing flesh.

My stomach clutched, my frame froze and my throat closed. He dropped the book, shot up straight and dashed down the aisle the opposite direction from me.

At his movements, I came unstuck, quickly turned on my boot and raced down my side, clearing the shelves and seeing him darting down the stairs. No, *jumping* down them three steps at a time, taking him down in two big jumps that made my heart jump with him because I feared he'd harm himself.

"Please! Stop! You're not in trouble!" I shouted. "Promise!" I kept shouting as I ran down the steps after him. "I just want to talk!"

Out the door he went and out the door I went after him, down the sidewalk to town.

The pavements were cleared, my boots had low heels and I belonged to McLeod's Gym. I didn't do those boot camps they had at McLeod's because they weren't at times I could attend (not to mention, I'd heard about them and they scared me). But I did go four times a week to spend half an hour on the Stairmaster, treadmill or rowing machine.

"A body takes care of itself or a body finds they don't have a body no more."

This was more of Dad's wisdom. So I took care of mine.

This meant, I might not be ready to attempt my first Iron Man, but I wasn't in bad shape.

Even with all this going for me, I was no match for the boy. He sprinted three blocks, gaining more and more, darted around the corner into town and by the time I darted around it after him, he'd disappeared.

I stood there, breathing slightly heavy, my gaze scanning the area to find any trace of him but he was gone.

"Darn," I whispered, hoping I didn't scare him into never coming back at the same time knowing that was not all I should do.

He was nine or ten and regularly beaten by someone. Bullies or, God, I hoped not, family. I knew it. And I had to do something about it.

I stood in the cold without a coat, my breaths coming out in visible puffs, my mind sifting through my possible next steps.

First, I had to get back to the library. I was the only one on, which meant there was no one there except patrons.

Then I could do two things.

One, I could call my dad, tell him what was happening and lay the problem on his broad shoulders, knowing he'd look into it then promptly do something about it.

Two, I could be a grownup, not call my dad to hand over a burden that wasn't mine but was all the same and I could go to the police station, report what I'd seen and hope they'd do something about it.

The problem with that was, Chace Keaton worked at the police station.

The boy's nose, eye, cheekbone and lip came into sharp relief in my mind's eye, and I closed my actual eyes as I sucked in breath.

I opened them and turned back to the library knowing what I had to do.

I should note, not liking it.

But knowing it.

*   *   *

Chace

It was quarter to seven when she walked in.

He'd applied for the job in Carnal upon graduation from the academy. It was the only place he'd worked since earning his badge, and he'd worked there thirteen years.

And not once had Faye Goodknight walked into the police department. Not even when Rowdy Crabtree brought her father in on that trumped-up charge for drunk and disorderly when Silas Goodknight had just been in Bubba's, a place he didn't frequent but he wasn't a stranger. Silas had been celebrating a friend's fiftieth birthday. Silas, nowhere near drunk and definitely not disorderly, spent the night in the tank. His wife, Sondra, had come in to make bail and pick him up.

Fortunately, the charge didn't stick. And none of the Goodknights knew this but the reason it didn't was because Chace intervened with Fuller, talking him down about targeting another well-respected, well-liked citizen. He'd explained Fuller already had enough talk in town about what was done to Walker, he didn't need more speculation. And worse, he didn't need to rile up Goodknight who had demonstrated, repeatedly, he was not the kind of man to go away quiet, lick his wounds and fight another day. He was the kind of man who would go down fighting, which meant he'd take others with him.

Fuller had, surprisingly, relented and set up Crabtree to take the hit of a bad arrest.

Now she was here. And he saw her eyes skid through him at his desk while they scanned the room and she moved to reception.

He figured she was there at that time because the library opened at ten and closed at six.

He also figured she was there at that time because she expected him *not* to be there.

Whatever reason she was there, he should leave it be. He knew he should leave it be.

But he couldn't help but think it was no coincidence that he'd not spoken to her directly once in all the years they'd lived in the same town, now they'd spoken twice and she was there.

So he didn't leave it be.

He got up and started to the reception desk.

Her clear blue eyes skittered to him when he was five feet away and he felt the touch of them like it was real. A hand curled around his neck. Fingers gliding into his hair. Soft, light, sweet.

That kind of real.

Fuck.

She just had to look at him, that was it, and he reacted.

He continued on his path to the last place he should be.

Close to Faye Goodknight.

"Everything all right, Faye?" he asked when he got there.

"She's got a report to make," Jon, the officer on duty at the desk, answered for her.

Chace didn't take his eyes from Faye. "About what?"

Jon answered again, humor in his tone now, "We haven't gotten that far."

Chace's body and mouth made a decision and carried it out again before his brain caught up.

And this was, stepping to the side and opening the low, hinged, wooden gate, eyes still on Faye, mouth saying, "Faye, you follow me. Jon, I'll handle it."

Her teeth appeared in order to bite her lip, she hesitated a moment then she moved to do as he asked.

Chace felt Jon's eyes on him but he didn't glance in his direction. It wasn't worth the effort. First, whatever this was, he was going to handle it and he had rank on Jon so Jon had no say in the matter. Second, Jon had a big mouth and even if Chace threatened him, Jon would run that mouth. It wasn't worth the effort to do more than threaten him. So whatever Jon was thinking about Chace intervening would be all over the station by tomorrow morning at eight o'clock. And Faye looking the way she looked and Chace showing at reception before she even had a chance to explain why she was there, he knew exactly what would be all over the station by tomorrow.

This last, he didn't give a fuck about. Enough words had been whispered about Chace over the last six years. This no longer affected him.

He led Faye to an interrogation room, opened the door and kept it open with arm extended, his nonverbal invitation for her to precede him. She glanced at him then lifted a hand to tuck her hair behind her ear as she looked away, ducked her head and walked by him.

He'd seen her tuck her hair behind her ear, often. And he'd always thought it was cute.

Seeing it close up, it was, like everything he was noting about Faye, a fuckuva lot cuter.

He stepped in behind her, closed the door and leaned his back against it, crossing his arms on his chest.

"Um...you might be mistaken," she started, her eyes moving to the door behind him before lifting to his. "I'm not certain this needs privacy, Detective Keaton."

"I thought we decided on Chace."

She blinked and her head gave a slight twitch. "What?"

"I want you to call me Chace, Faye."

"Right," she whispered, her eyes on him having changed so she wasn't simply meeting his but studying him.

"Now, what doesn't need privacy?" he prompted.

"I..." She started, paused then continued, "See, there's this..." She paused again, adjusted her torso in a way where it seemed she was trying to straighten her shoulders but failing as her eyes drifted away and she went on, "The thing is..." She trailed off, stopped and he watched as her teeth came back out. This time, they caught her lower lip on the outside then pulled in, teeth gliding over her lip and disappearing.

Christ, everything she did, having no clue she was doing it, was not only unbelievably sexy but her having no clue she was doing it was precisely why her doing it was unbelievably sexy.

"Faye," he said softly, her gaze shot back to his and she spoke again, this time quickly.

"There's a boy," she began. "I don't know, nine, ten years old. He comes into the library and steals books."

"I see," he murmured then guessed, "You don't want to get him into trouble but you also can't have him stealing books."

"No," she shook her head, "he returns them."

Chace blinked.

Then he asked, "What?"

"He returns them," she answered and kept talking in a rush. "I mean, since he steals them instead of checks them out, I can't know if he's returning all of them. But, for months now, he's been coming in once or twice a week and once or twice a week I'll have two or three books in the return bin that were never checked out. So, since I have no record what he took, I can't know if he returns them all. But he's a slip of a boy and although his jacket is big, he can't lug out dozens of books. And I've had my eye on him. So if he's stealing loads, I would notice. He isn't stealing loads so, I'm not sure, but I think he returns all of them or, uh..." she faltered then finished, "the vast majority of them."

"If this is true, I'm uncertain how there's a problem."

She pulled in a visibly deep breath.

And then she let it out while informing him quietly, "He's being beaten."

At that, Chace straightened from the door, but he didn't move from it as he whispered, "Beaten?"

She nodded.

"How do you know?" he asked.

"Well, the bruise on his cheekbone I saw. And the other one around his jaw. And then there were the ones on his wrists. But today," she swallowed, took a half step toward him, stopped and sucked in another breath before going on, "today, it was bad."

"How bad?"

"Eye swollen shut, bruises on his face, nose swollen and a gash on his lip that isn't being treated."

"Fuck," Chace muttered.

"It's worse," she whispered, and Chace nodded to her to go on. "He...well, he's very thin. And he's not clean, as in, *way* not clean. And his clothes don't fit him. And he's very, very thin."

"You said that," Chace noted quietly.

"He's so very, very thin, Chace, it bears repeating," she said quietly back.

Chace held her eyes and repeated his muttered, "Fuck." Then he put his hands on his hips and asked, "You know this kid?"

She shook her head.

"Speak to him?" Chace continued.

She shook her head again but replied, "Every time I've tried to approach, he runs away. I tried again today and chased him. He was terrified. He outran me then disappeared."

Jesus, she'd chased him? The town's pretty, curvy, quiet librarian chased a kid?

He verbalized his question. "You chased him?"

"Yeah, out of the library and into town. He disappeared the minute he turned onto Main Street. Well, not the minute, seeing as I was half a block behind him, but close after. And I told him he wasn't in trouble but he still ran."

"You chased him." It was a statement this time.

"Yeah," she answered anyway then he watched her body give a small jolt and she whispered, "Oh no, was that the wrong thing to do?"

"Sorry, honey, but you gotta know in case the opportunity comes up again. A kid being beaten and malnourished, which gives us an indication who's likely beating him, and not taken care of, which pretty much solidifies who's beating him, should not be chased. It's clear he's not livin' a good life. It's likely that life is filled with a good deal of fear. And him borrowin' library books outside of acceptable practice says to me whatever's happening at home means he doesn't trust anyone so he takes every opportunity to dodge connecting even if it means checking out a library book."

As he spoke he saw her eyes had grown wide, her lips had parted and she was staring up at him with that appealing wonder she'd stared at him with yesterday morning.

And alone in a small interrogation room while discussing an abused child it was far more appealing.

Then she whispered her cute, "Oh."

At this point he was seeing his error at giving them privacy. Top to toe, she was an itch he'd wanted to scratch for a long time. Faye Goodknight talking and reacting two feet away, her voice coming at him, her face expressive, her scent filling the room, she wasn't an itch.

She was a craving.

Chace buried it and asked, "He keeps coming around?"

She blinked and asked back, "What?"

"This kid, you said you've tried to approach, the times you didn't chase him down the street, he kept coming back?"

He saw her bubblegum lips twitch but she nodded and added her, "Yeah."

"Right," he muttered, reaching into his jacket pocket to pull out his phone. "He comes back, you don't approach. You call me."

"Call you?"

"Yeah," he bent his head to his phone and activated it, saying, "I wanna get a look at him. See if I know him or who his kin might be. Maybe find a way to make my own approach."

"He doesn't look familiar."

Chace lifted his head and looked at her. "You lived here

your whole life, Faye, but still, it's likely I've met more folk around here than you have."

"This is true," she said softly.

Christ.

Cute.

"Give me your number," he ordered.

She blinked.

Then she whispered, "What?"

"Your phone number. Give it to me. I'll call you, you'll have mine you can store in your cell."

"Can't you just give me yours and I'll program it in my cell?" she suggested.

"I could. But, darlin', things the way they've been…" he trailed off, shook his head and let that speak for itself. She might live in her books but the shit that's gone down, he knew from the limited conversations they'd had, had not escaped her notice. "I'm not big on surprises. You need to call me, when my phone rings, I like to know what I'm dealin' with before I answer it. I got your number, it'll come up on caller ID."

She nodded and pressed her lips together before she said quietly, "That makes sense."

Then she stood there staring at him.

"Faye, your number?" he prompted, and her body gave a slight start.

"Oh," she whispered. "Right." Then she gave him her number.

Chace punched it in and hit go. Her purse rang and he heard her making the moves to pull her phone out but he disconnected the call before she answered it. Then he hit buttons and programmed her into his phone while he heard her hitting buttons programming him in hers.

This meant access to Faye Goodknight's voice whenever he wanted it.

Fuck.

He buried that as he shoved his phone back in his pocket and looked again at her.

"I also need you to bag a book he's stolen and bring it to me," he told her.

Her head cocked slightly to the side and she asked, "Why?"

"'Cause he might have hit the system. We can lift prints, we might find out who he is, which might lead us to where he is."

"Oh," she again whispered, then another, "Right. Okay. I'll do that."

"Try not to handle it too much."

"Uh...Chace, our books, at least some of them, are handled a lot."

"We'll sort out what we find, don't worry about that."

She nodded again.

"I need a physical description of the kid too. I'll give it to the boys. They can keep their eyes peeled."

More nodding then she described the kid and his behavior. Nothing she said struck him as familiar to any kid he'd seen. Seeing as everything she said was not good, if he'd seen him he would have noted him.

When she was done speaking, he started.

"I'll talk to the boys, see if they've seen anything or heard anything. I'll also do some digging to see if any reports were made. Way things were, they could have been ignored or buried. I'll do what I can to uncover it if they have. Tomorrow, I'll call Child Protective Services to see if they've had any reports we haven't acted on or any at all. I'll also swing by the school to talk to the principal and ask him to talk to his teachers to see if any of them have concerns, either reported or unreported. In the meantime, you bag a book he stole and call me. Tell me when you can bring it in. When you do, I'll have an artist here who can take your description and give us a picture we can go on. That all good with you?"

"A police artist?" she asked, again looking at him with that expression of adorable, effective wonder.

"A police artist, yeah," he answered, expending not a small amount of effort to ignore her look. "You might not think you're good at describing someone but they're trained to pull it out of you and they're good at what they do."

"A police artist," she whispered.

"Yeah," Chace replied.

"And fingerprints." She was still whispering.

"Yeah, Faye, got no clue who this kid is. Gotta do something to find him, find out what's happening to him and put a stop to it. We don't have a name. We don't have an address. So we have to work with what we've got."

She was *still* whispering when she repeated, "Put a stop to it."

Now Chace was confused. She seemed stunned. Not in a bad way, that wonder was still clear in her expression. But stunned all the same.

"Uh, yeah, Faye. That's why you came here and reported this, isn't it? To put a stop to bad shit happening to a kid. So, let's set about doin' that, yeah?"

He stopped speaking and she said nothing, just stared up at him, those blue eyes big and locked on him.

But Chace was done. Done with this conversation. Done with gathering info and giving detail on what they were going to do. And especially done with being in a private room with the town's pretty librarian looking at him like he parted the Colorado River so she could get to the other side without the unnecessary hassle of getting wet. Something only her own personal miracle worker could offer her.

But Faye Goodknight was not done.

He'd know this when suddenly she was not two feet

away but in his space. So far in his space, her soft body was pressed the length of his, her arms were around his shoulders, one hand curled around the back of his neck, fingers in his hair, putting pressure on to bend his head. And last, her mouth was pressed hard to his.

What the fuck?

He put his hands to her hips to push her away, his mind filled with how he could do that as gently as possible when her tongue came out and the tip touched his lips.

And at that, Chace's body and mouth made another decision before his mind could catch up. This being his arms closing around her tight, his mouth opening over hers, his tongue spiking out, pushing hers back into her mouth and then he kissed her, very hard, very wet and very, very deep.

She didn't taste like bubblegum.

She tasted like bubblemint. Sweet and fresh and fucking fantastic.

He kept one of his arms locked tight around her waist while he slid the other hand up her spine, her neck and into her hair.

Fucking hell, silk.

Better than he imagined.

Better than he could even dream.

He bent forward slightly, arching her over his arm, forcing her body deeper into his and she moaned a sweet, soft moan against his tongue.

It was the best thing he'd ever tasted in his life.

In some faraway, vague recess of his mind that wasn't intent on her body pressed against his, the feel of her hair in his hand, the taste of her on his tongue and what all that was doing to his body, he realized she had no clue what she was doing. She was along for his ride. A willing, eager participant, giving, opening herself to him and doing nothing more but letting him take what he wanted.

It was, by far, the best kiss he'd ever had.

And on that thought, his brain caught up to his mouth and body and he tore his mouth from hers as he curled his fingers into her waist and shoved her back roughly.

She retreated three steps, her body not in control with the force of his shove, before she righted herself.

But she wasn't feeling his shove. She hadn't even processed the fact she was no longer in his arms.

She was staring at him, rose in her cheeks, mouth soft and swollen, lips parted, eyes hooded, visibly affected by his kiss, which meant she wore the fact that she was supremely turned on all over her face.

Just from one kiss.

It was a fucking good look.

It was the kind of look a man would get once and then fight and die to have aimed his way on a regular basis.

Fuck him.

Fuck *him*.

"What the fuck was that?" he clipped, and she blinked but that look didn't leave her face.

"What?" she whispered.

"What...the fuck...*was that*?" he ground out.

"I—" she started, blinking again, but he didn't let her continue.

"Don't do that shit again, Faye," he growled, took a step toward her and pointed in her face. "Do not do that shit again." He dropped his hand but put his face where his hand had been and kept growling. "I don't know what bullshit game you're playin', following me around, suddenly everywhere I am. But straight up, I'm not playin' it. You got some romantic idea I'm a wounded soul you can heal with..." he shook his head and flipped out a hand, "your limited charms, think again. I already told you, I do not want your concern. I do not want your company. And I do not want your inexperienced bullshit fumbling. Trust me, I had in my bed the master at that shit and she got nowhere. And you, just now, got as much as you'll ever get. Get this in your head, Faye, all I want from you is for you to leave me the fuck alone."

He didn't allow the look on her face to register. He didn't know what was happening with her. What he did know was, for her sake, he had to make his point clear. And if that meant being a dick, he had to be a dick.

So he was a dick.

He turned around and prowled to the door.

But at it, he braced, turned back and looked at her. He ignored the pain back in her features and the fact that it was magnified to such an extreme, if he wasn't set on ignoring it, honest to Christ, it would have brought him to his knees.

"You get a book, you call Frank Dolinski. I'll brief him, he'll be your point of contact from now on," he informed her, turned, yanked open and strode through the door, through the station and straight outside where he walked to his truck.

And while he did this, he didn't give one fuck that Jon's eyes followed him the whole way nor did he care what that would mean tomorrow would bring.

CHAPTER THREE

Drift Away

YOU'RE GIVING UP?!?!?

I stared at the message box on my computer and sighed.

Yes, I was giving up. A week ago, Chace had laid it out. I didn't get it. I wasn't experienced enough to know. It felt for a good while there, when his arms were around me tight, his lips locked to mine, his hand in my hair, that he was into kissing me...

Kissing me.

And oh, my, fraking Lord, what a *kiss*.

And to be that good, it seemed he had to be into it. Into me. Like Lexie said. *Way* into me in a hungry-heart, longing, soul-destroying-if-you-can't-have-it, put-your-life-on-the-line-to-get-it kind of into me, well, *into me*.

Then I suddenly wasn't in his arms and he was making it perfectly clear he was not into me.

Not at all.

Not even a teeny, tiny bit.

And I had a wise father who liberally shared his wisdom, a wise mother who shared her wisdom through deed rather than action and I also had a master's in library science.

I was no dummy.

I got it.

So I was giving up.

I lifted my hands to the keyboard and typed to my on-line friend Benji, *We weren't getting anywhere anyway.*

We were! He typed back. *It has to be someone in the Elite who hired the hit. And we've already discovered some of the players! The money behind the corruption. The money that paid for a clean hit. We have to keep digging.*

I'd met Benji on a forum celebrating everything that was the new *Battlestar Galactica* or, as Benji called it, "The best television show fraking *ever*."

I disagreed. I loved *Battlestar Galactica* but *Firefly* was by far and away the best television show *ever*, which made its midseason cancellation an act (I thought) of sacrilege. Fortunately, they made a movie about it. And also fortunately, Nathan Fillion moved on to another awesome show, *Castle*.

But nothing topped *Firefly*.

Nothing.

Years ago, my relationship with Benji had gone off-forum and grown so I'd introduced him to my other on-line friend, SerenityWash. I'd met her on a *Firefly* forum, and that was her screen name. Me thinking she was a "her" was the fact that she could perv on Nathan Fillion for hours in a way that I wasn't sure but I thought could not be gay love. Serenity and I were friends, close. We'd "known" each other years and we messaged each other all the time, talking about life, jobs, family, thoughts, feelings, emotions, but I didn't know her real name, her gender, where she lived or anything tangible about her. All of this she gave hints at but at the same time guarded like it was a state secret. So I never knew if the hints were real or if she was trying to throw me off track.

SerenityWash was her screen name, the name of the spaceship in *Firefly*, *Serenity*, plus her favorite character from the show, Wash.

Benji's screen name, by the way, was AdmiralAdama-forPresident. Seeing as this was a pain in the behind to type out, I'd made him give me his real name. And I knew he was a man since he perved on Number Six from that show in a way no woman could.

He'd also told me his full name was Benjamin, and I didn't know any girls named Benjamin so I was thinking his gender was not in question.

Over the years, I'd kept them up to date on the goings-on in Carnal. I'd also shared my long-distance, unrequited love for Detective Chace Keaton. They'd gotten interested, especially when things heated up and finally exploded. That included the news that Misty Keaton was dead and her husband was free to be, they hoped, with me.

They'd stayed interested, maybe unhealthily, and talked me into doing the same. And the unhealthy part about this was that they were both good at computers. They lived on the fringe of society, devoted themselves to on-line communities and geek television. They were always gearing up for then rabidly attending any geek convention that came their way. They also indulged in such other pursuits as, say, hacking and amateur sleuthing.

This led me to my middle-of-the-night trip, one of many, to the scene of the crime. I, of course, had no clue what I was looking for. Serenity, of course, watched *Bones* and told me you could catch a murderer by examining dirt. I didn't have three doctorates in entomology, botany and mineralogy like the fictional Jack Hodgins did on that show, nor did I have a space age lab to take a sample to be tested, so I had no idea what they expected me to do with the dirt at Harker's Wood. I did, however, live in Carnal and, head in a book, fingers on a keyboard with on-line friends, eyes trained to geek TV or not, I still knew a lot of the bad guys seeing as they were police and made their presence smotheringly known. So this also meant I knew most of them were idiots. And idiots couldn't commit murder and get away with it.

So up to Harker's Wood I went when no one could see me. I looked around, combed that wood so thoroughly that by now I knew it like the back of my hand.

But I never found anything.

I also, like Benji and Serenity, never gave up.

Until now.

I hadn't shared the recent events because both of them were openly hoping that our activities would reach a desirable conclusion, make Chace take notice of me and then, promptly, fall head over heels in love with me.

Obviously, this wasn't going to happen.

So now it was time for us to stop trying to do what we were never going to do anyway. Even if Benji had hacked into the Carnal Police Department's computer server and

Serenity had somehow managed to hack into and follow along with conversations and text messages on more than a dozen cell phones.

And what we were trying to do that we'd never do was find Misty Keaton's murderer.

Furthermore, even before the recent unpleasant and confusing (but unfortunately, for several beautiful moments, also excruciatingly exciting) Chace Encounters, I was getting worried.

This was because Serenity was turning up names that my own lame Internet searches showed were wealthy, powerful people. Big money. Old money. Judges. Businessmen. Politicians. Power brokers.

Serenity was convinced that the now-dead ringleader of a dirty band of dirty cops, Arnold Fuller, had these guys in his pocket. And Serenity was convinced that even though Fuller was very dead, a man like him couldn't yank the chains of men like that unless he had the goods on them. And last, Serenity was convinced that these goods did not die with Fuller.

They were out there.

She also thought that if we found Misty's murderer, we'd find this. In the brouhaha that followed Ty Walker's exoneration and the exposure of corruption in Carnal, none of this came out.

So Serenity was convinced there was another shoe that would drop and the best way for a shoe to drop without causing any damage was to aim it yourself.

As you could imagine, this did not fill me with glee. It didn't even fill me with trepidation. It filled me with the desire to run screaming from this pet project and never look back.

Alas, Benji and Serenity were dug in. Fortunately, Serenity's real identity was hidden so far behind a wall of her computer cunning that it was likely no one could hack it.

And Benji lived in England so, hopefully, the long reach of Colorado money and power wouldn't extend that far.

But I was done. Chace had called my charms "limited" and my kiss "bullshit fumbling" so I wasn't actually done. I was *done*. I didn't want any reminders of him. Luckily, I worked in the library, a building, to my knowledge, he'd never stepped foot inside of in thirteen years. And since I was the only paid employee at the library, I figured it was safe to say he never had and therefore never would. And I wasn't going back to the diner. I was also giving up La-La Land Coffee. This stunk. Shambles and Sunny's coffee was awesome, and Shambles's baked goods were to die for.

But these were the only times my path could cross with any regularity with Chace Keaton's so until the burn of his words faded away, I was avoiding them.

Benji and Serenity, I couldn't control. They were adults (I hoped) and they were far from stupid. Maybe less involved in the real world even than I was but not stupid.

And for my part, I'd just keep warning them.

Benji, we weren't, I typed. *And I'm not comfortable with what we're uncovering and you shouldn't be comfortable with it either. It's really none of our business. Things are good in Carnal again. I have a strong feeling, a very strong one, we should let this sleeping dog lie.*

But what about Chace? Benji typed back, and I closed my eyes.

Then I opened them in order to lie again.

He has a girlfriend.

What!?!?!?!

I pulled in a breath and kept lying.

Yeah. I saw him with her the other day. They look really close. She's super pretty.

OMG! Why didn't you say anything?!?!?

I just needed some time to give up a dream.

Oh Inara (this, by the way, was my screen name because Nathan Fillion's character was in love with the character Inara on *Firefly*—actually, my full screen name was Inara000 since there were a gazillion Inaras out there) *don't say that. Is this thing new with him? Maybe it won't work out.*

That isn't part of caring about someone, Benji, even if you care about them from afar, hoping they won't be happy. He wasn't happy with Misty. Now he looks happy with this new lady. He's moving on. I should too.

Don't give up hope. You never know, Benji replied.

No, what I know is, I've been home from college for seven years and he hasn't noticed me. He's been a widower for seven months and he hasn't noticed me. This means he's probably never going to notice me. I have a life to live too, Ben. And I should probably start living it.

My eyes remained on the screen as nothing came back from Benji for a while then it did.

I'm sorry, Faye. But you're probably right. Still, I hope you find someone spectacular because you deserve that and when Chace Keaton finally gets his head straight and notices you, then he can feel a little of what you're feeling now, knowing you're happy and that happy isn't ever going to be with him.

I wouldn't hold my breath for that to happen.

This I did not share with Benji.

A Benji that, reading his words, I was reminded of all the reasons why, even though I'd never met him and probably never would, I loved him.

Instead, I typed, *It's getting late here, Ben. I need to go to bed.*

Right, he returned, *I'll let you go. Back tomorrow?*

Probably, I answered, and I probably would be back tomorrow. Sitting in my apartment at my computer talking to people I knew well but had never met. Nor would I probably ever meet, seeing as they were social misfits.

Like me.

Twenty-nine and never been laid. I'd hardly ever been kissed, and I was pining for a man I'd never have who was real and another one who was a fictional character on a long-since-cancelled television show.

"Yep," I whispered as I typed, *Later, Ben.* "I need to get a life."

I read his farewell then shut down my computer.

Then I wandered to my couch.

There was one thing in my life that could be considered kickass. This was my apartment.

It was the space over Holly's Flower Shop on Main Street. This meant, on frequent occasions, it smelled like flowers. It also meant I could walk to work. Considering my car was a dark green junker Jeep Cherokee my dad handed down to me seven years ago upon my graduation from college, being able to walk to work and anywhere else I needed to go in my narrow life was a good thing.

My apartment was all one room, mostly. Four thin but tall arched windows in the front facing Main Street. All the walls were exposed red brick. The floors were beaten-up wood planks that, before she rented it to me, Holly had refinished so, although they were distressed, they were also gleaming and gorgeous. I'd thrown a bunch of mismatched, multicolored, multi-shaped but pretty and bright rugs here and there to warm up the room.

There was a kitchen at the back delineated from the room by a high counter with stools in front of it. It was big because the space was big. It had lots of ivory-painted cabinets with nicks and scratches in them that looked cool rather than beaten up and some of the cabinets were glass fronted so you could see my vivid collection of stoneware displayed. It also had a huge island in the middle and lots of counter space. The kitchen was awesome.

Next to the kitchen was a small utility room. It was tucked in the nook created by the wood-paneled room that bit into the space that was a big bathroom.

The bathroom had a pedestal sink and a deep, fabulous claw-footed tub that was the dreamland of tubs for people (like me) who liked to take baths.

By the windows at the front was my bright pink, slouchy, pillow-backed couch and three comfy armchairs (one royal blue, one aubergine and one bright teal), all with ottomans surrounding a variety of pretty but random mismatching tables. I read a lot so I needed a lot of different choices of where to read. With my seating area, I had it.

In the middle of the space sitting on a large, thick area rug in a rich forest green was my queen-size bed. It had scrolled, ivory-painted iron head- and footboards and wide but not deep ivory-painted but distressed nightstands on each side. One nightstand had a big lamp with a fluted glass base. The other had a lamp on it that was round, matte pink ceramic that looked like punched-out eyelet, the bulb inside it so the lamp threw pretty patterns on the wall when lit (like now). The bed had bunches of pillows of all shapes and sizes, soft sheets I indulged in that cost a fortune but felt great and a down comforter covered in a mint green cover with purple, pink and blue flowers on it.

The wall to the side of the bed close to the seating area was filled with shelves that had my extensive collection of books, my stereo, CDs, DVDs, some framed photos and geek items like a small-scale model of the *Serenity* ship from *Firefly* and a frame with a mounted chakram, Xena, Warrior Princess's awesome weapon.

The wall to the other side had a huge, antique wardrobe that my dad had to dismantle and put together to get it in there.

The wall opposite the shelves by the living area held my big, awesome shabby chic desk, computer and its paraphernalia. On the other side, between the front door and bathroom, was my antique distressed dresser. It had on top another fabulous lamp with a delicate, etched crystal vase I'd bought for a song because it didn't work but I bought it because I knew my dad could fix it. And he did.

Nothing matched, not even the stools around the kitchen counter. I had random, quirky bits and bobs here and there, decorating surfaces and walls. If I had to give the look a name, I'd call it "Distressed Mountain Girlie Kickass Chic."

And I loved it.

Which was good, I thought as I wandered to my couch, snatched up my iPod and threw myself down on it on my back, since I spent so much fraking time in it.

I stared up at the ceiling, smelling my candle burning (apple) and snatching up one of the many packs of gum around my house, unwrapping a piece and popping it into my mouth.

Bubblemint. I loved the taste, rejoiced when I discovered it, was addicted to it and chewed it all the time, even after midnight on a Thursday while I lay on my couch wondering what on earth I was going to do with the rest of my life.

It was likely that tomorrow Lexie, Laurie, Krystal or a mixture of them or all of them would be in the library. Not to mention they could bring the rare but plausible additions of their other friends, Wendy, Maggie, Stella, Betty, Sunny, Avril, Amber, Jazz, Kayeleen or God forbid, the crazy Twyla, who scared me more than Krystal.

I'd been blowing them off now for a week, telling them I was busy with library stuff. Seeing as we were having increasingly frightening but strangely vague funding issues, this, thankfully, was not a lie. But it also meant their occasional visits became a lot more frequent and one, the other or several of them, together and separate, had been in the last two days back to back.

Laurie and Krystal had told me that word was buzzing through town, which meant Bubba's biker bar and Carnal Spa then reaching out to the moon, that I'd gone to the station and talked to Chace.

Word was, from their sharing it with me, correct. That word stated that I had gone in to make a report. Chace and I had been behind closed doors for ten minutes. Chace had stalked out, looking pissed, and immediately gone to his SUV. Then I had wandered out moments later looking like I'd been slapped and quickly exited the premises without looking back.

At this news, I'd lied and told them it wasn't true at all. I told them about the boy I'd seen (and killed two birds with one stone by asking them to look out for him and call me if they saw him) and that was why I went there. Nothing had happened. Chace was looking into it and in the meantime I'd given Frank Dolinski a book and an artist had sketched a (very good) picture of the boy. All this done while Chace was absent from the station.

They didn't buy it, and although I had to admit I liked that they came around, I knew the pressure would increase and I wasn't looking forward to that.

But being the librarian in a small town wasn't nine hours a day, Tuesday through Saturday, of fun and laughter. Them coming broke up the day. They were funny. They were open, real and, unlike me, normal. And they liked me, which felt nice. It wasn't like I didn't have any friends. But all my friends from high school had either moved away or were in committed relationships so I didn't have much in common with them. We spent time together, just not very much. My other friends were accessed through a computer keyboard.

So it felt nice to feel like a part of their group.

I just didn't want to share about what happened with Chace. Maybe I would, one day, when it didn't hurt so much to think about it. Maybe I'd invite them over for dinner and margaritas and we'd get hammered and I'd spill the beans.

That sounded like a good idea. An open, real, *normal* thing for a girl who had a life to do. Have her girls over, dinner, drinks, drunkenness and confessing your most mortifying, painful life moments so they could tell you all men are losers and make you another drink.

I popped my earphones in and since I should be winding down rather than gearing up, which was where my thoughts were taking me, I put on one of my unwind playlists.

This worked until it came up in the queue.

Ella Mae Bowen's rendition of "Holding Out for a Hero."

Lying there like I did all the time, alone, late at night, in my kickass but lonesome apartment, her beautiful voice filled with longing, singing words I'd never really listened to, hit me like a bullet tearing clean through my flesh leaving a raw ache in its wake.

I didn't even try to control the tears that filled my eyes. I didn't feel the sting of them in my nose. I just let them fall as the ceiling above me went watery and the longing in Ella Mae's voice, the beautiful yearning of the words, ripped me to shreds.

I'd seen Chace Keaton at sixteen years old—incidentally, Ella Mae's age when she recorded that song—and I convinced myself I found my hero and he was always there, just out of reach.

But he wasn't just out of reach and if I kept hoping, kept reaching, eventually his fingers would close warm, strong and firm around mine.

He was just plain out of reach.

He lived in the same town but he was miles and miles and miles away.

When Ella Mae was done, I played her again.

And again.

Then again.

Then, tears in my eyes, I got up, blew out the candle and walked to the distressed, whimsical set of hooks Dad had mounted by my door. I grabbed my long, pastel green scarf and wrapped it around and around my neck, this pressing the cords of the earphones to the skin under it.

I replayed it as I grabbed my pine green wool pea coat, tugged it on, maneuvered the iPod around while I buttoned it up, nabbed my mittens that matched the scarf and pulled them on. Then I grabbed my keys.

I listened to it playing as I pulled open the door and walked out, locked the door, shoved the keys into my pocket and took off down the stairs that led to the back alley and my Cherokee.

I replayed it as I rounded the side alley and walked swiftly, shoulders scrunched, arms held up in front of me, hands clasped, through the fierce, arid cold that dried the tears on my face.

I replayed it when I turned off Main Street and walked through the quiet, dark streets to the elementary school. I listened to the words yet again as I slipped through the opening in the chain link fence and headed to the playground.

I was listening to it when I stopped at the swing set, lifted my mittened hand and rested it on one of the high swing set poles and dropped my head, pressing my forehead against my mitten. Listening and aching and knowing that there was nothing worse in the whole, wide world than the death of hope.

And I was listening to it when a hand wrapped firm and strong around my bicep but I also heard my low, surprised cry ringing in my head if not in my ears when I felt the touch and that hand didn't hesitate to whip me around.

Then I stared up at Chace Keaton's angry face.

What the frak?

I blinked up at him and I did this twice before I realized his mouth was moving.

He was talking to me.

"What?" I asked, automatically talking very loudly over music he couldn't hear.

His head jerked, his eyes narrowed even as they moved all around the vicinity of my head. I felt his hand leave my arm then suddenly Ella Mae was gone because he'd lifted both his hands and pulled out my earbuds.

Then I heard him growl, "Jesus, it's worse."

I wasn't following. I hadn't gone from denying my lonesomeness to understanding it to the core of my being, letting go a dream, feeling that ache throb through me, beating at me in a way I knew I'd feel it forever to standing in the cold in the elementary school playground staring at an angry Chace Keaton.

"What's worse?" I whispered.

"You, takin' a walk alone in the dark of night in a town full of bikers who like to get drunk, rowdy and laid and doin' it with your earphones in and music so loud you couldn't hear someone approach even if he was wearin' a fuckin' cowbell."

He was right, of course. I could actually hear Ella Mae now, and the earbuds weren't even in my ears.

Quickly, with my thumb, I paused my iPod but I replied to Chace, "Bikers are friendly."

"No, Faye, they're not."

"But I've been living here my whole life and so have a bunch of bikers. They are."

"Yeah, the ones who live here don't shit where they live. The ones who come here from other places don't give a fuck where they shit. 'Course, this would mean that something happened to you, the local bikers would have to throw down, seeing as someone harmed one of their own, so wherever they tracked the others to, all hell would break loose. After you created that nightmare, in the meantime, you wouldn't be doing too fuckin' good."

"You curse a lot," I whispered, and his head jerked again just as his eyes narrowed again.

"What?" he clipped.

"Nothing," I muttered and bit my lip.

His eyes dropped to my lips then sliced back up to mine.

Suddenly my hand was caught in a strong, firm grip and tugged while he stated, "I'm walking you home."

Since his hand was tugging mine and his body was tall, lean and muscular and it was moving, I had no choice but to follow it.

But I did protest as my feet moved double time to keep up with his long strides, "That's okay. Really. It isn't far and I won't listen to music."

He stopped abruptly, jerking my hand, which made me stop abruptly, and he bent his neck so his handsome face was an inch from mine.

His eyes were angry.

No, furious.

I stopped breathing.

"I'm . . . walking . . . you . . . home," he said low, slow, each word deliberate.

I did the only thing I could do. I nodded.

His face started to move back then his eyes narrowed again and, to the further detriment of my ability to breathe, it got even closer. His eyes moved over my features then they came back to mine.

"You been cryin'?" he asked, his voice low still but now soft.

I stared up at him and it hit me that he'd pulled us closer to the sidewalk where there were streetlamps so he could see me.

"No."

There it was again!

Another lie!

Chace called me on it and he did it again in that low, soft voice that made his normally deep attractive voice deeper and far, far more attractive.

"Honey, I got eyes."

I really liked it when he called me honey. He'd done it twice now and both times felt like gifts.

Of course, he probably called everyone honey if they were female. So it wasn't a gift. It was throwaway. Meaningless.

I pulled in breath and straightened my shoulders.

"Okay then, Chace. I have been crying. But the fact I have and the reasons why I was are none of your business. So if you're fired up to do your duty as an officer of the law and make sure I'm safe, then walk me home. But, if you wouldn't mind, I'll pass on the interrogation."

"There's the backbone," he muttered.

"What?" I snapped.

"Nothin'." He was still muttering as he moved away, yanked on my hand and we started walking again.

I wanted to ask what he was doing roaming the streets in the middle of the night but I didn't. I wanted to ask where his SUV was since I scanned for it as we walked through town in the cold and didn't see it, but I didn't do that either. I wanted to ask him to let go of my hand, but I didn't do that either.

I just walked at his side with my hand held firm in his big, warm one and I promised myself I wouldn't do anything stupid and dramatic. Like let my emotions and a beautiful, soul-wrenching song send me out into the night on an ill-advised walk. Which did nothing to clear my head seeing as I listened to the song that was wrenching my soul repeatedly while I did it.

In fact, I was deciding (dramatically, of course) from then on in, as we rounded the side alley to get to the back alley that led to my apartment, that I was listening to nothing but upbeat music for the rest of forever. I was so intent on deciding this that it didn't occur to me that I wasn't leading Chace to the alley where I lived.

He was leading me.

We'd turned into the back alley and got four steps in when we heard a crash.

Chace's arm instantly jerked mine, pulling me back. He stepped forward and in front of me as he let go of my hand and his went to the gun at his hip.

But I saw, peering around him, a head pop up from the other side of the Dumpster that was behind the Italian restaurant.

I knew that head.

"Holy frak!" I shouted. "That's him!"

The boy from the library took off at my voice, and I didn't hesitate to take off after him.

"*Jesus, Faye!*" Chace roared from behind me but I kept right on going, arms pumping, feet sprinting.

I heard the beat of Chace's boots then I saw him pass me and keep after the kid who darted around the corner of the side street. I watched Chace make the turn after him then I turned after them and saw Chace make another turn down Main Street.

I followed and saw Chace, well, chasing the kid down Main Street.

"You're not in trouble!" I yelled. "We just want to help! It's okay!" I kept yelling as the kid made a quick dash up a side street and disappeared, Chace still after him, thus, seconds later, turning and disappearing too.

I made the dash as well and saw them racing up the side street.

Two blocks up, Chace was nearly on him when the kid put his hands to a fence, catapulted himself over and dashed through someone's yard.

Chace didn't delay in following him and disappearing into the yard.

Once I made it there, it took me four tries to get over that fence and I eventually had to heft my ass on it and swing my legs over. I had a feeling I tore the seat of my jeans when I did but I dropped to the other side and took off after them.

I lost them in the dark backyard, stopped and tried to listen over my labored breathing, hoping I'd hear a noise that told me which direction they'd gone.

I heard nothing.

I stayed there a long time.

I still heard nothing.

Frak!

It hit me I was in someone's backyard after midnight and I shouldn't be. It also hit me that Chace was chasing after some kid and not only had I lost him but he'd lost me. Therefore it hit me I had no idea what to do.

I gave it some time just in case Chace came back, hopefully with the kid so we could get him warm, fed (he was Dumpster diving!) and talk to him, but Chace didn't come back.

So I quickly retraced our steps (avoiding the fence and belatedly noticing it opened at the drive and taking that route, which I should have taken earlier). I went back jogging just in case Chace had the same thought as me and was headed the same way. I also did it scanning, hoping I'd catch sight of one, the other or, better yet, both.

I didn't.

What I did was go to the bottom of the stairs that led up to my apartment in the back alley, paced and waited.

I did this for about ten minutes. I had my iPod and my earphones detangled from my clothing and shoved in the back pocket of my jeans by the time I saw Chace round the corner of the side alley and prowl toward me.

Believe it or not, men could prowl. I knew this by the way he was doing it.

He was five feet away when he ordered low, angry and confusingly, "Ass up the stairs."

"What?" I asked.

"Get your ass up the stairs, open your door, in your apartment."

That seemed like a good idea since it would be warm up there so I turned, raced up the stairs, dug out my keys, yanked off my mittens and opened the door.

I went in and Chace followed me.

He also slammed my door.

I tossed my mittens across the room to a chair, turned to him and my first thought when I took him in fully was, *Uh-oh*.

"You chased him again," he remarked quietly.

"I, uh…didn't think."

"Kid's terrified outta his mind and not only did you chase him, you shouted at him."

I pressed my lips together.

"In the dark," Chace went on.

I shrugged my shoulders up and kept them there.

"In an alley," Chace continued.

I made no move or noise.

"In the cold," Chace kept going.

I dropped my shoulders and unpressed my lips but slid the bottom one slightly to the side so I could bite the end.

"After midnight," Chace (hopefully) finished.

"Uh…" I mumbled but had no idea what to say. All that was true and, looking back, seemed more than slightly ridiculous.

"Kid like that knows this town like the back of his hand. Kid like that, fear that huge, he'll fight and scratch and die before anyone he doesn't know lays a hand on him. Kid like that needs care and communication. He needs to feel safe.

He does not need anyone chasing him and shouting at him. He won't hear your words, just your tone. And he'll know what chasing means and he'll do everything in his power not to get caught."

"So that's why you didn't, uh...catch him?" I asked stupidly.

"That's why," he answered shortly then elaborated. "He hit the dark of that backyard, he was vapor."

"Oh," I whispered thinking, maybe, he was actually still in that backyard and hiding.

"Get that outta your head," Chace broke into my thoughts. "I went back and looked. He's gone."

"Oh," I repeated on a whisper, now thinking it was weird Chace Keaton could read my thoughts.

"Jesus, Faye, you want me to help this kid, you gotta help me help this kid. And makin' him more scared is not the way to go about doin' that."

"Okay," I agreed quietly then hesitantly asked, "So, um...what *is* the way to go about doing that?"

"I don't know. Seein' him, that is not a kid who's escaped an abusive home. Or it's not the only shit in his life. He's terrified, of what, I have no clue. But whatever it is, it's huge or at least it is in his head. We have to find some way to establish trust so he'll let us approach or he'll come forward."

"Food," I said instantly, and his head jerked.

"What?"

"Food. I'll put out food. And...and...a coat!" I cried. "He needs a coat. I'll go buy him one. I'll put it out by the Dumpster."

"Honey, he's not goin' back to that Dumpster. Not again. Not ever."

"Oh," I whispered as my mind raced and I came up with another idea. "At the library. By the return bin. He returns his books. He hasn't been back in a week because, well, I chased him last time and he hasn't returned any books either. But he will. He always does. I'll put food and a coat out by the bin. And...and...more books. I'll find ones like he likes to take and I'll put them out there. With a note telling him he can find what he needs there and if he needs anything he's not finding, to leave a return note and it'll be left for him."

I watched Chace jerk up his chin before he said, "That's a good idea."

I grinned at him and said, "Thanks."

His eyes dropped to my mouth, it seemed strangely that his body went still then his eyes came back to mine and he asked instantly, "Why were you crying?"

I felt my grin die and I took a step back, murmuring, "Chace—"

"Why were you crying?" he repeated.

I took another step back saying, "I don't think—"

My heart started to beat harder when he took a step toward me and he asked again, "Why were you crying, Faye?"

I started actively retreating as Chace started actively advancing and I said, "I think I told you that's none of your business."

"Faye, why were you crying?"

I hit the foot stand of my bed and was forced to stop.

Chace didn't stop until he was toe to toe with me, neck bent, eyes locked to mine.

"I'll ask one more time, honey," he said gently. "Why were you crying?"

I felt it prudent, considering his proximity, to answer.

So I did.

"I was listening to a song that made me cry."

His brows went up. "A song that made you cry, leave your house in the dead of night and walk to the elementary school playground?"

To this, I offered lamely, "It's a good song."

His eyes moved over my face as his lips whispered, "It's a good song."

I held my breath unsure what was happening but I was sure what was happening to my heartbeat. It was escalating. And my skin, it was tingling. And my blood, it was firing.

I stopped holding my breath and pulled in a needed one.

Then I straightened my shoulders and said quietly, "I'm home safe now, Chace. You can go."

His eyes came back to mine and he didn't go.

Instead, he asked, "What song was it?"

No way in heck I was sharing that.

"Dobie Gray's 'Drift Away.'"

There it was again. Another fraking lie!

His eyes lit and his mouth twitched before he asked, "The song that moved you to tears and drove you into the cold night was a song about a man who gets through by listening to rock 'n' roll?"

I was realizing I really needed to pay more attention to lyrics when I answered with another lie, "Yes." Then to add validity to something that was nowhere near valid, I added, "My favorite part is when he sings while people clap."

And right then, in my apartment, I watched Chace Keaton throw back his handsome head and burst out laughing.

Seeing it, hearing the deep richness of it, my hands went behind me and curled into the iron of my footboard so they could assist my legs in keeping me standing.

I was prepared to ask him to leave when he stopped laughing (not that I wanted him to stop laughing, *ever*) but he got there before me by tipping his eyes back to mine and ordering through his laughter, "Put it on."

I blinked and my chest seized.

Therefore I had to force out my, "What?"

His eyes scanned my apartment, spied my stereo then came back to me.

He tilted his head to my stereo and repeated, "Put it on."

"Put what on?" I asked stupidly.

"'Drift Away.'"

Oh God!

"Um...I'm kind of tired," I informed him.

"Faye, honey, you just ran through a very cold night chasing an abused, terrified kid. You're not tired."

There it was, him reading me again.

"Um..."

"But I bet that song will help you relax and unwind."

He was right. It would. It was on my unwind playlist for that very purpose.

"Uh..."

"Put it on."

"Chace, I don't—"

"You don't, I find your iPod and I'll do it."

That got me moving for two reasons. One, this would require a body search, and my iPod was at my bottom. I didn't want Chace Keaton's hands anywhere near my bottom. Second, the song it was set at was "Holding Out for a Hero" which meant if he had my iPod, he'd catch me out in the lie and know, possibly, what really was making me cry.

So I slid out from in front of him, unbuttoned my coat, shrugged it off and threw it on my armchair. Then I unwound my scarf and did the same with that. Finally, I dug into my back pocket, pulled out my iPod and set up the song.

The strains of the guitar hit the space as I turned back to see Chace had taken off his coat, thrown it on my bed and he was leaning a hip against the footboard.

He looked good standing anywhere.

But he never looked better than standing right there.

Really, seriously, how was this happening?

"Forgot how much I like this song," he said through the music.

"Told you it was good," I muttered.

At my words, he suddenly pushed away from the bed and came at me.

I had to make a split-second decision. Run from the apartment (and I'd just taken off my coat), race to the bathroom and lock myself in, retreat again even though I had nowhere to go or hold my ground.

I took longer than the split second to make my decision and thus ended up doing the last and therefore was an available target when he reached down and grabbed my hand.

He yanked it firm but gentle and I flew toward him.

His other arm slid around me and suddenly I found myself, after midnight, in my apartment, dancing with Chace Keaton.

It wasn't just a close-to-each-other, hips-swaying dance. He swung me out, twirled me around, threw me wide and wound me back in. He was sure in his moves, strong, confident, and my body just moved how he wanted me to move. It didn't feel stilted, I wasn't nervous.

I just moved where he guided me like we'd danced together countless times. It felt natural. It felt right. It felt *great*.

So great, the song was so awesome, I got into it and started grinning, aiming this at him whenever my eyes caught his, which were always on me.

The slow bits, he held me close and swayed. The faster bits, he moved me around and when the clapping came, he pulled me close, his neck bending, his lips finding my ear and he whispered, "You're right, honey, this is definitely the best part."

My hand was resting on the hard wall of his chest, my head tipped back, his came up and we locked eyes.

Then I whispered, "See?"

He smiled.

I drowned.

Then he twirled me out when the tempo shifted up but we finished close, hips swaying. His arm was around me, his hand in mine holding it to his chest. My other hand was resting lightly on his shoulder. His jaw was pressed to the side of my hair and my eyes trained to the strong column of his throat.

The song faded away, our hips stopped swaying, but he didn't let me go.

I had no idea what was happening, how it came about, but that didn't mean I didn't close my eyes and commit every nuance of that moment to memory.

Then he said quietly in my ear, "For a long time, a long fuckin' time, Faye, nearly six years, I thought it was certain I'd never have anything as beautiful as the last three minutes. Thank you, honey, for giving that to me."

Once he'd dropped this confusing, exquisite bombshell, he moved away, went to his coat on my bed, tagged it, sauntered to my door and walked out of it, closing it behind him.

Not looking back.

CHAPTER FOUR

The Cherokee and Coffee

IT WAS FOUR days (well, technically three) after Chace Keaton said beautiful but bewildering words to me and sauntered out of my apartment.

In other words, it was Tuesday morning at eight thirty,

which was an hour before I had to get to work, preparing to open the library and I was in my Cherokee staking out the return bin in hopes of seeing the boy.

I was there on Tuesday because the library wasn't open on Mondays.

Also because I hadn't had time to come earlier.

This was because I was catching up on sleep, cleaning my house and going two kinds of shopping—grocery and for some kid I didn't know. My time was also spent having dinner with my parents including helping my mom make it and watching two movies with them after it. Not to mention, in order to keep my mind off things, I'd been to the gym twice and worked out for an hour rather than half that.

Further, I had a marathon session with Serenity to try to talk her down from uncovering dirt on scary, rich power brokers (this, incidentally, failed). I also had a marathon phone conversation with my sister Liza who lived in Gnaw Bone and was fighting with her husband (again). Though, not for the first time, even hearing it from Liza, I sided with Boyd. This wasn't unusual but I didn't tell Liza that. Not only that I sided with Boyd but also that it wasn't unusual I sided with him and maybe she should stop being such a drama queen.

That said, what did I know? I'd never even had a boyfriend. I was not in any position to be a marriage counselor.

So instead I played my normal role, the sister-bitching listener.

In the time between Chace leaving me Thursday night (or, more aptly, Friday very early morning) I'd gone out and bought the boy a new coat as well as a hat, scarf, gloves and three pairs of thick wool socks. I'd also guesstimated sizes and bought him two pairs of new jeans, two chunky, warm sweaters and some underwear.

With this, I added a pint of milk, three bottles of water, a package of bologna, a package of American cheese slices, a loaf of bread, a box of granola bars, three apples, a bunch of bananas, a cucumber (he wouldn't eat it but I had to make the effort of getting what my dad called "roughage" in him) and a ginormous bar of Hershey's chocolate (which he probably would eat).

I'd stuffed them in easy-to-carry bags and laid them out with some books that I didn't get from the library but bought. With this, I left a note I wrote that told him all of that was his, he could keep the books, more would be there on Wednesday and if there was anything he needed, all he had to do was write me a note, tell me what it was, put it in the return bin and I'd get it for him.

Now I was watching, having gone into the library the night before and checking the bin (he hadn't returned anything), hoping he hadn't returned anything since I checked. Also, I was hoping he'd show so I could get a better look at him, see which direction he came from and maybe, surreptitiously, follow him when he left.

I was focused on this and solely on this.

Because if I didn't focus on this little boy I did not know but I did know needed me (or someone), I'd focus on my weird night with Chace and freak right the frak out.

After tossing and turning, finally getting to sleep in the wee hours of the morning only to drag through work on Friday, so exhausted, I took the alarming news without reaction that the library might, just *might*, be forced to close because of funding issues, I decided this was my best course of action.

Life was happening all around me. This boy was alone in the cold, getting beaten up by someone and Dumpster diving. And I might lose my job and the town its library.

Both of these last were tragic for me, only one for the town.

This was tragic for me not only because it was my job, it was the only thing I ever wanted to do. I loved that library.

Since I could remember, Mom took me there to check out books. Since she did this, she told me her mom did the same with her when she was a little girl. And since I could get there on my own, I went there to get them.

I stayed there to read them. I did this because I loved it there, the feel, the smell of books, the quiet. Most of all I loved the serenity that came from being alone in a world of books at the same time not being alone because the world was around me, some of it real, the vast majority of it worlds all their own, contained on pages bound to a cover.

I didn't know what I'd do if Carnal Library was closed and not just because it was my paycheck.

So I didn't have time to worry about the confounding, mixed-message-giving Chace Keaton.

This was precisely the thought I was having when I heard my passenger-side door open.

My body jerked, I let out a small cry and my head whipped around to see none other than Chace Keaton climbing in wearing jeans, a fantastic western-style belt with an even more fantastic buckle, a canvas jacket lined in fleece, cowboy boots, a pearl-snap denim shirt with western-style stitching and carrying two white coffee cups from La-La Land. I knew at a glance that Sunny had either prepared the coffee or the cups because, in purple marker on the side, a bunch of flowers were drawn all around, and Sunny drew flowers. If the mood struck him, Shambles drew moons and stars.

"Take this," Chace ordered apropos of nothing, like sharing why he was in my car outside the library at eight thirty in the morning with two coffees.

He was extending a cup.

Automatically, my mittened hand reached out and took it.

He settled in, slammed the door closed and kept being bossy.

"For God's sake, Faye, it's twenty degrees out there. Turn on the truck."

"I'm on a stakeout," I informed him, and his eyes came to me so I finished, "I think it's against the rules to have the car running during a stakeout. The noise will give you away."

"Yeah, I guessed that you were on a stakeout. News flash, darlin', since you don't drive to work and your car is the only one in the lot, your sweet ass is in it and you aren't hiding, I don't think our street urchin is gonna miss you. This means he's gonna get nowhere near this place so you might as well turn on the truck so you don't freeze that sweet ass off."

That was two "darlin's."

And when did my ass turn sweet?

"Chace—"

"Turn on the truck."

God, he was bossy and annoying in the morning.

"Chace!"

He leaned into me and said quietly, "Baby, turn on the fuckin' truck."

Oh God.

Baby was nicer.

Like, by *a lot*.

I put my coffee between my knees and turned on the truck.

"What does it take? Around a year for this heap to warm up?" Chace asked before taking a sip from his coffee.

"It's dependable," I told him, taking my coffee from between my knees.

"Jeeps are. That being said, this should have been put out of its misery about ten years ago."

"It's fine."

"It's a heap."

"It's *fine*, Chace," I snapped then kept snapping, "What are you doing here? You're blowing my cover."

His eyes came to me and his lips were tipped up at the end.

Oh jeez.

His handsome lips on his handsome face tipped up looked nice.

"Blowing your cover?" he asked.

"I think you're endowing our street urchin with bigger powers than he has. He's just a kid."

"He's a kid living on the streets, which means he's in survival mode. Since no one, including teachers, knows who he fuckin' is, that means he's survived awhile."

This was news.

"The teachers don't know him?" I asked.

He shook his head and took another sip of his coffee, which reminded me to take a sip of mine.

Hazelnut latte. My favorite.

"Nope," he answered after he swallowed. "Asked the day after you reported seein' him banged up, principal approached his staff. Went back with the sketch, no one recognizes him. Fingerprints were a bust too."

"No one?"

"Nope."

"How can that be?" I asked.

"He doesn't go to school?" he asked back but it was an answer.

"Oh," I whispered, his eyes dropped to my mouth and his lips tipped up again.

I liked that.

Frak.

Before I could get my wits about me, Chace spoke. "What's in that haul?"

"Pardon?"

He tipped his head to the library, taking another sip of coffee so I took one of mine and looked to the library.

Then I looked back at him when he asked, "Those bags by the return bin. What's in them?"

"A new coat, hat, scarf, gloves, three pairs of wool socks, two pairs of jeans, two warm sweaters, some underwear, a pint of milk, three bottles of water, bologna, cheese, bread, a box of granola bars, three apples, bananas, a cucumber and a ginormous bar of Hershey's chocolate," I shared. Chace stared at me without saying a word and he did this awhile so I finished, "He won't eat the cucumber but Dad would be disappointed in me if I didn't add roughage."

"Christ," he whispered.

"Don't start," I commanded. "I know I shouldn't have added the chocolate but he's a kid. He should have a treat."

He kept staring at me without speaking and he did this another while and he did this in a way that made me weirdly nervous. The weirdly part was that I was nervous in a *good* way so I did the only think I could think to do.

I kept talking.

"By the way, I've been thinking on things, Chace, and you chased him too."

"What?" he asked quietly.

"Thursday night, or Friday morning…whatever. You chased him. You told me I shouldn't but you did too."

I got another lip tip. It made me more weirdly nervous in an even better way and he muttered, "True enough. Though, I started out chasing you."

I felt my brows go up. "You were chasing me?"

"Yeah, I started to chase you but the way you were goin' after him, hell-bent for leather, it occurred to me you would not be best pleased I caught you and stopped you. I didn't want to deal with that backbone of yours getting any stronger if you were denied what you wanted. Especially in the middle of the night with you in an emotional state, in the throes of dealing with hearing Dobie Gray's undeniably kickass but, no offense to you, honey, or Dobie Gray, in my opinion not cry-worthy song. It also occurred to me you *would* be pleased I caught the kid for you so I went after him instead."

It occurred to *me*, right then, that he was teasing me. Just a little bit but he still was.

And he said straight out he went after the boy for me, which was super nice.

This made me more nervous, the good kind, so, of course, I kept talking.

"Right then. Also, I will point out, when we first saw him, you put your hand to your gun. So it could be me shouting at him that terrified him. But you have to admit it could also be you not only having a gun but putting your hand to it when you saw him. Then you chasing him and being bigger, stronger and faster than me, and, I'll repeat, doing this in the possession of a weapon."

"I'll give you that too and it'd suck, I freaked the kid out, but no way I'm gonna be in an alley in the middle of the night or at any time with a pretty woman, hear a crash, know an unidentified person was in the alley and not go for my gun. So, I get the chance, I'll apologize to the kid. What I won't do is apologize to you."

Holy frak!

Not only was my ass now sweet, I was now a pretty woman.

What was going on?

No, no, I didn't want to know. Chace could be sweet or quiet or soft and then he'd switch off, go remote, get mean or walk away.

I wasn't going to go there. Not again.

So I went somewhere else.

"I know you find it hilarious that Dobie Gray moves me but, for your information, life is pretty crazy right now. Not to mention I'm worried about some kid I don't know, like *super* worried, so even the littlest thing might set me off. Including Dobie Gray."

This, of course, was me defending my reaction to a lie I'd told him about a song I wasn't listening to, but I thought it was my best course at that moment.

It was, I would find, not.

His brows drew together and he asked, "Life is pretty crazy?"

Fabulous.

More proof lying got you into trouble in a variety of ways.

"Yes," I answered, luckily not a lie, and said no more.

"*Your* life?" he inquired, sounding incredulous. I shifted my booty in my seat and squared my shoulders all while I watched Chace shift slightly up in his. His eyes lit and he muttered, "Christ, here we go. Backbone."

At his mutter, I got it.

And it irritated me.

Therefore, I snapped, "Is it *that* surprising I have a backbone?"

"Well…yeah."

"Why?" I kept snapping.

"Baby," he said softly and gave me another baby and it was soft so I felt my heart skip, "you live in a book."

I ignored my reaction to him calling me baby and replied, "I might do that but I still live and to live, walk, talk, breathe, eat, you have to have a backbone."

"I think, pretty much, of all of that, you need it just to walk," he returned, lips tipped up again. He was teasing me again, I liked it again but still, I felt myself glaring.

I was uncertain if I'd ever glared at anyone who wasn't related to me.

But I was certain I was glaring at Chace Keaton right then.

"Are you making fun of me?" I asked sharply.

"No," he answered, his lips still tipped up.

"Then why are you grinning?"

"'Cause you're cute and you're cuter when you get pissed though that's debatable since you're cute a lot."

Now I was cute?

What was going on?

I felt my brows snap together and I asked, "Do you have multiple personalities?"

"Not that I know of," he answered instantly.

"I suggest you get checked out," I shot back, then watched as he threw back his head and laughed.

I took an angry sip of coffee. Even delicious La-La Land Coffee, and Chace looking and sounding gorgeous while laughing, didn't make me any less peeved so I was glaring at him still when he stopped laughing.

I was also ready for him.

"Why are you here, bringing me coffee?"

He answered immediately, "At first it was 'cause I saw you sittin' here in the cold so I got you a coffee and came to tell you that you didn't have to sit here in the cold since I set up cameras."

He lifted his coffee cup but his long, attractive index finger (yes, he even had an attractive index finger) was extended and pointing through my windshield. I followed it and screwed up my eyes to look and, indeed, there they were. In the upper corner of the library, three cameras pointed in different directions aimed around and at the return bin.

"Feeds go to a tape," he continued, and I looked back at him. "Interns at the station can scroll through 'em. They see the kid, they alert me or Frank. We got an image of him, it's better than the sketch, we might be able to get a hit on missing persons or runaways in a national database. We get a direction coming or going, I can put up more cameras, different places, different angles, find out which direction he heads here from and if he goes back the same way."

"Oh," I whispered.

"That *was* why I'm here bringing you coffee until you told me your life is pretty crazy," he went on. "Now I'm here to listen to why your life is pretty crazy."

"It's nothing," I blew it off.

"It's something if Dobie Gray sets you into the dark night putting yourself in danger in order to brood."

"I wasn't in danger," I retorted.

"Faye," he said softly, "I know you know not too long ago we had a serial killer who lived undetected among our own and did it for a good spell. I also know you know that recently, serious shit went down that rocked this town and I'm guessin' you, like everyone, is waitin' to see if more will come of that. And, honey, more might come of that so you have to have a mind to your safety."

"More might come of that?" I asked quietly, adding onto my mental list of things to do when I got home. I needed to message Benji and Serenity and implore them to give up their long-distance sleuthing.

"You show me yours, I'll show you mine."

At his words, I felt my eyes get wide and I breathed, "What?"

"Crazy life," he stated as his explanation, and I got it.

I decided I might as well tell him. It was becoming clear that along with multiple personalities, Chace Keaton cursed with alarming frequency and was bossy and annoying in the morning. He also was obstinate, but not just in the morning.

"There are rumors that due to budget constraints, there are going to be cuts and one of those cuts is Carnal Library. They're thinking of closing it down entirely."

I watched his eyes flash right before he noted softly, "You'll lose your job."

"And the town will lose its library," I replied.

"Shit, Faye," he whispered.

"So, yeah, crazy stuff. Now, you show me yours."

He shook his head and asked, "Is there something we can do?"

"Who can do?"

"You, me, the town," he answered.

I shook my head but said, "I'm asking. We can conceivably fund-raise, go for grants and it doesn't cost a mint to keep a library running but it isn't a drop in the bucket either. There are things we've needed to do awhile and haven't had the money, such as upgrade our computers which are five years old and see a lot of use. Carnal has some money in it, a few private donors who, if feeling generous, might help out but if they don't, local fund-raising might not be enough."

"Petitions?" he asked and I shrugged.

"No idea."

"Wouldn't hurt," he told me. "Get one made up, I'll take one to the station. You can give Lexie one, she'll get signatures at the salon. Stella, the garage. Krystal, Bubba's. Maybe they see the community backing the library, they'll look elsewhere."

"That's nice, Chace, but the elsewhere they'll be looking to cut is at the schools or the police station. If people know that, the library is screwed."

"Honey, they've had consultants in and deemed Carnal police was overstaffed. They're keeping us at two detectives, twelve officers, the cap and no chief. Admin pool is cut back from four to two and they've dumped the position of receptionist, putting a uniform on desk duty. The Town Council is taking over as chief and the cap will report directly to him. That's a loss of ten personnel. Just Fuller's salary was over six figures, his inner sanctum also were overpaid. They're saving a fuckload on that."

"Is your job safe?" I asked quickly, and I watched his mouth get soft.

But his tone was strange, it sounded slightly self-deprecating when he answered, "Yeah, no way they're gonna get rid of the savior of CPD."

"Chace," I whispered but said no more because I didn't entirely get what he said or, more to the point, how he said it because he *was* the savior of the CPD. People were dying, his wife being that people, and others were getting framed and doing time for crimes they didn't commit. Chace and Frank Dolinski had taken grave risks working undercover locally for Internal Affairs in order to witness, document and uncover the corruption that had infested CPD and kept the entire town of Carnal under the thumb of a small-minded, bigoted, self-important tyrant for over a decade. Everyone knew that.

"I'll look into this library shit," Chace offered, taking me from my thoughts.

"What can you do?" I queried.

"Ask around. Find out why CPD cut back spending by hundreds of thousands of dollars and, on the heels of that, we're gonna lose our library."

"You don't really have to do that," I told him.

"You're right. I really don't. But I'm gonna."

I drew in breath.

This was nice too.

Then I whispered, "Okay," and after that, I took a sip of coffee.

He took a sip of his and aimed his eyes out the windshield.

"Now," I started carefully, "you were going to show me—"

"Fuck," he muttered, and I saw his eyes were focused on something.

"What?" I asked, turning my head and whispering, "Holy frak," at what I saw.

The boy was by the return bin. He was crouched, looking through the bags I left him.

I held my breath and I didn't even notice my hand shooting out and blindly finding Chace's. Not even when his fingers closed around mine.

We sat, still, silent, watching and holding hands as the boy found my note, read it quickly and shoved it in the bag. Then he shoved some books into the return bin and snatched up all the handles on the bags. Darting a glance left and right but not behind him where we were, he crept around the front of the library and disappeared.

"I'm gonna follow him," Chace muttered, and I heard his door open.

My hand clenched his and he stopped folding out of the truck to look back at me.

"Don't scare him," I whispered.

"I won't, baby," he whispered back, squeezed my hand, let it go then angled out of my SUV.

He closed the door and I watched him jog to the library and around it until he disappeared.

My eyes shifted to the dash and I saw he'd left his coffee cup there.

I looked to mine, the one he bought me.

I felt the heat pumping in my car, making it warm and cozy.

My eyes went back to his coffee cup and my mind decided I really should get that bronzed. And mine (when I was done). And maybe my passenger seat. And possibly my hand that he squeezed.

Then it hit me all that just happened, Chace showing up with coffee, us talking and it seeming normal if you didn't count him calling my ass "sweet," me a "pretty woman," telling me I was cute and teasing me, that was.

It was like we were friends.

Friends who danced at midnight.

Jeez, I needed to stop hiding and have the girls over for dinner and margaritas as soon as fraking possible.

That was, after I figured out if I should call Chace in an hour or two and find out what he found out about the boy.

*   *   *

Chace

Chace walked up the street, eyes on the library.

He'd never really noticed it, even knowing Faye worked there.

Now, knowing she might lose her job and the town might lose its library, he did.

An attractive building. Red brick. There was a concrete plaque over the door that stated it was built in 1902. Six steps leading up to the double front doors. Four large paned windows on either side. The shrubs and grass in front of it now covered in snow and large tufts of snow covered the four large urns, two at the top of the steps, two at the bottom that he had vaguely noticed were filled with healthy flowers in the summer months.

Eyes on the urns, he wondered if, in the previous summers, Faye planted them.

As he was wondering, her pretty, cute, bossy voice filled his head.

Don't start, I know I shouldn't have added the chocolate but he's a kid. He should have a treat.

Chace grinned to himself.

She'd kitted out that kid with the amount of food and clothes a lot of underprivileged kids would kill for, runaways definitely would. And books. She hadn't bought him a coat, some bologna, bread and pop and was done with it. She'd gone all out. She then staked out the return bin, still looking out for him.

Chace's grin got bigger.

He was being fucking stupid, he knew it. He should steer well clear. He knew that too.

But he didn't give a fuck.

The minute he saw the anguish in her eyes under the streetlamps and knew she'd been crying, he stopped fighting it. He'd chewed on it over the weekend. He was distracted during his dinner with his mom in a way she noticed and asked about it, but he carefully skirted the issue and didn't tell her.

But he knew, even before he drove by the library that morning and saw her in her Cherokee, something that provided him a golden opportunity to get in there, that he was no longer going to try to fight her pull.

So he stopped trying.

He should take better care of her. He should leave her to find a good man who could focus on her, their lives, the family they'd build. A man who didn't have so much baggage sometimes it was hard to haul his ass out of bed in the morning, it was so fucking heavy. Who wasn't caked in the filth he swam in for a decade. Who didn't come from a dysfunctional home that added more baggage to an already crippling load. Who didn't detest his father. Who didn't have to put energy into protecting his delicate, oversensitive mother. Who didn't have a dead wife who he didn't love but he also didn't protect and therefore her last experience on this earth was having her mouth raped.

But he wasn't going to do that.

Right now, Faye was worried about this kid. Right now, she had shit on her mind that sent her into the dark night. Shit he now knew meant she might lose her job, which meant, for a librarian in a small town, she was fucked. To get a job in her profession, she'd have to move. A move that would take her away from her family and hometown. Or she'd have to find a different occupation. Right now, she had no man to take her back. She had a few friends and a good family but that wasn't the same as having a man take your back.

This meant, Chace decided, he was going to be the man who took her back.

It was a weak decision and it was wrong. It was an excuse and a lame one. And it was highly likely once she found out everything about him it wouldn't end well.

But in his mind's eye he saw her face get adorably angry and heard her musical but irate voice ask, *Do you have multiple personalities?*

Seeing it, hearing her voice, he also decided he didn't give a fuck that he was weak and what he was doing was wrong.

He was still going to do it.

And in doing it, he was heading back to the library and not his truck so he could tell her what had happened with the boy, instead of doing what he should do and go to work.

But as he was jogging across the street to the opposite corner where the library was, his head turned so he could look to her old, beat-up Cherokee in the side parking lot and his peripheral vision caught on something. So his head turned further and he saw his burgundy GMC Yukon still where he parked it on the street. He also saw a man he knew, a man he detested only slightly less than his father, leaning against the grille, arms crossed on his chest.

Shit. Fuck. Jesus.

This was something he wanted to ignore but couldn't. It was time to have words, state where he was with this shit in a way that couldn't be misinterpreted and hopefully, but doubtfully, move on.

He stopped jogging and started walking, eyes trained to the man, feeling his jaw get hard.

Clinton Bonar, his father's associate, which meant lackey, kept his eyes trained to Chace as he approached. He was wearing shades but Chace still felt the man's eyes mostly through the nasty prickle on the back of his neck he always felt when he was around his father, his father's cronies or their minions.

He stopped a foot away and looked down the two inches he had on the man.

Clinton didn't speak, didn't even tip up his chin in greeting.

Chace didn't tip up his chin but he did speak.

"Dad back from his sick fuck fest?"

Clinton didn't move but asked, "Isn't it time you got over that, Chace? It's far from unusual for a man or a woman to have certain penchants."

"Wrong, Bonar, I know Dad's penchants and they are very unusual."

"He's a virile man with a great deal of energy even at his age."

"He's a married man at his current age and was six years ago and for the last thirty-seven years."

"A man needs what he needs and if he can't get it at home, he'll find a way to get it."

Chace jerked up his chin. "Dad certainly does that."

Clinton shook his head. "I'm uncertain why we're talking about this."

"Then I'll do you a favor and fill you in. That would be because I'm remindin' you that whatever the fuck he sent you here to do, I am not gonna do."

"We've been getting that impression considering you aren't answering or returning our calls."

"Then you're getting the right impression. I don't want to hear from you and I don't wanna speak to you. *Any* of you."

Clinton pushed away from Chace's vehicle so he was standing, not leaning, and said quietly, "There's unfinished business."

"Yeah, you've told me more than once," Chace replied. "And I've told you, it's not *my* unfinished business. It's yours."

"You know that isn't true."

"You're not catchin' this, man, but with me not talkin' to you or any of your buddies, it *is* true."

Chace watched him take a calming breath in through his nose before he continued, "We are aware that Darren Newcomb gave a copy of your father's tape to Tyrell Walker and Mr. Walker made copies and gave them to a variety of residents of Carnal. We wish for those tapes to be collected."

"Good luck with that."

Clinton ignored him and kept going. "Newcomb's also in possession of a variety of items we need returned."

"Good luck with that too."

Clinton shook his head. "I don't think you're understanding me, Chace. Newcomb has approached all of my colleagues, sharing he has these items and his intentions. He's received remuneration for their return and has reneged on his part of that deal and asked for more remuneration. This cannot go on."

"I can see you got a big problem there, Bonar, and I know you boys are thorough so I know you know this but I'll tell you all the same. Newcomb lost his job, he's a disgraced cop, no way in fuck he's gonna find another position anywhere and his daughter has leukemia. He has no insurance but he does have a strong desire to do whatever the fuck he can to keep her alive. The shit he has to do costs a fuckin' whack and is never ending unless, God forbid, she dies or she beats that shit. So my advice, settle in, because he's gonna take you for a long ride."

"We all agree it's unfortunate Newcomb's family is suffering and we hope the outcome is a positive one. That being said, my colleagues feel they should make their own choices as to what charities they'd wish to receive their donations."

"Then they shouldn't have done stupid, fucked-up shit and got caught doin' it by Fuller and his band of asshole brothers. That's also their problem and not mine."

Bonar leaned slightly forward, Chace's body went alert so Bonar wisely leaned right back but did it speaking. "I'll remind you, your father is one of the men who might, if he stops paying, be exposed."

"And I'll remind you I don't give a fuck."

Clinton continued, "He's exposed then your mother learns about his..." he paused, "inclinations. If you find them unsavory, a man, a police detective, imagine what it would do to Valerie."

Chace leaned in this time and even seeing Bonar's body go alert, he didn't lean back. "You got me with that shit years ago. I swallowed that bitter pill and jacked my life doing it."

"If this is true, why did you approach IA and offer yourself to go undercover?"

"That pill wore off, Bonar, and when it did, I couldn't live with that shit anymore."

"You made a lot of powerful men very vulnerable doing that, Chace. They don't like to feel vulnerable."

"I don't give a fuck about that either."

"You made Valerie vulnerable."

Chace successfully fought back the urge to suck in a sharp breath and the stronger urge to grab the man by his fancy-ass silk tie and slam him to the hood of his car, before he replied, "Then it's time I had a chat with my mom. It won't be pleasant and it'll fuck her up but it's better comin' from me than from the media or one of your goons."

"Chace, you are not understanding me and you need to understand me. My colleagues find this situation untenable, they want it to be over and they have the means to see to that in ways you will not like all that much."

"Is that a threat?" Chace asked.

"You know these men don't make threats."

"Then here's the same, you or they fuck with my mother or me, what I do they won't like all that much."

"Because of Trane, we understand that Valerie and you are off limits. That said, there are a number of citizens in this town you love so much you'd betray your own father to protect it. These men will not mind doing what they have to do to get what they want and laying waste to this town in the process. Starting with Tyrell and Alexa Walker."

Feeling his blood heat and his palms itch, Chace took a step into him, getting chest to chest, nose to nose and forcing Clinton to press himself back into the grille of the SUV.

"You fuck with Ty or Lexie, you fuck with me. You fuck with anyone in this town, you fuck with me. Those men wanna lay waste to Carnal, they gotta get through me first. Something you forget, Bonar, I may have left home, I may have become a cop, but for seventeen years, I was at the hand of Trane Keaton and I learned every trick he has. To protect what's mine, make no mistake, asshole, I'll use them."

"Calm down, Chace," he replied placatingly.

"Fuck calm," Chace growled. "My father gettin' off on sick-fuck, jacked-up kink made *my* life a livin' hell for far too long. I'm clear. I'm stayin' clear. You tell your boys to stay clear, man up and take whatever's gonna come to them."

"We're simply asking you to have a conversation with two men. Walker, to get him to collect his tapes, Newcomb, to get him to deliver on his part of the bargain. Very simple."

"Gettin' either of those men to do that is not about havin' a conversation. It's about usin' a strong arm and I've done that for you and your boys. I'm done doin' that too."

"As you've brought it up, at this juncture, I unfortunately have to remind you that you have, indeed, acted as an enforcer for my colleagues. If this was leaked, you'd find the questions asked by your superiors very uncomfortable and you'd undoubtedly lose your standing in this town as its saving grace hero."

"It's not a role that fits, you know why since you and your *colleagues* jacked my shit. So leak it. I'll take it."

"It's conceivable this would make the news. You were held up as the poster boy for bravery against corruption. The media enjoys building a hero. But they enjoy it more, tearing him down. It could destroy your life."

"Clue in, asshole, my life's already in the toilet. Not only would it be a relief but, I don't think you get this, I know my father's plays but I am not my father or any of the men you work for. I got a pair. Shit happens, I don't hide behind my money and men like you. I deal. Dish it out. I want you to. I already live under a cloud. Nothin' you or those douchebags you work for, who keep you in your expensive suits and shoes and haircuts, could do could make it any worse."

"You are very wrong, Chace."

"Try it and see."

Clinton held his eyes and Chace let him.

Then he said quietly, "There could come a time when Trane can't protect you."

"Let that time be now," Chace invited. "I don't want that piece of shit's protection."

"This is the wrong decision," Clinton whispered.

"No," Chace did not whisper. "Your boys are runnin' so scared at the same time thinkin' their money and position can buy them anything, they haven't been payin' attention. Your first move is against Ty and Lexie, you'll create a shit storm so extreme it'll never blow over. Not only is Ty Walker a man who has taken enough and is not about to take any more and will do what he's gotta do to protect himself, his wife and the family they're makin', he's a man who's got some serious power at his back. He stubs his toe and it looks suspect, the full force of the media, Samuel Sterling and whoever Sterling can round up will be all over your asses. I got their back and I'll have it any way I have to have it, even if it means throwin' myself on my sword. Think of that in your strategy sessions. And since I'm handin' out advice, Darren Newcomb is a racist asswipe, dirty cop who beat his wife so badly, the only play he gave her was for her to leave him and her kids. But he loves his daughter. He'll go down for her. You fuck with him and any chance he has to help his daughter beat that shit eatin' away at her, he'll make it ugly. So counsel your boys to take on a new charity and learn to hope Newcomb doesn't get greedy. You see his daughter through that shit, deal with him after. He deserves it. His daughter does not."

"I'll take this under advisement and share it with my colleagues."

"Good call."

"But you haven't addressed the matter of your mother."

Chace couldn't beat it back this time and sucked in breath.

If his mother knew about his father, it'd kill her.

She'd been a beauty her whole life, even now, at age sixty. She came from money, had been spoiled but it didn't make her like Misty, grasping and entitled. Nothing could beat his mother's sweet. It was how she was because it was who she was.

She loved and adored her son.

She loved and worshiped her husband.

Trane Keaton was a lot of things and not one of them was good. Except the fact that in his sick way, he felt the same about his wife. Like Chace, he handled her with care, like she was exactly what she was, a delicate, fragile thing who gave nothing to the world but beauty.

But she wasn't perfect precisely because she was fragile. The kind of fragile it took medication to strengthen or it would come flying apart. The kind of fragile that, before the meds and even sometimes after them, led to episodes that were at best unpleasant and at worst, especially when he was a kid, terrifying.

Fuck, she'd had a bad break that put her into treatment after reading an article about a little girl who'd been kidnapped, molested and murdered. As terrible as that shit was, she totally couldn't deal.

Finding out her husband was unfaithful to her repeatedly throughout their marriage and *how* would end her.

Chace knew that. His father knew that. But it was Chace knowing it that bought them his cooperation, until he couldn't stomach cooperating anymore because he couldn't even look in his own eyes in the mirror.

His threat to tell her had been a bluff at the time and Clinton knew it. But now, as he had when he made the decision to approach Internal Affairs and offer to assist in exposing the corruption in Carnal, Chace had to weigh his mother's mental health against the well-being of an entire town.

And he loved her a fuckuva lot.

But Ty and Lexie Walker had been through enough in their lives and they had a baby on the way.

Just they tipped the scales.

The rest sent them crashing.

"You force my hand, I'll do what I have to do. I do what I have to do, I'll deal with the fallout but *you* will deal with my father," Chace replied.

Again, Clinton's shades stayed locked to Chace's eyes.

Then he murmured, "Please step away."

"I will, I get your assurances I don't see you again or hear from any of your crew of assholes."

"I cannot guarantee that, Chace."

"That's unfortunate," Chace whispered.

Clinton continued to hold his eyes long moments before he requested quietly, "I'm asking you to step back."

Chace drew in breath at the same time he realized he couldn't do what he very much would like to do. Use his fists to provide Clinton Bonar with the experience Darren Newcomb's daughter was very familiar with, and that was a prolonged hospital stay.

His only play was to step back and walk away.

So he stepped back and walked away. The direction he walked was toward the library.

"This isn't finished," Clinton warned his back.

"It never is," Chace muttered, not knowing if Clinton could hear him and not giving a fuck if he could.

He watched the library coming closer as he thought of dancing with Faye after midnight to a fantastic fucking song while she smiled at him and let him hold her close. He'd sat in her truck, smelling her perfume, watching her expressive face, hearing her sweet voice using a variety of different tones that were as expressive as her face.

He'd bought her coffee. He'd watched a kid who had nothing grab five bags full of what he would consider gold that Faye Goodknight gave to him out of nothing but kindness.

He'd had a good morning, his first good morning in a really long time, that his father and his bullshit had turned to shit.

And that was exactly what he felt as his long legs ate the distance from his truck to the library. Shit. He smelled it. He felt it. He tasted it in his mouth.

He had to get rid of it.

He knew only one way to do that. Only two times in fucking years he'd smelled nothing but sweet, felt it and, only once, tasted it.

Dancing with Faye and kissing her.

The library wasn't open yet but he still wrapped his fingers around the handle of the front door and pulled.

It opened.

Thank fuck, she was in and hadn't locked the doors.

He walked in, vaguely seeing the layout, the shelves, the books, smelling that smell that only libraries had but his focus was on scanning the space.

To the right, the long checkout desk.

From a door behind it at the back left, Faye came out.

"Hey," she greeted in her sweet voice. "Did you see where he went?"

Chace didn't reply, he stalked to her.

When he started moving, she dipped her ear to her shoulder, her head jutting slightly forward, her face going from curiosity to scrutiny.

"Are you okay?" she asked quietly.

Chace rounded the side of the counter.

Cute, tight skirt that skimmed her hips, cupped her ass and hit her knees. Her low-heeled, brown boots. A scoop-necked tee under a cardigan. Skin displayed above the neckline of the tee highlighting an unusual and attractive three-tiered necklace. Auburn hair falling in sheets over her shoulders and down her chest, a hank of it at the top, right of her forehead pulled to the side in a cute bobby pin. Makeup subtle and appealing.

She looked like a librarian who had good taste in clothes and a light but expert hand with makeup. Her own style, a style that did nothing to emphasize the obviously attractive features of her face or frame and because of that, they contradictorily accentuated them. It was a style that worked for her in a huge way.

And it had been working for Chace the same way for a long fucking time.

"Chace," she said, still talking quietly, "did something—?"

She stopped talking abruptly when it became clear to her that he wasn't going to stop coming at her.

She took a step back.

Too late.

He was on her, he rounded her waist with an arm and twisted them so he was moving her backward toward the door she'd come out.

"Oh God," she whispered, hands coming up to rest light on his chest, eyes wide and staring in his. "Is the boy okay?"

He didn't answer.

He moved her through the door, reached out a hand, grabbed it, slammed it, turned her sharply then moved in so she was pressed to it.

"What are you—?"

She stopped talking abruptly this time because he tightened his arm around her waist and yanked it up, yanking her into his body. His other hand drove into her silken hair at the back of her head. Then his fingers cupped her head and tipped it to the side. He slanted his head to the other side and slammed his mouth down on hers.

She made a noise of surprise, her body tense against his and he thrust his tongue between her lips. Without a choice, they opened, another noise of surprise filled his mouth but he ignored that one too, carried on with what he was doing and took her mouth.

She tasted like bubblemint again. This time he knew why since his tongue encountered the gum.

Sweet, fresh, clean. Fucking *clean*. Beautiful.

God, nothing more beautiful.

He deepened an already deep kiss, needing it, and she gave it to him. The tension flowed from her body, it melted into his, her hands slid up his chest, one curving around the back of his neck, fingers going into his hair. The other one slid around his shoulders and held on tight.

Then she gave more, pressing deeper, her tongue timidly sparring with his, her fingers flexing into his scalp, her arm holding tighter. He took it, pulling her close even as he pressed her back into the door, forcing her soft curves to mold to his frame.

When he felt it start to take over, when he knew he'd lose control if he didn't stop, he stopped.

Tearing his mouth from hers, he tipped his head to rest his forehead on hers, his eyes opening to see, up close, hers drifting open in a cute, sexy flutter and he whispered, "Bubblemint."

She blinked slowly. No, *languidly.* Like she was shaking off a dream she didn't want to let go.

Then she whispered back, "I'm addicted to it."

Chace couldn't bury the groan that escaped his throat as he slid his cheek down hers and buried his face in her neck.

Her perfume was flowery but there was a hint of vanilla mellowing it. Sweet and fresh.

And clean.

The woman in his arms was addicted to gum. Not crack. Not kinky sex. Not booze. Not shopping. Not nagging a man or controlling him.

Gum.

Fucking gum.

He smiled against her neck.

"Chace," she called, a tremor in her soft, now somewhat husky voice. Uncertainty, a hint of fear. He felt her body tightening, preparing, bracing, not knowing, as he'd taught her not to know, what was coming next but knowing it could be unpleasant, and his head came up.

"I lost him on Cheyenne Street," he announced.

She blinked, faster this time before she whispered a stammered, "Wh...what?"

"Figure he made me though I don't know when. Had him

through town, up Navajo, down Ute, he was moving quick but not in an obvious hurry. Nervous, scouting, but like it was his normal routine, not afraid. He turned down Cheyenne and he was wind."

"Oh," she whispered, disappointed.

"Seein' as I don't know when he made me, he could live out there and he caught on I was followin' him and disappeared on his way home or, if he made me earlier, he purposefully led me off track."

Her head tipped slightly to the side and she reminded him, "He's nine or ten, Chace, and again, you're acting like he's a criminal mastermind. He's just a kid."

Fuck, it was whacked, it was his name but he loved it when she called him Chace in that voice of hers. It went clean through him every time and when it went through him it went in a fucking good way.

"He's a street kid," he reminded her back.

"Yes, a street kid, not a criminal mastermind."

He gave her a squeeze and dipped his face close to hers at the same time he dipped his voice low and said, "Baby, I'm a cop. Just trust I know what I'm talkin' bout. Yeah?"

"Yeah," she whispered immediately, and it wasn't lost on Chace that that wasn't the first time he called her baby and, after, she immediately gave in.

He filed this away for future reference then asked, "What's next in your scheduled haul?"

"My scheduled haul?"

"For the kid."

"Oh," she said quietly then, unfortunately, her hands moved but fortunately they only moved so she could cock her arms to her sides and rest them flat on his chest so she moved but didn't move away. She then kept talking. "More food. Cereal this time, I think, so I'll need to get him more milk. Maybe a bowl, plate, spoon, fork, knife and a sleeping bag just in case he's sleeping rough." Her eyes drifted away and she muttered, "I'll go to the mall tonight after work. I promised him another stash tomorrow." She focused back on him. "And I'll write another note. Introduce myself, tell him a little about me. So, you know, maybe if he starts to get to know me he might begin to trust me."

"My turn," Chace replied. "I'll get the food and the sleeping bag and I'll bring it, pizza and beer to your place tonight. I'll be there at seven."

That got him another blink and when she was done he saw it bought him that look of hers, eyes wide, lips parted, shock, wonder, fucking cute.

"Pizza and beer at my place?" she whispered.

"Seven," he didn't whisper but said that one word firm.

Her chin suddenly tipped down so she could look at her hands on his chest. Then her eyes darted around as her body got tight and he knew she was finally realizing where she was and therefore belatedly freaking out.

To contain this, he kept his one arm tight at her waist and slid the other hand out of her hair but did it gliding his fingers through it then feeling it drift over his hand as he wrapped his other arm around her shoulder blades.

"Faye," he called and her eyes darted to him.

"What's happening?" Her question was quiet.

"Honey, cast your mind back," he urged gently. "Two minutes ago, I was kissin' you. Three days ago, I was dancin' with you. You know what's happening."

She shook her head and stammered, "I...I..." With visible effort she pulled it together and went on, even quieter this time, "The last time I kissed—"

Chace cut her off, "This time I kissed you."

"Is there a distinction?" she asked.

"I told you I didn't like surprises. You surprised me. I didn't react very well."

Her spine straightened. He saw it and this time felt it and her eyes narrowed when she agreed, "No, you really didn't."

What he did fucked her up. He knew it then, he knew it now. He hated it then, he hated it now. He was lucky as all hell to be standing right where he was and he knew that too.

But since he was and she wasn't throwing a shit fit, pushing him off or shutting down, he took that as a sign and powered through.

"You're right," he whispered, holding her narrowed eyes. "I really didn't."

She put slight pressure on his chest and snapped, "You're giving me mixed messages, Detective Keaton."

It was the wrong thing to say.

Hearing her call him that, denying him something he'd come to love in the span of two weeks, thinking for years he'd never get his shot to hold the town's pretty librarian in his arms just as he was doing right then. What he'd just endured with Bonar, all that coming back up. Faye being angry, pulling away. Something he'd been keeping a tenuous hold on for a long fucking time snapped inside him and he instantly decided to power through a different way.

He put not slight pressure on her entire body, his arms tightening, his frame pressing her into the door, his face getting close and he growled, "Right then, here's one that isn't mixed. Do not call me Detective Keaton. To you, I...am... *Chace*."

"Oh..." she breathed then kept breathing when she finished, "kay."

"Okay what?" he prompted.

"Okay, Chace," she whispered immediately.

"Good," he kept growling, "we got that down. Now we'll get this straight and not mixed. You know my shit's fucked up. I'm workin' on that. You popped up with bad timing once and surprised me another time. I didn't handle either of those well. The shit I'm workin' through, I cannot promise I'll do any better. What I can promise is I like the way you dress. I like the sound of your voice. I like the way you smell. I like that your hair feels the way it looks, like silk. I like the way you taste. I like that you got a backbone. I like it when you get scared of me. I like it when you stand up to me. I like it that you care as much as you do for a kid you don't know jack about. I like it that you have no clue how to kiss but still, the two kisses I've shared with you are the best I've ever had. By far. I like all of that more than is healthy for me but especially for you. But I like it so much, I'm gonna ignore that and hope like fuck this doesn't get jacked like everything else in my life has a tendency to do. I like it so much I'm willin' to take that risk. I like it so much that I've decided you're gonna take that risk with me. And I'll make that straight too. I'm not asking you to take that risk, I'm tellin' you you're doin' it. That means I'll be at your place at seven with pizza, beer, a sleeping bag and food for our kid."

He moved infinitesimally so his mouth was a breath away from hers and he could smell her gum. The look on her face, the feel of her in his arms and the smell of her gum cut clean through him like it always did.

Then he finished but he did it on a whisper.

"Now, baby, are we straight?"

"Yes," she whispered back, proving, after his caveman speech, the baby thing worked fucking great.

"Good," he muttered, fighting a grin.

"I don't like beer," she announced quietly.

"What do you like?"

"Wine."

"What kind?"

"With pizza?"

"Yeah."

"Red."

"Dry or sweet?"

"Dry."

"You got it, honey."

The tip of her tongue came out to wet her bottom lip, his lips were so close it grazed his and when she tasted him, her body gave a soft jolt and her tongue disappeared. But it was too late, he felt that score through him and pressed her deeper into the door.

Her fingers curled into his jacket and she went on in a whisper, "I don't like pineapple on pizza."

"Works for me because I don't either."

"Okay." She kept whispering, bit her lip, let it go and admitted, "You're kinda freaking me out."

"Good."

She blinked again and her voice was pitched a half octave higher when she asked, "Good?"

"Faye, darlin', you're on your game, I'm fucked. I keep you off balance, I got the upper hand. What I can tell, with you, I'm gonna need the upper hand."

"I, uh…that sounds…um…are you sure that in a, uh…" she stammered, exposing something he already knew, that she had absolutely no clue how to play a man, the game or be in a relationship and that was cute and hot too. She finally finished, "That doesn't sound good."

"My job in that is to make it good for you."

"Oh," she breathed and he again fought a grin.

Then he asked, "You get that?"

"No," she admitted softly.

She didn't, he knew it, and that was also cute and hot.

"You will," he muttered.

"All right," she muttered back.

"Seven," he stated.

"Seven," she agreed, nodding once.

"I gotta go."

"Okay."

"Before I go, give me that mouth," he ordered and watched her eyes get wide.

Cute.

Hot.

"Pardon?"

"Baby," he whispered. "Before I go, I want your mouth."

He felt her tremble in his arms. Then he felt her body slide up his as she came up on her toes.

Then she gave him her mouth.

Chace took it and kept doing it until it was close to out of control. Only then did he stop, lift his lips, kiss her nose and step back. He pulled her from the door and held her loosely until he knew she was steady on her feet. Then he gave her stunned, soft, pretty, turned-on face a smile before he walked away, not looking back.

CHAPTER FIVE

Chocolate Peanut Butter Sundaes

I WAITED UNTIL the afternoon when my Tuesday volunteer, Mrs. Bagley, came in to help out before I went to my office and grabbed my cell phone.

I'd spent all morning trying to decide who to call. I was closest to Lexie and knew her the longest but she'd made it clear she wanted me to try things with Chace so I didn't think she could be objective. Krystal could maybe be objective but I wasn't sure about that. She seemed kind of hard, not to mention, even though I knew deep down she was good people, she frequently scared me. I didn't know the rest of the posse enough to share.

This left Lauren.

But choosing Lauren wasn't a process of elimination so much as her being the best choice.

I didn't know what it was but there was just something about her that was special. Something that made you know she'd have your best interests at heart. Listen. Advise thoughtfully. She was more mature, experienced. It wasn't that Lexie and Krystal weren't all that but they were more opinionated.

I needed someone to really *listen* and, after they did, advise.

In the end, I was pleased to know I chose well and made note of it for (hopefully) future counseling sessions as things (hopefully) moved forward with Chace.

When I called her, I could hear the bar sounds in the background but when I asked her if she had time to chat, I heard them fade then go clean away after she said yes.

So I told her everything to the minutest detail that happened between Chace and me. And it was fair to say I remembered the minutest detail.

Through this, she listened.

When I was done, I asked quietly, "Well?"

"Was there a question, honey?" she asked quietly back.

"Yes," I told her. "Should I have pizza with Chace?"

There was humor in her voice when she replied, "I thought that wasn't exactly a choice."

"It wasn't *then*," I replied. "When he was pressed up against me after kissing me and being all...I don't know... *intense* and growly and manly and saying nice thing after nice thing all, well...intense, growly and *manly* which made him sound like he really, *really* meant them. At the same time acting like the alpha male who just beat the rest of the world's alpha males in hand-to-hand combat and after had climbed up a mountain of their carcasses and was thumping his chest and grunting, 'Faye, my woman!' It's hard to say no *then*. *Now*, when he's not around, I'm remembering all the times he didn't say nice things and I'm reconsidering."

Lauren burst out laughing.

I had to admit it was kinda funny.

At the time, it was also more than kinda hot.

But, because of the last part, I didn't laugh because that was more than kinda scary.

I did wait for her to finish before I whispered, "Laurie, he kinda freaks me out."

"Yeah, Faye, honey, I get that," she whispered back then went on in a gentle voice. "I also get why. I'll tell you this, a girl is any kind of girl to you, she'll have your back. She'll listen and she'll give advice and she'll do her best to do well at both. But what you have to get is that the only advice she can give is from experiencing her own dramas or listening to her other girlfriends' dramas and watching them play out. In the end, though, your girl and her friends are not you and the men in their lives are not Chace. So you have to learn something difficult. How to pay attention, think, read signs at the same time listen to your heart. Sometimes these can be contradictory, and that's where your girls can help. But, in the end, you have to pay attention to all of that, make your decision, do whatever you have to do and if your girl's any kind of girl, she'll have your back then too. No matter what happens."

"Okay," I said softly, thinking that was nice and all but not entirely certain that it helped a whole lot.

Luckily, Lauren wasn't done.

"That said, I'll tell you about Tate and me. The part that coincides with what might be happening with Chace is that a long time ago, Tate's life was derailed. Totally. It was unexpected and he didn't handle it well. Not because he isn't smart, strong or a good man, just because life can sock you in the gut, wind you and before you get your breath back, it can turn to shit and then two decades later, you find you're still stuck in it. He got stuck. He pulled it partly together but he didn't pull it totally together until he found me."

I drew in breath and Lauren must have heard it because she went on quickly.

"This is not to say I believe only a woman can heal a man or at this early stage with things with Chace you need to take on the burden of healing his wounds. The man, or woman, has got to want a better life for themselves. They have to want to get past their issues. They also have to be willing to share that load. If they don't, a woman can work and slave and she'll never get anywhere. But if they want that better life and are willing to work at it, finding someone who genuinely cares, who wants to help, who is honest and thoughtful and generous and, Faye, the hardest but sometimes the most important of all, *forgiving*, can do wonders to assist along this journey. What I will say is that along the way that care, honesty, generosity and forgiveness can grow into love and love, honey, real, nourishing love, I truly believe, can heal anything. Because if you love someone, you'll want a good life for them and for yourself and you'll do anything to make that happen. That's what Tate and I found. It wasn't easy, we both had our issues, but we finally recognized it, and I know he'd fight and die to keep it and I'd do the same."

Wow. That was so awesome for her.

"I love that you have that, Laurie," I whispered.

"I love it too, Faye," she whispered back. "But I'm not done."

"Okay," I replied, pleased because all that was good too and I was glad she had that with Tate. I felt it kinda had something to do with Chace but I still was unsure.

I heard her take a breath then she said, "What happened

to Tate was an accident. A fluke. What happened to Ty was not. He was purposefully targeted, had his power stripped and some men, that isn't good. Some men, they don't bounce back. Lexie has told me a bit, Tate is tight with Ty and he's told me a bit too. I don't know all that went down with that so I don't know if what I'm guessing happened is what happened. But Lexie and Ty had some issues and this had to do with Ty struggling with having his power taken away. He's a man and men think they have to do what they have to do even if it's not the right thing to do. Some men lose sight of the fact that their women are there to support and protect them too. Ty lost sight of that and he nearly lost Lexie. I think what happened with Chace is more like what happened to Ty."

I felt goose bumps rise on my skin and I asked, "How?"

She didn't hesitate to answer.

"It isn't a secret that he didn't marry Misty for love. I don't know what happened with that either. I just know it seems he was forced to do something he did not want to do. I don't know Chace Keaton except in passing. But I live with a man like him and am surrounded by them. That could not have gone down very well. He had his power stripped too."

"Oh God," I breathed because I hadn't thought of it like that but now, thinking of it, and kinda knowing him, I knew it could be true.

"Yeah but worse for him, he's that kind of man and he's also a cop. He's taken an oath to serve and protect a bunch of people he knows and an even bigger bunch of people he doesn't know. I think he's established with what he's done at the CPD that he takes that oath seriously. So I think we can take it as read that his protective instinct is finely honed. I think we can move on from that that regardless if Misty was his wife because she or someone forced that on him, she was still his wife. *His.* If a man like Chace Keaton puts his ass on the line to protect an entire town, I cannot imagine it sits well with him that, right under his nose, his wife was shot to death, he liked her or not."

"Oh God," I breathed again even though I already guessed this. Laurie saying it out loud made it clearer, harsher and far more sad.

"And the way he treated her, on top of his power being stripped as well as her being killed, I figure all of that is tied up with him feeling not a small amount of guilt that he didn't look after her. When Dalton McIntyre was hunting women in our area and Neeta went down, Bubba lost it because he'd been partying so much, he wasn't seeing to Krystal. Out of that came a reconciliation and marriage. You know Jim-Billy who comes into the bar?"

Everyone knew Jim-Billy. Everyone loved Jim-Billy. He was a sweet old coot who lost his wife in a sad way, he never got over that so he spent nearly all his time at Bubba's. He also almost lost his life saving Lauren from a psycho. Everyone loved him because he was a sweet guy but when he saved Laurie, everyone started to adore him.

"Yeah, I know Jim-Billy," I told her.

"Well," she went on, "Jim-Billy's wife died in a house fire when he was on the road, and he blames himself because he didn't change the batteries in the smoke detector when no one knows if that would have helped, if she could even have been saved. I got over what happened to me easily because I had Tate, but he beat himself up for a while because he felt he didn't protect me. Men take this shit personally. They think they can stop it when they can't. It's likely what happened to Misty was going to happen no matter what Chace did. But Chace won't see it that way. He liked her or not, he's probably taking it personally."

"So what you're saying is, Chace has a lot of demons," I surmised.

"Yeah, honey, that's what I'm saying," she replied. "But I'll tell you more. First, a man like that is worth care, honesty, generosity and forgiveness. Second and most important for you right now, a man like that does not have a woman kiss him and he doesn't like it and he kisses her back. If he doesn't like it, he'll set her away. If he likes it, he'll kiss her back. He liked it when you kissed him, Faye. Maybe too much to deal with when he's dealing with demons the size he's got. But he most definitely liked it."

I liked that.

A lot.

So much something mortifying and painful became not so much of either.

I didn't tell Laurie this.

I just whispered, "Okay."

"I'll also tell you that if a man like that wants a woman to leave him the fuck alone, he does not go after her in the dark in order to walk her home. He does not chase a kid for her. He does not dance in her apartment with her at midnight. He does not bring her coffee. He does not kiss her. He does not enumerate all the things he likes about her including the kiss he insinuated he didn't like. And he especially does not make a date for pizza."

Her voice dipped quiet.

"Bottom line, baby, he likes you. Not a little, a lot. He's struggling with shit and he's taken that out on you. I know the insults he hurled at you stung, boy, do I know. I also know some men, or at least men like that, are not real good with exploring their feelings. So stuff comes out of their mouths they can't control and don't mean. With Chace, I don't know, it could be even more. It could be his head is such a mess, he wanted to protect you from that and was trying to push you away by being deliberately cruel when he didn't mean a word of it. Now, what you need to do is read the signs, listen to your heart and decide if you want to offer this man care, honesty, generosity and *forgiveness* and have pizza with him."

She hesitated, let that sink in then went on, still talking quietly but now gently and giving me the honesty.

"It could all turn bad, Faye, it could, no doubt about it. But it could all end up being better than you ever dreamed. That's your decision. That's your risk. Straight up, if I was in your shoes, I'd take your risk. I'd do it again and again and again. I'm not lying. I'd relive every minute I've shared with Tate, even the ones when things were insane or they hurt or they were confusing, and I'd jump for joy if I was offered the opportunity to do it on a continual loop for eternity."

"Wow," I whispered.

"Exactly, honey, *wow*," she whispered back.

"I think I'll have pizza with him," I decided and heard Lauren laugh softly.

Through it, she said, "I think in a couple of weeks or months or however long it takes for you to break through, I'll bake you a cake to celebrate. Just you, me, cake, champagne and both of us smug in the knowledge that we set the world to rights while your world was tilting crazily."

I hoped I got the chance to eat Lauren's cake.

I really, really did.

"I'll take you up on that and bring the champagne," I told her.

"It's a deal," she replied.

I took in another breath and stated, "Now I have another problem."

She hesitated before she asked, "And that would be?"

"Well, what do I wear for pizza at my place?"

At that, Lauren again burst out laughing.

This brought me to now, after work, in my apartment, at two to seven wearing what Lauren suggested I wear. Something comfortable but not something that said I didn't care enough to make an effort. A nice pair of jeans. My most kickass dark brown leather belt. The plum scoop-necked, long-sleeved top I wore to work. The three-tiered necklace with the tiny spiky bits that hung down and the silver hoop earrings that I also wore to work.

I'd taken out the bobby pin and brushed my hair. I'd sprayed perfume in the air and ran through it because I wanted to refresh the scent but I didn't want it obvious I refreshed the scent and I had no clue how to do that. So I tried the spray-in-the-air and run-through-it route and I was hoping it worked.

I'd done my breakfast dishes and wiped down the counters. I'd made my bed that morning but I still made sure the pillows were extra fluffed, the comforter was on the bed perfectly right and smoothed out. I'd tidied away my packs of gum. I'd stacked books. I'd lit candles. And I'd adjusted my unwind playlist (temporarily) to take out "Holding Out for a Hero," attached my iPod to the stereo and pressed play.

I'd also typed out a new note for the boy and printed it.

I was pretty certain I'd made the right decision to be in my tidied house in nice jeans, with a subtle refresh of scent, soft music playing and candles burning instead of being in Wyoming by the time Chace got there.

This did not mean, considering this was only the fourth date in my life, my first date with Chace, the man I convinced myself I was in love with thirteen years ago and it was happening in my apartment where my bed was an open part of the décor, I wasn't a nervous wreck.

I was.

Totally.

And completely.

Being thus, I dashed to the kitchen, nabbed a piece of gum and started chewing it.

Then I spied my *Firefly Serenity* model and my Xena chakram and I wondered if Chace watched geek TV shows.

I couldn't envision Chace watching TV at all. Even when he was having lunch at the diner, he brought work with him and worked while he ate. Even when Lexie sat with him, they talked, he smiled, she laughed and he still worked through it. Maybe he didn't watch TV at all. Maybe he did and he only watched gritty shows like reruns of *The Wire* and *Homicide: Life on the Streets* and never missed an episode of *Southland* watching the whole time, nodding his head thinking they got it spot on.

My eyes went to the clock on my nightstand and I saw it was two after seven.

Frak! He was late.

"Okay, all right, just two minutes. Maybe my clock is fast," I muttered to myself, coming to the realization I was chewing gum.

Chace had thoroughly, deeply, expertly and very, very effectively kissed me while I had gum in my mouth that morning. This didn't mean, when I sorted out my head, it didn't mortify me after he was gone that I had gum in my mouth when he kissed me.

"What am I thinking, chewing gum?" I was again muttering to myself, which I was pretty certain was a precursor to insanity.

I went to the kitchen bin, hit the top, it slid open and I spit out my gum.

A knock came at the door while I was engaged in this activity, therefore I sucked in a breath that was part air, part gum saliva and instantly started choking.

Oh God! I was going to die of choking while Chace stood outside with food for the boy, a sleeping bag, pizza, beer and wine and I'd never get my first date!

I rushed to the cabinet, grabbed a glass, filled it with water from the tap and sucked it back, calming the choking when another knock came at the door.

I slammed the glass down, ran to the door, pulled off the chain, flipped the dead bolt and threw it open to a narrow-eyed Chace who took one look at me and asked, "Heard you choking, are you all right?"

"You're beautiful, a good kisser, this is our first date, my bed is in the room, I'm nervous as all heck and I just thought I was going to die choking after spitting out gum so no, I'm not all right."

Yes, that's what I blurted, word for word.

Chace stared at me.

I stared back both wondering if I could will myself to melt like the Wicked Witch in *The Wizard of Oz* and if that was what Laurie meant by honesty or if it was a tad over the top.

These questions were answered when, first, I didn't melt. And second, Chace took a step in, dumped a big bag with a sleeping bag in it on the floor, caught me with one arm see-ing as the other one was holding up a pizza box and yanked me into his frame.

I collided with some force so my head tipped back, which was advantageous for Chace seeing as his was coming down and suddenly his mouth was on mine.

Then his tongue was in my mouth.

In the end, when he lifted his head, my arms were around him his neck, I was plastering myself to his long, hard frame and I didn't care at all my bed was about ten feet away.

Swimming through the happy daze his kisses created, I focused on him to see his eyes warm and sexy and moving over my face and I heard him ask quietly, "Still nervous?"

"No," I whispered.

"Good," he muttered. "Now take the pizza, honey. Serve it up. I'm starved but I have to go downstairs to get the rest of the shit."

"Okay," I replied but didn't move.

"Baby, you gotta unwrap your arms from my neck to take the pizza," he prompted, his lips tipped up.

My eyes fell to his mouth.

I really, really liked his lips tipped up.

Those lips said, "Faye," and his arm gave me a squeeze.

My eyes darted back to his, my arms slid from around his neck and I muttered, "Pizza, serving it up."

He let me go. I took the pizza.

Then his fingers trailed along my hip as he said, "Be back in a second."

I nodded to him feeling his fingers trailing on my hip like they were still there even though he was gone.

Jeez, I had to get myself together.

I decided to do that by serving up pizza. I had the place-mats on the counter in front of the stools, the plates, red pepper flakes, Parmesan cheese, salt and pepper all on the counter and was pulling down a wineglass when he got back.

I stared.

Chace walked to me carrying five grocery bags.

"Uh...not sure buying the entire store for that boy is good, Chace. If he's living on the street, the rest of the home-less population in Carnal will fall on him like vultures," I remarked.

Chace made it to the kitchen, hefted up the bags and they made a loud, multi-clattering, cacophony of thumps when they landed.

Then he turned to me. "Got one homeless guy in town, darlin'. He calls himself Outlaw Al. He celebrated his seven hundredth birthday this year and looks it. You talk to him, he'll swear he was the one who shot Billy the Kid. Every feral cat in Carnal will claw you soon as look at you but of any day or night, one or a dozen of 'em will be curled into Al like he's their momma. He has two teeth. And I don't see good things for his dental future since Shambles and Sunny built a small lean-to behind La-La Land so he'll have some protection from exposure. He was much obliged for this effort. Moved in while Shambles was still hammering in the nails. He mostly stays there except when it's his time to howl at the moon. And Shambles gives him baked goods he doesn't sell. I think our kid'll be good."

I stared at him.

Then I asked, "You know all of that about a homeless man called Outlaw Al that I've been living in this town near to my whole life and not only never heard of, but have never even seen?"

Chace shrugged off his jacket, tossed it on the island, moved to me and got close. I shivered when he lifted a hand and his eyes watched it pull the hair over my shoulder before it moved to curl around my neck. His eyes came back to me and he kept telling me about Outlaw Al.

"I know, you give it to him, he'll give his cats wet cat food but he prefers tuna. As for himself, canned corned beef, Vienna sausages, Spam, chili, ranch-style beans, Shambles's day-old baked goods and Colt 45." His lips tipped up and he finished, "Your dad wouldn't approve but no roughage."

"How do you know all that?"

"He told me and when I give him shit, he gives me orders for shit he actually likes. So I buy him shit he actually likes because, homeless or not, he dumps it if he doesn't like it."

"You buy Outlaw Al food?" I whispered, and learning this knowledge, seeing the sleeping bag, the bags of food, knowing about the cameras on the library and the all-out effort to find one lone runaway boy that Chace was spearheading even though he supposedly handed off to Frank—with all that, I could swear that Ella Mae was singing "Holding Out for a Hero" straight in my fraking ear.

"Me, Frank, Betty and Krystal," he answered and Ella Mae muted.

I blinked then asked with disbelief, "*Krystal?*"

His lip tip turned into a full-fledged grin, he bent so he was closer to me and he shared, "She's hard on the outside and that's the God's honest truth. Tough as nails. No one gettin' through unless Krystal herself opens the gate. But inside, honey, always on the inside of anyone, you'll find something else. Some people let you in right away. Some people you gotta dig. Some people never let you in and give you a show that's a total lie. Some people, like Krystal, you gotta earn a place inside. And Krystal's inside is soft and sweet and good."

"Has she let you inside?" I asked quietly.

"Not for thirteen years. Then, six months ago, I came home after a day that was shitty for me when the rest of the town was celebrating huge, walked through a slew of reporters to get to my door and found her sittin' in my dark living room. She broke in at the back. She was drinking my vodka. The first thing she said to me before she poured me a glass neat was, 'You done good, Keaton.' We shared a shot in silence and she climbed out my bedroom window. I'm not sure that's inside but I think, with Krystal Briggs, that's as good as it's gonna get."

"With Krystal Briggs, I think that's huge," I whispered, his grin turned to a smile and I got lost in it before he turned away.

He went to the bags. I pulled myself together and went to the cutlery drawer.

My ears perked up when he said, "Anyway, some of this shit isn't for our kid. It's for dessert."

I grabbed forks, knives and the bottle opener, asking, "Dessert?"

He was pulling stuff from the bags and taking it to my fridge as he answered, "Chocolate peanut butter sundaes."

That sounded *awesome*.

"What's that?" I asked, looking over my shoulder at him moving around my kitchen (and liking what I saw) while setting out the silverware.

"Ice cream, loads of syrup, a huge whack of peanut butter, whipped cream, ground peanuts and cherries. My ma used to make 'em for me."

Simple but undoubtedly amazing.

I mentally subtracted one slice of pizza from my evening's intake and added another "whack of peanut butter" to my dessert intake as I reached for the bottle of wine he'd put on the counter.

I was preparing to open it when I found my hands empty of wine and corkscrew and my head tipped back to look at Chace to see he had both.

"My dad didn't teach me a lot. One thing he did teach me was that a woman doesn't pour her own drink," he explained.

Ella Mae started singing in my ear again.

"Oh," I mumbled.

"Set out the pizza, baby," he ordered gently. "I'll take two slices to start."

"Okay," I kept mumbling then set out the pizza.

I hefted my booty on a stool while Chace poured my wine. He set the glass by my plate, grabbed a bottle of beer out of the six-pack, put the rest in the fridge, used the bottle opener end of the corkscrew to open his beer then he joined me at the counter.

I stared down at the pizza taking it in for the first time. It appeared to be meat lovers in the way that Outlaw Al liked canned meat. That was to say I saw pepperoni, sausage, bacon, hamburger, ham, pancetta and what appeared to be chorizo. It also had mushrooms, olives and peppers.

I was celebrating the fact that I was still only twenty-nine and had yet to suffer from heartburn as I nabbed the Parmesan cheese and started sprinkling.

It hit me we had silence as it hit me I was the hostess at the same time it hit me that it was kind of important Chace found me interesting. Part of being interesting was being a good conversationalist. We'd never really had problems talking but we'd also never been in a normal situation that would require normal conversation.

I was suddenly nervous again.

Therefore I started talking.

I did this to my pizza as I cut into it.

"You said your dad didn't teach you much. Are you two not close?"

"I hate him with everything that's me."

I blinked at my fork spearing the pizza and my knife sawing at it, turned my head and looked at Chace to see he was not a fork-and-knife pizza person. He had the slice in his hand and he was chewing.

"You *hate* him?" I whispered.

Chace swallowed and aimed his eyes at me.

"With everything I am."

"That's, uh...definite," I noted.

"Yep," he agreed then bit off another mouthful of pizza.

I went back to mine, muttering, "Sorry, I shouldn't have asked."

I'd forked it into my mouth when Chace asked, "We gettin' to know each other?" And I looked at him again.

I chewed and nodded.

He nodded back and kept talking. "Then that's somethin' to know about me. Hate my dad. Tight with my ma but she's sensitive. A little flighty. She forgets shit, gets wound up about it, gets clumsy, breaks things, gets wound up about that then she takes a pill or has a drink, lies down for a while and it's all good again. It's just her. When she's not like that, she's sweet and loving. She does a lot of charity work because she likes it and means it. It isn't a way to pass the time and get in the society pages. She genuinely wants to help. She doesn't have a lot of friends not because she's not friendly. But because she doesn't have the constitution to put up with people that are full of shit, users, manipulators or backstabbers and there's a lot of those in her circle. So she focuses her energy on people who matter and give good energy back. She isn't stupid but she doesn't always do rational shit and most of the time it's funny but some of the time she gets herself jacked up, which also gets her wound up."

He took a bite of his pizza chewed while I watched, swallowed while I watched then finished.

"She loves me, I love her. I don't get to spend the time I'd like with her 'cause she lives two hours away and my father is an asshole so if he's there, I'm not. And she makes fuckin' good sundaes."

"Well, there you go," I said quietly and he grinned.

"There you go," he mumbled and took another bite of pizza.

I turned my attention back to mine and had shoved some in my mouth when he asked, "Your folks?"

I looked at him, chewed, swallowed, put my knife and fork down and grabbed my wine. After I took a sip, I put my elbow to the counter, held my wineglass aloft and answered.

"My dad is awesome. He's wise. He's funny as all get-out. He loves me. He loves my sister. He loves my brother even though he wants to kick him up the backside a lot. And I love him. My mom is also awesome. She's wise but in a quieter way than Dad. Same with her being funny. She loves me. She loves my sister even though she wants to wring her neck a lot. She dotes on my brother which I'm no psychologist but I think that's why he does stuff that makes my dad want to kick him up the backside a lot."

"Where do you fit?"

"Middle," I told him. "My sister, Liza, is three years older. My brother, Jude, is three years younger."

I took a sip of wine while Chace grabbed his second slice and asked, "Why's your dad wanna kick his ass?"

I put the wine down and went back to my pizza, answering, "Well, he doesn't anymore. Jude joined the Army a year ago. Dad went to the Catholic Church when he enlisted and did a hundred Hail Marys in gratitude and we're not Catholic."

I heard Chace chuckle, shoved pizza in my mouth, turned my head and smiled at him while chewing.

"So why *did* your dad wanna kick his ass?" he amended his question.

I swallowed and told him, "Because Jude was a pain in his and everyone else's. I love my brother. He's a fun guy. He's *the* fun guy. But he takes zero responsibility for anything. He got kicked out of college. He got fired from his first three jobs. He's lived in four states in six years. He's had seven thousand girlfriends. All of them nice, sweet, smart and beautiful and any of them we met, the family loved them. A winning combination that's hard to find. But Jude tossed them aside like they were skanky, drunken, one-night stands he picked up at a Blue Öyster Cult concert when he was blotto and woke up to a fifty-three-year-old woman who'd been drinking a bottle of vodka for breakfast and smoking three packs of cigarettes a day since she was thirteen."

Chace's body was shaking, his mouth was grinning and his voice held a deep tremor of humor when he remarked, "That's quite a description."

"I read so I have a vivid imagination," I explained.

"No," he replied quietly, his voice holding a different kind of tremor that sent a thrill gliding over my skin. "You're Faye so you're cute."

"There's also that," I said, going for breezily but it came out wheezily.

His hand shot out, hooked me behind my neck and I found my body moving toward his as my eyes stayed glued to his until they were forced to close when his head descended and his mouth touched mine.

As fast as it happened, his hand clenched into my neck, guiding me back to settle on my stool and he let me go.

But the beautiful tingle of his lips brushing mine remained.

He took a bite, chewed and swallowed. I sawed off a bite, put it in my mouth, chewed, swallowed then went after my wineglass.

"So Jude's good?" Chace took us back.

I nodded, returned my glass to the counter, grabbed my pizza crust, gnawed off a bite and looked to him to see he was reaching for another slice.

I swallowed and kept sharing.

"He took to the Army. Called Dad, they had a man-to-man heart-to-heart and Jude explained stuff to him. Apparently, Jude needed discipline. He really likes it. He wants to be career Army. Noncom officer. And we're not talking corporal but a sergeant major. He's really into it. I guess I shouldn't be surprised. Dad did a stint in the Marines, was really proud of it and talked about it all the time while we were growing up. Jude was big into sports so he knew how to be on a team, follow the lead from a coach but still be a leader within the team. I guess his last rebellion was joining the Army, not the Marines, but Dad isn't complaining."

I took another bite of crust as Chace asked quietly, "You worry about him?"

I shook my head while chewing and swallowing and answered, "Funny, less now than I did before. Before, he didn't have a squad of brothers at his back. Now he does. That doesn't mean I don't worry but I'm happy Jude found something he's into, a place he fits, a place he belongs. So I focus on that."

"Smart," Chace muttered, and I gave him a small grin and went back to my crust.

Chace fell silent and I did too. This had the unfortunate effect of making my mind wander. Where it wandered to was that he stated plainly he hated his dad and he also immediately jumped all over helping the boy. I worried there was a correlation there and I worried through half my second slice.

"Gone quiet," Chace murmured, and I pulled in breath, put my cutlery down, grabbed my wineglass and looked at him.

Before taking a sip, I asked, "The cameras, Chace, a good idea but does CPD usually expend those kinds of resources for an unknown kid they don't know what's happening to him?"

"Feed tapes will go to the interns because they need shit to do. Cameras are not CPD's. They're a buddy of mine's. So it isn't CPD resources being used since they aren't paying the interns."

"You seem to be going all out for a boy you don't know," I noted quietly and cautiously as I set my glass aside and his eyes came to me.

Then his body turned to me.

"So are you," he noted back quietly.

"Dad says, a wrong is just wrong no matter who's doing it or who it's done to. If you know someone's doing wrong, you do what you can to right it. If you don't, you're no kind of person he'd want to know. And I want to be the kind of person my dad wants to know."

"Right," he replied but said no more.

"So that's why I'm doing it. Why are you?"

His brows went up slightly and he answered, "Faye, honey, I'm a cop."

"But you're going all out," I reminded him. "Are things, um . . . slow at the station or something?"

He grinned, leaned slightly toward me and said, "No. I'll admit, I'm not goin' all out for this kid just because I'm a cop. I'm doin' it because it means somethin' to the town's pretty librarian."

I held my breath as my heart fluttered and Ella Mae started singing in my ear.

"Now," he continued, "what I'd like to know is what you were *really* asking."

Laurie said care, honesty, generosity and forgiveness.

I didn't know if what I was going to ask fit into any of those except "honesty" but I hoped it also fit into "care."

"You hate your dad," I said gently.

He shook his head, leaned closer and put a hand to my leg, sliding it up so his pinkie pressed against the bend in my hip, and I tried to focus on his words and not his warm hand on me or where it was when he spoke.

"My dad's a dick. Lookin' back at my life, he was hard on me, too hard, hard in a way I'd never be to a kid but I was not mentally abused. He's got a way he sees life and men and how they conduct themselves and we do not see eye to eye on that. That's okay when you're a kid. But when your son starts becomin' a man and he doesn't do one fuckin' thing to lose your respect, you should give it to him including respecting the points of view he's developing and the ways he's beginning to look at the world. My dad didn't do that. He wanted me to be who he wanted me to be and refused to accept anything else. I guess I'm like him in that way because I refused to be anything else but the man I wanted to be. This meant we clashed. I skipped a grade and left for college when I was seventeen. Never went home again for more than a week or two, even for summers, found jobs that would take me away. This was because he never quit pushin' it. I never quit pushin' back."

"That doesn't sound fun," I whispered because it really didn't and I didn't like it that he grew up like that.

"It wasn't," he agreed.

"I'm sorry." I kept whispering.

"I am too," he replied then carried on. "Got worse as I got older because he never got over it. He hated me bein' a cop. Still does. Came to visit in order to tell me just that. Not regular but more than once and once was one time too many. Life happens, shit happens and it came to my attention more of the man he is and it's not good. He cheats on my mom. He does it repeatedly. He's done it since the beginning. I'm not down with that."

I pressed my lips together to hold back the words that hit the tip of my tongue and Chace, exhibiting again he could read my mind, read it.

I knew this when his hand went away from my leg but only to go under my stool and yank it his way, twisting at the same time so I was facing him. Then he pulled his stool closer to me, his legs splayed wide so they surrounded mine, his hands came to either side of my neck and he pulled me to him so our faces were close.

I put my hands on his (very hard, fraking heck) thighs because I didn't know what to do with them then I didn't have to think about it because he spoke. When he did, he did it quiet, gentle, honest, scary and sad.

"Things go good between us, one day I'll share in full about all the shit that's gone down with me including me and Misty. But you live in this town, it's a small town and it is not lost on me that people talk and a lot of that talk the last six years has been about me and Misty. What you have to know now, us startin' out, knowin' or thinkin' what you do about me and her and how I behaved, wonderin' if you wanna take a chance on me is that I didn't love her. I married her because I had to and it's gonna sound whacked and confusing as all fuckin' hell but I did it to protect my mother. Misty knew, goin' in, because I told her that I had no intention of being a husband to her in any way."

His fingers gave my neck a squeeze and he leaned even closer to me before he kept going.

"*Any* way, baby. We didn't sleep in the same bed. I didn't kiss her good morning or good night. We didn't eat dinner together. I didn't tell her when I was goin' or when I'd come home. I didn't make love to her, not once after we were married. Before it, I had her but what we did was never makin' love. There's a difference and she never got that from me. I told her straight up our marriage was a piece of paper. She wanted that out of the deal she bargained for and she got it. But she didn't get me. As far as I was concerned, she was a roommate I didn't like much."

When he stopped talking, I felt it necessary to comment so I did.

"You're right, Chace, that is confusing."

He grinned, it wasn't with humor but something else. Something I didn't get. Maybe sadness. Maybe bleakness. Whatever it was wasn't good so my fingers automatically gave his thighs a squeeze.

When they did, he kept talking.

"This isn't easy to explain. And I gotta tell you, honey, I'm feelin' both fuckin' thrilled I got the chance I never thought I'd have to do it and lost because I have no idea how to do it and make you understand somethin' that, from the outside lookin' in, did not look good. So I'll just do it straight up. I didn't see it as cheatin' on her because in my heart I wasn't married to her. She meant nothing to me. She trapped me. She did it willfully. She used a way that was seriously jacked. It put my family in harm's way and in some fucked up place in her head, she thought after she could make me fall in love with her once she had me legally bound to her. I knew her before, in town, in bars and in my bed. She knew the man I was. How she could think for one fuckin' second she could pull that shit and win me, I don't know. But she did. Then she quickly learned different. I was not nice to her. While she was breathin', my thoughts were, she bought that. She didn't want it anymore, she could walk away and demonstrate she had some good in her and give me the gift of lettin' me be free.

But I'll admit right now, I was not nice to her partly to make her leave me fuckin' be. When she wasn't breathin', the way I treated her fucked with my head. She was not a good woman. But no woman, good or not, deserves to be shot dead."

"That's true," I whispered.

"It is," he agreed.

"Chace?" I called. I did it softly but I did it like I didn't have his attention when he was so close, he was practically all I could see and it couldn't be argued that I had his complete attention.

"Yeah, baby."

"I don't know if you heard the talk. Or I don't know if someone talked to you about the talk going around town. But you should know that everyone knew something like that happened. And you should know no one blamed you for what you did when you were married to Misty. You should also know everyone always liked you. They wanted better for you. Including me."

I watched in awe as something washed over his features, something warm yet raw, beautiful but hideous and I felt my chest burn witnessing it.

Then he closed his eyes and pulled me to him so our foreheads were touching.

That felt sweet.

Way sweet.

Beautiful.

I kept talking and he opened his eyes and moved me an inch away as I did.

"You should also know that no one liked Misty but they all agree. They didn't like her. They figured she trapped you. Everyone knew she lied about Ty Walker. They thought that was crazy and mean and they couldn't wrap their heads around it. But no one wanted her shot dead."

"Good to know," he murmured.

Since his voice was quiet, his hands were warm and strong and we were so close, I felt it safe to keep going.

So I did but haltingly.

"I can't... I don't... I mean, I don't know all that went on and I can't imagine what it feels like, to be trapped like that, and I really hope I never do. But pretty much anyone in your position would do the same thing so if you're blaming your-self or feeling guilt about any of that because Misty came to an unexpected dire end, you really shouldn't."

"Wish it was easy as that, honey," he whispered.

He felt guilt.

Frak.

"I do too," I whispered back then forced a smile at the same time I gave his thighs another squeeze and shared, "But I'll let you in on a girl secret. A lot of things feel better after a chocolate sundae. So, I bet, you add peanut butter, chopped peanuts and a cherry, it might not sweep all that clean, but it'll help if only for a little while."

I hardly got the "ile" out in "while" before one of his hands slid up into the back of my hair and instead of us just being super close, we were super, *ultra* close because he was kissing me.

Chace tasted of beer. It was the only time I'd ever tasted beer that I absolutely *loved it*.

I leaned into the kiss, letting the happy haze Chace cre-ated whenever his mouth was on mine drift over me. When he ended it, one of my hands was holding tight to the side of his neck, the other pressed deep into the hard wall of his chest and I was breathing heavily.

It seemed to take a year for my eyes to open and I did not care even a little bit because when they finally did, Chace was smiling a small, warm, beautiful smile at me.

Then he was speaking.

Or, in his Chace way, gently ordering.

"Eat your pizza, baby, so I can make you a sundae."

What could I say?

Except, "Okay."

Which was exactly what I said.

Then I did exactly what I was told.

And I did it knowing that it was no skin off my nose to eat the pizza so he could make me a sundae since his sundaes sounded *awesome*.

But I also did it knowing I'd walk to the ends of the earth hand in hand with Chace Keaton and all he had to do to get me to do it was kiss me deep, smile at me, hold my hand and call me baby.

CHAPTER SIX

Do You Like My Dress?

Six oh three in the morning, the next day

I STRUGGLED UP from sleep when I heard my house phone ringing. My heavy eyes shifted across the expanse of my piles of pillows to peer groggily at my alarm clock and see it was three after six in the morning. I didn't have to be to work until nine thirty. Therefore, unless I went to work out before work, I was never up this early and everyone who knew me knew it.

This could mean bad things and, with drowsy trepidation, I grabbed the phone out of its charger, beeped it on, put it to my ear and mustered up a, "'Lo."

"Mornin', baby."

Oh my. It was Chace sounding drowsy too. No, correction. That would be, it was Chace, his deep voice sounding husky, soft, *sexy* drowsy.

Wow.

"Hey, Chace," I whispered. "Is everything okay?"

"Just wanted to know what you sounded like when you woke up in the morning."

Oh.

My.

Even still sleepy, I felt my blood start to fire and my belly dropped, which caused a tingle between my legs that also tingled down my thighs.

He went on, "And sounds like I woke you up."

"Yeah," I told him, still, for some reason, whispering. "You did. I'm never up this early."

"Never?"

"Well, never if I'm not working out. But I usually can't muster up the energy to get out of a warm bed in order to go work out so I turn off the alarm, go back to sleep and go to the gym after work."

He said nothing.

I kept talking.

"I have good intentions though."

He again said nothing.

So I called, "Chace?"

His voice was deeper, huskier, softer and way, way sexier when he told me, "Sorry, baby, I'm back at you in a warm bed. What else did you say?"

My vaginal walls contracted and my nipples started tingling as I whispered in answer, "I forget."

That was when I heard his deep, husky, soft, way, *way* sexy chuckle.

God. I was going to have an orgasm just listening to him chuckle!

"You staking out today?" he asked and I wasn't following. I was concentrating on my body and memorizing the sound of his voice in the morning.

"Pardon?"

"Our kid, honey. After you lay out the stuff, you staking out?"

"Yeah."

"I'll bring the coffees."

My heart fluttered.

He'd bring the coffees.

This meant I'd see him again. And soon.

"Eight thirty?" he continued.

"Sounds good," I replied in a vast understatement.

"See you soon, darlin'."

"Soon, Chace."

I listened to him disconnect. Then I put the phone back. After that, I smiled at my pillow. It was then my body caught my attention again and there was nothing for it. I reached to the drawer of the nightstand. As I was doing this, it occurred to me that I might have had the same effect on Chace as he had on me. It also occurred to me that he might do much what I intended to do because of it.

This meant when I pulled out my vibrator, my self-induced orgasm was off the charts.

The best.

By *far*.

After I was done, I put my toy away, stretched languorously and smiled again as I snuggled into my pillows.

It was early. I was awake. I had time.

I could relive the night before.

So I did. Happily.

After we got deep during pizza, Chace led us firmly out of deep. The good news was, after our conversation, there wasn't any residual heaviness underlying the evening. The other good news was, for the rest of the night, neither of us had a problem talking.

This, I had to admit, was mostly due to Chace guiding the evening. He asked more about my family. He asked about my schooling. He asked about my time in Denver and the grueling schedule I had, going back to Denver on the weekends to do my master's coursework while working at the library in Carnal. And he taught me how to make chocolate peanut butter sundaes that were exactly all their name cracked them up to be.

After that, with his arm light around my waist, he perused my shelves, my DVDs, my CDs, my books and the rest. He teased me about my chakram in a sweet way that wasn't mean at all. It made me feel warm all over not to mention he made it clear he thought my geekiness was cute. He laughed when I cracked a joke. He told me when we watched TV he got to pick (suffice it to say, I was not wrong about *Southland*). He asked what "frak" meant and I explained it was how they said the f-word on *Battlestar Galactica*, which made him roar with laughter. The best part about that was I got to watch.

He also showed me what he got the boy. Deli turkey and Swiss that he put in one of those disposable but reusable plastic storage tubs. Three bottles of different-flavored energy drink. A box of Lucky Charms and one of Golden Grahams. More milk. Grapes washed and in another tub. A bag of washed, prepared baby carrots. Six different kinds of candy bars. A pack of paper plates, another of paper bowls. A set of camp cutlery. And a really nice Swiss Army knife. It was thoughtful and generous and as we went through it, Ella Mae started singing to me again.

After that, we sat on my couch, Chace arranging us so we were sitting but also (yum!) cuddling and he told me more about his mom. It was clear he loved her. He didn't lie when he said they were tight because the things he said made it clear she loved him too. The only damper on the evening (though I didn't expose I thought this, I just listened and smiled) was that it also sounded like she was mentally unstable. Strangely, Chace didn't dance around it and the matter-of-fact way he described it made it sound disturbingly normal. Then again, maybe it wasn't strange seeing as, for him, clearly since he could remember, it was a fact of life.

But I had to admit, it disturbed me. A father who was too hard on him, not a good role model when he was young and more not one when he was older whom he detested and a mom who wasn't just flighty and sensitive but, perhaps, mentally ill didn't sound good.

I had a close loving family. My dad was a character. My mom was a nurturer. My sister was a drama queen, but loving. My brother was a rebel, but also loving. I was a dreamer, a geek and shy, but, I hoped, loving.

I couldn't wrap my mind around how Chace grew up. And the fact that he had no brothers or sisters (something Chace told me his mom couldn't do, something else that distressed her to an unhealthy extreme) made me sad. I'd lay down my life for Liza and Jude. They felt the same.

But no one had Chace's back.

The more I learned, the more it seemed that this was *ever*. No one *ever* had his back. Not growing up. Not now. Not Misty. Definitely not his dad. Not even his mom who loved him, but depended on him. She was so frail, he had no choice but to do everything he could, even as a kid, not to depend on her.

These thoughts fled my head when Chace stopped our conversation on the couch and started kissing me. This didn't last as long as I would have liked and got nowhere near past kissing. This was kind of a relief because I had a sense he understood I wasn't experienced but I wasn't sure he knew the extent of my inexperience and I wasn't all fired up for him to know (just yet). But truthfully, it was more of a disappointment because, seriously, he was a good kisser and I was definitely into it. So into it, when he stopped it in a sweet way and in an equally sweet way announced it was time he was getting on, I was thinking that I could do nothing but just kiss him for eternity.

His leaving was not a relief, just a disappointment.

I didn't share that, I just nodded.

He got up, pulled me out of the couch and walked me to the door. He put on his jacket. Then we made out more by the door.

He stopped that too (way too soon), kissed my nose in that sweet way he did in my office and murmured, "I'll call you tomorrow."

"Okay," I breathed.

He smiled.

Then he was gone.

I'd had four dates. Not a vast amount of experience.

Still, I knew that was not a good date.

It was a great one.

I knew this because it got heavy. It got deep. But it was also light and fun. He was interested in me, didn't mind showing it and digging to learn more. He didn't mind that I showed I was interested in him and, when I cautiously dug, he was open and honest. We laughed. We cuddled. We made out.

And chocolate peanut butter sundaes were the bomb.

Lying in bed thinking of our night, I sighed.

The last thing he did last night was promise to call.

The first thing he did this morning was keep his promise.

That was when, in bed, I smiled.

Then I threw back the covers and got out.

*　　*　　*

Eight twenty-nine the same day

I jumped when my passenger-side door was thrown open but I didn't cry out this time.

This was because I knew when I turned my head, I'd find Chace.

And this was what I found.

I smiled at him, accepted the heart flutter that witnessing his return smile gave me and saw he was in much the same outfit as yesterday. But under his jacket, he had an oatmeal wool crewneck sweater on over his jeans shirt, a jeans shirt that was a lot more faded. It looked good against his tanned skin so I hoped one day I'd see all of it.

It must be said that Chace's clothes were cool. He always looked like he'd walked straight from the pages of a beer advertisement marketed toward wannabe cowboys, rodeo stars and country singers. But with him, the way he walked, held himself, his extreme masculinity, his height, the lean muscle evident under his clothes, it was not a case of the clothes making the man.

Not even close.

It was the other way around.

He was extending my coffee, I took it and he hefted himself in while I examined the cup.

Sunny or Shambles was branching out. In teal, purple, hot pink, tangerine, lime and yellow marker were stars and hearts with fat, colored-in swirls around them. It actually was kind of a mini coffee cup work of art.

"Faye."

My head came up from examining my coffee cup as my heart again fluttered at Chace saying my name in a soft voice.

The instant my head came up, he tagged me around the back of the neck and pulled me to him.

Then he kissed me.

This was a new one.

I had very limited experience kissing. In fact, the kisses I'd shared with Chace more than doubled the kisses I'd had my whole life. I liked them all (Chace's, that was).

Including this one.

His mouth moved over mine then opened slightly so I followed suit. Then his tongue slid in, not a thrust, not an invasion but a lazy stroke.

My belly melted, my blood heated and I nearly lost my coffee.

He broke his mouth from mine but only moved about a millimeter away.

"Mornin'," he whispered, his deep blue eyes looking into mine.

"Morning, Chace," I whispered back and watched his eyes smile.

His hand took its time sliding from my neck, taking my hair with it in a way that felt like he was enjoying running it through his fingers.

Then he sat back in his seat and his eyes moved to the library.

I took an unsteady breath and took a sip of my coffee.

Another hazelnut latte. It didn't occur to me yesterday but it occurred to me then that he had to have asked Sunny or Shambles what my usual was and got it for me.

A nice thing to do.

Having this thought, my eyes moved to the library too. I'd gotten smart and parked on the street but on the side opposite the library, about a house down. I'd also kept the heat pumping. But before this, I laid out the stash.

"I take it, you're here, no sign of him yet," Chace noted, eyes to the library, lifting his cup to his mouth and taking a sip after he was done talking.

"Nope," I replied and watched him take a sip.

It wasn't that I hadn't noticed. I *way* had. But having had those lips on mine and now sitting in my truck with him so close and no drama happening, it hit me in a way it never had before how attractive his lips were. The bottom one full, little sexy ridges in it, the top one well formed, more ridges, a perfect match.

It also hit me how square and strong his jaw was and that I'd never seen it, not once, with stubble on it. Not even a hint.

But I bet he'd look good with stubble.

Then again he'd look good with anything.

It further hit me that he had very cut cheekbones. So cut, they hollowed out his cheeks. Since he had a perfect, straight, strong nose, blond hair and blue eyes, that jaw, those lips, his cheekbones and those hollows adjusted his Man Category. Without them, he'd be the cute boy next door.

With them, he was the rugged, rural mountain town cop who'd seen it all, wasn't impressed by much and didn't take any shit.

It seemed strange, yet hot, that he dressed well, had a nice SUV, never had stubble, obviously took care of his body but yet his thick, dark blond hair hinted at unruly. It was swept back from his face in a natural way that didn't suggest use of product. I'd seen, on occasion, when there was wind and I'd noticed him outside, that locks of his hair would fall on his forehead. Or when I'd happened to see him running and he was sweating, I'd seen his hair plastered there. But usually, it looked nice, neat, taken care of.

But there were bits of it that curled around his ears and his strong neck. Unruly bits that curled in as well as out. A hint of wild. A hint of unkempt. Just that barest hint he needed a haircut but in a way, if I was asked, I'd get down on my knees and beg him not to do it. In a way that those unruly curls made me want to reach out, take hold of one and tug.

My belly melted again.

Chace's head turned to me.

"Got bad news."

I blinked at his words that took me out of my very pleasant thoughts.

"What bad news?" I asked.

"Made plans last weekend with a buddy of mine. Goin' to Deck's tonight to catch the game. Which means I can't take you out to dinner."

I didn't know we were going out to dinner. Even so, this news was fairly devastating since now I did know but we weren't going so that was a huge bummer.

"Deck?" I queried.

"The cameras?" Chace for some reason queried back.

"Uh..." I mumbled, uncertain of my response to that, and his lips tipped up.

"He's my buddy who had the cameras. He's a private detective, among other things. Lives in Chantelle. He helped me install 'em Friday night."

I felt my brows go up. "Among other things?"

"Actually, he isn't a private detective. He just tells people he is. What he really is is a little scary. I ignore what he does because I'm a cop and if I didn't I'd probably have to arrest him. We're tight, have been since high school. He moved back this way about two years ago. Before that, by his account, he lived about everywhere. Since I think he's not exaggerating but downplaying it, I figure he's lived about everywhere and, except for getting an audience with the Pope, done about everything."

This Deck sounded interesting.

I didn't share that. I just muttered, "Oh."

"I'd cancel but Deck can be a dick when you cancel. He also doesn't invite the boys over unless he intends to go all out. His own homemade beer that's really fuckin' good.

Mexican layer dip and brownies that he makes that are even better. No joke. The man is six foot four, two hundred twenty pounds of muscled bulk and he makes dip and brownies. It's a spread. And it's a hassle puttin' up with his attitude, you don't show. So, I'm gonna show. But I'll call you before you go to bed. I'll make a reservation at The Rooster. We'll go there tomorrow night. Can you be ready by six thirty?"

No, I couldn't be ready to go to The Rooster at six thirty.

The library closed at six. Shutting everything down didn't take forever but I wasn't out until at least a quarter after. That meant I was home just moments before six thirty.

The Rooster was my favorite restaurant *ever*. It was a fancy steak joint in the mountains about a half an hour away. The views were amazing. The steaks melted in your mouth. The prices were astronomical but you'd sell your kidney without blinking just to trail your finger in their tri-peppercorn sauce and lick it clean.

I'd eaten there five times, all special occasions, and I'd never had anything that I didn't consider the best I ever had. This was saying something since Denver had some amazing eateries and I partook copiously while living there when I was at Denver University and going back for my master's.

It was also one of the only places close by where you could dress up. Even in Denver, jeans were acceptable practically everywhere and considered formal attire in some circles depending on your top and footwear. But in Denver, women, and men, found their occasions to run the gamut of gorgeous apparel.

In the mountains, this was few and far between and in our area, The Rooster was one of the only places you could get by with going for the gusto.

On my first going-out-on-a-date well...*date* with Chace, I wanted to go for the gusto.

But I couldn't go for the gusto if he was showing up

on my doorstep about a nanosecond after I got home from work.

So no way I could be ready by six thirty.

I still said, "Yes."

Chace didn't reply. He just studied me.

Then he demonstrated yet again he could read my mind.

"How about this, can you be ready at seven thirty?"

That was *way* better.

"Yes," I whispered on a small smile.

He grinned before he looked away, lifted his coffee cup but said to the lid before he took a sip, "Lookin' forward to the show you got planned, baby."

Panic instantly oozed from my every pore.

I liked my clothes. They were nice. Good quality. I thought they suited me. I had a few good getups for when I went back to Denver to meet friends or my family had special occasions that called for a little effort. And when I made an effort, I didn't mind making a statement. Though, only a minor one.

But I had not one thing to wear on a date at The Rooster walking in on the arm of all the beauty that was Chace Keaton.

My mind quickly flipped through my options and this time, it settled on Lexie.

Krystal wore tank tops even in the winter. She might put a cardigan over them if she was heading outside, but even when it was super cold, that was all the effort she put into covering up and keeping warm.

Lauren always looked good. She used to be some executive but it was clear since she hit Carnal she'd embraced the biker babe lifestyle. This included her wardrobe if, compared to the vast number of other biker babes who lived in the vicinity, she injected a healthy dose of class.

But Lexie used to be a buyer at a department store. She

wore high heels all the time, even high-heeled boots in the winter. Her husband was not a biker, he was a mechanic. A mechanic who owned a Dodge Viper and lived in one of the swank condos in the hills on the south end of town. Not to mention they were currently moving into an enormous house in an even more swank development in the eastern hills. I didn't see him often but when I saw him with Lexie, he didn't look like he could be in a beer ad. He looked like he could grace the cover of *GQ*. So Lexie didn't embrace biker babe chic or mountain girl cute comfort. She always, but always, looked phenomenal.

So I hoped she was free to go with me to the mall that night on an emergency mission.

"Incoming," Chace muttered as I made mental plans with Lexie and took a sip of my latte.

My eyes snapped up and I saw the boy stealthily rounding the building. I noted immediately even from our distance that the eye wasn't swollen anymore, the bruises were fading but not gone and the cut on his lip was still noticeably angry. He'd received a thrashing. Over a week and the evidence was still there.

The only thing that made me feel better about this was he was wearing the coat I gave him, the hat and the new jeans. But it was nippy. He really should put on the gloves and scarf.

I watched as he took his time and, as he did, he looked through the lot and surprisingly straight at the spot I'd been parked in yesterday, like he expected to see us there.

Like he'd seen us there yesterday.

Strange. Very strange. So strange it sent my body sliding toward Chace's. My shoulder bumped his and, without taking his eyes off the boy, his arm shoved behind me and rounded my waist.

My hand went out and my fingers curled around his thigh.

We watched in silence as he approached the bags, crouched by them but he didn't take time to dig through. He just grabbed them and motored to the back of the library, around and he was gone.

"Made us," Chace muttered, and I turned my head to look at him.

"What?"

He dipped his chin and twisted his neck to look at me; it hit me then how close he was but I didn't move back.

Not a centimeter.

"Made us even before he grabbed the shit yesterday," he answered. "My guess, just now, he scouted the area, didn't see us on the street so he made his approach from the direction he came from. This means he led me off track yesterday. He approached from the front, left around the front, headed toward town. Approached from the back this time, thinking we aren't here. Wherever he goes, he approaches the library from the back."

"Um . . . aren't you going after him now?"

He gave my hip a squeeze, I read the command, pushed back into my seat and Chace looked out the window, his profile contemplative while answering.

"No. Want him to feel safe. Don't want him to think it's a trap. He needed that shit yesterday. He knows he can outrun us or lose us. He saw us before he even returned the books. Maybe he knew he could get away, didn't want to waste the effort of walkin' here from wherever to return the books. Maybe he thinks we're no threat. No fuckin' idea. But now I think we should keep a distance, keep givin' and hope he takes you up on your invitation and gives back. Writes a note. Gets comfortable. Gets to know you. Maybe he'll approach us."

This sounded like a good plan.

Or at least it did until Chace hissed, "*Fuck*," with a lot

more emotion than he'd been talking with a mere moment before.

"Chace?" I whispered but his eyes didn't leave the library.

"Saw it yesterday, saw it clearer today," he replied.

"What?"

His eyes turned to me and I caught my breath at the anger I read in them. I was stunned that his seemingly mellow mood had shifted in an instant.

"His face, Faye. That's a week of healin'." He shook his head and his gaze moved back to the library on another, "*Fuck.*"

I reached out a hand and curled it on his knee, leaning into him, whispering, "Chace."

He shook his head again once but spoke. "Not eatin' right, no medicine, no water to clean, probably doesn't even know to do it. That'll all delay healing but that doesn't mean that kid didn't get nailed. He got fuckin' nailed. Nine years old, slinkin' around for food, Dumpster diving, I'm across the goddamned street and all I can do for his sake is sit on my ass, watch and wait."

Entire verses of "Holding Out for a Hero" crashed in my brain.

As they did, I squeezed his knee and called softly, "Honey."

Instantly, his head turned to me but I was so focused on his anger for the boy, I didn't see the expression on his face.

"He's got food. I'll put medicine out tomorrow and tell him how to use it. Shampoo, soap, a washcloth, a towel, suggest he finds someplace to clean up. Urge him to eat the fruit and veggies. Maybe buy some vitamins and ask him to take those too. We'll take care of him and then we'll get him."

"I know we'll get him, darlin', and that'll be good. But who I really wanna get is whoever fucked him up."

I pressed my lips together because he said that like he meant it a whole lot.

Then I unpressed my lips and replied quietly, "I want you to get him too."

His eyes moved over my face before coming back to mine and he whispered back, "Then I will."

I smiled at him.

He leaned in and touched his mouth to mine.

Unfortunately, he leaned right back and said softly, "Gotta get to work."

"Right," I replied.

"Call you before you go to bed."

I smiled again and repeated, "Right."

His eyes dropped to my mouth before they came back to mine, he leaned in several inches and whispered, "I'd take that mouth, but that'd mean I'd be makin' out with you in your car on the street. The town's pretty librarian doesn't need that kinda talk."

This was disappointing.

Until he finished, "Least not yet."

I smiled again.

Chace awarded me a return smile.

Then he took off and I drove my Cherokee into the lot, parked and went to the library.

*　　*　　*

Nine fifty-five that night

I was on my back on my couch, feet in the seat, knees to the ceiling, apple candle burning, snapping a piece of bubble-mint in my mouth, the last glass of the wine Chace brought the night before mostly consumed and sitting on a table beside me.

I had my Nook in my hand and I was reading.

Lexie was luckily free. Her friend Wendy was not on shift at Bubba's so she came with us to the outlet mall. They were both not only free but also beside themselves with glee that we were going to the mall because I was going out with Chace. Lexie especially. She was delighted and didn't mind showing it.

This felt good.

It also felt hopeful.

I liked my clothes but contradictorily, I wasn't a shopper. Luckily, I knew what I liked and I knew where to get it so my shopping experience was as narrow as my life had been (that was to say, as narrow as it was a couple of weeks ago).

Lexie and Wendy took me to the outlet mall and opened up an entire world to me.

This was why I came back not only with an outfit that even I thought was fan-freaking-tastic to go out with Chace in but also four other bags of clothes, shoes and (it made me blush but that didn't mean I didn't hope it wouldn't eventually come in handy) sexy undies and nightgowns.

They were having the time of their lives and I did too. I didn't know shopping could be such a blast. But with those two, it totally was.

Now I was home, unwinding, trying to read at the same time wondering if Chace liked dogs and/or cats. Since Holly didn't mind pets, I'd been thinking now for months about getting one or the other. This was what was on my mind when my phone rang.

It was the house phone again so I twisted, grabbed the handset from the charger by the couch, beeped it on and put it to my ear.

"Hello?"

"Hey, baby."

My bent knees fell to the back of the couch, I felt my eyelids go half-mast and I licked my lips.

Yes, all this from a greeting.

"Hey, Chace," I whispered. "Having fun?"

"It's a game, honey, not a parade."

My head cocked to the side at his words and tone and I asked, "That isn't fun?"

"Not when my team is losing."

"Oh," I muttered then inquired, "Who's your team?"

He hesitated and I heard sounds in the background of a TV clearly on a sporting event before he replied, "The Nuggets, Faye."

Right, of course.

"Basketball," I mumbled.

"Yeah, honey. Football's done in January."

I was still mumbling when I replied, "I heard something about that somewhere."

His team-losing grouchiness faded and I knew this when I heard his chuckle.

"You could be watching the Avalanche," I pointed out.

"Avs are on the road. West Coast. Deck's tapin' it. That's next."

"Oh," I whispered then, "Long night of male camaraderie."

"Deck doesn't break out the beer, dip and brownies unless there's serious shit to watch."

I was with Deck. All that effort should be for something.

"Deck sounds interesting," I noted.

"Yeah, he is, and every breathing female thinks the same thing."

A small, short giggle escaped me and I asked, "Pardon?"

"The amount he gets means he's either a good-lookin' guy or he's got the ability to hypnotize women that's undetectable but highly successful though the purposes he uses it for are nefarious."

"Ah," I replied through a smile, "breaking that down, he's hot."

"I can't make that call but I'm a detective so evidence suggests this is true."

I laughed softly and I knew Chace listened to it because he didn't speak again until I was done.

"You gettin' ready for bed?"

I blinked and looked at the funky clock mounted on my brick wall that I found in a cute shop in Glenwood Springs as I asked, "Bed?"

"Bed," Chace replied.

"It's ten o'clock," I told him.

"When do you go to bed?"

"I don't know, midnight?"

There was silence.

"Uh, when do *you* go to bed?" I asked.

"If I'm not drinkin' beer and eatin' homemade brownies, ten."

"Early to bed, early to rise," I whispered.

"Late to bed, lazy in the morning," he whispered back.

"I'm not lazy." I kept whispering.

"Baby, give me that. The thought of you, lazy in bed in the morning is a good one."

That got a full-body shiver and a quick mental inventory of my junk drawer to see if I had fresh batteries for my vibrator.

"I'm not sure this is fair." Yes, still whispering. "You being at Deck's with beer and brownies, me being here and you being sweet and um...other things."

"Other things?" His voice was teasing.

"Yeah, other things." My voice was soft.

"Fuck me," he muttered then kept muttering the weird words. "Cute. Hot."

"What?"

"Nothin', darlin'. It sucks but I'm gonna let you go. Boys're givin' me looks which means they're listenin'. That means they're gonna give me shit so I should probably not hand them more to give me shit about."

I didn't know if saying it was right or wrong because of how much it exposed about how much I didn't want to let him go.

I also didn't care.

This was why I suggested, "You could move to another room."

"Yeah, your sweet voice for any longer, the other room I'm gonna move to is your one-room apartment. That right there from the grins I'm gettin' bought me a load of shit so I'm gonna let you go."

"Okay," I said quietly.

"When you get to sleep in three, four hours, sleep good."

Teasing again.

God, I loved that.

So much, I laughed softly then I replied, "When you finish male bonding and get home, you sleep good too, Chace."

"Will do. 'Night."

"Good night, honey."

"Fuck me," he whispered, and it was a surprise so I blinked then asked, "What?"

"Nothin', baby. Talk to you tomorrow."

"Tomorrow, Chace."

"'Night, darlin'."

"'Night, Chace."

He disconnected and I beeped off the phone. Then I brought it to my lips and smiled against it.

Huge.

*   *   *

Six oh four the next morning

My home phone rang.

I drifted up from sleep, tipped my eyes to my clock and smiled a sleepy smile.

Then I went straight for the phone.

"'Lo," I whispered.

"Baby," Chace whispered back.

I snuggled deeper under the covers even though his voice made me way warm and cuddly.

"Hey, honey," I said soft. "You get home okay or are you deep in the mountains recovering from a ceremonial male bonding ritual after killing a bear?"

I got a husky, drowsy, sexy chuckle that made me feel warmer and way cuddlier then, "I got home okay."

"Good," I muttered.

"You sleep okay?"

"Mm-hmm," I mumbled.

This got me nothing.

I waited.

Still nothing.

"Chace?"

"I'm here."

"You were quiet," I told him something he knew.

"You sound half asleep."

"I'm not," I kind of lied.

"Maybe not, honey, but you sound it."

"Oh."

"I'll let you go after you tell me if you took care of our kid."

"All good," I said softly. "Bottle of ibuprofen, kid's multi-vitamins and some Neosporin. The other stuff I told you I'd do yesterday. Some more food to keep him stocked up. Another note telling him how to use the ointment and to get a wash if he can."

"You don't need me to pop 'round the store to pick any-thing up?"

"No, honey."

"All right, baby. Now go back to sleep."

"Chace?"

"Yeah?"

"In the note, I told him a little bit about you. Just who you are, that you're cool, he has nothing to worry about and you're helping me look out for him. Was that okay?"

"Yeah, Faye. That's fine. Go back to sleep."

I didn't want to go back to sleep. I wanted to talk to him until the earth started revolving around the moon.

I didn't tell him that.

I said, "'Kay."

"See you later, honey."

"Later, Chace."

He disconnected.

I beeped off my phone.

I didn't think I could get back to sleep.

But I did.

*   *   *

Eight thirty-two that same morning

My eyes on the return bin, Chace's coffee on my dash, mine in my hand, my car parked on the street, I waited for the boy and Chace.

I'd texted him to say coffee was my treat. He'd texted back to give me his order and tell me he'd pay me back when he got to my Cherokee. I texted him back and asked him if he knew what "my treat" meant. He texted me back with, *Baby, I'll give you money when I get to your SUV.*

These were simple words on a phone display but I still could read the tone.

My text back was, *Oh, all right.*

I expected that would be the end but I got a one-word reply.

Cute.

God, Chace Keaton was fraking *awesome*.

My cell rang. I pulled it out of my purse and saw the display said, "Chace calling."

I felt a little thrill shiver over my skin and took the call.

"Hey."

"Hey, honey. Bad news. Got a callout. I can't do the stakeout with you today."

That was a huge fraking bummer.

"Okay," I replied.

"I'll be at your place tonight, seven thirty."

"Does seven thirty mean our reservation is at eight?"

"Eight fifteen, in case we hit traffic or weather."

"Will this mean you'll turn into a pumpkin on the way back, considering we'll probably get home past your bedtime?"

Silence then, "Now she gives me smartass and it's still fuckin' cute."

I smiled.

The boy showed.

"Oh my God!" I exclaimed on a muted cry. "He's back."

"How's he look?"

I studied him as he made his careful way to the return bin. "He's wearing my coat, new jeans. The hat. He really should wear the gloves and scarf I bought him. It's cold. I'll put that in my next note." Then, quietly, "Lip still bad."

"He uses the Neosporin, it'll help."

"Yeah."

I listened to Chace sigh as I watched the boy make it to the bags.

"He get 'em?" Chace asked.

"He's going for them now."

"Good," he muttered then, "Gonna let you go. See you tonight."

"Tonight, Chace."

"Later, honey."

He disconnected.

I watched the boy walk away with the bags.

I gave it time, secured Chace's coffee (latte, triple shot) and then drove into the lot.

I took Chace's coffee with me into the library and I drank it after mine. This meant I was wired all morning.

Or it could be my date with Chace that night that made me wired.

It didn't matter.

It felt like I was dancing on air.

*   *   *

Seven thirty that evening

"Frak, frak, frickity frak, frak, frak," I muttered, looking at myself in the full-length mirror on the inside of my wardrobe door.

This wasn't me.

It was hot.

But it wasn't me.

I was wearing a sweater dress the color of a green olive, a color that Lexie told me would work for me in a big way with my coloring, and she was not wrong.

The dress was awesome. Formfitting (very), it went down to just above the knee, had a deep, wide vee in the front that exposed the skin of my chest and collarbone but only a hint of cleavage. The sleeves were tight all the way down and went past my wrists. And there was some vertical detailing in the knit that was sensational. It made me look taller at the same time it accentuated my curves. There was more of it around the waistline so it gave even more of a sense of an hourglass figure than I already had, and one could say my figure was extremely hourglass.

In a moment of idiocy, I'd looked up straight hair hairstyles on the Internet to get ideas. When I got home, I did a bit of fluffing, spraying, tousling and teasing, the last just at the top back, and swept just the hair at the top of my forehead back about an inch, securing it with dark brown bobby pins. But the fullness and teasing at the back gave it a sex kitten vibe that even I had to admit looked really good.

I'd added more makeup than I usually used, deepening it a bit, some green around my eyes but not going overboard because I never felt comfortable with a lot of makeup caked on. But with the hair and dress, the effect was astonishing.

I had on silver hoop earrings that were long and an intricate five-tier silver necklace that was a mixture of green, brown, purple and dark blue beads, small silver balls with some short silver spikes.

It all wasn't me. Yet it was, just not in the me sense of me but in the *Me!* sense of me.

It was the boots that did it. Dark brown, patent leather with a pointed toe, four-inch spiked heel and a super-thin strap around the ankle with a tiny buckle at the side that made my ankles look delicate and gave a classy, stylish rock 'n' roll look to the boots.

They weren't hot. They were *smokin' hot.*

The whole getup made me look sexy.

It made me *feel* sexy.

I liked it a whole lot while at the same time it freaked me out a whole lot more.

Because I wondered what Chace would think about it.

And I hoped like all fraking heck that he'd like it.

A knock came at the door and I jumped.

Oh God, he was there.

Frak.

I closed the wardrobe door and secured it with the little latch, sucked in a huge breath and walked across my apartment belatedly thinking I should have had a glass of wine (or two) while I was getting ready.

I pulled off the chain, undid the dead bolt and opened the door.

Chace was wearing a heavy denim western-stitched, slim-fit shirt that looked like it was once black but then it had been left out in the elements for a year and after dragged behind a truck for a thousand miles so it was now a dark, distressed gray. Once this was accomplished, it clearly had been blessed by a tough-as-nails ninety-year-old cowboy who could still lasso a steer going flat out on his horse and this blessing happened during a sacred rite like all clothing that was kickass should be.

Over it, Chace wore a well-tailored black wool sports jacket. Dark blue jeans. Black cowboy boots and a black tooled leather belt with a silver belt buckle with a subtle cow's skull imprinted on it.

My mouth started watering and I had to curl my hand around the edge of the door to remain standing because my legs started trembling.

I lifted my eyes to his face and whispered, "Hi."

At my voice sounding, his eyes, pointed down and aimed around my breast/midriff area, shot to mine.

Then, one second I was standing in the door, the next second I had my back against it, Chace against my front, one of his arms around my waist, one in my hair, cupping the back of my head and his tongue was in my mouth.

This was another, different kind of kiss.

I thought the one in my office was deep, thorough and heated.

It had nothing on this.

It wasn't only the delicious tongue action. There were heads slanting this way and that (both of ours). Hair being gripped (only mine) and gripped in a sexy way that pulled at my scalp rough but gentle and so hot I felt the area between my legs get wet. Hands were doing a lot of roaming (three of them, one of Chace's, both of mine under his sports jacket).

It was wild. Abandoned. Rough. Wet. Intense. Fiery. Thorough. Exquisite. Heart pounding. Blood singing. Soul rocking. Life altering.

Luscious.

When Chace tore his mouth from mine, I actually felt it take a supreme effort for him to do it. His strong hand was cupping my behind. His other one was fisted in my hair. One of my arms was cocked, forearm and palm pressed flat against his lat, pulling him to me. My other arm was wound around his back, hand fisted in his shirt. Our breath was coming heavy, fast, mingling as it brushed our lips.

I slowly opened my eyes and at what I saw in his, another rush of wet surged between my legs and my fist in his shirt tightened.

Undone by the kiss, forlorn that it ended, mindlessly and idiotically I asked the first question that popped into my head.

"Do you like my dress?"

Chace's head jerked even as he blinked. When his features righted he stared down at me half a second before his hand went out of my hair, his other one slid up my back and both of his arms closed around me super tight. He bent his head, shoved his face in my neck and burst out laughing.

I decided to take that as a yes.

*   *   *

Eleven seventeen that night

"I gotta go, baby," Chace whispered against my lips.

We were making out, standing just inside my door. We'd arrived back about ten minutes ago. I still had my coat on, Chace his jacket. When we stepped in, he'd closed the door but immediately pulled me into his arms.

Dinner was fabulous (not a surprise). Conversation was easy. Smiles were frequent. Laughter the same.

In the car there and back, I found out Chace listened to country (also not a surprise) and it was good country.

Now the night was over.

And I really, really didn't want it to be.

Still, I whispered back, "Okay."

Chace didn't move, not even his lips that were still a breath from mine.

"Good mornin' call tomorrow."

Goodie!

"Okay."

"My turn for our kid but I didn't have time to do anything."

"That's okay. On my lunch hour I bought him some more books, some comics, a flashlight, some batteries, a toothbrush, toothpaste, a few packs of gum, more water and some more candy bars. I also wrote the note and added a notepad and some pens so he could write back."

I felt Chace's smile against my lips at the same time I saw it in his eyes.

"I'll take the weekend," he offered.

"All right," I accepted.

"We'll win him, Faye."

"Yeah," I whispered.

"Want that mouth again before I go, baby. Soft this time," he whispered back.

"Okay," I breathed, got up on my toes and touched my lips gently to his hoping I was doing it right.

Then I moved back.

The gentle look in his eyes told me I did it right and I felt like the queen of the world.

He lifted his lips to kiss my nose, his arms gave me a squeeze then he let me go.

He turned to the door, had it open and was walking out when I called, "It was a really good night, honey, thank you."

He turned back to me, his beautiful blue eyes hit mine and his face was solemn.

"No it wasn't, Faye," he replied and my heart squeezed. Then he finished quietly, "It was a fuckin' great one."

At that, my heart flipped.

Chace closed the door.

I stared at it.

Then I sucked in breath.

After that, I twirled, skip-danced to my bed, flopped back on it and smiled at the ceiling.

Huge.

CHAPTER SEVEN

Hazelnut Half-and-Half

"'Lo, honey."

Like every morning since the first, Chace's dick, already hard, jerked at hearing Faye's cute, drowsy, husky voice answering the phone.

"Mornin', baby," he replied.

"Catch any bad guys last night?"

It was Saturday morning, a week and two days after their date at The Rooster. Their dinner at the Italian place in town the night before had been cut short when he got a callout after someone got home and found their place had been burgled.

He and Faye had had a week and a half of early morning phone calls where she was cute, sleepy, innocently sexy and oftentimes funny. A week and a half of coffee and stakeouts, watching the kid grab bags of food, water, books and other items Faye or Chace deemed he needed. They'd had a week and a half where they'd had dinner together every night, going out or eating in at Faye's place, where she cooked.

Chace was not surprised but that didn't mean he wasn't pleased to discover that, like the way she dressed, groomed, kept and decorated her house, she had a subtle flair with cooking.

It was stick-to-your-ribs, no-frills home cooking.

It was also exceptional.

That was, they had dinner every night except four times. One, when she went to have a pre-scheduled dinner with her mom and dad. Three, when she went to the gym and worked out.

One of those, he'd had to work late as well so he'd met her for a drink at Bubba's, a place she'd never been but was greeted like a regular by Krystal and fucking Twyla, the butch waitress who put the fear of God in most men but acted like Faye was her BFF. Chace was surprised at this but started chuckling when he saw that Faye was even more startled by Twyla's behavior. Then, just like Faye, she warmed to it and by the end of the time they were there, she and Twyla were gabbing like long-lost sisters. He'd walked her home after, made out with her just inside the door and left her about eight hours before he wanted to.

Two of those nights, he left her to it. He did this to cool things down, not for her, for him.

Too much of her would push him to push her to go too fast.

She was like a drug and as the days, and especially the nights, wore on and she became more comfortable with him, being in his arms, having his tongue in her mouth, his hands on her and hers on him, she was making it very clear she was willing to explore. She was gaining experience, trying things out, becoming more confident and getting restless. She was also making that last obvious. She wanted more, and how she communicated that was phenomenal. So phenomenal, he had to cool it off so he wouldn't lose all control.

Before and during Misty, he had an active sex life with a variety of partners. He was not a player. He was straight up with the women in his life, and many of the women in his life were just that, women in his life. Prior to Misty, he dated, he had relationships, he worked at them if he thought they held promise, but none of them felt right.

Mostly this had to do with the fact that the first time Faye caught his attention she did it in a big way he couldn't ignore. He hadn't known, until seeing Faye, the kind of woman he was looking for, but one look at that auburn hair, those crystal blue eyes, the curves she didn't hide but also didn't display, her skittish behavior, shy smile and the dreamy look on her face made a lasting impression he couldn't shake.

But he wasn't done enjoying variety and, at the time, she was very young, clearly inexperienced and would require time and care that he had every intention would lead to commitment so he held off on approaching Faye.

Too long, it would turn out.

But hopefully not too late.

After Misty, the possible fruition of his relationships was curtailed for obvious reasons, and although he had them, the women who took him to their bed knew there'd be an end. He enjoyed it, they enjoyed it but they both kept distant because both knew there was no future.

Before and during Misty, all of this had been regular.

Ironically, since Misty, he'd only had two women. One he'd dated and fucked for a month and then ended it. He did this because she made it abundantly clear she was hoping for more and Chace was not in the head space to give it to her. The underlying desperation he felt from her reminded him of his dead wife. It wasn't calculating like Misty, it was just desperate and it didn't settle so it eventually put him off. The other was a leftover from his time with Misty who opened her door and bed to him any time he made the call. It was sporadic. It was random. It wasn't frequent. But it was regular.

The last time he made that call was three weeks before he saw Faye in Harker's Wood.

That meant he'd not had a woman in six weeks.

This was a record.

This was also making the carefully controlled necking he'd been using to initiate Faye torture. Exquisite torture but torture nonetheless.

Their morning phone calls, something he fucking loved, was a form of exquisite torture too.

Luckily, when they were done, he was in bed, hard, and could do something about it.

Which he always did.

Today would be the same.

Tonight, though, was the night.

Tonight after Faye finished work she was coming to his place for the first time and Chace was making her dinner.

She wasn't leaving until Monday.

She didn't know that and he was not about to freak her out and tell her to bring a toothbrush and an extra pair of panties.

Tomorrow morning he'd leave her in his bed and go get them for her.

"Yes," he answered her question.

He got silence then, "Pardon?"

"Got 'im."

More silence then, "Already?"

"Lenny Lemcock tries to stay on the wagon," he started in answer. "He also frequently fails. When he fails, he needs to get so drunk he doesn't remember anything for a month. This requires money. Money, since he doesn't have a job and lives on disability, he has to steal. Took one look at the house, knew it was Lenny seein' as he leaves a mess as his signature. He also leaves prints. Didn't even have to lift a print though to know it was him. He hangs in seven different establishments. I found him at the fourth, three sheets to the wind. He's in the tank and unfortunately for Lenny, since this is about strike seven and although the guy is funny, can charm a snake and has proven that repeatedly by charming a variety of judges, the last time he appeared, he got the warning. No more second chances. He's fucked. He'll dry out doin' time and my callouts for burglaries will drop drastically."

"Do you know everything about everyone in town?" she asked quietly, residual sleep and a hint of sweet wonder in her voice.

"Only the ones who do fucked-up shit."

"And Outlaw Al," she added.

"Al lives on a diet of canned meat cut by canned beans. His residence is a lean-to in an alley. His best friends are twenty-five feral cats, and he can pack all of his belongings in a shopping cart and not one of them is something anyone in their right mind would want. All of that is fucked-up shit. Just not the annoying kind."

He heard her quiet, musical laughter and, like he always did when he heard it, he savored it.

When he lost it, he ordered gently, "Right, baby, time for you to go back to sleep."

"Okay, honey."

He closed his eyes as that went through him.

He loved her calling him Chace.

But her calling him honey was something else. Something pure. Something magical. Like the first snow of the season falling at night. You wake up to it, make coffee, wrap up in a jacket and scarf over your pajamas, tug on thick socks and sit outside on your porch, drinking coffee that makes your insides warm but seeing your breath puff out in front of you, the air coming out clean and going in cleaner.

It was a little common miracle but even common, that made it no less miraculous.

The first time she'd done it, it felt like he'd been touched by the hand of an angel, and he hadn't gotten over feeling that every time she'd done it since.

He opened his eyes and asked, "You got the directions to my place?"

"Yeah," she replied softly, and that went through him too. "I think I'll be there around quarter to seven."

"All right, honey."

"You sure I can't bring anything?"

"Just you."

"Okay, Chace."

That went through him too, always.

"Go back to sleep."

"Okay."

"Later, baby."

"'Bye, Chace."

He disconnected, tossed his cell on his nightstand and rolled to his back, his eyes going to the ceiling.

Misty had slept in the master.

Chace had slept in the guest room.

A month after she died, he'd gotten shot of his old bed that she slept in and bought a new one. Spent a whack on a mattress that felt like sleeping on a firm cloud. It was spectacular.

Tonight Faye would be in that bed with him, her hair, her scent, her body, her crystal blue eyes all a pillow away.

A clean bed, unsullied by the garbage that used to be his life.

His bed.

He shoved his hand behind his head at the same time he lifted his knees and wrapped his other hand around his cock.

Then he closed his eyes and went through one of the many scenarios he'd be taking Faye through in the coming months. This one involved a lot of Faye using her mouth. He took his time. He did it stroking lazy at first, firmer and faster later.

And when he was done, he came hard.

*   *   *

Three hours later, after jacking off to Faye, making coffee and having breakfast and a run, Chace, showered, in jeans, a dark blue twill shirt, a heavy wool denim marl sweater and thick wool socks, was sitting on the rocking chair on his front porch. He had a hot mug of coffee in his hand, his feet up on the top of the railing in front of him, his eyes pointed out at the plain.

Chace lived in a four bedroom ranch-style house at the southwestern end of Carnal. He owned fifteen acres and not one of his neighbors owned less than three times that. Therefore, from his front porch, he couldn't see any of his neighbors' homes. Just the valley plain they lived on, the trees dotting the plains and shrouding the houses, the hills surrounding the area, the mountains beyond that and, in the distance, the town of Carnal.

Carnal looked farther away than it actually was. Seeming small across the plain, it was only a ten-minute drive.

Chace's mother's parents had set up a trust for him that he could access when he was twenty-five. To buy this house and land, he'd accessed part of it for a hefty down payment that would leave him with a mortgage manageable on a cop's salary. Living room, dining room, family room, huge-ass kitchen, butler's pantry, walk-in kitchen pantry, two and a half baths, study and four bedrooms, the master having one of the bathrooms and a big walk-in closet. There was an old-fashioned front porch, a large square deck out back and a massive two-car garage that could easily fit two SUVs, two snowmobiles and an ATV.

The rest of the money, he never touched.

This was because, since he could fathom the concept, he decided he'd have three kids. This was mostly because he'd never had a brother or sister and he wanted one, the other, or, better, what Faye had, both. Not having it, he decided that whatever kids he had, they'd have siblings and live in a house full of people, noise and love. Therefore, the rest of that money he'd set aside for their college educations. If they wanted to go to trade school, be beauticians or plumbers or got into Harvard or Stanford and became doctors or lawyers, he didn't care. Whatever it was, they wouldn't worry about paying for it.

He'd done this because his father refused to pay for Chace's education because Chace hadn't taken business courses but instead law and political science with a view to becoming a cop, not an attorney. In his usual fashion, Trane Keaton tried to use money to manipulate. Chace just got grants, loans, worked while taking classes and during the summers, paid his own damned way and took whatever courses he wanted.

He didn't complain, it was no use, and he had to do it to get what he wanted. But it wasn't easy. He remembered the late nights studying, the exhaustion in classes and dragging himself to work after them, and he'd paid off his last student loan five years ago. He wasn't going to put a child of his through that.

He also, back in the day when he allowed himself to think of this shit, didn't intend to marry a debutante or socialite with a daddy who could spend a mint on her wedding. He'd marry who he fell in love with, and whoever she was, she would have the wedding of her dreams even if Chace had to use his trust fund to help her. So the money was left alone for that too.

Last, his house was fucking fantastic. Big rooms. Lots of windows. Lots of places to be inside and out. Fabulous views. It'd been dated when he bought it so he updated all the baths, the kitchen and the flooring. His mother wanted to decorate it so he let her but went with her to guide her hand. Shopping was something he could give or take, usually give, but his mother loved to do it, she loved to be with her son, he enjoyed being with her so it was something they could do together. He couldn't say he wanted to do it again. He could say it turned out well.

That said, the woman he decided to put in his house would be encouraged to make it a house she wanted to live in. If she wanted a new state-of-the-art kitchen, the trust would cover it. If she wanted to add on a room where she could sew or knit or whatever the fuck (in Faye's case, a place where she could have quiet to read), he'd use the trust to give it to her. Whatever it was, she'd have it and he kept the money aside for that purpose as well as the two others.

A family, a wife who had what she wanted, a home.

All Chace ever wanted. Something his grandparents, both dead, would have been pleased as fuck he used the money they gave him to have.

When Misty lived there, she'd put her stamp on it. This was another attempt to win Chace, making what she said "his house theirs." Along with all her other attempts, this backfired.

She hadn't worked when they were married but Chace didn't give her money to keep herself. The money she had was from nefarious sources. It was soiled money.

They did not share her soiled money in a joint account. She bought herself what she wanted and Chace had no input.

When she'd died, Chace was left with everything. Her money, her belongings, all of it. He'd given it all away. Her parents took her personal belongings and the rest went to a couple different charities.

His thoughts made him sigh. He took a sip from his coffee and scanned the landscape he had long since memorized but it didn't mean he didn't still gain some peace or wasn't quietly moved by the scenery.

This was a feeling he liked having back. He'd lost it when Misty was in the house, a place he escaped as often as he could. He didn't sit on his porch and drink coffee when Misty was around. He didn't take the time to gaze at the view when he was coming or going. He dreaded coming home and he was always in a hurry to leave.

Taking another sip of coffee, as usual whenever his mind was on Misty, it drifted from her to when Chace had approached IA. He informed them of what was happening at CPD, his willingness to make it stop, and he'd taken his pay packets to them.

Every officer on Arnie Fuller's personal team got a packet once a month, the size determined by what they could fleece from local businesses and blackmail out of power brokers. Chace had accepted his because it would have been suspect if he did not.

He was a willing foot soldier as far as they knew.

He drew the line at approaching local businesspeople and forcing their donations to the Carnal Police Widows and Orphans fund. He also drew the line at being a blackmail go-between. He explained this to Arnie by showing him the wisdom of folks in town thinking there might be one or two honest cops on the payroll. Arnie had fallen for it so of all of the muck Chace had to swim through and the other filth he had to turn a blind eye to, at least he was clean of that garbage.

But he'd placed every envelope in a safety deposit box in a bank in Chantelle and handed all of them over to IA when they'd launched the undercover investigation.

There was nearly fifty thousand dollars in those packets. Six years of being on the take. IA made sure it was leaked to the media that Chace had turned in his money. They set him up as the poster boy for all that was good and right in law enforcement. They wanted no one to have any doubts so they set about making that so, using Chace to do it. Although it was true, in fact, everything they shared with the media was true, just selectively chosen as to what they'd share, it wasn't anyone's business. The way they shared it made it seem like he was some sort of white knight with a sword endowed with mystical powers, which he was not.

Luckily all that had died down, as it usually does, the infested personnel had been fired or incarcerated and replaced, and the town seemed to be settling, slowly but they were doing it.

Which brought Chace to his plans for the day. Grocery shopping for the weekend and his meet with Tate Jackson.

Tate was part owner of Bubba's bar but he was mostly a bounty hunter. He had once been a cop. So when the citizens of Carnal had a problem they couldn't trust the police to handle, they went to Tate. Tate, a good cop who never got dirty under Arnie's rule, a good man, always did what he could.

Since Chace's unexpected meeting with Clinton Bonar, Tate had been out of town after a skip. Chace had phoned him and told him they needed a meet as soon as he was home. Frank Dolinski knew about Bonar. To cover his bases, Chace needed Tate to know as well as a select few other men in town.

Tate got home yesterday.

They were meeting that afternoon.

On this thought, and another sip of coffee, something caught the corner of Chace's eye and he turned his head to gaze at the lone road that wound through the ranchland around his house. Seeing as the area between Carnal and the base of the mountain where Chace lived had only one road, Chace knew every car or truck that came down that road. Living there eight years, he even knew the vehicles of friends and family members.

This was not one of those vehicles.

It was a black Jeep Wrangler.

Chace reckoned he knew who was in that Wrangler.

The Goodknight family was a Jeep family. Faye, Sondra and Silas all drove Jeeps of varying ages.

Silas drove a black Wrangler.

Watching Faye's father's approach, sipping coffee, preparing for what was to come next, vaguely it occurred to Chace that Faye and Sondra, when it came to cars, were like mother like daughter. Their cars were not new. Faye had never upgraded hers that he knew of. Sondra took over Silas's vehicles when he was done. By the look of her and the way she acted the times he saw her, no nonsense, busy and active, she probably didn't care what she drove just as long as it got her where she wanted to go.

Chace watched Silas drive through the double-wide opening in the white picket fence at the end of his lane that led to a fenced-off enormous backyard. The rest of his land was unfenced. He liked the land, the space, the quiet, the peace. He didn't give a fuck if the livestock of his neighbors wandered onto his land. If they chewed the grass it meant Chace didn't have to mow the shit.

But that white picket fence was what sold him on this property, and he sanded it and painted it once every two years. Any time there was a repair needed, he saw to it as soon as he could, and he walked the fence occasionally just to check. The house was big, you could build a family there, you could add to it if you needed more room. But that long, white, rectangular line of fence surrounding it, delineating it, creating a yard, circling and highlighting the house made it seem like a home.

Chace waited until Silas made it to the end of the lane and stopped close to the house before he took his feet off the railing. He rose as Silas threw open his door. He walked to the top of the steps and leaned a shoulder against the white-painted porch post as Silas made his way up the cleared-of-snow flagstone walk Chace laid six years ago.

"Mr. Goodknight," he called when Silas was halfway up the walk and Silas, eyes to his boots, lifted a hand and kept up the path.

Only when he stopped at the bottom of the steps did his crystal blue eyes rise to Chace.

"Call me Silas, Detective Keaton," he invited.

Chace jerked up his chin and returned, "Chace."

Silas jerked up his own chin then tipped his head to Chace's coffee mug. "Got more 'a that?"

As answer, Chace turned and walked to the house, opening the storm door, the front door and moving through, turn-ing to hold the storm door open for Silas to follow.

He did and in they went, Chace leading the way over the oak floors that led to the back of the house that he'd laid four years ago when Misty was on a two-week vacation to visit a friend in Maryland.

Left side, a big dining room with rectangular table. The room had hints of western, hints of country, all of it with an underlying class that was all his mother.

Right side was what his mother liked to call the formal living room. Chace wasn't formal so the room had two com-fortable burgundy couches facing each other with more hints of western, none at all of country, which his mother referred to as "the formal part."

Chace moved through a deep, wide archway as he led Silas into the vast space that made up a big kitchen and fam-ily room.

The kitchen had an island in the middle with a five-burner stove and so much counter space it served as a kitchen table that could comfortably seat a family of eight. The island was a showstopper but so was the massive picture window over the sink at the back of the house.

The family room had an enormous sectional, three sides that were essentially three full couches. Big flat screen TV. Shelves filled with books, CDs, DVDs. And a stone hearth fireplace in the corner.

Off the kitchen leading toward the front of the house was the pantry, a hidden entry to the dining room and doors to a utility room and the garage.

Straight ahead from the wide hall that flowed from the front of the house to the back, there were double-wide French windows that led to the back deck.

Chace went directly to the coffeepot, asking, "How do you take it?"

"Seein' as Sondra ain't here, three sugars and a healthy dose of half-and-half."

Chace put down his mug, opened the cupboard and reached for another one as Silas continued to speak to his back.

"On me all the time, Sondra is. Her dad had a heart attack so she's got it in her head I'll have one. I run two miles a day. Do my sit-ups, pull-ups, push-ups every day. Work outside most of the time. Got ten acres to take care of. And three kids that may be grown but that don't mean I don't lend a hand. I do all this so I can enjoy half-and-half and sweet in my coffee. She doesn't see the balance."

Chace poured coffee and gave him the bad news. "I don't have half-and-half. Just milk."

"You don't have half-and-half?"

His tone was off in a way that Chace couldn't read but it still set him on edge. Or *more* on edge.

He looked over his shoulder at the man even as he reached for the sugar.

"No."

Silas Goodknight locked eyes with him and announced, "My Faye, she puts half-and-half in her coffee. Hazelnut flavored."

There it was. A feeler.

Chace and Faye were not seeing each other on the sly. By now the whole town knew they were dating. Regardless, Faye had told Chace that she'd told her folks they were seeing each other when she was at dinner at their place last weekend.

Now Silas Goodknight knew that his daughter was not waking up and making her coffee at Chace's house.

Chace mentally added hazelnut flavored half-and-half to his grocery list and replied to Silas, "Buy her coffees at La-La Land, Silas. Know she likes hazelnut. Haven't had occasion to see her usin' half-and-half."

Silas held his eyes a moment before murmuring, "Right."

Chace turned away, prepared Silas's coffee and handed the mug to the man before returning the milk to the fridge, tagging his own mug, turning toward him and resting his hips against the counter. Silas had the side of his hip to the island.

Neither man spoke as they both sipped.

Finally, Chace cut to it. "What brings you out this way, Silas?"

Silas moved his gaze from contemplating the view out the picture window to Chace.

"Been meanin' to do it for a while so decided to do it. Wanted to tell you I admire what you did. That kinda thing doesn't take bravery, it takes balls. Big ones. Not a lotta men would make the decision you made and carry it through. The kinda thing that was happening beats a man down. Most men think they have two choices and all the others took one of those two choices. Either he joins in or he cuts his losses and moves on. You didn't do either 'a those. You saw wrong bein' done, stomached it for as long as you could then set about rightin' it. Took guts. Took balls. Not a lotta men have either. You do. I admire that."

"Obliged but not sure I agree," Chace muttered politely. Surprised this was his opener, not wanting to be on this subject, he braced because he had a strong feeling Silas didn't seek him out to share gratitude a week after he found out Chace was dating his daughter.

Silas's focus grew intense and his voice went quiet when he returned, "Then you'd be wrong, son. Arnie Fuller was a pissant as a kid. His dad was an asshole. His granddaddy was an even bigger one. Then he got himself a uniform and he was no less a pissant. But a pissant with a badge is not a good thing. Grew from there 'cause, see, that man had no way to go except bein' an asshole like his kin. Problem was, he was better at it than both of 'em. You may not have been here then but you know it grew and how it grew. It wasn't bad when you started but that kinda shit is always bad, just the level of shit you gotta negotiate rising. Got to the point we were all drownin' in it. You and Dolinski cleared that away. Not one man before you, even Tate Jackson, took that on. Two decades of shit at a rising level. So, I disagree with you not agreein'. You did a thing no man before you would do, and a lot of people are grateful."

Not wanting to talk about this but definitely wanting to shut it down, Chace accepted the gratitude with a chin lift then he took another sip of coffee.

Silas took a sip of his and his gaze returned to the window.

Silas didn't speak. Chace didn't either. This stretched on awhile and Chace tired of it.

"Silas, there more you wanted to share?"

Silas's eyes cut to him and he didn't hesitate lowering the boom.

"I don't want you datin' my daughter."

Chace felt his body go solid.

Fuck, shit, there it was.

Fuck.

Shit.

"Silas—" he started.

Silas lifted a hand. "Grateful, son, told you that. But I'm an honest man so I came here to share that gratitude and lay it out. I wish you happiness. You deserve it but not with my daughter."

"That doesn't sync, Silas," Chace said quietly.

"I get that. But I'm guessin' you also get me," Silas returned quietly. "See, Chace, I pay attention. Knew the kind of man you are the minute I laid eyes on you. Don't know the story. Know it's not a good one. It's none of my business and I don't wanna know. So I'm not askin'. What I do know is my daughter's a dreamer. She hides those stars in her eyes but you don't gotta look deep to see 'em. As her father, I want her to live out whatever dream she's cookin' in that pretty head 'a hers. I also know that you married a woman under the eyes of God and even if you didn't wanna have your ring on her finger, it was. Then you went about your business like you hadn't made those vows under the eyes of God. I figure you had your reasons but whatever they were, I'm a man, a husband, a father and I want good for my daughter. I hope somewhere inside you that you get me when I say that no matter what the reason, breakin' that vow to your wife, to God, don't sit good with me when it comes to you spendin' time with my girl."

"We were married by a justice of the peace," Chace shot back immediately when Silas stopped talking and he watched Silas blink.

"Come again, son?"

Chace straightened away from the counter and held the man's eyes.

"At the time, didn't think I'd have another shot. What I did know was that if I married a woman I intended to love and cherish until death did us part, I'd be happy to stand in front of a preacher in God's house and make that vow with the intention of keepin' it. Misty wanted a church wedding. She did not get one for precisely that reason. I was not going to make a vow in God's house that I intended to break. So I didn't. Now, if I'm lucky enough to find a woman I love and cherish, I will make that vow to her and to God to stand by her side in sickness and in health until death do us part. And if that woman happens to be a woman I chose, a woman I actually love and cherish, make no mistake, Silas, when I make that vow, I'll mean it."

He took in breath, Silas opened his mouth to speak, but Chace beat him to it.

"And I want you to know, I don't take offense. You're right. I get you. You just don't get me. I even appreciate you comin' here, lookin' after your girl. You're also right, what went down is none of your business. I'm not gonna tell you what that is, not ever. What I can promise you is that, if what's bloomin' between me and Faye keeps takin' root, grows and blossoms, she will know everything. I will not keep anything from her. It'll be up to her to make the decision whether she wants to stick with me on this path I'm on tryin' to get back to the man I wanted to be. When she learns, if she decides to share that with you, that's her call. I won't get in the middle of family and how they communicate. I won't ask her not to share. I'll let her decide what she needs to do. I'm fortunate her folks are the folks they are 'cause I already know without havin' to ask that you and your wife won't share if Faye does."

"Tryin' to get back to the man you wanted to be?" Silas asked softly.

"You swim in filth, Silas, it seeps in through your pores."

At that, Silas shifted away from the counter and whispered, "Son, you cannot take that on."

"Too late. I did that when I married Misty. I'll give you a little. I got caught in that trap six years ago. I worked with IA for fourteen months. I reckon you can do the math."

"But—"

Chace talked over him. He had shit to do. He didn't want to talk about this. Even with a good man like Silas Goodknight deserving his time, reminding him he wasn't good enough for Faye and why, he had no intention of backing off.

"I didn't take offense and I hope you won't either when I say I'm not gonna back off Faye. She's pretty, she's sweet, she's kind and she's funny. She makes me laugh. She gives me hope. I already know it's selfish to be with her and I don't care. Haven't ever had the beauty she brings to my life, Silas, and six years ago I lost the hope I ever would. Selfish or not, I've experienced it now so I'm holdin' on. No way I'm lettin' that go. But because I respect the man I know you are, including the fact that you're the kind of father who created that beauty, I'll give you somethin' so you can walk away with a little peace of mind. I'll bend over backward, tie myself in knots and break my neck to do what I can to return the beauty she's giving me. This isn't God's house but it cannot be denied my house is in God's country so you can take that as you will when you get that vow."

Silas Goodknight stared at Chace without saying a word but Chace saw his eyes working. He just had no chance to prompt him to spit it out or find some way to shut this down because his cell rang.

He yanked it out of his pocket, looked at the display and muttered a distracted, "Sorry, need a minute," as he set down his coffee mug, took the call and wandered to the sink as he greeted, "Hey, baby."

"The boy wrote us a note!" Faye screeched in his ear.

Chace blinked at the landscape out his window. "What?"

"The boy wrote us a note! His name is Malachi!"

Jesus, Malachi? What the hell kind of name was Malachi?

"He says he likes Snickers," she went on excitedly in a quick rush. "He says the sleeping bag is super warm. He says he wants to read *Holes* and he wants the next *Harry Potter.* And he says he was able to get into the showers at the campsite north of town and take a shower! Isn't…that… *awesome*?" she finished on a cry.

"Yeah, honey," Chace agreed on a smile.

"We broke through!" she exclaimed.

"Yeah," he repeated.

"It was in the return bin. My hands were shaking when I read it. Heck, they're *still* shaking."

Christ, she was cute.

And she was right. It was awesome so Chace made a decision.

"Steppin' it up," Chace told her.

She hesitated before she asked, "What?"

"Done with sittin' in your SUV watchin' him grab his stash. Monday, I'm in my truck on the street, you're standin' by the return bin. If you can talk to him, good. I think this is a sign he might be willin' to slip through that opening we created. Your mission will be to get him to come into the library and talk to us both. We get his story. We feel him out. See what he'll give us. See if he'll trust us and trust that CPS can look after him."

"Don't you think it's too soon?" she asked anxiously. "He just wrote us a note."

"Faye, honey, we been doing this for near on two weeks and he's sleepin' rough. We're givin' him shit but he's still takin' care of himself and he's a little kid. He needs a roof over his head. Hot, good food in his belly. A guiding hand. Schooling. We can have no idea how long he's been out there. He isn't safe. We gotta get him safe, and not in three weeks. If we can manage it, Monday." She didn't respond so he prompted, "You with me on this plan?"

"Uh...okay," she answered with zero enthusiasm.

Clearly, she wasn't with him.

"We'll go cautious," he said quietly. "I might be a threat. You hopefully won't. So it's you at the returns. He doesn't want to go into the library, you give him an alternate option. A home-cooked dinner and a hot shower in a real bathroom on Monday night. No strings, he can walk away. But we'll talk to him while he's eatin' and do what we can to make him not want to walk away. You good with that?"

"Um . . . sure."

Still hesitant, no enthusiasm, worried.

"Baby," he tried gentle this time, "we're not gonna swoop down on him, cuff him and throw him in a cage. Ask him what his favorite meal is. Promise him you'll make it. You make it, the way you cook, him livin' rough, he'll love it. We broke through. Now we push the advantage."

"Get to him through his stomach," she whispered.

"It's worked so far," he replied and heard her soft, melodic giggle.

"Okay, Chace," she agreed more firmly.

"Okay," he said through a smile.

"I'm bringing champagne over tonight to celebrate," she declared.

"I'll pick some up today, you just bring you."

A pause, this one slightly annoyed then, "Chace, I *can* afford champagne."

She was right and she was wrong. She had a junker car, lived on the cheap in a rental that was kickass but mostly because she made it that way and, until recently, she walked pretty much everywhere she needed to go unless it was to the mall, her parents' or her sister's.

He'd been looking into the shit with the library and her salary was a matter of public record. She had a master's degree and got paid just above half of his salary. It wasn't poverty line but it also wasn't what you'd expect someone with that level of education and increasing experience to get. She ran the library. Her job description was three pages long. Budgets, accounting, acquisitions, promotion, programs and managing a volunteer staff that Faye had told him numbered five. She was a one-woman show. Her salary was peanuts for that level of responsibility.

Chace had found this disturbing, especially with the threat of closure. He didn't know a lot about it but he was looking into it and it didn't look good, particularly with the cutbacks at CPD. In fact, it hinted at further corruption in the Town Council, which would surprise him and annoy him. They didn't need any more of that shit and he didn't want to have to deal with it. He just hadn't had the chance to dig deeper.

So she could afford champagne but not only would he rather she spend her money on the kid, dresses and boots like she wore to The Rooster, he was the kind of man who took care of his woman. Furthermore, he was going to the grocery store. He wanted her at his place to eat and then do other things, not making stops before she got there.

"Faye, I'm goin' to the store in about ten minutes. No need for us both to go," he pointed out. "I'll get champagne."

That bought him a quiet, sweet, "Oh. Right. Of course."

Chace grinned at the window again.

"Well, I suppose I should climb down from cloud nine and get to work," she remarked, and he heard it as he often did. Even when she was cute, sleepy and hot on the phone in the morning, she didn't like to let him go. She didn't say it flat out, even tried to hide it, but it was there.

Chace liked that.

"Get to work and I'll see you tonight."

"Okay, honey. See you tonight."

"Later, Faye."

"'Bye, Chace, and…'" she paused then whispered, "Malachi. Yay."

She wasn't cute. She was fucking cute.

Through his grin, he muttered, "'Bye, baby."

He disconnected, turned and his body gave an involuntary start, a reaction he showed and couldn't bury, an unusual occurrence.

This was because, first, he'd forgotten Silas Goodknight was even there.

And second, Silas Goodknight was smiling at him huge.

"Right!" Silas stated smartly and put his mug on the island with more force than needed. "That's that. I'll expect you and Faye over for dinner next Saturday night. Be there at six. Sondra likes flowers, pink ones. Just tell Holly, Holly'll know what to do. Or tell Faye, she'll know what to do too. Other than that, bring you and a big appetite. Sondra may bitch about me takin' care of myself but that don't mean when company comes, she don't like to show off."

As Chace processed going from Silas's surprise visit the reason for which was to tell him he didn't want Chace dating his daughter to Silas asking Chace and Faye to dinner, Silas moved toward the front door.

With no other choice, Chace followed him.

They were outside, Chace at the top of the steps opening his mouth to give his farewell or say something else altogether, Silas at the bottom when Silas turned, locked eyes with Chace and beat him to speaking.

"Don't know the path you're on to the man you want to be. Do know that in any man's life, the journey includes dark places we find ourselves in where we don't wanna be. I get that you were in a dark place. I get you were there for a good while. I also know you made your way out. I don't understand why you don't think you've found the light and I won't ask. You already told me you won't share. I get that too. I probably wouldn't either. But I know from the way you spoke about my daughter, the look on her face when she was talkin' to me and Sondra about you last weekend, what she told us you were doin' for that boy she took to lookin' after and what I heard just now on the phone, you've already found that man. You just haven't realized it yet."

As Chace stood in the cold in his jeans, shirt, sweater and socks staring down the stairs, Silas lifted a hand and finished, "See you next weekend."

Then he sauntered down Chace's walk to his Wrangler.

Chace watched him give another short wave through the windshield before he did a three-point turn and drove down the lane.

Chace continued to stare after him as the Wrangler turned left and motored toward Carnal.

Then he grinned and muttered, "Fuck me," before he turned on his foot and walked back into his house.

*   *   *

As Chace drove up the drive to Tate Jackson's house in the hills, he noted Tate had the company that Chace suggested he have. Deke's beat-up pickup truck. Wood's Ford F-150. Ty's Land Cruiser. And a Cherokee Chace couldn't place but he suspected it was Holden Maxwell's considering Chace suggested Max get a call.

Deke Hightower was a drifter but he had a strict path that he drifted between. Carnal to Sturgis. He lived simple. Beat-up pickup. Harley. Roof over his head. Jeans on his ass. Food in his belly. And beer at Bubba's or the All American Roadhouse in Sturgis, whisky if he felt like living it up. He took odd jobs along the way in order to facilitate this life. The man was rough, monosyllabic and enormous in height and breadth. This hid the fact that he was smart as a whip. But he didn't try to hide the fact that he was loyal. He had Tate's back when Tate and Laurie were getting to know each other and all that went down with that. He had Ty's back during his drama.

Coal "Wood" Blackwood owned a share of the family-run garage in town. They specialized in Harleys. His father started it, built it up and now anyone who lived in a two-hundred-and-fifty-mile radius who had the funds to get their bike worked on at their garage brought it to Pop and Wood's. Wood's father, Pop, was a devoted Harley man who saddled Wood with a biker son's biker name that surprisingly Wood, considering he was also a biker, refused to answer to and everyone called him Wood unless they wanted his fist in their groin. Rumor had it he'd spent his teenage years and early twenties spreading this message wide and now no one called him anything else. Not even "Mr. Blackwood."

Chace parked, walked up the steps and down Tate's deck to the door while taking in the conifers all around dusted with snow.

Tate was a mountain man to Chace's plains man. Tate got his quiet and peace from being surrounded by nothing but trees.

Even before the shit that went down with him, Chace liked the openness of the plains, the vistas panoramic, the opportunities to make a surprise approach nonexistent.

Tate liked seclusion. You had to know where you were going to find Tate's house. If you happened on it by accident or design, he had the firepower and willingness to use it in order to encourage you to explain why you'd wandered his way and get you to move on if he didn't like your answers.

Chace hit the door and opened it without a knock because he saw the men sitting around the dining room table just inside. The owner of the Cherokee was who Chace expected, Holden Maxwell. Not a local, he owned a construction company in Gnaw Bone. However, he was a friend of Ty's and his wife was an attorney. She was the attorney who acted as Ty's attorney so he, like everyone, was not unaware of what had gone down. Although not intimately involved, he still had ties.

"Beer?" Tate asked as Chace closed the door.

"Yep," Chace answered.

Greetings were exchanged by chin, eyes or words as Chace took his seat at the table and Tate put a beer in front of him.

As Tate reseated himself, Chace asked, "The women?"

His eyes went to Ty who answered.

"Lexie and me moved into a huge-ass house last week. Furniture we got filled about a sixteenth of it. We also got a fuckload of money in the bank, courtesy of the State of California. This means Lexie, Laurie and Maggie are shoppin' for furniture. It also means, by tonight, I'll have to hire an architect to add onto my already huge-ass house because we'll have more furniture than we can fit in the fuckin' place."

Chace felt his mouth twitch. Lexie definitely liked to shop, this was well known. But what was funny was the fact that Ty was bitching when he didn't give one shit Lexie was out dropping a load of cash. First, they had it. Second, he'd lasso the moon if it made his wife happy.

Chace muttered, "Right," and took a sip of beer. Then his eyes went around the table and he started, "Got shit to do and got shit news. Wanna brief you, get the shit part done and then get on with the shit I gotta do."

More chin lifts, Chace took another sip of beer and sat back in his chair before he went on.

"Got a visit from one of my father's men. Man's name is Clinton Bonar. You may know him," Chace stated, his eyes not missing Tate's flashing with recognition. "You might not. My advice, you get the chance, don't. He introduces himself, walk away then five seconds later, call me. He's an asshole and of all the varieties of asshole there are, he's at the top of the scale of the worst there could be. Unfortunately, the last time I saw him, he was an asshole with a message."

Chace took another sip of beer and continued, sharing what Bonar shared, and as he did the alert but relaxed vibe in the room lost the relaxed part. This came especially from Ty when Chace mentioned his father's tapes.

So when Chace finished, he did it eyes on Ty and he did it quietly.

"I do not give a fuck you have them. I also don't give a fuck what you do with them. What I ask is that if you intend to use them, you give me a heads-up so I can do what I can to soften the blow for my mother. Me requesting you being here was not me doin' what Bonar wanted. I do not intend to be the errand boy for those assholes. I'm outta that shit. No more. I'm just sayin' this so all of you can keep your eyes and ears open, be aware, be cautious and report to me or Frank anything that concerns you. Frank and the cap know all of this. Whatever happens, we agree, we deal with it openly, within protocol, as a matter of police business. Maybe they'll see the wisdom of backing off and dealing with Newcomb quietly. Maybe a storm is brewing. We just need to be vigilant."

"Not gonna use those tapes," Ty declared when Chace stopped talking.

"Like I said, don't care what you do with them," Chace replied.

"Not gonna use 'em, don't even fuckin' want 'em. Got a kid comin', don't need shit like that in my house. I'll collect 'em, give 'em to you. That way, at least you're clear with your dad and they think of doin' somethin' stupid, Lexie and I are outside their warpath," Ty returned.

"You do not need to buckle to these men," Chace told him quietly, and Ty leaned across the table toward him.

"I'm not bucklin' to those motherfuckers." His deep voice rumbled firmly. "I do not want that shit in my house. I have no use for it. I got a wife who don't need any more bullshit, and handin' over some sick-ass sex tapes is a small price to pay for keepin' her clear of that shit. I have no intention of fuckin' with your mother's head. We both been forced down a murky road together, you and me, and as we moved down that road, we didn't know we had company. When shit got extreme, you had my back. You also had my wife's. So I'm also doin' this for you. What I'm not doin' it for is those motherfuckers. But they can think I am. I don't give a fuck.

They don't factor in my life and once those tapes are out of it, the last nuance of them is too."

Chace saw his point, seeing as it was hard to miss, and nodded.

"Am I the only one here that thinks that maybe a full frontal assault to teach a lesson that the town's not gonna be fucked with anymore is the way to go?" Deke asked, and this was not a surprise. Deke behaved himself in Bubba's because if he didn't, he'd get an ass full of buckshot from Krystal's shotgun. But Carnal to Sturgis was paved with bars that saw Deke's blood or, more often, blood he caused to flow hit the pavement in parking lots. He was not a man to sit on his hands or back down from a fight.

His question got two "Yeahs," one from Wood, one from Chace with a "Uh…yeah, Deke. It's only you," from Tate.

Ty just grinned at him. Max grinned at the table.

Then Max looked at Chace. "You need me to give Mick a heads-up about this?"

The Mick he was talking about was Mick Shaughnessy, the top guy at the Gnaw Bone Police Department.

"You wanna do that, it'd save me time," Chace answered. "He has questions, tell him he can give me a call."

"Will this reach to Gnaw Bone?" Max went on, and Chace kept his gaze.

Then he replied, "It happens. Yes. Two men vulnerable in Gnaw Bone. One sits on the Town Council. One has an office down the hall from your wife."

Chace watched Max's face get hard then he whispered, "Fuck."

"Don't know what they got on him and don't know who Darren's squeezin'. Just know he's made payoffs in the past and he's provided free legal advice," Chace informed him.

"This does not make me happy," Max informed Chace.

"It wouldn't make me happy either," Chace agreed. "But my understanding is, Nina put out her shingle and shares office space with George but she didn't partner with him. If Newcomb's after George, then he's runnin' scared. He'll do all in his power to keep this from Nina. My guess only, she's legally and financially clear, unless he's outed and dishonored, she never has to know and there's no need to drag her in. She's your wife, your call. But you tell Mick. He'll have her back."

Max pulled in breath through his nose before he sighed and sat back. What Chace knew of Max, by that evening, both Mick Shaughnessy and Nina Maxwell would know. What Chace knew of Nina Maxwell, by Monday, George Nielson, a prominent attorney in the area, would have the side of her tongue, something feared widely since she knew how to use it, and possibly he'd be looking for new office space. She'd moved in with him when she'd moved to Gnaw Bone to marry Max. Still, she'd get the offices. Nina Maxwell was also not one to back down from a fight. She fought on the side that was right and she rarely lost.

"Right, so, our shit storm might not be over. Bad news but fuck it, we've been livin' with worse," Wood said at this point. "Now, what I wanna know is," his eyes came to Chace and his lips surrounded by his goatee twitched, "are you seriously datin' the town's librarian?"

At this point, Chace sighed.

"Saw her with him at Bubba's," Deke confirmed then said with emphasis and a scary grin, "*Tight*."

"You think I'll man up while you trash-talk Faye, I'll shut that down now," Chace said low, and there were more lip twitches.

"Is it possible to trash-talk Faye?" Tate asked then went on, his lips surrounded by a full on beard curved upward, "Pure as the driven snow."

Fuck.

"Been around," Wood muttered, grinning at Tate. "Done a lot. Never been down a road no one's ever taken."

Fuck.

"Sweet," Deke whispered, his grin aimed at Chace.

Chace took a healthy slug of beer this time as he rose. After he found his feet, he put the bottle on the table and announced, "Now I'm shuttin' this shit down. Thanks for the beer and the time," he said to Tate then moved his gaze through the men before he began to leave.

"You don't get it, Keaton," Ty's voice stopped him, and his tone made Chace look back. "Clean pussy therefore undoubtedly sweet pussy, we're happy for you, man."

"Not sure I like you referring to Faye as 'pussy,'" Chace warned, not giving that first fuck Ty had five inches and a shitload of bulky muscle on him.

"Lex don't like it either but she got used to it. You will too," Ty replied.

"Terrific," Chace muttered, not thinking in a million years that Ty Walker would be his bud. Now after getting the Walker style you're-in-my-posse statement, he was at odds with how he felt about it.

"He's not lyin', Chace," Tate said quietly and Chace looked to him. "That works out, pleased for you. You get a good woman in your bed, life has a way of straightening itself out."

"Road can't be murky, it's got light shinin' on it," Ty added. Chace shook his head, not at odds with how he felt about Tatum Jackson and Tyrell Walker, two of the biggest badasses he knew, demonstrating signs they were pussy-whipped and didn't give a shit.

"She's got any friends, I'm on the market," Deke put in at this point, and Chace was done.

To communicate this, he lifted a hand, dropped it, moved

to the door and the sounds of deep, low chuckles followed him out.

It took him two steps to shake that shit off.

Firstly, because it wasn't nasty or jacked so it wasn't worth getting irritated at.

Secondly, because he had a shitload of food at his house including a bottle of hazelnut half-and-half.

CHAPTER EIGHT

Cats and Dogs, Birds and Bees

I DROVE TO Chace's place attempting to control my breathing. This was because I was near on hyperventilating.

And this was because tonight was the night.

I'd decided.

Tonight I was going to give Chace my virginity.

Chace didn't know this yet, of course. It was my decision. Although I was fraking nervous, I was sticking with it.

I'd made this decision for a variety of reasons.

Firstly, because I'd fallen in love from afar with Chace at sixteen and now we were dating. I'd known for thirteen years he was the man I wanted to give it up to. Therefore, even though we hadn't been dating long, considering I'd been into him for thirteen years, I figured it was high time I got down to doing that.

Secondly, because I was twenty-nine, I finally had a boyfriend so it was also high time I got laid.

And last, because with all the necking and early morning

phone calls, Chace a touch away or his voice, sleepy and sexy coming to me over the phone or his tongue in my mouth, for the first time in my life, I *needed* to get laid.

The problem with this was, I had no clue how to go about doing that.

I knew Chace was experienced. I knew this through living in the same small town as him as well as experiencing firsthand that, well, experience albeit limitedly. Men had to get some too (I thought), and he was around me enough he couldn't be getting it elsewhere (I hoped). So I didn't really get why he wouldn't allow it to go beyond necking.

My only thought was that, Chace being Chace or who I was getting to know as Chace, was smart, he was experienced and putting both of those together he knew or figured out I was not. So, being Chace, a good guy, he was taking things slowly. Not to mention, I wasn't exactly like the other women I'd known he'd been with. It wasn't (outside of Misty) like they were all loose. They just weren't like me. I'd grown up in Carnal, my mom and dad had too, not to mention they were well known and well liked. Maybe it was a respect thing.

Whatever it was, I was going for it.

But before I went for it, I needed advice.

This time, I didn't even have to think about it. At a quiet time in the library, I'd grabbed my cell, moved to my open office door, stood in it with eyes directed into the library and I'd called Krystal. Quickly and succinctly I explained my dilemma while trying and likely failing not to blush.

Krystal's response?

"I'll be there in five."

This was both a relief and made me even more nervous.

Those nerves escalated when she wasn't at the library in five. She arrived in fifteen. My heart started palpitating when I saw her stroll through the door with Twyla.

Now, I liked Twyla and the night I had drinks with Chace at Bubba's, Twyla had demonstrated (surprisingly) that she liked me too. Every girl always had openings for new girls in her posse, and one could say I had more openings than most since my girl posse for years had been limited. Unless you were the type of woman to steal boyfriends or clothes, all girls were welcome.

It was just that Twyla didn't seem like one of the girls. This was mostly because she was known throughout town as being able to best just about anyone at arm wrestling and I wasn't talking her engaging in this activity with other women. Though, I'd heard this wasn't unheard of, it just took her a lot less time to win. She also was known to be a former Marine. And last she was known to hold great disdain for all things girlie. So being in a girl posse didn't seem to be something she'd desire.

Then again, she was a girl and every girl, even me, knew that men were awesome for some things but others, no one but another girl would do.

My current situation being a prime example.

I just wasn't certain this instance was one of those that Twyla could be helpful with.

Further, I was not fired up by the idea of everyone in Carnal knowing intimate details of my life, including my life with Chace. That made me uncomfortable, for me, but it also made me uncomfortable because Chace had been the topic of a lot of discussion for a long time. Before that happened, he seemed a man who liked to live quiet. That choice had been taken away from him. Now, when he could get it back, I thought he should.

When they made it to the checkout desk, both scanning the vicinity to see there were no patrons close, I decided to start.

And I started with a lame, "Uh..."

Krystal's eyes sliced to me and she answered my unasked question. "She wouldn't hear no for an answer. Don't know how she knew. My side of the conversation was five words. She just did. I tried to talk her out of it. Ten minutes, didn't work, pissed me off so I just came. She followed." Krystal then looked to Twyla. "By the way, the time we're here, you're not gettin' paid for bein' there."

Twyla was a waitress at Krys's bar. By the look on Twyla's face, she didn't care that she'd lose her probably not-very-exciting waitress wages.

She didn't respond to Krystal. She looked to me and stated immediately, "Throw yourself at him."

"Holy frak," I breathed, my lungs seizing at the thought.

"Are you *nuts*?" Krystal hissed, leaning into Twyla.

"Do I look nuts?" Twyla returned, and unfortunately the answer to that was yes, she did.

It wasn't that she was built like a truck, which she was. It wasn't this because she was entirely comfortable in her frame, she worked it and thus it worked for her.

It was that she wore her hair in a female mullet. A male mullet was bad enough. A female mullet, well, I wasn't the keeper of all things fashionable and felt people should do what they liked but I also knew what everyone else did. That a mullet was one place no man or woman should ever go.

Krys gave up on Twyla and looked to me. "Do not do that. Talk to him."

Twyla stopped looking at Krys and her eyes came to me. "Do not talk to him. Throw yourself at him."

"Stop telling her that," Krys snapped at Twyla.

Twyla crossed her arms on her chest and looked back at Krystal.

"You get I like girls," she stated, but it was a prompt.

"Yes," Krystal replied.

"And I like girls who do things like wear mascara and lipstick."

"I know your partner, Twyla, you both were at my house for Bubba's barbeque spareribs three weeks ago," Krys returned.

"Right so, I like girls. And I've liked 'em all my life. I was a Marine. I've shot a gun. I own five of them, guns, that is. I watch the Nuggets, Avs, Broncos and Rockies. I've never in my life worn a skirt. I wear a sports bra because with these babies," she circled her bosoms with a pointed finger before dropping her hand to the checkout desk, "I got no choice. God saw fit to grant me an A cup, no way. Since I'm a C, I'm fucked. I have never worn mascara. I do not own a blow dryer. And I get off on goin' down on chicks. Now, which one, you or me, has more in common with Chace Keaton?"

I had to admit, she had a point there.

Krystal had to admit it too, even though I could tell she didn't want to. I could tell because she opened her mouth and closed it.

Twyla looked at me. "Throw yourself at him."

Krystal closed her eyes, dropped her head to look at her boots and her honeyed locks fell forward to hide her face.

I whispered to Twyla, "I kinda already tried that."

Krystal's head shot up as Twyla's eyebrows did the same.

"No go?" Twyla asked.

"He, uh... shuts it down or, um... redirects it but um... mostly shuts it down and concentrates on kissing."

"He know you're a virgin?" Twyla asked.

"Um..." I answered, not knowing until then that Twyla knew I was a virgin.

"How much neckin' you do?" Twyla requested details when I was unable to go on.

"I have little experience but it feels like, on a scale of one to ten, one hundred and fifteen."

Krystal grinned.

Twyla kept up her interrogation. "So, you had little experience before him?"

I nodded.

"On a scale of one to ten, how much experience did you have?" Twyla pushed.

"Point two five," I replied quietly.

"He knows you're a virgin," Twyla muttered, and my heart jumped, not pleasantly.

Krystal punched her in the arm. "Now you're freaking Faye out."

"Uh, just to be clear, the throw-yourself-at-him bit already freaked me out," I shared.

"So what's on tonight?" Twyla asked, ignoring my share.

"Dinner at his place, the first time I've been there," I told her.

"Bring panties and a toothbrush. Then find a way to tell him you brought panties and a toothbrush." She suddenly clapped, I jumped and she finished, "Done."

"Oh my God, that's actually a good idea," Krystal whispered, and Twyla's eyebrows shot up again, this time in affront.

"You think I walked five blocks in the Colorado Mountain March cold for no reason?" Twyla queried. "I'm a lesbian who can jack most motherfuckers up. I know non-lesbians who can do the same. You bein' one of 'em, I might add, though you do it with a shotgun in your hand. Same freakin' thing. But bein' a lesbian don't make me not good at advice."

I made mental note of this and added Twyla to my phone tree for when I experienced a relationship emergency.

"I didn't say that you weren't," Krystal retorted.

"Felt that way," Twyla shot back, Krys's eyes narrowed and she leaned in.

"Now you're being sensitive. I'll remind you, *Faye* called *me*," Krys stated.

"Maybe so, but when there's a problem, it's all hands on deck," Twyla returned.

Krystal had no retort, looked stymied and also looked angry that she was. Not unusual, just scarier than normal.

I decided to wade in. "Just an FYI," I said to Twyla. "I've added you to my relationship emergency phone tree."

Twyla grinned huge at me.

"Great," Krys muttered. "I finally get my shot, I get bumped because Twyla horned in."

I blinked at Krystal because she sounded genuinely aggrieved.

It then hit me that Krystal Briggs had let me in. Not like she had Chace. *In* in. She cared about me. She wanted to help. I was past the hard outside layer that kept everyone out and was in the soft, warm center.

Which made me feel warm inside too.

"Don't worry, Krys, her bein' a virgin and him bein' the kind of man he is, I'm sure you'll get your chance," Twyla assured.

I suddenly didn't feel warm inside anymore.

"What kind of man is he?" I whispered, and Krys and Twyla both looked at me.

Then they both said at the same time with the same emphasis, "*All* man."

I felt a shiver. It wasn't a bad one. It wasn't a good one. It was a nervous one.

"Right, so I *was* freaked out. Now I'm nervous."

Twyla tossed her hand in the air and stated, "You been seein' each other awhile, that man's been seein' to you in that while, not pushin' things, goin' slow, keepin' it controlled, you got no problem."

"This is true," Krys said, leaning into me. "No kidding, Faye. That says a lot."

I felt slightly better.

I still needed guidance.

"Um, so, how do I work in the panties and toothbrush? I mean, it's not something I share over dinner," I pointed out, trying not to blush but feeling the heat.

"He's got his tongue in your mouth," Krys began, "and he'll have his tongue in your mouth. You're on the couch, and you'll be on the couch. When he takes his tongue out of your mouth, find a way to whisper it in his ear. That'll speed things up."

"*Real* quick," Twyla agreed on a short nod.

Oh man. I was beginning to waver on my tonight's-the-night decision.

Twyla must have seen it because she leaned in. "He's done good by you. He's done good by this town. Word I hear, he's pretty solid. So far, he's taken care of you. He was way into you the other night. I may be into women but I spent a lotta time around men. You saved it awhile, you wanna give it away, you could do worse. But, honest to God, not sure you could find better."

I smiled at her because that made me feel *much* better.

Unfortunately at that point, a patron approached the checkout desk with an armload of books. Fortunately, Krys and Twyla hung around long enough for them to vow to me they wouldn't breathe a word about our discussion to anyone. One thing could be said of the two of them, if they vowed, which they did, they'd keep it.

And last, since I hoped I'd be unavailable the next morning, I asked them to take care of Malachi. Krys jumped on that, took my list of things I thought he'd need, promised to stop by the store and leave the bags by the return bin the next day.

So there I was, in my car on the road that led to Chace's house. A road I'd only been on a few times in my life because there was no reason to go down it since it led to a dead end at the foot of the mountain and had nothing but a bunch of ranches on it. Those times I'd been on it were while driving around with kids in high school for no other reason than to pass time and listen to music loudly on the stereo.

I'd changed purses because I now had clean panties, my toothbrush and I'd added face wash, moisturizer, deodorant and one of my sexy new nighties so I needed a bigger one. I thought it best to be prepared. If I was spending the night, I didn't want to sleep in makeup. Slept-in makeup looked awful in the morning.

I also had my sexy undies on and, just in case, had been wearing nothing but those every time I saw Chace, which meant every day since I'd bought them. I'd changed out of my work skirt and into jeans, brushed my hair and done the run-through-a-spritz-of-perfume routine. I was chewing on a piece of bubblemint because Chace told me in a growl during a make-out session he loved the way I tasted. So if bubblemint was an addiction before, suffice it to say it was an obsession now.

And I was nervous as all fraking heck.

His house came in sight and I knew it was his because he told me it was the only one surrounded by a white picket fence. He also had the porch light on and there were some bright floodlights at the side of the house that were lighting up the lane and the drive.

I grabbed the wrapper, spit my gum in it, balled it up, threw it in my cup holder, deep-breathed and turned in his drive.

I parked, set the parking brake and when I went for my door, I saw the door to Chace's house open. Chace, in jeans, a shirt and a kickass sweater, was walking out of it.

The deep breathing stopped working.

I managed to grab my bag, throw open the door and jump out. I slammed the door and walked up the cleared path, my eyes to Chace. He was standing at the top of the porch steps following my progress with his eyes at the same time looking outrageously hot. I figured this last wasn't because his outfit was better than any other I'd seen him in because it wasn't. Nothing beat the outfit he wore to The Rooster. Not even when I saw the faded jeans shirt in its full glory.

It was because I was hoping I'd very soon see him out of his clothes altogether and I figured it would be a good view.

I kept deep breathing, stopped at the foot of the steps and looked up at all his gorgeousness.

Nervous, fearing I'd pass out, I said the first idiotic thing that came to mind and luckily it was just idiotic and not mortifying.

"Do you like dogs and cats?"

His head jerked and I watched his eyes, warm on me even in the cold night, blink.

"What?"

"Dogs and cats. Do you like them?" I pressed on regardless of the fact it made me sound like an idiot. I'd started down this road. I had to follow it to its fruition. Hopefully, though, it was less a road and more like a short lane.

"Will my answer affect whether or not you'll come into the house to eat?" he asked back.

"No," I answered then added a partial truth. "I'm coming in because I'm hungry."

"Then cats, yeah, if they're the friendly kind who don't mind being petted and don't act like they own you rather than the other way around. Dogs, yeah, without any conditions," he finally answered.

"I've known a lot of friendly cats but I don't know any

who don't act like they own you rather than the other way around," I shared.

"Then cats, no," he amended his answer and continued with his own question, "Baby, you wanna tell me why we're standing outside talking about cats and dogs?"

I didn't because a smarter conversation would be about birds and bees.

I didn't share that.

Instead I said, "I'm thinking about getting one. A cat or a dog, I mean."

"Is my answer a deal breaker?"

"In what sense?"

"In the sense that if I say no, I don't like one or the other, you won't come into the house and eat."

"I already answered that."

"Yeah, darlin', but I said no to cats and you haven't come into the house yet."

"Oh, right," I whispered.

I fell silent.

So did Chace.

He broke it.

"Faye, we're still standing outside."

That was when I blurted, "I was leaning toward a cat."

After that was when Chace threw his head back and roared with laughter.

I liked it but still, I bit my lip.

When his eyes dipped down to me, he said through his waning laughter but he said it gently, "Baby, climb up the fuckin' steps."

I climbed up the effing steps.

I didn't get to the top before Chace bent low and took my hand so the last two steps I did it hand in hand with his.

He started to guide me across the porch to the door and I spied two rocking chairs with a table between them.

White picket fence. Nothing but plains and ranches and mountains all around. It was darkening dusk so I couldn't see but I already knew the views from his house would be astounding from every angle, the kind you would never get used to.

Those rocking chairs would be perfect to sit in and read for hours in the summer. Or sit next to Chace and do absolutely nothing and be happy doing it.

Somehow, this thought and how beautiful it was made me tug on his hand, turn slightly into him and go up on my toes.

His body gave a slight jerk as if he was surprised but he still stopped with me and bent his head as if he knew I wanted his ear.

Which I did.

Because, into it, I jumped the gun and let it all hang out.

"I brought clean panties and a toothbrush," I whispered and held my breath, not moving, not even to breathe.

Chace didn't move either. Not a muscle. I didn't even sense him breathing.

Oh God. Oh frak. Oh *God*.

Then suddenly Chace moved and he did it to let go of my hand, bend low and I was flying through the air but doing it safe in his arms, one of them behind my knees, one of them around my waist.

I automatically curled an arm around his shoulders, tipped my head back and I did this last just in time for his mouth to take mine.

Holding me, he opened the storm door and carried me over the threshold kissing me.

So I guess I did it right.

*   *   *

A phone was ringing.

It wasn't the first time. In fact, it was the third.

I heard it but I didn't care. And I didn't care the other two times either.

This was because I was on Chace's bed, in Chace's bedroom, with Chace's mouth on mine, his tongue in my mouth, his hand down my pants and I was *this close* to coming.

This had happened fast, starting with the kiss Chace gave me while carrying me all the way to his bed. It was like the kiss he gave me before we went to The Rooster. Wild. Abandoned. Fiery. Exquisite.

Luscious.

But it was more *luscious* because he was doing it *carrying me to his bed*.

You couldn't get more luscious than that.

He kept kissing me as he bent a bit, the light went on and he lay me on my back in his bed, immediately following me in.

I knew he wasn't controlling this. Not even close. I knew this when his hands went up my shirt and I felt them for the first time, warm skin against skin.

I liked this so I reciprocated, tugging his shirt out of his jeans and my hands pushed inside.

But I liked what they encountered more. Oh my fraking Lord, I liked it a lot more. Hot, smooth, hard with lots of interesting planes and bunches and ridges to trail my fingertips over and discover.

My touch had an astounding effect, and that was Chace's hand gliding from my waist to my ribs and curling around my breast over my bra. Nearly instantly when his hand reached this destination, his thumb slid firm over my hard nipple.

No one but me had ever touched me there and suffice it to say, Chace doing it while kissing me, lying mostly on me, his firm, hot skin under my hands while in his bed, sent shafts of fire through me the likes I never experienced. The likes I didn't even know existed. The likes I liked a whole heckuva lot.

So much I tore my mouth from his on an arched neck, whimpering moan.

This also had an astounding effect, and that was both of Chace's hands going to my jacket and yanking it down my arms. Then he pulled me up and jerked it away, tossing it to the floor.

After it went my shirt.

This might have freaked me out if his mouth hadn't found mine, my back hadn't again found bed and his hand hadn't again found my breast and, last, his thumb hadn't retraced its path then gone backward for another swipe.

I wasn't wrong that the first time was magnificent because the second and third were just as fraking good. So good, I arched my back and whimpered into his mouth, my hands tugging his sweater up.

Chace got the message I didn't even know I was sending. I would know this when he tore his lips from mine, arched away from me, put his hands behind his shoulder blades, ripped his sweater off and tossed it aside. My shaking hands immediately and instinctively went to the buttons on his shirt. I got one undone before his back bowed, his body shifted, I lost purchase on his shirt, his hand lifted my breast and his mouth closed on my nipple over my bra.

Okay, oh frak, okay, the thumb swipe, magnificent. His mouth, *sublime*.

My back arched so deep, it left the bed and a low, long, quiet moan rose out of my throat then I had his mouth back on mine, his hand and thumb back at my breast. I got another rough, wild, deep, wet, *long* kiss and I was already lost. But at his kiss, I knew I never wanted to be found.

My hands were moving. Having minds of their own, they went everywhere they could find, touched everything they could reach, took in as much as they could get. Including running over his hard behind, one hand rounding his hip and then it happened.

Not even thinking, just acting on instinct, so turned on, so out of life and into Chace, my fingers grazed the hard evidence of arousal.

I gasped into his mouth because I liked it. Not a little, a lot. It wasn't a surprise. But it was a gift, knowing I gave him that, feeling it, knowing that was all for me.

And wanting it.

Chace growled down my throat.

Oh my fraking, fraking *Lord*, but I liked that a whole lot more.

His hips jerked away, his torso came up, my eyes slowly opened and his hand went to my belt. I felt it tugging as my hands went back to his shirt.

I clumsily managed to get two more buttons undone before the zip went down on my jeans and I heard Chace's gruff, thick, deeper-than-normal voice call, "Faye."

My eyes moved to his and not even knowing why, just feeling the word come from deep in my soul, needing to say it, needing him to get it, I whispered, "Please."

His hot eyes holding mine, his hand slid in. *Straight* in. Inside my panties, fingers curving around, his middle one pressing in and my hips left the bed to push into his hand as my eyes closed. I felt my lips part, but mostly I felt nothing but how unbelievably *awesome* it was to have Chace's hand down my pants.

"Fuckin' beautiful," I vaguely heard him mutter then when his finger moved and I started to understand what heaven felt like, I equally vaguely heard him order, "Want that mouth, baby."

My chin tipped down instantly and he took it.

Oh jeez. That was better. *Tons* better.

Unable to do anything else, my fingers curled into his shirt tight. I held on and gave him my mouth, felt what he was doing with his finger and I held tense, my whole body, like if I let go, it would shatter.

He stopped kissing me long enough to murmur against my lips, "Move with me, Faye, your hips. Don't fight it, give in to it."

My brain couldn't process much but my body obviously heard his words because my hips started working with his hand. Sliding back to his forth, forth to his back and that was *a whole lot better.*

"Chace," I breathed against his mouth.

"That's it," he whispered against mine.

Already built, it started pulsing, throbbing, it was going to explode.

I quit breathing.

Chace stopped his finger moving, slid one inside... *inside*... that would be inside *me*... and I gasped but then let no more air in or out.

"Faye, honey, *breathe.*"

I did what I was told and breathed, his finger slid out of me and started doing what it was doing before and his mouth took mine again in a kiss.

Through this, the phone rang twice.

Now I was there. I was there. I knew that feeling. I also knew it was going to be better than ever. The best. The absolute best.

I tore my mouth from his because I couldn't take his tongue anymore. It was all too much, too much goodness. I shoved my face in his neck and gasped as it happened. Driving through me, making me clutch on tight, shove my face deep, buck my hips against his hand, the heat of it rushed through me, burning me to a cinder.

I was right. It was.

The absolute best.

When I came down, slowly, lazily, it felt like it took years and I didn't care if I lost that time, it felt that good, the phone had stopped ringing and I was no longer on my back but on my side. My leg was thrown over Chace's hip and one of his arms was tight around my waist, holding me close to his body. His other hand was in my hair, tucking my face in his throat. Both of my hands were still clutching his shirt.

My breathing started evening out, my fingers relaxed, my hands went flat against his back and I heard Chace gently ask the top of my head, "How you doin'?"

I was fine. I was beyond fine. I could die right there and be happy. Not, of course, that I wanted to do that but that was just how fine I was.

"I'm good," I whispered.

"Good," he whispered back.

I pressed deeper into Chace and his arm got tighter around me.

Then I closed my eyes tight and called, "Chace."

"Right here, honey."

I pressed my lips together and then I did what I had to do. I announced, "There's something you have to know."

"I know it."

I blinked at his immediate answer, this action leaving my eyes open, but I was so surprised at his quick response, I didn't have it in me to notice I was staring up close at his very attractive throat, which was an opportunity I would normally take time to savor.

Then I asked, "You know it?"

"Yep."

"You know what?"

"That I'm the first man to have his hand down your pants and later, I'm gonna be the first man who does other things to you too."

Yep, he knew it.

Oh God.

I closed my eyes again and dipped my chin, uncertain whether to be embarrassed or whether, from his tone, which was gentle, quiet but straightforward, not to be and his hand curled warm around the back of my neck.

I felt his lips on the top of my hair.

There he whispered, "Faye, darlin', I want you to hear this and get it, what you just gave me was the most beautiful thing I've ever been given in...my...*life*. What you'll give me later I know from what I've already had, not just now but since I've known you, will be even more beautiful. With me, anytime, anywhere, you're safe. But of the anytime and anyplace you're with me, the place you're safest is right here, in my bed. You never have to be embarrassed. You can ask questions. You can react how you want. You can be who you are. If I'm doin' something you don't like, you can stop me. Nothin' will ever happen in this bed that you'll be uncomfortable with. I swear to you, baby. You're safe here and you always will be."

These words were awesome.

But still.

I took in an unsteady breath, opened my eyes and started falteringly to ask his throat, "You don't think that I...I mean, that I haven't...uh—"

He cut me off to say firmly, "No."

"But, at my age, the fact that—"

"No, Faye."

I took in another unsteady breath and whispered, "Really?"

His fingers gave my neck a gentle squeeze. I read his message and pulled in another halting breath before I gave him what he nonverbally asked for and tipped my head back.

His was already tipped down and his eyes immediately captured mine.

My teeth immediately captured my lower lip. His gaze went to my mouth before coming back to my eyes.

"You didn't hear me, which means you didn't get me," he said softly.

I let my lip go and mumbled, "Um..."

He dipped his head closer, touched his mouth to mine and pulled back half an inch before he whispered, "Baby, you gave that to someone else, it wouldn't be mine. Now it's mine. No one can ever have it. It'll always be mine. I love it. I think it's beautiful. So I absolutely do not think the town's sweet, cute, pretty, shy librarian who held on to that for as long as you did then gave it to me is anything but really fuckin' good."

I could tell by the seriousness mingled with serious warmth in his eyes he meant that. All of it. All he'd said.

Every word.

And because he did, I smiled at him.

His eyes dropped to my mouth before they closed slowly. That warm, raw thing I'd seen over pizza and deep conversation our first date was sweeping through his handsome features before he did what he did that night. Eyes closed, he tipped his head forward so his forehead was touching mine.

"Chace," I whispered, watched his eyes open and his head went back.

Then he announced, "Time to feed you."

I blinked. His body moved as if he was going to move away from me but my arms tightened around him.

"Chace," I called again, he stilled and looked at me.

Then something else hit me and since I had his attention, I had to say something about it.

So I did, but I didn't say it.

I stammered it.

"I...uh, well, um...you know...uh, that is," I finished on a rush, "what about you?"

His features cleared and it was then he smiled at me.

It was a new smile. Wicked.

And also wicked hot.

Oh my.

Then he said quietly, "Just had my hand down your pants, honey, still gotta know, how real can you take it right now?"

"Real?"

"Real."

I didn't know the answer to that question.

But he told me I was safe in that bed and since Chace stopped giving mixed messages, I'd never felt unsafe around him.

So I invited, "Sock it to me."

He kept smiling his wicked smile, but it was now tinged with amusement. He rolled partly into me so I had no choice but to go to my back. He was partly on top of me and he pulled one arm from around me to plant a forearm in the bed beside me.

Then he looked down at me, dipped his face back to close and he said gently, "Later, for you, I'm gonna take my time. I'm gonna do everything I can to give you everything you need to prepare to take me. What I couldn't know is if you take care of you. If you don't, like it just did, it could go fast for you so this wouldn't give me time to prepare you. Now," his lips tipped up, "you're good. It'll give me the time I need. Then it'll be good again for you and also for me."

Okay, maybe I wasn't ready for that kind of real. I knew this because I felt my cheeks warm.

Still, I mumbled, "Oh. Okay."

Chace chuckled so I knew he didn't miss my blush. He bent and brushed his mouth against mine before he lifted away again and whispered, "We'll work up to straight talk about sex."

This seemed like a good idea.

"I'd appreciate that," I whispered back.

Chace's body shook a little with his amusement. I didn't have the chance to feel much of it because he rolled over me then pulled me out of bed and onto my feet.

It was at this point I realized my jeans were undone and I was wearing nothing up top but my emerald green, satin, demi-cup bra with the little, tight diagonal pleats across the cups and tiny edge of dove gray lace.

Chace was bent to tag my shirt off the floor and my hands quickly went to my jeans.

He straightened, his eyes dropped to my torso and stayed there as his hand came out to offer me my shirt and I got the zip up.

"Take that, I'll do this," he ordered, his hand not holding my shirt coming out to curl into my waistband and he tugged me to him.

I bit my lip, took the shirt and started to pull it on.

It was over my head and Chace's fingers had done up my button and were working my belt when he muttered, "When we work up to straight talk, I'll tell you exactly how I feel about your bra."

Oh my fraking Lord.

Well, one thing about that, it was good to know the bra was a worthwhile purchase.

I yanked my shirt down and avoided Chace's eyes.

He finished with my belt but used a finger hooked in the buckle to tug me even closer, and the intimacy of this sent my eyes skidding to him.

"I'll amend my statement in a way since you're safe with me anywhere but especially in my bed and also especially in this room," he told me the instant he got my eyes.

"Uh...okay," I whispered, happy to hear it, even if it was mostly a repeated statement though not getting why he said it.

Chace, who had demonstrated often he could read me, read me. I knew this when he kept talking.

"What I'm sayin', Faye, is, you're avoiding my eyes because maybe you're embarrassed or feelin' shy and uncertain about what to do next."

His hand came up, shifted my hair off my shoulder then curled around the side of my neck. But his eyes never left mine throughout this or when he used his finger hooked into my belt buckle to pull me even closer and his face dipped to mine.

"I like you," he whispered. "I hope you're gettin' that. I like all I know about you, even what I already knew that you were gonna tell me earlier. That bein' that no one's been in there. That is, no one now but me. And last, I like knowin' the town's cute, sweet, pretty, shy librarian who I'm datin' wears sexy underwear." His smile hit his eyes, which were all I could see, and he went on, "I like it a lot, baby. A fuckuva lot. So you got not one thing to be embarrassed, shy or uncertain about. Yeah?"

"Yeah," I whispered, giving him a small, relieved smile because I was relieved and not in a small way.

"Good," he whispered back, lifted his chin, kissed my nose then let go of me in the two places he had hold of me but grabbed my hand and pulled me out of the room.

Seeing as my eyes were closed since he was kissing me and carrying me on the way to his room, on the way out of it, I could finally take in his house.

Which, as he moved me through it, was really nice. It was an extension of him. Masculine (very), good taste and western.

It was also massive. We kept going (and going and

going!) and then finally hit an enormous room that was both family room and kitchen. They were enormous in their own right but put together they were *massive*. Not to mention his sectional, which was like I'd never seen before. It was, essentially, three full couches. *Three*.

I figured Misty lived here with him but I didn't figure he lounged on his couch with her watching TV, mostly because he told me he spent zero time with her if he could help it. This meant that couch had been a couch for one. Which was crazy.

"Uh...you have a lot of room," I noted as he led me to the kitchen.

"Yep," he agreed.

"This is a lot of room for just one person," I remarked as he stopped me by an island that could act as a guest bed for three adolescent children. Just pump up an air mattress, toss it on top and hope they didn't roll off.

He didn't reply to my remark.

Instead, he asked, "You drink red or white wine with tacos?"

I looked to him to see he was standing at his fridge. "Tacos?"

"Ground beef, packet seasoning, store-bought shit to put on top. I'm not a cook. Don't like doin' it. But gotta eat and when I eat, I like to eat shit I like. If it comes out of a packet, so be it. They might not be Rosalinda's or even close. But they don't suck. So, we're havin' tacos."

"I like tacos," I informed him though I liked Rosalinda's Mexican food better. You had to drive to Chantelle to get it, but Chantelle wasn't very far and Rosalinda's was so good, it was worth the trip. When I didn't drive to Chantelle but I had a taste for tacos, I used the packet stuff too. So I decided to inform Chace of this fact. "I also make packet tacos, FYI."

"Good to know," he muttered, his lips tipped up then, "Red or white?"

"Red."

He moved to a bottle of wine sitting on his counter.

I moved to a stool, pulled it out and hefted my booty on it.

"Room to grow."

This was Chace. I stared at his back at his weird comment that came out of nowhere as he shifted to the side to open a drawer and pull out a corkscrew.

"Pardon?"

He nabbed the bottle, turned to me and his eyes locked on mine in a way I forgot how to breathe.

"Room to grow," he repeated then explained. "Another thing that sucked about life when my future included Misty. Didn't think I'd have what I wanted and what I wanted was why I got this place. I bought this house to put a woman in it then plant a family in it. So it's big because I want three kids. Room to grow."

Holy.

Frak.

"Room to grow," I whispered breathily, unable to tear my eyes from his.

"Yep," he answered firmly then asked. "You want kids?"

"Uh...yeah." I was still whispering and it was still breathily.

"How many?" he went on.

"Three."

Yep, still whispering. Yep, still breathy. Also, incidentally, it was the truth.

Chace smiled.

I quit breathing.

I forced my eyes from his and took in the bottle of wine.

Then I asked, "Didn't you get champagne?"

"Fuck," he muttered and my gaze went back to him. "Forgot."

I was disappointed and tried to hide it but I still inquired, "You forgot the champagne?"

"No," he answered, putting the bottle of red back on the counter. "You leadin' the night tellin' me you had a clean pair of panties in your purse, I forgot that I bought champagne at all."

I bit my lip even though I got a little happy niggle that I was able to make him forget anything.

He grinned and I had a feeling, the way he did it, that he read my mind.

I had no time to react to this because he walked down a back hall and disappeared.

He came back with two trumpet-shaped champagne flutes that had cute teeny, tiny little horseshoes etched around the bottom just above the stem. I didn't know how but they managed to be classy and cool rather than looking kitschy like some of that kind of thing could look. Perhaps it was the etchings, which were precise, almost elegant and not cartoony. Perhaps it was the quality of the crystal, which was so clean and fine it showed prisms in his overhead lights. Whatever it was, they were awesome.

Chace set them on the island by me, his manner like they were no better than plastic, and headed back to the fridge as I offered, "Anything I can do to help?"

He turned with the bottle of champagne, the fridge closing behind him, and had his mouth open to speak when we both heard a knock on the door.

His eyes went in the direction of the front door. They were narrowed under drawn brows and his jaw had gone hard. It was kind of a scary look. But my eyes dropped to his shirt, which was untucked, the three buttons I'd unbuttoned were still unbuttoned and I saw a sprinkling of reddish brown chest hair. Not a thick mat of hair but a short, sexy *sprinkling*.

By sexy I actually meant unbelievably *fraking* sexy.

My mouth started watering.

Chace would undoubtedly not think chest hair was sexy, but I knew whatever he was thinking were very unsexy thoughts when he growled, "Fuckin' shit," put the bottle on the counter by the glasses and came to me.

He ran his fingers through the length of my hair at the side, bent and whispered, "Be right back." Then he kissed my forehead, his fingers left my hair and I twisted on my stool to watch him prowl (oh jeez, he was prowling) to the door.

Even with him prowling and impatient, my eyes watched him move, his broad shoulders not even close to being hidden by his shirt, his long legs in his jeans, his arms loose at his sides and it was, as ever, a good show.

Over dinner at my place that week, he'd told me he was a swimmer and ran track in high school and kept it up since then. He swam at the YMCA in Chantelle twice a week, ran five miles twice a week, ten miles once a week and had weights at his house where he did weight training twice a week.

This effort paid off for him in a big way, and since he maintained his body and pushed it on occasion, he knew what it could do and the way he walked, in total command of his frame, communicated that.

I had a feeling with that and what had happened in his bedroom, this boded well for what Chace referred to as "later." A shiver ran up my spine the likes I'd never felt before but I liked it a whole lot.

I smiled to myself and my eyes drifted to the champagne. I needed a drink. I'd had a Chace's-hand-down-my-pants orgasm. That definitely called for champagne. I wanted to open the bottle but from our very first date, if

Chace was with me, I'd not poured myself a drink or bought myself one.

It was then it occurred to me that Chace was kind of old-fashioned. He had no trouble with me cooking for him and serving up the food. But he didn't want me to pour my own drink. He helped with dishes if he was at my place but he was strictly a dry-and-put-away man. Strictly as in, there were clearly boundaries. Men didn't wash. They dried and put away. Men didn't serve up food. They poured drinks.

It was definitely old-fashioned.

It was also weirdly hot.

"Jesus, are you fuckin' serious?" I heard him ask in what had to be a rude greeting then finish, "Jon, I'm off duty. Very fuckin' off duty, and this would be why I didn't answer the fuckin' phone."

Right, Chace was cursing more than normal. He was pissed. I knew this but I had a feeling his pissed-ness had increased after finding out who was at the door.

"I know that but we need you on this one, Chace, or I wouldn't be out here. You're our most experienced detective," another voice sounded.

"Frank might have passed the test only a few months ago but he's been around these parts since birth, clean and on the job awhile. He'll do fine," Chace told him.

"It's a murder, Chace."

My breath left me and my body stilled.

"Fuck," I heard Chace clip.

"Darren Newcomb," Jon told him.

Suddenly, all the way from the front of the house, a white-hot current of electricity streamed through.

It was so intense, I twisted woodenly on my stool to face that way as Jon went on, "Brother, sorry, so sorry, brother, but he was found on the access road up to Miracle Ranch about ten feet from where they found your wife. And, buddy, this sucks, I hate to share this shit, but Newcomb was done just like her."

At these words, my body having a mind of its own, I ignored the terrifying current still streaming and moved quickly through the massive kitchen to the hall.

I saw through the hall that the front door was open, storm door closed. The uniformed policeman who was at the reception desk when I went to the station was standing just inside Chace's lit foyer. Chace's body was still and his jaw in profile was hard, both in a way that made my heart clench.

Jon's eyes cut to me when I moved through the hall then they cut to Chace. I saw them drop to his shirt, taking in the opened buttons, and they came back to me. He shifted uncomfortably, likely reading into the situation somewhat inaccurately since the action wasn't interrupted but reading accurately there was action.

This would normally mortify me.

But my focus was entirely on getting to Chace.

Which was what I did. Immediately, I moved into him. His arm came up in a distracted way, curling around my shoulders as I fitted my front to his side and my arms moved to circle his middle.

"Honey?" I called as he stared silently at Officer Jon.

When my word sounded, his body jerked slightly, he looked down at me and muttered, "Go back to the kitchen, darlin'."

"I'm good here," I refused gently, giving his middle squeeze.

He dipped his face close and repeated quietly, "Go back to the kitchen, baby."

I pulled in breath, squared my shoulders, held his eyes and repeated (kind of), "Chace, honey, I'm good *here*."

"Backbone," he murmured, his gaze drifting around my head and shoulders then it sliced to Jon. "Send someone to check Harker's Wood. I'll get Faye sorted and then I'm on my way."

Oh God. Holy frak.

Harker's Wood.

I'd heard of Darren Newcomb but I didn't know how. His name was just familiar.

But whoever he was, this had something to do with Misty.

"Frank's already on that. Got a cruiser headin' that way. Frank's with the body," Jon replied.

"Call him, tell him I'll go to the body first. The wood second. Anyone on the family?" Chace returned.

Jon shifted uncomfortably again as he shook his head.

"Fuck," Chace muttered then, "Right. Body, wood, then I'll go to his family."

I didn't like that but even if I didn't, it was his job. Unfortunately, murders were happening in Carnal on an alarmingly frequent basis. Well, that wasn't true. Just Tonia Payne, a waitress who was killed by Dalton McIntyre. Then there was Neeta, Tate's old girlfriend though she didn't live in Carnal, she was just murdered by McIntyre who did live in Carnal and also did *all* his killing here. And, of course, Misty Keaton. But still, that was three people I semi-knew in the last few years when I'd lived there near to my whole life without a one.

Though I suspected even if you informed a hundred families a loved one had died or something bad had happened, it would never get any more fun.

"Right, Chace," Jon muttered then he looked at me. "Sorry, uh...Faye, is it?"

Like he didn't know. I'd been with Chace at the Italian place, The Rooster and Bubba's. The talk hadn't come to me but I was no dummy. The town was buzzing.

Anyway, I'd given him my name at the police station three weeks ago.

"Yes, Faye." I offered my hand but stayed close to Chace, with my other arm wrapped around his back. "Jon?"

"Jon, yeah." He took my hand and gave it a squeeze while giving me a small smile appropriate to an introduction on the heels of giving the news that someone had been murdered. "Sorry to interrupt but, uh . . . nice to meet you, formal like."

"You too, Jon," I said quietly and pulled my hand away.

He let it go and looked up at Chace.

"See you, um . . . there," he murmured, dipped his chin to me then walked to the door.

Chace gave my shoulders a squeeze. I read the command, dropped my arm and he followed Jon.

"Later," he muttered, Jon looked over his shoulder at Chace, jerked up his chin then took off.

Chace closed the door and turned to me.

"I'll just uh . . . go, um . . . find my purse and head home."

I was thinking about where my purse might have gotten to so I jumped a little when I felt Chace's hands settle on either side of my neck and my head tilted back to catch his eyes.

Then I caught my breath at what I saw.

"Please, honey," he whispered, "make tacos. Eat 'em. Watch television. Do whatever. But however it ends, when you go to sleep, crawl into my bed."

Oh God.

I blinked, my belly warmed, my heart skipped, my hands came up to curl around his wrists and my mind couldn't decide whether to be scared, excited or freaked.

"Chace—" I whispered back, not sure what else I was going to say but not getting the chance to say it.

His hands squeezed my neck, gripping firm but not hard. His face got closer. "Please, Faye, whatever this is, when I get home from it, I want to slide into my bed with you bein' in it."

"Okay," I agreed quietly, and it was Chace's turn to blink. "What?"

"Okay," I repeated. "I'll stay. I'll eat tacos. I'll watch TV. If you're not home, I'll go to sleep in your bed."

His head moved away an inch but his voice was still soft when he asked, "Easy as that?"

"You want me here?" I asked back.

He didn't answer that. That raw warmth washed through his face and he murmured, "Christ, Faye."

I finished as if he answered yes.

"Then I'm here."

His fingers gripped harder and he clipped a guttural, "Christ, Faye," that hurt to hear but for some reason felt good all the same.

I squeezed his wrists. "Go, so you can get back. I'm hungry so I have to cook." I rolled up on my toes and concluded, "I'll leave the champagne for tomorrow."

It was then his hands at my neck gave me a rough jerk toward him but he didn't kiss me. His hands left my neck so his arms could close around me tight.

And he hugged me.

I closed my eyes, wrapped my arms around him and pressed my cheek to his chest because it felt good.

It also felt bad and this was because I knew he was feeling something ugly and I couldn't protect him from it. The only thing I could do was sleep in his bed as he asked. And that meant so much to him; he man-communicated it with a hug.

And really, if you communicated that way, who needed words?

That said it all.

I hugged him just as tight or as close as I could get seeing as he was stronger than me.

This lasted not long enough for me before I felt his lips at the top of my hair and he said, "Dresser, middle right are my tees. Tag one when you go to sleep, yeah?"

I nodded though I didn't know about that. I'd brought a sexy nightie. I now had a conundrum. The sexy nightie (for Chace) or his tee (for me).

I didn't choose before he kissed the top of my hair, gave me a squeeze and let me go.

But I felt the tips of his middle three fingers light under my chin and I again did as he silently commanded and gave him my face.

"This probably won't go quick but I'll get home soon's I can."

I nodded.

His fingers slid like a whisper over my jaw making the skin of my neck and cheek tingle in a good way as he whispered, "Thank you, baby."

"You're welcome, honey."

He grinned, a small grin that didn't reach his eyes. Then he bent his head and touched his mouth to mine.

I got another mouth touch after he went to his bedroom, I went to the kitchen and started rooting through for dinner fixin's and he came back wearing his sweater, jacket and boots.

He left.

I made tacos. I ate tacos.

I put the leftovers in one of those reusable but disposable tubs that Chace, upon inspection, seemed to have a lot of.

I watched his big flat-screen TV.

When the clock was about to strike midnight, I took off my makeup, moisturized, brushed my teeth, put on my sexy nightie and slid into Chace's bed.

I thought I'd never get to sleep, what with where my body was resting. A place it had never rested in twenty-nine years, not only it being Chace's bed, but *any* man's.

But his mattress was the fraking *bomb*. It felt like a firm cloud.

So, seconds after my head hit one of his pillows, I was out like a light.

CHAPTER NINE

Worth the Wait

I SWAM UP from sleep, feeling warm, delicious, my eyes fluttering open and closed as I felt weird sensations at my back and waist.

My eyes kept fluttering as a warm body fitted itself to the curve of mine, a strong arm circled my belly and pulled gently back so my warm body fit snugger into the one behind me.

Chace was home.

"Honey?" I called, my voice barely audible.

His arm around my belly gave me a squeeze. "Go back to sleep, baby."

God, he really felt nice. Everything felt nice. His awesome mattress. The down comforter over us. Pillows that were just the right mixture of firm and yielding. The warm cocoon we were in. Chace the length of me, holding me close.

Then where he'd been, why he'd been there and the nuance of Misty that was attached to it penetrated. My eyes quit fluttering, my consciousness quit doing the same and I came awake.

"Are you okay?" I whispered.

"Go back to sleep, Faye," he whispered back.

I lay there in the curve of his body, beyond comfortable, warm, safe, having had a nice night in a nice house and not being out in the cold dark investigating a murder and telling a family someone they loved was dead.

Then I moved my hand to his at my belly.

When I asked it this time, it was firmer.

"Chace, are you okay?"

His fingers extended out, mine fell through, his caught mine, lacing them and he closed both of our fingers tight.

Then he said quietly, "No. But I'll be all right after I sleep."

I pulled my hand from his but immediately turned in his arm.

He immediately adjusted with my body's movements as he started, "Faye—"

I wrapped my arm around his waist, pressed close and asked, "Do you need to talk?"

"I need to sleep," he answered.

"Maybe you should talk," I suggested quietly and cautiously.

"Actually, baby, what I need is sleep."

"It was bad," I whispered.

"Yeah," he whispered back.

Oh jeez.

"So you should talk," I urged softly.

"Honey, you're sweet but what I need is sleep."

"You should get it out."

His arm around my waist tightened and his voice got a little impatiently growly when he said a warning, "Faye."

"It isn't good to sleep on stuff, Dad says so," I pressed.

"Your father is a wise man but I'm not bein' nice, shieldin' you. It's late and I really need sleep."

I pressed closer to him and whispered, "You bury stuff, it can fester."

"Faye—"

"You have to work it out."

"Faye, honey, seriously—"

"You don't want to talk, then work it out another way. Make love to me."

His body went completely still, he said not a word and I was with him on both counts.

Did I actually say that?

I would find that I did when in an instant I was on my back and Chace was on top of me.

"You serious?" he whispered.

No. I wasn't serious. I was crazy.

Though, one couldn't argue with the fact the weight of his big, heavy, warm body felt good on mine.

"Yes," I whispered back.

"You ready for that?"

No. I absolutely was not ready.

Though, again, his big, heavy, warm body felt good on mine.

And, well, I hadn't forgotten the conversation with Lexie, Laurie and Krystal and how they'd all had to unfuck a man and they'd done it (partially) by, well, fucking him.

Tonight, Chace had what was fucking him up come back up.

So...

Frak!

"Yes," I whispered.

"You sure?"

He was reading me even in the dark.

"Yes," I repeated quietly. My hands moved up the bare skin of his back, liking the feel but attempting to communicate I was sure.

"Faye, baby—"

He needed to get a move on. If this was going to happen,

it was him who had to start it. I'd proven I could follow. I sure as heck couldn't lead.

In order to facilitate this, I demanded quietly, "Kiss me, Chace."

"Fuck," he growled, and my hand slid into his hair.

Seriously, his hair felt *great.*

This gave me courage so I lifted my lips to his and whispered, "Kiss me, honey."

He slanted his head and kissed me.

Then, about a second later, he proved me correct.

I was great at following.

His kiss was not wild and abandoned. It was soft, sweet but still deep. He was starting slowly and I went with him, my hands moving on his skin, retracing their path from earlier, memorizing the feel of him, loving every inch.

His hands moved on me too, down my sides, a light touch that was still somehow firm and definitely warm. Or, at least, it warmed me.

As his hands moved up after going down, his mouth slid to my ear and he whispered, "What're you wearin', baby?"

"I, uh...came prepared," I whispered back, felt him smile against my neck then his tongue ran the length of it as his hands slid back down the silk of my nightie.

I shivered.

Chace's mouth came back to mine.

More slow, sweet kisses. More lazy, unhurried stroking. Then his mouth moved back to the side of my neck, worked there and I liked that. God, it felt beautiful. It moved to my throat, down and his tongue dipped into the dent at the middle of my collarbone. Something about that felt so sweet but so decadent, it quivered through me and I shifted restlessly under him.

Slowly, his mouth moved back up my neck as his hand moved to span my ribs.

When his lips hit mine, he asked quietly, "More?"

"Yeah," I answered quietly back.

His hand moved up and cupped my breast.

My mouth moved before I told it to and this was to murmur, "Oh yeah."

His thumb slid over my nipple.

My hands stopped drifting and my arms closed around him.

His mouth took mine in another kiss, not as slow, not as lazy, more heated, more demanding.

I gave. My tongue moving against his as Chace's hand slid down, under the hem of my nightie and up. Then it was skin against skin, cupping my breast, his thumb doing a swipe.

God, even more beautiful. Perfect. My back arched slightly to press into his hand, he growled into my mouth and the kiss got even more heated and demanding.

I kept giving, my hands moving on him again, faster, covering more ground, one moved down over his behind.

Chace's thumb stopped swiping, his finger met his thumb and he rolled.

Oh God, that felt *great*. So fraking great, my hand clenched his behind, I tore my mouth from his, shoved my face in his throat and whimpered.

Chace's voice was thick, hoarse when he asked, "More?"

"Yes," I breathed then, "You."

"What?"

"What do I do for you?"

I felt his neck bend and in my ear he asked, "You trust me?"

"Absolutely," I whispered my answer instantly.

"Christ, baby," he whispered back then, "Follow me."

I didn't know what he meant until his hand moved out of my nightie. It found my arm, pulled it from around him, slid down and took my hand. Then he moved my hand to his side, in, over his ribs, across the ridges of his belly and down.

I held my breath.

Chace felt it and I knew this when he murmured, "Breathe, baby."

I breathed.

He slid my hand down, down, down and in. I felt the crisp hair. I turned my head, pressed my lips to his neck then he took my hand down and his fingers wrapped mine around his hard cock.

Oh God, I liked that.

Holy frak, I *liked* that.

That was mine. That was for me. And it felt *awesome*.

I touched my tongue to his neck and my hand instinctively squeezed.

In return, his teeth nipped the skin of mine and he growled, "Want your mouth."

I turned my head and gave it to him.

He took it. His hand on mine stroked down, then up and down again. My thumb slid in a circle around the silky tip.

So silky, vaguely I wondered how something so hard could feel like satin.

It didn't matter because it was beautiful and it was hot. God, so *hot*. Amazing. Touching him was almost better than him touching me (almost).

At my touch, Chace groaned into my mouth.

Hotter!

"Chace," I whispered against his lips, my body pressing upwards, my legs moving restlessly. His hand pulled mine gently away from his cock, up over his belly and around his back while his lips went to my ear.

"Faye, baby, right now, I'm gonna taste you. This means my mouth is gonna work between your legs. You're gonna come in my mouth, honey, then I'm gonna take you. You ready for more?"

Oh heck yes.

"Yeah," I whispered.

"Cute, hot, fuck," he whispered back. Then he did as he said, moving down, not fast, not slow, his mouth on me, his hands on me, pulling my nightie up under my breasts, tugging down my panties, he slid off to the side.

His lips made it to my belly where he kissed me then he pulled my panties down my legs. I lifted my knees to assist, he yanked them free of my ankles then they were gone.

He positioned his hands on the insides of my knees, putting mild pressure there as he urged gently, "Open for me."

Hesitantly, hot, bothered, excited, restless but also a little scared, I did as he asked.

"That's it," he whispered.

I felt his lips on the inside of my knee where his hand was then they moved down the inside of my thigh, down, down. I tensed. I braced, my legs started trembling as his lips made their journey.

Then he was there.

God.

Oh God.

God, God, *God.*

That was . . . it was . . .

Indescribable.

My fingers curled into the sheets, my feet went into the bed and my hips moved with his mouth.

One of his hands moved under me, cupping my behind, helping me, pulling me up as the fingertips of his other hand slid feather light on the inside of my thigh.

Okay, this was better than his finger (maybe). This was fan-fraking-*tastic.*

Tremors chased themselves down my legs, my belly

dropped, my breasts swelled, my fingers clenched the sheets and then it happened.

"Honey," I whimpered, my back arched, my neck arched, it rushed over me, tore through me and I came.

Really, fraking *hard*.

Still coming, vaguely, I felt his lips brush my belly. I felt his hands close my legs. Then he was gone.

I was swimming out of it when he was back, his hands back at my knees, pressing and he didn't have to urge me this time. They opened for him as my eyes fluttered open and I saw his shadow on his knees between my legs.

One of his hands was at my knee, drifting down the top of my thigh, his other hand was doing something and before I got myself together, he fell forward between my legs into his hand at my side. Then he dropped down to a forearm and I had his weight.

I liked this too.

No, loved it.

He felt fantastic.

His head came down, his lips to my neck and he whispered, "You good?"

"Oh yeah," I whispered back and felt another smile.

Then he said softly, "I'll go slow, baby. No matter what, no matter that we're here, you need me to stop, I'll stop."

I had absolutely no clue what he was talking about. As far as I was concerned, he could do whatever he wanted.

Regardless, since he seemed to be waiting for answer, I said, "Okay."

"Okay," he said against my neck, then I knew what he was talking about because I felt him guide the tip of his cock against me.

He hesitated for just a moment.

And I got it. I understood.

And he was going to get it.

And he was going to get it because it was his.

I turned my head so my lips were at his ear and I urged, "Take it."

Under my hands it occurred to me that his body felt weirdly like it was straining.

"Take it," I repeated softly.

I felt the tip nudge inside.

"I'll go slow," he replied, his voice so low it was like a groan and he eased out then he eased just the tip back in.

"Come inside, Chace," I whispered.

"You're so tight, baby, don't wanna hurt you."

My arms grew tight, my thighs pressed into his hips and I told him the truth.

"Honey, come inside, take it, it's yours."

"Faye—"

"Now."

"Baby—"

"Please."

His hand moved from between us up my belly and around, to become an arm around my waist and he slid in a little deeper.

Okay, oh God, that felt good.

His lips moved up my neck and his cock slid even deeper.

Okay, right, wow, that felt better.

His tongue moved down my neck and he slid in deeper.

Oh God, all right, even better.

He slid in deeper and then he, again, stopped and eased back out.

Wow, wow, fabulous.

"Chace," I whispered, my hands drifting over the skin of his back. "Do you need me to do anything?"

"No, baby." His voice was low, hoarse, beyond thick, sounding pained.

"Come inside," I breathed in his ear. "Take me, honey, I'm yours."

That did it.

He surged up, his mouth came to mine as my body settled and I felt him inside, all the way, full of him, connected to Chace. Finally.

Beautifully.

Me full of Chace, the best feeling in the whole fraking world.

"Fuck, baby, I gotta move," he groaned.

"Move," I encouraged and he moved, his thrusts controlled, fluid, rhythmic and very, very nice.

Oh God, why hadn't I been doing this for longer?

As he moved, his thrusts going faster, still controlled, his arm moved from around my waist, in over my belly and down and I felt his thumb right where I didn't know it needed to be until it was there.

Oh God, seriously, I'd been *missing out*.

My mouth opened under his as my hips surged up.

"Wrap your legs around me, Faye, hold on tight," Chace ordered, I wrapped my legs around his hips and his thumb pressed deeper and circled.

Holy frak.

"Yes," I breathed into his mouth.

His tongue slid into mine.

He moved. He pressed. He circled. His tongue matched his thrusts. My skin tingled. Tremors shot through my system. My blood, already fired, went molten. I kissed Chace back and my hand slid down to cup his behind and urge him to give me more.

He gave me more, faster, harder, oh yes, amazing.

Chace tore his mouth from mine, buried his face in my neck and I heard both of our heavy breaths as he groaned into my skin, "Jesus, fuck, so sleek, so tight, fuckin', *fuckin'* beautiful."

"Honey," I breathed, the word hitched in the middle because his thrusts had increased in power and were jolting my body. My hand not at his behind slid up his spine, into his hair and fisted in an effort to hold on.

I gave another hitched breath, this one for a different reason and I continued to receive Chace's thrusts but his forearm went out of the bed so I also took his weight. His hand went to mine at his behind, his fingers curling around my wrist, he pulled it away, up, slid his hand into mine, laced our fingers then, still thrusting, he planted his forearm back into the bed but holding my hand.

Holding my hand.

Holding my hand.

Hard. Tight. Fingers laced.

Like he'd never let go.

Suddenly, like a shot, it hit me, my legs and arms tensed and I cried out as I came again. Not harder, not longer but for some reason way, *way* sweeter.

When I came down, his thumb was gone, his arm shoved under me, his hand curled around the back of my neck and his mouth came to mine as he kept thrusting, deeper, deeper, God, I loved having him inside me.

Then his hips bucked into mine, stayed planted, he groaned into my mouth and I loved that even more.

Nearly instantly, his lips left mine, slid across my cheek and I heard his labored breathing in my ear as I felt mine even out.

We were lying in the dark in the middle of night but everything about that moment I felt with a clarity I'd never had before.

Everything.

His weight on me, our bodies connected, his hand warm at my neck, fingers wrapped firm around the back, our fingers laced in the bed, his breath sounding in my ear, drifting across my skin, his weight on me, his thick, soft hair in my hand, my legs wrapped around him.

I hoped I never forgot that, any of it, not any of it, for the rest of my life.

I'd given Chace Keaton my virginity like I'd decided I wanted to do at the age of sixteen.

He took it and, before, gave me two orgasms and during, gave me another one.

And when I had mine and he had his, he held my hand.

Overwhelmed by all of it, the beauty of it, having what I'd dreamed of for years, having it be better than my dreams in a big way, the tears hit the backs of my eyes. I didn't even try to stop my mouth when my head turned so I could find his ear.

"When I was sixteen, I saw you and when I did, I was young, romantic, and it might sound stupid but the minute I saw you, I knew I wanted to give that to you. I knew it was only you. I waited thirteen years, honey. It was worth the wait."

His body stilled over mine and my heart clenched.

Oh frak, that was too much.

Oh frak! Maybe the first time couples did it, they didn't share deep, romantic secrets.

Frak!

His hand slid from my neck as I tensed, uncertain what to do, unable to escape him seeing as he was on me and *in* me. I had nowhere to go and no hope of getting there even if I had somewhere to go.

His body shifted slightly then the light came on.

I blinked at the sudden brightness.

Then I focused.

When I did, I stared.

The tears pooled in my eyes instantly at what I saw and mere moments later, slid out the sides.

Because his eyes were gazing in mine. His beautiful blue

eyes, in his handsome face, on top of his amazing body. The eyes of a man who was all man.

And they were wet.

Oh my fraking *God*.

His hand came to my jaw, cupping it, his thumb sweeping across my cheekbone but he didn't watch his thumb. His eyes never left mine and he didn't hide it, he didn't fight it.

I gave him my virginity.

He gave that to me.

It was the most beautiful gift I'd ever received.

Then he whispered, "I wanna see to you. Will you let me do that, Faye?"

I'd let him do anything.

Anything.

Even though I had no idea what he was talking about.

"Yes," I answered.

His head dropped and, his lips on mine, he whispered, "Thank you."

Then he touched his mouth to mine, gently, slowly slid out and he saw to me.

This being, he rolled out of bed, carefully gathering me in his arms and taking me with him. He then carried me to the bathroom and set my booty on the vanity counter. It was dark, only the light from the bedroom lighting the space. I saw his semi-shadow moving around as he turned on the taps of the tub. Then he moved to the little room that held the toilet, I heard it flush and he came back into the room.

The subdued light shone on his naked body and I had my first glimpse of all that was Chace.

It was no less beautiful than my thirteen years of imagining made it out to be, broad shoulders, wide wall of chest, defined collarbone, muscled thighs, ridged abs, slim hips, cut hip bones.

But the sexy sprinkling of chest hair that spread out

under his collarbone, over his pectorals, ribs, belly and led to the thicker hair above and around his beautiful cock was a bonus I didn't expect.

He stopped in front of me at the basin, gently pulled my nightie from under my booty and I held my breath as I lifted my arms and he tugged it off.

Before I could be embarrassed about being naked in front of him, he lifted me in his arms again and set me on my feet beside the tub. Then he guided me and we climbed and settled in together, Chace behind me, his legs surrounding me, knees bent, me reclining between them back against his chest as the tub filled with hot, soothing water.

"Just relax, Faye," he urged gently, his arms circling me, one at my ribs, one at my chest.

"Okay," I whispered, and it wasn't a lie. It was impossible not to relax in that shadowed room, in that hot water with Chace all around me after having two orgasms.

"You're beautiful, baby," he said softly in my ear, one of his hands gliding over my belly. I suspected, through the shadows and over my shoulder, he was looking at me.

God, I hoped he thought so.

"Okay," I repeated quietly, not as sure about that one.

"All mine," he muttered. "Christ, finally, all mine."

I closed my eyes, pulled in breath and relaxed deeper against his chest.

I felt him shift, his lips at my neck he kept muttering, "Thirteen years, all mine."

That meant something, what I said to him. I knew it. Since after I said it, he showed me by making himself vulnerable to me, I knew it had to mean a lot.

But his words made me realize it meant *a lot*.

And that meant *a lot* to me.

I swallowed and turned my head toward his lips. They touched my forehead then his arms gave me a squeeze.

The tub filled.

When it was time, Chace moved us both forward and turned off the taps then settled us back. When we were settled, his hands glided over my wet skin, light, sweet, soothing, lovely.

The water, the orgasms, Chace and his hands, any vestiges of tension left me. I melted into him in the semi-dark.

His hands stopped roaming, both his arms wrapped around me and we sat in the tub, silent, together.

That was, we did until I drifted off to sleep, my arms over Chace's, my head turned, my forehead tucked in his throat.

I didn't know if I was asleep for an hour or two minutes before we were up then I was *up* as in, again cradled in his arms.

He was gentle and quick with toweling me off and pulling the nightgown over my head.

He did the same with himself but quicker then I was back up and he was carrying me to the bed where he lay me. I watched in sleepy fascination as he pulled on a pair of burgundy flannel drawstring pajama bottoms.

Drowsily, I decided he was hot naked. He was hot in clothes. He was also hot in pajama bottoms.

Not a surprise.

He came to my side and switched off the light then I heard it as he rounded the bed and I rolled as he did. The bed moved as I watched his shadow enter it. He flicked the covers over us and he stretched out on his back.

But he didn't settle on his back because I felt his hand shove under me and I was hauled to his side. His arm curled me close, pressed tight down his side and I had no choice (not that I would take another one) but to rest my cheek on his shoulder and snake my arm across his flat abs.

"So you're a cuddler?" I whispered.

"No," he replied.

I blinked at the shadowed planes and angles of his chest. "Uh…"

"Or I wasn't until about two seconds ago."

My belly melted and my heart flipped.

"You move away from me, Faye, you'll be right back where you are right now," he warned, his voice quiet, soft but low and serious.

Weird.

Hot and sweet.

But weird.

"Okay," I whispered.

"You stay close," he ordered.

"Okay, honey."

"Okay," he muttered, and his arm around me got tighter.

My arm around his gut gave him a squeeze.

He fell silent.

I stared at his chest.

Then I called, "Chace?"

"Yeah?"

I licked my lips.

Then I said quietly, "Thank you for making that beautiful."

He said nothing.

Then he rolled into me, pressing a knee between my legs so I was forced to hook one around his hip and both his arms gathered me close and held me tight.

"Sleep, baby," he whispered, and now his voice was quiet but hoarse.

"Okay. 'Night, honey."

One of his hands slid up my spine and into my damp hair then it slid through.

And back.

Then he whispered, "'Night, baby."

His hand slid through my hair.

And again.

Moments later I fell asleep pressed deep and held tight to Chace Keaton.

CHAPTER TEN

Halfway Gone

CHACE'S EYES OPENED and he blinked away sleep.

The strong Colorado sun was fighting his curtains and, as usual, winning.

Chace felt his body get tight.

Something was wrong.

He stared across the pillows at the empty bed.

He was on his side, one hand shoved under the pillow at his head, his other arm thrown wide.

No Faye.

Instantly, it felt like a hand reached in and gripped his gut in an iron-tight fist.

Not a man prone to fanciful thoughts, not one he could recall in his life, it still hit him that the way his life had swirled down the toilet, it wouldn't be a surprise that the last three weeks had been a dream. A cruel, twisted dream.

A taste of sweet.

The touch of an angel.

A trace of a miracle.

Then gone.

He smelled bacon frying.

The moment he did, he rolled, threw back the covers,

angled out of bed and prowled out of the room, down the hall, through the arch and toward the kitchen where he took five steps then stopped dead.

Because Faye Goodknight was standing at his stove at the island.

Faye Goodknight.

In his house.

In his kitchen.

At his stove.

All this the morning after she gave him her virginity and spent the night in his arms in his bed.

She was wearing the shirt he wore yesterday. It was unbuttoned and only partially covered the sexy-as-all-fuck sapphire blue silk nightie that had thick lace at the top and, he'd seen last night but couldn't see now, another rim of thick lace at the hem as well as deep slits up each side. A nightie the likes of which he figured no virgin would wear. The likes his ex-virgin was definitely currently wearing.

Her head was turned slightly to the side to take a sip from one of his coffee mugs.

But her eyes slid to him and she didn't take a sip.

She lowered the mug to the counter by the stove and snapped, "You spoiled the surprise."

"What?" he whispered, unable to make his voice louder but she still heard him because she answered.

"I'm making you breakfast in bed." Her eyes moved the length of him then came back to his. "Or I *was*."

Her words and her tone jerked him out of his stupor and he kept prowling toward her.

Her pretty, makeup-less face lost its mock annoyance and she stared at his advance, her body turning toward him as he rounded the island. She looked like a doe caught in head-lights, just as terrified, just as frozen and just as cute.

She forced out a, "Chace—" but that's as far as she got

before he hooked her at the waist with an arm and yanked her into his body. He drove his other hand in her hair, cupped her head, tilted it to one side, slanted his then he took her mouth.

When he did, he took his time.

He didn't break the kiss until he'd had his fill.

Or his fill for now.

When he lifted his lips from hers, he opened his eyes to see hers follow suit far more slowly. She did this often. Chace liked it. It made her look like she was waking from a really good dream.

He slid his hand down to curl it around the back of her neck and he whispered, "Mornin', baby."

She blinked and he watched her lick her lips, his gut clenching a good way this time, a fucking good one, and she breathed, "That sounds a lot better in real life."

Chace grinned.

"Not that it isn't good on the phone," she hastened to add.

Chace's grin turned into a smile.

"Or that the phone isn't real life," she continued.

Chace just kept smiling.

"Just that it's better in person," she finished.

Chace's body started shaking with his chuckle.

He might be amused but she was absolutely not wrong.

He bent his head, pressed his face in her neck and whispered against her skin, "You feelin' okay?"

"Yeah," she replied and his arm gave her a squeeze.

"Inside," he clarified gently. "Okay?"

"A little achy," she told him quietly. "Not a bad achy. Just a heretofore unknown, um...achy."

"Bath didn't help," he muttered.

For some reason, his words made her relax deeper into his frame.

After this, her soft musical voice came at him, still quiet. "It isn't bad but I'll take some ibuprofen with breakfast."

He lifted his head and looked down at her in his kitchen, his shirt, his arms in the morning.

He was wrong.

Or maybe it was just that yesterday, she was fucking pretty.

Today, she was beautiful.

And today, she was his.

She tipped her head to the side.

"Do you have any?"

He wasn't following.

"Any what?"

"Ibuprofen."

Right. She was achy.

"Yeah," he answered.

"Good," she muttered, her eyes drifted to the side and then came back to him. "Bacon, honey."

"Right," he whispered, bent his neck, kissed her nose and let her go.

She turned to the bacon.

He moved to the cupboard where he kept his vitamins and painkillers.

"So, making lemonade out of lemons, now I get to ask you since you're awake instead of springing it on you," she started. "Do you like poached eggs?" He grabbed the bottle of ibuprofen, looked at her as he closed the cupboard and saw she was grinning at him over her shoulder. "I make world-class poached eggs."

Chace felt his lips tip up. "World-class?"

"Well, they haven't been sanctioned thus by a Cordon Bleu panel but my dad calls them that."

He moved in behind her, slid an arm around her, hand gliding over his shirt and hitting the silk of her nightie at her belly as his other hand put the bottle by her coffee mug.

In her neck he muttered, "Yeah, I like poached eggs."

That got him a breathy, "Good."

He kissed her neck and moved away to get himself a mug for coffee.

"Honey?" she called as he was pouring it. His head turned her way to see her face soft, her ear dipped to her shoulder, her crystal blue eyes intent on him. "Hazelnut half-and-half," she went on quietly. "Thank you for thinking of that. My favorite."

Clearly, her father hadn't phoned since his visit and briefed her about their plans for next weekend. Or if he did, he understandably didn't share that part.

Chace was going to have to tell her about Silas Good-knight's visit. He'd intended to do it last night.

He'd do it that morning.

After he very quickly ate her world-class poached eggs.

And after he, not very quickly, ate other parts of her.

Then he'd tell her.

*   *   *

Something Chace learned about Faye the night before was that, with very few inhibitions and minimal coaxing to get her beyond them, Faye trusted him and had zero issues with giving herself to him, giving in to what he was making her feel and enjoying the fuck out of it.

This was something that held true that morning after poached eggs, coffee and enough light, non-taxing conversation to ascertain that she was, indeed, comfortable with him in his house, his shirt and her nightie.

Which meant he was open to picking her up, carrying her to the couch and making short work of getting her excited and squirming under him so he could pull off her panties and give her a very hot, very long orgasm using his mouth between her legs to do it.

But something he learned about Faye that morning after

he made her come, moved over her, settled them both on their sides, held her as she came down and their after-oral-sex whispers went from little bits of nothing to him telling her about her father's visit was something that surprised him.

That was that Faye Goodknight had a fucking explosive temper.

It was, like everything about her, cute.

But it was also seriously volatile.

He learned this when he shared about her father and felt her body go rock solid in his arms as he watched her eyes narrow.

His arms around her tightened in an effort at containment when he quit talking and she asked in a quiet voice that was not her usual sweet, cute quiet but a dangerous quiet, "Pardon?"

"Honey, it's okay," he assured her. "He was doin' his duty as a dad and it ended well."

She said nothing for several long seconds.

Then, as if he didn't speak, she repeated, "*Pardon?*"

"Faye—"

He got no further because she tore out of his arms, sitting up abruptly. She rolled the half an inch she had to the edge of the couch, which meant she nearly fell over the side. Moving quickly, if angrily, she somehow managed to get her feet under her, straightened up with her head bent, whipping around, taking her gleaming sheets of hair with it so they flowed with her movements.

She did this while she demanded to know, "Where's my fraking purse?"

"Faye—" he tried again as she bent over, snatched up her sexy green satin panties and clumsily pulled them up her legs, nearly tripping, cute as all fuck.

Chace, head in his hand, elbow in the couch, watched with not a small amount of absorption as her heart-shaped ass appeared briefly before she settled the panties on her hips and his shirt fell over her again, hiding her from his view.

Through this, she cut him off and kept ranting.

"I'd kill him but I love him so that's out. This means he gets the edge of my tongue. I mean, I like hazelnut half-and-half, but I cannot *believe* he showed at your house unannounced to say what he said! Now where's my *fraking* purse?"

She was stomping, heading toward the arch, her neck twisting this way and that. She spied something and changed directions jerkily, coming back his way as Chace got up on a forearm in the couch.

"Faye, honey, calm down. It was not a big deal."

She snatched the phone out of the base that was on the table over the side of the sectional and her eyes sliced to him.

Oh yeah. Totally fucking pissed.

And totally cute.

Chace fought back a smile.

"It is to me!" she snapped loudly, bent her head, her hair fell forward and he heard his phone beeping because her thumb was jabbing at the buttons.

Chace pushed out of the couch, got to his feet and rounded it as he watched her put the phone to her ear and start pacing.

"Mom," she said into it before he got to her, "I want to talk to Dad. *Immediately.*"

Since he didn't make it to her in time, Chace decided to settle in and enjoy the show. So he rested his ass on the back of the couch, stretched out his legs, crossed them at the ankles, his arms on his chest and did just that.

"Yes, there's something *wrong*," she continued, still pacing. "Let me talk to Dad."

There was a pause while she halted in a stilted way and stared obviously unseeing out his French doors.

Then she went on, "I *know* it's time for church. I don't *care* if you're late. This is important. You can sneak in the back."

Another pause to let her mother speak before she carried on.

"I don't care if Dad's favorite part is singing the hymns at the beginning of the service, I told you, this is important." Pause then a hissed, seriously pissed, "*Yes*, it's about his visit to Chace."

She listened again as she yanked her hand through her hair, pulling it back, her body jerked with agitation and she started pacing again but when her hand went out of her hair, it fell right back around her face.

She was cute. She was being funny. She looked fucking fantastic pacing through the space between his kitchen and living room in her sexy nightie and his shirt, her long legs on display, her hair swinging around. Not to mention, his stomach was full of her damned fine food and the taste of her was still in his mouth.

All this meant Chace was amused, relaxed and content.

Therefore he was completely unprepared for Faye rocking his entire fucking world.

"That was not fraking *cool*, Mom. It wasn't *cool*. Dad doesn't know and it's none of his business but I'll tell you since you won't let me talk to him then *you* can tell him, Chace has been through enough. He doesn't like surprises. He doesn't need hassle. And I won't stand for it!"

Chace felt his body get tight and he stopped watching her and started staring at her.

"Yes! I know that fraking means the f-word, *Mom*. In a television show! I'm the one who told *you*, remember? When the Cylons explode our world and we're aboard a spaceship in a ragtag convoy trying to stay alive and find Earth, you can take me to task for saying the word *frak*! Until then, no and definitely not *now*!"

She halted facing his French doors again and stared out as she listened.

Then she spoke again.

"Right, well, don't hold your breath for that, Mom, seeing as I'm going to be a kickass fighter pilot like Starbuck so I'll be out in my Viper most of the time, fighting the Cylons to keep you alive so you won't have time to give me a lecture about cursing."

Another pause, this one lengthy.

Then, "I don't care. It's not good that he shared his thoughts about Chace *to Chace*, thoughts he had because of town gossip. That's not good. That doesn't say nice things about *Dad*, not *Chace*. It was judgmental and uncalled for. But it's more, Mom. It doesn't say good things about *me*. Because it says Dad doesn't trust *me* to be smart enough to see past the hot guy Chace is to who he *really* is *underneath*. That would be a good man I can trust, who takes care of me, makes me feel safe, makes me feel good, teases me, likes me for me and who's worth my time. Even if Dad had concerns about Chace, he should know *me* better than that. I may be a dreamer, Mom, but you raised me, so did he so I'm not a stupid dreamer. I'm just *a dreamer.* And I'll point out he should have showed Chace respect not only as a man but as the man everyone in this fraking town knows him to be but also Dad should have shown *me* respect by keeping his mouth *shut*."

She fell silent but this didn't last long.

"No, I still want to talk to him. Tell him to call me after church. I have a few things to say."

An even shorter pause.

Then, "Okay, and just so you know, I'm angry but still, if I found you were an unknown model of Cylon, I wouldn't kill you because you're my mom. But I would find you a habitable planet and dump you there. I'm also angry enough to dump Gaius there with you. He's brilliant but he's annoyingly arrogant, smug, a total jerk, completely self-serving and unpredictable. You'd hate him. So that tells you just how angry I am at you for not letting me speak my mind to Dad. Enjoy church and I'll see you next Saturday."

Then without waiting for a response from her mother, she beeped off the phone and whirled to him.

Once she had his eyes, she snapped, "God!"

Then she clamped her mouth shut and glared at him.

Chace studied her, her cheeks pink, her eyes heated, thinking, with that hair, he shouldn't be surprised her temper was fiery.

He studied her thinking that he was feeling something he didn't quite get, didn't know what it was because he'd never felt it before. He just knew that whatever it was was huge and it was good.

She took him out of his thoughts when she said quietly, "Chace, I'm so sorry Dad did that."

"Faye," he called softly. "Come here."

"Give me a second," she replied. "I'm fighting the urge to throw your phone across the room."

She was too far away and what he was feeling was too big so he pulled out the big guns.

"Baby, come here."

She came to him immediately.

Chace buried a smile, uncrossed his arms and ankles, bent his knees so his feet were to the floor but his legs were open and he leaned forward, reaching for her hand when she got close. He took the phone out of her other hand, tossed it to the couch and guided her between his legs. When he had her where he wanted her, he let her hand go but both of his arms circled her loosely though not loose enough not to communicate he didn't want her pressing close. As she always did, she got the message he didn't need to verbalize, leaned her body into his and looked into his eyes.

"We got a problem," he murmured.

"I know," she agreed.

"Actually, *you* got a problem," he told her.

"I know," she agreed again. "I have an overprotective father who I'd like to kick in the shin."

Chace gave her a squeeze and shared his thoughts. "He did right. I took no offense. Honest to God, I had a daughter whose first boyfriend had my reputation, I'd do the same fuckin' thing. Wouldn't think about it, wouldn't give a shit she got pissed. I'd make my thoughts known, feel him out and make sure he knew he had in his hands something precious. It ended good. I understood why he did it. I admire him for doin' it and it shows how much he loves you. And, I'll repeat, I'd do it myself. So quit bein' pissed."

As he spoke, the anger shifted out of her face, her eyes went from heated to warm and her body relaxed deeper into his.

When he was done speaking, she asked softly, "So what's my problem?"

"Faye, seriously, you're hilarious when you're angry." He grinned at her, one of his hands trailing up her spine and into her hair as he continued, "This does not bode well for you, baby, 'cause you ever get that pissed at me and you start talkin' about Cylons and bein' a fighter pilot, I got no choice but to laugh, which'll likely make you more pissed."

Her lips twitched and she whispered, "Likely, seeing as Mom laughed through nearly that whole conversation and that only annoyed me more."

Chace didn't doubt it.

"What's a Cylon anyway?" he asked.

"Robots that look like robots, the scary kind with a red eye that flashes back and forth, but there are other models that look so much like humans they're nearly undetectable from real humans. This means they're very dangerous because they can infiltrate the human world and even if you cotton onto one of the models, since they look and act so much like humans, you never know what they're up to. You might *think* you can trust them but you can never be sure."

He felt his lips tip up. "Which one of your shows is this from?"

"*Battlestar Galactica.*"

His hand cupped her head, pulling her face closer to his as he whispered, "Honey, you are one serious geek."

"It's a good show," she whispered back.

"Right."

"You might like it."

He doubted that.

She read his doubt and pushed, "Seriously, Chace, Admiral Adama is your type of guy."

"Should the unfortunate event occur that I'm in a full-body cast and unable to move for months, there's no sports on TV and I've rewatched reruns of *Friday Night Lights* so often, I can quote them, you have permission to introduce me to Admiral fuckin' Adama."

At that, she gave him a soft giggle then her eyes dropped to his mouth. Her ear dipped toward her shoulder, the smile faded from her lips and her hand at his chest trailed up before she whispered a very hesitant, "Chace?"

"Right here, baby," he whispered back, his gaze moving to her bubblegum lips.

"Um…earlier…" she trailed off and didn't start again.

His eyes moved back to hers. "Yeah?" he prompted.

"You got to…I mean, I got to…but, you know, you got to…and then you didn't get to…" she stammered then stopped again, but he got it and his arm around her tightened.

"You're achy. We're givin' it a day or two."

Her hand had curled around his neck and her thumb came out to stroke his jaw when she whispered, "Isn't there some other…I mean, could I…or you that is, um, could you teach me to…" she pulled in an unsteady breath and her eyes left his lips and looked into his, "use my mouth?"

His dick started getting hard, his hand in her hair spasmed and his stomach got tight.

"You ready for that?" he whispered, hoping to Christ she was.

"You ready to teach me?" she whispered back.

The answer to that was fuck yes.

He didn't give her that answer. He held tight and fell back, twisting so he landed on his back in the couch, taking her with him so she landed on him.

Then he pulled her head toward him but shifted it so her cheek slid down his until he had her ear.

"Do whatever you want, whatever comes natural. Pointers, suction is important. Movement is too. Adding your hand is hot. Always check your teeth, and the tip is the most sensitive so payin' special attention to that occasionally means payoff for me." His arms gave her a squeeze and he finished with, "Yeah?"

"Yeah," she breathed in his ear, squirming on top of him.

She liked that. She was working herself up.

And he liked both.

Christ.

Never would he expect this to come this soon. But he was not complaining.

"Go for it, darlin'," he encouraged, he heard her pull in a deep breath then he felt her lips at his neck. Then her tongue. She moved down and, so as not to take her attention, he carefully reached for some toss pillows and shoved them behind his head in order to watch.

Then he watched as Faye got sidetracked by his chest, seemingly fascinated by studying it, running her hands over his skin and chest hair but her light touch and the trail of her crystal blue eyes felt so fucking good, Chace wasn't going to complain about that either.

The same with his abs, which contracted at her touch, something she noticed and it brought those clear blue eyes to him.

Heated again, turned on, lips parted, wonder, cute, sexy, fuck.

"Keep goin'," he urged, his voice deeper and rougher than normal, she gave him a small smile that cut through him straight to his dick.

Then she put her mouth to his abs and down, down, she pulled the string on his pajama bottoms, yanked them down and she had him.

She slid to the side, pulling his bottoms off and she took him.

Chace didn't know what to expect. He'd never gotten head from a woman who hadn't done it before. But experience was clearly unnecessary when there was off-the-charts enthusiasm. Not to mention she obviously memorized every word of advice he'd given her and he knew this because she put it into practice brilliantly.

When he was close, he yanked her up his body but took her hand, wrapped it around his cock and they both finished him off together.

When he came down, the look on her face told him she liked what she'd caused. So much, even with the mess on his stomach, he moved her hand with his into her panties and used her finger against her clit to finish her off, doing that together too.

He knew she liked what she'd done and what they'd done together because even though he'd given her a climax not long before, this didn't take long.

When her eyes fluttered open as she was coming down and then after he kissed her, he took her to his shower so they could both clean up.

*   *   *

It was after their shower.

After Faye located her purse, which had fallen off her arm when he carried her to his bedroom. He must have kicked it after she dropped it since it was in the living room. She had found it the night before to get her shit to get ready for bed and left it there but clearly in her anger forgot she did.

She searched for her purse in one of his clean tees so it was also after she located her purse, dug out and tugged on another pair of sexy panties, these ruby red. After that, Chace caught her in his arms and told her he appreciated her jewel-themed underwear collection, something that made pink hit her cheeks and him chuckle.

It was after she did the breakfast dishes that her cell rang. After Chace listened to her side of the slightly less irate conversation she had with her father, which was no less hilarious but far more confusing. She went on about someone called Walter, who apparently had a chunk of his brain cut out but who would also never disrespect his son called Peter, even though Peter wasn't really Walter's son but an identical person Walter kidnapped from an alternate earth. From her side of the conversation, it was clear her father found her analogy just as confusing as Chace did. Chace didn't try to swallow down his chuckles because the whole thing was so fucking hilarious he knew he wouldn't succeed. And he had no problem enduring Faye's annoyed glares because those were equally hilarious.

It was also after she finished the call with an exasperated but nevertheless heartfelt "Love you, Dad," which didn't include her threatening to dump him on a habitable planet with an asshole, that she explained to Chace her analogy was from a show called *Fringe*. After this she spent a little time explaining the show and zero time attempting to convince him he'd like it since, from what little she said and since she knew him, she also knew she had no hope of achieving that.

It was after she made him lunch, they did the minimal dishes and she suggested they relax in front of the TV. This filled him with dread and he didn't hide it, which made her laugh, wrap her arms around him, lean in deep, tip her head way back and promise in her sweet, soft, musical voice she wouldn't lead him astray.

Therefore, he'd agreed.

So it was also after she found he had Netflix and convinced him to try the TV show *Psych*. She told him it wasn't geeky but hilarious. He'd agreed mostly because she was in his house, wearing nothing but his tee and ruby red panties, he was in track pants and a long-sleeved thermal and he didn't much give a fuck what they did just as long as she was close when they did it.

Which meant it was also after she found one of her favorite episodes, turned it on and they settled stretched out on the couch, Chace with his back to the back of couch, head in his hand, elbow in the couch, Faye tucked in front of him in the curve of his arm, head on a toss pillow.

And last, it was after he was relieved to find she was right about *Psych*. It wasn't geeky. There were no spaceships, alternate universes or fantastical explanations for ridiculous plot devices. It was just damned funny and, to top that, clever.

So it was then, when the episode ended, she reached to the big square coffee table that sat surrounded by his sectional, hit the button to take them back to the Netflix menu, she turned on her back in front of him and gave him her crystal blue eyes.

"So?" she asked, and he grinned down at her.

"You were right, baby, not geeky, just funny."

She grinned back. "Isn't Shawn the bomb?"

The guy was funny but that wasn't the word Chace would use.

Still he said, "Yeah."

She turned his way and got up on her elbow, head in her hand and suggested, "Maybe you need a fake psychic detective at the Carnal Police Department."

Chace chuckled, carefully tangling his legs with hers, an intimacy like all of them that he'd cautiously initiated with her that she took without reaction except to allow it and settle in.

And as he did this, he replied through his chuckle, "He's just hyper-observant with an understanding of detective work. That's kinda my job so we already have one and that would be me except the fake psychic part."

Her eyes slid to the side and she mumbled, "Oh, right."

Which was so cute, he had to lean forward and touch his lips to hers.

So he did.

As he was doing it, his cell on the coffee table rang.

Faye twisted her neck to look over her shoulder at it but Chace tightened the arm already around her waist, leaned into her, let her go to reach and nab his phone then brought them both back.

He looked at the display and let out a sigh.

Then he looked at her and said, "Hopefully this won't take long, honey, but I gotta take it."

"Okay," she murmured, and he took the call he didn't want to take.

When the phone was at his ear, he said, "Keaton."

"Chace, hey. Sorry to disturb your Sunday."

It was new Carnal detective and Chace's co-poster boy hero in saving the CPD, Frank Dolinski. A good guy. A smart cop. A local since birth. A police brat who wanted exactly the same things in life that Chace had wanted before his life turned shit. To earn his badge. To go about his business respecting it. To stay true to his oath to protect and serve. To find an attractive wife who cooked well, gave great head, made him laugh frequently and could shoulder the burden of his coming home from a bad day.

During his tenure on the force, unlike Chace, Frank stayed clean through the entirety of it. This didn't mean he didn't have to look the other way but he also didn't hide the fact that he didn't like it. This made him not Arnie's favorite person. It also showed he was courageous. He'd approached IA some months after Chace did, but he did what he could inside to try to turn boys back to the right side. But when Ty Walker was coming up for probation and it came clear that hell could easily break lose when he got it, Frank decided he had to do what many cops had a great deal of trouble doing.

Turn on his brothers.

Last night they'd had a discussion with the cap, who decided that Frank should stay as primary on the Newcomb case. The kill site being Harker's Wood, the dump site the access road to Miracle Ranch, too many similarities to Misty's murder, Cap felt Chace was too close to it. He also felt Frank needed the experience. Last, they all knew Frank would get nowhere. The investigation into Misty's murder had been purposefully jacked, but Chace conducted his own. There were few leads and the ones there were went nowhere.

But the men of the department knew Chace was still looking so Chace handed over all he had to Frank and Cap told him to take Frank's back.

Frank, Chace and the cap had another conversation about Clinton Bonar's warning and what this move against Newcomb meant. This meant Bonar would get a visit. It also meant other powerful men with motive would be approached too. All strictly protocol. All following standard investigative procedures.

So last, this meant things were going to heat up in Carnal and Frank, the cap, Chace and a new, inexperienced force were going to have to do what they could to make sure no one else got burned.

Chace did, however, have to go with Frank to Newcomb's sister to inform her that her brother was dead. It was she who had called the station Saturday morning to say he hadn't come home the night before and she was looking after his kids so she expected him at nine. She waited as long as she could before all-out panic ensued. She knew he was into bad business, something that couldn't be missed because he was fired from CPD for his participation in Arnie's corruption but had stayed out of jail due to his willingness to testify. CPD knew he was vulnerable. Thus began the search.

Chace had been the one to tell Tonia Payne's parents their daughter was dead, including, at their insistence, how she'd died, and her death was uglier than most. He'd also informed Misty's folks. Throughout his career, not regularly but too fucking often, he'd had bad news to give about car wrecks and arrests.

This was less fun than all of that shit and none of that had been pleasant. This was because Newcomb's wife had taken off, whereabouts unknown, which meant his kids, one of them gravely ill, had lost their last parent.

Newcomb was a moron, racist, wife-beating, asshole pig. He played with fire for understandable reasons but should have been smart enough to know that when he got burned, the ones who would live with the scars were his kids.

He wasn't that smart.

And now they were fucked.

"How's it going?" Chace asked a question he knew the answer to.

They had DNA on this guy from his semen. But the samples were deliberately tampered with, the tampering explained away as a "mistake." In fact, they were so tainted, they couldn't even run them.

Reports were probably not in yet but it was doubtful they'd find semen on or in Newcomb. Possible but doubtful.

They didn't even have slugs. Misty was done by a gun stolen by one of Carnal's own in an effort to frame him. From visuals on Newcomb, he was done close range with a high-powered assault rifle. Overkill. But this meant the shots were through and through. It also was a likely reason why Newcomb didn't fight or attempt to flee. A man carrying an assault rifle undoubtedly struck an imposing figure. If you tried to run, if that rifle had a scope, you'd still be fucked. So this time, the killer collected the bullets and shell casings, leaving them with next to nothing.

That was what they had. Next to nothing. No locals at either site reported seeing vehicles in the vicinity. No bullets, shell casings or DNA that could be found unless something came up on tests run at the lab. Nothing except footprints, which, from preliminary investigation of both scenes, kill site and dump site, was all they got this time too.

"We know he wears construction boots," Frank answered. "But since every third guy in this county wears motorcycle boots, cowboy boots or construction boots, that narrows our suspect pool down to about two thousand guys."

Chace could hear the frustration in Frank's voice and he understood it. He wanted to get this guy for four reasons. The guy was a murderer likely times two, at the very least, and he needed to be stopped. CPD had a nasty case file open and unsolved that fell on them during a time when it was infested. Frank wanted to make an important bust because it would look good. And he wanted this off Chace's shoulders and he was one of the few men who knew it was weighing there. Not because Chace had shared. Because Frank worked side by side with Chace and Frank was observant.

"He's not local, Frank," Chace said quietly. "He's a professional. He could be from anywhere."

"Yeah," Frank replied quietly, then in a normal voice, "Old Man Harker'd pitch a fit, he knew this shit was goin' down in his wood."

Frank was not wrong about that. Old Man Harker died seven years ago, luckily before the major garbage started piling up at the CPD and they found a serial killer lived local. He'd given his wood to the town before that, he was that proud of it and he loved Carnal. Knowing blood had been spilled and mouths had been raped in a spot where Harker and many others in town thought a miracle had occurred, he'd lose his mind.

Luckily in this instance, he no longer had a mind to lose.

"This isn't why I'm callin'," Frank went on.

"Yeah?" Chace prompted.

"Like you asked when you called in yesterday, had the interns run the name Malachi. They report nothin' comes up. No one is lookin' for this kid. Or at least, if they are, they haven't reported him missing."

"Could be a fake name," Chace muttered.

To which Frank asked incredulously, "Malachi?"

"The kid reads four, five books a week, Frank. So yeah, Malachi."

At this, he felt Faye's hand press into his chest and he dipped his chin to look at her to see he had her full attention.

Thus he muttered into the phone, "If you don't have any more, Frank, appreciate the call but gotta go."

To this, Frank asked searchingly, "Faye still there?"

Jon had opened his big fucking mouth.

Not a surprise but damned annoying.

"Gotta go," Chace repeated.

"Right," Frank murmured, a smile in his voice, and Chace couldn't see it but he bet it was knowing.

Jesus.

"Thanks for the call," Chace told him.

"Not a problem. Enjoy the rest of your Sunday with Faye," Frank replied.

He definitely would.

And yeah, Frank's smile had been knowing.

"Later," Chace gave his farewell.

"Later, buddy," Frank gave his and Chace disconnected.

"Malachi? A professional?"

She didn't even wait for him to toss his phone on the table, which was what he did before answering.

Once he'd shifted into her, did that and brought them back, he told her, "Asked the interns to run the name Malachi, see if anyone reported him missing. They did. Nothing."

"What does that mean?"

"It could mean a lot of things, honey. What it means most is that we gotta talk to this kid. He's not registered in school. He's not reported missing. He's like a ghost, and kids aren't ghosts unless serious bad shit is going down. We gotta push the breakthrough tomorrow and get him talkin'. You gonna be up for that?"

She nodded immediately and Chace ran his hand up her back, pulling her closer as he did and dipping his face to hers.

"You gotta go gentle but you gotta get a good result. If you don't, I'm steppin' this shit up another way. We need him safe. We need him fed. So, it sucks, baby, but we need him in the system."

She slid her bottom lip to the side and bit it. She often bit her lip. She often licked her lips. He'd learned to read why she did both. He didn't see the slide and bite often, but it usually meant she was very nervous, feeling more than her normal shy or a little bit scared.

"He'll be okay," Chace assured gently.

She let her lip go and asked quietly, "What does stepping stuff up mean?"

What it meant was setting Deck on the kid. Deck would find him. Deck wouldn't be outrun because he wouldn't give up. And Deck would likely scare the shit out of the kid.

He didn't tell her that.

Instead he said, "I'm still figurin' that out. But we'll hope we break through tomorrow. Yeah?"

She nodded.

Then she changed the subject.

"A professional?"

He shook his head and told her softly, "Police business, honey. Can't talk about that."

"The murder last night," she guessed.

"Yeah," he answered, and she pressed in closer as her eyes went from holding his to studying him.

"That was unfun," she whispered.

"It was but it's also something I can't talk about," he replied.

"It brings up Misty," she pushed, and Chace sighed.

"Yeah, baby, it does."

"You should—"

"No," he cut her off.

She pressed in closer, opened those bubblegum lips of hers to say something and serious as fuck, she got closer, in his tee, with him on his couch, she pushed it, he'd give her anything she wanted.

So he had to shut this down.

"Give me this," he said quietly and quickly she shut her mouth. "This day with you after what you gave me last night. This one day, you and me and food and TV and champagne with the hamburgers I'm makin' tonight and all of it good. All clean. All normal. All right. No Misty. No murder. No history. None of that garbage. Just us. You had what you had to give me last night to give once and I had it to get once. We shared that and it was beautiful. So let's keep it beautiful, just us for a day. Tomorrow we can try to talk to abused kids and let the world back in. Today, tonight, give me," he tightened his arm around her and finished, "*this*."

"Okay," she whispered immediately, and he hadn't even had to use the word "baby."

Chace stared down into those blue eyes in that pretty face with those extraordinary cheekbones, all of it surrounded by her fantastic hair, looking up at him with warmth and understanding in her eyes, and he knew in that instant he was falling in love.

Christ, he could have none of the beauty that met his eyes, her heart-shaped ass in his bed, the gift of her virginity and only have her giving in last night and just now when he needed her to and calling her folks to ream their asses about hassling him and it would have started happening.

But he had all of that and her being a geek, her imagination, her humor, her immense care for a kid she didn't know and fuck him, he wasn't teetering. He was halfway gone.

Ty and Tate had this. One was a brunette. One was a blonde. Neither of them was shy.

Both of them gave this.

Jesus. He got it.

And he had it in the curve of his arm.

Fuck, he wanted to make love to her.

Fuck.

He couldn't without maybe causing her pain.

So he did what he could. He kissed her. He did it soft, he did it long, he got his hands up her shirt and she got her hands up his.

When he broke the kiss, he asked her softly if she wanted popcorn and to watch another episode of *Psych*. She grinned at him huge because she did.

Before they settled back in the couch with a bowl of

microwave popcorn and cans of soda, he informed her she was again spending the night.

Not that it was a question.

But her answer?

She directed another huge-ass smile at him.

Then she whispered, "Okay."

CHAPTER ELEVEN

Round Two

Six oh three the next morning

"Baby, wake up."

I drifted out of sleep, my eyes opening and at what I saw, I was certain I was still dreaming.

Chace, sitting on the edge of the bed in a pair of those long, loose running shorts and one of those skin-tight running shirts that had the awesome stitching and a collar that went halfway up his neck, both navy blue.

How had I never seen *this*? I'd been avidly watching him for *years*. I'd even seen him run, and this was on numerous occasions. He was usually wearing track pants and one of those tops with the half-zip at the throat (an outfit that was also awesome but not near as awesome as this one) or loose running shorts and a tee. Granted, if I got a look at him somewhere mid to end of run, his shirt was plastered to him with sweat. Which, for Chace, was a good look.

Still.

This was *much better*.

I pried my eyes from the muscles outlined rather spectacularly by his shirt and blinked at his face.

When he had my eyes, he spoke softly. "Goin' for a run. When I get back, I'll take a quick shower. We'll hit the store, pick up some shit for Malachi and grab a coffee before we go to the library."

I wasn't keeping up. I was in a haze from sleep, doing that sleeping next to him (which was yummy) and him looking super, double-dose hot in the morning. I couldn't process the English language.

Therefore, I murmured, "What?"

He grinned and that didn't make things better.

Then he leaned deeper into me so his grinning, handsome face was close. And, incidentally, so was the skin-tight shirt and the muscles it covered.

Therefore there was no way I would process his, "I'm goin' for a run. We got shit to do when I get back and not much time to do it in so get your shower, I'll grab a quick one when I get home and some food and we'll move. Yeah?"

As he spoke, my eyes drifted down his chest and when he stopped speaking, some part of my brain registered it was my turn so I asked, "How do you get a shirt that tight on?"

"Faye," he called, and my eyes floated back up to him. When they hit his, his eyes moved over my face and he muttered, "Fuck, you this cute and sleepy when I talked to you all those times on the phone?"

"Probably," I answered since it was a question but it also likely wasn't the truth. He wasn't looking hot sitting on the bed with me when I was talking to him on the phone. He was somewhere else just sounding hot. Now I had both.

"Fuck it," he muttered like he wasn't talking to me then carried on, "I'll run after work."

That was when I found my sleep-warm body plucked out

of bed and dragged across his lap. He twisted, rolled and then I was back in bed but not under the covers, under Chace.

I blinked up at him again.

"You wanna know how I get this shirt on?" he asked.

"Yes," I breathed.

His mouth came to mine, his eyes looking into mine and he whispered against my lips, "Then take it off."

I was sleepy, this was true. I was hazy, this was true too.

But even so, I was up for that particular challenge.

Definitely.

                    *   *   *

Eight fourteen that morning

I wandered dreamily into La-La Land Coffee hand in hand with Chace Keaton.

I was dreamy because he gave me an orgasm with his mouth but this time he also used his fingers *at the same time*. It was *awesome*.

I was also dreamy because after that, I started to give him an orgasm with my mouth but ended up giving him one with my hand *all by myself*. I kissed him while I did it. *I kissed him*. And it sounded and felt *nice*.

I was further dreamy because after that we had a shower and I talked Chace into grabbing breakfast at La-La Land.

This wasn't hard to do.

I just said, "Let's save time, skip breakfast at home and get something from Shambles and Sunny."

Since his soapy hands were on my naked wet skin and his eyes were watching his hands move, he answered on a distracted mutter, "Works for me."

Watching him watching his hands, I figured I could ask him to build me a model of the Sistine Chapel with minia-ture true-to-life detailing then a shed we could display it in, advertise it and sell tickets and he would have said, "Works for me."

I liked this. It made being naked and wet with Chace in the shower not weird or embarrassing.

It made it a lot of other things. Like beautiful. And it made me feel a lot of other things. Like desired. Cherished.

And *powerful*.

I made a mental note of this for future reference.

Last, I was dreamy because Chace and I went to the grocery store before La-La Land. I didn't know why this made me feel dreamy. It was an everyday thing, going to the grocery store. But somehow doing an everyday thing, just like the day before, lazing around and watching TV, seemed magical when I did it with Chace.

This didn't mean it wasn't relaxing the day before. Sometimes fun, sometimes sweet like when he chuckled at the antics of Shawn, Gus, Lassie, Juliet and the crew from *Psych*. I loved it that he liked that show and I loved hearing his comfortable, laid-back laughter. I didn't suspect he was comfortable and laid-back a lot. I didn't suspect he laughed a lot. I didn't like either. It might be characters on a TV show giving it to him, still, I liked that he had it.

So even though we just picked up bits and pieces for Malachi and we weren't there long, for some reason I knew I'd remember that first trip to the grocery store with Chace for the rest of my life. Like a fantastic vacation. A special birthday party.

A wedding.

This dreamy feeling stuck with me as I entered La-La Land for maybe the thousandth time, but this time the first time with Chace (which was also special) and it stuck with me in a big way.

I saw Shambles immediately. He was wearing a pair of those round, John Lennon glasses with bright green shades in them. He had a rainbow-colored tie-dyed bandana tied around his forehead, the top of his shaggy blond hair bunched weirdly at the top and hanging low to his shoulders out the bottom.

He took one look at us, his arm shot straight in front of him, his finger pointing back and forth between Chace and me and his mouth started moving to say loud words.

"You! *With* you! *Together! Groovintude!*" Then he dropped his arm and shouted, "Sunny! Baby! All those coffees to go separate and now they're here together! Proof! Our sweet Faye landed the hot police guy!"

This was the exact time my dreamy feeling ended and heat hit my face.

Sunny ran in from a room at the back as Chace, reading me again, dropped my hand and slid an arm around my shoulders, pulling me protectively close to his side. With no other choice and because it felt good, I slid my arm around his narrow waist.

Neither of us was able to say a word.

This was because Sunny clapped while jumping up and down and shouting, "*I like!*"

We made it to the counter (unfortunately) and Shambles looked at Chace, "No offense to your brethren, dude. There are other hot local federales but none as hot as you."

"Shambles is a guy," Sunny leaned in to inform me of a fact I knew, "but he's comfortable in his manhood so he's capable of spotting hotness and has no problem sharing his opinion. He's not my style," she jerked her head at Chace, "but I think every member of the sisterhood would agree on some level your guy is a hot guy."

This was not in doubt.

"Um..." I mumbled.

"I appreciate the compliment but I think you both get Faye's a little quiet so I'd also appreciate it if for her sake you'd be a little more cool," Chace said in a quiet voice that nevertheless held authority at the same time it was weirdly gentle.

I tipped my head back to stare at his profile, amazed he could pull this off at the same time not surprised at all.

"Right," Shambles whispered like he'd been shushed in a library and not gently told off by a hot guy cop. Then he looked at me and he said, "Sorry, Crimson Stargazer."

By the way, if you were a regular, and Sunny and Shambles liked you, they gave you a hippie name. I knew this because, while getting to know Lauren and Lexie, I learned that they called Lauren "Flower Petal" and they called Lexie "Midnight Sunshine." Usually they just called me "Star" for short like they called Laurie "Petal" and Lexie "Midnight."

They were weird. They were hippies. They were the only hippies I knew so I didn't know if they were weird hippies. What I did know was that they were sweet.

"It's okay, Shambles," I said, smiling at him.

"It's cool you read 'cause reading is cool," he went on softly. "It's cooler you're not reading and, instead, standing close to a hot guy."

No truer words were ever spoken.

My smile got bigger.

Shambles smiled back.

Then he jumped as he whirled, moving to his espresso machine and crying out, "Hazelnut latte and triple-shot latte, coming up."

"We need breakfast, Sunny," Chace said, and she jumped to the case filled with Shambles's homemade baked goods.

"I see you're having a good effect on the hot guy already, Star," Shambles said to me while fiddling with that coffee grinder thingie. "He never gets anything out of the case. The only alternate he orders is one of my smoothies with a scoop of protein powder. The only reason I *have* protein powder is because he and Midnight's hubster ask for it in their smoothies."

"The hot guy has a name, Shambles," I said quietly, smiling through it and hoping I didn't sound like I was being mean. "His name is Chace."

Shambles, showing he took no offense, threw a goofy grin over his shoulder at me and replied, "We know his name but I'm the kinda guy who calls 'em as he sees 'em."

Well, there you go.

"Lapis Bravery," Sunny, at this point, murmured under her breath.

"Perfect," Shambles murmured back.

"What?" I asked and Sunny's eyes tipped to me.

"Lapis," she said softly, "his eyes. Bravery," she hesitated and I felt my throat get thick before she finished, "*him*."

That *was* perfect. If there ever was a hippie name for Chace, that was it.

Chace didn't think so and I knew this when I felt his body get tight and he asked, "What the fuck?"

I looked up at him. "Your hippie name. I'm Crimson Stargazer. Lexie is Midnight Sunshine. Sunny is Sunray Goddess. And you're Lapis Bravery."

"I don't—" he started, but I gave his waist a squeeze and shook my head once.

His jaw got hard and he shut up.

I looked into the display and ordered a blueberry muffin with brown sugar crumbles on top. Chace took the fun out of it by ordering a carrot muffin made of whole wheat flour, which was the healthiest thing in the display.

Chace paid and I didn't even go for my purse. This was because Chace *paid*. I learned that lesson already. In fact, I learned it the third time I tried to text him saying coffees were my treat at stakeouts and he'd texted back:

Baby, I pay. The end.

There you go.

The end.

We gave our farewells and were walking back to his truck (we'd dropped mine at my place before shopping) when Chace started, "Faye, I'm not big on—"

I stopped walking abruptly and stopped him with me on a tug at his waist (we still had our arms around each other).

Chace looked down at me and I whispered, "Don't."

"Baby—"

I shook my head and turned into him, getting up on my toes. "Baby works for you, honey, but this time, please, don't use it. You're that to people in this town. You're bravery. I don't know why you don't like it, why you get that weird look on your face and tone in your voice when it comes up. I want to know and hope I will, when you're ready to tell me. But let them have that. In this town, after what went down, people need to believe that. And Sunny especially."

Sunny, too, had been kidnapped and stabbed by the serial killer Dalton McIntyre. Arnie Fuller had not instigated a search for her even after Tonia Payne had already been killed. It was Tate and Wood who went looking for her and called in the police to assist with the search. She had been quiet for a while after that. Now she was back to her normal self.

So everyone needed to believe there was bravery behind the badges that protected that town.

But Sunny needed to be a true believer.

Chace stared down at me and a muscle ticked in his square jaw. But he didn't say anything and this I correctly took as him giving in.

I pulled in a breath and hoped I was doing the right thing when I tipped further up on my toes and kissed that jaw.

I did it right.

I knew this when he sighed, his arm got tight around my shoulders giving me a mini-hug then it loosened telling me to step back and get a move on.

I stepped back, adjusted to his side and got a move on.

But this didn't mean I didn't worry about what just happened. I wasn't wrong. Chace didn't like being a local hero.

Any man should be humble. I knew this because my dad said so.

But that wasn't it.

It was deeper, darker.

And I hoped he'd one day share it with me so I could throw some light on it.

*　　*　　*

Nine sixteen that morning

I watched Chace's door open on his Yukon and then I watched him fold out, slam it and saunter to me.

Malachi hadn't shown. He was never this late.

Ever.

I bit my lip as Chace approached and saw Chace's eyes drop to my mouth.

When Chace stopped in front of me, he shared his guess. "He either saw you standin' there and decided not to approach or he's late."

I threw out an alternate guess. "Or something's wrong."

Chace lifted a hand, pulled my hair off my shoulder then curled his fingers around the side of my neck, ordering gently, "Don't jump to that conclusion, darlin'."

I bit my lip again.

Chace kept talking.

"Maybe it's too soon for him. You told me Krystal said she'd take yesterday's shift. If Krystal said she'd do that, she did it. There were no bags here when we got here. So he came yesterday. Today you're here, visible. Maybe he's not ready for a meet."

I stopped biting my lip and nodded.

Chace kept going.

"I should have signed in over an hour ago. I gotta go."

I'd never thought of that. He told me his schedule pretty much adhered to when crime was committed, but his scheduled hours were eight to five with every other weekend on call. We'd been staking out the return bin for two weeks so this meant he'd been late to work every day for two weeks.

I tilted my head to the side and asked, "Are you going to get into trouble because you're late?"

"Cap knows about Malachi and the stakeouts. I got my phone, they need me, they know where I am, so no. But I'm never in this late so now I gotta go."

I nodded.

"What're you gonna do?" he asked.

"Um...walk home, get changed, get in my car and come back, see if the bags are gone. Park on the street and watch awhile if they aren't."

Chace nodded this time. "You want a ride?"

I shook my head. "No, a walk will do me good."

His hand gave me a squeeze and then he asked a question I really, *really* liked.

"We doin' your place or my place tonight?"

He wanted to see me again and soon.

Yippee!

After celebrating inside, I contemplated his question. His house was better than mine. So was his kitchen. But my house had my clothes in it. I wasn't one of those people who knew what they were going to wear throughout the week. Not even the next day. I usually stood in front of my wardrobe for ten minutes making my selection the morning of.

Though, I was assuming his question of my place or his

meant not only where we'd be meeting and eating but also sleeping.

Maybe I was wrong.

But I hoped I wasn't.

Belatedly and hesitantly, I answered, "Mine."

"Good," he muttered, dipping his head to touch his mouth to mine then moving back a scant inch. "There's a piece of furniture in your house that's on display I been lookin' forward to tryin' out."

He was spending the night.

Yippee!

I moved into him, his hand slid to the back of the neck and he gave me a kiss that wasn't a touch on the lips.

When he moved away again, he didn't let me go but he did say, "I'll run after work. I'll be at your place around six thirty."

"Okay, I'll see you there."

"Right," he murmured, moved in for the lip touch again then moved back and gave my neck another squeeze. "Later, baby."

"Later, Chace."

He let me go and I watched him walk to his truck.

I walked to the sidewalk as he drove off. He gave me a raised hand flicked out to the side as he drove past. I waved.

Then I did what I told him I would do. I went home, changed, got in my car and went back to the library.

The bags were still there.

I didn't like this.

I drove around, parked on the street, waited and watched.

At ten thirty, I was bored, I had a house to clean, groceries to buy, a gym to visit and a hot-guy boyfriend to feed and entertain that night.

So, giving one last look at the bags waiting by the return bin, my heart heavy and my nerves rattled, I drove home.

*   *   *

Eleven forty-eight that night

I powered down my Nook, shifted carefully and set it on my nightstand. Then I reached to turn out the light.

Chace was behind me in bed, sleeping.

I liked this.

We had a good night. Dinner and light conversation. Chace teasing, me laughing. Chace laughing when I worked at making it happen. We did the dishes. I read, my back pressed to the couch, my front pressed to Chace's side, my Nook resting on his abs, Chace on his back, eyes on the TV so Chace could watch the game.

The game ended, Chace muttered, "Meet you in bed," which I took as my cue to get ready for it.

This I did, wandering out a little nervously in a satin nightie that was a cream so creamy it was pearlescent. No lace, simple, elegant and short. I did this nervously because the minute I left the bathroom, I saw Chace's eyes lock on me.

I made it to the edge of the bed, started to put a knee in it but my knee didn't hit bed. This was because Chace, lounging on his back, did an ab curl, lunged and I was on my back in bed, Chace on me.

"My girl and her sexy nighties," he murmured with easy-to-read appreciation, and this was due not only to his tone but his hands roaming over the satin.

Then he kissed me.

Before I slipped into the haze of Chace's kiss, I made a mental note to call Lexie and have her round up Wendy so we could go back to the mall. I hadn't bought that many nighties or underwear.

I needed to stock up.

Hanky-panky commenced though Chace again didn't make love to me.

"Tomorrow," he muttered against my lips, and I was about to tell him I felt perfectly fine but his hand moved into my panties to cup my behind.

That felt *nice*.

Righty ho! Tomorrow it was.

And that night, I wasn't disappointed.

But when we were done, I also wasn't sleepy. As I commenced after hanky-panky talk and this went on for a while, it came clear Chace was. He didn't tell me to shut up but I could read in his voice he was tired.

So I told him quietly, "I'll let you sleep, go to the couch and read."

"Read here," he returned.

"The light—"

His arms around me gave me a squeeze. "Read here, baby. I'll be all right."

"Okay," I whispered.

And that was what I did. He didn't lie. He was all right. I checked about fifteen minutes after I started reading and he was asleep on his side, one hand shoved under his pillow, one arm cocked in front of him on the bed.

I took this opportunity to study him since I'd never seen him sleep. His long, dark brown lashes resting at the tops of his cheeks. His handsome face relaxed and no less handsome. His big, powerful body shut down.

Studying him, I wasn't surprised to note he exuded extreme hotness even when he was unconscious.

Pure male beauty.

After I set the Nook on the nightstand, I turned out the light and settled in, my back to him, thinking maybe I should adjust my sleeping schedule to his. The last two nights, I fell asleep in his arms. It was nice having him here with me in my bed. But it was better cuddling with him before I fell asleep.

Bath didn't help.

His words the morning after I gave him my virginity filtered through my head.

So much was happening and all of it was so huge, I didn't think of it at the time, why he did that, guided me to the bath.

I wanna see to you. Will you let me do that, Faye?

He thought he would cause an ache and he did it to alleviate the pain.

My heart settled, I smiled against my pillow just as Chace's arm wrapped around my waist and hauled me across the bed. He didn't tuck me to him, he tucked me *under* him, his body curved into mine but it also tilted into mine so it was pressed deep into me.

He did this the night before too.

I liked it then.

I liked it no less now.

"Done?" he muttered, his voice sleepy sexy.

"Yeah," I answered, my hand sliding down his arm to curl around his wrist at my belly.

"Good book?" he kept muttering.

"Yeah."

"Good," he continued muttering.

I snuggled deeper into him.

His arm around me tightened.

I sighed.

I felt his arm relax and his weight settle into me.

He was asleep.

My eyes drifted closed and I became the same.

*   *   *

Ten twenty-three the next night

I gasped as Chace gathered me in his arms, rolled and I

found myself still connected to him but sitting up and straddling him.

Oh my fraking *Lord.*

He'd lifted the ban on sex. We'd done a lot of really fun
stuff before he finally connected with me again. And I was
enjoying it, on my back, wrapped around Chace with Chace
thrusting sweet and rhythmically inside me.

I was enjoying it *a lot.*

Now I didn't know what to do.

Chace was up too, sitting under me in my bed. His hand
moved up the satin of my nightie, up my neck to my head, he
cupped it and tipped it down so his lips had my ear.

"Move, honey," he whispered, his arm around my waist
giving a gentle pull up.

"Move?" I breathed.

"Ride me," he urged. Just those two words tore through
me, sending shivers in their wake. "Go fast, go slow, do what
you want but don't lose the tip."

Ride him.

Okay, um...I was a virgin before Chace but I'd seen
television, movies, read romance novels. I knew there were
more positions than missionary.

Chace was introducing me to a new one.

So I pulled up.

Not much fun.

I slid down.

Oo, *better.*

I tried it again.

Yeah, the down was better but to get it, you had to have
the up.

So I did it again.

I found my rhythm and then I found I liked my rhythm a
whole lot better when it was faster. I also found I liked my
rhythm a heckuva lot more when I added allowing my hands

to roam Chace's skin and my mouth and tongue to roam his neck.

Instinctively, I discovered something *awesome* and that was, on a downward glide, if you ground in, pressing deep, shifting your hips around, that...felt...*great*.

It didn't only feel great to me, it felt great to Chace too.

I knew this when he growled against the skin of my neck, his head went back and his lips ordered, "Faye. Mouth. Now."

I lifted my head and gave him my mouth.

Incidentally, I did this on a downward glide and grind.

Fraking phenomenal.

Chace's hand slid from my waist up my side, over my ribs to my breast. His fingers curled around then one finger and his thumb honed in on my nipple, squeezed then rolled.

I slammed down on Chace, ground in, ripped my mouth from his, my neck arched back and I came hard on a gasp that melted into a whimper.

While I was still doing that, Chace whipped me to my back, wrapped my legs around his hips and drove in way faster and harder than he had the other night. Way faster and harder than I rode him.

Still coming, my body jolting, Chace thrusting, I couldn't be sure, it had never happened before, not even close but either I started coming again or my orgasm lasted a really long time.

It still ended before Chace's began so, although I did it hazily, I got to watch.

Fabulous.

After he came down, he buried his face in my neck but unlike the first time, he didn't stay planted. He moved in and out, slowly, four times (I counted) before he slid in to the root and stopped.

There was something about that that was immensely sweet,

gently giving something to me while at the same taking something from me, which meant I also had something to give.

I loved it.

One of his hands glided down my nightie at the side and he murmured against my skin, "Next time I take you, baby, I want you naked. You think you'll be ready for that?"

What I thought was, once he started, I didn't think much of anything. If I was lucid, I probably wouldn't be. Since I'd not be lucid, I would.

The other thing I thought was, it was unbelievably sweet that he asked.

So I whispered, "Yeah."

"Good."

My arms gave him a squeeze.

His head came up and he looked down at me, one of his hands moving to slide into the hair at the side of my head, his thumb coming out to do lazy, soft circles at my temple.

That was unbelievable sweet too.

"Came with just my cock," he noted quietly, and his words made me blink into his handsome, sated face.

"What?"

"Seein' as I'm still inside you, I'm hopin' you can take it real, just for now, but not a lotta women come just from takin' a man's cock."

Seeing as he was still inside me, I'd just come twice or I'd had a really hard, long one and I'd have to get used to real eventually, I gave it back.

But hesitantly.

"Seeing as uh...*before* there was your finger action at my, um...then your finger action between my...you know, and then *my* hand action at—"

I shut up when he grinned and whispered, "I get it, Faye. You were primed."

I relaxed underneath him, grinned at him back and muttered, "Yeah."

"Like that," he kept whispering.

I was confused. My opinion was, there was a lot to like, as in, all of it.

Which part did he like?

"Uh…" I began, his grin turned into a smile, I started drowning in it then he did something *amazing*.

He rolled us so he was on his back, I was on top of him, straddling him and we *stayed connected*.

Oh wow.

I blinked down at him while both his hands came up to either side of my head, his fingers sifted in my hair, pulling it back then holding it there at the same time managing to use the rest of his arms hold me.

"I like it all, honey. Fuckin' brilliant, showin' you things, watchin' you react, get excited, get confident, try your own thing. But what I meant was, I like it that you can find it just takin' me." He used my hair to pull my lips to his, his brushed mine then he gently tugged my hair to pull my head back and he finished, "A fuckuva lot."

"That's good," I whispered because it really was.

His hands moved behind me and I would know it was to transfer my hair into one when my hair stayed back but one of his hands drifted down my spine to rest on the small of my back before he said gently, "We gotta get you to the doctor."

This was not a comment I expected so I felt my brow furrow and my head tip to the side.

"Why?"

"Birth control, darlin'."

"But I'm on birth control."

Chace blinked up at me before he stared.

Then he asked, "What?"

"I'm on birth—"

I stopped speaking abruptly because I finally lost the haze and snapped back into real life.

When I hit my twenties, my periods changed. They'd always been regular, light cramping, nothing too bad. Then they stopped lasting four days, started lasting two because they became heavy, the cramping intense and sometimes I'd get minor headaches that weren't debilitating but they weren't fun either.

It was the cramping that was bad. Month after month, for the first day, it was awful. I'd have to sit in a hot tub and take large doses of ibuprofen even to make them manageable. If I didn't start at night, I would have to miss class when I was in college or even miss work when I was working. If I did start at night, it would take so long to get the cramps to go away, my sleep was interrupted and I'd be a zombie at school or work the next day.

When it came down to missing or zoning out during work, I eventually went to the doctor. She put me on birth control and *voila!* Back to regular periods, cramping and headaches gone, flow normal.

I'd never gone off the Pill and I'd never used it for the purpose it was intended because I'd never needed it. So I never thought of it that way.

Until now.

"You're on the Pill?"

Chace's voice took me back to him at the same time it reminded me this was not a story I wished to share.

"Uh…"

His hand at the small of my back became an arm around my waist and he said low, "Faye."

"Yes," I whispered.

His brows drew together. "There a reason?"

"Um…"

"Faye, bein' real, my dick is still inside you," he reminded me. "This is not only shit we can talk about. It's shit we *have* to talk about."

"Uh…"

"Honey—"

"I had really bad periods, I take the Pill and it regulates them so they're not bad anymore," I said in a rush.

"Right," Chace replied matter-of-factly then concluded, "Excellent. Next time I get you naked and I get *you*, no condoms. All you. Fucking brilliant."

He let my hair go, gave me a squeeze with both his arms, lifted his head off the pillow and touched his mouth to mine.

Then he rolled me to my back sliding out of me, bent his head, kissed my shoulder and muttered, "Be back."

He rolled again and angled out of the bed. I dazedly watched the muscles of his back and shoulders move as his arms swung loosely at his sides (along with watching other, um…parts of him) because he was walking to my bathroom.

Okay, well, I guessed I didn't need to be embarrassed about discussing my period with Chace.

Good to know.

I rolled the way he rolled, hung over the side of the bed, reached out and nabbed my panties. I had them on and was sitting on my booty in the bed, knees to my chest, arms around my calves, back against the pillows I'd shoved against the headboard when Chace came back out.

One could say I had no problem with *his* nudity. Even lucid. This could be because his body was like a walking, moving, blood-flowing-in-its-veins work of art. Or it could be because he didn't have any problem with it and that communicated something to me.

Whatever.

I didn't.

There was something marvelous about him climbing

naked in my bed after making love to me that would make even the biggest prude not be embarrassed.

He pulled the covers up to his waist, put his forearm in the pillow and tipped his eyes up to me.

"I'm worried about Malachi," I announced, and his face went soft.

"Knew this was comin'," he muttered.

He would since I texted him four times that day to give him status reports on the bags that Malachi had not been by to pick up. Not yesterday's stash. Not today's.

I twisted my torso to him, letting go of my legs, positioning them in an "S" beside me and leaned into him.

"Two days, Chace, and he hasn't come to get his stash. This time, I wasn't hanging out. This time, we were in your truck on the street," I reminded him.

"Maybe he made us in the truck," he suggested.

"Or maybe he saw me standing there Monday and he freaked out and he's not coming back. When I left this evening, all the bags were still there."

"It's gonna be okay, Faye," he assured me quietly.

I shook my head. "Something's wrong."

"Maybe but it's going to be okay."

I stared at him.

His arm came out, hooked me around the waist and pulled me down and in the bed so we were facing each other.

"I made a call," he informed me.

I got up on my forearm so we were face to face.

"What call?"

He studied me before he sighed and said, "Deck."

I felt my brows go up. "Deck?"

"Deck's between jobs right now so Deck's got time on his hands. When Malachi didn't show this mornin', I gave Deck a call. He's gonna find him."

"Oh God," I breathed.

Chace's arm got tight around my waist. "Baby, it'll be okay."

"Deck sounds kinda crazy," I whispered.

"He is. He's also not stupid. He knows this kid's been abused, Dumpster diving and scared outta his mind. He'll go soft."

"But—"

His arm got tighter, shifting and tugging me so I had no choice but to come off my forearm since I was back to the bed, Chace looming over me.

"He'll go soft," he whispered.

"You're sure?" I whispered back.

"Yeah."

I took in a breath, let it out and nodded.

"In the meantime, we keep doin' what we're doin'," Chace went on.

I nodded again.

"Now, you gonna read or sleep?"

This meant, I assumed, Chace was tired. Then again, it was past his bedtime.

"Read," I told him quietly, and he grinned at me.

Then he bent his head and kissed me, one of his sweet, soft ones, open mouth, lazy stroke of the tongue. My toes curled, both my arms went around him and the fingers of both hands went into his hair.

When he ended the kiss, his lips didn't leave mine and he murmured there, "Read."

"Okay," I murmured back.

He lifted up, kissed my nose and moved a hint away.

I rolled to my side of the bed and grabbed my Nook.

Chace's light went off.

I turned on my Nook and read. An hour later, I turned it off, set it on my nightstand and turned out my light.

I barely settled into bed before I was hauled into and mostly under Chace with his arm at my waist.

"Done?" he mumbled sleepily.

"Yeah."

"'Night, baby."

"'Night, Chace."

His arm gave me a squeeze.

I snuggled into him.

His weight settled into me.

I closed my eyes and went to sleep.

*   *   *

Ten oh seven at night, three days later

"Chace."

"Fuck, baby."

"Chace!"

"Give me that mouth."

I gave him my mouth. Half a second later I moaned my orgasm into his.

When I was done doing that, his hand cupping my head shoved my face in his neck and he kept powering up.

I was back to his headboard, my legs around him holding tight, my arms around his shoulders doing the same. He was on his knees, his hand was at my behind holding me up and his other hand was in my hair, his arm holding me close.

And he was powering deep, his hips driving up, slamming into me.

Seriously, sex . . . was . . . *awesome.*

One of my arms left his shoulders so my hand could drift down his back to his behind and clench in so I could feel the muscles there working.

Sublime.

"Jesus, fuck," he growled into the skin of my neck through grunts.

I was learning to recognize the signs. He was getting close.

I held on tighter.

"Jesus, fuck, so fuckin' tight, tight and sweet," he was groaning now through his grunts.

I loved that. So much, I ran my tongue up his neck.

He powered up harder, hips bucking, hand clenching my booty, other hand fisting in my hair and I heard as well as felt his deep, guttural groan against my skin.

Yeah. Seriously.

Sex . . . was . . . *awesome*.

His breathing settled and his hand let my hair go to slide down and curl around the back of my neck.

I held on tight and didn't move a muscle.

"Town's pretty, cute, sweet librarian wears sexy-as-all-fuck underwear, sexier nighties and gets off on getting banged, back against the headboard."

I blinked into his skin.

"What?"

Chace didn't repeat himself.

Instead, he asked, "How long after I planted you against the headboard did it take you to come, baby? A second?"

I pulled my head back to stare at him.

He pulled his back to grin at me.

"Are you teasing me?" I asked, uncertain how I felt about this.

"Yeah," he answered. "Though, I will point out, I'm teasin' you but it's the God's honest truth. Got you up there, you went wild."

I felt my eyes narrow and I snapped, "Well, it was hot."

"Yeah it was. Got hotter when you went wild for that whole second before you came."

I kept snapping but the only thing I could get out was, "Chace!"

"It's true."

"It wasn't a second."

"A second and a half," he amended, *slightly*.

"It wasn't a second and a half!" My voice was rising.

"That's not true. Totally a second and a half, no more."

"I'm uncertain how I feel about you teasing me when I'm naked," I shot back.

His smile turned wicked. "Naked, seriously fuckin' wet with my cock still inside you, you mean."

I felt my cheeks heat, I looked over his shoulder and muttered, "Whatever."

"Jesus, wettest I've ever had along with the tightest," he went on, and my eyes cut back to him.

"Chace!"

He pressed me into the headboard, his face got close, his smile died and his eyes went intense. "What you got to give, Faye, here," his hips pressed into mine, "clean, pure, all fuckin' mine and that's beautiful right there. But the rest, how wet you get, how tight you are, you goin' wild for me like you did just now, baby. *Fuck*. You gotta know, coupled with the other, that's beauty that's off the charts."

Hmm. I liked that.

A frak of a lot.

I bit my lip.

His eyes dropped to my mouth and his grin came back.

Then I was on my back in the bed with him on me, giving orders. "Gonna let you go. You're gonna go clean up, come back and round two."

My eyebrows shot up.

Round two?

We'd never gone a second round.

"Seriously?"

"Not on duty tomorrow," he reminded me.

"Well, I am," I reminded him. "I have to work."

His grin stayed fixed and he reminded me right back, "Yeah, but your day starts at nine thirty. You can sleep in."

This was true.

I held his eyes.

Then I whispered, "Round two?"

His eyes got intense and he whispered back, "Oh yeah."

Oh.

Yeah.

"Okay," I breathed, he bent his head to touch his mouth to mine then rolled off.

I skedaddled off the bed and to the bathroom to prepare for round two.

And yeah.

Seriously.

Sex was awesome.

*   *   *

Twelve fifteen that night

I lay in bed snuggled into Chace's side, his arm under and around me, hand under my nightie drifting a short path up my spine and down to the top of my undies, my arm around his gut, cheek to his shoulder, top leg tangled with both of his.

We'd had almost a week of us being all the us we could be.

He worked, I worked. He ran or swam or did weight lifting, I went to the gym. We had dinner together. We walked to Bubba's from my place after dinner once to have drinks. He watched sports, I read.

He did not, however, watch any of my shows and stood firm on this even when I semi-begged him to give *Supernatural* a go telling him Dean Winchester was most assuredly his type of guy. Although I gave up, I decided next week I'd try again. Dean and Sam could lapse into heartfelt man conversations and there were demons and ghosts and a variety of apocalyptic storylines. But still, I figured Chace would get into it mostly because they drove a kickass Impala. And all men (or most men and the men who were all man were most of them) liked cars.

Anyway, I had last week's episode taped. Since I was spending all my time with Chace, if he didn't watch it with me, when was I going to get my dose of Dean and Sam?

The sex was regular (after the ban, morning *and* night!) and got better and better (deliriously so). As Chace guided it, I became more confident and we got to know each other better, in bed and out.

It had been another wonderful week.

Brilliant. Fabulous. Amazing.

The only pall was Malachi.

He hadn't shown all week and daily I asked for reports from Chace about what Deck was uncovering.

Deck, so far, had found nothing.

Chace had also come up with zip. This included him expanding his search by contacting every school in the county and every surrounding county to see if a boy called Malachi was enrolled.

Nothing.

"Kid's a ghost," Chace had muttered, and his tone eloquently underlined he didn't feel this was good.

I didn't either. How could he not be on the register of *any* school in *five* counties?

"I'm worried about Malachi," I muttered into the dark silence, and Chace's hand stopped drifting and his arm curled tight around me.

"I know, baby," he whispered.

"This amount of time, he's running out of food."

"Deck'll find him."

I lifted up and looked down at him in the dark. "Chace—"

His other arm reached across his body and I felt his hand cup my cheek.

"Faye, baby, Deck'll find him. Nothin' we can do. Not right now. You need to sleep. You got work tomorrow. Tomorrow night, we got your family. And Deck's stymied. He doesn't like to be stymied. Not ever but definitely not by a nine-year-old kid. This was a favor he was doin' for me. Now it's his mission. He won't give up, Faye, and he'll find him."

I sucked in breath.

He was right. There was nothing we could do after midnight on a Friday night. I had work the next day and we had to face my family tomorrow night.

This was supposed to be a dinner for Mom, Dad, Chace and me. Then Liza found out about it (Dad and his big mouth). Now she and Boyd and her kids were coming and it was a pre-birthday bash for her son, Jarot.

Don't ask me about the name Jarot. I *told* her he'd be teased and called "carrot," and he was. She loved the name and she was Liza, when she loved something she was perfectly willing to pitch numerous fits to get it. So Boyd gave in mostly to shut her up. Luckily, he gave in after demanding the right to name their second kid. His name was Robert. Suffice it to say, Robbie didn't get teased on the playground.

Then again, Robbie was a bruiser.

Jarot played with Legos all the fraking time and Liza, Boyd *and* Dad were convinced, with the stuff he built, that he was going to be an architect.

He was almost nine.

Robbie had been sent home from school three times for punching kids in the nose.

He was six.

No one said what they thought Robbie was going to be mostly because the optimistic choice was the next Great White Hope in the boxing ring. But the practical one was he was going to be a drug dealer's enforcer.

"Oh, all right," I gave in on a mutter then settled back in.

Chace's hand at my cheek sifted back through my hair before it fell away and his hand at my spine went back to drifting.

I relaxed.

"We'll find him, Faye."

It was quiet but it was a promise.

I pressed closer.

He knew I was worried and he didn't like it.

But I knew he was worried too. Although I didn't want him to be, I liked that he was for a kid he didn't know.

"Okay, honey."

"Sleep," he urged.

"Okay."

"'Night baby."

"'Night, Chace."

His hand quit drifting and his arm gave me another squeeze then his hand went back to drifting.

As it moved, my mind quit drifting and my eyes closed.

Then I did as Chace urged. Tucked close to him, I slept.

CHAPTER TWELVE

Family

FAYE'S FIDGETING BESIDE him in his truck caught his attention so Chace reached out a hand and tagged hers. He linked their fingers and pulled their hands to his thigh.

They were on their way to her parents' house and she was

anxious. This was, she told him when he gently pressed it out of her, not because she was worried about what they would think of him. But what he would think of them.

"They're a little um…nutty," she'd said.

"There's good nutty and bad nutty. My guess is they're good nutty," he'd replied.

She gave him a cute but dubious look and went on.

"And loud."

Chace didn't reply.

"And opinionated," she continued.

Chace just grinned at her.

"And in your business," she carried on.

Chace's arms, already around her, tightened and his grin got bigger.

"I'm kind of the black sheep. I mean, they all read but none of them are shy, um…*at all*," she kept going.

"You love them?" Chace had asked. When he got her nod he finished quietly on a squeeze of his arms, "Then I will too."

This served to calm her and earn him a smile.

But about a minute ago, his assurance wore off.

Once they got there, she'd settle in and be okay.

As for Chace, he wasn't worried. Getting the invitation to dinner from Silas Goodknight after he came for his visit and the reason he came for that visit, Chace figured he did something of which Silas approved.

As for the other Goodknights, Faye liked him and he reckoned that was all he needed. If they were good people and they loved Faye, both of which he knew was true, they'd either look deep to see what Faye saw in him or they'd bury their feelings so it wouldn't distress her. Of what he already knew about them around town and from Faye's talk, he already knew he liked them.

Therefore, he wasn't driving to dinner concerned about how the dinner would go.

No, he had a variety of other things weighing on his mind.

The first was Malachi.

As far as they could find, the kid didn't exist.

This came from Chace checking Colorado Vital Records and finding nothing on a Malachi of their Malachi's approximate age being born in the state of Colorado. It also came from Chace contacting local and not-so-local schools. Chace, Frank and Deck pulled favors with folks they knew and looked into the school systems in and around Aspen, Grand Junction, Glenwood Springs, Montrose and even as far away as Denver. Although several Malachis were enrolled, none of them matched their Malachi's age.

Chace, Deck, Frank and other officers asked around town to see if anyone not only had seen Malachi recently but also if they'd seen him before. Except for a few folks reporting they thought they might have, it was nothing concrete and, outside of maybe noticing him, they had no more.

It wasn't surprising that he was good at being invisible.

It was surprising that it appeared he didn't exist at all.

Chace could see him roaming but not very far. In that day and age, folks didn't pick up kids and give them a ride without having concerns, asking questions and usually reporting it or straight up taking the kid to the authorities. So although Chace could see him making his way to Carnal from another town, even another county, he couldn't imagine he got there from Denver much less another state.

He'd set an intern on it and there was no one of his name or matching his description on the missing person's database.

This and his disappearance did not bode well. Even if Faye and Chace freaked the kid out with Faye standing by the return bin on Monday or he'd made them sitting in the truck, the kid had to eat and they'd backed off. Faye kept his stash outside by the return bin even when they weren't watching. She'd also posted a laminated note on the side of the library asking anyone who discovered the bags to leave them for Malachi.

They'd been left for Malachi. She left the library half an hour before and reported to him they were there. For the last week, every time they came back in the morning, they were still there.

This left plenty of time for him to sneak to the library when he knew they weren't watching.

It could be he'd noticed or heard somehow that Deck was on his trail. But since Deck hadn't even picked up a scent and the kid made no connections with anyone but Faye, Chace couldn't fathom how.

The kid was nine or ten and as far as Chace knew didn't have superpowers or the capacity for clairvoyance. He was in survival mode and would take chances in order at the very least to eat.

The longer he remained gone, the more Chace's, and Faye's, concern escalated.

But this was not the only thing weighing on Chace's mind.

The town had not surprisingly not rejoiced at Darren Newcomb's murder.

It wasn't that he was well liked. He was roundly hated. But it was the same as Misty. No one felt he deserved that and, further, no one felt his kids did.

They were braced for whatever might come next after what had already happened. It didn't take someone with the powers of deduction akin to Sherlock Holmes's to know that Newcomb's murder might be the tip of the iceberg.

As a matter of course in the investigation of Darren Newcomb's murder, Newcomb's home had been searched and Clinton Bonar and the men he'd worked for had received visits from Frank.

It was also not a surprise that they found Newcomb's house had been tossed and whoever tossed it did a thorough job. Almost the entirety of it was destroyed. Couch cushions torn open. Mattresses slashed. Carpet pulled up. Linoleum ripped away. Dresser drawers broken. Even pockets in clothing turned inside out or ripped out completely.

Whether they found what they were looking for was anyone's guess.

Chace had visited the scene. Even though Frank was primary, that didn't mean Chace wasn't still looking for his unwanted but dead wife's murderer.

What he saw made him come to some conclusions.

Newcomb and Misty's murderer, if they were the same person, knew that when he did Misty his tracks would be covered by the dirt at CPD. That didn't mean he wasn't careful with everything but his semen. With Newcomb, he left them nothing. Whoever tossed Newcomb's house also left nothing but a mess. No prints. No one had heard anything or seen anything. Then again, Newcomb lived local but removed, up in the hills at the east of town. The closest house was a wood away. Easy not to hear or see a thing.

Still, Chace didn't think the killer did the search. He reckoned the man got in, did his thing and got the fuck out. Whoever went through Newcomb's house took their time. A man with one, possibly two local murders on his hands would not hang around.

This meant Bonar and the Boys had a team working Carnal and therefore shit hitting the town was shittier.

Further, Bonar and the Boys were not thrilled to get visits from Frank.

This was communicated through voicemail by Bonar *and* Chace's father. He'd ignored both calls and listened only to Bonar's message. He deleted his father's without listening. This was because, from experience, he knew that even the man's voice set his teeth on edge in a way that could stick with him for days.

But he'd replied to Bonar in a text: *Threat was made against Newcomb to a police officer. This was reported. Murder investigated by the book.*

This was all he said, he felt it said it all so he intended to say no more. After receiving this text Bonar had called him three times. Chace had answered the calls then immediately ended them without even putting the phone to his ear, taking away Bonar's opportunity to leave a message.

He gave up.

But Chace knew *they* hadn't.

Chace knew Newcomb was a moron, racist pig who beat his wife but he was not stupid enough to keep the shit he had on those men at his house and he was a good enough father not to want it close to his kids. Where he kept it or who he gave it to either still had it and were in danger or it had been found and the threat was over.

Frank was looking into the former and not coming up with much.

They'd have to wait and see if it was the latter.

If this wasn't enough to make his thoughts heavy, there was more.

The library.

Chace had made five calls to the president of the Town Council asking for specifics about the future of the library and when the library's possible closure would come up for public discussion at an open council meeting.

Although all his calls and messages were taken by Cesar Moreno's assistant, Chace had not received a call back.

Chace knew Cesar Moreno, the Town Council president. He knew him as a good man, a family man and a devoted husband. The kind of husband who still held hands with his wife even though they'd been married eighteen years. The kind of father who was always at his three sons' baseball games. The kind of father who doted on his only daughter like she was a princess.

In fact, his daughter's quinceañera last year was such a huge event, it was still talked about. Well attended, most the town invited, no expense spared and all of the traditional ceremonies, such as the Thanksgiving mass, the donning of the crown and the changing of the shoes were performed.

Chace knew Cesar well enough he was invited to the quinceañera but since Misty was still alive and he'd have to bring her, as he usually did when they received an invitation as husband and wife, he declined attending.

Cesar knew Chace enough to understand.

Misty had been devastated. She liked a good party, a chance to dress up and a further chance to strut around on Chace's arm. This was why he very rarely gave her those opportunities. That and he couldn't stomach spending time with her.

Cesar had also kicked in the instant shit went down at CPD. His hands were tied when Arnie was at his zenith of power, and he didn't like it. But he was smart enough to keep quiet about it in order to protect himself and his family from being targeted and he did what he could within the council and as an advisor and leader in the town.

Therefore, the moment he could begin clean up, he did. Openly, honestly, quickly, no red tape and a great deal of communication. The goal was to communicate to the town that the storm had passed and it was a dawn of a new day. Chace knew he threw himself into this including spending countless hours engaged in reorganizing the department, searching for replacement personnel, hiring and working with consultants and holding town meetings to gather feed-back and keep citizens informed.

So his non-response to Chace was a surprise Chace didn't like and further didn't get. From what he knew of Cesar, he was a civic leader, a cultural leader, a respected businessman and a decent family man. He was honest, direct and approachable.

This was not his MO at all.

And Chace didn't like it.

"Please don't curse."

Faye's voice took him out of his thoughts and he asked, "What?"

He felt her eyes on him so he glanced at her before looking back at the road as she repeated, "Please don't curse in front of my family."

"Faye—"

Her hand gave his a squeeze and he felt her body lean toward him as she went on, "You should be you, of course, but Dad's a deacon at church. He mows their lawn and trims their shrubs in the summer. Mom designs the Sunday programs. And Mom gets mad at me when I say 'frak' and that isn't even a real curse word. But she feels the meaning behind it is enough. I'm twenty-nine but she *still* hands me guff without hesitation."

He gave her hand a squeeze back and replied, "First of all, meetin' your family, I'm not gonna swear. Second, there'll be kids there so I'm not gonna swear. And last, when your dad came for his talk, he swore. Repeatedly. One thing your kid doin' it, she's a girl, a pretty one at that, as a parent, you feel you can tell her off for it no matter what her age. But a man talkin' to a man, they'll say what they like."

"Dad cursed when he talked to you?"

Her tone was cute, breathy, disbelieving and Chace grinned through the windshield.

"Yep."

"Really?" she whispered.

"From memory, he said 'asshole' more than once, 'shit' more than once and if you count 'pissant,' he said that more than once too. There might be others and I don't recall him droppin' the f-bomb but he sure as fuck didn't shy away from colorful language."

"Holy frak," she breathed, and at that Chace smiled through the windshield.

Then he quit smiling and dropped his voice low to assure her, "Baby, it's all gonna be good."

"Well, you got Mom. I've never seen a bouquet of flowers this big."

She was not wrong.

Chace hadn't ever bought flowers for a woman and seen the results so he didn't know a fifty-dollar bouquet was that huge. He frequently sent flowers to his mother. But he called in the order and rarely saw the result since he rarely went home. Further, he spent seventy-five dollars on his mother's flowers. Which, from the arrangement currently lying across Faye's lap that Holly at the flower shop made up, with a gleam in her eye after he told her how much he wanted to pay, meant his mother's were likely enormous.

So it was no wonder his ma always called beside herself with joy when she got them. He thought she was just being sweet.

"It's going to be all right," he told her as he turned down the road northwest of town that led to the Goodknight house, a road nearly directly opposite where Chace's house was located at the south.

"Liza will probably be inappropriate one way or another," Faye stated, which meant she either ignored him or was so deep in her anxiety, she hadn't heard him.

"Faye," he squeezed her hand, "it's gonna be all right."

"And she might have a drama or...you know, just so you know, she isn't averse to fighting with Boyd in front of people. Even the kids. If it gets rip-roarin', she'll tell the boys to go to another room, but she doesn't care who else witnesses it."

"Faye," he gave her hand a gentle jerk then held it tight

and strong, "I want this to go well *for you* but, no offense to your family, I do not give a shit about it. I don't go to sleep with your family. I don't wake up to your family. I give a shit about *you*. But, honey, that said, honest to God, I'll like them. I know this because I've lived in the same town as them for thirteen years and I *already* like them. Gettin' to know them better means I'm just gonna like 'em more. That goes south for some fucked-up reason, it doesn't change the fact that I'll be goin' to sleep with you and I'll be wakin' up with you and the rest of it, we'll deal. Yeah?"

She didn't reply.

Chace had to let her hand go to make the turn into her folks' drive and he did both as he prompted again, "Yeah?"

He got no reply until he halted behind a silver Toyota 4Runner.

When he did that, she blurted, "You come from money and you handle elegant champagne glasses that had to cost a mint like they're plastic."

His head turned to her to see her face was pale and plainly anxious in the dash lights.

Fuck.

This was a surprise.

Fuck.

He put the truck in park, switched off the ignition and lights and turned to her.

"Come here," he ordered quietly.

"I'm right here, Chace."

"Come here," he repeated.

"But, I'm—"

"Baby, *come here*."

She leaned deep into him, stretching across the cab of his truck and resting a hand on his thigh.

He lifted a hand to the side of her neck, slid it back and up into her silken hair and he pulled her two inches closer.

Then he said softly, "I make almost double what you do and live in a ranch-style, four-bedroom house on fifteen acres south of town. I got a manageable mortgage because my ma's folks left me a trust. That trust isn't a fortune but it's a whack. I dipped into it to get the house I wanted to live in and build a family in. I will not touch it again until I get married and have kids. Only then will it be used to make my house a home and to give my kids an education. It will be used for nothin' else unless, God forbid, there's an emergency."

He pulled her an inch closer even as he moved an inch closer to her and kept talking.

"I got a small nest egg that I do what I can to make bigger just because it's smart. I invest in a retirement plan that will augment my pension because when I'm done and livin' the good life, I'd like that good to be better. I take two vacations a year, both to bodies of water where I can fish 'cause I got ski slopes all around and I can go boardin' whenever the fuck I want. I wear jeans and cowboy boots and I'll trade up this truck this year because it's four years old so it's time. I'll eat at The Rooster for a special occasion but even though that food is the shit, I'm just as happy with Rosalinda's and that is no joke."

He moved his other hand to curl around hers on his thigh and kept quietly going.

"My mother bought me those glasses, darlin'. That was the first time they were ever taken out of the cupboard she put 'em in. There is other shit in that house Ma got me she thought I had to have and probably all of it is expensive because she can afford it and that's her way. There is absolutely *no* shit in that house that belonged to or was purchased by Misty. What those glasses say *was* my life. I walked away from it when I was seventeen, I never went back, I'll never go back and I don't miss it. I don't give a fuck about champagne glasses. They *could* be plastic for all I care. They break, they break. *You* broke, I'd care. Champagne glasses, no. Now you got it all so are you with me on this shit?"

"Yes," she whispered, her eyes peering deep into his.

She was with him so he gave her the rest of it.

"I already know that family in there is better than the one I grew up in, honey," he whispered back. "Money and status don't mean shit. It's character that means somethin'. My father doesn't have that. Your father does, he married a woman who has it and together they built a family that has it. You're nervous and twistin' shit in that pretty head of yours to make you more nervous. Stop it. This is gonna be fine."

"Okay," she said quietly.

"Now you got a job ahead of you and that's to try real hard not to be cute. When you're cute, it makes me wanna kiss you in a way a deacon at a church, who still curses just not in front of his daughter, will not like. Since you're cute all the time, this is gonna be hard for you. But I'm askin' you to try."

Her bubblegum lips twitched then she replied softly, "I'll try."

Staring at her mouth, he muttered, "And you'll fail."

"Chace—" she breathed, and his eyes shot back to hers.

"You're bein' cute," he warned.

Her ear dipped to her shoulder and her brows inched together.

Cute.

"I just said your name."

"All it takes."

Her head righted, her eyes went hooded, her lips parted and she gave him her look.

Then she gave him more cute and he was fucking thrilled to take it.

"Seriously," she whispered, near reverent, beyond adorable, "you're fraking *awesome*."

He loved it that she felt that way.

And he hoped to Christ she always would.

Chace grinned before he used his hand to pull her close and dip her down so he could kiss her nose. They could have an audience but she was chewing gum. He tasted her, especially with the additional element of bubblemint, they wouldn't head inside for fifteen minutes.

Then he pulled her back and stated, "Let's go in."

She nodded, started to move away and he let her go.

He waited for her to round the truck before he took her hand and guided her to the lit front door.

He'd been out this way on numerous occasions when he was in a cruiser on patrol and for a variety of business during his tenure at CPD. The road that led to the Goodknight house did not dead end at the hills west of town but meandered up them and through the mountains. There were ranches off that road, a couple of units of rental condos for residents and for vacationers and, higher up the mountain, a few large homes owned by wealthy residents or kept as second houses to wealthier non-residents. He'd long since known where the Goodknights lived mostly because, after he'd spotted Faye, he put that one with the one of their name on the mailbox on the street and got two so that house hit his radar.

Their house was split level and, by the look of it, built in the '70s. Likely family room, dining room, kitchen and other common areas on the lower level, living room and bedrooms up top or vice versa. Seeing as from the road you couldn't see an elevated deck leading off the upper level but instead a dug-out patio leading from the lower one, he was guessing the family areas were down below.

As they made their approach, they were, surprisingly, not greeted at the door. Instead, Faye let them in without knocking and while Chace was closing the door to the March evening Colorado cold, she shouted, "We're here!"

That was when it began. Something Chace thought he was prepared for.

Something he was not.

A night in a normal, average family home with a normal, average family that was nutty, loud, opinionated but funny, immensely close and teasingly loving.

They were still standing on the stone-tiled landing that had a half flight of stairs leading up to an open space living room to their left and a half flight leading down straight into a kitchen right in front of them. Upon Faye's shout, two boys, her nephews, Jarot and Robbie, came racing up the steps. The older one had dark brown hair with a hint of red. The younger one had Faye's hair.

He thought they were racing to greet their Aunt Faye but he would immediately discover they weren't when they both came to rocking halts in front of him, tipped their heads back and spoke in unison...loudly.

"Show us your badge!" Jarot demanded on a shout.

"*Gun!*" Robbie screeched.

Apparently, it had been shared with the boys he was a cop.

"Um...can Detective Keaton show you his badge after you say hello to your Auntie Faye, I introduce you to Detective Keaton and maybe he gets a drink, sits down and relaxes?" Faye suggested in a practiced-sounding tone that was mixture of mild exasperation and "aren't my nephews adorably naughty?"

"Right," Jarot backed down, moving toward Faye and allowing her, with a soon-to-be nine-year-old's obvious reluctance, to give him a short hug and an even shorter peck on the cheek.

"*Gun!*" Robbie repeated on a screech, ignoring his aunt completely.

"Robbie! Mind your manners!" a woman reproached, and Chace's eyes went to the stairs.

Chace had seen Faye in town with her sister, Sondra and Silas, and it was her sister, Liza, who was approaching.

God had seen fit to grant Faye with her father's unusual blue eyes and her mother's unusual auburn hair. He'd seen fit to grant Liza Newman with her mother's dark brown eyes and her father's dark brown hair. Both were nice but Faye's combination was a knockout while Liza's was simply appealing.

That said, she was attractive but her hair was cut short. A style that she wore well and it suited her but it was something Chace did not often find appealing. She'd had two children but her ass and tits were less abundant than her sister's on a frame that both women inherited from their mother. Same height, same tiny waist, body meant to be hourglass, not streamlined. This meant she took more than passing care of herself and therefore likely dieted. She didn't look gaunt or in a bad mood because she needed a sandwich since she'd only had a protein bar between breakfast and now. But it wasn't a look that Chace found appealing either.

Last, Faye was wearing a little jeans skirt through the belt loops of which she'd threaded a bright scarf that she'd tied off to one side in a bow. Up top, she had on a dark green, lightweight sweater under a canvas jacket. The sweater fit well and its neckline had bits that draped in interesting ways making the sweater do what only Faye could naturally do. It hinted at skin and curves without highlighting either at the same time drawing your attention to both.

She was wearing a pair of cowboy boots he'd never seen before that were sweet in their own right but even sweeter on Faye. Fawn suede heavily embroidered with bright stitching. The stitching included yellow and orange that was random detailing, there were some green-stitched vines and last there were vibrant pink flowers.

In her outfit, Faye looked what she was: a native Colorado mountain girl who worked in a library and her native was *native* seeing as a line of her people had been there for thousands of years.

Her sister was in wide-legged black slacks that fit tight on her narrow ass, a complicated blouse she got either in Denver or New York City and a pair of high, spike-heeled, shiny black shoes that probably cost more than Faye's entire outfit. Her makeup was somewhat heavy and her hair took her far more time than Faye's to arrange. This was partly because Faye's hair dried in the gleaming straight sheets so she didn't have to do anything but shove a bobby pin in it somewhere if she felt the urge. It was mostly because Liza not only spent time on her hair but her entire appearance and it looked it.

Normally, Chace didn't like to spend time with women like this mainly because he didn't find them attractive and they usually proved to be the kind of women who thought he would, in a big way.

But when Liza made it to the top of the stairs, her eyes came to him and they were warm, there was an outgoing, friendly smile on her face and her appeal ratcheted up significantly.

It ratcheted up more when she stuck out a hand toward him, saying in a welcoming voice, "Chace, awesome to meet you. Been looking forward to it since I heard you were dating my baby sister."

He shook her hand and replied, "Liza. Good to meet you too."

She let him go and nabbed both her boys by the tops of their heads, tousling their hair, "These are my two crazy bugs, Jarot," she tousled his hair again, "and Robbie," another tousle for Robbie. "Boys, say hello to Detective Keaton then back downstairs with the both of you."

Jarot raised a hand in a quick wave and muttered, "'Lo, Dee-tective Keaton." Then he did as he was told and raced away.

Robbie stared at him and repeated, "Wanna see the gun."

"Sorry, bud, didn't bring my gun," Chace replied on a lie since he did but it was in his truck.

Robbie kept at it. "Then wanna see the badge."

Liza's hand slid down to the back of his neck, she bent over him and ordered, "Badge later. Now, say hello then go downstairs, honey."

He looked at his mother and narrowed his eyes, clearly peeved.

Then he looked back up at Chace and said a sulky, "'Lo," before he also raced away.

Liza looked back at Chace, sharing, "I tell myself he's in a stage but this is denial. He's my baby and I spoil him. I should probably stop doing that but I can't. So his future wife will have to sort him out and I'm just going to enjoy myself."

Faye got close, leaned into him and up in order to whisper, "This is not a good plan."

"As usual, I agree with my girl Faye," a deep male voice came their way.

Chace looked to the stairs to see a shortish, stocky, prematurely graying, good-looking man walking up them wearing a welcoming smile and a mountain man uniform of jeans and a flannel shirt that clashed violently with his wife's apparel. He also looked like a man who didn't give a fuck. He was who he was and she was who she was and even though they didn't go together, taking them in it was clear, in their way, they fit.

He had his hand up before he made it to Chace but only continued talking when Chace's hand gripped his.

"Boyd Newman," he introduced himself, still smiling.

"Chace Keaton," Chace told him something he already knew not only because he was seeing the man's sister-in-law and this was undoubtedly reported to him but because everyone in the county knew who he was.

"Good to meet you, man," he gripped Chace's hand tight but not combative, just friendly, then they broke the hold.

"Uh... you want to let the man come down and get a beer or what?" Silas called from the bottom of the stairs.

"I'll take your coats," Liza muttered, and Chace moved to Faye to help her with hers before giving it to a now-beaming, didn't-miss-the-help-with-her-sister's-coat Liza.

Then he took off his own and gave it to her. She tucked both under her arm and moved to a door on the landing that was clearly the coat closet.

Faye grabbed his hand and walked him down the stairs at the bottom of which she let him go because she had no choice, seeing as Silas engulfed her in a bear hug that included several hearty claps on the back and a couple of swings. He let her go and stuck out a hand to Chace.

Chace took it and got a, "Chace, beer, bourbon, vodka or what?"

"Silas. Beer," Chace answered.

Silas let his hand go but lifted his, clapped him stoutly on the arm, moved away and Sondra was there.

"Chace, happy to have you here," she beamed up at him, offering her hand. Chace took it and squeezed while wondering if, when Faye got older, her hair would turn that attractive silvery white just around her face like her mother's was. He also hoped it would.

No fancy clothes for Sondra Goodknight, as ever. Also no makeup.

Nice jeans. A turtleneck sweater that became her figure, and it was a soft beige color that became her complexion. A chunky, low-hanging necklace made of silver, turquoise and coral that looked vintage and was definitely Native American. Stocking feet.

Family dinner. Family time. Family. No high heels. Just

wool socks and because her daughter's boyfriend was there for the first time, she threw on a necklace.

Yeah, he liked Sondra Goodknight.

"Good to be here, Sondra," he muttered.

She gave him a bright smile much like Liza's, he let her hand go and Faye moved in for a kiss on the cheek and to hand her the flowers.

"These are from Chace, Mom," she told her mother, Sondra took the bouquet and her eyes went to the flowers then to him and they were even warmer.

"Pink. Perfect," she said softly then finished, the gratitude gentle in her voice, conveying the feeling behind the words without overdoing it, "Thank you, Chace."

He lifted his chin.

She grinned at him and announced, "I'll put these in water and there are a few things to finish up in the kitchen. Go in and sit a spell." She turned to her daughter, lifted a hand to touch Faye's cheek lightly and then whispered softly, "Pretty as a picture." She dropped her hand but tipped her head toward the family room and went on, "Take your man in to get comfortable, honey. Your dad will bring in his beer."

Faye grabbed his hand and led him to the right, directly toward a couch in the family room.

Chace followed, his mind consumed with Sondra's soft voice saying *Pretty as a picture*.

Light touch. Loving comment to her daughter delivered in a quiet way that was practiced but that made the compliment no less heartfelt. Instead, it amplified it. Stocking feet. Comfortable in her home. Wanting you to be too. She appreciated the flowers, made that known but didn't go overboard in a way that would make Chace ill at ease.

As these thoughts swiftly moved through his head, Chace couldn't help but think what it would be like when Faye eventually met his mother.

Valerie Keaton wouldn't be wearing wool socks and a beautiful Native American necklace. She'd be in a brand-new outfit that would cost more than Faye earned in a month. She would praise Chace, no doubt, and act loving and sweet. She'd also be nervous, likely clumsy because of it, embarrassed because of that and, finally, overly apologetic. She'd also try too hard and therefore manage to smother Chace *and* Faye in her efforts to make Faye like her at the same time convince Faye that Chace could move mountains.

Except Misty for reasons he couldn't avoid, Chace had never taken a woman to meet his mother, not only because there wasn't a woman he'd had that was important enough to meet her but also because his ma would work herself up about it. Chace took great pains to avoid working his mother up even before his life went to shit for the ultimate pain he took to avoid just that. An unnecessary meeting with a woman not important enough for it wasn't worth it.

Faye Goodknight would most definitely be meeting Valerie Keaton. Chace already knew this. But, until that moment, he hadn't been dreading it.

Now he was.

He barely got his ass in the couch and his woman arranged in the curve of his arm before Robbie was standing in front of him.

This time, he smacked his hand on Chace's knee and demanded, "Badge!"

Chace uncurled his arm from around Faye, leaned forward and pulled his badge out of back pocket. As he was doing this, Liza handed Faye a glass of wine and his beer.

But she also leaned in and whispered low but loud enough Chace could hear, "My baby sister finally got laid."

He felt Faye stiffen at his side even as he felt his own gut get tight, sensing her embarrassment.

Robbie, missing this or more likely focused, snapped, "Badge!" again with another smack on Chace's knee.

Liza went on, "Written all over you, babe. *Awesome.*"

Liza moved away, grinning to herself and making big eyes at Faye.

When he noted Faye was glaring at her sister with narrowed eyes, deciding to be annoyed, not embarrassed, Chace decided for her sake to ignore it and concentrate on her nephew.

So he flipped open his badge for Robbie who instantly tore it out of his hand.

Faye handed him his beer and muttered, "Too bad you didn't bring your gun."

Yep, annoyed.

And cute.

Chace grinned.

Robbie heard Faye and agreed with, "Yeah! Gun!"

"No, gun, Robbie. Shut your trap about it, kid, jeez," Boyd ordered, coming in carrying a bottle of beer and taking a seat in one of the four armchairs scattered around the space. This gave Chace a clue why Faye, who lived alone, had more armchairs than anyone he knew.

Robbie whirled on his father and fired back, "Shut *your* trap."

Boyd's face changed to the dad look no kid wanted to see and his voice was rumbling when he said one word.

"Robert."

Robbie scrunched up his face then wisely stopped giving attitude, dropped his head and got lost in his study of Chace's badge.

At this point, from nowhere, Jarot popped up in front of him.

"You ever shoot anyone?" he asked.

"No," Chace answered.

Jarot looked crestfallen and Robbie's head snapped up showing he thought his brother's line of questioning was more interesting than Chace's badge.

Jarot perked up again and asked, "You ever shoot *at* anyone?"

Since he had, albeit only with the intent to warn thus miss, Chace looked at Boyd who now had his wife sitting on the arm of his chair and he got the entire story with one glance.

Liza was sipping her wine and gazing at her son as if he just masterfully played an entire piece by Chopin on the piano and did it using nothing but the power of his mind.

Boyd had his eyes aimed at the ceiling.

No help there.

Faye, luckily, chimed in.

"Jarot, honey, maybe this conversation can happen when you're twenty-five."

Chace felt his lips tip up but Jarot just looked to his aunt, back to Chace and didn't give up.

"You ever *get* shot?"

"No," Chace answered.

"Shot at?" Jarot persevered.

Chace was silent because he had. This was the time he shot back as a warning, missed, scared the wired junkie out of his mind, as was his intent, and the junkie dropped his gun. This he was not going to tell Jarot *or* Faye.

Faye read his silence and her body got tight beside him so he lifted his arm and curled it around her again.

"Jarot," she said softly when Chace had her tucked close.

Jarot again changed tactics. "Arrested anyone?"

"Yes," Chace answered.

"*Lots* of them?" Jarot kept up his interrogation.

"My fair share," Chace told him.

"*Cool*," he whispered.

"Hey," Robbie spoke up, and Chace looked at him to see his head tipped to the side and his face screwed up. "Why you holdin' Auntie Faye?"

"Because she's my girlfriend," Chace replied.

His upper lip scrunched up into his nose and he said with disgust, "*Auntie Faye* is your *girlfriend*?"

"Robert," Boyd clipped, and Robbie whirled on his father.

"She's gross!" he shouted then immediately shared the reasons behind his opinion. "She gives sloppy kisses!"

"Only to you, honey," Liza told him, and her dancing eyes went to Faye before she went on, "Hopefully, she gives Detective Keaton other kinds of kisses."

"All kisses are sloppy," Robbie retorted with authority then finished, "*and* gross."

"Trust your father on this, boy, they aren't," Boyd informed him with true authority that Robbie completely missed.

"They are," Robbie disagreed. "I know 'cause Molly keeps givin' 'em to me at recess and they're gross."

"Molly's Robbie's *girlfriend*," Jarot shared then looked to his brother. "*Molly and Robbie, sittin' in a tree, k...i... s...s...i...n...g*," he sang, grinning an evil kid grin at his brother.

Chace was surprised that song endured but apparently it had.

Robbie leaned into his brother, face screwed up again but a different way this time, "Shut up, Jarot!"

"*You* shut up, Robbie," Jarot shot back, leaning in.

"I'm having all girls," Faye whispered, and Chace swallowed down a chuckle but did it on an arm squeeze for Faye.

Then he called, "Yo," and both boys looked at him. "Robbie, give me back my badge." Robbie looked ready to decline this order until Chace removed his arm from around Faye again. After a quick head to toe of Chace whereupon he correctly ascertained Chace could take him, he then thought better of it and jerked Chace's badge his way. Chace took it but didn't flip it closed. Instead he showed it to them and asked, "This cool to you?"

Both boys nodded their agreement avidly, eyes aimed at his badge.

Chace flipped it closed and got their eyes aimed at his face.

"You'd be right. It is. Man has this, he doesn't say girls are gross and he also doesn't tell anyone to shut up. Even his brother. Even when his brother is teasin' him. It's cool because he's cool. You don't get one of these unless you can be cool. Now, can you two be cool?"

"I can be cool," Jarot offered immediately, and Chace reckoned he could but Robbie clearly had to think on this awhile.

"Robbie?" Chace prompted, and Robbie looked at him.

Then Robbie proved he might be a cuss but he was an honest one.

"Maybe," he answered.

"How about you be that way just for tonight?" Chace suggested. "No more callin' your Aunt Faye gross."

Robbie's head tipped to the side again and he sought clarification, "Can I call her gross if she kisses me?"

"No," Chace answered.

Robbie's mouth moved around for a bit before he asked, "Can I fight with Jarot?"

"No," Chace repeated.

Robbie's mouth moved around some more as Chace buried his urge to laugh.

"Well, I'm bein' cool," Jarot put in at this point, back straight, voice haughty, looking down his nose at Robbie. "'Cause if I am, Dee-tective Keaton'll put a good word in for me when I become a cop. And the first person I'm arresting is," he leaned toward his brother and finished, "*you*."

"You aren't arresting me!" Robbie shouted.

"I am!" Jarot shouted back.

"Jesus," Boyd muttered.

"What's with the shouting?" Silas shouted, walking into the room carrying his own beer. He stopped and looked down at his grandsons. "What? A man gets his shoutin', fightin' kids outta the house only to have his *kids'* shoutin', fightin' kids come into it? Yeesh. Give an old man a break," he said to the boys.

"But Jarot said he's gonna arrest me," Robbie defended himself.

"He probably will, you don't clean up your act," Silas returned. "A good time to start is now. Your grandmother's settin' the table. She could use some help."

Faye made a move to get up at the same time Liza did but it was Faye who said quietly, "I'll help, Dad."

"You'll sit your keister down, visit with your old man and the boys will help their grandma," Silas returned then he looked down at Jarot and Robbie, his brows up, "Boys?"

Jarot shuffled out.

Robbie hesitated.

"Robert," Boyd warned.

Robbie shot his dad a rebellious look before he shuffled out too.

Chace returned his badge to his pocket and put his arm around Faye again.

Silas settled into another armchair.

"Just so you know, she might be quiet and she's always been cute as a button but both of these hid the demon within," Silas informed him, not leading into it even a little, and Chace did his best not to stare. "There's a temperament behind that hair, son. So, my advice, don't catch it from Faye."

"Totally," Liza agreed.

"You guys," Faye put in, shifting uncomfortably at his side.

"Don't act all innocent," Liza told her then looked at Chace, "She chased me around the house with scissors."

"I did not!" Faye returned heatedly. "*You* did that to *Jude*."

"You *so* chased me around with scissors. *Jude* chased *you* with the fire poker."

He felt Faye turn to look up at him, he gave her his gaze and she confirmed, "This actually happened."

"And she actually chased me with scissors," Liza took their attention by repeating.

"Liza, I did *not*," Faye retorted.

"You totally did," Liza fired back.

Faye gave up and tried something new. "You were a hair puller."

"So were you," Liza returned.

"Of course I was, because *you* were. It called for retaliatory measures and that was my only choice," Faye replied.

Liza gave up on Faye and looked to Chace. "She also mixed all my makeup together."

Faye didn't give up on Liza and leaned toward her. "That was because you told Danny I had a crush on him."

Liza's eyebrows shot up. "So?"

"I didn't have a crush on Danny!" Faye shot back. "I had a crush on his brother Dillon! Danny thought I liked him so he kissed me *in front of* Dillon." She flounced back in the couch, throwing out a hand. "And there went my shot at Dillon."

"Like you'd take that shot," Liza muttered the God's honest truth.

"No, but if Dillon had, I would have taken *that*," Faye returned on an out-and-out lie.

"Now I'm glad I got boys," Boyd said to no one.

"Who's Dillon?" Chace asked Faye and, for some reason, Liza found this hilarious, and he knew this because she burst out laughing.

"Nobody," Faye muttered, glaring across the room at her sister.

"Cutest boy in school," Liza answered and Chace looked back to her. "Or *was*. Now he's got a beer belly the size of Texas, is thirty-one years of age and is working on wife three, kid five and still thinks his stuff doesn't stink because he was captain of the football team fourteen years ago."

Jesus, Chace knew the guy.

"Dillon Baumgarner?" he asked.

"You know him?" Liza asked back.

He did, unfortunately. The guy was a dick who, Liza was right, had a huge gut and thought his shit didn't stink. Regrettably, he was able, with a bewildering frequency, to convince women of this fact. He went through them like water, whether he was committed to one legally or not. This wasn't the only reason he was a dick. He was just a dick.

Chace didn't share this.

He just looked at Faye, fighting a grin and saying quietly, "Good you held out, honey."

Liza burst out laughing again. Boyd chuckled. Silas smiled at the both of them.

At this point, Sondra walked two feet into the room and announced, "Soup's on. Come and get it."

Then she walked right back out.

Apparently, Sondra spoke, everyone listened because instantly they all made a move.

But as they started out of the room, Silas caught up with Chace, Chace's arm around Faye, Faye returning the gesture and Silas shared, "The scissors, Faye's right. Liza chased Jude with 'em."

"See?" Faye directed this at her sister's back.

"Though," Silas went on, "she got the idea from Faye."

"Did not!" Faye snapped, her head twisting so she could aim her glare at her father.

"Sweetheart, you did it," he returned then looked at Chace. "Got in trouble for it, sat in the corner for half an hour because of it and then wrote a report for her second-grade teacher about it which caused the woman to call her mom and me into school."

They walked through the kitchen into the dining room at the other side of the house and Silas kept sharing.

"She didn't know what to do with herself. Said the report was work well beyond any seven-year-old she knew. Also said she was alarmed that it was about parental cruelty. We convinced her our Faye had a vivid imagination. Since she'd noted this already, luckily she wasn't hard to convince."

"The scissor story," Sondra muttered, obviously over-hearing.

"Chace is getting the lowdown," Boyd shared then looked at Chace. "Settle in, man. Happened to me ten years ago. Took 'em around two dozen visits to burn the stories out. I didn't know whether to think I got hold of a hot one or move to a different state."

"Faye's stories will be better because she's got that shy-and-retiring gig going on," Liza put in as she fussed over Robbie's napkin in his lap while he shoved at her hands and glared at the side of her head. "No one would ever expect her temper matches her hair."

"Learned that myself thirty-four years ago but my teacher was her mother," Silas added, seating himself at the head. "Knew, my baby girl came out with that red fuzz on her head, I was in for trouble. And I was not wrong. Though, half the time she's rantin', it's about fathers with chunks cut outta their brains or Darth Vader and I don't know what the heck she's on about."

"Uh…does anyone mind if we stop acting like I'm fifteen and Chace is my high school boyfriend you're all trying to scare to death and maybe remember to act our ages?" Faye suggested, glaring at her father at the same time motioning to a chair, which Chace took as her telling him to plant his ass in it.

"No," Liza denied immediately.

"Nope," Silas took a second longer and did it while shaking his napkin out at his side and grinning at his daughter.

"I didn't do this to you," Faye retorted to Liza as she situated herself by the chair next to his therefore Chace moved to pull out.

She tossed a small, distracted grin at him before taking her seat.

"No, you didn't. But you side with Boyd on all our arguments so *this* is payback for *that*," Liza returned.

"How about this," Sondra, seated at the foot of the table, started. "I just spent an hour cooking, an hour before that baking a cake and half a day cleaning my house. I'd like to enjoy the meal and my family. I wasn't all fired up about this banter when you two were teenagers. Now I like it less. So how about we eat and act like adults. Does that work for anyone but me?"

"It works for me," Faye stated instantly.

"It would," Liza muttered.

"Liza," Sondra said in a tone much like Boyd had used with his boys except feminine. Clearly it was just as impossible to be denied because Liza's face immediately assumed a thirty-two-year-old woman's pout that made her look nearly as cute as her sister, just more sophisticated, and Chace finally got an idea of why Boyd liked it in there.

This was more evidence that Sondra spoke, people listened. The banter ended.

Chace missed it.

It wasn't ugly or hurtful. It was reminiscing, nostalgic,

teasing and although heated, there was a different kind of warmth under that heat. It was a warmth that Chace had never felt before. An affectionate kind that said these were shared memories and, regardless of their alarming nature, there was no love lost. They'd just morphed into amusing anecdotes that provided opportunities for teasing but fond banter that would leave no one with hard feelings.

It wasn't the first home of his girlfriends' parents that he'd visited. It wasn't his first such dinner.

But it was the most interesting one and he'd never felt as comfortable.

Food was passed around and Chace took in the flowers he bought that Sondra had put in the middle, a silent but thoughtful indication of her gratitude. Liza looked after Robbie who was at her side. Faye kept an eye on Jarot who was at hers. Sondra kept an eye on both her grandsons as they flanked her.

Surprisingly, even Robbie minded his manners at the table. Clearly, it was a free-for-all the rest of the time but when he was at his meal, he was to be quiet and behaved and he was.

The food was delicious and it was also familiar since Sondra obviously taught her daughter how to cook.

This made him feel comfortable too.

The conversation was light, easy and flowed naturally. Chace was pulled in from the start, Silas and Boyd talking sports and, in an experienced way, Sondra, Liza and Faye remained silent but not removed while they did it.

Chace participated in a discussion about the Avalanche with the men while listening to Faye remind her mother that spring was nearly on the Rockies and asking her if she'd help again that year with flowers at the library.

So that answered that. Faye planted those flowers with her mother.

There was something about that, knowing daughter and

mother worked side by side to create beauty for a building that didn't belong to them but instead the town, that also made him feel strangely comfortable.

Conversation naturally turned and again this turn was affectionately heated as it became political and the politics at the table quickly outed themselves, those being strictly segregated by gender. Men, staunchly conservative. Women, resolutely liberal.

Through this, Chace remained neutral by keeping his mouth shut until Boyd threw up his hands, looked right at him and begged, "Man, help us out here. Even out the friggin' numbers."

"Boyd, don't say frig!" Liza snapped.

"Why?" Boyd clipped back.

"The boys!" she hissed.

Boyd looked to Jarot.

"Jarot, buddy, what does frig mean?" he asked.

"Boyd!" Liza kept hissing.

"Uh…" Jarot looked mystified then, game and clearly unaffected by his parents' heated words, he tried, "Frig means, um… *frig*?" he asked in answer.

"See?" Boyd bit off to Liza.

Liza glared at him and then looked at Jarot. "You're right, honey. Frig just means frig. Now, please don't say that at school or, well… *ever.*"

"For goodness' sakes, it's just frig," Silas entered the conversation at this point.

"Dad!" Now Liza was snapping at her father.

"Oh my God, Dad," Faye whispered, also to her father.

"He's a boy." Silas shrugged. "Boys, you gotta give on some things."

"Here we go," Faye muttered to her plate and Chace looked at her to see her chin tucked in her neck and her eyes focused with keen attention on her food.

"Um...I'm sorry?"

This came from Sondra and he'd been at this table once, the dinner wasn't entirely consumed, the birthday cake to come was deep into the horizon, therefore he didn't know Sondra but for less than an hour and still, Chace read her tone was dangerous.

"Now—" Silas started but Sondra cut him off.

"Don't even go there."

"Sondra—" Silas tried again.

"No," Sondra interrupted again. "There are not different rules for girls and boys, Silas. You tried that with Jude and I didn't like it then. You can't try it again with Jarot and Robbie."

"No offense, Sondra, but, personally, I don't give a frig if my kid says frig and he's my kid," Boyd interjected.

"Well, *personally*, I *do*," Liza retorted. "And he's my kid too."

"You girls don't like it, never did," Silas started as if it was all the same to him. "But no matter, things are just different between boys and girls, men and women. That's the way it is, that's the way it'll always be."

"Oh, frak," Faye muttered to her plate again.

"It is not!" Liza said in a near shout.

"Love you, Liza darlin', but it is," Silas replied.

Liza's eyes sliced to her sister. "Please, God, tell me this one," she jerked her head at Chace, "is enlightened since these two," she jerked her head at Boyd and Silas's end of the table, "are *not*."

"Well, uh...Chace is a little old-fashioned," unfortunately Faye shared. "He won't let me pay for anything and he never lets me pour my own drink."

"Good man," Silas muttered on a nod to Chace.

"Right on," Boyd muttered, grinning at Chace.

"Gentlemanly behavior will never be old-fashioned,"

Sondra chimed in, her eyes on Chace. "I'm pleased to know you're a gentleman, Chace. But, no pressure, if things should progress and your children someday sit at this table, I hope you will not be okay with them saying *frig*."

Chace didn't get a chance to reply, which was good since he didn't intend to do so. This was primarily because, if he and Faye had boys, he didn't care if they said frig but if they had girls, no way in hell. He knew by the conversation half the inhabitants of that table of legal drinking age would not take to that very well.

But he didn't get the chance to reply because Sondra's eyes cut to Faye and she concluded, "Or *frak*."

"I like frak!" Robbie shared at this point then unfortunately for his aunt, went on, "It's fraking great!"

"Frak," Faye whispered and Chace put some effort into not doing what he had an overwhelming desire to do, burst out laughing not only at Faye's whisper and Robbie's comment but also at Liza *and* Sondra turning infuriated eyes her way.

Boyd was feeling what Chace was feeling and Chace knew this because he didn't bite back his laugher. He just roared with it.

Silas grinned at his grandson.

Liza and Sondra opened their mouths to say something but it was then that Chace's phone rang and every eye at the table came to him.

"On call, need to take this," he muttered, pulling it out of his back pocket. "My apologies. I'll take it in the other room."

He saw a couple of understanding nods before he got out of his chair and looked at the display on his phone. He hid his confusion at what he read as he hit the button to take the call.

Then he walked with swift, long strides around the table

toward the kitchen and put the phone to his ear, saying, "Keaton."

"Man, shit, fuck, man," Deck said in his ear, and Chace's gut clenched as he walked faster to get to the living room.

"What?" he demanded low.

Hesitation then, "Fuck, man."

"Deck," he clipped quietly and stopped in the living room. "Give it to me. What?"

"Found your kid," Deck said, his tone was not good and Chace's clenched gut twisted.

"Talk," he ordered.

"Talked to the old guy in the alley."

"Outlaw Al?" Chace asked.

"Yup, if that's the old guy in the alley lives behind the coffee place. Talked to him before. Man was three sheets. Talked to him tonight, he was only two and made some sense. Sees the kid around. Followed him once. Told me where to go. There's a reason why I couldn't catch wind of him, so off the beaten track, there is no track. Found him in a shed, east side of town, up in the hills a fair ways. Shed's gotta be about two hundred years old by the look of it. Long forgotten. Definitely not in repair. It provides some protection against weather but that's it. Got a roof on it, holes in it, snow inside, but it's somethin'."

"Cut to it, Deck," Chace growled.

"There's also a reason he didn't come to you and your woman," Deck said quietly.

"Say it."

"Kid's fucked up, brother. Face fucked up, arm fucked up, look of it, broken and his leg looks like it was caught in a trap. Saw the blood trail in the snow. Drug himself back home to this shed from wherever he got nailed. Had to pry himself loose with his hands, means they're fucked up too, still got his gloves on, mangled, brother, and a dried, bloody mess. But, a week of him in that shed alone, injured with no medicine…" He pulled in an audible breath. "Got a pulse on him, weak but it was there. Called an ambulance. He was lucky he had that sleeping bag or he'd be gone, hypothermia on top of trauma and maybe shock. Other than that, he was fucked. Dragged shit close to him to eat, get water but I suspect he gave up on that days ago. Not eatin', not drinkin', leg, arm, hands and face fucked up, he was unconscious, Chace. Couldn't wake him so maybe even comatose. They're takin' him to the hospital now. I'm in my truck, followin' them. County."

"Faye and me'll be there in twenty," Chace told him immediately.

"Right," Deck replied.

"Do me another favor. Call the station. Get someone up to that shed. Follow that blood trail. I wanna know where he was comin' from, he got caught in that trap. I want them to follow his footprints in the show. We haven't had snow since last week. They'll show where he went and where he came from. Leads to anything of interest, they don't approach. They tell me. Once I get Faye in my truck, I'll call myself to confirm your communication. But I want them on the move now."

"Right," Deck repeated.

Chace started moving back to the dining room while he muttered, "Thanks, Deck."

"No thanks, brother. Shoulda gone back to the homeless guy days ago."

Chace stopped in the kitchen and said firmly, "You didn't. But you found him. Now he's getting help."

Deck was silent a moment then, "Yeah."

"See you in twenty," Chace stated.

"Later, brother," Deck murmured.

"Later," Chace replied then disconnected.

He sucked in breath.

Then he moved to the wide opening that led to the dining room and all eyes came to him.

He only had eyes for Faye.

"Faye, baby, I need to talk to you a second," he called gently.

She only had eyes for him too and hers were wide and scared.

He watched her face pale and her lips form the silent word, "Malachi."

But it was Silas who spoke out loud.

"Everything okay, son?"

Chace tore his gaze from Faye and looked to her father.

"No."

At his word, Faye shoved back her chair and rushed around the table.

When she got close, he caught her hand and moved with her to the family room. He heard murmurings from the other room but he was focused.

When they stopped in the family room, Silas, Boyd and Sondra were with them.

He ignored that and moved into Faye. Lifting a hand to slide the hair off her shoulder, he then curled it around her neck and dipped his face close.

"Deck found Malachi. He's been injured. It's not good. They're takin' him to County now so we need to go, baby."

"I'll get our coats," she replied immediately, broke from him and ran to the stairs.

"I'll come with," Silas announced.

Chace looked to the man. "It's not—"

"I'll come with," Silas reiterated, holding Chace's eyes a second then he turned to his wife.

Before he could speak, she gave him what he, their daughters and their grandson needed.

"Jarot will get his cake then I'll be there," she whispered.

Silas nodded then followed his daughter.

"You need anything, man?" Boyd asked and Chace shook his head.

"We'll call, we do," he muttered.

Boyd nodded.

Liza showed at the opening to the room. "Is everything okay?"

Boyd moved to her, murmuring, "Later, babe, let's get back to our boys."

Chace watched Liza look searchingly at her husband but she made not a peep as she followed him out of the family room through the kitchen toward the dining room. Boyd slid his arm around his wife's shoulders, Liza reciprocating with one around his waist.

Sondra moved to Chace, lifted a hand, curled it around his bicep and squeezed while peering into his eyes, her ear dipped to her shoulder, her eyes warm and worried.

Faye ran into the room both carrying his coat and yanking her hair out of the collar of hers.

She came to a rocking halt, offered his coat to him and whispered, "Let's go, honey."

He nodded, took his coat, turned to Sondra and said quietly, "Dinner was great, sorry to cut it short."

She gave his bicep another squeeze before she let him go and whispered, "Drive safe. Call us if there's news. I'll see you in a while."

He nodded again, shrugged on his coat while Faye gave her mother a hug. Then he took her hand, guided her to the stairs and held her hand tight when it seemed she was trying to fight against sprinting to the car.

They got in, got on the road and Silas's Wrangler headlights were in his rearview mirror when he took her hand, linked their fingers and pressed them to his thigh.

"It'll be okay," he whispered.

"Okay, Chace."

"He'll be all right."

"Okay, honey."

His fingers gave hers a squeeze.

Hers squeezed back.

Then he let her go and reached for his phone.

After he called the station and confirmed his orders, Chace broke the speed limit on the way to the hospital.

CHAPTER THIRTEEN

Sweet

"SWEET."

Deck spoke so quietly, Chace could barely hear him over the crunching snow.

Chace didn't process the word because his mind was consumed.

It was consumed with the fact that they'd been walking through the dark wood at the bottom of the eastern hills that flanked town and they'd been doing it for ten minutes. The last five, they'd steadily been moving uphill.

Since leaving Sioux Street, the eastern most street that edged the town, they'd had nothing but trees, rock, snow and bitter cold.

It wasn't fun for him, a fit man in his thirties. The idea of Malachi making this trek to get what he might need from town filled him with unrest. Or more than he already had. He knew the kid was hiding, but finding his spot in the middle of nowhere filled with snow, cold and wild animals, some of which were dangerous, took it to a different level.

Chace's mind was also consumed with what he left at the hospital.

When Chace, Faye and Silas arrived, they were working on Malachi with urgency and they weren't allowed to see him.

He flashed his badge and asked for reports when they had them and this got them a visit from an ER nurse five minutes later. She'd made the visit to garner information about Malachi, such as possible allergies to medicines and why he was in the state he was. Unfortunately, they couldn't tell her jack about medicines but at least they were able to fill in some of the blanks about the state he was in.

Before she left, she'd explained they were concerned about malnutrition, dehydration and infection, not in that order. They'd lucked out and found a vein and were pumping him with fluids and antibiotics, warming him up and cleaning his wounds to assess the extent of damage.

By the time Chace left with Deck to meet the officers at the shed, have a look at it and its surroundings himself, Sondra had arrived and a doctor had come to make his report.

Malachi's humerus was broken. It had already begun to knit so they'd had to put him under, rebreak it and set it. They'd also lucked out that Deck's unpracticed eye saw nothing but mess. Malachi had apparently cleaned his wounds as best he could with, what they were guessing from what they could smell on his sweater, the shampoo Faye had given him. He also had antibiotic ointment on the worst of them, Faye's Neosporin. It was good he'd cleaned his wounds and used the ointment but treatment had been delayed, infection was still a concern so they were pushing strong IV antibiotics.

He was in the critical care unit because they still had some concerns that infection had set in and they reported they had minor worries that he might lose his fucking leg *and* his fucking hands.

The hospital had a policy that only family members could attend patients in critical care and therefore, at first, they were denied a visit. Chace explained the circumstances including the fact that it was jacked, but Faye was the closest thing the kid had to family and the only person who they knew who had spoken directly to him in weeks. The doctor relented instantly knowing, even if nurture came from someone he hardly knew, nurture was nurture.

Chace and Faye were let in to see him, and at first sight of his small body with tubes stuck in him, his hands wrapped, his face bruised and still swollen, his arm in a sling, the covers taller around his dressed leg, Chace thought Faye would fall apart. Many people would, men or women. Fuck, Chace had to suck in breath to hold it together.

But she didn't. She moved directly to him, ran her fingers lightly through his hair and bent right to his ear.

"It's Faye. Chace and I are here, Malachi. We're here. We found you. You're safe now," she whispered. "You're safe, honey. You just need to get better. We're here and you're safe."

Chace found a chair and moved it to the bed before he put his hand to the small of her back. She was still bent over Malachi running her fingers through his hair but when she felt his touch, her neck twisted and she caught his eyes.

"Sit, baby," he whispered.

She nodded and sat then pulled the chair closer, stretched out an arm and wrapped her fingers around his bicep.

Chace gave her a moment then slid the hair off her shoulder and bent close.

"Gonna see to business."

Her head twisted so she could catch his eyes again and she immediately nodded without uttering a question.

But she whispered, "Come back."

"I will," he promised. "I'll send your mom in."

She nodded again and turned back to Malachi. "Chace has to go, Malachi. But he's coming back," she whispered.

"Give me some room, darlin'," Chace muttered, Faye's head jerked to look at him then she moved back in her chair and Chace moved in, leaning over Malachi.

He curled his fingers around his bony shoulder and bent close to his ear. "Stay strong, buddy. You're good. You got folks lookin' out for you now."

He gave him a gentle squeeze, pulled back and looked to Faye to see now, she had wet in her eyes.

He wanted to comfort her but he sensed if he did, the hold she had would unravel.

So he moved in to kiss her nose, pulled back half an inch, locked eyes with her and whispered, "Be back soon."

"Okay, Chace."

He shifted away, cupped her jaw in his hand, slid the pad of his thumb over her bubblegum lips then he let her go and walked away.

He gave a brief report to Deck, Silas and Sondra, sent Sondra in and told Silas what he and Deck would be doing. They exchanged phone numbers. Then Chace followed Deck to Sioux Street and into the wood.

Long moments after Deck muttered the first word either of them spoke during their trek, Chace asked, "What?"

"Your woman," Deck answered. "Sweet."

He was not in the mood to be given shit about Faye.

"Deck—" he started in a warning tone.

"No shit, Chace. Not what I meant. She's sweet. Pretty. Great hair. Great ass. Great fuckin' boots. This shit fuckin' sucks, that kid, the state of him, what you're gonna see when you get to that shed, brother, nothin' good about it. So bad, it's beyond bad straight to disturbing. So now, you think of what you left back at that hospital. Because, seriously, man, when we get up there, you're gonna need good thoughts the like of your girl."

Chace was already preparing himself for what he'd see.

Now he knew it was worse.

Fuck.

Deck wasn't done.

"Lined up two hundred women, told me to choose the one for you, I'd choose the one back there. Settin' myself up for what I'm gonna see again, gonna hold on to the knowledge that a year ago, my boy had one serious fuckin' bitch sleepin' in his bed and he was sleepin' in his guest room. Now, when he's done with this shit, tonight, tomorrow, until he does the smart thing and makes it legal and then until he dies, he's got that sweet in his bed. Don't flip out, I know it's new between you two. I also know you are no dumb fuck. You got that kinda sweet, you're gonna make it legal. Since I don't have sweet to go home to, I'll hang on to the fact that my brother, who's always deserved it, finally does."

Deck and Chace had shared vows of brotherly love over Deck's dad's stolen beer they consumed in Deck's basement when they were freshmen in high school the first time they got drunk off their asses.

Since then, through a lot of good times and bad, that love grew.

These kinds of words from Deck were rare but they were as real as the feeling behind them. Deck detested Misty, fucking hated Chace's father and not just recently and he knew the whole story. So they were also not surprising.

They also gave fair warning of what he was going to see.

They walked in silence for a few more minutes before men's voices could be heard and the beams of high-powered flashlights like the ones Deck and Chace were using to light the way could be seen.

"Keaton and Decker," Chace called to inform them of who was approaching.

They got a "Yo," and a "Hey" back from two of the four uniforms on duty, Dave and Terry. Both were new recruits. Dave, a three-year veteran who moved to Carnal from Idaho to be closer to his nearly new wife's family in Gnaw Bone seeing as she was pregnant and had three sisters and thus they had four built-in babysitters, including her mom. And Terry, a fresh recruit out of the academy, hailing from Fort Collins.

Deck and Chace met them in the snow outside a dilapidated shed about the size of a big bathroom. The men huddled, kept their lights low in their hands, aimed up but away from faces, lighting the conversation.

"Didn't pull in lights, Chace, 'cause it'd be a pain in the ass to haul 'em up here but also because we might wreck tracks if we did," Dave informed him and Chace nodded.

"Got in a good look around, though," Terry added. "Did the best we could not to disturb anything. Not that there was much to disturb."

This was not good.

Chace nodded anyway.

Avoiding the shed for now, he asked, "What'd you find?"

"Not hard to find the trap," Dave told him and went on to explain, "seein' as the blood trail led from it to him." He dipped his head toward the shed.

"Two hundred yards, I figure," Terry shared quietly, careful with this knowledge because of what it said and Chace braced so his body wouldn't jerk.

Two hundred yards. Two fucking football fields. A long way to go with a broken arm, two mangled hands and a fucked-up leg.

A long way to go.

Jesus Christ.

"Able to walk the first fifty." Dave's voice was also quiet. It got quieter when he continued, "Had to drag himself the rest of the way."

Chace closed his eyes and dropped his head.

He shouldn't have let it go the way it did. He should have tracked him or set Deck on him sooner. He shouldn't have given in and gone slow. He should have pushed it.

He didn't.

Jesus Christ.

"Trap's old," Terry carried on, Chace opened his eyes and looked at him. "Probably set years ago and forgotten. Rusted. Snowed over. The kid couldn't have seen it even if he was movin' in daylight. Pure bad luck he happened on it."

Malachi seemed to have a lot of bad luck.

But this bit of it was on Chace.

"He's big on invisibility, Chace," Dave put in. "Couldn't find a lot of tracks and, we get lights or come back in daylight, we'll know more but seems like he covered them. We went a fair ways, large perimeter, got some animal tracks, only thing we got is a few leadin' toward the trap he probably hadn't yet covered and was in no state to mess with and the tracks leadin' from the trap to the shed. Lots of disturbed snow around the trap."

"Found some drops look like blood," Terry stated. "Leadin' to the trap comin' from the hill, northeast."

"He was beaten before he hit that trap," Deck muttered.

"Yeah?" Dave asked.

"Leg was fucked up by the trap but his arm was broken and his face was a mess. Trap didn't do that," Deck told them.

This got nods.

But Chace was thinking of a kid who had been beaten, his arm broken but still had the presence of mind to cover his tracks in the snow.

Who the fuck was beating him, who was he hiding from and why?

These questions were strangely exclusive at the same time inclusive. Somehow, whoever got hold of him got the chance to do it.

But they didn't know about this place. He kept this a secret.

So how did he keep getting beaten?

Terry looked to Chace. "You want lights brought up?"

Chace looked at his watch then his gaze went to Terry. "Not tonight. Tomorrow morning, we'll come back up, get a better look around in the daylight, follow that blood, see if we can get anywhere with that."

Dave and Terry nodded.

Chace reluctantly turned to the shed.

"Bad shit, man," Dave murmured. "Popped Terry's cherry, steppin' into that."

Terrific.

"Won't sleep tonight," Terry mumbled, glancing at the shed then back at Chace. "How old was he?"

"He *is* nine, maybe ten," Chace replied.

"Is, right, is," Terry mumbled again, this time quickly then he asked, "He good?"

"No," Chace answered.

"Right," Terry muttered.

Chace studied Terry a moment and decided not to tell him there'd be other sleepless nights. Memories of this and new memories. Traffic accidents. Domestic disturbances. Child abuse. Suicide. Overdoses. Small town didn't mean small crime. Even with a clean department. He stayed the course, made it his career, he'd have enough to haunt his sleep for the rest of his life.

Unless he found a good woman to sleep beside him.

On that thought, Chace turned to the shed to create the

next ghost that would haunt his, a ghost only the likes of Faye Goodknight could beat away.

He felt Deck move with him and they both trained their flashlights on the door. Rickety, planks warped. Lots of space in between and not only on the door. There was a wind, snow, it'd rush through and settle inside.

It wasn't much but for a desperate kid, it was better than nothing.

The door hung drunkenly and it was a miracle it held. The shed wasn't built in this decade or the last. It was, like the trap, unused and long forgotten. A great hiding place in the summer. A desperate one in the winter.

He carefully pulled open the door, stepped inside and held his body tight as he swung the flashlight around and tried not to breathe in.

"Remember, kid was here awhile, man," Deck whispered behind him.

The smell eloquently stated that. So did the state of the sleeping bag. Malachi had been unable to move so a week's worth of bodily mess was visible to the eye and reeking in the small space. The sleeping bag had been zipped open and thrown wide to get him out so the inside was visible and stained with not a small amount of excrement and urine and copious amounts of dried blood.

Chace moved the flashlight around the area and his eyes followed the beam. Malachi had set up his sleeping area against one side of the shed. Under the sleeping bag were some thin, torn pieces of fabric. They looked heavy, they were definitely discarded. Likely from someone's trash. These were under his sleeping bag, which meant, until Chace and Faye gave him that bag, they were all he had. Chace couldn't even make out if they were blankets or rags. What they were were definitely not enough to shield him from the cold.

At the top of this mess, a small, round cushion, definitely a castoff, stuffing coming out, soiled, dirty.

His pillow.

By the pillow, a bag of bread torn open as if by fumbling hands, blood on the plastic, blood stark on the scattered white of pieces of bread. Eight bottles of water, empty. Six energy drink bottles, empty. The shampoo bottle sitting on its side, blood on it, top not on, shampoo leaking out. The tube of Neosporin, no cap, squeezed dry. Two apple cores. An empty bag of baby carrots with blood smears. Four banana peels, not peeled off, ripped open, teeth marks visible on the inside skins now brown. He'd gnawed the meat out. The bottle of ibuprofen, blood on its sides, unopened. Possibly too difficult to get the cap off with torn-up hands and a broken arm but the pain was bad enough, he'd tried. A milk jug opened and on its side, milk still in it, its sour smell mingling with the foul odor. The flashlight Faye got him was among this mess, on its side, the light pointed toward the sleeping area, no beam coming from it now.

He moved his light across the back wall and felt his gut get tight.

Six milk crates, plastic, probably stolen from behind the grocery store. Three upended and against the dirt and snow at the floor of the shed. Three sitting on top holding their precious contents away from the dirt and wet. One held the carefully packed remnants of food and drink Chace and Faye had given him. One held his sparse collection of clothing, folded precisely, organized carefully. One held the other bits and pieces, the stacks of paper plates and bowls, his camp cutlery, bottle of vitamins, toothpaste, toothbrush, the packs of batteries Chace bought him to go with his flashlight.

Last, closest to the sleeping area, was a little table that was obviously a castoff Malachi had collected, probably, from the state of it, resting against trash bins at a curb.

His nightstand.

On top of it, his books and comic books. Carefully, almost reverently arranged and Chace knew if he approached and looked closely, they'd be methodically organized.

His prized possessions, close at hand for when he lay in that bag and read.

His prized possessions, close at hand just because they were prized.

Chace sucked in breath to tamp down the surge of feeling moving quickly, freezing his insides, and he shifted his beam through the space. Nothing much else, no furniture, some drifts of snow that came through the holes in the ceiling or the openings in the planks.

But in the corner opposite the sleeping area, assisting greatly in the stench, a hole was dug. As it was close to the door, Chace only had to take one step to look in it and see it was excrement and it was dug down deep. There was a large pile of dirt beside it. The boy shoved dirt on top, probably to aid in getting rid of the smell.

He didn't see to the call of nature in nature.

He did it there.

And he did it there because he didn't want anyone to find it elsewhere.

His fear of discovery was so great, he lived with his own shit.

He lived with his own goddamned shit.

Chace moved his beam across the dirt along the wall.

There were three other piles, dirt loose on top, small mounds.

Fucking shit, he'd been there awhile.

Fucking shit, *he'd been there awhile*.

"Jesus Christ," Chace whispered.

"Brother, he's safe now, got sweet sittin' right beside his hospital bed," Deck said quietly from beside him.

"Jesus Christ," Chace repeated.

"I fucked up with the homeless guy, I gotta let that go, and Chace, man, you gotta work past this and let it go," Deck went on.

Chace stared at the hole.

Deck was silent, giving him his moment.

Then he stopped being silent.

"Do not let CPS get their hands on this kid," Deck whispered.

Chace nodded, his eyes still on that fucking hole.

"Whatever drove him to this desperation, do not set his ass in the system," Deck went on and Chace turned, cutting his eyes to his friend.

"He's not goin' into the system."

Deck held his gaze.

Then he nodded.

Chace's phone rang and he pulled it out as he walked around Deck and got the fuck out of that shed.

Once he was breathing clean air again, he took the call and put it to his ear.

"Keaton."

"Chace, Silas," Silas replied. "Listen, son, visiting hours are over and they made Sondra and Faye leave the room. Sondra's got Faye in her Cherokee, we talked her into leavin'. Nothin' she can do sittin' in the waiting room, and whatever she can do tomorrow she'll do it better if she gets a little rest. We're takin' her home."

"Right," Chace muttered.

Silas said nothing.

"I'm still at the shed, Silas," Chace told him when this silence stretched.

"Okay, son, but you didn't answer my question," Silas stated.

Chace blinked.

What question?

"Sorry, didn't catch the question."

"We're takin' Faye home."

"Got that."

"Son, I need to know *which* home we're takin' her to."

Jesus.

Was the church deacon Dad of the virgin girlfriend he'd deflowered asking him which bed he wanted to sleep in with his daughter that night?

"Yours or hers?" Silas continued.

Fucking hell, he was.

Chace quickly processed this and the question and figured Faye would want familiarity around her.

"Faye's," he told Silas.

"Right. You gonna be long?"

"I'm leaving in five, trek to Sioux is about ten minutes, bit more and then I'll be there a couple minutes after that."

"Right. We're idling, ready to leave now. We'll probably arrive around the same time. See you there. If you get hung up, see you tomorrow."

Tomorrow?

He didn't ask.

He just said, "Right, Silas."

"If I'm not there when you get there," Silas continued, his voice soft, "see to my girl. Like her momma, Faye is, in a lotta ways and not just hair and temper. She can stand strong through a lot of shit, son. So strong you won't even know inside she's sufferin'. But inside she's sufferin'. And now is one of those times. You gettin' me?"

There it was. The reason Silas Goodknight didn't mind Chace sleeping beside his daughter.

"I'm getting you, Silas," Chace replied quietly.

"I reckon you are," he muttered then, "'Bye, Chace."

"Later, Silas."

Chace disconnected.

Deck, Terry and Dave got close but it was Dave who spoke.

"What do you want done with the shit in there?"

"You take pictures?" Chace asked.

"Yeah, about a hundred of 'em," Terry answered.

"Good," Chace said on a jerk of his chin. "The milk crates, the books, bring them back to the station. Careful with those books. Keep them as they are however you gotta do that. I'll come and get them when he can have them at the hospital and I want him to have them as he keeps them. Yeah?"

Dave gave him a nod and a "Yeah."

Chace looked at Deck. "I gotta get to Faye. They've left the hospital."

"Right, Chace. I'll help the boys here with the kid's stuff."

Chace nodded, gave a chin dip to Dave and Terry then turned back the way he and Deck came.

He walked through the dark, quiet night, the moon silvering the snow, the trees shadows, the only sound his boots crunching through the icy ground cover.

But the only thing he saw was the inside of that shed.

And he still smelled it.

He needed Faye.

Deck was right and he was wrong. He couldn't use the thought of her to get past what he saw.

He needed her.

And Malachi, whoever the fuck he was, needed everything.

*   *   *

Chace blinked away sleep and the first thing he saw was the soft, light blue sheets of Faye's bed.

In other words, he saw sheets because Faye wasn't in bed with him.

He sat up and turned in order to angle out of bed but stilled when he saw her on her couch. She was wearing his sweater, her knees to her chest under it, stretching it out. She had on a pair of bulky, thick socks. Her neck was twisted, her chin resting on her arm which she had laid along the back of the couch, her eyes aimed out the window lit by the first kiss of dawn.

She looked her usual cute but he also saw something in her profile he'd seen on her face before, once. Something he saw years ago. Something he didn't remember until he saw it just then.

It was one of the few times they'd been in the same place at the same time and she'd caught his eyes for brief seconds before she quickly looked away then moved away.

It was right after he'd married Misty.

It was sorrow.

The memory, what he now knew it meant and her look sliced through him like a blade just as her head turned and her eyes caught on him.

She bent her neck, rested her cheek to her knee but held his gaze.

"I love this town," she whispered.

"Come back to bed," he whispered back.

"Lived in it most my life, left to get educated, came back as quick as I could."

"Back to bed, honey."

"I want to go places, see things, do things but always come right back here."

"Bed, darlin'."

"You saved this town." She kept whispering and he felt his entire body get tight.

"Faye, baby, come back to bed."

"I don't know what secrets you hold but whatever they are, I'll always believe you saved my town."

"Come to bed, Faye, or I'll come and get you."

"You need to save him, Chace." She was still whispering, her cheeks getting red and not because she was embarrassed but because she was fighting emotion.

Chace was done.

He threw back the covers, stalked to her, plucked her out of the couch and carried her back to bed. He planted her in it, joined her there, pulled the covers over them and gathered her in his arms.

She shoved her face in his chest and one of her hands under his body so both of her arms could close around him tight.

"If he loses his hands—" Her voice was thick, scratchy, hard to hear.

"Stop it," he ordered gruffly.

She sucked in a breath that broke and Chace pulled her closer.

Last night, Sondra and Silas had still been at Faye's when he got there because they'd arrived minutes before. They all shared a drink and talked quietly in Faye's seating area before her parents felt comfortable with the state of their girl and left him to see to her.

Close, long hugs were exchanged between Faye and her mom and dad. Chace got a shorter one, but a close one, from Sondra and a firm handshake with a couple claps on the arm from Silas.

After they left, Chace had poured Faye another glass of wine and opened himself another beer and she'd interrogated him about what he found and where it was.

He'd told her nothing and, as she kept at it, reiterated she didn't need to know.

When she gave up, she did it by looking in his eyes and saying quietly, "I already know just because you won't tell me."

She likely didn't and therefore he was glad she gave up.

He got her another drink. To relax her and in an effort to perk her up, he told her he'd watch the show she'd been begging him to watch.

It worked. She gave him a small smile and even acted a little excited as she sorted out the TV. She also fell asleep halfway through the episode.

Chace, however, didn't. Luckily she fell asleep before he had to admit that, although it had an edge of geek, the show about two brothers who were on a self-appointed mission to save the world from a variety of phantoms, demons and monsters, whose best friends were an angel who wore a trench coat and a redneck who always wore a beat-up baseball cap, wasn't all that bad.

She woke slightly when he moved to take them to bed. So she groggily got ready and joined him there then slid straight back into sleep, curled close.

Chace didn't follow her for long hours.

Now was now, Chace holding Faye in his arms while she struggled against tears.

He tipped his chin down and against her hair told her, "Honey, let it go. Nothin' wrong with tears."

"If he wakes up, I don't want him to see my eyes red and face blotchy," she replied, her voice still thick, which meant her throat was still clogged.

"*When* he wakes up, Faye, all he's gonna see is pretty. Trust me, he's a guy, I'm a guy, that's all we see."

She shook her head as best she could seeing as her face was in his chest then she tilted her head back and caught his eyes with her brightened ones.

"Stop being sweet," she whispered.

Never, he thought, caught in her crystal blue eyes.

He pulled her up so they were face to face.

Then he offered her an out.

"You want something to think of, not the vast pile of shit that all of this is?"

"Please," she answered softly.

"I don't know his story. I don't know who his people are. How he got where he is and how he is. I also don't care. We gotta think about how we're gonna engineer this situation so he goes from where he is now to somethin' good. I don't mean possibly well-meaning foster carers because there could be a 'possibly' in that. I mean *somethin' good*. That goes without saying that if CPS gets him and can't place him in foster care, he doesn't go to a fuckin' home for boys."

Her entire face brightened and she stated immediately, "I'll take care of him."

Chace knew he'd get that.

So carefully, gently, he told her, "That isn't going to happen."

"Chace—"

"Faye," he cut her off, "I'm a cop on a recently cleaned up local police force. I can finesse this but I gotta use that finesse aboveboard in a way questions won't be asked and that kid gets what he needs. And, baby, I know you'd give him what he needs but right now you do not have the ability to do that since you live in a one-room apartment over a flower shop."

Her nose scrunched up because this point was valid but she didn't like it.

She still gave in to it.

"Right."

"I got room but I'm also a single man who's got a girl-friend who spends the night and, I'll repeat, the finesse I gotta use has gotta be aboveboard so I can't just take a kid under my wing without goin' through certain motions. And my sleepover girlfriend might be frowned upon if I do."

"Mom and Dad," she said immediately.

"Yeah," he replied. "Or Krystal and Bubba or Tate and Laurie."

"Or Boyd and Liza," she threw in.

"Right, or Sunny and Shambles," he suggested.

"We need to make calls," she whispered.

"We need to make calls."

"Who first?" she asked.

"Your mom and dad."

She grinned, the sorrow shifting totally out of her face. "They'll say yes."

He already knew that.

"Yeah," he murmured.

Her grin turned into a smile. "They'll be great with him and we can see him all the time."

He knew that too.

"Yeah," he repeated.

"I'll call them now."

He twisted his neck, looked at her alarm clock then looked at her.

"It's just going six thirty."

"They'll be up."

"Will they be up and in the disposition to discuss takin' on a kid when they not too long ago got their house all to themselves?"

"Yes," she replied immediately.

He figured that was true too.

"Give me a kiss then grab the phone."

She smiled even bigger so he felt it on her lips when she gave him her mouth.

When he broke the kiss, she moved in to give him another

light one before she rolled out of his arms and reached for the phone.

Chace rolled out of bed and moved to the bathroom.

By the time he walked out, she was sitting at the side of her bed, off the phone, her dancing eyes came direct to him and her mouth moved.

"They said yes."

Then she smiled big.

Chace smiled back.

Then he walked to the kitchen and made his girl breakfast.

* * *

"Chace, I get you but I haven't had time to assess the situation fully yet. What I already know—" Karena Papadakis started.

She was a child welfare officer and she was standing with Chace outside the Critical Care Ward.

"He's a deacon at the church," Chace cut her off to say. "She designs the Sunday programs. He mows the church lawn. Seriously, Karena, Sondra Goodknight won't even let her twenty-nine-year-old daughter say 'frak,' a made-up curse word from a sci-fi TV show. They'll do good by this kid."

He'd already told her he wanted her to place Malachi with the Goodknights, and she was rightly and not surprisingly balking due to procedure.

"They're older," Karena replied quietly.

"Yeah. They are. Which means they've already raised three kids so they know what they're doin'. One of those kids is the mom of two boys. One's the town librarian who has a master's degree. The last one's in the Army serving our country," Chace returned.

"They don't have foster certification," she told him.

"Then get it for them," he told her.

"It would require home visits, foster parent classes—" she began.

"The state he's in, Karena, he's not gonna be discharged tomorrow," Chace pointed out. "You have time and what you already know about that kid and the more you'll find out, I know you, you'll bust your hump to fast-track it."

He was not wrong about this. There were people who found jobs. Karena Papadakis found her calling. Her caseload wasn't exactly light but it also wasn't what a person in a similar position in a city would be. This gave her plenty of time to do her job the way she'd probably break her back to do it even if her caseload was double. And that was, with care.

She held his eyes and then cautiously reminded him, "Medical reports say this kid may be special needs. The history you gave me tells me he already is."

"You know I won't let that kid down. You don't know this but you can take my word my woman won't let him down. They're her parents. She's got nephews close to his age. Her sister lives in Gnaw Bone. You place this kid with the Goodknights, he goes from livin' in his own shit in a shed in the middle of nowhere to livin' in a modified Brady Bunch house ten minutes out of town with a good, close family who, I assure you, can handle special needs. These people got so much goodness, Karena, they can handle anything."

"Chace," she said softly, "I've heard what you and Faye Goodknight have been doing for this boy but—"

She stopped speaking, her body jerked and her eyes went over his shoulder so Chace twisted his torso to see Silas bustling up.

"Heya," he dipped his chin to Karena on a grin when he stopped at their side and muttered a further. "Sorry to interrupt."

Then he turned to Chace and jerked up a box Chace didn't get a good look at before he kept speaking.

"Lookee here, Chace." He shook the box. "After church, me and Sondra went real quick to the mall. My Faye says Malachi likes to read lots and since his hands are messed up, got him one of those fancy-shmancy eReaders." He shook the box again. "Guy at the electronics store, he said all he's gotta do is press a button on the side to turn the page. They even had little stands he can set it in to hold it up so he doesn't have to hold it himself. So we got him one of those too. 'Til he gets his hands back, he can keep right on readin' 'cause I figure he can press a button." He lowered the box, dropped his head and studied it, murmuring, "Gotta turn it on at the bottom with a slide doohickey but I figure Sondra, Faye, she's around, or me could set him up to get him goin'."

Sondra caught up, didn't seem to notice Karena at all and lifted a bag toward Chace. Chace also didn't get a chance to look at it before she dropped it and started talking.

"PJs," she announced. "Warm ones. You think they'd let him put them on?" she asked then didn't wait for an answer and turned to Karena who she hadn't yet met and informed her, "Those hospital blankets are thin. He needs warm jammies." Then her head jerked this way and that, caught on something and she moved quickly away, muttering, "There's the nurse. I'll ask her."

"I need a plug," Silas said at this point. "Gotta charge this puppy up."

Then he took off.

Chace watched as Silas moved away, his head down, his eyes obviously scanning for an outlet. Then Chace saw Sondra standing with an African American woman who was not a nurse but Malachi's doctor. She was wearing scrubs, her long, glossy black hair pulled back in a thick ponytail, and both of them were looking at a pair of navy blue flannel little boys' pajama bottoms with airplanes printed on them, smiling.

Chace looked back at Karena.

"I'll fast-track it," she mumbled, her lips twitching and she moved away, hand in her purse to pull out her phone.

It was Sunday and Karena Papadakis, a woman he'd worked with more than once, had taken his call and left her family to meet with him at the hospital.

Now she was making more calls to colleagues who also probably didn't work on Sunday.

Chace grinned at her back as she walked away.

Then he moved toward Silas to help him find a plug.

*   *   *

"I'm sorry, Detective Keaton, this is awkward but I've asked you here because unfortunately we have to have this conversation," the hospital administrator started. "Now that that boy is past urgent care, as he doesn't have insurance, we need to discuss—"

"Don't worry about the hospital bills," Chace interrupted her. "I'll be responsible for them. If there's a specialist that can confer with Dr. Hughes who can assist in saving his hands and foot, please advise her that she has the go-ahead to seek assistance with his case."

The administrator blinked then rallied to inform him, "Dr. Hughes is an exceptional pediatric critical care doctor. We're lucky to have her."

Chace held her gaze, nodded and replied, "Glad to hear that. But if there's more that can be done for him, I want it done. Even if he has to be transferred to another hospital."

Quickly, she gave him information he didn't give a fuck about. "We're a fully equipped Level II Trauma Center. The only one in the mountains outside Loveland and Grand Junction."

"He's beyond trauma care," Chace reminded her.

"We're an excellent facility," she pressed.

"I believe you. I still want everything that can be done for Malachi done," Chace returned.

"It's my understanding the boy cleaned the wounds and treated them. Gangrene didn't set in. He may lose some mobility but the threat of him losing them entirely is over."

"Ma'am," Chace leaned slightly toward her, "for an indeterminate amount of time, that boy has been livin' in a shed in the woods by himself with no light, no heat and the toilet he used was a hole he dug himself in the corner. He does not need to endure that only to endure learnin' to live without a limb or, possibly, losin' some use of a limb. I get you got pride in your hospital. What you need to get is that I got the funds to see to it that boy gets the best care he can get. So I'm askin' you to help me get him that. If you don't, I'll find a way to do it myself. Now, please, talk to Dr. Hughes and save that kid's hands and foot."

She held his gaze and whispered, "I'll speak with Dr. Hughes."

"Obliged," Chace replied.

She got his point loud and clear and he knew this when she reached directly for her phone.

Chace gave her a nod, got out of the chair he was sitting in opposite her at her desk and walked out of her office. As he did, his phone rang.

He pulled it out, looked at the display and took the call.

"Keaton."

"Blood's a dead end, brother," Deck said in his ear.

Deck had called earlier informing Chace he'd be with the officers who combed the woods that morning. Now he sounded like he was in his truck.

"Nothing?" Chace asked.

"Few drops like they said, leadin' northeast. Then they

disappeared. Maybe he saw them and covered them. Don't know. Just know there's nothin'."

"Tracks?"

"None of those either," Deck replied. "Wind, snowmelt and settling, even efforts to cover them disappeared. The only thing we found is a trail leadin' to the north side of town, goin' in at the Carnal Hotel end and another leadin' toward the library. Both sets, deep, back and forth, packed. But, you didn't know he was out there, could be anyone's since there were so many of them, packed in the snow with snowmelt wiping out individual prints so now it's just a trough in the snow. But when he got close to the shed, he started to erase them. Smart kid. Didn't know the trajectory, didn't know the shed existed, which probably no one knew, by the time he made the effort to get rid of his trail, it could lead anywhere. No one would know where he was heading."

Chace stopped at the elevator but stood to the side and didn't tag a button.

"Your take?" he asked quietly, and Deck answered immediately, knowing what Chace was asking.

"No fuckin' clue. Cops say in those hills there are two housing developments, one upscale, one middle income, and a bunch of older, individual residences not contained in a development. Beyond that, mountain's too steep to build homes. Even so, cops say, and I could see for myself, it'd be near on impossible for him to climb up to any of those residences. Slope of the hill gives way to sheer rock face. I'm gonna grab some lunch then go back and look around more, see if there's some opening where he could climb. If there is, see what it leads to and if he didn't bother to cover those tracks. It was me, I was nine and someone was beatin' the shit outta me, I'd be gone. I wouldn't stay close. But for whatever reason, he went back for more. None of his prints, no one else's either. No one found him at his shed and did that shit to him then left him there. So, I had to go with my gut, he was stickin' close for a purpose. What that is, no fuckin' clue."

"Siblings," Chace whispered.

"Say again?" Deck asked.

"Could see him getting beat because someone caught him stealing food or just plain stealing. That'd be jacked but the town is known to have a few mountain families who take care of their own business in an old-world way. Those families live outside town, in the hills or up deep in the mountains. It'd be a surprise but I could see it happening. But Malachi is a smart kid, he'd learn not to get caught again, and Faye says she's seen him on numerous occasions with visible evidence of abuse. Personally, I've seen it twice. So that's not it. Also could be he went back to someplace familiar to get food or clothes, got caught, got beat. Or it could be he went back to check on something he cared about, a brother, a sister, got caught, got beat. He wasn't hiding that shed just from the general population of Carnal. He was hiding his tracks down from wherever he came. He was hiding from whoever's at home. He's hiding from everyone."

"You need to get your boys to run the occupants of those residences," Deck muttered.

"Yeah, but I already checked Colorado Vital Records. Deck, kid doesn't exist. Not local. Not in the entire state."

Deck was silent.

Then he said out loud what Chace was thinking.

"This is dark, brother."

"Nope," Chace returned, "black."

"Pitch," Deck whispered, and Chace knew Deck was thinking what he was thinking.

Two scenarios.

One, serious hill country, jacked shit where a family existed somewhere in those hills, had minimal contact with the real world and this included procreating and not birthing their babies in a hospital that had records or sending their kids to school.

Two, Malachi and possibly one or more blood or practical siblings had been taken from their real families and were being raised on the quiet by some seriously hill country, jacked person or people who hid them from the real world for nefarious reasons and in order not to be exposed.

Chace had been in that town for thirteen years. Even if there was someone in the hills that lived quiet and eschewed society, they had to mix in some ways. If this escaped his notice, Frank had grown up in that town. He would know about them, he would talk about them, they'd be on cop radar or there would be talk in town. Chace could see people in Carnal letting folks live their life as they saw fit even if they didn't agree or thought it was whacked. Half the residents were multi-generation hardcore bikers who had been attracted to that town pre–Arnold Fuller as a haven for those who sat a Harley and lived that way of life. So they appreciated this considering they'd chosen a way of life that wasn't exactly mainstream. That didn't mean they wouldn't talk.

This left option two. Malachi had been snatched by someone not right in the head. This meant he could have come from anywhere. This meant he could have a family out there looking for him.

"I'll eat, go back, comb those woods," Deck offered, breaking into his thoughts.

"I'll call the station," Chace replied.

Deck hesitated before he asked quietly, "How's he doin'?"

"Hasn't regained consciousness and they're a little concerned because he should have by now. Even so, Faye's been readin' to him almost all day. Got her out twice to get a cup of coffee in her and so she could eat some food when her sister came by with lunch she made. Her mom took over while she was gone. She's back in."

"What're the doctors sayin'?"

"Can't say, he's not awake, not movin'. The update though is that the scare is over about him losin' his hands and foot. Mobility is in question. Color's better though."

"Right."

"I'll let you know, anything happens."

"'Preciate that."

"Get lunch, Deck. Speak soon."

"Later, man."

"Later."

Chace disconnected and shoved the phone in his pocket.

Then he tagged the elevator button to go up and check on Faye and Malachi.

*   *   *

It was time to go, visiting hours were over, the nurse told him. He appreciated her telling him so it would be him that would be the one to go in and tell Faye she had to give it up for the night.

He washed his hands and moved through the ward to the open door, hearing her voice coming soft. She didn't read staccato, she put emotion into it like a true storyteller, or as best as she could while needing to be quiet in that ward.

He entered Malachi's room on the thought that someday she'd read to their kids that way.

Therefore, he had a small smile on his face when he saw Sondra first, sitting in the corner, and her eyes snapped to him as she raised her index finger and put it to her lips.

With this warning, Chace rounded the closed curtain slowly, silently and stopped dead.

This was because Faye was sitting by the bed, bent over her book, focus entirely on it but her arm was stretched out and she had her fingers curled around Malachi's forearm.

And Malachi's light brown eyes were open, his head

slightly turned on the pillow and his focus was entirely on Faye reading to him.

But even with the bruising on his face, it was plain to see he thought God had sent an angel to his bedside to tell him a story.

Chace felt his throat close and held perfectly still.

Then Malachi's eyes shifted to him and his entire body got visibly tight.

"Faye," Chace called gently, she stopped reading and her head came up.

But as she began to turn her head to look at him, she saw Malachi.

He saw in profile as her face got soft and her lips parted right before she whispered, "Malachi."

His eyes shifted to her with barely a movement of his head.

She rose to a squat above her chair. Leaning in partially she kept her voice at a whisper when she said, "Hey there, honey. You sure took a long nap. We were getting worried. Welcome back."

He just looked at her.

"I'm Faye," she told him. "But you know me, don't you?"

He didn't say a word or move his eyes from her.

Faye kept going.

"That's Chace, I told you about him. Chace Keaton. He works at the police station. He's a detective. He bought you your Swiss Army knife and your sleeping bag and some of your food. Remember?"

Malachi didn't move or speak.

Faye didn't give up.

"Over there, that's my mom. Her name is Sondra Good-knight. She brought you some warm pajamas that they said when they move you out of here, you can wear."

Malachi kept looking at Faye a second then his head

turned on the pillow for a glance at Sondra before he looked back at Faye.

Sondra got up, got close to the bed, Malachi's eyes moved back to her and she reached out two fingers to touch the blanket by his side but not him.

"Nice to meet you, Malachi," she said gently. "Now I'm going to go get the nurse. They need to know you're awake. All right?"

Malachi didn't answer. Sondra looked to Faye then to Chace then she moved slowly out of the room.

Chace took a step toward the bed but stopped when Malachi's eyes shot to him and his body stiffened.

Faye noticed it too. She came up fully out of the chair but stayed bent to him.

"He's okay, honey. Chace is a good guy. I promise. He's a good guy."

Chace forced his voice to very quiet when he said to the both of them, "I'm good right here. Malachi can tell me when he's okay with me bein' closer."

Faye had turned her head his way and she nodded then she looked back at Malachi.

"See? Chace is a good guy, honey. You can trust him but he's such a good guy, you can take your time doing that and he'll be patient. Promise."

The nurse came in and she was smiling at Malachi. "Well, look at you, awake and showing us your pretty brown eyes."

Malachi watched her warily as she approached his bed until Faye straightened and his eyes cut back to her in a way that made Chace's body get tight.

"I called the doctor," the nurse said. "She'll be in soon and, I'm sorry, but we'll need room, Malachi will need privacy and visiting hours—"

"It's okay," Faye cut her off. "We'll give you what you need."

She leaned back down to Malachi, Chace braced and it happened when she told him, "I'll be back tomorrow to read—"

His body knifed up, his bandaged hand darted out and batted at the book in her hand, which fell to the mattress, then he lunged toward her and rounded her neck with his arm with such force, he took her torso into him at the bed.

"Fuck," Chace whispered, starting toward the bed, but the nurse was on them and looking at Chace.

"Get another nurse."

Chace turned instantly and moved to get the nurse, not wasting any time, and when they rushed back, Faye was sitting on the bed, bent deep into Malachi, his arm still tight around her neck and she was murmuring to him.

The other nurse approached immediately.

"Maybe you can explain this attachment," she whispered.

Chace didn't delay. "She's been feedin' him and keepin' him in books. They met five minutes ago for the first time but that doesn't mean she's not the only thing he's got."

"Right," she whispered, and moved toward Faye and Malachi.

Chace approached cautiously and was careful to stop where he'd stopped before, no closer.

"I'll be back, buddy," he heard Faye whisper. "Tomorrow. First thing. I promise."

Malachi didn't say anything and kept his arm tight around her.

The nurses stared over the bed at each other, clearly uncertain whether to intervene or allow Faye to pull it off.

"Okay," Faye whispered. "This is what I need, honey. I need you to look out for yourself a little while longer, and right now that means I'm worried about your hands. I don't want you harming yourself. You have to let me go so the nurses can look after you and the doctor can see you. I need that from you, Malachi. Tomorrow, I promise, honey, swear, cross my heart, I'll be back. Until then, you…are…*safe*. Totally safe, Malachi. I wouldn't lie to you about something as important as that. Promise. Do you believe me?"

No sound, no movement, everyone was still for several long moments then Malachi's arm relaxed and he lay back in bed.

"Thank you, sweetheart," Faye whispered then moved to her feet while stretching her arm out to put the book on the nightstand and Malachi became agitated again.

His eyes on the book in Faye's hand, he banged his elbow repeatedly in the bed while his legs shifted under the covers and strange, animal-like noises sounded low from the back of his throat. The nurses moved, one to put a hand on his shoulder, one to put hers gently to his legs.

"What, buddy?" Faye asked, and he shook his head back and forth, slamming his elbow into the bed, continuing to make those noises. "Malachi, please, honey, stop doing that. You'll hurt yourself. Calm down and talk to me. What?"

Sheer intuition made Chace move swiftly. Not closing in on the bed, he rounded Faye at the back, pulled the book out of her hand then leaned into her, taking her with him, using her as Malachi's shield against him as he shoved the book under the boy's flailing arm and tucked it to his side.

Malachi's arm instantly stopped moving but shifted to trap the book tight there and he settled.

"You want your book," Faye whispered.

Malachi took in a deep breath, his eyes locked to Faye.

Then he nodded once.

Jesus, this kid had been fucked up.

Jesus.

A feeling he did not like gnawing at his gut, Chace straightened away from Faye and caught the gaze of one of the nurses.

"Do not take that book away," he ordered, and she nodded instantly.

"You see," Faye said quietly to Malachi. "You'll have that until you have me again. Okay?"

Malachi held her eyes and didn't move.

She ignored this and whispered, "Okay."

Then she lifted her hand and ran it through his hair before she straightened away.

"See you soon, honey," she said softly.

He swallowed, his eyes darted to the nurses then back to Faye.

Then he nodded.

"My brave Malachi," Faye whispered, reached out a hand, touched his bicep then she looked through the nurses, bent, grabbed her purse, smiled at Malachi and, finally, her hand found his and closed around it so tight, he felt pain.

"Later, buddy," Chace murmured, and Malachi looked to him but said not a word.

They passed Dr. Hughes who was hurrying in and so intent to get to Malachi, she only jerked up her chin at them on her way. Faye didn't notice. She walked out, her neck twisted to look back at Malachi.

She finally lost sight of him and looked forward but she didn't speak.

Chace led her to her parents. The instant they stopped close, Silas spoke.

"Rosalinda's. My treat. Liza, Boyd and the boys are meetin' us there."

Chace stayed silent, letting Faye decide their evening plans.

"Sounds good," she said quietly.

There was her decision. She needed family.

So she'd get it.

"Right," Silas muttered, taking all that was Faye in carefully as Sondra silently did the same, then Silas looked up to Chace. "Liza and Boyd have hit the road. So should we. Meet you there."

Chace nodded, got a clap on his arm from Silas, a smile from Sondra after she kissed her daughter's cheek. They followed them to the elevator and walked out to the parking lot together.

Sondra and Silas separated from them to head to the Wrangler and they both did this on waves.

Chace jerked up his chin as Faye waved back and he walked with her to the passenger side of his Yukon.

"Beep, honey," she muttered, her eyes on the door, but Chace used his hand in hers, his other hand going to her waist to assist and he turned her, back to the truck and moved in.

Her surprised eyes lifted to his.

"Assure me you're all right," he demanded.

"I—"

"He's fucked up, Faye, and that was intense. But he's nine. He's got you, he's got me, your parents, your family, a doctor who I've been told is highly skilled and gives a shit and nurses who handle him with care. Once he's outta there, he's got everything when he had nothing. He's young enough that no matter what fucked-up shit he's endured, he can be guided out of that into trusting something good. It's new. He freaked. He's latched onto you. But that will subside, darlin'. We'll work it and he'll be okay."

"Chace, I'm fine. Just hungry."

He blinked at her words and calm tone after her hand nearly crushed the bones in his then he studied her face in parking lot lights.

After he did this awhile, he told her, "You cannot keep shit buried. We got a long row to hoe with this. You give him strength, you unload on me the shit that causes in you so you can give it to him. Starting now. Deal?"

She leaned into him, got up on her toes and whispered, "Chace. I'm *fine*."

"Baby—"

"Except I need a burrito. Stat."

Chace stared at her.

She lifted her hand and curled it around the side of his neck.

"Two days ago," she said softly, "not knowing where he was and the state of him, I was *not* fine. Now he's messed up but he's safe and I know where he is so, I promise, honey, I'm...*fine*."

She held his gaze as he tried to read hers.

Then she stopped giving him time and stated, "Feed me. If you don't, all the way to Rosalinda's, I'm explaining the entirety of the history of Angel, the vampire with a soul given to him by gypsies as punishment for him killing one of their own. This history will range from *Buffy the Vampire Slayer* through to *Angel*, his own TV show. I'll also add my opinions on why they should never have cancelled *Angel*. I'll tell you now, this is multi-part and doesn't all have to do with the fact that David Boreanaz is hot. And, if you delay, I might even have time to get into why I think Joss Whedon should be recommended for sainthood."

She had her moment.

Now she was fine.

So Chace dug into his jeans, pulled out his keys and beeped the locks.

Faye grinned.

Chace bent his head and touched his mouth to hers.

They heard a short honk of a car horn and they both turned their heads to see Sondra and Silas in the Wrangler driving past, Sondra giving them a wave.

Faye waved back as Chace reached around her to open her door.

He closed it after she climbed in.

Then he rounded the hood, folded in and took his woman to have a meal with her family.

*   *   *

She was finding it even though Chace was going slow, gentle, loving the feel of her, the smell of her, the sounds she was making.

But he knew by the noises, the way her body was shifting under his, the way she was tilting her hips with each stroke to get more of him and the fact that she wrapped one leg around his ass and pressed the inside of her other thigh against his hip that it was building.

He slid his lips from her neck over her jaw to take her mouth in a deep, slow kiss as his hand found her arm, slid down and wrapped around her wrist to pull it from around him. He twisted his hand, linked fingers with hers then pressed their hands into the bed, also moving so his forearm would take his weight.

He kept kissing her, thrusting deep but sweet and slow as he moved his other hand to find her arm and pull it from around her. Sliding his hand down to hers, he shifted it to her side, pressing her hand flat against her skin, gliding it up, in, up then, his hand over hers, he cupped her breast with it.

His thumb moving hers, he rubbed it tight over her hard nipple.

And he got it. Her hips jerked, she gasped against his tongue, her leg tightened around his ass and she came.

Fuck, he loved that about her. Fast and hard or slow and sweet, she found it with just his tongue, her nipple and his cock.

Sometimes just his tongue and cock.

He moved faster, kept kissing her, thrusting harder and she took him, tipping up for him, giving him all of her as she kissed him back until he thrust deep, stayed planted and poured himself inside her as he groaned down her throat.

Fucking magnificent.

When he came down he found she was running the tip of her tongue along his lower lip, something he liked, something he liked to do to her, something he taught her.

Then again, he'd taught her everything.

She was his in every way she could be, his in a way most men never got a shot at.

His.

Yes.

Fucking magnificent.

His tongue gently pushed hers back into her mouth so he could kiss her deep, slow and long before he let her mouth go and trailed his lips back to her neck.

She'd wrapped her arm around him again and she moved her foot that was in the bed in order to wrap her leg around the back of his thigh.

Their hands were still linked in the bed beside her.

He'd fucked a lot. He'd also made love. It couldn't be said there weren't women he'd cared about that he'd shared quiet moments like this with, as close as they could get.

But none of them felt like Faye. None of them smelled like her. None of them tasted like her. None of them curled their fingers between his quite as tight. None of them felt nearly as sweet wrapped around him, their soft bodies pressed under his, taking his weight. None of them, after taking her, made him feel clean and like everything was right in the world as long as her body was in his bed.

Not one.

Not even close.

"So, debriefing way late, dinner with your family went good..." he paused, "both times."

He muttered this against the skin of her neck, felt her

body give a soft jerk of surprise under his then he heard a soft giggle escape her throat.

That felt good. It sounded good. Like everything was right in the world, just because they were together in his bed, even when everything was not.

She'd give him that if she was twenty-nine or seventy-nine and he knew that right down to his soul.

He lifted his head and looked down at her to see she was smiling.

"Maybe for you," she replied. "I found it annoying."

"Just so you know, I get a second, I'm hiding the scissors," he informed her.

"That actually didn't happen."

He grinned and dipped his face close. "Faye, you're lying."

Her eyes shifted side to side before she muttered, "Well, if it did, I blocked it out."

They came back to him when he stated, "*That* I believe."

"I'm the middle child," she began to defend herself. "Liza and Jude always ganged up on me."

"That I believe too."

"So, *if* I were to wield scissors, it was probably necessary. Self-defense."

"That, sorry to say, darlin', doesn't jive."

She rolled her eyes and muttered, "Whatever."

"Baby," he called softly and when she looked back at him, he told her quietly, "Told you I'd love 'em."

Her eyes went hooded, the tip of her tongue slid out to lick her lips then she whispered, "Good. I'm glad."

He'd seen her tongue so he dropped his head to retrace its path.

When he lifted his head, her eyes were still hooded but the look on her face was entirely different. A look he was coming to know. A look he liked.

"You want more, baby?" he asked gently.

Her teeth came out to bite her bottom lip briefly before she let it go and whispered, "You have to go to work tomorrow."

She lost her mind when he had his mouth between her legs. Even just coming, it'd take him fifteen minutes, she'd come just as hard or harder and he'd still get decent shuteye.

Worth it. Absolutely.

He bent his neck, kissed her earlobe and, in her ear, ordered in a whisper, "Go clean up. Come back, I'll give you more and eat you."

Her head turned slightly so her lips were at his neck even as her three limbs convulsed around him and her fingers laced with his tightened.

"Yeah?" she whispered.

Fuck, he was still partly hard inside her, just came and his dick still twitched at that one, breathy word filled with want from his girl.

"Yeah," he whispered back.

"Slide out, Chace," she breathed, and slowly, he slid out.

Slowly, she slid her lips up his neck.

Change of plans. Eat her until she found it. Then fuck her until he did and hopefully she did again.

He kissed her shoulder and rolled off.

She gave him a small, semi-shy grin then hustled her ass to his bathroom.

When she came back, not yet completely comfortable with her nudity in front of him, she was wrapped in his robe that was on a hook on the back of his bathroom door.

His mother bought him that robe post-Misty. Somehow when she was over, she'd discovered his old one was gone, this being because Misty, in the beginning, had taken to wearing it. So when her shit went, his old robe went too.

Another woman had worn the robe Faye now wore. He

didn't like that and made a mental note to get rid of it and get another that was just hers.

She left it on when she crawled into bed.

Which meant he got to take it off.

This he did ten minutes later.

Ten minutes after that, after he'd made her come, he was back inside her to find it himself.

And just like Faye always did, she found it again too.

CHAPTER FOURTEEN

He Was Gone

CHACE WAS OUTSIDE the station putting the crate with Malachi's books in the back of the Yukon when his phone went.

He slid the crate in, straightened out of the truck and grabbed his phone.

The display said, "Faye calling."

He hit the button and put it to his ear.

"Baby."

"*He moved his fingers and toes!*" she screeched in his ear.

Chace dropped his head and smiled at his boots.

That morning, he'd gone for a run, come home, dragged his girl out of bed and into the shower then he'd taken her to La-La Land. They got breakfast while Faye filled Sunny and Shambles in on all things Malachi. He left her on the sidewalk outside La-La Land with a kiss. He was going to his truck and driving to the station. She was walking the two

blocks to her place to change then go to the store to get Malachi treats and last, to the hospital.

He'd separated from her a little over two hours ago. After
a briefing from the boys that coincided with the two he had
from Deck the day before, he'd asked the interns to modify
their search to include missing siblings. Then he'd taken care
of some business and now he was on his way to the hospital
to check in and get Malachi his books.

He was doing this because the kid had nothing. Those
books, the way he had them organized, meant something.

So Chace was going to take them to him.

"They said he ate all his breakfast even though they
had to help him and he's been awake all morning," she told
him. "He hasn't spoken yet but when I walked in *he smiled
at me*."

She said this like her favorite movie star walked off the
red carpet, picked her up in his arms, carried her to his lim-
ousine and drove off into the sunset with her.

"Great, honey," Chace muttered.

"They're moving him to a normal room now. But they
say they're only keeping him another day," she stated.

"Karena is meeting with your parents as we speak, Faye."

"I know, Mom called and said that's why they're not here.
Is that going to go okay?"

"Yes."

"Sure?" she pressed.

"Yeah, baby, I—"

He stopped speaking because he felt a nasty prickle on
the back of his neck. There was a presence with him. Not a
good one.

His head came up and he saw his father walking his way.

No.

Shit. Fuck.

No.

"Chace?" Faye called as Chace stared at his father who was staring at him.

He turned, lifted a hand and slammed the back to his truck, assuring her, "It'll go fine."

"Is everything okay?"

She read him instantly even on the phone. He wondered, distractedly, if it was that obvious or if that was how far he'd let her in and he decided it was both.

"Yeah," he lied, shifting around the side of his SUV. "I'm comin' to you now. Bringing his books."

"I don't think he can hold them yet."

"Maybe not but he'll want 'em."

She was silent a second then he got a quiet, sweet, "Yeah."

"Chace," he heard his father's terse voice call as he yanked open his door.

"Gotta go," Chace muttered into the phone.

"Oh, right. Okay, see you soon," Faye said in his ear.

"Chace!" his father clipped.

"Who's that?" Faye asked.

"No one. Gotta go, honey," he whispered, angling up into the truck. "See you soon."

"Soon," she whispered back. It was hesitant. She knew he was lying since someone was calling his name. It sucked doing it but he disconnected quickly as he tried to pull the door closed.

This didn't work because Trane Keaton was standing in his door hand on it, firm and strong, holding it open.

Chace's eyes went to his father.

In the many jokes life had to play on him, it saw fit to make him look like his father. Same height. Same build. Same hair. Same eyes. There was barely any of his mother in him, even though she was blonde and blue-eyed. He got what he got from his father. He'd heard it from his father's cronies since he could remember.

Spitting image, Trane.

So Chace knew in thirty years, he'd look like his father.

Straight, lean, the strong features and good looks he'd been fortunate to be endowed with hardly faded. He was the kind of man whose looks enhanced with age, then, as that advanced, grew interesting, still retaining the handsome, the strong, the vital.

If Trane Keaton was another man, Chace would look forward to this and appreciate his father gave him good genes.

Instead, he dreaded a lifetime of looking in the mirror and remembering his father.

"You're not returning my calls," Trane accused, his voice hard, his face angry. He was pissed he had to make the trek from Aspen. Pissed his son didn't do his bidding. Pissed to see Chace in jeans, a shirt, sweater, coat and boots with a badge on his belt folding into a Yukon when he should be wearing a five-thousand-dollar suit folding into a BMW.

"No, I'm not," Chace confirmed then ordered in a cold voice, "Step back."

"I need to speak to you privately and immediately."

"You aren't gettin' this, Dad, but that is not gonna happen."

"You aren't *getting* this but that is not *going to* happen."

Jesus, he was thirty-five and the man was correcting his fucking English.

"Step back," Chace growled.

"You live with rednecks, Chace, but you don't have to sound like them," Trane returned, voice superior and fuck, but Chace hated that and Trane talked like that all the time.

"Got somethin' to do, step back."

"Personally, I blame Jacob Decker. I should have put a stop to you spending time with him when you both were at school. Your mother wouldn't hear of it. Now I hear he's back."

Chace's body went solid.

He was making a point and not the usual one.

Deck hated Chace's dad. Trane Keaton returned the favor.

Deck won a full scholarship to the private school Chace attended but he didn't come from money. His father was an electrician. A skilled trade but not acceptable in the life of the Aspen Keatons. It didn't matter that Deck had an IQ of one fifty, a certified fucking genius. He was not good enough for Chace. When Deck didn't go on to cure cancer or help the government create space age weaponry but used his superior reasoning and higher intellect to do shit that was a little fucking scary, Trane felt this was proof positive he'd been right all along.

But this wasn't the point Trane was making.

He was telling Chace they were keeping an eye on him.

Not a surprise but an annoyance. Deck could definitely take care of himself. When, in the flash of an eye, you could calculate your height, weight, muscle mass, the poundage behind your swing, aim and connect knowing exactly what kind of damage you'd inflict to wherever you connected, you could seriously fuck someone up. This wasn't theoretical. When they were in high school and college together, Chace had seen it firsthand. Jacob Decker never got bested, not only because he was freaking tall and seriously strong but because he was fucking smart.

But if Trane and his band of assholes got impatient, they could aim at anyone to make their point to Chace.

Deck was in that firing line.

He made a mental note to phone Deck on the way to the hospital and repeated, "Step back."

Trane's eyes locked to his son.

"And, if you see Faye Goodknight any longer, your mother will want to meet her."

Trane stepped back then. This was because Chace angled out of the car and he had no choice.

But Trane didn't retreat, just gave him room so Chace, unfortunately, ended up nose to nose with him.

"You don't breathe her air," he whispered.

"You'll never learn it's not advantageous to wear your heart on your sleeve," Trane replied, sounding put out that Chace had not learned one of the many useless lessons he'd tried to drill into him when he was a kid.

"Wore it for Ma. Anyone who wants to get at me knows I'm that kinda man. Got nothin' left to hide. The thing you don't get is, that kinda man is the kinda man a real man wants to be so there's nothin' *to* hide."

"Foolish?" Trane's voice was snide.

"Protective." Chace's was firm.

"If you give it all away, Chace, you're not protecting yourself."

"It isn't me I'm gonna protect."

"Therein lies your faulty strategy."

"No, see, the kind of man you are expends his energy to save his own ass. The kind of man I am doesn't do shit to have to worry about that and instead he works his ass off to keep those worth his efforts safe. So the message I'm sending is, I give a shit about someone, you do not fuck with them or you fuck with me."

"And is Faye Goodknight worth those efforts?"

Chace didn't reply.

Trane kept his eyes locked to his son's for a while then he muttered, "At least she has a master's degree."

They'd looked into Faye.

This wasn't entirely unexpected. It was sooner than he would have guessed. It was also annoying.

"Faye doesn't exist for you and she'll exist for Ma when I decide she does," Chace told him.

"Then I'm sorry to disappoint you further, Chace, since I shared with your mother over breakfast this morning that you're seeing someone. I thought it wise, since I learned you'd had dinner with her parents at Rosalinda's last night."

Chace felt a muscle in his cheek jump.

"Things are progressing swiftly," Trane noted quietly.

Chace held his gaze and kept his jaw clenched.

"Valerie will give it time. She won't want to pressure you. My guess, you have about fifteen minutes before you get her call to ask you and Faye to dinner."

Fuck.

Fuck.

"She's very excited," Trane continued then his lips twitched and the piece of shit had the balls to finish, "She never much liked Misty."

Chace was done. "You gonna move back or am I gonna have to drive over you?"

"We haven't had our talk."

"A talk we're not gonna have. Two seconds. Move away or I roll over you."

Trane held his eyes.

Then his changed slightly and he whispered, "You know I didn't like that happening to you. You also have to know I didn't want you to see what you saw."

"It happened. I saw it. All your money, you can't undo it."

"You need to look after the Walkers," Trane advised quietly.

"They're lookin' after themselves. Ty is gettin' me your tapes. I'll text you when you can send a lackey to pick them up."

It was barely there but Chace was close enough to see the relief flash through his father's features.

Then he said, "Newcomb."

"By the book."

"Chace—"

Chace leaned into him so their noses were almost touching.

"By the book, Dad. Call off your goon squad. This shit is not gonna go away unless you pull your fingers out, pay attention and stop makin' your problems everyone else's."

"They're getting impatient," Trane whispered.

"That hasn't escaped my notice, seein' as a man's dead."

Trane opened his mouth to speak but when he did, Chace's gut roiled in a sick way because he had to give the bastard something.

"Don't," he whispered and the way that word came out, Trane shut his mouth. "For Ma, I'll give you this warning. You say shit right now, I will walk right into that building and report it. So don't. Don't give indication you have knowledge about a murder and a break-in. Help me help Ma and keep your fuckin' mouth *shut*."

Trane held his eyes for long moments but he didn't speak.

Chace was done.

"Ma calls, I take Faye to her, you are not there," he told his father.

"She won't like that," Trane replied quietly.

"Make some excuse and make it a good one. That won't be a problem. You're a practiced hand at that."

Trane shook his head. "She wants us to be a family, Chace, and if this relationship with Faye Goodknight progresses she'll want that even more."

"Then get creative because she'll get that from me, from Faye, but you will not be involved."

"Regardless of the outside situation, I agree with your mother. You're my son. If you marry this woman—"

Chace cut him off to growl, "She's not 'this woman.' She's Faye."

Trane nodded, his eyes flashing, Chace's words giving it

away but he let it alone and carried on, "You marry Faye, you have children, those will be my grandchildren."

"You'll have not one thing to do with them either."

A flinch.

Jesus.

The asshole flinched.

"Chace," Trane said softly before Chace could process the flinch, "I made a mistake. Men make mistakes."

"My dead wife shoved shit up your ass in order to blackmail you so she could maneuver her body into *my* bed," Chace clipped, Trane flinched again and Chace went on crudely, going in for the kill. "I get a man might like ass play. Your kind of play, I *don't* get. You're correct. I'm your son. Means you're my father and I should never have seen my father doin' that shit. It's entirely fucked up in a way so jacked it can't be described that we're even *having* this conversation. Then you got nailed after you got off, protected your ass and set mine swinging. *That* is not a father. Takin' us back to earlier, *Dad*, a good man, a *real* man, he fucks up, he lets his ass swing so his son's doesn't. You not only didn't protect me, you pulled me right into your shit. So, breakin' that down, you're my father but you also are *not*. That means, when I put a ring on Faye's finger and yeah, Dad, I said *when*, you will not be her father-in-law and you sure as fuck will not be a granddad to our kids. Please, God, do one fuckin' thing for me in my life as your son. Give me that. Give my woman that. And give my kids that."

Done, he turned, angled up into his truck and slammed the door.

Without looking at his father, he shoved the key in the ignition, turned it, put it in gear and threw an arm around the passenger seat, looking over his shoulder to back out.

He didn't scan to see where his father was when he pulled out of the station parking lot.

He did, five minutes later, pull out his phone to take his mother's call.

She was in a state but luckily a good one. So excited she was babbling.

"I'll get Donatta to cook! All your favorites! Oh, Chace, darling, I'm so pleased you're finally healing after Misty. This is *excellent* news and I *cannot wait* to meet her. I'm just *certain* she'll be *fabulous*."

What she both did and didn't mean was, after Misty, anyone would be fabulous. She didn't mean it nasty. It was nonetheless true.

When she actually met Faye, she'd be beside herself and undoubtedly the next day would go shopping. For what, it was a toss-up, but Chace guessed baby shit first, wedding shit second and expensive presents for Faye that would convince her she had Keaton Love third. She'd hide the baby shit and wedding shit and she'd be in Carnal the day after to lay the expensive shit at Faye's feet.

Fuck.

As he'd done his whole life, he gave in because he didn't have it in him to burst her bubble. He did manage to delay this dinner for three weeks. They needed time to settle Malachi. He needed time to prepare Faye for the dinner. Last, he needed time to prepare for it himself.

She was disappointed at the delay but she was eventually getting what she wanted so she hid it, just not well.

Chace disconnected with her, connected with Deck, gave him the heads-up and then he pulled into the hospital parking lot. He grabbed the books, headed in, got Malachi's new room number and went to his room.

He stopped just at the door when he saw what was happening inside.

Malachi's color was definitely better. He was wearing the pajamas Sondra had bought him. He was awake, alert, his hair cleaned, the bruising on his face fading and he was smiling at Faye who was sitting in a chair beside his bed and had her hands up in front of her.

"Are you *this* old?" she asked, moving her fingers around, flashing numbers at him that Chace couldn't entirely see because he could only see her left hand but that hand opened wide and fisted three times. In other words, he counted fifteen on just one hand.

Still smiling, Malachi shook his head.

"Okay, how about *this* old?" Faye went on.

More flashing of hands. More of Malachi smiling and shaking his head.

Her voice got softer, sweeter and she asked, "How about this old?"

Malachi's eyes dropped to her hands, they shifted to her face and, the smile still in place, he nodded.

"Nine," she whispered then, "I have a nephew who's going to be nine this week. His name is Jarot." She leaned in and shared conspiratorially, "But when you meet him, you can't tease him and call him 'carrot.' He doesn't like that."

Malachi's smile got bigger but it fled his face when his eyes darted to the door and he saw Chace.

Faye twisted in her chair and she aimed a smile at him.

He smiled at her then looked at Malachi. "You're good, buddy. I'm just here to bring your books."

Malachi's eyes dropped to the crate Chace was carrying and stayed there as Chace rounded his bed, giving it plenty of room as he went to the windowsill.

"I'll set them up here and you can tell Faye where you want them after I'm gone," Chace muttered.

He moved to the deep windowsill, set the crate down and carefully arranged the books as they'd been arranged in the box, keeping them in order and placing them as Malachi had had them in the shed.

When he turned back to the bed, he stayed at the window and saw Malachi's eyes on the books, going up and down, counting, reading, assessing they were all there. Chace also saw, on the hospital table positioned over his bed, the book Faye had been reading him last night as well as a row of plastic-wrapped Snickers bars that had been opened, two empty wrappers showing he'd dug in.

"I'm gonna steal Faye a second, talk with her and then I gotta go back to work," Chace told Malachi and the kid's eyes shot to him. "You need me to pick anything up when I come back after work?"

Malachi stared at him then shifted his eyes to Faye.

"Malachi isn't up to talking yet, honey," Faye said quietly, and Chace looked to her. "You have to give him yes-or-no questions," she advised.

When Chace looked back to Malachi he saw a hint of fear in his face and tenseness in his body. This said loud and clear he wasn't up to communicating with Chace at all.

When Faye spoke again, Chace would know she'd read this as well.

"Chace is staying over there, sweetheart," she said gently. "He would never hurt you. He was the one who sent his friend to find you so we could get you to the hospital, make you better then take care of you. But we both get things are a little scary now. Still, he's willing to do a favor for you so maybe you could help him out by letting him know what you want like you do with me. Just nod your head but to Chace. Okay?"

Malachi held her eyes for some time then, what Chace assumed was a yes, he looked at Chace.

So Chace asked, "Do you want a cucumber?"

Malachi's head jerked slightly, his eyes flashed then, thank fuck, his lips twitched before he shook his head no.

"Broccoli?" Chace went on and he heard Faye's soft,

quiet giggle but he didn't take his eyes from Malachi, who again shook his head no.

"Twix?" Chace continued and Malachi pressed his lips together and nodded. "Strawberries?" Another nod, another eye flash, the kid liked strawberries. Finally, quieter, Chace asked, "Have you read *The Lion, the Witch and the Wardrobe*?"

His lips parted, he liked that a fuckuva lot better than strawberries, and he shook his head.

"When I was your age, bud, that was my favorite," Chace shared. "You want Faye to read that to you?"

He bit his lip but nodded his head.

"I'll pick it up," Chace muttered.

Malachi just stared at him.

Chace gave him a smile then looked at Faye and asked gently, "Can I talk to you a minute?"

She nodded, turned to Malachi and got out of her chair but bent slightly over him. "I won't be gone long and then I'll be back and we can talk some more."

He held her gaze and nodded.

She reached out, touched his cheek lightly, going in slowly, but the touch was fleeting before Chace watched her profile give him a gentle smile and she whispered, "Be back soon, sweetheart."

She moved, Chace rounded the bed at a distance feeling Malachi's eyes on him so he gave him a flick of two fingers and a wink and walked out with Faye. He stopped her outside his room so Malachi could see her through the window by the door.

Her eyes were searching and he knew her mind was still on their phone conversation when she asked, "Is everything all right?"

"My dad paid me a surprise visit," he shared, saw her body give a small, surprised jolt as her brows shot together and he moved into her, curling his arms loosely around her. She lifted her hands and rested them lightly on his chest as he muttered, "It's okay."

"Why did he visit you?" she asked.

"Why does he do anything?" Chace evaded. "Mostly to be an asshole."

"Is your mom okay?"

He nodded. "She's good. Got a call from her too. We're invited to dinner, three weeks."

"All right," she replied hesitantly, her eyes still searching his face.

"It'll be okay. Dad won't be there," he assured her.

She continued studying him before, for him, she let it go by whispering, "I'm sorry, honey. I don't know what went down but I do know it's unpleasant seeing him. So I'm sorry."

Chace gave her a lift of his chin and changed the subject. "Those books, they're special to him. My advice, talk to him, put them where he wants them. He'll probably want them close, and tell the staff to leave them be."

She nodded.

"Should we be concerned about the fact he's not speaking?" he asked.

"I don't know yet. They're having a child psychologist come up and have a chat with him after lunch. They say at this point that it isn't really surprising considering how he was living and how he was found. He's not refusing to eat. He's communicating nonverbally. He's not agitated. Except for not talking, he seems to be in good spirits. He does have some hesitation around the nurses but they're going gentle and he settles pretty easily. He doesn't seem to like men very much so it isn't just you. They have a male nurse on this ward, he came in, Malachi didn't like it. He noted it immediately and assured me he isn't coming back."

That said a lot but Chace didn't share what it said.

Faye went on, "We'll know more when the psychologist speaks to him. But they've examined him and it isn't physically that he can't talk. Whatever's holding him back is psychological."

Chace nodded and asked, "Word from your parents?"

"All good. The house passed inspection. Apparently the spring schedule of foster care classes started last Saturday so they've enrolled Mom and Dad. But they're going to place Malachi there tomorrow. Dad's at work during the day but Mom works at home and can be around twenty-four/seven, which they said is good. So it's all in place."

Silas was a geologist who worked for an environmental consulting company based in Chantelle. Sondra was a part-time bookkeeper who did the books for a variety of businesses in town, including the Italian restaurant, Holly's Flower Shop and La-La Land Coffee. She worked at home, available to Malachi. Perfect.

"You'll wanna be there tomorrow," Chace guessed, and he knew it was accurately because Faye immediately nodded.

"I already called my volunteers. I'll open up and get them sorted then the two of them are going to handle things. Mrs. Bagley has closed for me before. She has keys. That's good too."

"Right," Chace muttered then he told her, "I'll pick up some stuff for him, the book and bring it here after work but, darlin'," he pulled her slightly closer and dipped his face to hers, "your mom comes, you gotta give him time alone with her. Start teachin' him to trust her. You don't have to be gone hours but he's gotta get used to her without you around. Okay?"

She nodded but she did it scrunching her nose. She had to do it, she knew it but she didn't have to like it.

"He's good now, Faye," Chace said quietly. "Family. Food. Movin' his fingers and toes. All the books he can want on that thing Silas bought him and to hold in his hands. He'll be all right."

"Yeah," she whispered, leaning into him, her expression clearing.

He dipped his face closer to kiss her nose and when he moved back, he murmured, "I gotta go."

"Okay."

"He says he wants somethin' else, call me and I'll pick it up when I go out."

"Okay."

"See you here later tonight."

She grinned and whispered, "Okay."

"Your bed or mine?"

Her face got soft, her body melted into his and she asked back, "Which one do you want?"

His mattress was better. Her sheets were the softest sheets he'd ever felt in his life. Therefore, a toss-up.

But her place was closer to La-La Land, which meant he had more time with her in her bed and her shower before they headed for coffee.

"Yours," he answered.

"'Kay," she breathed and that was so cute, he bent his head and kissed her quick but open-mouthed, sliding his tongue inside to taste her before he broke the kiss and again lifted his lips but this time to kiss her forehead.

Over her head, he saw Malachi watching them from his hospital bed. And, fuck him, Chace would never have guessed, not in a million years, that Malachi would watch Chace holding Faye, talking to her, whispering with her and kissing her and that would buy him what it bought him.

But when his eyes caught the boy's, it was slight, it was hesitant but it was there.

The kid smiled at him.

Thank fuck.

Chace smiled back.

Then he gave Faye a squeeze and looked down at her. He saw that she was looking over her shoulder into Malachi's room and she looked back at him, hesitant too but happy, her lips parted, a bit of her cute wonder shining through and then she smiled huge.

Chace smiled back, gave her another squeeze and a, "Later, Faye."

"Later, honey."

He glanced at Malachi before he let her go on another smile and walked away.

*   *   *

Chace felt Faye's hand run lightly down the skin of his side, he blinked sleep away and saw, strangely, the light was on and she was turned to him.

She'd been reading. She read most nights and he loved that. Loved the fact that for years, he saw her nose in a book and now he had her in bed with him in one of her little nighties, close enough to touch, her nose in a book. The time he spent knowing she was going to be his, the years he spent knowing she never would, he'd not thought of that. Being in bed beside Faye while she read. But having it felt like a gift. It was maybe whacked to think about it like that but he didn't care.

He liked it.

But she usually turned off the light and settled in. When he felt it, he pulled her into him.

Now the lights were on and she was facing him, her hand on him.

His hands moved so his arms could curve around her and he pulled her to him.

His voice sounded sleepy when he asked what he always asked, "Done?"

"Uh..." she hesitated, "yeah."

Her hesitancy and the change in normal circumstances made Chace focus on her.

"Everything okay?"

Her body shifted against his, her legs moving restlessly, and all sleep left him because she did this and often. But usually she did it when his mouth was on her, his hands on her.

She was turned on.

What the fuck?

"Faye," he called and she bit her lip.

Then she pressed her body against his, tucking her face into his neck and she whispered, "There was...uh, in my book, you know," her legs moved against his and she finished so low he barely heard her, "a really good sex scene."

Chace smiled.

Oh yeah, she was turned on.

And now he was too.

"Hook your leg over my hip, baby," he ordered and she instantly complied.

He instantly slid a hand over her hip to her belly, down, between her legs then he shoved his thigh up, trapping his hand against her.

Dripping.

It must have been a good sex scene, she was totally primed.

He shifted a finger and her hips jerked as a small, low, sexy noise drifted up her throat.

Totally primed.

His dick started getting hard.

Then something occurred to him.

"You read sex scenes a lot?" he asked quietly.

"Um..." She didn't answer, which was her answer.

She did.

He pressed his finger in tighter and her hips started moving with it.

His dick got hard and started throbbing.

"What'd you do before me?" he whispered into her hair. She pressed her tits into his chest, her face deeper into his neck and ground her hips down on his hand and thigh.

What she didn't do was answer.

"You got in this state, Faye," he pushed gently, "what'd you do before me?"

Her hips undulated with his finger and he heard her breath come faster.

She still didn't answer.

His finger stopped moving and he cupped her between her legs.

She whimpered, pressed closer and pushed her hips against his hand.

Phenomenal.

"Faye," he growled.

"Toy," she whispered then quickly, "Chace, your finger."

But he was caught up in visions of Faye touching herself with a toy.

Good ones.

Really good ones.

"Where is it?" he asked, his voice low, gruff.

Her hips kept pushing and now her hands were moving with agitation over his skin.

"What?" she asked.

"Your toy. Where is it?"

Her head tipped back and oh fucking yeah.

She was turned on. Huge.

"Why?" she whispered.

"'Cause I'm gonna use it on you," he whispered back.

"Nightstand," she answered immediately, so hot, so cute, she wanted that and she wanted it bad.

Fuck. Amazing.

He dipped his head and took her mouth in a long, wet, deep, wild kiss then twisted just his torso to hold their position, hoping to Christ it was in the nightstand at his side.

It was.

He didn't hesitate to turn it on and position it.

Like he expected, she reacted violently to this but in a good way, pressing her tits deep in his chest, holding on tight, her nails scraping the skin of his back, her face soft, lips parted, hips jerking against the vibrator.

And he got to watch.

It was fucking brilliant.

His voice now hoarse, when she was close, he asked, "How'd they do it?"

"Wh-what?" she gasped, her hips now jerking.

Christ.

Hot.

"In your book, baby," he prompted, and she tried to focus on him but failed. He pressed the toy harder to her clit, rolling it and growled, "Faye."

"All fours," she panted.

Jesus.

Fuck yes.

"You want that?" he pushed. They'd never done that. She could definitely get wild but he was still initiating her to sex slowly.

"Yes, please," she breathed, her hips bucked, her head shifted back, lips parting and she came for him.

He didn't delay, turned off the toy, threw it aside, rolled her to her belly then pulled her hips up and positioned, thanking Christ she'd done what she'd done only once before and that was start reading without putting her panties back on.

Then he drove in.

He was so far gone, she was so slick and still pulsing with her orgasm, it didn't take him long. Still, she'd just found it but, all Faye, all his, she could get wild. So as he pounded into her, she lifted one hand to curl her fingers around the iron of her headboard and found it again. Her head jerking back, her hair flying, her ass tipping to the ceiling, she came hard and loud, crying out with it, it sent him over the edge and he joined her.

Coming down, he took her slow, gentle, his hands moving over her sweet ass, her hips, the smooth skin of her back, her sides, her ribs under her nightie. Then he pulled out, dropped to her side and hauled her over him so she was on top. He shifted, yanking her covers over both of them then he rounded her with his arms.

She breathed against his neck, her body so loose and sated, she gave him all her weight.

He took it because it felt fucking great.

Finally, she whispered, "I don't get it."

"Don't get what, darlin'?" he asked quietly.

"I've been doing that for a while and you still do it better than me."

For a second, Chace's body tensed just thinking yet again of Faye touching herself.

Then his arms got tight around her and he burst out laughing.

When he was done, he noticed her head pressed tight into his neck just as he noticed her body was no longer loose but taut in his arms.

His laughter died but his arms stayed tight when he called, "Faye?"

She didn't answer.

His hand slid up her spine to glide into her hair and he called again, "Faye, honey? You okay?"

"You know I have a toy," she whispered.

Fuck, she went so wild for him sometimes he forgot this was all new to her.

"Lots of women have toys," he told her quietly.

She didn't answer.

"Nothin' shameful about it," he went on.

She was silent.

He used his arm around her to pull her up but even when she was forced to take her face out of his neck, she avoided his eyes.

"Faye, baby, look at me," he whispered, and it took her a couple of seconds but she did it. When he got her eyes, he reminded her, "You do not have to be embarrassed with me."

"I—" she started and, his hand in her hair, he pulled her face closer to his.

"That was hot," he kept whispering and she bit her lip. "*Really* hot."

Her eyes went side to side before lighting on his again and she whispered, "But I—"

He rolled her to her back, his chest pressing her to the bed and kept his face close to hers when he went on, "Seriously, Faye, honey, that...was...*hot*. I came within minutes of gettin' inside you and I made love to you before I fell asleep. I love makin' love to you, baby, fuckin' love it. But we just fucked and I gotta tell you, I love that too. I like takin' you sweet. I like takin' you slow. I like fuckin' you hard. And I like thinkin' of you touchin' yourself. I like knowin' all that wild was layin' in wait for me and you kept it under control by takin' care of yourself. That's hot too. *Unbelievably* hot. Everything about you is hot, honey. You got nothin' to be embarrassed, ashamed or worried about because you're the best I ever had. All of you. All we share. The best kiss. The best orgasm. The best lovemaking. And seriously the best fuck."

She was staring up at him, eyes wide when he finished and she whispered with disbelief, "Really?"

"Oh yeah," he whispered back with feeling.

"But...how?"

"I don't know how, you just are."

"That's...it's...I—"

He pressed into her and said firmly, "Faye, it's true."

"But...*when*?"

He felt his brows draw together before he asked, "When what?"

"When was uh...you know, your best orgasm?"

"The first time with you."

She blinked. Cute but also kind of annoying. Annoying because he gave it to her then, showed it to her straight out so she had to fucking know.

"Seriously?" he asked.

"Seriously *seriously*?" she asked back breathily, which meant doubtfully.

"Faye," he started, "first, no one had been in there and you'd just come. I'd never been inside a woman that tight and wet, which in and of itself meant it was gonna be good for me and it really fuckin' was. But also, no one had been in *you*. That meant you were mine. I didn't take it. You *gave* it to me. You couldn't miss that meant somethin' to me so yeah, seriously, comin' inside you the first time you took me was the best orgasm I've ever had." He hesitated then finished firmly, "By far."

"Seriously?" she whispered, still dubious and now he was getting pissed off.

"Yeah, Faye, seriously," he replied shortly and she stared.

Then he watched as wet filled her eyes.

Fuck.

"Faye, what the fuck?" he asked.

"I...I..." she stammered, "I want to be good at it. For... for you so you...you'll keep liking me."

He stared down at her.

Then his torso collapsed on hers because he couldn't hold it up due to the fact that he was roaring with laughter.

He heard her wheeze and, still laughing, he rolled them so he was on his back again and she was up top. He kept laughing as he lifted his hands and pulled her hair away from her face as she studied him, a look on her face he couldn't quite read but didn't give a fuck he couldn't.

"Shit," he muttered, still chuckling, "that was fuckin' funny."

"I'm being serious," she whispered.

"I know, honey, that's why that was so funny."

Her stare turned to a glare and he started chuckling again. So she snapped, "Chace!"

When she snapped, he snapped. His hands in her hair at the sides of her head cupped her so he could pull her face to within a half an inch of his.

"First up," he began, his tone deadly serious because he was deadly fucking serious, "I'm not lyin' or handin' you a line. I'll say it one more time. You're the best I ever had. I don't know why and I don't care why. It's just true and I figure it's because it's you. Second, and a lot more fuckin' important, you don't bury shit like this, concerns you have, fears that run deep and not talk to me about 'em. You don't go about life with me like all is good and you're settlin' in and harbor shit deep that eats at you. You lay it on me so I can help you let it go."

"Do I get to return that favor?" she asked instantly.

"What?" Chace asked back.

"You're harboring stuff deep that eats at you. Do I get you laying it on me so I can help you let it go?"

Fuck, how did she maneuver this?

Fuck, he'd walked right into it.

"Faye—" he started and she yanked her head back, pushing up.

"I get it. The answer to that is no," she muttered, but he rolled with her so he was again on top and when he had her contained, he saw it was Faye now who was angry but he also saw she was hurt.

Fuck.

"Give me time," he whispered.

"I am," she whispered back.

"It'll all be yours, Faye, I promise when the time is right, when I can face it, when we're strong and you can face it, I'll give it to you."

Her head gave a slight jerk and she was still whispering when she asked tentatively, "You're not testing me?"

He blinked then asked back, "What?"

"You, it's…whatever it is, is uh, *deep* and if you don't, um…intend for there to be a, um…future for us then you wouldn't want to—"

Christ, he was a fucking idiot.

He dipped his head, touched his mouth to hers and stopped her talking.

Then he lifted his head so he was a breath away and he shared softly, "Faye, I'm fallin' for you."

Her hands were at the sides of his ribs and he felt her fingers dig in as her eyes got big. "What?"

"You heard me."

"Chace—"

"Straight up, this is the man in your bed. I want in there, Faye, and when I get in there, I'm gonna dig in deep so when I share my shit that's so dark you'll be blinded by it and you'll wanna run to the light, you can't because I'm so deep, you can't let go."

She was breathing heavier as she stared at him before she said quietly, "Nothing about you can be that dark, Chace."

"It can 'cause it is."

She shook her head. "I don't believe that."

"Good, keep not believin' it so I can dig in there and when I give it to you, you can't let go."

"It's not that dark," she pushed quietly.

"This is the only warning you get, Faye, 'cause you don't kick my ass out right now and you sleep beside me tonight, tomorrow I just keep digging deeper but it's no lie. It is. It's as dark as it can get. Dark and ugly."

"That isn't true."

"It is."

"It *isn't*," she stressed. Chace opened his mouth to speak but her hand shot up between them and she pressed the tips of her fingers against his lips and went on. "I'll tell you why I know. Because what you just told me you were doing, you wouldn't do. Not to me. Not to anyone. You wouldn't make me care for you only to hurt me. You know whatever it is, I can handle it. Because if you didn't know that, didn't believe it, you would not be here right now. That isn't the type of man you are, Chace, and I don't care what you think, I know who you are. I don't know who you *think* you are but *I know who you are*. I also know nothing you can tell me will make me think differently."

Jesus, he fucking hoped so.

She wasn't done but she moved her fingers from his mouth to cup his jaw before she kept talking.

"I'm glad you like me. I'm glad to know you're not sharing with me not because you're testing me but because of why you explained you aren't though that's crazy but, whatever. Take your time. I'll be here and after, I'll still be here. And I'm glad you thought that was hot. Because I read a lot of romance novels and my toy got a lot of um...uh...you know, *use* before you so, um...you're going to get a lot of um...*use* now too."

Chace Keaton stared down at Faye Goodknight, her head against the pillows of her bed, her body under his and he wondered how in *the fuck* six years of misery led him to all the promise that was her.

He'd wanted her for years not having any fucking clue how much of her there was to get, how deep it ran or how sweet it was.

"Now," she went on, taking him out of his thoughts, "I need to clean up and get some sleep. Malachi is getting sorted tomorrow and I need to be on my game. You can take from that I'm not kicking your ass out. I'll tell you now, I do have a temper so that doesn't mean you won't one day be sleeping on the couch. I know this because Dad did this on occasion and I *am* a lot like my mom. But your behind will never be out. And you can take from *that* that I'm falling for you too. But you know that since you know I already did it thirteen years ago. I'm just glad to know now I picked really fraking well."

His heart pounding in his chest which got tight, his hands moved swiftly, framing her face, holding it steady and his voice was thick when he whispered, "Do not say that shit unless you mean it."

Her hands moved to frame his face too and she whispered back, "I wouldn't. You know it. I held out for a hero and I don't give a frak if you don't think you're one. I *know* you are and even if you weren't one to the whole town, you're one *to me* and you can take that to the fraking *bank*."

Fuck.

Cute.

Sweet.

His.

That constriction in his chest relaxed and when he asked, "Take it to the bank?" his voice was suddenly light and her eyes narrowed.

"Don't tease me when I'm being serious and we're talking deep."

"Sorry, baby, you just said I could take something to the bank. No one says shit like that except cops in '70s cop shows. You talk like that I have to give you shit. Got no other choice."

She started glaring and then she started bossing.

"Get off me. I'm leaking and I don't like to sleep in a wet spot."

"When do you ever have to sleep in a wet spot?" he shot back.

"Well…never," she answered. "But I don't want to start."

Cute.

Sweet.

His.

Christ.

He dipped his mouth and touched hers.

When he lifted away, he whispered, "All right, clean up."

She shifted under him, muttering, "Fine."

But as she moved, his arm circled her waist, detaining her, and her eyes came back to his.

"I know what you think," he started to warn gently. "I know why you think it but you made a decision just now so when you get it all from me, darlin', and you decide to run, you gotta know I'm not letting go."

"Fine by me," she replied immediately, lifted up, brushed her bubblegum lips against his then rolled out from under him.

Her short chocolate brown satin nightie glided down to settle over her ass as she got out of bed and moved toward the bathroom. Chace watched it then watched it move under the fabric until she disappeared.

Then he rolled to his back, her toy rolled into him so he tagged it and replaced it in her nightstand. After, he again settled on his back but this time he lifted his hands and covered his face, pressing the pads of his fingers into his forehead and digging deep.

He did this hoping with everything he was that Faye didn't lie.

He did this hoping what she read in him was true. Not that he was who she thought he was because he knew he wasn't.

But that she could take the dark he had inside him without breaking free to run to the light, leaving him behind in black.

He dropped his hands when he sensed her coming back and watched her walk across the room and turn out the light before she climbed in bed.

The instant the covers were over her, he reached to her and pulled her into his arms, face to face.

She hooked a leg over his hip and pressed deep.

"Faye?" he called.

"Yeah," she answered quietly.

"No way in hell no matter how pissed you get I'm sleepin' on the couch."

"We'll see," she replied, still quiet.

"We won't. We work it out before we sleep or you suck it up. You do not sleep without me." He paused then finished, "Ever."

"Whatever," she muttered, pressing closer.

This meant she was done with the conversation.

It also meant she was giving in.

Then again, she always did when it was important.

He pulled her even closer knowing one thing.

He wasn't falling anymore for Faye Goodknight.

He wasn't halfway there.

He was gone.

CHAPTER FIFTEEN

Potatoes

I LOCKED UP the library and moved to the steps, on my way home.

It was Wednesday. It had been a week and a day since they released Malachi from the hospital.

As seemed to be the case since Chace came into my life, this time had not been uneventful. Not even a little bit. It had been eventful and busy.

But surprisingly, Malachi settled in with Mom and Dad relatively well. He had some issues with Dad and the first night I left, he got agitated, very much so, so I didn't want to leave. But Chace and Dad took me aside and told me something I knew logically but didn't like all that much. This being that I was doing him no favors hovering when he had to get used to his surroundings. So I left with Chace. And I didn't like that either.

Chace took me home, poured me wine, and he stretched out on my couch and watched some game. As he did this, his lips were tipped up because I was pacing and fretting, something he thought was funny, something I did not. Then I called my parents an hour after we walked through my door only to have Dad tell me Mom was reading Malachi *The Lion, the Witch and the Wardrobe* and all was fine.

It took two days for Malachi to settle with Dad.

It would be the weekend before he let Chace in.

This was on Saturday when Mom and Dad were at Liza

and Boyd's for Jarot's official ninth birthday party. It was decided it was too soon to introduce Malachi to Jarot and Robbie, much less a bunch of other kids, so Mom and Dad, Chace and I were taking turns looking after Malachi and going to Jarot's party.

I had another volunteer look after the library for me in the afternoon and Chace and I were taking the first shift. They were leaving the party early and we were going later.

By this time, the bruising around Malachi's face was gone, he was getting around on his leg very well and the bandages were off his hands because Dad decreed, "They need air." That didn't mean Mom didn't gunk them up with Neosporin three times a day. They were healing really well and within a couple of days he had no problems holding the Kindle Dad bought him even with one arm in a sling.

He loved it. Mom downloaded a shed-load of books on it and he was always in a chair or on the couch, eyes glued to it but his fingers hitting buttons, testing it out, seeing what it could do. He messed it up a couple of times so Mom and I had to sort it but he learned from what he did and by the weekend, he knew more of how it worked than I did my Nook.

Chace had noticed his fascination with this so on Saturday, while I was at work in the morning, he'd gone and bought Malachi a portable Nintendo and a few games.

Although Malachi no longer got visibly anxious around Chace, he still held back from him. So when we got to Mom and Dad's, I gave him the game but told him Chace bought it. Then, not knowing much about it, I fumbled my way around showing him how to use it.

Obviously, and fortunately, I fumbled too much. This meant Malachi got impatient and gently pulled it out of my hands and carefully wandered to Chace, handing it to him.

I tried not to cry as, without a word or making a big deal of it, Chace crouched beside him and explained how to load the game cartridge and use the Nintendo while Malachi stood close, head bent, eyes riveted to it. Then Chace handed it to him and, get this! He *leaned into Chace* as his thumbs tentatively moved over the game.

It...was...*awesome*!

As I deep-breathed, Chace let him do this, watching him test out the game then he slowly straightened, guided Malachi to a chair and sat him in it, Malachi's head bent to the game the entire time.

It only came up when Chace started moving away. Malachi made a noise in his throat, slammed his elbow in the arm of the chair so Chace went back, asking quietly, "What is it, buddy?"

He bumped the arm of the chair with his elbow twice, his eyes on Chace, and they didn't leave until Chace sat his booty on the arm of the chair and stayed close while Malachi's head bent back to the game. Sometimes he'd lift it up and point at things so Chace would show him what to do. But he didn't let Chace leave him until he had it down and was absorbed in it. And more, with great patience, since sitting there watching a kid play a video game probably badly couldn't have been barrels of fun, Chace didn't leave him and acted like he could sit there for forever.

This was awesome too, a heart-melting awesome that I didn't know what to do with so I just felt it and let's just say it felt *great*.

Half an hour later, Malachi came into where Chace and I were sitting at the kitchen table. He still had the Nintendo but also the other game and he handed both to Chace.

Then he *again* leaned into Chace as Chace ejected the game, set up the new one and showed him as he told him what to do.

And he *stayed* leaned into Chace, his thumbs on the game, his head bent to it as Chace and I resumed talking, me with a huge, fraking grin on my face, Chace often shaking his head at me in that way he did when he thought I was doing something cute, his lips tipped up.

Eventually I had to come down from my high when Mom and Dad got home and we had to go to Liza and Boyd's.

But half an hour later, my high came back with a *whomp* when Chace and I walked through Liza and Boyd's door and Jarot and Robbie raced to him. Both grabbed a hand, hauled him in, but it was Jarot who shouted to his gaggle of friends, "This is my new Uncle Chace and *he's a cop*!"

Thus commenced Chace showing his badge around. This bled into Chace somehow getting conned into giving kids piggyback rides. And this somehow devolved into Chace being wrestled to the floor with a slew of nine-year-olds, near nine-year-olds and Robbie's three six-year-old friends' flailing arms and legs being mostly all I could see.

"Okay," Liza whispered in my ear, she'd sidled up to me and at the glance I spared her after tearing my eyes away from Chace under a pile of kids she went on, "I get him. He's hot. He's the kinda hot a woman would forgive a lot of asshole, he's *that* kinda hot. But he's that kinda hot *without* the asshole part, which is a plain miracle. So you giving it up to him, baby sister, I get it." My eyes went back to her and she was grinning at me like a lunatic as she finished with emphasis, "*Totally.*"

I looked back toward Chace who had managed to untangle himself from the pile of kids and was standing. But he had Robbie dangling down his back with his arms around Chace's neck, giggling his behind off and Jarot under his arm, shouting through his own giggles, "*I'm gonna be a cop like Uncle Chace and arrest a bunch of bad people!*"

My belly melted, my heart flipped and I whispered, "I hope we have all boys."

"Oh no," Liza whispered back. "Man like that, you've got to give him a princess."

This thought made my belly melt more, my heart flipped then flopped and my eyes went to my sister.

"A princess," I breathed.

"Another one," she said gently then lifted her fingers to twitch my hair. "He's already got one."

God, seriously, I fraking *loved* my big sister.

I grinned.

She grinned back.

I would learn that night that Chace spending an hour allowing himself to be the grown-man personal toy to my nephews didn't affect his stamina.

It was a great lesson to learn.

I walked toward Main Street, my mind moving back to Malachi, who had yet to speak his first word.

The child psychologist who saw him in the hospital said that this was not unusual and we shouldn't be overly concerned. She said it was clear he had endured multiple traumas and had intense trust issues. Providing him stability and nurture, making him feel safe, gently forcing him to express himself in a way he was comfortable with and communicating to him verbally with great regularity would eventually break down whatever issues he had and he would again speak. She warned that he should not yet be asked about what led him to his hiding hole or who or what he was hiding from. He needed to be shown he was safe and he could trust those around him. When he was, and with her in attendance, questions could be asked.

But this also meant she wished to see him regularly, and Mom took him to the hospital for a twice-weekly schedule of appointments. There had been no breakthroughs, and Chace kept reminding me that whatever had been going down with him had been happening for a while so we couldn't expect him to snap into normal little-boy behavior in a few days or even a few weeks. Chace told me I needed to give it time and be patient.

I didn't like this either but I had no choice. It couldn't be said that Malachi wasn't adjusting. He was now close to me, Mom, Dad *and* Chace. He didn't talk but he did smile, touch and find his ways to say things he needed to say.

So I was giving it time and trying patience.

The psychologist also noted that his socialization skills were not advanced and she pointed out the obvious that now was not a good time to enroll Malachi in school. Therefore, Mom looked up home schooling on the Internet and went to the school to talk to some teachers. She also sat with Malachi and discovered what we knew. His reading was off the charts and he knew his numbers, had some basic math skills, in other words, he knew how to add small numbers. But other than that, not much.

This meant she'd begun to initiate him to some lessons without letting on she was, such as asking him how many Tater Tots he had then, after he ate two, asking him how many he ate and how many he had left. She also sorted some art stuff for him, giving him paints, colored pencils and paper and setting him up with them at the kitchen table when she cooked. She would begin a full-fledged home schooling program once she, Dad and the psychologist felt he was ready to be assessed by a teacher so they knew where to start.

The only surprising and alarming thing with Malachi was that Mom and Dad shared that it seemed he'd never seen a television set. As he had company and that company was reading to him at the hospital, we hadn't had the occasion to turn on the set in his room when he was there.

When Dad turned their set on, they said Malachi freaked.

The same, they reported, with phones and radios.

This knowledge made Chace's jaw get tight in a way I knew he wouldn't explain. I also knew he was doing his thing with his brethren, including his brothers in arms and Deck, all trying to find out why Malachi was as Malachi was and what happened to him. I'd learned the night we found Malachi that Chace didn't intend to share this with me and I also understood he didn't because he was protecting me. So much was going on with Malachi, with life, with us, I decided to let him have this play.

For a while.

Soon he'd learn I wasn't a fragile doe he had to protect. Or at least I hoped it was soon.

In other words, Malachi was good. He was in a bed every night with a full belly, as many books as he could get his hands on, a video game he played constantly and no more fear of TVs, phones or radios. He had people he trusted. His smiles came often and we'd all even heard him laugh. The doctor reported his hands and leg were going to be fine with no loss of mobility and I had to believe with the way he adjusted to his new circumstances, everything would with him eventually.

He also had tons of clothes and shoes and Mom and Dad, Chace and I had a big envelope full of checks and cash.

This was because I told Sunny and Shambles about Malachi, not to mention the cops who went to that shed, they all started talking and word about Malachi flew through the town of Carnal.

There was a reason I loved my town and that reason became apparent when word got out about our boy.

Everyone I knew, Lexie and Ty, Lauren and Tate, Bubba and Krystal, Twyla, Sunny and Shambles, Wood and Maggie, and a bunch of people I didn't know came to the library or the station and brought Chace or me clothes, shoes, belts, hats, socks, underwear, pajamas, coats, baseball mitts, Nintendo game cartridges, books, you name it...and money. Money for his hospital bills, money to help Mom and Dad and not a little bit of it. Within a few days, we had over five thousand dollars. That day, Mrs. Bagley gave me a check that took us well over ten.

Carnal took care of its own and wherever Malachi hailed from, he was claimed as one of theirs. They heard about him and they did what they could. Some gestures were small. Others, grand.

All beautiful.

I was thinking this as I walked up the stairs to my apartment, knowing Chace was there. Tonight was the first night since Malachi was released from the hospital that we weren't eventually heading to Mom and Dad's to check in. This was Chace's decree. Our night. Alone time. Just a night, just Chace and me.

The Sunday after Jarot's party, we'd taken the next step in our relationship. He'd given me the key to his house and a garage door opener. I'd given him the key to mine. We spent time at work, at Mom and Dad's with Malachi, doing our everyday things like Chace going to Chantelle to swim, me going to the gym, so the day could end in either one of our beds. But the day always ended with us together in whichever one it turned out to be.

Although Chace had not yet shared his dark secrets, I knew even more now with how he was with Malachi, my nephews, the easiness he had with my parents, the way he was with me, that whatever they were wouldn't faze me.

I was in love. Not with an idea. Not with a dream. With a good man who had demons but treated my parents with respect, young boys he barely knew with kindness and generosity and me like I was the most precious thing on earth.

Knowing he was at my house making twice-baked potatoes to go with steaks he'd broil, I didn't bother with the key. I turned the knob and walked into my apartment, grinning to myself, looking forward to a just us evening and not having that first fraking clue I was walking into a very different Chace.

I closed the door, saw him standing by my computer, hands to his hips, looking hot.

I started to smile but the smile died and confusion reigned when he spoke.

"I've got a girlfriend?"

My head dipped to the side. "What?"

"I've got a girlfriend," he stated, and something about the way he stated it, something in his tone, the look on his face, the line of his body, made me brace.

"Uh…" I hesitated when he said no more, "I think so. Her being me."

He jerked his head to my computer and what he said next made me realize when I braced, I didn't brace enough.

"Your friends Benji and Serenity think somethin' else."

Oh no.

Oh frak!

I totally forgot. Things had been so busy, I'd been spending so much time with Chace, at Mom and Dad's, it had been weeks since I had a full on conversation with either of them.

I had sent a few emails, just cursory updates and reminding them I hoped they'd backed down from their sleuthing.

But I hadn't shared about Chace partly because I didn't have time for big explanations. But also partly because I wanted to keep him to myself and I wanted to make sure it would last, that it was real before I told them. I did this because I'd have to admit I'd lied to them about Chace having a girlfriend. I also did this because when they heard, they'd be angry I lied to them but over the moon that Chace was with me. And I didn't want them to get excited about something that wasn't all I'd dreamed it would be, dreams I'd shared with them *for years*.

There it was yet again. Lying always, *always* got you into trouble.

"H-how—?" I started, and Chace cut me off.

"Got on to check the game time, barely got that fucker booted up when screens popped up. They're pissed, baby. *Seriously.* You haven't been available to them but you haven't been forthcoming *why*. And they got things to share," he leaned toward me and the way he did made me lean slightly back even though he was ten feet away, "about *the Elite*."

Uh-oh.

"Chace—" I whispered but said no more because he lost it.

I knew he lost it because he roared … yes … actually … *roared*, "*Have you lost your fucking mind?*"

My heart started thumping in my chest.

"Chace—"

"Take your goddamned coat off and get away from the door," he growled, and my head jerked.

"Wh-what?"

"Take," he took a step toward me and I stepped back, "your," he took another step and so did I, "*goddamned*," another step for him and me, "coat off."

"Why?" I whispered and kept retreating as he made it to the door and stopped.

I then watched in fascinated horror as he flipped the dead bolt and set the chain then turned to me.

"Do it, Faye."

"You're kind of scaring me," I said softly.

"Yeah?" he asked, tipping his head sharply to the side. "Good," he bit off to finish.

"It's not good," I whispered.

"Oh yeah, it is, honey," he whispered back. "You should

be scared of me right now. You should be scared of me because I am extremely pissed off. And I'm extremely pissed off because you and your band of misfits have been doin' something so fuckin' stupid I can't even explain to you how stupid it is. And the reason it's stupid is because it's dangerous."

"Chace, it—"

He interrupted me to rap out, "It what?"

"We—" I tried again but he cut me off again before I could say two words.

"You what?"

"Please let me speak."

He didn't.

He leaned forward and thundered, "*Misty got dead because of those assholes.*"

"I know," I whispered.

"So, she got dead, you and your two buddies thought it was smart to play with that kinda fire? Jesus fuckin' Christ, Faye, how could you be so goddamned stupid?"

"I told them to back off," I said softly.

"Well, they didn't," he fired back. "They got names, Faye, they got *a lot*, and *all of it* they should not have. They should not know. I do not know those two but I know *you*." He lifted a hand and jabbed a finger at me. "And I *like* you. I didn't fuckin' *like* my wife but I still didn't want her on her knees, terrified, a cock forced in her mouth, her face raped before she got holes blown into her. So if that shit happens to *you*," he jabbed his finger at me again, taking a step toward me before rocking to a wooden halt, "I...will...lose...my... *goddamned mind*!"

But I was frozen, head to toe, so it took a lot of effort to force out my, "What?"

"Yeah," he ground out. "Semen on her face, darlin', in her stomach. No one knows but a bunch of cops, most of them dirty, and me, the same *and* her fuckin' husband. Last thing Misty did on this earth was give a blowjob and not one she wanted to give. Before he fuckin' took her life, he fucked her goddamned *face*."

My entire body started shivering as I stared at him and tried to process this horror.

"That why you were up there that night we met?" he asked, and when I stared at him blankly, shivering, shocked at this new knowledge, he barked, *"Answer me!"*

I jumped and whispered, "Ye-yes."

"Jesus fucking *Christ*!" he yelled, turning, he swiped my perfume bottle off my dresser, shifted and with a scary, powerful sidearm throw he threw it across the room so it shattered against the bricks at the other side of the apartment.

I blindly took quick steps back, going at a diagonal and slammed my side into the kitchen counter. My body registered the pain so I stopped.

His burning eyes scorched back to me and he clipped out, "This world, Faye, the one you actually live in is not a fantasy."

"I...I know," I said softly.

"Bad shit happens."

"I know," I repeated.

"Happily ever afters are not fuckin' guaranteed."

"Chace—"

"You can be you, good, sweet, kind, generous, loving and *still* get your face raped and holes blown through your beautiful body and no hero's gonna ride in and save you from that shit because you'll be fuckin' *dead*."

"Pl-please calm down, Chace, and let me explain."

"There is no explanation for this stupid fuckin' shit, Faye," he fired back, and I stared at him.

Then I squared my shoulders and whispered, "There is."

He studied me a second before he threw his hands out to his sides and invited sarcastically, "Dazzle me."

"I was doing it for you," I told him softly, and he shook his head, moving toward me but I stood my ground.

"Wrong answer," he growled.

"It affected you, Misty's death. I saw it, how it upset you and, you know, I, well, I had a crush on you before—"

I stopped speaking because suddenly he rushed me and before I knew it both his hands were on either side of my head, his face was all I could see and he whispered, "Shut up."

I didn't shut up.

I kept going in a whisper.

"I didn't like to see you suffer."

His hands pressed in and he clipped low, "Shut up, Faye."

I didn't shut up.

I kept talking.

"I wanted it to stop."

"Shut it."

"I wanted it to stop. I wanted you to be free."

His face got closer and he growled, "Shut it."

I again didn't shut up.

I gave him all of me.

"I wanted you to notice me."

He used my head to yank me into him then one of his arms closed around me so tight I couldn't breathe, his other hand curled around the side of my head, pressing my cheek to his chest, and he bit out, "God damn it."

My fingers curled into his sweater at his sides and I kept at it but I had to do it on a breathless wheeze. "It was stupid. I knew it when Benji and Serenity started turning up stuff so I tried to stop them—"

His hand flexed into my scalp but his arm around me loosened slightly as he whispered in a voice that seemed torn out of him, guttural, leaving damage in its wake, "Seriously, Faye, fuckin' shut it."

I shut it.

He held me close and I held on to his sweater for what seemed days before I felt him shift but only his head so his lips were at the top of my hair.

"Fuck me, what am I gonna do with you? Even when I wasn't with you, you tried to take my goddamned back," he muttered there, and it was not a question for me so I decided not to answer.

His hand slid from the side of my head to my jaw, he tipped my head back and I hesitantly looked into his face, relieved to see he was no longer pissed way the frak off but that didn't mean he wasn't openly troubled.

"You fucked up, Faye."

I slid my lower lip to the side and bit it before letting it go and whispering, "I think I got that."

"Now is not the time to be cute," he warned.

I pressed my lips together.

He closed his eyes and pulled breath in through his nose.

Then he opened his eyes and ordered quietly, "You get on your computer and you talk those two down. I don't give a shit what you gotta do. Get their promises. Get them to vow on whatever geek shit you guys hold sacred that they are not gonna do one more thing on this gig. You have to, you tell them I'll hunt them down and arrest their asses for whatever bullshit I can dream up with illegal wiretaps and hacking. Then we hope they haven't got on radar. And we hope more they haven't put *you* on radar. Because knowin' that shit happened to Misty when my ring was on her finger, I didn't want it there or not, eats at me every fuckin' day. That shit happened to you, it'd kill me but not before I hunted down the man who did it to you and I made sure he was dead. I am not jokin', not even a little bit. So get on your computer and sort their asses, baby, and do it now."

Cautiously, my heart beating hard even as it hurt, for him and for Misty, I asked, "Did that really happen to Misty?"

"Question and answer time is *after* you sort those two. Not now. Go, Faye, and don't make me tell you again."

One could say he was being supremely bossy in a way I did not like.

Still.

Eats at me every fuckin' day.

Frak.

Misty.

So instead of sharing with him I didn't like him being that kind of bossy, I whispered, "Right."

I let his sweater go, he let me go and I hustled across my apartment, taking my coat off as I went.

I threw it on an armchair then I sat in my desk chair.

On the screen I saw either Benji or Serenity had started a three-person chat and there was a line of *Faye, you there?* over and over again.

I scrolled up, saw Chace had entered the conversation pretending to be me which wasn't cool but I decided to share my thoughts about this when he hadn't just lost his mind.

I took a deep breath and I put my hands to the keyboard.

Actually, guys, you were talking to Chace. Now it's Faye and I'm here.

Nothing then, *What?!?!?* This from Serenity.

And *What the frak?!?!?* This from Benji.

Typing hesitantly (yes, you could type hesitantly), I shared, *Chace and I are kinda together.*

More nothing then, *What?!?!?* This from Serenity.

And *What the frak?!?!?* This from Benji.

Oh jeez. Here we go.

Well, actually, Chace and I are more than kinda together. We're REALLY together. And now he knows what we've been doing since he was here and turned on the computer. Your chats popped up. He joined as me. You spilled the beans and he's a little peeved. That was me finishing on an understatement.

You got to be fraking kidding!!! This was Benji.

OMG! What the hell?!?! This was Serenity.

I typed a bunch of stuff, explaining my lie (I hoped). Explaining Chace and I getting together. Telling them about Malachi and all that went down. Finally explaining why Chace was pissed, including the scary, alarming, heart-breaking new info about Misty but skirting over Chace being terrifyingly angry. Though not skirting over it too much in the hopes that they'd understand and finally back down.

So, to end, it seems this might put me in harm's way. Chace doesn't like that much so you have to stop or he'll arrest you or end up on a hunt to kill the man who violated and killed me. Obviously, if this is my possible end, I'm also asking you to help with not making that happen and backing down. I finished.

There was again nothing until Serenity popped up with, *It's kinda not cool he pretended to be you.*

I'll talk to him about that later after I assure him I won't end up riddled with bullets in a ditch because we're being stupid. I replied.

That was when Benji came in with, *I cannot fraking BELIEVE you two are TOGETHER!*

I can't either, I shared.

Is it good? Benji asked.

How to answer that?

I decided on, *On a scale of one to ten with ten being how good I was sure it would be, it's about seven thousand, six hundred, and twenty-three.*

Whoa. Serenity typed. Then, *Righteous.*

Fraking AWESOME!!!! Benji put in.

So, seeing as I'm with the man I've been crushing on for forever and it's that good, I'd like to keep it that way WITH-OUT him being pissed at me. Can you help me with that? I asked.

No probs, Benji answered instantly.

Then nothing.

Serenity? I prompted.

We're close. She pointed out and I sighed.

Maybe, maybe not and maybe we're close to me coming to an untimely demise because we stuck our noses into something we shouldn't. I returned.

Inara, I get you, but there's still a murderer to be caught. Serenity replied like catching murderers was her job. Which it could be, I didn't know. I just knew this particular murder wasn't her job to solve (maybe).

Serenity, girl, stand down. Benji urged.

Serenity, honey, you are where you are, wherever that is, and I'm here. Someone is already DEAD. Someone else might have recently got dead because of this. I do not want to be strike three. This isn't real to you but I'm living it. What we're doing, from Chace's response, tells me I could be in the path of destruction. You might be enjoying this but it isn't fun for me. The fear I've been feeling as you've been uncovering things hasn't been fun for me either. Something I already told you. Last, Chace was seriously pissed and although it wasn't cool he pretended to be me with you two, honestly, in a weird way, he had the right to be. I get you but please get me. Back down. Promise me. Stop everything. For your sakes, for my sake and also for the sake of Chace and me. I begged.

Nothing from Serenity until, *Oh, all right. Whatever. I'll stand down.*

Swear on any possible future, no matter how slight, that Nathan Fillion could kiss you, the universe would take that opportunity away if you keep up with ANY of this. I pressed.

Yeesh, Inara, I said I'd stand down. Serenity evaded.

Swear. I demanded.

Nothing then, *Fine. I swear on losing the opportunity to kiss Nathan Fillion that I'll stand down.*

I sighed with relief because that was so big it was *huge* but I typed, *Thank you.*

Is he there now? Benji asked.

Yes. I answered.

What's he doing? Benji asked, and I looked to the kitchen to see Chace was doing something at the counter.

Cooking dinner. I answered.

Sah-fraking-weet. Benji replied.

Pictures, sister, seriously. He's yours, you're tight, we want files. Serenity ordered.

I could do that.

So I replied. *Okay but I have to go. I'm hungry and Chace might still be a little mad.*

Go! Benji urged and finished on, *Pictures!*

Inara? Serenity on-line called.

Yes? I on-line answered.

Cool for you. I get you holding it close. But I'm really happy for you. Serenity typed.

Me too, darling. Benji added.

Thanks, guys. I replied wishing one day I'd meet them at the same time knowing it was a high probability I wouldn't which sucked because they were cool and really, when you got down to it, the best friends I ever had. So I finished with, *Sorry I've not been around. I'll keep in better touch.*

Girl! Serenity shot back. *Nathan was in my kitchen cooking dinner, I would NOT be on the computer talking to you.*

This was true. She wouldn't.

Friends fit in your life, Benji added. *They don't take away from you living it.*

Seriously, really, I hoped one day I met these guys.

Love you guys. I told them.

Right back at you. Serenity told me.

To the moon and back. Benji said.

I sighed.

Go to your guy. Serenity urged.

Okay, later, guys. I agreed.

Later, Inara. Benji said.

Later, Faye. Serenity typed.

I closed the chat and went off-line without looking to see what went down when Chace impersonated me partly because I didn't want to know and partly because it might make me mad and we'd had enough of that for one night. Then I made a mental note to reprogram my chat software so it didn't log me in on startup.

Out of the corner of my eye, a glass of wine appeared with Chace's fingers around the bowl. I watched him set it on my Wonder Woman coaster and then tipped my head back to look at him.

"Did they vow on Luke Skywalker's lightsaber that they'd stand down?" he asked. I saw he was no longer pissed, there was a teasing light in his eyes, but that didn't mean he didn't still look troubled.

"Something like that," I mumbled, dropping my eyes and reaching for my wineglass.

I felt the tips of Chace's fingers under my chin so I looked up at him again. The second I caught his eyes, he demanded softly, "Assure me they're done."

"They promised me they're done," I assured him just as softly.

"Okay," he muttered, leaned in and touched his mouth to mine.

Then he straightened, turned and sauntered to the kitchen while I watched and sipped my wine.

He hit the kitchen and called, "Deal is, I bake the potatoes and broil the steaks. You twice-bake the potatoes. Potatoes are baked, darlin'. You're up."

"Chace," I called back.

He closed the fridge his head was in, came out with a beer and his eyes came to me. "Yeah?"

"Promise me you'll never speak to me and scare me like that again no matter how pissed you are at me."

I saw his beer disappear as both of his hands went behind the high counter that cut the kitchen from the other space but his eyes didn't leave me when he ordered, "Come here, Faye."

"Promise me," I pushed.

"Baby, come here," he called gently.

My body started to move but my mind shut it down and I repeated, "Promise."

He held my gaze and I let him.

Then he spoke.

"You fucked up, Faye," he told me, still talking gently but loud enough for me to hear across the apartment.

"I know," I agreed.

"He raped her face. I'm not a woman, I can't call it but I'm guessin' that isn't much better than violating other parts of her."

I *was* a woman but I luckily didn't know either. That said, my guess, it wasn't.

"I didn't know that," I reminded him.

"You knew she was dead," he returned.

I did know that.

I remained silent because he had a point. But I stayed where I was because I felt I did too.

We held each other's eyes in silence and this lasted a long time before Chace ended it.

"Never hurt you." His voice was soft but firm. A vow.

"You scared me," I told him.

"No, honey, *you* scared *me*."

"What?" I whispered but he heard it because he answered.

"Anything happened to you, I don't know what I'd do."

"Chace—"

"You in my life, me livin' in hell, feels like I've been touched by an angel."

I stopped breathing.

Was he serious?

"Anything happened to you, I don't know what I'd do," he repeated.

He was serious.

I forced air in my lungs.

Chace kept talking.

"See them in my head, her footprints in the dirt on the trail. She was wearin' heels. She stumbled. She fell. He drove her on. Her knee prints in the clearing where he violated her. They were yours, those were your last moments, no drama, no joke, I'd lose my mind."

"It haunts you," I said softly but he again heard me.

"Damn straight. I didn't want her but that didn't make her not mine."

Oh God, Laurie was right.

I stood and reminded him, "You didn't kill her, Chace."

"I didn't protect her either."

Oh God. Laurie was *so* right.

"Has it occurred to you that you couldn't even if you tried?" I asked.

"Yeah, Faye, but I also didn't try," he answered instantly.

Oh *God*.

I reminded him of something else. "She trapped you into marriage."

"That make it okay she died that way?" he asked swiftly.

"Of course not," I answered just as swiftly.

He studied me a moment before asking, "You're so okay with Misty gettin' done the way she did and me holdin' no responsibility for that, why are you so far away?"

At that, I moved to him, I did it quickly, setting my wineglass on the counter as I rounded it and went right to him. He turned to me as I got close and I fitted my front to him, rested my hands on his chest and tipped my head back to look right in his eyes.

"I suppose," I began to give in, "since I'm not doing anything else as stupid as being the de facto ringleader of a band of amateur computer sleuths, I won't have to be worried you'll get that pissed at me again so I also suppose this conversation is moot."

He lifted a hand, slid my hair off my shoulder then wrapped his fingers around the side of my neck, his other hand still curled around his beer on the counter and his lips twitching as he noted, "Bet I'm the only man banging a woman in Carnal who uses the words 'de facto.'"

"This is likely," I murmured, and his fingers at my neck gave me a squeeze.

His voice was low and serious when he ordered, "You forget what you know about those men, who they are, whatever they uncovered and shared with you."

I nodded.

"You tell anyone about that shit?"

I shook my head.

"Think hard, Faye. Lexie? Lauren? Even Twyla?"

I kept shaking my head and whispered, "No, Chace. No one. I even lied to Krys, Lexie and Lauren when I let it slip about going to Harker's Wood and I never lie. Or um, I very rarely lie." God! No more lying! "No one knows," I concluded.

"Right," he muttered.

I took in a breath then I leaned deeper into him and asked quietly, "How do I help you let go the responsibility you feel for what happened to Misty?"

"Don't get dead like her," he replied immediately.

"Okay," I whispered, hoping a frak of a lot I managed that then went on, "But other than that."

His eyes moved over my face as his hand slid up to my jaw then his thumb slid over my lips before going back and he answered, "No fuckin' clue, baby."

I was still whispering when I told him, "I hate that happened to her."

"Me too," he whispered back.

"I don't know what happened but maybe, if she was playing with fire, with Arnold Fuller, what she did with Ty, maybe it was she who got herself burned."

Chace pulled in a breath.

Then he admitted softly, "She was playin' with fire."

There it was. A little of his "dark." Not much but a little. Thank God.

"She didn't deserve it but it isn't your fault," I told him softly.

"Okay, Faye."

"Seriously, Chace."

He dipped his face close to mine and he whispered, "Okay, Faye. Seriously. You're right and you don't even know how right you are. She got messed up with people she thought she could play, she made her deal, didn't get out of it what she wanted, rethought things and the people she'd fucked along the way and wanted to do right. They knew she was wavering. They took her out. Lucky for Ty, she wavered and fell the right way before they gave her the ultimate fuck in more ways than one. So yeah, they could have done her in my house and they'd have found a way to do it without me bein' able to stop it. Okay. I'll work on lettin' it go. Now can you smush up the fuckin' potatoes and add shit that makes it taste good so we can eat before you go to bed at midnight?"

"Yes," I answered.

"Good," he muttered.

I pressed my lips together, fighting a grin, hoping I got through even a little bit and I started to move away but his hand sliding back down to my neck and curling in a way that got my attention stopped me.

"I'll do everything I can not to get that pissed at you again," he promised on a whisper, looking me straight in the eyes.

My heart skipped.

Yes, I was precious to him. He had a right to be pissed. I had a right to be scared. But I knew he'd stop it before it happened again and he'd do it for me.

Touched by an angel.

Yes.

I was precious.

"Thank you, honey," I whispered back.

"Potatoes."

"Right."

His fingers dug in as he dropped his head and touched his mouth to mine before he let me go, I moved away and turned my attention to the potatoes.

*   *   *

"You gonna memorize the pattern of my chest hair or are you gonna get off me and read until two in the morning?"

At Chace's question, I stopped doing what he said I was doing, running my eyes and fingertips over his chest hair, and I tipped my head back to look at him.

I was on top of him wearing one of my nighties. He was under me, not wearing anything. He'd made love to me. I'd cleaned up, come back to bed and climbed on top of him. Thus commenced my avid perusal of his awesome chest hair.

"The house smells like my perfume," I said quietly, and this was no lie. I'd cleaned it up while Chace did the dinner dishes (even washing!) but the smell was still strong.

"I'll buy you another bottle tomorrow," he muttered, his hands moving over my skin low on my back and my booty. He'd slid up my nightie to gain access and, as ever, this felt nice.

"Chace," I whispered then didn't know how to go on so one of his hands dipped low and cupped my behind.

"Promised I'd try not to get that pissed again," he reminded me softly.

"It isn't that," I told him.

"What is it?" he asked.

I took in a breath and let out the words. "You impersonated me with my friends."

"Yep."

I blinked.

That was his reply. *Yep.*

"But—"

"They were all over you and didn't lead in slow. First it was about me and how you *weren't* with me but I was with someone else and it degenerated from there. I get why you'd be pissed but I think you get why I did what I did."

"How would you feel if I did something like that to you?"

"I was doin' somethin' fucked up, like lyin' to my friends about you or puttin' my life in jeopardy, I got caught out, I hope I'd have the balls to own it and take my licks."

This fraking sucked because it was a really good answer.

I had no idea I scrunched my nose thus communicated this to Chace until his body started to shake under mine, his arms closed tight around me in order to slide me up and I focused on his face to see he was smiling.

When he got me face to face with him, he left one arm angled across my back, hand cupping one cheek of my bottom. But his other hand lifted and he tucked my hair behind my ear, his eyes watching before his hand cupped my jaw and his thumb stroked my cheekbone and lips.

When he started doing this, he asked gently, "Why'd you tell them I was with someone else?"

"Well, um...because, uh—"

"Faye."

Frak.

"It was after that kiss at the station that went bad," I said quickly.

I saw his eyes flash with remorse but I powered through.

"They knew I'd been crushing on you for a while. The whole mission with finding out who killed Misty was about easing your pain and getting you to notice me. So, I had decided I was going to avoid you at all costs after that happened at the station and that meant avoiding discussing you with them. So I lied and said you'd moved on. I didn't share when things happened for us because I wanted to make sure it was real and good and might last before I blew up their pretty bubble. We've never met but we care about each other a whole lot so I didn't want to blow up a bubble that would just as quickly burst."

"This bubble isn't gonna burst, baby," he whispered, and my body melted into his.

"I hope not," I whispered back.

His eyes dropped to my mouth as his thumb slid over my lips and he muttered, "Best kiss I ever had."

My head tipped to the side and his eyes came back to mine as I asked, "Pardon?"

"In the station. Best kiss I ever had."

I melted more into him and whispered, "Chace."

"Fought the pull of you. Lost."

Oh God. I liked that.

"Honey," I breathed, my hand sliding up his chest to his neck.

"Was comin' home from Deck's, saw your lights on, late. Didn't even think about it. Stopped and sat in my truck on the street lookin' up at your apartment, wonderin' what you were doin' up so late. Five seconds later, there you were on the street, oblivious to everything. Told myself not to follow you. Followed you. Fuckin' glad I did."

"You knew where I lived?" I whispered.

"Knew where you lived. Knew where your parents lived. Knew what you drove. Knew where you worked. Knew what you ordered at the diner. Knew everything I could know about you."

Oh my God!

That was *huge*.

My fingers dug into his neck and I kept whispering when I said, "Chace." But I couldn't think what else to say.

"Best thing I ever did, goin' after you," he whispered back. "Got my dance with you. Led to different kinda dances with you. Best thing I ever fuckin' did."

His words affected me so deeply, since I couldn't hold it up anymore, I dropped my head and buried my face in his neck.

His hand at my jaw slid back into my hair and his head turned so his lips were at my ear.

"Love your hair, Faye," he murmured.

And I loved everything about him.

Absolutely everything.

I didn't tell him this. I lay on top of him, feeling the power of him under me, the warmth of his hand on my behind, his fingers sifting through my hair and I memorized every nuance of it.

Finally, Chace broke the silence.

"You gonna read or fall asleep on top of me?"

"Fall asleep on top of you," I muttered into his neck.

His hand fisted gently in my hair, his fingers dug into the flesh of my bottom and he replied, "Works for me."

It worked for him.

Touched by an angel.

I sighed. After a while, my thumb running back and forth under his jaw in a mindless caress stopped, this telling Chace I was asleep.

*   *   *

Chace

Chace stared at the ceiling, Faye curled into him, asleep after he'd rolled into her and took her to his side to turn out her light, taking her with him when he twisted to turn off his.

The Elite.

A good nickname.

This meant her friends knew who these people were.

What they didn't know was that these people made it their business to know everything.

Everything.

Most especially everything that might make them vulnerable.

"Fuck," he whispered, Faye stirred and he forced his body to relax.

She settled.

Chace didn't.

CHAPTER SIXTEEN

Perfect

I WAS IN a dither.

A fraking dither!

It was a multi-faceted dither starting with the fact that Chace would be at my place in fifteen minutes to drive me to Aspen to have dinner with his mother. It was Saturday night and I'd again left the library early, leaving it in the hands of a volunteer so I would have time to come home and get ready.

It also had to do with the fact that it had been nearly three weeks since Malachi got out of the hospital and even though in every way he was a normal kid, so far as interacting with Jarot and Robbie in a (somewhat) healthy way, he still hadn't spoken a word (this being the unhealthy part of how he interacted with Jarot and Robie).

Now even the psychologist was concerned. Everyone was. Even Chace couldn't hide his concern. Malachi was communicating a lot more, this being writing things down on a notepad. But he wasn't talking.

My dither further had to do with the fact that Chace and I had been together over six weeks and even though all that was good, no, fraking *great*, he hadn't shared his "dark" with me. We were cool. We were *awesome*. But that bomb was always below the surface, and I never knew when the fuse would be lit and it would blow.

And my dither had to do with the fact that last week, Chace's temper boiled over again. But this time, luckily, it wasn't directed at me.

It had to do with the fact that he finally tracked down and confronted the president of the Town Council, Cesar Moreno, about what was going on at the library and why Moreno was avoiding him.

I knew Cesar and his family, we weren't great friends but everyone in town knew him. He was a good guy. His wife, Isabella, was one of those ladies who was a lady, all class, soft-spoken but still sweet and approachable. Both his boys were fantastic baseball players. He was a great Town Council president. Even my dad liked and respected him.

But when Chace found him, unfortunately, he didn't hand Chace any bull.

What he told Chace was that he was avoiding him, and thus me since everyone in town knew I was with Chace, as he dealt with the issue "in-house." This issue was that there was a member of the council who wanted to close the library not because of funding issues. This was what they were telling me to prime me just in case things got out of hand. But because there were books in the library that she deemed "inappropriate," including the *Twilight* series, *Harry Potter* (due to them having such "heathen" topics as vampires and magic) and a variety of art books that Cesar told Chace she described as having "nudie boobies."

Cesar did not share who she was.

This did not mean Chace didn't blow his stack to Cesar *and* me.

"We don't need a fuckin' powder keg like this one on top of all the other shit happening in this town," he'd growled, prowling through his family room, his phone in his hand while I sat on his sectional, drinking wine, keeping my mouth shut and watching him.

He'd made this statement in between calls to whom I surmised from his side of the conversation were Tate, Wood, Krys, Ty and my dad.

In other words, lighting the match on that powder keg his own danged self.

But it was the call to my dad that alarmed me. Dad would lose his mind if he knew the library was in danger of being closed down and why. Not only because his daughter would lose her job but because he abhorred censorship.

I was not wrong about Dad losing his mind. Chace got off the phone with him and my phone immediately rang.

It said, "Dad calling," and his greeting was a shouted, "I didn't do two tours with the Marines only for my hometown to close down the library because of nudie boobies!"

I tried not to laugh anytime anyone said the words "nudie

boobies" but I didn't succeed at this and thus often got scowls from Chace whenever it came up, seeing as Chace didn't think anything was funny about this situation.

Needless to say, Dad was angry but Mom was quietly angry, which was *way* worse. Therefore, Cesar Moreno got a visit from her the next day. Also Krys and Laurie created petitions, and they were now all over town.

Cesar was not pleased. The bulk of the work cleaning up the police department was done but he needed a break and not another huge drama on his hands (this he told Dad). But also he had hope that he could nip this in the bud without it blowing up into a huge deal. That said, considering the fact that whoever this woman was had not backed down in weeks, that hope was dwindling.

So now it was a huge deal and it was also on the docket for discussion at the next public Town Council meeting.

As for me, I was concerned, definitely. But I felt that if I let that concern show, Chace, Dad, Mom and all my friends would get even more up in arms about it than they already were, and they were seriously pissed. So I decided to leave Cesar and the rest of the council alone, attend the meeting, put out petitions in the library, urge people to sign them and hope.

This wasn't all I was in a dither about.

Neither Chace nor his colleagues nor Deck had found out what had gone down with Malachi, *and* whoever murdered Darren Newcomb had not been found. Although Chace didn't talk with me much about either of these, I could sense both were disturbing him, and this escalated daily.

Not to mention the fact that Chace didn't seem at all thrilled about going to dinner with his mom. He did, however, communicate with me that it wasn't about me.

It was, "She is how she is and she's gonna be a fuckuva lot *more* than she is, tryin' hard to make you like her. Heads up, darlin', this will *not* be fun in *any* way."

I already knew this from the way he talked about her and I didn't share that I thought it was sweet that he worried about her *and* me. It would be what it would be. Then it would be over.

This led me to the last part about why I was in a dither.

This being that I was wearing a little black dress, my first little black dress ever. Lexie, Laurie and Wendy went shopping with me to get it (and more sexy undies and little nighties to stock me up, Chace had seen all my others, repeatedly).

It fit like a glove from below my breasts to the top of my knees with a slit up my back nearly to my behind. It had tiny little sleeves created by panels that attached to the empire waistline and went up over my shoulders. My back was totally covered but in an enticing vee created by the panels, cleavage showed. I had a pushup bra that enhanced the cleavage and was seriously sexy to boot.

Further, at lunch I'd gone to Carnal Spa, and Dominic, stylist to all Carnal babes, had given me a new hairstyle. He didn't take much off the length but he cut in choppy layers that gave my hair what he called, "Personality and flow, dahlink." It was layered along my neckline and he'd cut a thick, long, sassy bang in. He did a lot of sifting his fingers through my hair and I bought some goo he told me would "separate and define" so it would lay "*perfect*."

I had to admit, I thought it looked fantastic. I didn't look like the shy, virgin, town librarian anymore. I looked like the stylish town librarian who was regularly getting banged by the town's hottest cop.

I was also wearing a pair of sex-on-heels, strappy stiletto gold sandals that even turned *me* on wearing them.

Lexie, Laurie and Wendy assured me the entire getup was elegant, classic and stylish.

Standing by my wardrobe taking in all that was me in the

mirror on the back of the door, not just my shoes, my dress and my hair but also my smoky makeup, I wasn't so sure.

Yes, it was elegant, classic and stylish. It was also sexy as all frak, and I wondered not only what Chace's mom would think of me but also Chace.

Especially the hair.

He told me flat out he loved my hair but he didn't have to say that. He was always finding reasons to touch it, tuck it behind my ear, move it over my shoulder, run his fingers through it. It wasn't like it was no longer there. It was just that it was . . . *different*.

There was a knock at my door, I jumped and whirled toward it, my brows drawing together.

Chace never knocked since he had a key.

I looked at the thin, graceful, gold watch on my wrist that my parents gave me when I graduated from college and saw that Chace was early.

Then I went to the door, flipped the dead bolt and pulled it open, asking, "Did you forget your key?"

My eyes went up, up, up and I found myself staring at Chace's best friend, Deck.

I had met Deck, once, at the hospital when Malachi was brought in.

Therefore, I was in no state to appreciate all that was him.

Now that there was no drama at hand I had the opportunity to appreciate all that was him and we'll just say there was much to appreciate in quantity *and* quality.

"Babe," his deep, rumbling voice tumbled down at me, "before you open the door, you should ask who's there."

I blinked.

His eyes moved from my hair to my coral-painted toes back up to my hair.

Then he muttered, "Fuck."

"Uh . . ." I muttered back.

His eyes did a head to toe to head again and he repeated, "Fuck."

So I repeated, "Uh…"

He seemed to jolt himself out of his stupor and his hazel eyes came to me.

"Got a minute?"

Actually, at my calculation I had twelve but that didn't mean I was fired up to have my boyfriend's seriously hot guy best friend in my house for a surprise visit.

"Sure," I told him, and stepped back.

He moved in, all of him, all his height, his muscled bulk and his mess of seriously longish, thick, dark hair. He didn't need a haircut two weeks ago. He needed it two months ago. It curled and flipped around his ears and down to the collar of his jeans shirt, a heavy hank of it resting on his forehead falling past his eye.

I'd had the not-frequent, but also not-rare, always-happy occasion to reach out and tug at Chace's curls, and those occasions had included when he was in his truck beside me, on the couch beside me and in bed beside me. When I gave into this whim, it bought me one of three responses. Chace's lips would tip up but he'd otherwise ignore it (driving). He'd turn to me and smile (on the couch). Or he'd turn *into* me and kiss me hard (bed).

Deck's hair made your fingers itch not only to tug at those curls and flips but also to run through it.

Repeatedly.

And take your time.

I licked my lips as he closed the door and I moved toward the kitchen asking, "Would you like a beer?"

"No, my boy's gonna be here in a few so not gonna take that time, Faye."

I stopped and looked at him, confused, uncertain and a little worried.

"Okay," I whispered and saw his eyes travel over me again, something that was beginning to freak me out.

When they hit my face he said quietly, "Couldn't've picked better for him."

"What?"

He held my gaze and he answered straight out. "You're perfect for him. Every inch. Sweet and class. Pleased as fuck for him, he found you."

I wasn't freaked out anymore. Or I was, just in a nice way.

"Thank you," I said quietly, liking it a whole lot it seemed I had Chace's best friend's approval.

"Tonight, babe, it's not gonna go good."

I blinked.

Then I asked, "Pardon?"

"Chace told me you were goin' to Aspen. So I know about tonight. What you need to know is, his mom's a mess. Whatever Chace told you, it's worse. She's a good woman but she's not a well one."

I didn't know what to do with this. Not the knowledge, which I'd already figured out. The fact that it seemed he'd come there to impart it.

"I, um...from what Chace has told me, I've already figured that out," I informed him.

"Do not let whatever happens there freak you so you take off."

Oh my God! What the frak?

"Um..."

"They know what it is. It's not hereditary. Chace is solid. His dad's a total dick but, mentally, the man is solid. He's fucked in the head but only 'cause he's an asshole. It's just her. It doesn't run in her family. Some chemical imbalance. But it's only her."

"Oh, uh, okay," I whispered.

He took a step toward me. "Whatever you hear, whatever

you see, whatever he says, do not let it freak you. Tonight or *any* night."

He was beginning to freak me and not the little bit of freak I was feeling, a *whole lot of it*.

"Deck," I said softly.

"He needs you," he said softly back.

Oh God.

"The dark?" I whispered.

"What?" he asked.

"The dark," I said louder. "He says that there's—" I stopped abruptly and took him in at the same time it hit me all that was happening and the fact that it wasn't right even if it was Deck. So I squared my shoulders and went on, "You know, I...it's very cool that you're here, taking his back. I'm guessing from why you're here, what you know, what Chace has said, he's tight with you. But I don't know you and even if I did, I wouldn't be comfortable talking about Chace behind his back. So, although your intentions are admirable, I'd like to request that this conversation stops here."

He held my eyes and this lasted what seemed like years.

Then he whispered, "Perfect."

I bit my lip.

"You gonna tell him I was here?" he asked.

I let my lip go and answered softly, "Yes."

"Perfect," he replied then he moved to the door but stopped at it and turned to me. "Know this, babe, something goes to shit and it ends between you two, you'll never find a better man. Not ever. You may think you will, he may convince you that you will, but you will not." He paused then finished softly, "Ever."

With that parting shot, he jerked his chin up at me, opened the door and disappeared.

I realized I was holding my breath.

Then I realized I had yet another reason to be in a dither.

"Fraking great," I muttered.

*			*			*

"You okay?" I asked softly into the cab.

We'd hit the Aspen city limits ten minutes ago and were winding our way up a mountain road filled with seriously exclusive properties.

My dithers had not totally died except one.

Chace fraking *loved* my hair and he loved, loved, *loved* my dress and shoes. He made this perfectly clear using his mouth but not to form words. He also used his fingers and I'd had a very quick, very hard orgasm while pressed into the wall beside my front door caused by Chace's hand down my panties coupled with Chace's tongue in my mouth.

So that was one down.

I hadn't shared about Deck because Chace seemed tense and I didn't want to make him more tense *and* pissed or worried so I decided to tell him about Deck later.

So I was focused on one dither and that was Chace being tense about dinner.

"I'll be happy when this shit is over," he answered.

I would too, for him.

"She's gonna have the spread, honey, someone cookin' for her, someone servin' us. She'll go all out," he warned me.

I'd never been served in a home before by anyone other than the owner of the home. It would be weird but not torture.

So I replied quietly, "All right, Chace. That actually sounds kind of cool."

He turned into a handsome, curving drive that was lit on both sides with those lights that rose out of the turf. "Food'll be rich, complicated and there'll be a lot of it. You don't like somethin', don't be polite and eat it. Just eat what you like."

"Okay, honey."

He kept winding up the drive to a large, rambling house

set into a mountain backdrop lit full on by lights at the front. The brick was a lovely mixture of whites and pinks. The landscaping, even under the melting April snow, was supremely attractive.

"She's in your space, you're uncomfortable, give me a sign and I'll take care of it."

"I'll be fine, Chace."

"Don't worry about what I'll think, just give me a sign," he reiterated while he parked.

He turned off the ignition, I reached a hand out and curled it around his thigh and his eyes came to me.

"I love you."

Every centimeter of air in the cab of his truck went still as he stared at me by the dashboard lights and I stared back at him.

I said it.

I meant it.

I meant for him to get me and it.

But I wasn't planning on it.

Still, I had to roll with it.

"You love her. I'll love her because I love you and not a crush love like I was feeling for thirteen years. A real love for a good man who teases me and makes me laugh and makes me feel safe and holds me close at night and watches way too much sports and not enough geek TV and gives me amazing orgasms, one of which I had before walking out of my house this very night." I paused, he said not a word, I struggled against having a heart attack and then finished lamely, "And you can take that to the bank."

Then I wasn't in my seat.

My seat belt flew back and I was hauled across the cab, my booty wedged between Chace and the steering wheel, his hand was in my hair, his other arm was tight around me, his lips were crushing mine and his tongue was invading my mouth.

Okay, so, he liked it that I loved him.

Good to know.

I melted into him, rounding his neck with my arms, pressing into him and let him have everything he wanted to take. Apparently, he wanted to take a lot because the kiss lasted a long time. It went from heated to scorching and it was one of those times I felt Chace's effort to tear his lips from mine when he eventually did.

But he didn't let me go and put me back in my seat.

He buried his face in my neck and breathed.

"To sum up," I wheezed, my breath still coming fast, my heart turning over with happiness, "stop worrying, honey. Everything will be *just fine*."

"You're a fucking miracle," he whispered against my skin and I closed my eyes.

I loved that he thought that about me.

"I'm a woman," I whispered back.

"You're an angel."

God.

God, I loved him.

Totally.

"Okay, but I'm yours and I think God frowns on some of our more miraculous activities, activities I enjoy so perhaps we can keep that title on the hush-hush and I'll just be your woman."

He lifted his head and looked down at me through the subdued light. I felt his eyes gentle on me, saw his face was soft and relaxed before he whispered, "Works for me."

My ploy, which included me sharing life-altering emotion, worked.

I grinned.

He grinned back, bent his neck, touched his mouth to mine then shifted me, depositing me back in my seat.

He turned the SUV lights off and he was at my door by

the time I hopped down, which meant he had a steadying hand on my elbow when I did. That hand slid down so his fingers could lace in mine as he pulled me out of the door and slammed it. Then he walked me across the dry, very black blacktop asphalt to his front door.

Weirdly, it seemed the snow had been trimmed at the side of the drive, it was so perfectly removed. So I guessed when you had gobs of money you had money to spend on people manicuring your snow.

Interesting.

The door was thrown open before we got to the semi-circular set of eight steps (I counted) that got narrower and narrower until we hit the top. Another dither died when I saw the elegantly attired, extremely attractive blonde woman with a soft updo wearing a light pink cocktail dress and high heels smiling gleefully at us.

I wasn't overdressed. Fraking brilliant.

"Chace, my darling, and *Faye*," she gushed, stepping out into the chill night air and throwing her arms wide. "I've been on pins and needles all day. No!" she cried, "all *week*."

I smiled up at her then grew a little concerned because she wasn't big, I wasn't big but Chace *was*, she wasn't moving and her step would not hold all three of us unless we huddled together like a miniature football team.

This problem was sorted when we made it to her and she threw herself in Chace's arms, forcing him to let my hand go and round her with them, thus not taking up much room.

"Ma," he muttered.

"Chace, my beautiful boy."

That was sweet.

He pulled back but she didn't. Her arms went from around his shoulders so her hands could frame his face and she beamed up at him a second before letting him go and turning to me.

"Faye," she said, throwing her arms wide, which meant one of them slammed into Chace but although he shifted (as best he could which meant one of his cowboy booted feet had to step down a step) she didn't seem to notice.

I moved quickly into her arms in order to conserve space and gave her a tight hug.

"Mrs. Keaton," I whispered in her ear then pulled back but not out of her arms. "Chace talks about you all the time. I'm so pleased to finally meet you."

She dipped her chin bashfully and fluttered her eyes and really, even though she was older, she worked it.

Then her eyes moved over me and something changed in them that wasn't bad but it wasn't altogether good either.

"You're a beauty. A *true* beauty. Natural." Her arm left me and her hand lifted as if she was going to touch my hair before it fell away and she moved minutely back. "Red. I thought a blonde would suit Chace better but I was very wrong."

"Thank you," I murmured.

"And please, call me Valerie. Mrs. Keaton sounds so... so..." her eyes slid to the side before coming back to me so she could finish, "*stuffy.*"

"Valerie it is then," I replied on a smile.

"Ma, you think we could move inside?" Chace prompted.

She jumped away from me, clasping her hands in front of her, and I fought the urge to reach out to her in case she tumbled over the step to the inside.

"Of course, of course, let's get you inside and those coats off. I'm *dying* to see Faye's dress. From what I can see, it looks *beautiful.*"

I heard Chace sigh as I felt his fingers curl around my elbow, we moved in behind her and all stopped in a huge foyer with a massive chandelier hanging down over it, the gazillions of crystals dancing prisms everywhere.

"Enrique," she said to a man wearing a white shirt and dark slacks standing close by, "please take Faye and Chace's coats. We'll take drinks in the sitting room. Faye, what would you like to drink?"

Chace was helping me out of my long, cream wool coat as I shifted my little black clutch from hand to hand and answered, "A glass of white wine."

"Excellent," she smiled at me then her eyes went to Chace, "Beer, darling?"

"Yeah, Ma," Chace muttered, handing our coats to Enrique.

Taking in Chace without his long, black wool overcoat, the skirt around my hips, hand down my panties orgasm, I had to admit, was helped by the fact he was in a very well-tailored, dark blue suit with an open-necked blue shirt the color of his eyes. His belt buckle with the suit was subdued western but still western and the cowboy boots were all Chace. Still, like his mother and I, he made an effort and, as was his way, succeeded wildly.

Enrique moving off with our coats, Valerie led the way to the "sitting room," which was the most formal room I'd ever been in in my life. It was done in soft pinks that were nearly cream and just plain creams. Even in a room that formal I took my cue from Valerie and Chace who settled in like it was your everyday family room, Valerie in an armchair, Chace and I side by side on a couch.

As I was tucking my purse next to me, Valerie said, "I didn't know what you liked, Faye, and Chace told me you seemed to like everything except pineapple on pizza. But we're not having pizza so I told Donatta to do it up but avoid pineapple. I hope you brought your appetite."

"I always do," I replied on a smile. "But just so you know, I like pineapple just not on pizza."

"Excellent!" she cried with more excitement than was

needed then clasped her hands in front of her again and leaned from her pinky-cream armchair toward Chace and me on the creamy-cream couch and she noted, "Chace tells me you're a librarian."

"I am," I confirmed.

To which she exclaimed, "I love books!"

I laughed softly and shared, "I do too. It's kind of important to like them when you spend all day around them. What's your favorite book?"

This was a mistake. Huge. Though I couldn't fathom why.

Still, I saw it. She sat back sharply, her face grew pale, the fingers of her hands in front of her started fidgeting, her eyes darted to Chace and she looked suddenly terrified.

I felt my body get stiff at her reaction but Chace prompted quietly, "Your favorite book, Ma."

Her eyes skittered to me then back to Chace and she whispered, "I..." but stopped.

It then occurred to me that she was worried what her favorite book would say about her. She wanted me to like her and she wanted this so much, she was terrified of just being her.

"I have lots of favorite books," I cut in, and her eyes came back to me so I smiled gently and went on. "Let's see, there's Rosamunde Pilcher's *The Shell Seekers* and *Oryx and Crake* by Margaret Atwood. Then there's *Fried Green Tomatoes at the Whistle Stop Cafe* by Fannie Flagg and *Skinny Legs and All* by Tom Robbins. I could go on and bore you for hours," I told her. "And I haven't even started on the romance novels."

The fear left her face and she leaned toward me again. "Oo, I like Carly Phillips."

I leaned toward her, smiling big. "I do too. She's awesome. *The Bachelor*," I told her one of my favorites.

"*The Playboy*." She gave me one of hers.

"*The Heartbreaker.*" I one-upped her.

She sat back again but this time grinning, "Those Chandler brothers..." she trailed off, needing to say no more.

"I know," I agreed.

"Where's my beer?" Chace asked.

I looked to him and burst out laughing then I looked back at Valerie and said through my laughter, "I'm sure you know this but Chace watches *way* too much sports on TV. I'm trying to expand his horizons by introducing him to my television shows but he's reluctant. I'll admit, my shows are geeky, Valerie, but they're *awesome*. So I guess romance novels are *way* out of his realm of exciting dinner conversation."

She smiled at me and replied, "Then we'll endeavor to find something Chace likes to discuss."

"Do you know the Avs chances at the Stanley Cup this year?" I asked.

"No," she answered.

"Then perhaps we can talk him into explaining ballistics," I suggested, and it was Valerie's turn to burst out laughing.

Enrique came in with a tray of drinks and as he handed them around, Valerie wiped a non-existent tear of laughter from her eye and belatedly replied, "I fear, Faye, as interesting as my son is, if he explained ballistics, *I* would find it outside the realm of exciting dinner conversation to the point I'd fall asleep."

"Luckily your furniture is comfortable because I probably would too. Though I'd be worried I'd get my makeup on it if I stretched out to take a ballistics-induced nap," I told her.

"Then we'll retire to the less formal family room when Chace tells us about ballistics," she told me. "I don't mind makeup on my furniture but the furniture in there is much more comfortable."

"Two sleeping women in cocktail dresses. Terrific. Let's do that. You can sleep, I can put on the game," Chace muttered, and my eyes shot to Valerie.

"See!" I cried.

"I do indeed," she replied, grinning at me.

I took a sip of my wine, swallowed and lifted the glass to her. "This is delicious, Valerie."

"Do you know wine?" she asked.

"Not even a little," I admitted. "Just what I like to drink."

"Then you *must* go to Napa. You don't have to know wine to go to Napa. You just have to like it," she told me.

"Sounds the perfect vacation destination," I replied, she grinned again, seeming relaxed and looked at Chace.

"Lovely, darling. Faye enjoys wine like I do." She lifted her own wineglass. "Such a bother, Misty and all her cocktails. I never quite—"

Chace got tight at my side. Valerie got visibly tight across from us, her face paled and fear filled it again.

I instantly forged into the awkwardness and did it gently.

"I grew up in Carnal, Valerie, I knew Misty and that was very sad. But Chace and I are up front about things." *For the most part*, I thought but did not say, and went on, "But that was a while ago and Misty's not here to drink cocktails and although that's upsetting, we're here to enjoy wine and each other's company so we should learn from the loss of a young vital woman and do that."

"Of course," she muttered, looking uncomfortably at her knees.

"Valerie," I called, and her eyes skittered to me. I leaned forward when I got them and continued, "We don't know each other but we already have something important in common and that is we both care a lot about Chace. Please don't think you have to handle me with care. He thinks the world of you and shares it. So I knew I would too. I hope I win you over tonight so we can find out if we have more in common than Chace and Carly Phillips. But we should start that being open with each other and letting it shine through. Don't you agree?"

"You're very forthright," she said softly.

I wasn't really. I was just being forthright then for her *and* Chace.

"I hope you don't mind that," I said softly back.

"Not at all, Faye," she whispered.

"Good," I whispered back then carried on. "Just so you know, I'm normally very shy and quiet. But when the town's most handsome cop turned his eye my way, I got a little sassy."

She gave me a small grin and kept whispering to say, "I can imagine that happens."

I gestured to myself with my wineglass. "Living proof right here."

"Uh…do I exist in this conversation?" Chace asked, Valerie sat back, I sat back and Chace's arm on the back of the couch instantly moved to curve around my shoulders.

"Sorry, we were having a moment," I muttered, suddenly kind of embarrassed.

His arm curled me toward him so my eyes were forced to lift to his and when they did he murmured, "Yeah." But it was a "yeah" filled with approval.

He followed this with a lip touch.

I squirmed at his side and when his mouth left mine, I whispered super soft, "Your mom."

"Don't mind me," she chimed in, and Chace didn't uncurl me even though we both looked to Valerie to see her again beaming. "I think a man who's confident in displaying affection is very attractive, even and especially my son. Therefore this is something I taught him."

So I had her to thank.

I'd find another time to do that.

Instead, I just grinned.

Chace uncurled me and asked his mother, "Are we gonna eat in this millennium?"

"Chace, so impatient!" she snapped without any rancor whatsoever but on a doting smile.

"Not impatient. Hungry. I've been in an SUV for two hours and it's eight o'clock."

"You should have had a snack," Valerie admonished.

"Ma, Donatta doesn't serve anything less than three courses and her shit's the shit. I was not gonna have a snack and ruin it. But I am gonna gnaw off my own arm in about two seconds if Enrique doesn't show with some crackers and cheese."

"You shouldn't say the s-word," she told him.

"Does you tellin' me not to curse mean Enrique's not on his way with crackers and cheese?"

"Foie gras," she muttered.

"Well, clap or somethin' and get him to get a move on," Chace ordered, his lips tipped up, meaning he was teasing and Valerie looked to me.

"Have you noticed he can be annoying?"

"Um..." I mumbled then shut up.

"Smart, baby, don't answer that," Chace murmured on a shoulder squeeze.

"Her non-answer *is* her answer and it was affirmative," Valerie informed him.

"But it doesn't count because it wasn't verbalized," Chace informed his mother.

She rolled her eyes.

I smiled at their back and forth.

Chace got impatient.

"Seriously, Ma, pâté isn't my top choice but it's food. We gonna get that before Faye and I have to move in?"

She scowled at him then called loudly yet still daintily, "Enrique! You can serve the foie gras now."

"Fuckin' brilliant," Chace muttered.

"Chace!" Valerie snapped.

"Chace!" I semi-snapped.

"Not fuckin' brilliant," Chace muttered again, grinning.

I looked to Valerie. "He swears way too often."

"We're in accord over that, my dear," she replied snippily, still scowling at Chace.

Enrique walked in.

"Fuckin' brilliant," Chace muttered again, uncurling his arm from around my shoulders and leaning toward the tray instantly as Enrique set it on the table in front of us.

I looked to Valerie and rolled my eyes.

Valerie looked to me and did the same.

Then I sat forward to get my foie gras because Chace might not find it a top choice but it was one of my favorites in the whole world.

*   *   *

Dinner went great.

Then it happened.

We were in the less formal family room which was, indeed, less formal but it was still more formal than I was used to. I was thinking that I was glad the material of my dress had a little stretch because after that dinner, I needed it.

Not including the foie gras, it was four courses of rich, complicated food and not those elegant, minimalistic, rich, complicated food portions but vast portions even my mother would balk at serving. Nevertheless, it was delicious but it was *filling*.

Wine flowed freely and Valerie relaxed. Between my forthrightness and Chace's teasing, she already seemed relatively comfortable by the time we headed to the opulent dining room, its table laid with china, silver and crystal that was so delicate and refined, I suspected the Queen of England would find it a little daunting.

We'd only had one incident during dinner. This being that the flowers I'd ordered through Holly were gracing the table and Valerie calling my attention to them and expressing her gratitude so often that, in the end, I was running out of ways to say, "You're welcome."

Chace noticed this, it seemed to make him tense and eventually he muttered to his mother gently, "Ma, she gets it. You like 'em. Let it go, okay?"

At this, she got a bit fidgety and I thought she'd knock over her wineglass but I again forged into the breach, making some comment about Chace's horseshoe champagne glasses and how much I liked them. She beamed at the compliment, relaxed and settled in.

In fact, by the time we made it to the family room, I was wondering what all the drama was about. Sure, she seemed nervous, she seemed very much to want me to like her and have a good time and Chace seemed unhealthily attuned to it but it wasn't that bad.

Until suddenly, out of nowhere, when we were sitting and chatting in the family room, me finishing my last glass of wine knowing it was getting late and the drive was long so we'd be leaving soon, Valerie's eyes lit up. At the same time a wave of something immensely unpleasant flowed from Chace, filling the room.

Seemingly oblivious to Chace's emotion, Valerie set her glass aside, clasped her hands in front of her, her eyes shot back and forth between Chace and me and she instantly gave me the information I needed to understand what was going down.

"Trane is here!"

Uh-oh.

I tensed with Chace as Valerie babbled on, "He said he

was tied up, most likely wouldn't make it." She looked at me. "I was devastated. I *so* wanted you to meet him and Chace's father *so* wanted to meet you. I more *so* wanted Trane to meet you after I actually *met you* and you're *so very charming*. And now," she beamed between Chace and me, "he's here!"

She then shot to her feet and rushed from the room without another word.

I turned to Chace but as I was doing this, he got to his feet, hauling me up with him, announcing on a growl, "We're leavin'. Now."

I nodded and didn't say a word. I just bent and grabbed my bag as I went on alert because I could feel from his vibe that what would happen next would not go well.

I was not wrong though I had no idea how bad it would get. And I would have no clue that bad wouldn't happen until much later and it would be *very* bad.

We were coming into the foyer when we met Valerie and Trane.

I was not surprised to see, considering their money and Valerie's barely diminished by age looks, that Trane's father was also very dignified and attractive.

But I was surprised to see the resemblance Chace had to his father. They weren't mirror images of each other, Trane's hair had some gray mingled with the blond. But they were the same height, same build and Chace's eyes were the same color as Trane's. Although Chace was younger, the power and strength of his frame and stature not faded as Trane's somewhat had, there were more than a few similarities.

I didn't really get the chance to process this for, upon being in his father's presence, that emotion flowing from Chace ratcheted up around two dozen levels making it hard to breathe. But even though he couldn't miss it, Trane barely glanced at his son before he eyes lighted on me.

He sent a familiar but less natural and warm smile my way as he approached us.

"Faye," he moved toward me as I felt Chace, already close, weirdly start crowding me, "what a delight. So pleased I made it home in time to meet you."

Not knowing what to do considering everything about Chace screamed I should run for the hills but Trane was giving me a welcoming smile while Valerie stood to the side beaming with obvious pleasure, I simply locked my body but allowed Trane to take my hand.

It was when Trane touched me, the stifling emotion rolling off Chace hit the danger zone, but I was caught. I could do nothing but allow Trane to lift my hand and touch his lips to my knuckles even when Chace's arm slid around my waist, his fingers digging in and his mood blanketing the room.

I hadn't been around rich people so I couldn't know, maybe they kissed fingers as a matter of course, but even if Chace wasn't being weird, I wouldn't have liked him kissing my knuckles. It was debonair, I'd seen it happen before in movies but it also was a bit creepy. Furthermore, he couldn't miss Chace's possessive claiming tactics that shouted *stand back!* Thus he couldn't miss he was putting me in an extremely awkward position and that wasn't nice to me or his son.

Trane straightened and dropped my hand but didn't release it when he continued to ignore his son and looked in my eyes. For my part, I was again caught, wanting to put pressure on my hand for him to release it at the same time thinking that might be rude.

"You're lovely. What a shame I wasn't able to be there while you graced my table."

"Thank you," I whispered.

"Let her go," Chace growled low enough his mother

wouldn't hear but his father definitely did because he let me go.

His eyes cut to his son.

"Chace," he greeted. "You're looking well."

"We're also leaving," Chace replied, moving me around Trane toward his mother. I could hear the effort it took him to modulate his voice when he spoke to her. "Sorry, Ma, but we have to hit the road."

Her face fell instantly showing she wasn't disappointed, she was devastated.

Thus she leaned in beseechingly. "Couldn't you stay for just one more drink so Trane can relax and chat with you and your charming Faye?"

"No," Chace replied tersely, not to mention rudely, leaned in, kissed her cheek then moved back and told her, "I'll call. Maybe in a coupla weeks you can come to Carnal, spend the weekend."

"But—" she started but Chace's arm gave my waist a squeeze, I took his meaning and moved forward.

"Lovely dinner," I murmured, curling my hand reassuringly on her upper arm and leaning in to touch my cheek against hers. "I enjoyed it very much, the food," I moved back, caught her eyes and gave her arm a squeeze before I finished, "and especially the company."

She grabbed my hand and leaned in too and she did this in order to throw me right under the bus.

"Please, Faye, talk to Chace. Just a drink. The whole family," she pleaded.

She wanted that, badly, and I knew Chace was not going to give it to her.

I was saved from having to reply when Chace moved me firmly away from her and stated, "We gotta go."

He then instantly guided us toward the front of the foyer, stopping at a door and opening it.

"Just a drink. Fifteen minutes," Valerie urged, her tone edging toward desperate.

Chace came out with my coat but his eyes sliced to his father. I fancied I knew him well, but you didn't have to know him well to know he was telling his father to shut this down. Now.

Trane read this and moved to his wife, murmuring, "It's late, love. They should be making their way."

Her voice was rising to the point there was a hint of hysteria in it when she returned, "Fifteen minutes! That's all I ask. Fifteen minutes with my family all together."

"Fuck," Chace clipped under his breath.

He'd helped me on with my coat so I was unfortunately free again to forge into the breach.

"It really is late and it's also a long drive. I've had to work today, your food was delicious but with that, work, wonderful wine but lots of it and good company, I'm afraid I'm dead on my feet. I'll probably fall asleep in the car." I smiled at her. "Not to mention, it's past Chace's bedtime. So, to be safe, we should be getting home. It really was so lovely meeting you and," I turned my eyes to Trane, "having the chance to meet you too." I looked back at Valerie. "And I hope you take Chace up on coming to spend the weekend. I can show you my library and make you dinner."

Her face moved like she was fighting tears, Trane shifted into her and slid his arm along her waist, this seeming to give her the strength to fight the tears back and nod.

"Of course, you're right, Faye. It is late and you and Chace should be on your way," she whispered with clear disappointment.

I approached her and took her hand. "I hope to see you again soon."

"Yes," she agreed, her hand limp in mine but I still gave it a squeeze.

"Faye," Chace called shortly, I looked over my shoulder at him and nodded.

I looked back at Valerie, letting my eyes move through Trane and I said, "Thank you for a lovely evening."

"My pleasure," she muttered, her eyes beyond me on Chace, her melancholy obvious, extreme and alarming.

Chace ignored this, claimed me by grabbing my hand and his only farewell was, "Ma. I'll call."

He didn't say one word or even look at his father.

Then we were out the door, down the steps and hoofing it to the Yukon. Chace bleeped the locks, walked me to my door, yanked it open and practically picked me up to plant me in the passenger seat.

I barely cleared my feet from the door when it was slammed and Chace was prowling around the hood.

I looked to the front door, saw Valerie and Trane there, his arm around her shoulders, her look despondent, his blank. I lifted my hand and gave them a happy wave that I hoped didn't look stupid or, worse, forced.

Chace angled in, started up the Yukon and executed a tight turn in the large space of the front drive and we were on our way.

He, incidentally, didn't wave. He didn't even glance at his parents.

I gave it time and when we were close to hitting Aspen proper, I whispered, "Chace—"

"I hate him, you know that," he cut me off to say curtly. "I love her, you know that too. You wanna sleep on the way home, sleep. But I do not wanna talk so if you're not sleepin', do me a favor and give me quiet."

I bit my lip.

Then I gave him quiet.

And I endured his heavy mood all the way home without sleep not having any idea the worst was yet to come.

CHAPTER SEVENTEEN

Always

IT WAS VERY late when we hit my apartment, after one in the morning.

The drive had been silent, Chace's mood not lifting, not in the slightest.

The very much shorter walk up my stairs to my apartment had been silent too.

I was wandering the space, turning on lights, trying to decide what to do, what to say and wishing I could go to the bathroom and call Laurie, Lexie, Krys or Twyla to ask when Chace spoke.

"Headin' home."

I was standing on my side of the bed, turning on the light but at his words, like a shot, my back went straight and my eyes cut to him standing in his coat by the door.

Since the night he took my virginity, we never slept apart. Not once. We never even went to bed without the other.

Not once.

I didn't have a good feeling about this.

"What?" I whispered.

He didn't repeat himself.

Instead, he said, "You go on to your folks tomorrow without me. I'll call you Monday. Maybe Tuesday."

Monday?

Maybe Tuesday?

A chill slid over my skin even though I still had my coat on but I didn't move a muscle and stared at him.

He finished, "Later, Faye."

Later, Faye?

No kiss. No touch. No darlin', honey or baby.

Just *later, Faye*.

He was at the door when I called on a stammer, "I... you... Chace, what's going on?"

He turned at the door and leveled his eyes on me. "Need space, you do too. This is happening fast. Too fast for me, where I am. Too fast for you, this bein' your first relationship. Just slowin' us down, givin' us time, takin' that time to sort my head."

Sort his head?

What was there to sort?

My heart started pumping so hard, I could actually feel it.

"I... I don't... it doesn't *feel* fast," I told him cautiously.

"Well, it is," he told me firmly then he was done and I knew it when he started to turn back to the door, muttering, "Call you Tuesday."

He didn't move in slow motion but it felt like he did as thoughts collided in my brain.

Lots of them.

Too many.

Weeks of them.

And they did this so fast it felt like my head was going to explode.

Then I felt my shoulders square with a snap and I stated, "You'll call me Tuesday."

He looked back at me and, sounding impatient, he confirmed, "Yeah. That's what I said. I'll call you Tuesday."

"I've seen you every day, slept beside you every night for weeks and all of a sudden I not only won't see you but I won't hear from you for two days."

"Right," he replied.

"You told me I wouldn't sleep without you," I reminded him and finished, "ever. Now you're saying I won't sleep with you for two days?"

A muscle worked in his jaw but he didn't speak.

My heart started racing.

I changed tactics.

"What if I don't want to wait until Tuesday?" I asked.

He shook his head. "Faye, it's late. I'm wiped. We'll talk Tuesday."

"Would it matter to you that I'd rather you didn't leave right now but we either talk about whatever's obviously seriously bothering you or you allow me to see to you in other ways?"

"No, it wouldn't because I'm tired. I been thinkin' on the way home and I'm tellin' you the way you can see to me is to give me space. So, you'll give me space and we'll talk Tuesday."

I'd give him space. He decided and that was it.

It hit me just then that Chace decided a lot and that was it.

And it also hit me that whenever my girlfriends told me their boyfriends needed space, they didn't need space, as such, they needed something else entirely.

So I made a decision, my first in our relationship.

"No we won't," I announced, and his brows drew together.

Then he took in a calming breath, clearly tamping down his irritation that he was dealing with his inexperienced girlfriend, and he explained, "When I say I need space, Faye, when anyone wants space, it's important to give it to them."

Oh no.

Frak no.

He might be my first pretty much everything but I wasn't seventeen and exploring the ways of the world. I was twenty-

fraking-nine, not stupid, I had my own opinions, my own
desires, my own needs and they were just as valid as his.

Last, I was suddenly so over this I could scream.

I didn't scream.

I invited, shrugging off my coat, "Great, take *a lot* of it."

He turned fully away from the door and asked, "What?"

"Take a lot of it," I repeated, moving and tossing my coat
on a stool as I made my way to the kitchen. "You want it.
You have it. But don't bother calling me on Tuesday."

His barely there patience slipped when he declared,
"Jesus, Faye, it's fuckin' late, I'm fuckin' tired. I'm tellin'
you what I need so you can read into that what I don't need is
a fuckin' drama."

"No drama." I pulled open a cupboard to nab a wineglass. I closed the cupboard, turned to him but didn't look at
him as I reached for the bottle of wine on my counter, finishing, "Just giving you space. Plenty of it."

"Fine," he stated as I squeezed the plastic thingie Chace
had shoved into the bottle last night and pumped the air out
of so the wine would keep, heartbreakingly sad I was doing
that because Chace had done it like he always did it and my
earlier decision meant Chace would never do it again.

"But don't call Wednesday," I told the wine.

"Jesus." I heard him clip.

"Or Thursday." I kept at it as I poured my wine.

"Fuckin' hell, Faye."

"Or Friday," I went on as I turned the bottle in my hand
to stop the flow without it dripping.

"Faye, this isn't a big deal."

Not to him.

But it was to me.

Though he obviously didn't care.

I set the bottle on the counter, lifted my eyes to him and
concluded, "Or at all."

His body went visibly solid and his mood again blanketed the room as his eyes locked on mine.

I kept talking.

"You're right, you didn't say it but I get it. I'm inexperienced. I need guidance in this relationship business. I don't know what I'm doing half the time." I took a sip of wine, held his gaze as I did, lowered my glass and swallowed. "But you don't have to know about relationships to know that no matter how wonderful a man may seem, how he makes you feel, it is not okay for him to keep things from you. It is not okay that, even though he's going through serious stuff in his head, he lashes out and rips you to shreds. It is not okay that, although he's more experienced than you, he doesn't guide the relationship but controls it with an iron fist. So you want time and I have no say in the matter? Take it. *A lot of it.*"

His expression shifted and at the shift, I braced.

"You're makin' a bigger deal of this than it is, honey," he said softly but didn't move toward me. "After what happened tonight, I just need some time to get my head together."

"What happened tonight?" I asked.

Chace didn't answer.

When it was important, Chace never really answered.

"Right," I muttered, my heart squeezing and it didn't feel good at all. I took a sip of wine and didn't get what women were always talking about in regard to drinking wine during heartbreak. It didn't make me feel even a little bit better.

Maybe I needed more of it.

Like, a case.

Chace didn't move.

"You aren't leaving," I prompted, pleased with myself that my voice didn't crack because tears were rushing up my throat.

"I'll call you Tuesday," he whispered.

I lifted my wineglass his way and invited, "You do that."

He didn't move.

I took another sip of wine.

When I lowered my glass, reading me yet again, he noted, "You're not gonna answer."

"Nope," I replied, sounding shockingly cavalier considering my insides were bleeding.

"Faye—" he started, taking a step toward me.

I shook my head and lifted a hand his way. "Unh-unh, no. Door's the other way, Chace."

He rocked to a halt, his chin jerked down and to the side in a motion that made it look like he'd been struck then he righted his head and reminded me, "You told me you'd never show me the door."

"I changed my mind," I fired back.

He studied me a moment while I hoped to all frak I gave nothing away then remarked, "You know my family's fucked up."

"No. I know your mother is mentally ill and I know this is not in her control, it isn't her choice. It's an illness like any other illness and it's nothing to get tense or be embarrassed about. If she had diabetes, cancer, it wouldn't reflect on her in any way. But because she is how she is, *you* are how *you* are, thinking I'll judge her or maybe both of you because of something out of either of your control. That's not nice and I don't like it."

"Faye—"

I interrupted him. "And I don't know about your father. You've told me some but not all, definitely not what would drive you to behave the way you did tonight. For your mother's sake, it seems a not difficult thing to do, putting up with him for fifteen minutes to shield her from that emotion. *He* seemed capable of doing that for her. But obviously, whatever it is runs deeper. And obviously, you don't intend to share it with me."

"It *is* deeper," he shared, just not much because he didn't go on.

"No kidding?" I asked, hiding my despair behind sarcasm.

"Give me time," he urged quietly.

"How much do you need, Chace? A year? Ten? Twenty?" I shot back, now hiding behind anger.

"It isn't pleasant," he whispered.

"So is a lot of stuff in life," I replied. "Clue in, I am not your mother. Yes, I read. And yes, I do it a lot. And yes, I did it before you because life can suck and living in a fantasy world is a lot more fun than living in the real world sometimes. This was not a weak choice, it was an informed one. The cops in my town were dirty, my father was getting pulled over all the time because he didn't like it and didn't mind saying it but didn't have the power to stop it. Innocent men like Ty Walker were being extradited states away to stand trial for murders they didn't commit. Women who weren't all that nice but still, that doesn't matter, were being murdered. My friends got cheated on by their boyfriends or dumped after they slept with them or lied to or broken up with for what seemed no reason at all. You know I can go on. There's not one thing wrong with saying, 'To hell with that garbage,' and immersing myself in worlds where happily-ever-afters *are* guaranteed or things are so fantastical, you know they're not real, even the bad stuff. But that doesn't mean I'm weak or fragile. It doesn't mean I'm incapable of living my life. Everyone finds things they enjoy so they can escape. I'm not a freak. Even you do it with your sports. Part of me likes that you want to protect me from unpleasantness but part of me feels like it's a slap in the face that you think I can't cope when I can."

He took another step toward me saying, "It's worse than you could expect."

"Okay," I returned instantly. "Maybe it is. But you not sharing tells me you don't trust me to be able to handle it. Which means you don't trust me to hold up my side of the relationship. Which means we don't actually *have* a relationship. I don't have to have had one to know that both people in a relationship have responsibilities for keeping it strong and making it thrive and part of that is taking each other's backs. You have mine but refuse to allow me to take yours. I've been cool. I've been patient. I've given you time. You want more, take it but don't drag me with you as you struggle with this crap, Chace. Because the longer we're together the more *you* should get to know *me,* come to the understanding I can handle it and trust me. You aren't even close to that. That tells me you won't be. So you want to keep your dark secrets, let them eat at you, fine. But don't make me watch it happen."

"So what you're sayin' is, hours ago, you told me you love me and now, I want a couple of days to get my head straight, you're breakin' up with me," he said low, a warning. A warning I no longer gave a frak about.

"Yes," I replied.

"Just like that?" he asked.

"No, it's never happened to me before but I doubt after I fell head-over-heels in love with a wonderful man who kept important things from me, I'll get over it just like that. I'll drink with my girls and cry and wonder if I made the right decision. Then another man will come along, he won't be as wonderful as my first love, but I suppose I'll eventually get over it and move on."

This was the way, way, *way* wrong thing to say and I knew it when the air went from smothering to stifling and Chace moved.

I tried to keep my cool as I watched him shrug off his coat and throw it over the footboard of my bed and I did this by sharing, "It's cold, Chace, and the door's the other way."

His eyes sliced to me and he clipped, "Stop that shit."

"What shit?" I asked

"The cold, remote Faye. It's shit," he answered.

"You're right. It is. It's a façade to hide the fact my heart is breaking. But, whatever. That isn't your problem anymore. Now, can I point out, you told me you need space but you're still fraking here?"

"Another man is not gonna come along," he informed me, and I stared.

Then I asked, "What?"

"You are not movin' on to another guy," he crossed his arms on his chest and finished, "Ever."

"That choice is not yours."

"Yeah it is," he returned swiftly. "You can't give away what's mine."

"You aren't getting this, Chace, but just now, I took it back."

"Can't take back what's mine either."

God! He wanted to go, why wouldn't he just *go*?

I had to shut this down.

"I thought you were tired," I reminded him.

"Thought of movin' on," he stated, and I was back to staring.

Then I thought I got it, it hurt but whatever. I had wine and, tomorrow, I'd call the girls and then, in about fifty years, I'd get better so I invited, "There's the door. Move on."

"Was this close to it," he continued.

"Chace—"

"Then you came back into town."

I felt my head jerk in surprised confusion.

Chace kept speaking.

"Decided with one look at you, I'd put up with it, all the shit that was gettin' worse at work 'cause my end game would be you."

Was he saying what I thought he was saying?

"The town's sweet, cute, quiet, pretty librarian in my bed, my ring on her finger, enjoyin' it as I taught her how to enjoy it, plantin' my babies in her, building a family."

Holy fraking *frak*!

He *was* saying what I thought he was saying!

No, he was saying *more*.

I stopped breathing.

He continued talking.

"One look, at the grocery store, you in the aisle, your nose in a book. Stared at you, so fuckin' cute, but I had no clue how you could shop and keep your nose in a book. But there you were, doin' it. You looked up, saw someone you knew, smiled at them and I knew eatin' all that shit at work would be worth it when I was ready to make my play. That cute in my bed. That hair. Those eyes. That smile. Definitely worth it. So I ate it, bidin' my time, gettin' the wild out of me so all I'd give you was sweet. You'd move to Gnaw Bone, Chantelle, I knew you would so I could kiss that bullshit good-bye, get myself out of it without takin' you away from the folks you loved when I claimed you."

Holy frickity fraking frak, frak, *frak*!

I forced air in my lungs.

Chace moved toward me and kept talking.

"Waited too long."

I watched him come to me, my heart beginning to beat harder and my feet no longer not moving because I was trying to be cool but because I was frozen solid with shock. He came to a halt one foot from me so I tipped my head back to look at him.

He lifted a hand, pulled the wineglass from mine and set it on the counter with an alarming-sounding *clink*.

I looked at the glass in a vague effort to ascertain that it wasn't broken then I tilted my head back to look back at him, mouth open but I didn't say a word.

He did.

"He touched you."

I blinked because I didn't understand his words.

"What?"

"He touched you," Chace repeated.

"Who?" I asked.

"My father. He wasn't only in your presence, you, my Faye, *mine*, cute and clean and sweet, he *touched* you. Took your hand, held it." He stopped speaking abruptly, sucked breath in through his nose then bit out, "Put his *mouth on you*."

Okay, now, what on earth?

"So?" I asked quietly when he said no more.

"He likes kink."

I blinked again because these words were unexpected and also I didn't know what they meant.

"What?"

"Kink," he ground out then, "sex, darlin', can get adventurous and you don't carry on with this bullshit play you got goin' on, we'll have time, I'll show you how and we'll explore that in good ways that we both like. But it can also get weird. To each their own. I don't give a fuck what someone does to get off. What I do not need to know is that my dad likes it weird and when I say weird I mean sick-fuck, turn-your-stomach," he leaned into me for emphasis even though he put undeniable verbal emphasis on his final word, "*weird*."

I didn't want to know this. I didn't want him to know this. I didn't know why he was sharing this. And I didn't want to know *how* he knew this.

But he told me.

"Misty and a girlfriend took an assignment from Arnie Fuller and they did that shit to my dad. They also taped it. They also blackmailed him with it. And I've seen that tape."

My mouth dropped open as my stomach clenched and bile filled my throat.

I closed my mouth to swallow it down.

Chace's eyes moved over my face and when they locked on mine, he whispered, "Yeah. That unpleasant enough for you, Faye?"

It definitely was.

"I—" I started.

"Gets worse," he cut me off, and I blinked again.

Worse?

How could *that* possibly get *worse*?

Chace told me.

"Her play, soon's you get over the shock of learning that jacked-up shit, you'd figure out. But still, I'll tell you. She used that tape to get money from my dad. Arnie used it to get my dad under his thumb and Misty used it more to get my ring on her finger. They played that tape for me and told me the way. Either I marry Misty and toe the dirty cop line or my mom sees that tape. So I wind up with a fuckin' *wife* who did my dad dirty in more than one way. I got that shit burned in my brain and her slut ass sleepin' in my fuckin' bed. Top that, through that shit, I know what they're doin' to Ty, I know why and I can't do one fuckin' thing to stop it or my mom pays. In the end for all I know, I got no shot at anything, Misty doesn't let me go or shit doesn't get cleaned up. No future. No family. No *you*. Nothin' that I wanted, wanted all my life, important things like a woman I loved in my bed and kids we made under the roof I provided by doin' good work I was proud of. Just a bitch in my bed and a dad who cheats on my mom and *how* he cheats a memory I will never, ever erase."

Oh my fraking *God*.

"Chace—" I whispered.

"You want more?"

My heart seized.

"More?" I breathed.

"Yeah, Faye," he leaned in deeper, "*more*."

I didn't but I would take it. Still, he didn't give me the chance to accept or refuse.

He kept right on going.

"Before Misty, before she did that to my dad, I was Frank. I did what I could for the citizens of this town knowin' things were gettin' ugly but keepin' my nose clean. I worked my brothers, hopin' they'd turn from the dark side. After they had me, after I saw that tape, I had no choice but to join their ranks. My mother saw that, tonight, she was good, tonight, you helped her keep it together but she saw that, Faye, trust me, she'd unravel. Hospital stay. My count since I could remember, she's had four. One lasted six months. This would destroy her. If by some miracle she got better, she couldn't live with him. Problem is, she can't live without him. Knowin' that, knowin' she had nothin' good to get out for, she might *never* recover. I don't want my mother in a hospital the next thirty years. I got no choice. Keep my mouth shut, take my envelopes filled with dirty money, look the other way and step up when they gave me an assignment."

"You returned the money," I reminded him quietly. "It said so in the papers."

"Yeah, but when my father's cronies, the Elite, got their shit in another mess, this mess involving Arnie, a mess that had to be sorted with muscle behind a badge, they sent me. With no choice, I went."

I didn't understand.

"Chace, I don't—"

"A man tried to horn in on Arnie's blackmail and extortion business and they sent me to talk him down. Except, to talk him down, I had to use my fists and with that tape in an envelope ready to be couriered to my mother, I had no choice but to do it."

I understood then and, involuntarily, my feet took me

a step back and, not that he could, but still, Chace didn't miss it.

"Yeah," he whispered, his face as hard and harsh as his voice, "see that dark gathering now, don't you, baby?"

"You went to Internal Affairs," I whispered.

"Yeah, I did. I took as much of it as I could stomach then I swung my mother's ass out there and went to IA. Fun choice, my mother's mental health or my ass."

"And the town," I added.

"Yeah, and the town. Detective Chace Keaton, the courageous hero who brought down a band of dirty cops. They hid the fact I *was* one. They hid the fact that for years I did shit or didn't do shit I should have when people were getting fucked. Not just a little, like your dad gettin' pulled over, which, by the way, Faye, I knew was happening but couldn't stop. But a lot, like Ty Walker losin' five fuckin' years of his fuckin' life rotting in a prison states away, doin' time for a crime he did not commit. Your dad said when a wrong's bein' done, you're no person he'd want to know if you don't do what you can to make it right. You live by that too, and I'm that person you don't wanna know."

"Chace, you *did* something," I reminded him.

"And, before, I did other things, Faye. I *was* that wrong."

"You were forced to be."

He shook his head. "A stronger man would not have been forced to be."

"Your mother—"

"I could have walked away," he told me.

"I wouldn't have," I returned instantly.

At my words, his body jolted.

I kept talking.

"Someone intended to harm my mom, dad, Liza, the boys, any of my family or someone I loved, I'd do what I could to stop it. Anyone who loves someone would."

"Even lie down with filth?" he asked, disbelief heavy in his tone.

"Whatever it took," I answered.

He shook his head. "No, darlin', easy to say, harder to do."

"I don't mean it was easy, I mean I would do it."

"You wouldn't."

"You can't know that."

"I can. You were raised by Silas and Sondra Goodknight. You would make the right choice. I was raised by Trane and Valerie Keaton. I made the wrong one."

"You made the *only* choice."

"In hindsight, everything seems clear, but at the time, it was not and I had choices. I just didn't make the right ones."

"You loved her and your hand was forced. It took you a while but you eventually saw your way clear and got the town clear and, incidentally, it's debatable if that was the right choice since I can assume it made her more vulnerable than she already is."

"And before that, Faye, I *beat* a man into givin' me shit he was holdin' over a bunch of men who didn't deserve that effort."

I felt my flinch and saw his face get harder when he caught it but I powered through.

"You did it for Valerie."

"I did wrong."

"You did what you had to do."

"Yeah, and it...was...*wrong.*"

But I'd had enough.

And so had Chace.

It was time to break through.

"God!" I threw up my hands, losing it. "Do you *not* understand that the power behind the love of your actions for your mother and, what you don't get, Chace, also for your father is a beautiful thing you should be *proud of*?"

His body locked.

I didn't catch it. I was on a mission and was already too far gone.

"Do you not think that I don't think that, if you loved me that much, if you turned your back on everything that was you in order to protect me, that I wouldn't love you *more*? Love you more because you loved me so much you'd do everything you could to keep me safe? Even going so far as losing *you*? But what you don't get, Chace, is that you never lost you. What *they* did was wrong. What *you* did was *right*."

Chace didn't move, not even to twitch and I still didn't catch it.

I was on a roll.

"If you made another decision because you were all fired up to be the man *you* had to be, to protect the future *you* wanted, *that* would have been selfish. The choice you had was no choice at all. Save someone you love from a breakdown or save a town and your own ass. You've lived your whole fraking life protecting her. You'd been conditioned since birth to make that play. But even so, you actually took the *harder* road to do the *right* thing even if it meant you were forced to do *wrong* while you were on that road. It was selfless, it was brave and it was *heroic*. More so because, God willing, Valerie will never know you had to do the things you did to protect her. So she's shielded from that too, knowing the way she is that she can't help meant her son went through that for *her*. So you did it knowing you'd not even earn her gratitude. You did it knowing all you'd get is shit but she'd have peace of mind."

Chace just stared at me, unmoving.

I kept ranting.

"If my father knew this, he'd admire you. If my mother knew this, she'd adore you. If the town knew this, they'd revere you more than they already *do*."

"Right," he said softly. "You think you got that figured out, then what about Misty?"

"What about her?" I snapped.

"She was my wife. I treated her like shit. I cheated on her and, in the end, I didn't protect her."

Not this again!

"Fraking heck, Chace!" I clipped. "She wasn't your wife, she was your albatross! Your prison warden. Ty spent five years behind bars. *You* spent *six* in a different kind of prison. It isn't even *sane* what she did to you, thinking you would get over it and fall in love or *attempt* to find even minimal contentment in that kind of arrangement. I couldn't wrap my head around what she did to Ty and I *really* can't wrap my head around what she did to *you*. It was the same and yet it was *worse*. You didn't like her so you didn't pretend to like her. You didn't marry her for love so you carried on with your life like she wasn't there. *She* bought that by doing... doing..." I faltered, too beside myself to find words then sallied forth, "what you would call seriously jacked-up shit. When she was alive, *you* didn't give her a thing she didn't deserve including what happened to end her life. That is also not on you whether you shoulder it or not. Shouldering it is your *decision*, not your responsibility, not your curse. Your *decision*. One you can also decide not to do. No one, but no one who thinks clearly, and they don't even have to love you like I do, would disagree with me."

"Baby—" he started on a tortured whisper but I was still gone.

"No!" I snapped, lifting a hand between us. "I'm not done. I know you're older and more experienced than me but what *you* need to know is that if you trusted me with that information about your father, as vile as it is, it would have given me the tools to handle tonight a lot differently. I could have avoided his touch so that wouldn't upset you and I could have smoothed our departure so your mother wouldn't get distressed. If I was aware of the situation, I could have finessed it. Which I will do in the future if we have a future that doesn't include me wanting to kick you in the shin or attempt to shake some sense into you even though you're bigger and stronger than me and if I can control my desire to punch your father in the nose!"

I was working myself up and getting louder as I carried right the frak on.

"I mean, I can't believe this! *This* is your dark? *This* is your big secret that's going to drive me away? *This* is what's eating you? The fact you're a good man, a fantastic son and when faced with impossible choices that would bring most men to their knees, you carry on being wonderful, taking care of runaway, abused kids, teasing your new girlfriend, making her feel like a princess and giving her amazing orgasms?" I leaned into him, eyes narrowed, "Seriously?"

Then I wasn't leaning into him anymore because I was over his shoulder, he'd turned and was prowling to the bed.

"Chace!" I snapped at his back. "I'm not done ranting!"

He bumped me on his shoulder. I sucked in breath as I flew through the air, landing on my back in bed and I didn't get another breath in me before he landed on top of me.

"You're done," he growled in my face.

"I am *not*," I hissed in his.

Then I was since he was kissing me hard and the fingers of one his hands were pulling down the zip at the back of my dress.

Okay, that kiss was good, better than most and they were all super good so that was saying something. Apparently, heightened emotions made for effective kisses.

Still, when he tore his mouth from mine, I ranted on, if a little breathlessly, "I'm not done straightening you *out*."

Chace's response was non-verbal. His body arced away

from mine and *whoosh!* My dress was pulled over my head, taking my arms with it. When it was gone, Chace's hand was on my belly, his eyes on my body.

"Knew it, that dress, you sittin' next to me all night, knew you'd give me this later," he muttered to himself, his hand gliding down my belly so his fingertips could trail the waistband of my panties.

He liked the undies. Nice to know but nothing new.

"Hello?" I called, and his eyes came to mine. "We're fighting, remember?"

Two things happened at once. Chace's lips came to within a breath from mine and Chace's hand slid into my panties.

I stopped breathing.

"Get ready, baby, you're about to get something new."

"And that would be?" I asked tartly (but still breathlessly which took the sting out of my tart, unfortunately), putting my hands on his shoulders, preparing to push.

"Make-up sex," he answered, his fingers in my panties moved in a way I liked and my belly plummeted and my fingers, instead of pushing (frak!) curled into his jacket.

I fought his pull and informed him sharply, "We aren't done fighting."

"Yeah we are."

"No we're not."

His middle finger slid hard over my clit and then glided deep inside and it felt so fraking good, I gasped, my hips jerked but the rest of my body melted under his.

I was hazy but I could still feel his lips smile against mine before he muttered, "Oh yeah we are."

Then he kissed me and we were.

Done fighting that was.

We weren't done with other things.

Sex, as I'd mentioned before, was *awesome*.

Make-up sex was *out of this world*.

Heightened emotion didn't only make for effective kisses, it made for effective *everything*.

I didn't think either of us held back during sex. Sometimes Chace controlled the intensity. It was rare but it could happen that I might get a little timid with nudity but Chace had a mind to that and never pushed.

But after you'd almost just broken up with your boyfriend whom you loved even though his best friend told you not to. After he'd shared with you he'd taken one look at you and knew he wanted to spend the rest of his life with you then let you into his deepest, darkest secrets that were way deep and scary dark. After that, you didn't think of anything.

Not anything.

But each other and using that emotion and anything else you had to make the bad go away and bring on the good.

And the good was *good*.

It was all hands, mouths, fingers, tongues, rolling, yanking at clothes, tugging at shoes, tossing them away, then clenching, scratching, licking, sucking, biting, positioning, gasping, groaning, whimpering and growling.

Then Chace took over and did me on my knees and two seconds before I would find it, he pulled out, dropped to his back beside me, yanked me over him and he made me ride him. Which I did, hard, my eyes on him hooded, my hips moving fast, grinding deep, my hands sliding over his chest.

Then I was on my back, Chace's hips pumping between my legs, he was up with one hand in the bed, arm straight, one of my knees hooked around it, the other hand between my legs, thumb right where I needed it.

And, oh God, it felt *good*.

So good I was *this close* again and it wasn't going to be good. It was going to be *fantastic*.

Chace drove in deep, stayed planted and ground his hips into mine.

"Faye," he growled, I forced my neck to right and tried to focus on him. "No one gets in here but me," he declared, making his point grinding deeper into me.

"Okay," I breathed.

"No one, Faye."

"Okay, honey."

He pulled out, slammed and ground in again. "Ever, Faye."

"Ever, Chace."

He pulled out, slammed and ground in and ordered, "Say it again."

"Ever."

Another slam and grind then, "My name, baby."

"Chace," I whimpered, shifting under him, so fraking, *fraking* close.

He released my knee and fell to his forearm in the bed beside me. It shoved under and his fingers curled around the back of my neck.

I instantly wrapped my leg around his hip, tipped my head up and, his lips against mine, he whispered, "Do you love me?"

"Yes," I breathed.

"Always?"

He wasn't thrusting hard and grinding deep. His rhythm was smoother, gentler, beautiful and I finally focused on him, my arms gliding around him to hold tight.

"Always," I whispered.

Chace slanted his head and kissed me, his tongue sliding into my mouth and I came.

I took him through it, after it and, when his thrusts grew faster, more powerful, driving deep, I felt it and loved it after he buried his face in my neck and groaned low against my skin.

He started gliding in and out and I took that too, loving it, before he slid in deep and stopped and one of his curls came to my attention. My hand moving of its own volition slid up his back, my fingers closed on it and I gave it a little tug, giving myself a little happy shiver doing it.

"Apparently," he started in a mutter, talking to my neck, "I wasn't tired."

I closed my eyes, let his curl go and circled his hip with my other leg so I could hold him tight with everything I had available to me.

"But unfortunately," he went on, "when you're way pissed, you lay off the geek references so you make way too much fuckin' sense."

That meant I got through.

Thank you, God, I got through.

I opened my eyes and dipped my chin so my lips were at the skin under his ear, the skin of my upper lip tickled by his unruly curls and I whispered, "Chace."

His head came up and I caught my breath at the look on his face, warmth, regret and something else, something huge, something that made my heart skip.

"I should have told you earlier. I should have trusted you. I should have read all the things you were sayin' to me with the way you were with me, for me and with Malachi and knew you could handle it. I was wrong, baby, and I fucked up. But I love you, Faye, and protection going hand in hand with love is all I know," he admitted quietly.

My chest depressed as my eyes started stinging.

What I saw on his face was love.

He loved me.

Loved me.

"You love me?" I whispered, just to confirm.

"Fell in love with you in a grocery store aisle and you didn't even know I was there."

"I probably did," I confessed, and his lips tipped up but it wasn't teasing and sweet, it was strangely sad.

"Then you did but I didn't know. You wanted me, I wanted you, I sat on what I wanted and fucked up my life."

"You didn't fuck up your life, Chace."

"If I moved on you when I wanted to, you'd have been in my bed the last seven years and Misty wouldn't have seen it. Ty wouldn't have—"

I squeezed him with all my limbs and whispered harshly, "Stop."

He shut his mouth.

I went on, "Nothing can change what happened but one thing *can* change and that's you feeling that the world is on your shoulders. Another thing that's all you know since your mom is ill and has been your whole life is thinking you're responsible for everything around you, that you can fix it, make it better or at least cushion everyone's fall. Your dad, when you were growing up, should have protected you from that too. Proving he's not only the worst father in the world but also the worst in history, he clearly didn't."

"I won't give him much, honey, but you live with that in your house, it's impossible to shield a child from it."

"That's debatable and you're right, I didn't live it, but am I right that he didn't try?"

Chace slid out of me, rolled us to our sides, pulled my hair away from my face but kept his fingers in it before he answered quietly, "You're right. He didn't try."

Both his arms closed around me tight, gathering me closer even as his hand didn't leave my hair but his legs tangled with mine and he carried on.

"Not to get you riled up again but I get him. It's different, girls and boys. A man will want his son to step up."

"Maybe so but I know I'm not wrong when I tell you it's different also between children and adults. Children aren't expected to step up until it's time to teach them to be adults.

But before you do that, you have to let them be children. It's a guess, but you never got that."

He closed his eyes and tipped his head so our foreheads were touching but not before I saw that raw look wash over his face and I finally got it.

And I hated it.

He opened his eyes, pulled his head back half an inch and confirmed what I just figured out.

"I never got that," he whispered.

I stared in his beautiful face, feeling his awesome chest hair teasing my breasts, his powerful arms around me, his heavy legs tangled in mine, his heat seeping into me. I took this all in and instead of it along with the end of our fight, the knowledge of his love, the lingering orgasm soothing me, I got pissed.

And when I say that, I mean, I . . . got . . . *pissed*.

So this was why I informed him, "You know, even Darth Vader had the good grace to *ask* Luke to join him on the dark side."

Chace blinked then his arms got tight.

But it was too late.

Way too late.

I was gone.

"I mean, they were fighting to the death and he cut off Luke's hand but still, he gave him the fraking *choice*."

"Faye—" he started, my name trembling with humor but this was lost on me.

Totally.

"But Trane Keaton?" I asked then immediately answered, "*Nooooooooo*. He doesn't ask. Just drags you right in. No hand extended. No, 'Chace, I'm your father. Join me on the dark side,' giving you the opportunity to say, 'Never!' Not for him. No. He just shoves you right in!"

"Honey—"

I tore from his arms but only to sit up, smack him in the chest and rant on.

"I mean, *seriously*? You saw a kinky sex tape he starred in! How can he even *look* at you much less *kiss your girlfriend's hand*? Gross! Darth Vader didn't *have* a girlfriend. He gave all his attention to quashing the rebellion! As he should!" I started yelling. "Until this moment, I never would have thought I'd say up with the Empire but, here I am, saying it! Darth had a mission and one had to ask oneself, considering the emperor was wrinkly and seriously ick, what the frak? But you could see deep inside Darth was struggling. Because deep inside he was Anakin. There's no Anakin in Trane Keaton!" I shouted then I found myself on my back in the bed with Chace on top of me.

"Baby, calm down," he whispered, grinning.

His grin was lost on me since I was focused on scowling and declaring, "I do *not* like your father."

"All right, darlin'."

"Darth Vader's a better father, which states *exactly* how bad your father is," I declared.

"Okay, baby."

"And let's just say it's good I'm not a trained Jedi because I'd get my lightsaber, jump in my T-65 X-wing Starfighter and hightail my ass to Aspen and *call him out* if I was."

His mouth twitch was also lost on me as he murmured through it, "Yeah, honey, that's good."

"He might still have it, even being advanced in years, but he'd be no match for a lightsaber," I added authoritatively.

"Probably not," Chace muttered.

I kept scowling.

Chace kept grinning but he did it with his body shaking on top of mine so I knew inside he was laughing.

"This isn't funny, Chace," I told him something he had to know *way* more than me.

"It wasn't, not for thirty-five years, it definitely wasn't. Then, two minutes ago, it became fuckin' hilarious."

I sucked in an annoyed breath.

Chace kept grinning.

I sucked in another annoyed breath.

Chace asked, "T-65 X-wing Starfighter?"

"The combat spaceship of the Rebel Alliance," I snapped.

"T-65 X-wing Starfighter?" Chace repeated.

"Have you seen *Star Wars*?" I asked.

"Yes," he answered.

"More than once?" I pushed.

"Yeah," he said, still grinning.

"Then, if you have, you know about the X-wing Fighter. Everyone knows about the X-wing Fighter seeing as it, Luke and the Force destroyed the Death Star."

"Yeah, baby, I know about the X-wing Fighter. I just had no fuckin' clue it was called the T-65 X-wing Starfighter."

"It's not classified information, Chace. You can read all about it on Wookieepedia."

His body started shaking again, as did his voice when he asked, "Wookieepedia?"

"Stop making fun of me when I'm pissed," I snapped.

"Wookieepedia?" Chace repeated, his body now rocking, taking mine and the bed with it.

"Stop making fun of me!" I yelled, slapping his arm.

Suddenly his hands framed my face, his body, my body and the bed ceased rocking and he had my full attention mostly because he was all I could see.

"I just laughed about my dad for the first time since I was sixteen and Deck and I talked trash about him in Deck's basement, gettin' drunk and Deck givin' me space to let off steam. Now, and probably forever, if the occasion arises, I'll look at my dad and see Darth Vader and wanna laugh my ass off rather than wantin' to rip his head off, somethin' I thought would be impossible. Until now. Now, after six fuckin' years of feelin' buried under shit, I see it through your eyes and finally feel clean. For the first time in six years, I feel free. I feel relief. I'm relieved to let that shit go. I'm relieved to know you got the strength to take it. I'm relieved to know you can be with my mom and make her at ease. I'm fuckin' beside myself you're in love with me. I'm pleased you know you get that back from me. What I'm not, baby, is makin' fun of you."

Oh yeah, I broke through.

"Okay," I whispered, my arms sliding around him.

"And I never would," he went on.

"Okay," I whispered, my arms locking tight.

"You're cute and you make me laugh and honest to Christ, lookin' back, except with Deck, I don't remember doin' it and feelin' it comin' from me free and clean all my fuckin' life."

Oh man. Seriously. I broke through.

"Okay," I whispered, tears again stinging my eyes.

"So let me enjoy laughter without slappin' my arm and gettin' all pissy when that laughter finally feels real."

"Okay," I whispered yet again then started deep breathing.

Chace stared in my eyes.

I stopped deep breathing and bit the side of my lower lip.

Chace's eyes dropped to my mouth as he murmured, "Wookieepedia."

I let my lip go and informed him, "Later when things are, um...less intense, I'll need your opinion on whether Greedo or Han shot first."

Chace's lips tipped up as his brows drew up and his eyes came back to mine, "Is my opinion a deal breaker?"

Nothing with Chace was a deal breaker.

Not anymore.

Still.

"Um..." I mumbled.

His hands at my head pressed in, his thumbs sliding over my cheekbones, one coming to land on my lips as his face got super close and the lip tip faded clean away before he whispered a thick, rough, "Fuck, Faye, but I fuckin' love you."

Okay, I didn't like curse words all that much.

But that sounded really, *really* good.

"I'm glad," I whispered back.

His thumbs moved back over my cheekbones then his chin lifted and he kissed my nose before he muttered, "Go clean up, honey, so we can get some shuteye."

I nodded.

Chace rolled off.

I walked to the bathroom, cleaned up, walked out, went to my dresser and pulled on a new nightie. This one super tight, stretchy and purple that had lace at the cups, was sheer everywhere else and I added the lacy, string-bikini panties that matched.

When I turned to walk back to the bed, Chace's eyes were on me but aimed low and they didn't move from my body even as I moved.

I lifted a knee to plant it in the bed and his eyes came to mine.

"Seriously?" he asked a question I didn't know the answer to.

So I answered, "Um..."

Chace lunged.

We didn't get shuteye for some time and when we settled, I had the nightie on but the panties were on the floor.

My apartment was dark, we were on our sides, face to face (or my face in his throat, his in the top of my hair), bodies tangled and I was two steps from dream world when he murmured, "Han shot first. Greedo didn't have a prayer."

This was the right answer.

Han Solo was badass and Chace knew it.

Therefore, because of that and other more important reasons, I fell asleep smiling.

CHAPTER EIGHTEEN

My Sister

CHACE BLINKED AWAY sleep, feeling Faye cuddled close to him, smelling her hair, her lingering perfume and seeing the late April sun streaming into her apartment.

His first response was to curl her, already close, closer.

His first thought was that weekend they were going to the mall so they could buy sheets like hers for his bed.

He liked her apartment, he liked the look of it, its vibe, its proximity to La-La Land and work, both his and hers, but he was done with it. Done with two places, two closets, two fridges to fill and morning conversations about which of their two beds they'd end the day in.

She could bring her look and vibe to his place.

He'd decided she was moving in.

This would likely be frowned upon by her mother and father and thus make Faye hesitate.

So he reckoned he best put his ring on her finger.

They hadn't been together very long so she could have a long engagement just as long as she spent that engagement with his diamond on her finger and her heart-shaped ass in his bed.

Thoughts of her ass sent his hand down to it.

She'd altogether stopped pulling her panties on before going to sleep. She slept in her nighties, something he liked. They were sexy. They felt good. They looked great. But he loved it that she'd shunned the panties.

Which meant, in bed, he always had an all-access pass.

He smoothed his palm over her ass as his other arm tightened around her waist, pulling her even closer. She stirred, tilting her head slightly back, her eyes fluttering, taking their time opening before he had her crystal.

"Hi," she whispered, and his hard cock twitched.

"Mornin', baby," he whispered back.

His eyes moved over her face.

He liked her hair like that. It did what she always did, the thick, long bangs highlighted her eyes, the layers down the sides did the same to the line of her neck. It was subtle but effective. It made her look more mature but still her age. It was stylish and it was unconsciously sexy.

She snuggled even closer, he ran his hand back over her ass, her hips pressed into his and she tipped her head back further, her eyelids going half-mast.

It was an invitation he took, bending his neck to give her a soft, short, deep kiss.

When he broke it, he murmured against her lips, "You wanna sleep in and I'll run? Or you wanna make love? Or do you wanna fuck?"

That got him a languid blink before she tipped her chin, moved in and he felt her lips against his throat.

It took her a while to pull it together and he was beyond fucking thrilled when she whispered a word she rarely used but one that never failed to affect him when her soft, quiet, musical voice wrapped around it.

"Fuck."

Oh yeah.

His fingers dug into her ass, his arm around her waist slid

up, his hand diving into her hair. He fisted it, gently pulled her head back and bent his to take her mouth.

This kiss was not soft or short. But it was deep.

Then Chace rolled into her.

Then he set about fucking her.

*   *   *

Chace moved with his empty plate to the sink where Faye was, making a mental note that he didn't have to buy a new robe. He'd dumped his old one and now at his place she grabbed one of his shirts or tees and since he had the same in her closet and drawers, she'd taken to doing that at her place too.

Which was what she was wearing now, one of his clean shirts, sleeves rolled up, hair wet from their shower, standing at the sink doing breakfast dishes.

He set his plate beside the sink, moved into her back and swept her hair aside so it was mostly hanging over one shoulder, just a sweet layering around her neck.

He dropped his lips there as he slid a hand along her belly

He kissed her lightly then moved his lips to her ear. "Nervous about tonight?"

The Town Council meeting to discuss the future of the library was that night. So far, she hadn't displayed much reaction to all that was happening. That didn't mean he didn't read her concern but she wasn't letting on she was panicked or freaked.

Then again, they had thousands of signatures on petitions, Cesar had hundreds of phone calls and even people from Chantelle and Gnaw Bone were getting into the action seeing as if Carnal's library fell, they'd lose that resource too. This included Nina Maxwell sticking her nose into things, and Nina didn't do things by half measures. This was why they had thousands of signatures on petitions. Nina had them circulating around the entire county.

Hands in the soapy water, Faye turned her head, Chace lifted his and she gave him her eyes.

"Not really," she said quietly. "Maybe I should be but I'm more worried about the fact that Malachi still hasn't spoken."

Reflexively, his hand pressed into her stomach.

He was worried about that too. As was everyone, including Malachi's psychologist.

This didn't only say worse things about what went down with the kid, it also tied their hands with finding who abused him. They had nothing. Zero. Unless they could get it out of him, that was going nowhere.

But recently, it was more.

He'd seemed to be settling. Silas and Sondra were making efforts at socializing him so he went with them to town for dinner, they took him to the library to see Faye, took him grocery shopping. He didn't seem comfortable with this. He was watchful, wary, but he did it and, like everything else, seemed to be settling into that too.

Except for not speaking and having unusual reactions to everyday things like the television, phones and radios, he was a normal kid. He liked video games. He liked books. He'd gotten used to TV, phones and radios. He paid attention to those around him, laughed, smiled and often bent his head and scribbled on his notebook to share a quip, what he was thinking, feeling or wanted. Which meant they'd learned the kid had a cute sense of humor, he liked *Modern Family* and he had a massive sweet tooth.

But what he shared was never deep. It was never personal. He was among them and a part of them but he held himself detached. Although he had definitely formed a bond with Silas and Sondra, the only people he didn't seem detached from were Chace and Faye. It took a while for Chace to get in but when he got in, he was *in*. The kid didn't latch himself to either of them but his eyes followed them around a room if they moved, he paid more attention to them when they were speaking and if they left a room, he eventually followed in order to stay close. It wasn't like he crawled into their laps but if they were with him, he was never far.

But even though they had that connection, he didn't share with Faye or Chace either.

And in the last week, he seemed the same yet still more distant.

Something was on his mind and even though they all, in their individual ways, tried to find out what it was, he wasn't sharing.

It was Wednesday, a week and a half after Faye and Chace went to Aspen. Over a month since they found Malachi.

It was time to push.

Chace moved from Faye's back, grabbed a dish towel, a clean plate in the drainer and started wiping. "I'll call Karena at CPS and his psychologist. Have a chat with them. See if they agree it's time to step this shit up."

Her head twisted to him and her hands arrested in cleaning his plate. "I don't want him alarmed, Chace."

"You think I'd do that in a million years, baby?" he asked gently.

He watched her draw in breath before she shook her head.

"No, I wouldn't," Chace confirmed. "Never. But he's gotta get better. He's gotta start school next year. He's gotta make friends and the only way he can really feel safe is if we can catch who fucked him up and deal with them so he knows they'll never hurt him again."

She sighed, nodded and went back to her plate.

Seconds later, she whispered to the plate, "I'll kill them."

"What?" Chace asked.

She rinsed it, put it in the drainer and went after the cutlery at the bottom of the sink.

"You find them, you keep them away from me. I won't be

responsible for what I do if I get near them," she threatened in her soft, sweet voice, which made Chace smile but he didn't let his amusement become audible. This was because he thought she was cute but she was also being very serious.

When he could keep the humor out of his tone, he promised her, "They'll be sorted, Faye."

"I hope so," she muttered, wiping down the cutlery.

"They'll be sorted."

She nodded to the sink, rinsed the cutlery and put it in the drainer. Then she moved to the stove to get the skillet and it occurred to Chace she felt this depth of emotion for a kid she didn't help create, she didn't carry in her womb, she didn't bring into the world.

Which meant when they eventually got down to making a family, she'd give this and likely more to their brood.

Something she had, always.

Something he never did.

Something he'd always wanted.

Something their kids would take for granted.

He'd fucked up, not sharing his secrets, not trusting in the strength she'd displayed since he met her, transferring on her in her shyness his mother's frailty. It might have been an understandable fuckup but it was a fuckup.

But they had it out, she helped him let it go and then she let it go. The next day it was Chace and Faye, no rehashing it, no searching comments, no penetrating looks. She was over it, she'd helped him over it, she was moving on and she took him with her. Except for the fact that they both understood the depth of their feelings for each other, their commitment to their relationship and that bringing them indelibly closer, drama over, onward.

That was going to be his life. Faye at his side. Faye at his back. Dramas, fights, they'd happen, they'd end and they'd move on. And his kids would have that too, all of it, her devotion, her strength, her brand of quiet but fierce protection and her ability to sort through the shit, lay it out and move on.

He put the last plate away feeling his lips tipped up as she scoured the skillet and he grabbed the cutlery to dry it as he watched her rinse the skillet, the water running over her hands.

Naked hands.

Yeah, he needed to put a ring on her finger.

Soon.

* * *

"I'm uncertain why you have a voice in this meeting, Mrs. Maxwell, you don't even live in Carnal," Mary Eglund asked, snippy and impatient.

It was eight seventeen in the evening and Chace was sitting in the Town Hall next to Faye and trying with decreasing success not to laugh his ass off.

This was because it was no longer a mystery and also not a surprise that it was Mary Eglund, known as a Jesus freak and not the handing-out-daisies-and-pamphlets kind, was behind the attempted library closure. This was also because, after a few opening comments by Cesar followed by a few inflammatory remarks from Mary, the floor was opened up.

Krystal Briggs got there first and tore the council a new one, swiftly and succinctly, and managed to do it without any cursing.

On her heels stepped up Nina Maxwell whose wrong side Chace decided never to get on because she might be passionate but she was also eloquent and she had an English accent so all that sass was tied up in some serious class.

She was also very pretty and when Chace could stop watching her, he watched Max watching his wife. Most of the time, Max was grinning. Some of it, he was shaking his head but doing it grinning. Some of it, he was trying to control the active toddler he had at his knee at the same time holding a sleeping baby cradled in his arm. All of it denoting he was pussy-whipped in that good way like Tate, Ty and now, Chace.

Cesar, Chace noted right off the bat, was playing this smart. He had no intention of shutting down the library. Mary had minimal support from the other council members, none of whom had said that first word. He was keeping his mouth shut, letting Mary have her meeting at the same time letting her dig her own grave.

Mary was digging it but Nina had handed her the shovel.

"You sit on the Town Council," Nina retorted. "Therefore I can only assume, as part of your duties, that you are aware of the funding sources of local amenities including the fact that taxpayer dollars from the entire county go to Carnal in order to keep the library doors open. Therefore, the citizens in Gnaw Bone, Chantelle and every town in this county have a right to be heard at this meeting."

"This is true," Mary shot back. "But the bulk of the funding comes from Carnal."

"I'd hardly describe the funding provided by Carnal as 'bulk' in any sense of the word considering your library is drastically under-resourced, needs new computers, is unable to keep on top of periodicals, purchasing books at the time of their release and their DVD collection is woefully dated," Nina returned. "If public records and my calculations are correct, the Town of Carnal will have a surplus in their budget this year so, as I see it, they shouldn't be closing *down* a resource but funneling more funds into the resources they already have."

"Jeez, she must have taken notes during our conversation," Faye muttered from beside him, and Chace pressed his lips together, using his arm already around her to pull her closer.

"Not to mention," Nina went on, "we're extremely fortunate to have a librarian managing *our* facility who has a master's in library science. She's worked there seven years. The Library Board has given her nothing but glowing appraisals and she gets paid on the lower spectrum of the salary range for someone who works five hours a week less than she does."

"As if she works those hours," Mary spat, and, at this surprising insinuation, both Faye and Chace straightened in their seats. "I've been paying attention and, recently, she's taken an exorbitant amount of time off."

"Holy frak," Faye muttered.

"I've read her job description," Nina retorted. "With her tenure, she's earned three weeks' vacation, four personal days and five sick days a year. With your estimation of 'exorbitant,' are you alleging she's taken advantage beyond this allotment?"

"I would *allege* she's taking advantage of her town-funded position most assuredly considering she's carrying on a blatant affair with a recently widowed man!" Mary fired back, and Faye shot straight at his side as a growl escaped Chace's throat that he couldn't but also didn't try to contain.

"Now see here!" They heard Silas shout and both of them turned to see him standing up from his bench on the opposite side of the room, his face red as a beet, his arms straight down at his sides in fists.

"Mary, I'll ask, with respect, that you keep your remarks directed to library business," Cesar cut in before Silas could lose it, speaking into his microphone, his face red as well, and he was visibly furious.

"It *is* library business considering this town through this council is providing the Library Board with funding to pay the salary of a fallen woman," Mary returned heatedly.

"Oh my God," Faye whispered as Chace's own hands balled into fists.

"Ms. Goodknight's personal life is not up for public debate," Cesar shot back even more heatedly. "And, Mary, I'm warning you, one more comment, I'll close this meeting and reconvene later. But that later will be after the members of the council meet to discuss your behavior here, likely censure you and, personally, if you say one more word, you have my promise that I'll take steps to have you removed."

"I think the words she's already said are enough for the council to consider taking steps toward her removal," Nina put in, standing at the microphone up front, and her words were heated too.

"Try it," Mary invited. "I think you'll be surprised at how much support I have. I'm not the only one who believes Faye Goodknight's recent behavior is well *below* reproach."

"That wouldn't be me!" Bubba Briggs boomed from the back.

"Or me!" Jim-Billy shouted from the front.

"Me either, you stupid cow," Stoney, the owner of one of the local bike shops, added loudly.

"Nor me!" Holly shouted.

Lauren shot up from her seat between Tate and his son, Jonas, and yelled, "You should be ashamed of yourself talking about our sweet Faye like that *in front of everybody*!"

Faye and Chace's heads jerked to behind them where Dominic, the owner of the local hair salon, was shouting, "Immediate impeachment!"

Their heads jerked back to the front to see Shambles standing two benches in front of them, yelling, "Dudette, know this, I have the right to refuse service and I never thought I'd do that to anyone *in my life*. But starting now, you can get your cappuccinos and chunky peanut butter cookies somewhere else! Talking about Crimson Stargazer like that when she's finally found a hot-guy boyfriend is just... plain... wrong but it's also serious *mean*."

"Great," Faye mumbled.

"I hardly think a *hippie* endorsement is doing your librarian any favors," Mary said to Shambles, her lip curled. "You'd do better to sit down, *Mr. Shambala*." When she said his name, she said it like it tasted foul.

At that, Chace knew something snapped in Faye and he knew this because she shot to her feet.

"Ms. Eglund," she called, and Chace braced as Mary Eglund turned her venomous eyes to his woman.

At the same time, so did everyone else.

When Faye got her attention, she spoke.

"You are entitled to your opinions about my personal life. You are also entitled to share them. You are further entitled to share them publicly. You doing it, how you do it and what you say actually says more about you than me. As does your snide tone directed at Shambles. But on the matter at hand, threats of the library's closure started before my relationship with Detective Keaton began and those threats occurred because of your concern about the content of some of the books in our catalogue. On that subject, I'll say that I have always accumulated a catalogue the Library Board approved as fit for this county. The books you cite as those that are inappropriate for our library and thus give cause for its closure are some of our most popular books for adults *and* children. I find it heartbreaking that these books that open up worlds of reading to children and young adults are not only questioned but are being threatened with removal. That you would use your personal agenda to eliminate something so valuable, so vital to a community as a library is beyond words. I've read to countless children in that library. Those with very little can come to that library and find something that costs nothing to entertain them in lives that are often lonely. The library serves as a gathering place for friends who share the love of books. It further serves as a resource for those who escape the pressure of everyday life, doing it by losing themselves in the written word. It serves as an avenue of gathering knowledge for those who could be planning a trip to Utah or researching their heritage, learning about the history of this country or how to make soap. Those walls and shelves contain works of art created by words and depicted in pictures. There are volunteers who are retired or stay-at-home moms who serve their community proudly and do it in that library. My mother took me to that library. Her mother took her to that same library. And I hope to God by the end of this night, I will have a future where I will take my children to that library. I will abide by the wishes of this community. What I won't do is sit silent while you turn your nose up at a kind man like Shambles and cast aspersions on the relationship I have with a good man whom I happen to love. If you close the library, that would be a tragedy. If you close it simply because you feel you have the right to tell others what they can read and see or because I fell in love with a kind, decent man and did it in a way in which you, personally, do not approve, that would also be a tragedy. But it would be a reprehensible one."

With that, Faye sat down.

And when Faye sat down, everyone shot out of their seats and cheered.

He heard Silas roar, *"That's my girl,"* as Faye ducked her chin into her neck, Chace wrapped his arm around her and, smiling broadly, moved his lips to her ear.

"Well said, baby," he whispered.

"I just told most of the town I was in love with you," she whispered back.

"Are you?"

Her eyes peeked at him from beneath her bangs. "Yeah."

"Then what's the problem?"

"Mrs. Maxwell, you can sit down." Cesar's voice could be heard over the hollering and applause. Chace and Faye looked up but he noticed Faye had more than a little pink in her cheeks when she did. "If we can have order, I'll invite anyone who is not in opposition of the library being closed to take the microphone," Cesar finished.

Everyone settled. Nina moved back toward Max who was sitting with their two kids in the front bench. She gently pulled the baby from him and settled in her seat and also in the crook of Max's arm. No one moved to the microphone, and Chace's eyes went to Mary to see hers narrowed on someone in the congregation and she was jerking her head to the microphone.

Chace looked through the crowd but the room was so packed, standing room only, he couldn't see who she was motioning to.

"No one?" Cesar called into his microphone.

When no one moved or even raised their hand, Jim-Billy shouted out, "Vote it, Moreno."

Cesar looked to his left then right then at Mary. "You've had your meeting, Mary, the council will now vote. All in favor of Carnal Library's closure, say aye."

Mary's hand shot up and she shouted, "Aye!"

None of the other council members moved. Mary glared at the one at her side then she glared at the one at the opposite end.

They avoided her gaze and kept their mouths shut.

Likely, they'd murmured remarks of alliance just to shut her up. Or maybe they didn't expect the force of the opposition. Whatever reason, she expected their votes to swing her way and they were not.

"Nays?" Cesar asked, and the other three council members cried, "Nay!"

"Right the ef on!" Bubba shouted from the back.

Cesar brought down his gavel then announced, "The Carnal Library will not close."

Another cheer roared through the crowd.

"Comments and feedback about the catalogue held at the library should not be directed to the Town Council but to the Library Board, which, thank God, I'm not a member of," Cesar finished over the noise. "Thank you for your attendance this evening. Enjoy the rest of it."

He barely got out the last word when Chace heard Silas shout, "Faye, sweetheart, you got Malachi?"

Chace felt his neck begin to prickle as Faye looked around and called back, "No, Dad. Thought he was with you."

"That was awesome!" Lexie showed at the end of their bench, dragging Ty with her and Chace distractedly noticed that only Lexie Walker could be heavily pregnant and still wear a stylish, skin-tight dress, high-heeled boots and look stunningly beautiful.

"It was," Faye replied but she sounded distracted too.

"Serious as fuck, Nina's the shit," Ty muttered. "Bitch never backs down from a fight."

"Don't let Nina hear you calling her a bitch," Lexie advised.

"No fuckin' way," Ty replied, grinning down at his wife. "She's got verbal claws so sharp, she'd shred me."

"Uh...have you two seen Malachi?" Faye asked them, she and Chace were both standing, looking around. Faye was craning her neck and speaking. "He came in with Mom and Dad. Blond boy? You know, the one Mom and Dad are looking after."

"Saw him," Lexie answered. "Don't see him now. And by the way, he's super cute."

"Yo, Keaton!" Chace heard his name called and turned to see Wings, one of the local bikers, fighting the crowds leaving or standing around and talking to get to him.

"Excuse me," Chace muttered, grabbing Faye's hand and moving her out into the aisle when Ty and Lexie moved out of the way. The second they were there, Wings made it to him.

"Little kid slipped this to me and took off," he said to Chace, and that prickle on his neck started biting. "Thought I'd wait until the end, you know, what with this bein' a big deal for Faye and all."

Chace took the note that had his name printed on the outside in Malachi's writing and opened it, Faye crowding him close and he could feel her tension.

It said in Malachi's handwriting,

She's here. It's safe to do it now.
I'll be at the shed.

Silas and Sondra pushed through, Silas announcing, "Our lil' bugger took off. Can't find him anywhere. I'll go to the restroom—"

"Note, Silas," Chace stated tersely, lifting up the note, Silas took it but Chace was looking around. He found Deck at the back, chatting up a blonde and he whistled. The second the sound pierced the air, Deck's neck twisted and Chace got his eyes. Chace jerked up his chin. Deck did too, coming his way.

"What? I don't get it. What's safe?" Silas asked, heavy concern threading his tone.

"Everything all right?" Ty asked.

"Who is *she*?" Faye whispered, and her tone, a tone he understood because he felt its cold crawling through his system, made Chace look down at her.

Before he could speak, he heard Deck say, "Yo. What?"

Chace looked at Deck and told him, "Something's going down with Malachi. At the shed."

"I'm on it," Deck stated immediately, turning to move the other way.

"I'm going too," Faye put in. Chace looked down at her and opened his mouth but she got there before him, squaring her shoulders. He knew by that and the worried look in her eye, he was fucked. "I'm going too," she repeated firmly.

"All right, baby," he muttered.

"Mary Eglund is a serious pain in the ass," Krys announced, making it to their huddle, Bubba following in her wake and Chace saw Tate, Lauren and Jonas also hitting their group.

"Something's going down with the kid," Ty told Tate.

"What kid?" Max asked from behind them. Nina, he and their kids had moved up the center aisle and were down the bench from them.

"We need to go, Chace," Faye whispered, grabbing his hand and holding it tight. "We need to go, go, *go.*"

She was losing it.

"You need help?" Tate asked.

"Yes," Chace answered, turning, positioning and taking Faye with him so they were facing all of them. "Malachi's his name. Silas, pass the note around," he ordered, and continued when Silas did as he asked. "Faye and I are heading to Sioux Street, eastern dead end where it meets up with Cherokee. Deck'll be there. We need men in that wood to fan out and look for him."

"What's this shed?" Max asked, looking up from the note Tate walked down to him.

"Ramshackle, 'bout a twelve-minute walk, if you do it sedate, going direct east with a hint north," Chace answered.

"He wants you at the shed, why do you need men in those woods?" Ty asked.

"Because there's someone in those woods who could hurt him. They have before, they'll do it again. He thinks it's safe. I wanna make sure it is," Chace responded, feeling Faye get more and more tense at his side.

"I'll call Deke," Tate muttered, turning toward Lauren.

"I'll call Wood," Ty stated, looking down at Lexie.

"I'll call it in to CPD," Max said, pulling his phone out.

"I'm with you," Silas declared then looked down at Sondra, yanking his keys out of his pocket. "You go home."

"Silas," she whispered.

"Go home, honey. Stay close to the phone," Silas replied.

"I want to look too," she told him.

"And he needs someone at home if he has to make his way there," Silas returned gently.

She nodded.

"Baby, you go with Sondra," Bubba said quietly to Krys, and Krystal, her eyes on Sondra, nodded as well.

"Chace," Faye's voice was trembling and her hand in his tightened so tight, it drew pain, "we have *to go*."

Chace nodded down into her pale face, he looked to Silas and he ordered, "Let's go."

And with a glance through their friends, they left.

*   *   *

"What you got?" Chace said into his phone as he moved through the slush, mud and over the wet rock of the thawing wood, hearing Faye moving five feet behind him at his right flank, Deck moving through the wet brush ten feet in front of him slightly to his left.

"At the shed, no Malachi," Silas answered in his ear.

"Sit on it, Silas," Chace ordered.

"Been sittin' on it forty-five minutes, Chace," Silas retorted.

"Sit on it longer," Chace returned.

"Rather be lookin'," Silas fired back.

"He approaches that shed, he'll need someone there he can trust," Chace informed him.

"That could be Faye," Silas shot back.

"Who're we talkin' about?" Chace asked shortly.

He got silence for moment then, "Damn it."

Silas knew Faye would no sooner sit at a shed and not be looking for Malachi than Chace would. Or, apparently, Silas wanted to do.

"Got you wrapped around her finger," Silas muttered in his ear cantankerously.

"You want that another way?" Chace asked, tiring of the conversation.

"Take your point." Silas kept muttering.

"Are we done?" Chace asked.

"Find him, son," Silas whispered then disconnected.

Chace shoved the phone in his back pocket and kept moving through the wood along the sheer cliff face. He saw Deck's light cutting the night in front of him as well as Faye's behind him. They walked in silence, following Deck's lead. In the last weeks, Deck had been out there at least a dozen times, combing the area north to south, climbing the rock face, following wildlife trails that led nowhere, finding nothing but getting the lay of the land. They'd been at it nearly an hour and were well north of town, beyond the town limits, moving slowly upward. If they walked another half hour and shifted west, they'd be on Tate Jackson's front deck.

They hadn't even picked up tracks.

"We're getting far away, Chace," Faye called, her voice tight.

Fear and concern.

"Keep lookin', honey," Chace replied.

"It's getting late," she told him.

"Keep lookin'."

"And cold."

He heard a sharp whistle and stopped dead, aiming his light toward Deck.

Deck was aiming his light to his fingers, two of which

were moving in a motion of walking then he swung his light to the forest floor.

He'd found tracks.

Faye rushed up to his side.

"Quiet, Faye, as quiet as you can be. Follow, stay behind me. Let's go," Chace ordered, Faye nodded then he moved swiftly and as silently as he could to Deck.

When they reached him, Deck continued to move through the forest.

Chace and Faye followed and Chace saw the tracks. At hearing Faye's quick intake of breath, he knew she saw them too.

Five minutes passed into ten and then Deck stopped abruptly, lifting up a hand.

Chace and Faye stopped behind him. Chace moved carefully to his side where he halted, using an arm to sweep Faye behind him and putting his hand to his gun at his belt.

There was movement.

"Lights," Chace murmured and turned his flashlight off, Deck's followed half a second later then Faye's went out.

They listened to the sounds of approach and Chace trained his eyes through the dark at where it was coming from. From the noises, he couldn't get a sense of what they were dealing with, child, adult or both. They didn't talk, didn't make anything but the noise of footfalls in the snow, mud and the brushing of branches.

Then they came clear. Chace knew Faye saw them the minute he did for she sucked in another audible breath.

Through the dark, Malachi in his new jeans and a sweater and he was holding the hand of a little girl, maybe five, six, in a thin, pale-colored nightgown, Malachi's coat hanging on her, barefoot, hair a scraggly mess coming out from under Malachi's hat, face dirty, thin as a fucking rail.

The children didn't notice them until they were four feet away. When they did, they rocked to a halt, their heads tipped back sharply and the girl whimpered in alarm, ducking behind Malachi.

Chace braced to run after them if they took off but they didn't.

Shocking the shit out of Chace, his eyes locked to him, Malachi shuffled forward two feet and stopped.

Then his face cracked in a huge smile and he whispered in a scratchy voice, "Finally got her. Rebecca. My sister."

His sister. His fucking sister.

Chace was right. There was a sibling. All he'd done was for her.

Faye leaned heavily into the side of his back and whispered, "My sister."

Then he felt her body buck and he knew she was fighting tears.

Chace had to hope she could hold it together as he leaned back a bit to give her the cue, she took her weight from him and he crouched low.

"Rebecca's got no shoes on, Malachi. It's cold, snowy and muddy. Can I carry her home?" he asked.

Malachi looked at Chace then twisted his neck to look at his sister then he looked back at Chace and nodded.

Chace carefully lifted one hand toward Rebecca, she cowered back behind Malachi and whimpered.

Malachi's scratchy voice came back. "It's okay, Becky."

"Doan wanna," she murmured.

More of Malachi's rough, quiet whisper. "He got me a sleeping bag."

"Doan wanna."

"He's nice."

"Doan wanna!"

"Becky, honey, look at me."

This came from Faye who had moved and was now crouching beside Chace.

She spoke again when Becky peered fearfully from around Malachi.

"I'm Faye. This is Chace," she motioned to him then she tipped her head up to Deck so both kids tilted their heads way back to look at Deck. "That gentle giant is Jacob Decker. It's cold, sweetheart, and you need some food in your belly." At the mention of food, Becky's eyes shot back to Faye and, at what this said, Chace's gut twisted. "You can walk with us, of course, but we'd get you warmed up and food in you a lot faster if you let Chace carry you."

There was nothing then, softly, "Gentle giant?"

"Yeah, he's big but he's sweet," Faye told her.

"What's he?" Becky asked, pressing into Malachi but jerking her chin to Chace.

"He's a white knight on a fiery steed except his steed comes in the form of an SUV and it's not fiery. It's burgundy."

Becky kept pressing into her brother then she whispered, "Did he buy Miah a sleeping bag?"

Miah?

Faye wisely didn't question the name. She just answered, "Yes, honey, he got him a sleeping bag and camp cutlery and candy bars and energy drinks and lots of stuff. That's what white knights do. They save damsels in distress but they also look after kids who don't have it very good."

Becky's eyes moved over Chace in the moonlight.

Then slowly she shifted out from behind Malachi, took two steps toward him and lifted her hand his way. Moving carefully, Chace reached out toward her.

Her little, pale fingers curled around his.

He cautiously moved forward and slowly swung her up in his arms.

Then he whispered, "Let's get them home," and moved swiftly through the wood.

"Take my hand, sweetheart," he heard from behind him,

and he knew Faye was looking after Malachi but Chace didn't miss a step.

But when her little, trembling body caught his attention, he stopped, put her down gently, shrugged off his jacket, wrapped it low around her in an effort to cover her legs and feet and lifted her back up.

While he was doing that, he heard Deck ask Malachi, "Piggyback?" which meant if Deck carried Malachi, they could keep up.

The scratchy voice came back, a hint of excitement in it, "Yeah."

Chace forged through the forest hearing them coming after him.

After five minutes he heard Deck's, "Gentle giant?"

Then he heard Faye's, "Shut up."

He did not smile. The girl in his arms was freezing, dirty, underfed and her brother just saved her from some unknown "she" who was at the town meeting.

Five minutes later he heard Deck's, "White knight on a fiery steed?"

Then he heard Faye's, "Deck, shut...*up*."

Then he heard Malachi's laugh.

Only then did he smile.

But it was not a big one.

*   *   *

Chace forced himself to drive slower than the speed limit on his way to the hospital. He did this to give himself time to control his fury.

He'd just left the station. They were processing Enid Eglund for homicide and kidnapping while her sister Mary blustered to the cap in the reception area.

As she did, Tate, Ty, Deke, Bubba, Wood, Max and Deck as well as half the Carnal police officers looked on with varying expressions of disgust. Chace was angry, having difficulty controlling it, but still he knew those men were there and not home with their women because they were worried they'd have to help him keep a hold on his shit.

He finally left when Ty broke into Mary's harangue, clearly a woman with a little power who thought she had a lot more and it was backed by God, and he did it with, "Bitch, give it up. Your whackjob of a sister isn't gonna fry even though she should, but she is gonna pay. You talkin' yourself sick and borin' everyone to death is not gonna stop it."

Mary glared at him, visibly fighting the urge to lash out but wisely not doing it considering it would have no effect, not to mention the fact that Ty was a six-foot-seven powerhouse and there were very few who had the courage to give him lip and fewer still were women. Lexie was one of the only ones he knew who did it and did it with regularity. That and the way she looked, Chace reckoned, were the reasons she warmed his bed with his baby inside her.

At this point, however, Chace decided he was done and mumbled to Frank that he was out of there.

Then he got the fuck out of there.

After getting the kids out of the wood, they'd taken Rebecca to the hospital first. While they checked on her, with Deck and Silas close (Faye was in with Becky), he'd spoken to Malachi, or, as they'd learned, Jeremiah and got the story as Jeremiah told it haltingly in his scratchy voice.

Jeremiah and his sister had been kept in a basement by a woman called Enid. They rarely saw the light of day and only when she forced them to do chores in her garden. They had little to eat. They were lectured often and for long-ass periods of time about God, the Bible and how they were both heathens for reasons Chace didn't get because Jeremiah was too young to understand and explain. Nevertheless, whatever they were was clearly jacked. And whatever they were, she told the children, they needed to be punished for it.

But Jeremiah had been cast out some months ago after Enid had, for some reason, declared him even more unholy than he already was and therefore unfit to be around his sister.

He was cast out but he went back in order to try to free his sister. Upon his returns, he was caught, beaten, sometimes bound and then beaten and cast out again.

He kept going back.

For his sister.

The last time, the worst time, when he was determined to get her because he knew Chace and Faye would take care of her as well as him, she'd broken his arm and, on his return to the shed, he'd been caught in the trap.

When he saw Enid at the town meeting, Enid being, Chace reckoned, the person Mary thought would back her play about the library, he'd seen this as his opportunity to get his sister free and he took it.

Incidental information he gave them was that he had not had his reactions to TV, radio and phones because he'd never seen them before but because Enid regularly lectured about the fact that they were the work of the devil. Enid informed the children, repeatedly, they were used to spread gossip and preach sin, she did not allow them access to any of them and she warned the children they'd land in hell if they ever utilized them.

He'd also shared that Enid had told them, again repeatedly, that grown men held evil. They were wicked, existed only to corrupt women and children to their wicked ways and should always be avoided. This was why he, at first, feared and shrunk away from men.

Further, he told them that Enid referred to him as Malachi and refused to address him by his given name, Jeremiah.

Jeremiah didn't understand the reasons for this thus couldn't share them. Why he gave them Enid's name for him, rather than his real name, he didn't explain, and considering the difficult information he was sharing, Chace didn't press.

However, Becky's name actually was Rebecca but Enid would not allow him to call her by her nickname and he only did so when they were alone. Becky was too young to understand the name change and never called him anything but his nickname, "Miah," for which she got in trouble but, from what Chace could tell from his faltering explanation, Jeremiah paid the price.

Last, he'd shared that he was not nine years old but eleven. His growth had likely been stunted by malnutrition or perhaps both children came from small parents. Regardless, he didn't do this to put them off the track. The way he haltingly explained made it seem he did this in order to hide his embarrassment at his lack of schooling which he expected they'd figure out, which they did but they had no idea, considering his real age, how bad it was.

In other words, the bitch wasn't a whackjob. She was a seriously fucked-up whackjob.

They didn't press him for more. He was worried about his sister and what he'd given them was already enough for him to relive for the time being.

Chace called in what he knew and it didn't take long for them to trace "Enid" to Enid Eglund who lived in that area, about a five-minute drive from Tate Jackson's house.

By the time units got to her house, she'd discovered Becky gone, panicked, read her time was up and had taken off. They put a BOLO out on her and one of Mick Shaughnessy's boys in Gnaw Bone nabbed her and brought her back to Carnal.

Becky was found to be malnourished to the point that her small stature meant Chace had underestimated her age. She wasn't five or six but eight years old. Her feet were scraped but other than that she was fine. Regardless, they admitted her for observation and a psych evaluation the next day.

Leaving Faye with her father and mother at the hospital, Chace went to the station and watched in an observation room full of men as Frank interrogated Enid Eglund. It took some time but things she said meant officers left the room to hit computers.

It all came together. Then, when confronted with it, Enid let it all hang out.

Enid Eglund had gone to Wyoming three years ago to attend a revival. Being seriously fucked in the head, she saw a young woman with two young children and no man. Clearly something about this made a woman living on the verge of snapping snap. She made assumptions, followed the woman home, murdered her in her sleep, kidnapped her two children, brought them back to Carnal and kept them in captivity.

She was a recluse, came to town to grocery shop and go to church, lived in the home she'd inherited from her parents and made meager money doing phone sales at home. No one really knew her but her sister and, from Mary Eglund's rant, even that spinster didn't know her reclusive spinster sister very well for she had no idea for three years Enid was concealing two children. Nor did she know, or admit to herself, the extent of her sister's insanity.

Enid was also convinced she was doing God's work, committing multiple felonies not only by the laws of the State of Colorado but against the Word of God, in order to save the children from a fallen woman and punishing them for their mother's perceived sins.

The murder and double kidnapping in Wyoming, obviously, had not been solved. It wasn't fresh, but cases like that never went cold if there was someone left who loved the ones who were missing and missing persons, unless found, were not deleted from the databases. Therefore, how the interns hadn't turned the children up in their searches, Chace didn't know but come the next day, he would find out.

But upon calling the authorities in Wyoming, they found that Jeremiah and Rebecca's mother was not an unwed mother full of sin, as Enid assumed, but a widow whose husband died in a car crash two months before she was killed by Enid Eglund. She and her husband were survived by parents who were still hoping their grandchildren were alive.

They would soon get really fucking great news.

Now, as Chace turned into the hospital parking lot, he had to give really bad news: all that went down with Jeremiah and the fact that, shortly, Jeremiah and his sister would be taken from them and returned to their grandparents.

He pulled in a deep breath as he parked and threw his door open.

Faye had told him that the hospital staff had agreed to them, and Jeremiah, sticking close to Becky. So Faye and her mom and dad were still there.

He moved through the hospital to the room number she'd given him but stopped one foot in the door.

Silas was asleep in a chair. Sondra was reading in another. Becky was asleep looking tiny in that huge hospital bed, and there was a cot opened next to it in which Faye was curled and asleep, cuddling Jeremiah close to her front.

Chace stood frozen, staring at his woman with her boy, so his body gave a slight jerk when Sondra's hand fell light on his arm.

He turned his head to her.

"Outside," she whispered, he nodded and moved back through the door which she carefully shut behind her.

She tipped her head back to catch his eyes.

"How bad is it?" she asked quietly.

"Brace," he whispered gently, and she closed her eyes.

When she opened them, he told her. He kept going even as

the tears formed and her lips trembled and he did because he knew she could hack it. She'd made Faye, she wouldn't break.

He was right. She didn't.

When he was done, she simply said softly, "Grandparents."

"They'll process her, call the local authorities in Wyoming and those boys up there will either head out with the news tonight or they'll wait until first thing in the morning. It's been years, Enid Eglund is a sick woman whose story is rambling and hard to follow, so likely they'll do DNA to make certain Jeremiah and Rebecca are who they think they are and tests will take a coupla days to run. That said, we got photos and, it's been years, they're older but there's no denying those kids are theirs. My guess, any grandparents whose kids are dead and grandkids were missin' for years, they'll be down here soon."

She nodded. She was a grandparent. She knew. But there was sadness in her eyes not only for what Jeremiah and Becky had endured, what they'd lost but that she was losing her boy.

"My play?" Chace asked, and she focused on him again.

"Don't take her away from them," she answered, knowing exactly his question.

It was Chace's turn to nod.

She turned to the room and Chace followed her.

Then, even though there was barely enough room, he took his jacket off, tossed it at the end of the cot then entered it carefully, fitting himself to Faye's back and wrapping his arm around her and Jeremiah.

She stirred, her neck twisting, her sleepy eyes coming to him.

"Sleep, baby," he whispered.

"But—"

"Sleep."

She looked at his face, her eyes roaming it. Then she nodded and settled back in.

It was uncomfortable as all fuck, he was on the very edge, but he settled in too.

He sensed Faye slide back into sleep and knew he probably wouldn't join her.

He felt eyes on him and his went to Sondra.

When his eyes caught hers, she whispered one word across the room, it spoke volumes and settled warm deep in his soul.

"Perfect."

Chace understood her and the enormity of her meaning.

But he didn't reply.

He dipped his chin to her, settled back in, closed his eyes, held his girl and her boy close and, moments later, found sleep.

CHAPTER NINETEEN

He Sent an Angel

"SON."

Chace turned from watching Faye playing Candy Land with Lexie, Krys, Twyla, Becky and Miah on the floor of the Goodknights' family room to see Silas standing at his side.

Actually, Lexie wasn't on the floor. Her pregnant belly wasn't conducive to being on the floor. She was lounging on the couch and Miah was helping her take her turns.

"You couldn't have gotten a good night's sleep on that cot," Silas went on. "Take my girl home, let her see to you, get some decent shuteye."

It was just past noon the next day. Becky had been released. Faye had arranged for cover at the library, doing it muttering, "Frak Mary Eglund and her lunatic sister. They want, they can fire me for taking more personal time." They'd shown up at the Goodknights with cars in the drive, these holding Lexie, Krys and Twyla with shopping bags full of clothes and shoes for Becky.

Becky had gotten a shower in and put on her new clothes. Like Miah, she seemed to be settling. Miah settled because he knew the Goodknights had a connection with Faye. Becky settled because her brother was there as well as food, clothes and a shower.

That didn't mean she wasn't skittish, wary and often didn't jerk her eyes to her brother sometimes for understandable reasons like someone walked into the room or there was a loud noise, sometimes for what appeared no reason at all.

The psychologist had seen her and briefed Chace, Faye and the Goodknights.

The trauma Miah had endured, being cast out and his focus entirely on biding his time to save his sister was why he'd chosen not to speak. It was likely from both the kids' behavior and things Miah had told them that he'd been looking out for his sister and shielding her as best he could from Enid Eglund's lunacy for years. As a survivor, he took the good coming to him from living with the Goodknights. As a kid, he took the care Faye and Chace gave to him and let it build trust. But in the end, his mind was turned to getting his sister free, he considered it his responsibility and he wasn't going to share it with anyone. Therefore, in an effort not to share at all, he controlled how he communicated.

The psychologist also told them they'd both need in-depth trauma counseling, and their reunion with their grandparents would need to be monitored by a professional. As the two only people he truly trusted in this world, this the psychologist understood from Jeremiah sending Chace that note and allowing him to care for his sister, Chace and Faye had to be there.

Upon hearing the news, the cops in Wyoming didn't wait to share with four of their locals that it was highly likely their grandkids were alive and in Colorado. They'd made their visits, waking them to share the news. Therefore, as expected, both sets were on their way and were expected to arrive at the station imminently.

Chace was conflicted. He wanted to be there to meet the grandparents but he didn't want to be away from Faye and the kids or take her away from them. He'd told her what had happened and her reaction had been much like her mother's except stronger. It tore her up what had happened to those kids and it tore her up knowing, although it was a good thing they'd be with their blood family, that doing so would mean Miah would be a state away.

So she was staying close.

Chace wanted to give that to her but he didn't want to leave her.

"I'll survive, Silas," Chace muttered.

Silas's eyes moved over Chace's face then they swung into the living room and finally he looked back at Chace.

"Right," he whispered then, louder, "I'm goin' into town. The kids' folks will be here soon and I wanna do what I can to assure them their grandbabies are in a good place and, least one of 'em for a spell, had folks lookin' out for him. Sondra's on the phone with Betty to get them rooms at Carnal Hotel. We wanted 'em to stay here while they're doin' their testing but the psychologist thinks that's too much for now. Miah feels safe here and Becky feels safe with Miah. That's fragile so we gotta see to it. But Liza's makin' a coupla lasagnas to bring over. The psychologist can show tonight so they can come and have the reunion soon's we can manage it.

Good one, with family and food, and my Liza makes a mean lasagna. But Liza'll drop 'em off and go. It'll be just you and Faye, Sondra and I, the grandparents, the psychologist and the kids. Sondra's bagged a coupla pop bottles the kids drank from and I'm takin' 'em in with me for DNA."

"All that's good. Thanks, Silas," Chace replied.

He watched Silas's expression change and read it instantly.

"Miss him," Silas muttered, his eyes drifting to Miah. "He's a good kid. Nice to have a lil' bugger in the house again." His eyes drifted back to Chace and when he spoke again, his voice was tinged with sadness but it was firm. "But they should be with family."

"They should be with family," Chace agreed.

Silas nodded. "Off with me then," he murmured and moved away.

Chace watched him go then his eyes went back to the living room when he heard laughter. It came from all the women and Miah but there was also a little giggle from Becky who was looking timidly at Faye.

Faye had made her giggle.

That was his girl. She could break through anything. Even shit this huge. He knew it since she'd done it for him.

He felt his lips tip up as his phone rang and he saw Faye and Miah's eyes cut to him and Becky jump, terror filling her features, her eyes cutting to her brother.

He automatically sent a reassuring smile their way, pulled out his phone and, for Becky's sake, stayed calm and acted like what he was doing was just what it was, normal and natural.

He looked at the display and, at what he saw, he figured he knew the reason behind the call.

He took the call and put the phone to his ear.

"Frank, they at the station?"

"They arrived twenty minutes ago," Frank replied. "We

got them sorted with coffees from La-La Land and some of Shambles's brownies. Gave them a briefing up to now. Took the DNA samples. Lab is primed to fast-track it. But, uh..." he hesitated, "not callin' about that, Chace."

Chace felt his brows draw together. "What're you callin' about?"

"You got privacy?" Frank asked.

Fucking shit.

"No," Chace answered.

"Get it," Frank said quietly.

Chace didn't look into the family room as he moved out of the doorway, up the stairs and into the living room on the top floor.

"Got it," he said to Frank.

"Right, well, brother...fuck," Frank started then stopped.

"Frank," Chace prompted impatiently.

At his prompt, Frank went on hurriedly, "Okay, man. We got an outta-town biker in holding, no big thing, pulled him over for reckless driving, he'd had a few, not over the limit, he was just jacking around. But when we ran his license, found he had a bench warrant on him, tickets he hasn't seen to in C Springs. But he's been in there with Enid most of the night and apparently, she's been rambling. Some of the shit she said he thought was more fucked than what seems to be her usual fucked. When he got breakfast, he told Jon. Jon told me. We pulled her outta holding and put her into an interrogation room and asked more questions. Took a while, brother, but got it out of her."

When he didn't go on, Chace asked, "Got what out of her?"

"The reason she cast Jeremiah out."

"And that would be?" Chace pushed when Frank again stopped speaking.

"Okay, Chace, shit, okay..."

"Frank," Chace clipped when he trailed off.

When Frank continued, he again did it quickly. "Apparently, Jeremiah got away. He'd been attempting escapes frequently with zero success but he made it clear. He was in the woods. Brother, from what we can tell, he was in *Harker's Wood*. What he saw there flipped him right the fuck out. So right the fuck out, he went back to the only thing he knew. He went back to *her*."

Chace's body went still as a statue and his mouth felt strange when it formed the words, "What did he see?"

"From what we can get from her, he saw a blonde woman givin' a man a blowjob."

Oh fuck, no.

Please God, no.

Chace closed his eyes and dropped his head.

"I think it was Misty, brother," Frank whispered. "Enid didn't see it, she wasn't there. She just beat it out of him and what he told her he saw, she lost what was left of her marbles and got shot of him, thinkin' he was makin' that shit up or that he was the son of Satan or whatever. But I reckon, and the timeline jibes, that he saw Misty and the man who murdered her. It flipped him, he went back to her because it was the only thing he knew, the only protection he had."

It would jibe, Chace knew it. Jeremiah was terrified when he was out on his own. Chace could see this fear coming from Enid, knowing his sister was still captive, but he could see it was more. He'd seen Misty's face get raped, probably sensed her terror, maybe saw the gun and possibly saw her murdered.

Fuck, he'd seen that shit.

Fuck, he still had to be holding on to that fear.

Fuck!

"He could be the key to finding who did Misty," Frank told him quietly then finished, "and Newcomb."

Chace opened his eyes and lifted his head. "Who knows this shit?" he rapped out.

"Uh, me, Jon, the biker and the video camera that caught my questioning."

"You tell Cap. And you tell Jon to keep his trap shut and make sure Jon gets that message. He runs his mouth, I'll lose my mind and the way I lose it he will not want. You make sure that biker thinks she's just a lunatic, and you don't share that shit with anyone else."

Frank was silent then, "They find out there was a witness—"

"Then Miah's fucked," Chace finished for him.

"Shit, brother," Frank murmured then, "but, department's clean."

"Shit leaks, like it does whenever Jon runs his mouth. This gets to the wrong ears, that kid just went from enduring a goddamned nightmare to runnin' scared the rest of his fuckin' life."

"Right," Frank whispered.

"I'm callin' his psychologist. Then I'm comin' to the station."

"Right," Frank repeated.

"You got shit to do," Chace told him.

"Right," Frank said again then he disconnected.

Chace drew in a breath. Then he drew in another one.

Then he walked downstairs to tell Faye he was going to swing by the station and come back with treats from La-La Land for the women and kids.

*   *   *

"You cannot be serious," Frank said to Dr. Carruthers, Miah's psychologist who was standing with him, Chace and the cap in Cap's office.

"Deadly," Dr. Carruthers returned immediately.

"He may have been the only eyewitness we got to an unsolved murder, a murder committed by a man who, it's highly likely, has killed two people on this patch," Frank shot back.

"Until the DNA tests are done, those children are wards of the state and therefore the state makes decisions about their welfare and to make those decisions they would consult with someone like *me*. When they consult with me, I will strongly encourage them not to allow the police, however gently, to interrogate a boy who's father died in a car crash, his mother was murdered, he'd been kidnapped, imprisoned, mentally and physically abused, possibly had seen a murder but definitely a sex act at an age where he cannot process this in and of itself. It was an act that was not consensual and finally, he lived on his own, taking care of himself on the streets and in the wilderness all while terrified about the state of his sister. So let us not waste time by calling in CPS only for them to ask me what I think and act on my recommendation. Just take my word for it now that you are not going to talk to that boy about witnessing an act of rape and a possible murder," Dr. Carruthers retorted.

"You can be there," Frank offered.

"And, in the future, if it's necessary for you to interrogate him, I *better be*," she rejoined.

"It wouldn't be an interrogation," Frank clipped.

"It won't be anything," Chace growled, and all eyes came to him but he was looking at Frank. "No way *in fuck* you're gonna talk to Miah. Not now. Not fuckin' tomorrow. Not next fuckin' week. Not until Dr. Carruthers gives you the go-ahead to do it and maybe not at all. Tonight he's gonna eat lasagna with the folks who looked after him and the grandparents he hasn't seen in three fuckin' years and he's gonna do it feelin' safe and looked after. Not remembering watching a woman get her face raped. You call CPS and you try to get to that kid and they lose their minds and let you, Frank, you'll have to go through me to get him."

"But it's Misty," Frank told him something he already fucking knew.

"Yeah, it's Misty. And yeah, I wanna know who did her. But I do not want to sacrifice whatever scraps of peace of mind we've managed to give Miah in order to get that fucker. He doesn't get to do Misty, maybe Darren and fuck Miah too. No fuckin' way. We'll find another way," Chace fired back.

Frank's face filled with disbelief before he reminded him, "You've been living and breathing her case for months."

"And I'll live and breathe not knowin' who did her but resting easy that my not knowing means Miah can put this serious as fuck shit behind him and move the fuck *on*," Chace returned. "Honest to God, Frank, I'm uncertain I *ever* want you to speak to him about this shit. His grandparents ask me, I'll tell them not to volunteer him. We'll find this guy another way. But, he was my kid, he went through that shit, I would not swing his ass out there. Even and especially if it meant protective custody. Even and especially because it might mean, if this guy is part of a bigger operation, witness protection. That kid had three years of his life seriously fuckin' jacked. You cannot stand there and tell me Misty and Darren are worth jackin' up the rest of it."

"A crime has been committed, it doesn't matter against who," Frank said softly.

"By my count, lots of 'em have and only three of 'em against Darren and Misty. The rest, Miah and Becky endured. They will not endure more," Chace replied.

"Someone has to stand up for Darren and Misty. And someone has to pay for what was done to them," Frank shot back.

"I agree. Absolutely. What I don't agree is that Miah is the one who's gotta help us do all that," Chace retorted.

Frank pulled out the heavy artillery. "This isn't the cop I know you to be."

But Chace was immune. "I'm not a cop. I'm a man who is also a cop. And I'm the man who bought that kid a sleeping bag when he was sleepin' in rags, taught him how to play video games and carried his trembling sister through the woods after he rescued her. And I'm content to be that man over bein' a cop."

"You're going to be an excellent father," Dr. Carruthers cut in at this juncture, and Chace looked to her.

"I hope so since mine is a jackass."

Her lips twitched and she replied, "Well, maybe so but you learned the tools somewhere, though," she went on to advise, "I'd curtail the swearing."

Christ, he'd heard that before.

He didn't respond. He looked at Cap.

"We done?"

Cap nodded then turned his eyes to Frank. "No Jeremiah, son."

"Cap!" Frank bit out sharply.

"You get antsy, disobey an order, you try to get to that boy or his grandparents to make your attempt to get through Chace, you gotta get through me first. Boy's had enough. We'll find this asshole another way. As far as we're concerned in this office, Enid Eglund's ramblings about what Jeremiah saw are just that: ramblings. This dies here."

Frank's back went up and he returned softly but irately, his meaning veiled but still clear, "That isn't the way of the law."

"There's dirty, Frank," Cap replied just as softly but not irately. "And there's compassion. This says not one thing about Misty Keaton or Darren Newcomb and who did them or this office's determination to find that man. This is this department deciding to act with compassion for a witness. You sleep on that and you'll see it clear."

Frank stared at Cap then Dr. Carruthers then Chace before he walked out.

"You got lasagna to eat, son," Cap told him then looked at Dr. Carruthers. "You do too."

"Right," she whispered, grinning.

They made a move to the door but Cap stopped him, calling, "Chace."

Chace looked back at him.

"Tragic, definition of it, all that's happened to those kids. You and your woman, you did right by them. I see you got ties and they're strong. 'Spect, what I know of Faye Goodknight and her family, they do too. This job, we see a lotta bad. Can get used to it. Can make you hard. Wear you down. But tonight, son, tonight you get somethin' not a lot of cops get. You get to witness what those kids' grandparents are considering a miracle. When they take Jeremiah and Rebecca back to Wyoming, you'll get to keep that along with the knowledge that you helped make that miracle happen."

"Right," Chace muttered.

"Help her deal. Give your woman that heads-up," Cap advised.

Chace held his captain's eyes thinking, fuck, but it was a shitload better working for this man than it was working under Arnie.

Then he nodded.

Then he followed Dr. Carruthers out in order to meet Miah and Becky's grandparents.

*   *   *

Chace opened the door to his truck to get in and get to Faye but stopped when he heard his name called.

He looked to his right to see Marc, one of their interns, moving toward him, his face pale, eyes troubled.

Chace knew immediately why. Marc had run the searches and Marc had heard about Miah and Becky.

Therefore, before Marc stopped and while he was opening his mouth to speak, Chace ordered quietly, "Don't."

Marc closed his mouth then opened it again to say in a tight voice, "I set the wrong parameters."

"Don't, Marc," Chace repeated.

"I didn't know he was eleven. I didn't think just to try a search outside—"

"Not your job," Chace cut him off. "Your job is to work and learn. My job is to help you learn. I didn't know he was eleven either. But I also didn't suggest it. I just expected it. Expected you to do somethin' you didn't know to do. It was my fuckup, Marc, not yours."

"I've been an intern for—"

"Doesn't matter," Chace interrupted again.

"If we knew, we could have—"

"Shake it off," Chace ordered.

Marc's eyes got wide but his tone was bitter when he asked, "Shake off knowin' I kept those kids from their grandparents for weeks, that girl held captive by a whack-job, all this because I didn't do somethin' as simple as do a search with a wider age range?"

"Yeah," Chace replied, and Marc blinked so Chace went on, "Listen, man, you want a career in law enforcement or you move on to anything else, you are gonna fuck up. Your superiors are gonna fuck up but you'll do the work and feel shit about it or they'll dump their fuckup on your shoulders. You wanna be a cop, sometimes decisions you gotta make either on the fly or during a long-term investigation are not gonna be the right ones. It'll happen because you're human. You gotta cut yourself some slack or, whatever you decide to do in this life, it'll drag you down. One thing you can learn now is when someone gives you an assignment and doesn't fully explain it, if they put that shit on you, that reflects on them. I gave you an assignment, I guessed the wrong age range and I made assumptions. You did what you were told. We both gotta live with that. But do not take that blame. Shake it off. Learn from it. And move on. Best you can do and it's what I'm gonna do."

Marc studied him then asked quietly, "You're not pissed?"

"I was yesterday. Now, seein' your face, seein' you give a shit, thinkin' on it, I still am. But at me. I had a bunch of shit goin' on in my life and didn't give my attention fully to this. I fucked up and I made you feel the way you feel right now and kept those kids from their folks. But they'll see them again tonight and soon, they'll be home and healing. It's over. We learn from it and move on."

There it was. Faye having his back and she wasn't even there. Faye teaching him he couldn't shoulder the world's burdens. Teaching him to give himself a break. Teaching him in a way he could teach a decent kid who wanted to do good deeds in his life the same lesson so he didn't take the world on his shoulders like Chace had done for thirty-five years.

Marc held his gaze. Then he nodded and said, "Next time, I'll extend the search."

Chace hoped like hell there wasn't a next time.

But he didn't say that. He nodded.

Marc lifted his chin, moved away and Chace watched him go.

Then he gave it a moment, forced himself to let it go, sighed, angled in his truck and headed to Faye.

* * *

Chace blinked away sleep knowing something wasn't right.

It was the dark before the dawn and he sensed as well as felt he was alone in his bed.

He lay still and silent, listening to see if Faye was in the bathroom.

He heard nothing so he threw back the covers, walked to his dresser, grabbed a pair of pajama bottoms and pulled them on. He moved through the dark, quiet house, finding nothing, seeing nothing until he noticed the front door open, the storm door closed.

He moved into the foyer, his bare feet silent on the wood, and looked out the door to see Faye in her nightie, one of his sweatshirts and a thick pair of his socks, sitting on a rocking chair like he sat on them, pulled up to the railing of the porch, feet up.

Her eyes were aimed at his plain.

It was near May and they were caught in a valley but it was still cold. Her legs had to be freezing.

He moved back through the house, pulled on his own sweatshirt and socks, went back to the family room to grab a throw and then down the hall to the front door.

Her head turned when he opened the storm door.

"Hey," she whispered.

"Hey," he whispered back, moving to her and throwing the blanket over her legs, tucking it around her hips before he nabbed the other rocker, pulled it up beside her and sat his ass in it.

He tipped it back, cocked his knees and lifted his feet to the railing.

He wasn't surprised she was here. She'd held it together for Miah so he could hold it together for Becky during dinner.

Therefore, it had gone well.

It had been the miracle Cap said it would be.

DNA tests were fast-tracked and pending but they already knew there was no denying it from the pictures. The meeting made that solid. Miah and Becky's grandparents recognized them the second they saw them and they were beside themselves, both women and one of the men breaking down instantly, necessitating Silas and Sondra leading them out to pull them together.

But they did, returned and they had dinner.

It had been a strange night.

That didn't mean it wasn't beautiful.

Three years ago, those four people thought they lost everything worth anything in their lives in the expanse of two months.

At the Goodknight table, they got some of it back, it was precious and they didn't even try to hide it.

There was definitely a spark of recognition for Miah, thus he seemed open to them in his distant way. Becky had been five when she'd been taken, her nightmare had just ended so she either didn't recognize them or couldn't yet process the fact that she did but she followed her brother's lead. Dr. Carruthers was pleased and approved another visit the next morning. Breakfast at the diner with Sondra and the grandparents.

Soon, they'd go home.

Faye had been welcoming and friendly to the grand-parents and supportive to the kids, openly loving to Miah as was her way and as affectionate to Becky as she could be. When they left, she'd been quiet.

Chace had given her that play.

On their rockers, he kept giving it to her. He let her find her time to end the silence and after taking that time, she did.

"It's over," she whispered to his plain.

"It's over," he agreed quietly.

"They love them." She kept whispering.

"Yeah," he replied gently.

"Loads."

"Yeah."

She was silent a long moment then, "Love heals."

She needed to believe that. Luckily, she was right. He knew this because she taught him that too.

"Yeah, baby," he whispered.

She fell silent.

Chace let her, eyes on his plain.

Then he heard her soft sob and it was his turn to have his play.

He got out of his chair and lifted her out of hers. She instantly curled into him, her chest in his, her face in his neck, her arms around his shoulders. He pulled open the storm door, kicked the front door shut and walked her to his bed. He lay her in it and joined her there, gathering her close as her body rocked gently and the tears flowed.

When she quieted in his arms, he tipped his head so his lips were at her hair and he asked, "You cryin' 'cause of all of it or somethin' in particular?"

"All of it, I think."

"You'll miss him," Chace noted gently.

She nodded and her breath hitched.

He gave her a squeeze.

She took in a shaky breath and whispered, "I'm glad they're nice people."

"Me too."

"Did you see the pictures?" she asked, and he gave her another squeeze because he did. Both sets of grandparents brought pictures.

Miah and Becky, their mom and dad. Happy family. Half of that gone.

"Yeah," he answered.

She pressed closer, burrowing in. The loss was too much to bear in the dark before dawn.

Chace gave it time.

Then he asked, "You get me?"

Her head tipped back and she caught his eyes. "Get you?"

Quietly, Chace explained, "For whatever reasons, life took away their parents and led them to a nightmare. Then God was done and He sent an angel to put a stop to it. That angel bein' you, a woman capable of performing a lot of miracles. Now, when I call you an angel, do you get me?"

Tears filled her eyes again, she dipped her chin, shoved her face in his throat and her body bucked with her sob.

She got him.

*   *   *

One week and two days later

Chace stood and watched Sondra give Becky a hug while Silas stood close to Miah, grinning at him, probably teasing him, but the despondency could still be seen around his eyes. Faye was standing beside Chace, smiling at her parents and the kids, but her sadness was a great deal more pronounced.

They were standing outside and the cars were packed.

The kids were going home.

"Chace," he heard and turned his eyes to Miah and Becky's paternal grandfather.

"Ezra," Chace muttered as the man got up close and stopped.

He tipped his chin and smiled at Faye then he looked up at Chace.

Then quietly, he said, "It's come to my attention, son, you covered Miah and Becky's hospital bills."

He heard Faye make a muted noise and felt her shift into him, her arm brushing his, her fingers curling around his, but she said nothing.

He hadn't told her. He also didn't intend to.

Shit.

"Yep," he replied casually, hoping that would end it, knowing from getting to know these people it would not.

Ezra nodded before saying, "We've been talkin' and we—"

Chace cut him off, "Don't worry about it," and Faye's fingers around his grew tighter.

Ezra's eyes grew wider. "But, that had to—"

Chace shook his head. "I have a trust fund. My grandparents gave it to me. They were good people. My grandfather worked hard all his life. He was a good man. If they knew the money they worked hard to earn went to that, they'd be pleased. Trust me. If they were alive, they'd do it themselves. Now, it's done. You got enough to see about setting right. But that's not part of it."

"That's too much of a gesture," Ezra replied softly.

"It wasn't a gesture," Chace returned just as softly. "What it was, if this makes it easier to accept, is me and Faye buyin' our way into those kids' lives. You're leavin' but this doesn't end, not for them, not for us. We wanna know they're growin' and doin' it strong but we also wanna know how. If you give that to us over the years then we're even."

Ezra stared up at him, his throat moving as he swallowed and Faye leaned into his side.

Then Ezra whispered, "We can do that."

"Good," Chace muttered and moved to shake the man's hand, this necessitating Faye letting his go.

After he shook his hand, Faye moved in for a hug and more hugs commenced, farewells, heartfelt keep-in-touches, forced smiles that were sad but nevertheless happy.

Finally, Chace watched Faye whisper something in Becky's ear while hugging her that made Becky giggle. It was a small one but it was a genuine one.

Then he watched her hold it together by a thread, her eyes bright, her lips quivering as she gave Miah a tight hug that lasted a very long time and was unusual in the sense that an eleven-year-old kid was just as reluctant to let go.

Watching it, Chace's throat got tight.

He touched Becky's hair in his farewell and she moved to her grandparents as Faye made a low noise in the back of her throat and let Miah go.

She straightened and ran her fingers through his hair before she whispered, "Call me. I want to know what you're reading."

Miah, his eyes also wet and getting red, nodded.

Faye bit her lip and stepped away.

Miah turned to him.

Chace began to lift his hand to give him a shake but stopped when Miah moved right into his space and curled his arms around Chace's middle.

At his touch, his less-thin body pressed to Chace's, his arms, neither of them in casts or bandages, around him, Chace's throat completely closed. He felt the wet in his own eyes and wrapped his arms around his boy, holding tight, bending his neck and closing his eyes.

"Sleepin' bag was warm," Miah muttered to his gut, his voice trembling.

Fuck. The kid was killing him.

"Good," Chace muttered back, his voice thick.

Miah held on. Chace did too.

Then Miah whispered, "Your hair."

Chace opened his eyes. "What, buddy?"

Miah leaned back but didn't let go, looked up at Chace with his red eyes and kept whispering, "Your hair. Lion's hair."

Chace didn't get it but forced his own smile and replied quietly, "Okay."

Miah let him go, Chace's arms dropped away, Miah's chin quivered but his eyes didn't waver from Chace's when he whispered, "You're my Aslan."

Aslan.

The Lion, the Witch and the Wardrobe.

Holy fuck.

The words like a sock in the gut, Chace's chest got tight and he crouched in front of Miah saying the only word he could think to say, "Buddy."

"I'm gonna be Peter." Miah was still whispering.

"Good choice," Chace whispered back, forcing it through the sting in his throat.

They held each other's gazes, Chace having no fucking clue what to say or do.

Then Miah whispered, "'Bye, Aslan."

Holy fuck. Fuck. Fuck. *Fuck.*

"'Bye, Peter," Chace whispered back.

Chace watched him pull in breath, look up at Faye then he turned and walked to his grandparents.

Chace moved to straighten and barely got his feet when Faye was in his space, her front pressed to his side, her arms wrapped tight around his middle. He slid an arm around her shoulders, Silas and Sondra moved close and they watched Miah, Becky and their family get into their cars.

They called good-byes, they waved and they stood in Silas and Sondra's front drive and watched as they drove off and they kept watching until there was nothing to watch anymore.

Faye moved first and when she did it was to get up on her toes and find his ear.

"Told you that you were a hero," she whispered, and Chace closed his eyes but she wasn't done. "I'm not the only one who thinks so, Aslan."

He turned into her, pulling her fully into his arms and burying his face in her neck.

He held tight.

She returned the favor.

They felt Silas and Sondra silently move away.

As he held her, feeling her body rock quietly with her tears, her wet hitting his neck, he held strong but he knew she could feel his own wet against the skin of hers.

And he didn't give a fuck.

CHAPTER TWENTY

Breathe

I BARRELED UP the steps and didn't bother inserting the key because I knew Chace was inside my apartment already.

I threw the door open, saw him in my kitchen, head tipped back taking a long draw from a bottle of beer and, as his eyes slid to me around the bottle, his chin dipping down, I shouted, "It's a girl!"

He dropped the bottle and asked, "What?"

I slammed the door, raced to him and threw myself in is arms with such force, he rocked back on a foot.

"It's a girl. A girl! Lexie and Ty had a little girl. Her name's Ella Alexi!" I cried, jumping up and down, taking him with me since my arms were around him and one of his was around me.

He grinned down at me, muttering, "Good news, darlin'."

"The best!" I exclaimed as I stopped jumping. "Ten fingers. Ten toes. Krys says she's got black fuzz on her head, already full of curls. I bet she's adorable."

"I bet." Chace kept muttering through his grin.

I shook him in my arms and shared, "I can't wait to meet her."

Chace was still grinning and muttering when he replied, "I bet that too."

"Krys says half-price tequila shots in celebration," I informed him.

"Only Krystal would celebrate the birth of a child with half-price tequila shots," Chace noted, and I smiled into his face because this was crazy, hilarious and true.

"Can we go?" I asked.

"Drink tequila?" Chace asked back.

"Yeah."

"You drink tequila?"

"No."

"Ever?"

"Um . . . maybe twice in college but, since then, no," I told him.

"Then . . . yeah. Absolutely."

I felt my brows draw together at his weird, firm answer. "Absolutely?"

"Baby, you happy and drunk, your place a couple of blocks from Bubba's and your bed ten feet from the front door, the answer to that is yeah . . . *absolutely*."

I felt my womb contract and bit back my suggestion that Chace, as he'd be buying since he wouldn't let me, should hit the ATM prior to us going out.

Instead, I got up on my toes, touched my mouth to his and moved away while asking, "Dinner first?"

"Yep," Chace answered. "What're we having?"

I opened the door of the fridge and pulled out the packet of hamburger, replying, "Packet tacos."

"Works for me," he muttered.

I set to work while Chace got me a glass of wine. Then I kept working while Chace sat on my counter and I took sips of wine and I told him my other good news.

"Library Board called. I have a meeting with them

next week. The Town Council has allocated more funding to the library and they've told me when we get it we'll get new computers and they're giving me a ten percent salary adjustment."

"Not on par with Lexie and Ty havin' a healthy baby girl but still, good news, honey," Chace commented, I looked to him and gave him a big smile since he was also smiling at me then I turned my attention back to the taco meat.

"Faye," he called when the meat was browned and I'd added the water and seasoning.

I looked back to him. "Yeah?"

"Turn it down," he ordered, and I dipped my ear to my shoulder.

"What?"

"Come here." He kept ordering and my head straightened.

"We're close. I just have to slice the lettuce and tomato," I told him.

"In a minute, turn it down, we got a problem."

Oh jeez.

I didn't like this.

We hadn't had a problem in a while.

It was Saturday, three weeks and then some since we'd met Becky.

Miah and Becky were back in Wyoming and, from daily reports, they were settling in, doing fine, seeing a local counselor and bonding with their grandparents as well as their aunts, uncles and cousins. They were living with their mom's parents with their dad's visiting daily. In fact, they had dinner together every night.

This meant the kids were surrounded all the time by people who loved them and showed it.

Good stuff.

Miah was still reading and doing a lot of it and I knew this because he called at least once a week to tell me what he read, what he thought about it, what he was planning on reading next and asking my thoughts on what he should add to his list to be read. He was still also playing his video games and I knew this because he called Chace at least once a week to talk to him about the games, his scores and other boy-to-man stuff.

At first it was weird getting used to a communicative Miah. But since he pulled his thumb out of the dam, there was a lot to flood through. It was like there was never a time when he didn't speak. He could gab for half an hour nonstop and if he was really excited about something, that shone through.

He seemed to be really excited about a lot of things and that way regularly.

Great stuff.

I missed him. Mom and Dad missed him. Chace missed him. But it was clear he was flourishing. So that helped us to be able to cope with missing him.

Anyway, we were all planning on taking a week's vacation to drive up there and spend some time with them. This was my idea and I wasn't certain how Chace would feel, our first vacation together, spending it with my parents, a couple of kids and four people we didn't know very well.

Chace thought it was great idea with one caveat.

"We get a hotel room, baby, in a hotel where your parents *aren't* staying."

Apparently, there would be other activities during our vacation.

Hotel room sex with Chace. Another something new.

Another something to look forward to.

More good that had happened was that Mary Eglund had slunk away, resigning from the Town Council after her sister's felonious activities had become public knowledge and, already disliked, she was now reviled. This was because she, one of the only people to have contact with

Enid Eglund, didn't see her sister's insanity and do something about it or find she was abusing two kids whose mother her sister murdered. Instead she spent her time being annoying and telling people how to live their lives when she should have been taking care of family business.

Rumor had it her house was on the market.

She wouldn't be much of a loss to the community.

Her sister, on the other hand, was currently enjoying her stay in a hospital for the criminally insane somewhere in Wyoming. I didn't like this, Chace didn't either. What she did to those kids, I felt, deserved worse punishment.

But there was no denying she was seriously, fraking 'round the bend. She'd been deemed unfit to stand trial and pretty much fit for nothing but loads of meds and incarceration among a bunch of other folks who were as tripped out as she was.

I didn't like it but I didn't dwell. She was locked away, perhaps not the way I'd prefer but she was still locked away and no longer a threat to anyone.

So there it was.

Onward from the slightly bad was further good.

Valerie had spent the weekend before visiting and except for a couple of times where she got nervous and fidgety, these being when she first met my parents when they came over to Chace's for dinner, it had been a really good weekend.

I liked her. She was cute and funny and, with Chace now far more relaxed with her, the visit had gone well. Except she brought me a pair of earrings, pearls surrounded by diamonds, their expense so obvious it kinda flipped me out but Chace told me to roll with it and, with no other choice, I did. I wore them all weekend even though they were way fancier than my outfits, but she seemed delighted I did so it was worth the fashion faux pas.

Trane had not been invited nor did he show. Valerie didn't mention him. Chace and I didn't either. I sensed an underlying sadness in Valerie that this was the case but I also saw her determination to enjoy Chace how she could take him so I did what I could to facilitate that.

I felt something lovely seep into me because I could see she saw Chace was happy, more relaxed, a part of my family and I sensed she liked that immensely. So although there was sadness, there was also ease.

Life was good. It had settled into normal. No dramas. No "dark." No nothing but work, food, family, sex, TV, books... life.

I didn't want a problem. We'd had enough problems.

I was enjoying good. Like, a frak of a lot.

So I didn't want bad.

But even so, I turned the burner down on the meat and moved to Chace though I did this on leaden feet. He spread his legs when I got close and I took that as my cue to move between them. When I did, I rested my hands on his thighs and he lifted one to shift my hair over my shoulder as the fingers of his other hand curled around the top of my hip. After he slid my hair away, he wrapped his fingers around the side of my neck, his thumb gliding over my jaw.

"Is it Miah?" I whispered. "Have you heard something?"

"No," Chace whispered back, his eyes moving over my face in a way I couldn't quite read.

It wasn't bad. But I wasn't sure it was good since it was so intense.

"Becky?" I went on quietly.

"Nope," he answered immediately and also quietly.

I pulled in a breath then cautiously put out there, "Has something gone down with Misty's case or, um... anything around that?"

"Nope," he repeated, and his hand left my neck to drop to mine on his thigh and wrap around it.

"Chace—"

His head dropped to watch his thumb move over my fingers as he muttered, "Naked, baby."

My head twitched at his weird word.

"Pardon?"

His eyes came to mine and he repeated, "Naked."

I felt my brows draw together and I asked, "Naked?"

He held my gaze even as he moved, his other hand leaving my hip to shove into his jeans pocket then he held my hand as his other moved to it.

My eyes tipped down as my breath stopped coming when I watched a simple but stunning diamond solitaire being slid onto my left ring finger.

"Naked," he whispered, and I sucked breath into my nose as I stared at the diamond now at the base of my finger. "You marry me, I'll add a band under that, cover you up."

I blinked as the sting hit my nose, the wet hit my eyes, but after I blinked, my gaze didn't move from that ring and I again stopped breathing.

"Baby," Chace whispered, his hand holding mine giving me a squeeze, "*breathe*."

I breathed.

His thumb moved over the ring and his beautiful deep voice came back at me, "Will you marry me, Faye?"

"Yes," I whispered so quietly it was like a breeze.

But I didn't take my eyes off Chace's ring.

His hand stayed curled around mine, his thumb firm at the base of his ring, but his other hand came to the side of my neck and slid up into my hair behind my ear.

"Will you build a home with me?" he whispered his question.

"Yes."

"A family?"

"Yes," I repeated, my breath catching just at the idea of that beauty.

"A life?"

My head tipped back, his beautiful blue eyes locked on mine, and everything he felt for me was shining from them, warming me to my soul in a way I knew I'd never, ever be cold.

Not again.

Not in my whole life.

"Yes," I whispered as the tears slid out of my eyes.

When they did, his hand slid out of my hair so it could cup my jaw and his thumb moved across my cheek to catch them as they fell.

"I love you, Faye Goodknight," he said quietly, looking deep in my eyes.

I sucked in a breath that broke twice before I replied, "I love you too, Chace Keaton."

His lips tipped up and his eyes grew super warm.

"Want you movin' in, baby," he murmured.

"Okay," I agreed immediately.

"Next weekend," he went on.

"Okay," I agreed, again immediately.

"We start buildin' our home, our life now so we can give it to our kids after that band joins your diamond."

My breath hitched again and I repeated, "Okay."

His eyes lit with a different light, one I loved just as much when he asked, "You gonna jump on-line and tell your geek squad you landed me?"

"Yes," I whispered.

"Kiss me and I'll finish the tacos so you can do that."

"Okay," I said yet again but stayed where I was and didn't move.

"Baby, kiss me," Chace prompted when this lasted a long time.

"In a second, honey, I'm memorizing this moment."

Raw flooded his features but this time, it wasn't pain.

It was beauty.

Then Chace's hand drove back into my hair, he pulled me to him and kissed me.

Ten minutes later, Chace finished the tacos and I got on-line to give the news to Benji and Serenity.

*   *   *

Krys didn't miss my ring when we wandered into Bubba's an hour later.

Therefore, Chace didn't have to hit the ATM. Any time he tried to pass a bill to her, she refused, and Chace could be bossy but if Krys was in the mood to refuse, you had no hope of winning.

There were a lot of hoots, hollers, claps on the shoulder for Chace, hugs for me as Krys and Twyla shared the news around the bar then told anyone who came in. One or the other of them got on the phone, which meant Tate and Laurie came in. Then Deke. Wood and Maggie came a little later. Deck wasn't far behind them. Sunny and Shambles hit the bar not long after. The flow continued as did the hugs and claps on the back and news spread so fast, I took a call from my father whose voice was thick when he told me we'd have a family celebration soon and he'd try to keep the news from Liza so she wouldn't do something dramatic to steal my thunder.

Although I would have liked to share the news with my family, I was too happy to care someone took away my shot and I was happier hearing Dad was happy.

Bubba jacked the stereo up and after a few songs, Krys took over the control of the iPod attached to it. She clearly was in a romantic mood and Chace was definitely in a romantic mood because even though no one was dancing, the minute Mazzy Star's "Fade into You" came on, he led me to an open space by the window, pulled me into his arms and we started swaying.

Before Chace, this would have mortified me.

In Chace's arms with his ring on my finger, the world faded away as I faded into him.

Krys followed this with Bad Company's "Feel Like Makin' Love," Bruce Springsteen's "Leah," the Cowboy Junkies singing the Velvet Underground's "Sweet Jane" then back to Bad Company for "She Brings Me Love."

Through all this, Chace held me close in his arms, I kept mine locked around him, our friends were close, part of our town looking on but there was no one who could penetrate our moment. We were in a sea of happy people celebrating love and babies and a town free to just be. But for me it was just Chace and for Chace it was just me.

And through it, holding me in a way I knew he'd be happy never to let me go, Chace proved he could hold me close and dance until the morning light.

Then she played it. Whether she remembered me telling her about it or whether it just came up, Krys played it.

Ella Mae Bowen singing "Holding Out for a Hero."

And when she played it, I decided it was time he knew.

So I pressed even closer so I could lift my lips to his ear.

"That night, it wasn't Dobie Gray," I whispered. "It was this song. It was Ella Mae singing this to me when I thought you weren't all I knew you to be, which is all the words to this song. Twenty-nine years, I held out for this. Then, half an hour later, you proved every one of these words true and every moment since then, you kept doing it. I'll take you thinking I'm your angel but you need to know you're my hero. Twenty-nine, honey, I held out for this. Twenty-nine years, I held out for you."

His face, already in my neck, burrowed deeper. His arms, already holding me tight, pulled me closer.

He said nothing.

But as he swayed me to Ella Mae, I sang with her in his ear.

And that moment in that bar in Chace's arms with me whispering his song into his ear telling him all he was and all he was to me, no matter the beauty that lay before us, no matter the beauty we created, I knew there would never be a moment more beautiful than that for me.

At the end of the song, Chace sealed that beauty by sliding his lips to mine then sliding his tongue into my mouth, sweet, gentle, soft, giving, letting me give.

Everything that was him.

Everything that was me.

CHAPTER TWENTY-ONE

Holding Out for a Hero

THERE WAS MOVEMENT at the other end of the bar and Chace watched a brunette leave the back hall and enter the common area from where the bathrooms were.

Faye had disappeared back there fifteen minutes ago and it was time to go home. It was time to go to bed. It was time to make love to his woman for the first time while she was wearing his ring on her finger.

Fifteen minutes was a long time for her to be gone. He was impatient. He wanted her alone. He wanted to keep dancing with her. He intended to dance with her until dawn but in a different way.

But the bar was packed, which meant there could be a line at the women's restroom.

He grabbed his beer, lifted it up, took a drag and on the way down his eyes caught on Tate.

Tate was just down the bar leaning two forearms into it, one hand curled around a bottle of beer. Laurie was at his side but she had an arm around his gut and her torso was draped over his back, leaning into Wendy who she was talking to and Chace couldn't see Lauren but Wendy was laughing.

Tate's woman might be draped over his back but his eyes were on Chace.

When he caught Chace's he lifted his beer and he tipped it out as his lips twitched.

Chace knew what that salute meant.

Tate knew what Chace was feeling. Not finding the right woman but finding the only one, the perfect one, the one that was meant for you. Then putting your ring on her finger, claiming her and knowing she was yours, no one else would ever have her, your bed would never be cold, you'd always have someone at your side or taking your back.

Tate Jackson knew how good that felt. He knew what it meant. He knew how important it was. He knew there was nothing better in the world.

Chace lifted his chin to him then watched as Lauren shifted to say something in his ear. Tate's eyes unfocused as he listened, his face got soft, his lips curved up then he turned his neck and Chace lost sight of him as he took his woman's mouth.

Yeah. Tate Jackson knew how good it felt.

At that moment, his phone vibrated in his pocket.

He pulled it out, not surprised it was vibrating even though it was late. Word was traveling fast. Good wishes were coming thick. Chace reckoned that day was significant for the town of Carnal. Ty Walker had moved on to the next step of good coming out of a life fucked by the men who'd fucked over the town. On the same day, Chace had too.

Chace looked down at his phone to see it was a text. He moved his thumb over the buttons to pull it up and when he saw it, his body went still.

We have Faye. As of now, she has four hours of air. You have that time to find and return the articles needed. If you don't, we won't tell you where to dig her out and she'll run out of breath.

After reading it, his lungs burning, Chace moved swiftly from his position at the bar and shoved through the crowd toward the back hall. When he made it to the mouth, regardless of the heaving bar, he saw it was empty.

He moved down it to the women's restroom.

He opened the door, a blonde at the sink turned and narrowed her eyes at him but he ignored her and called sharply, "Faye!"

"You cool, dude?" she asked.

He was absolutely not.

"Faye!" he clipped.

Nothing.

His eyes went to the blonde. "You seen a redhead in here?"

She looked at him and bent slightly to aim her eyes under the stalls, calling, "Any of you redheads?"

"Nope."

"Not me."

"He cute?"

None of them Faye.

Fuck.

Fuck.

Before she could answer, he swung out and moved quickly down the hall to the back and the emergency exit. He pushed the door open and heard no alarm. Outside in the alley there was no car, there was no one. There was nothing.

Fuck.

Fuck.

He moved up the hall, stopping at the mouth and tipping his head down to the phone.

Fifteen minutes, if they incapacitated her, had a car, they could be long gone.

He stared at his phone.

Four hours of air.

Chace kept staring at his phone.

Dig her out.

Chace continued to stare at his phone.

She'll run out of breath.

Memories collided in his brain.

Faye staring at him the first time she did it with that wonder in her eyes, on the sidewalk outside La-La Land when he apologized for being a dick. He didn't know it then but she did it because she had a crush on him and he was, also for the first time, close.

It affected her so much, just him being close, she stopped breathing.

So he'd whispered, *Breathe, Faye.*

And right before he wrapped her hand around his cock the first time they'd made love, she'd been holding her breath.

So he'd murmured, *Breathe, baby.*

And that very night when he'd put his ring on her finger.

Baby, he'd whispered, *breathe.*

She'll run out of breath.

Breathe.

"Chace?" Tate's voice came at him from close, his head jerked up and when Tate saw him, his face went from questioning to alert. "Christ, man, what's goin' on?"

"They've got Faye," he growled.

"Who?" Tate asked.

"The Elite," Chace answered tersely, those two words

raw, and he didn't see Tate's chin jerk back. He was moving toward the door, pushing through the crowd, vaguely hearing Tate shout men's names but his mind was scrambling.

Darren Newcomb was not a bud. Chace detested the man. He avoided him as best he could. He had no idea who he'd trust. He had no idea where he'd hide that shit. He had no idea who he might give it to.

"*Fuck*," Chace hissed, pushing open the door and hitting buttons on his phone.

He stopped outside, hit reply then typed in, *I'll find it, you'll get it but I'll need more time* and then he hit send.

"Chace, talk," Tate ordered and Chace looked up to see Tate there with Bubba, Deke, Wood, Jim-Billy and Deck.

"There's shit out there," he told them.

"We know," Tate replied. Always sharp, Tatum Jackson. He knew exactly what was going on.

"They want it. From their message it sounds like they've buried Faye somewhere. She's got four hours for me to find that shit and get it to them or she runs out of air."

"*Buried her?*" Deck growled, his big body tense, his mood drifting dangerously through the air, and Chace shoved his phone to his friend who took it but suddenly it all came clear and his eyes sliced to Tate.

"Tate, call Max. Get him to get to George Nielson, find him, drag his ass out of bed if he has to and find out what he knows or if he can find out anything. Max isn't up for that, I need a man to go to Gnaw Bone who is," Chace ordered, Tate lifted up his chin and stepped away.

His phone chimed and Deck hit buttons, then his eyes came to Chace. "They said you got four hours, no more," he told him, jaw hard, eyes glittering.

Chace looked at his friend. "That number, from the text, use your superpowers. Get a lock on it." Deck nodded, stepped back and pulled out his own phone. Chace looked to Wood. "You call Ty. I know it's shit on a night as good as tonight for him but we need to pull him in. He needs to connect with Dewey. Dewey knows everything about everyone. Get Ty to get Dewey on the move collecting intel. Dewey can find out or even has ideas, we need to know who may be in play and how they'll play it."

"Right, bud," Wood muttered and stepped away.

Chace reached out and yanked his phone out of Deck's hand then he took off running toward Faye's apartment.

"Fuck! Where you goin'?" Bubba shouted at his back as he ran and hit buttons on his phone.

He put it to his ear and listened to it ring. It rang four times and he was about to disconnect in order to reconnect and wake that jackass up when he heard his father's voice.

"Chace?"

"Dad—" he started, his breath heavy but Trane cut him off.

"It's nearly two in the morning."

"Shut the fuck up and listen. Your buddies lost patience. They've buried Faye alive. I got four hours to get the shit out there back to them or she runs out of air. Get your ass out of bed on the phone or in your car or fuckin' both and find out where Faye is."

"Buried alive?" Trane whispered as Chace took the turn into the alley toward Faye's apartment hearing footfalls behind him.

"Every second you waste is a second of air she does not have," Chace growled into the phone as he made the next turn into the back alley then he disconnected.

He sprinted up her steps hearing men taking them behind him. He yanked out his keys, opened the door and surged through. He ran straight to her desk, turned on the lamp there and hit the button for her computer.

"Brother, you gotta let us in on what's goin' on in your head so we can move out and find your girl," Deck told him as Chace searched through the shit on Faye's desk, yanking at it, his hands hitting shit he didn't need, it falling to the floor unheeded then he found it. Her address book.

He stepped away from the computer and looked at Deck. "That boots up, call up her chat and see if you can engage a guy named Benji or someone that calls herself SerenityWash."

He saw the other men all standing in Faye's apartment, all of them on their phones, then he bent his head and flipped through the address book.

Nothing on anyone named Benji. No entry with "SerenityWash."

Fuck.

"Chace," Tate called, and Chace looked to him. "I'm goin' to Newcomb's sister."

"Frank questioned her. She says she doesn't know shit," Chace told him.

"She says it but she might change her mind knowin' someone's buried alive so she might cough it up or she may know Newcomb enough to know where he hid it or who he gave it to then the boys can make the rounds," Tate returned.

"Go," Chace grunted and Tate went.

"Got Benji," Deck told him, shifting away from the keyboard and Chace moved in.

Bending over it, he typed,

You got Chace. The Elite have got Faye. They want the shit out there or she runs out of air. You got an idea of who they would contract this shit to?

He got back, *OMG! Runs out of air? What the frak does that mean?*

He typed, *Hold it together and think. I asked you a question. Answer it.*

Benji replied, *They communicate regularly with a man named Clinton Bonar.*

Fuck.

Right.

Bonar.

Chace straightened, threw his phone to Deck and growled, "Bonar. Call him," his eyes sliced to the men, "find him."

Bubba and Deke took off. Deck put the phone to his ear.

Chace went back to the keyboard.

What else? He asked.

I'm trying to engage Serenity. She was the one who found most of the stuff. But it looks like she's off-line. Benji typed back.

You got contact info on her? Chace pushed.

No. Benji answered.

A real name? Chace went on.

Sorry, Chace, no. OMG.OMG. Benji was losing it.

Hold it together. You got anything? Chace returned.

Faye told us to forget it all, delete it. I did. I don't know if Serenity did. But I'll see if I can restore anything from backups. I'll send it to her email and I'll keep trying Serenity, Benji replied.

Do that now. Chace ordered, got back an *Okay,* and he turned from the keyboard.

"Bonar isn't answering," Deck muttered, his head bent to Chace's phone, thumbs moving over it.

Chace prowled to Faye's house phone by the couch, snatched it out, engaged it, hit buttons and put it to his ear.

"Carnal Police Department, can I help you?" Terry answered.

"Terry, Chace," Chace replied. "Got a text, the men Arnold Fuller was blackmailing have arranged to have Faye Goodknight kidnapped and their text indicates she's been buried alive. I have four hours to get what's being held over them or she runs out of air. You talk to Frank to ascertain who they are, you, Frank and anyone else on duty gets the word out. Every one of those men are rounded up and brought in for questioning. Now. Tonight."

"Jesus, Chace," Terry muttered.

"That's a second of air Faye just lost," Chace bit out.

"Fuck, okay, but, my understanding, those men are all over four counties and all the way to Aspen," Terry told him.

"Then you better get on the goddamned phone," Chace growled then disconnected.

"Chace, bud, Dewey's meetin' me back of Bubba's," Wood called, and Chace got the chance to get a chin lift in before Wood walked out the door and the second he disappeared, Jim-Billy, Lauren and Krys were rushing through it.

"What's going on?" Krys asked.

"Ass at that computer. Faye's been taken." Lauren and Krystal gasped, Jim-Billy grunted but Chace just kept talking. "She has some friends who might be in contact through a chat. There might be emails coming through. Sit on that computer and call me if they give you anything."

Krystal ran to the computer, Lauren at her heels.

Jim-Billy called softly to Lauren, "Laurie, darlin', toss me your phone."

Lauren pulled her phone out of her pocket as Chace looked to Deck.

"Let's go."

"Where?" Deck asked.

"Bonar," Chace replied then he prowled out of Faye's apartment, his chest tight, his throat closing, his palms itching, fear and fury battling for supremacy and it was a crapshoot which would win.

And when.

Deck followed him out.

*   *   *

Faye

I turned the valve on the oxygen tank they left me, the flashlight they left me lighting my movements, my hands covered in blood from pounding against the wood surrounding me.

The air was getting thin.

I used up too much panicking.

I needed more.

I moved the plastic thingie so it covered my mouth and nose and breathed in.

Chace's words came to me.

Baby, breathe.

My eyes shifted to the note I'd found when I'd stopped panicking, pulled it together, surveyed my close confines, found the flashlight and the tank. It was resting against the wood at my side.

You have four hours. So does he. The phone has minimal charge. No GPS. You'll have enough time for one call. Use it if you need to say good-bye.

My eyes shifted to the phone they left with me.

Then they closed.

Ella Mae sang in my ear.

I kept my eyes closed.

I felt Chace's arms around me, his body pressed to mine, our hips swaying.

We were getting married. We were going to build a family.

I held out for twenty-nine years. I held out for Chace. I held out for a hero.

He would find me.

Chace would find me.

*   *   *

Chace

"I don't know *shit*," Bonar spat, eyes to Chace even though Deck had his limp body held up by his neck.

Chace sucked in breath, looked to his watch and remembered the time the text came through because it was burned in his brain.

Faye had less than three hours.

His eyes moved to Deck. "She has less than three hours."

Deck pulled back an arm and let fly. When he connected, the blood splattered against the wall behind them.

Chace's phone rang. He pulled it out and took the call.

"What?" he clipped into it as Deck leaned into Bonar, jerking Bonar to him with his fingers wrapped around his throat, and growled something low that Chace couldn't hear.

"Brother, we're pullin' them in and they're all lawyerin' up," Frank said in his ear.

Chace opened his mouth to speak but he heard in the background, "Charge them all with three counts of conspiracy to commit murder and book 'em."

Cap was there.

"We don't have evidence to support that," Chace heard Frank tell the cap.

Then he heard Cap mutter from close, "We'll worry about that later. Charge 'em, book 'em and give that to me." Then Chace had Cap direct. "Son, whatever mess you're out there makin', have a mind to me bein' able to clean it up."

Disconnect.

If Faye wasn't running out of air, he would have smiled.

Instead he tipped his eyes to Bonar, who was bleeding profusely from his nose, several cuts in his lips and the entire left side of his face was swelling.

Deck was localizing the damage and it looked like it hurt like a bitch.

Bonar's eyes shifted from Deck to Chace.

"I knew this was the man you were," he whispered, getting it wrong.

This was exactly the kind of man he was, but a man like Bonar would never understand the reasons why.

"Where is she?" Chace whispered.

Bonar grinned.

Deck shook him and his head flew back and forth like a ragdoll.

When Deck stopped shaking him, Chace repeated, "Where is she?"

"Compartmentalization," Bonar whispered through another grin.

Fuck, he didn't know. He might give the order but he would have no idea how it was carried out or maybe even by whom.

Chace felt movement and looked behind him to see Bubba walking into Bonar's bedroom.

He didn't delay. "Talked to Krys. Don't get this but I'll say what I get fast. Whoever that guy is Faye knows on the computer sent a load of shit. They printed it all out and everyone's been combin' through every word and digit. Shambles and Sunny showed. Wendy. Twyla. More. Saw a number that this one," Bubba jerked his head to Bonar, "called a lot. Traced it to some corporation in Denver. No name. But the dude on the computer has got skills. He locked on that number's GPS." Bubba lifted up his phone on which a text was displayed. "And right now, whoever he is, he's local."

Chace turned to Deck, jerked up his chin and then moved to the door.

"I'll be pressing charges," Bonar called after them and Chace stopped because he felt Deck stop.

"Motherfucker, bring it on. But know this, you call the

cops, I'll see to it that we're cellmates even if I have to make shit up. You've looked into me. You know my skills. Only difference will be, I'll make it so Chace and me'll be out *way* before you," Deck told him then he delayed no further and followed Chace as Chace left the room.

*   *   *

In his Yukon, Deck at his side, following Bubba who was exceeding the speed limit, fighting the excruciating pain in his chest, the sour in his gut, Deck's phone rang.

"Yo." Chace heard then, "Right," then a beep and, "Phone the texts were sent from, a burner. No shot at GPS."

Chace sucked in breath.

Then he drove.

Five minutes later, five minutes less of Faye's air, his phone rang.

He pulled it out, hit go and put it into his ear.

"What?"

"Son, you've had them arrested."

His father talking soft and quiet. Ma was asleep.

"Yeah? And?" Chace clipped.

"I can hardly talk to them while they're incarcerated."

"Maybe your lawyer can get word to their lawyers to be smart and start talkin'."

"I'm afraid they won't listen. What's happened tonight, it's been made clear I'm out of their loop."

"What?" Chace asked.

"You're off limits. Valerie's off limits. And when I met Faye, I communicated to them that *she* was off limits. I'm alarmed they've made this move. It isn't like them and I knew nothing about it."

"Well, you makin' that clear hasn't been all that helpful, Dad. My life got jacked. Mom doesn't know it but she was threatened with learnin' about your perversion. So the people whose asses you've been coverin' haven't been all that safe. Now, including Faye."

"I had no idea they were planning to target Faye, Chace. I had no control over the other. Fuller did that to you two," Trane reminded him.

"You let him," Chace shot back. "Now, as this isn't helpin' things, unless you got somethin' for me that will, we're done."

"You need to talk to Clinton," he advised.

"Already done. Compartmentalization. You know how he plays it. You got another name for me?"

There was silence then, "I'm not this man, Chace," he said quietly. "I'm not the man you think I am. The only reason I had that association with Clinton, not to mention the one I was forced to build with most of those men, is because that tape forced me into that association."

"Bonar's been on your team for a long fuckin' time, Dad."

"When this started happening and we became aware that the others were facing the same thing, we allied and Clinton's job description was adjusted accordingly."

"My woman, the woman whose finger I put a diamond on tonight, Dad, has less than three hours of air. You givin' me this history is not helpin' her one fuckin' bit. Now do you have shit for me that might help me?"

"Will the police be at my door soon?" Trane asked back.

There it fucking was.

"Don't know. Don't give a fuck. But honestly surprised you aren't already in custody."

"Your mother—"

Covering his own fucking ass.

As always.

As fucking always.

Because of that, Chace lost it.

"My woman has less than three hours of air," he thundered into the phone. "This is not about you, this is not about savin' your ass and this is not about protecting Ma. This is about saving the goddamned *life* of the woman I fuckin' *love.* So do not call me unless you got shit that will help *Faye.*"

"I'll keep doing what I can," Trane told him, and Chace disconnected without another word.

"You cool?" Deck asked.

"No," Chace bit out.

"Gotta find cool, brother. We're runnin' against a clock. You burn out, gotta be locked down, burns time. You gotta stay ice cold."

"Your woman's buried alive somewhere, probably fuckin' terrified, you have no fuckin' idea how to save her, you can show me how you remain ice cold," Chace growled.

"You do it knowin' this shit'll get done. You do it knowin' you got your boys at your back. You do it knowin' they will not give up and you do it not givin' up either."

Chace sucked in breath through his nose but the burn it brought seared through every inch of him.

"She delivered me," he whispered.

"I know that, Chace," Deck whispered back.

"She's better than a dream."

"I know it, brother."

"She's gotta be terrified."

"No she isn't. She's Faye and she's waitin' for you."

That cut through because, his Faye and her backbone, that was undeniably true.

Chace sucked in another breath and his phone went again.

He engaged it and put it to his ear.

"Keaton."

"Chace, Max," Max replied. "Jeff just arrested George

but I got to him first. He admitted he fiddled the figures on his taxes. Fuller found out because George's accountant was on his payroll. Not enough to make him an ugly target, just enough for him to pay the toll and toe the line. Since Fuller fell, George hasn't heard shit. He thought it all died and was shocked as shit when Nina got up in his face. This shit tonight has flipped him out. He has no idea what's going on and he had no idea there were others until it was all over. He's not in with this group, Chace. He was small time. Just a toy for Fuller."

Dead end.

"Right," he muttered.

"I'm on my way to Carnal. You got somethin' you need me to do?"

"Go home to your family. You wake Nina, tell her tomorrow she may be gettin' a call from me, this gets ugly."

"I'm an extra pair of hands, Chace," Max told him quietly, and Chace pulled in another breath.

"Then call Wood or Tate. They may be workin' something I don't know about."

"Right. Done," he muttered then he said, "Keep it together. Shit happens but more often than not, it tends to have a happy ending."

The damsel was in distress waiting for her happily ever after.

Fuck.

"Thanks, Max," he muttered.

"Later."

He heard the disconnect, pressed the button on his phone and drove.

*　　*　　*

Bubba rolled his truck off to the side but before he did that and Chace followed, Chace saw it.

Two cars in the ditch. By their positions, one had forced the other off the road.

He stopped, put his SUV in park and cut the ignition.

Deck was already out, Deke and Bubba out in front of him.

Chace jogged beyond Bubba's truck, rounded it and came to a rocking halt as a figure formed from the shadows.

Samuel Sterling. Self-made, African American multimillionaire. Friend of Ty. Good man.

But not a local unless Aspen was considered local.

Fucking hell.

"What the fuck?" he asked. Sterling stopped four feet away and put his hands up.

"Ty knew I was in the area. He received some information. He gave me a call."

He wasn't in the area. The minute Ty heard Faye was in danger, he decided all hands on deck, he'd made a call and Sterling moved out.

There were unmistakable noises in the distance and Chace looked beyond him into the dark, seeing nothing.

"It's my understanding you're an officer of the law," Sterling noted, and Chace's eyes cut to him.

"You got someone out there?" he asked.

"I recommend you allow me and my colleague to handle this," Sterling returned.

"You got someone out there?" Chace repeated.

"We acquire the information you need," Sterling said low, "and I assure you, we *will* acquire the information you need, you find your woman, she'll need you clean and free."

Chace moved toward him, starting, "I will not stand here—"

Sterling put a hand in his chest. Chace stopped, dropped his eyes to the hand in his chest then sliced them to Sterling's face.

"For your woman, you will," he whispered.

Fuck.

Fuck.

He would. He'd already swung his *and* Deck's ass out there tonight.

He had to let this be.

Fuck.

Sterling looked in his eyes. Then he dropped his hand, turned and disappeared into the darkness.

Deck, Bubba and Deke closed ranks.

The noises came from the distance.

Chace's hands balled into fists.

Deck looked at his watch then shouted, "As of now you got one hour and fifty-three minutes and we're forty-five outta Carnal! Get the lead out!"

He'd memorized the time of the text too.

Chace's phone rang. He engaged it and put it to his ear.

"Keaton."

"Chace, Wood." He heard. "Dewey got some names. Coupla guys who do dirty work for members of this Elite. Ty and Twyla are with me, we're on one. Gave the info of the other to Tate who's connecting with Max and they're on the other. Ty's texting you names and specifics now. You on the lead Krys and the gang got?"

"Sterling is," Chace said into the phone.

"Good. I'll tell Ty that connection worked. We'll keep in touch."

Then he was gone.

"Brief," Deck grunted when Chace beeped his phone.

Chace gave the short brief.

Then the men stood in the night and listened to the remote sounds.

Chace looked to his watch.

One hour forty-eight minutes.

"Fuck," he whispered, every inch of his body buzzing, everything that was him urging him to sprint into the distance and take care of business and he was using everything he had to stand where he was.

"Keep it together, brother," Deck whispered back.

"Fuck," Chace repeated.

"Ice, Chace," Deck muttered.

Chace's phone rang and he took the call.

"Keaton."

"Chace Keaton?" a woman asked in his ear, and his body jolted at the unexpected and unknown voice.

"Yes."

"Right, this is Ally Nightingale. You know me as Serenity."

Instantly, Chace turned on his boot and started jogging to his truck.

"Chace, what the fuck?" Deck called.

"Talk," Chace growled into the phone.

"She's buried in your backyard."

Jesus Christ. Jesus Christ.

His backyard. His fucking backyard.

The woman kept talking. "She's beyond your fence. Midline, seventy-five yards out. The ground will be disturbed. I got the stuff they were looking for and I handed it over to their contact two minutes ago. They gave me the details. I'm an hour out. I hope you're closer."

Chace angled into his truck already aiming the keys to the ignition.

"I'm forty-five minutes out," he told her deciding he was actually thirty.

"Righteous," she whispered. "She'll have an hour."

Deck angled in beside him as Chace threw the SUV in reverse, his door still open, Bubba and Deke jumping into the truck in front of him.

"See you there," she told him.

"See you there," Chace replied then threw his phone on the console without disconnecting.

When he shifted to drive, the forward motion of the truck slammed his door. Once he'd executed the turn, his cell careening, Deck's hand darting out to tag it, he put the pedal to the floor.

"She's in my backyard," he told Deck.

Deck's phone started beeping. He was making the calls. Chace drove.

* * *

Faye

I didn't know how much time I had.

And I didn't want to lose my shot.

I thought about Dad and Mom.

But when I turned on the phone, the display said low battery and my thumb automatically hit Chace's numbers.

I put it to my ear and after one ring heard, "Keaton."

God, I loved his voice.

I'd made the right choice. If I died here, the last thing I'd hear was his beautiful voice.

I took the tank from my face and whispered, "Hey, honey," then put it back.

"Jesus, fuck, Faye, baby," he whispered back. "You okay?"

I took the tank away and told him, "The phone they left me to say good-bye only has a minute—"

"I know where you are, darlin'. I'm on my way. Everyone's on their way. You got time. Be there soon."

I took the tank away and told him, "The tank's almost out."

"What?"

"I'm in the red zone."

"You got over an hour."

"I'm in the red zone."

"Faye, someone will be there soon."

"Okay."

"Soon."

"I love you Chace."

"Soon, Faye."

"Okay, I love you."

"I love you too, now someone will be there—"

The phone died.

I put the tank back and breathed.

I waited.

And I breathed.

I waited more as I breathed.

I did this until there was nothing left in the tank to breathe.

My mouth pulled in nothing.

My eyes fluttered closed.

Ella Mae sang in my ear.

*   *   *

"*Just fucking dig!*" I heard shouted in my dream.

My eyes fluttered, my mouth sucked in breath.

It got nothing.

Scraping.

Thumping.

My eyes closed.

Banging.

Loud, loud banging.

Wood splintering.

Air rushed in and, my body moving without me telling to do it, I shifted toward the weak breeze, sucking it in.

More banging, scraping, the sounds of something beating through wood, the piercing, scratching noise of someone tearing it away. I felt dirt shower on me, wood falling on me, air streaming in and I sucked at it, taking dirt in with it and choking.

Then I heard a loud thump and Chace's, "Fuck me, Jesus, fuck, fuck me."

A loud crack of a sheet of wood breaking then hands under my armpits and I was pulled out.

Out.

Air.

Clean air.

A lot of it.

No dirt.

I sucked it in.

"Give her to me," I heard rumbled and I was jostled, in different arms, my eyes opening and closing, my mouth sucking in air. "I got her. Give him a hand," the same voice ordered.

I was shifted then jostled and new arms closed around me, familiar arms, and then I was down, my ass in Chace's lap, his arm tight around me, his legs cocked, cocooning me, his other hand shifting my hair away from my face.

"You breathing, baby? Faye, you breathing, baby?"

I looked into his face and saw the bad kind of raw.

So I gave him what he needed to take it away.

"Yeah."

Before I could watch it melt away, he shoved my face in his neck, his voice thick and hoarse when he muttered, "Fuck me, fuck me, fuck me."

I looked over his shoulder and saw Ty, Tate, Wood, Deke, Twyla, Bubba, Deck and Nina Maxwell's husband dirty, filthy, mud caked up their arms, on their chests.

They'd dug me out with their hands.

I turned my face into Chace's neck and whispered, "You need to buy a shovel, honey."

His body went solid around me.

Then he shoved his face in my neck and burst out laughing.

*   *   *

Semi-lounging, semi-not on Chace's couch, hanging over the back of it, I looked out his back window.

On his deck illuminated by the outside lights was a beautiful, thin brunette who was having words with an extortionately handsome Italian American man. This was happening while a supremely good-looking black man with twists in his hair and another man, somewhat schlubby wearing Buddy Holly glasses and a t-shirt that I could appreciate that said, "All hail Khaleesi, bring on the dragons!" looked on.

"I told you once, I told you a thousand times, *Ren*, what I do with my life is none of your business! Stay out of it!" she shouted.

She.

That would be Serenity.

My Serenity.

Or a woman I met an hour and a half ago named Ally Nightingale. A woman, after she gave me a big, relieved hug, who told me she lived in Denver. A woman who unabashedly and thankfully did not stop poking her nose into murder and mayhem in Carnal when I asked her to.

The woman who saved my life.

Luckily, at her back, was a badass introduced to me as Darius Tucker (the black guy) and a computer geek that Ally admitted did all the keyboard work introduced to me as Brody (the *Game of Thrones* freak).

Following her on her self-appointed assignation to save my behind but doing it in order to ream her was a man I hadn't met since he laid into Ally the second he arrived. I did know from her shouting at him that he was called Ren.

Cool name.

Hot guy.

And he seemed seriously pissed at her, but it was in that way that Chace got pissed at me when he found out I did something crazy and stupid. That was to say, he was pissed because he was seriously worried she'd get hurt.

And it seemed Ally wasn't cottoning onto that.

It further seemed Ally "Serenity" Nightingale was not like me in a lot of ways and not just that she was thinner than me, taller than me and a brunette. But also she was the queen of backtalk and attitude.

I knew this when Ren shouted back, "Baby, you keep up with this shit, I'll chain you to my goddamned bed!"

To which she returned heatedly, "Try it, Zano, and I'll *kick your ass*!"

All Chace had to say was "baby" and I was all, "okay."

Not Ally.

Watching, it appeared Ally never gave in in her life, even to a serious hot guy who was threatening to chain her to his bed, which, studying him in all his tall, dark, hot-blooded Italian, badass gorgeousness, was no threat at all.

Jeez, she had this guy hot on her heels and she was perving on Nathan Fillion? I mean, Nathan Fillion was mega hot but this guy...amazing. And he didn't live wherever Nathan Fillion lived but he was right there, on Chace's deck, a foot away from Ally, shouting at her because he was worried.

I sensed movement, tore my eyes from the action, turned my head and watched Chace, hair wet from a shower, in clean jeans and a sweater, bare feet, walking to me, eyes to the window.

Infinitely hotter than the Italian hottie on the back deck.

He shifted in behind me and hauled my booty into his lap as his lower half twisted so one leg was on the couch, my hips were between his legs and through this, his eyes remained out the window.

"They still at it?" he asked.

I looked from Chace's handsome profile out the window to see Ren pointing a finger in the African American man's face, not a good move in my estimation but he didn't seem to be worried, as he shouted, "*You* should know better!"

Darius Tucker grinned.

Seriously, he was hot too.

"Yes," I answered.

"Should I intervene?" Chace asked.

There was a hot-blooded, pissed-off, tall Italian guy on the deck. *I* was steering clear. I'd had enough danger for one night.

"Would you want someone to intervene when you were concerned-pissed and shouting at me?"

"I'll leave them be," Chace muttered instantly and I grinned. "Just got a call from Cap," he announced, and my eyes went from the scene outside to him.

"Yeah?"

Chace's eyes came to me.

"He told me that apparently, while Ally and Tucker were playin' the Elite to get a lock on you, Brody was at CPD showin' them the trail. They may have got what Newcomb was holdin' over those boys, but two of them got fidgety and stupid. Direct links to the guy who nabbed you at Bubba's, and that shit ties in another man called Clinton Bonar who they're goin' out to pick up now. Some of that crew might breathe free but those two will go down for conspiracy and Frank says they already got warrants to collect shit on Brody's trail. Not to mention, Tucker and Brody are both connected to a private investigator in Denver called Lee Nightingale who's got links to law enforcement. So, the male PI Nightingale and his brother who happens to be a cop put their stamp on it, the shit he gave them direct may still be admissible."

"Did she know they were coming after me?" I asked, hoping she didn't and thus didn't warn me.

"Not until she got the same text I got," Chace gave me the right answer. "She and Brody were hacked in, following their communications so she was on alert because she knew something was going down. She got that text when I got it and she, Tucker and Brody hauled ass. They had a lock on who Newcomb gave the shit to and they motored direct to him. Took him down, got it, dropped Brody and made the connection to hand it over."

"So Serenity saved me and took two of them down," I whispered.

"It sticks, yeah," he whispered back.

"Wow." I was still whispering, my eyes drifting to the window.

Darius was looking at his boots. Brody was biting his lip and looking to the dark sky. Ren had Ally pinned against the railing of Chace's deck in a way I couldn't see her at all.

No one was shouting but Ren's body was still tight with fury.

And his booty looked really good in those faded jeans.

Seriously, I needed to have a chat with Serenity. She needed to wake up.

"Faye," Chace called softly, I tore my eyes from Ren's behind and I looked back at him. His hand came up and slid my hair over my shoulder then curled around my neck when he went on, "Samuel Sterling delivered your kidnapper to CPD."

Fraking *good*.

The creep.

"Okay," I whispered.

"Can you ID him?" he asked gently, and I bit my lip because I could.

He'd stunned me in the back hall of Bubba's and I woke up in that box but I saw him before he did it.

Chace didn't miss me biting my lip and whispered, "Fuck."

We hadn't spoken of it. Chace had made a call telling his colleagues that he'd let them know when I was okay to make my report and for the time being they were to steer clear.

They steered clear.

So it was all about the guys and Twyla giving me hugs (Twyla's being the tightest), making phone calls to let their women know I was good, them taking off, me showering, Chace showering and Ally and Ren fighting.

"Can we do it tomorrow morning?" I asked.

"Yeah, baby," he answered.

"Can I tell you about it tomorrow too?" I asked softly.

"Whenever you're ready, Faye," he answered softly.

"Did Krys and the girls tell Benji I was okay?"

"Yeah. He knows everything."

Good. Benji would be worried but I wasn't surprised to hear that he'd totally stepped up for me.

"I need to do something for all of them, say thanks for helping," I muttered, wondering what said "thanks for saving my life" and thinking, unless you were a gazillionaire and could hand out castles, pretty much nothing did.

"I think you breathin' is thanks enough," he told me.

"Yeah," I whispered because he probably thought right and luckily that cost a lot less than a dozen castles.

Chace's eyes moved over my face before they again locked on mine.

"You seem okay," he noted quietly.

Quietly back, I noted, "I am. I'm breathing."

Upon me finishing my last word, he sucked in breath as he closed his eyes, his hand shifting up and back into my hair, pulling my forehead to his.

"I knew you'd save me," I whispered, his eyes opened and he pulled his head an inch away.

"I didn't know," he whispered back.

"Well, I did."

"And I didn't save you. Serenity did."

At his words, I found his wrists with my hands and tugged them between us. He'd showered but there was still dirt in his nails and tears in his flesh where he'd pounded through and torn away the wood imprisoning me.

I dipped my ear to my shoulder, but held his eyes as I shook his hands and asked, "You didn't?"

"Faye—"

"Did you give up?"

"No, but, honey—"

"Would you have given up?"

"No, but I lost it."

"Of course you did, you love me."

"Deck had to hold me together."

"Of course he did, he loves you."

"Faye—"

"You pulled me free."

"Honey—"

My hands tightened on his wrists, I leaned in and whispered fiercely, "It was *you* who ended it, Chace. *You* that dug me out. *You* that pulled me free. You had help but *you* did it. That's my last memory of that nightmare. You pulling me free."

His eyes warmed and he opened his mouth to speak but I wasn't done.

"I'll let you in on a secret, honey. The knight who has serious chinks in his armor but never falls is the true hero. That means he's won battles and doesn't waste time polishing his armor so he can look good while he rides in parades that are tributes to his glory. He just drags himself back on his steed and keeps right on battling. And if he's the right kind of knight, he never rides alone. The best heroes inspire loyalty. The best heroes keep fighting the good fight, tirelessly, quietly. The best heroes always have scars. If they didn't, the heroine would have nothing to do. It's her job to help the hero let all that stuff go in order that her man can be strong enough to fight on but when he's with her he's free to just *breathe*."

His wrists twisted so my hands released them but he just captured mine in his own, pressing them to his chest and his voice was gruff when he asked, "You gonna breathe free, honey?"

"Lauren was kidnapped and stabbed by a serial killer and she told me she never lost a wink of sleep because when she slept she did it next to Tate," I told him and his brows drew together.

"Is that an answer to my question?"

"Yeah. See, what happened to me you feel is your responsibility because you feel it's your responsibility to protect me. But for me, I was freaked and I was in a box in the ground for a couple of hours. Now I'm not. Tonight, tomorrow, every night I'll sleep next to my knight with the chinks in his armor and his scars, knowing he'll always take care of me so I'll sleep easy. You won't, not for a while, and I'm sorry about that, honey. But you'll eventually notice me sleeping easy then you will too. But for me, it's over, you made that happen so I'm already free just to breathe and earlier, I bought a lifetime being free to breathe by accepting your ring. I may have needed an oxygen tank for a while but your fist went through that wood and moments later, I breathed clean and free."

"That's all it takes for you?" he asked, his voice back to gruff.

"Well, I wouldn't call it 'all it takes.' Not a lot of girls land a real, honest-to-goodness, larger-than-life hero. But, since I was lucky enough to do that then, essentially . . . yeah."

Chace stared into my eyes.

Then he let my hands go so his arms could wrap around me, the fingers of one hand gliding into my hair, he pulled me to him and took my mouth.

It wasn't a fiery kiss. It was a slow, sweet one.

Still, it created a burn.

I had my arms around his shoulders, pressing deep and it was getting good when we had to break it off and look out the window because Serenity screeched, *"Ren! Put me down!"*

Then we saw him prowl with a struggling Ally over his shoulder to the stairs off the deck. He prowled down them, rounded the deck and house and they went out of sight.

Darius and Brody watched this too in a very weird way like it was nothing new then they walked into the house.

Darius took us in and immediately lifted his hand. "Don't get up. We'll go 'round too. Just here to say good-bye and if you need us, we're checkin' into the hotel in town. Leavin' tomorrow."

"Right," Chace muttered.

"Cool to meet you," Brody called.

"Uh...you too," I called back even though it kind of wasn't due to the circumstances though it still was. Then I asked, "Is she going to be okay?"

"This Neanderthal act means he's gonna stop jackin' around? Yes," Darius answered. "She keeps pushin' him away and he keeps puttin' up with it? No."

Sounded like there was a story there.

Serenity was *so* holding out on me. Even more than I thought she was.

"My money's on Ally," Brody muttered.

"My money's on Zano," Darius muttered back.

Definitely a story there and it had nothing to do with Nathan Fillion.

Interesting.

"You sure you don't want a beer or something?" I asked and felt Chace's body tense around me.

"How 'bout we have a beer tomorrow when you haven't just been dug out of a wooden box covered in three feet of fresh dirt?" Darius asked back.

"That would probably be a more appropriate time for entertaining," I muttered.

That was when I felt Chace's body shaking around me at the same time both Darius and Brody grinned at me.

"Glad it all ended good. Later," Darius gave his farewell.

"Yeah, later," Brody gave his.

"'Bye," I called.

Chace gave them a chin lift.

They barely got the door closed before we were up, me in Chace's arms and Chace heading to the hall, down it and to his room.

He set me in the bed, put a fist in it on either side of me and leaned in so he was all I could see.

"Be back, two seconds," he whispered.

I nodded.

He left and I knew he was closing down the house for the night. I got proof when the light shining through the window from outside went out. It wasn't needed anymore anyway. Dawn was coming.

When he came back, I watched him take off his jeans and sweater and climb in bed beside me. Then he turned out his light, rolled over me and turned out mine.

When it was out, he shifted into me and gathered me in his arms.

I was wearing one of his sweatshirts, clean panties and a pair of his socks, all I'd tugged on after my shower.

He was silent.

I remained that way too.

Then I stopped remaining that way.

"Are you okay?"

No answer.

My hands slid up the skin of his back and I called, "Chace?"

"I'm in the red zone," he whispered.

His words, *my* words, words, the memory of them, the reason he was saying them making my heart clench.

I closed my eyes and pushed in closer.

"I'm okay," I whispered.

"You'd run out of air."

I opened my eyes. "For hardly a minute."

"You'd run out of air."

"It's over, honey."

His arms tightened around me and his voice was yet again gruff when he asked, "Can you really tell me after that shit happened you're okay?"

"I only had to wait for you, Chace. You had to look for me. What you went through is worse so, no. I'm not really okay but I'm not freaked about what happened to me. I'm upset about what happened to you."

"Jesus, baby, I'm okay."

"You aren't."

"You're here, you're breathin', you're in my bed, you're wearin' my ring, I fuckin' am." His voice was reassuringly firm as his arms were reassuringly tight.

Still, I pushed, "Promise?"

"Fuck yeah. I'm just worried you aren't."

"Well, I am."

"Could fuck with you."

"Maybe, but you'll be here."

"Could give you bad dreams."

"Maybe, but you'll be here."

"Could be okay then in a year, two, twelve, it'll sneak up and haunt you."

Jeez!

Sometimes a protective hero hot guy could be stubborn and annoying.

It was my turn to be firm. "Okay, maybe, Chace, but *you'll be here*."

He went silent.

Then he whispered. "Yeah, I'll be here."

Yeah.

He would.

In a year, two, twelve.

Always.

I snuggled closer and whispered back, "Yeah."

He went silent.

I remained that way too.

Then I again stopped.

"Tired?"

"Fuck no." Again firm.

"You want to talk?"

"No."

I snuggled even closer. "Make love?"

Without delay or a word, Chace rolled into me, his mouth hit my throat and his lips slid around and up my neck.

I took that as a yes.

"Fuck?" I whispered an alternate suggestion.

"Make love," he muttered against my jaw, and I grinned into the gathering dawn as Chace's hands moved under his sweatshirt.

Then I whispered back, "Works for me."

EPILOGUE

All That's You

One year and six weeks later

"IT'S NOW MY honor *and* my pleasure to pronounce you, Chace Keaton and you, Faye Keaton, husband and wife. You may kiss the bride."

My eyes slid from the reverend to Chace's.

His eyes were really, really blue.

They looked really, really happy.

Just like me.

I didn't know it happened until his mouth came to mine, his eyes open, so close, so very close, and his lips moved against mine when he whispered, "Faye, baby, *breathe*."

My breath rushed against his lips.

Then he kissed me.

When he was done, even with the cheering and clapping, he didn't take his mouth from mine as he whispered, "Bubblemint."

Against his lips, I smiled.

* * *

Ty

One year, five weeks and six days earlier

They should have seen it.

They didn't see it.

Or maybe they didn't expect it would happen coming from a man like Keaton.

But they weren't there like he was, watching Keaton digging her out with his bare hands, jumping into that hole, the agony of relief on his face when he heard her choke, the way he pulled her out, dropped to his ass and curled around her.

Ty was there. Ty had seen it. And Ty had felt that same relief when Lex called him after she'd been kidnapped by Fuller and when he'd seen her at the hospital.

So he knew when they brought the man who kidnapped and buried Faye alive through the station for whatever fucking reasons they brought him through, Keaton would not keep his seat and just watch.

He didn't.

Ty had never seen a man move that fast. Not in his life.

But one second Keaton was sitting behind his desk, the next he was across the room, the man against the wall, Keaton in his face, his hand wrapped around the asshole's throat.

The officers moved but Ty and Sterling were already in motion and they got there first and flanked Keaton.

Keaton was chest to chest, nose to nose with him and the man was choking.

"How's it feel not to have any air?" he whispered, face and eyes stone cold.

"Stand down, Detective," Sterling murmured.

"You left her three hours, not four," Keaton kept whispering as he kept squeezing the breath out of his captive.

"Chace." Ty inched closer.

"Three hours of air," Keaton hissed.

"Man, you are not doin' Faye any favors with this," Ty told him quietly. "She needs him to pay. Not you. Stand down."

Keaton held the man's eyes.

Ty inched closer.

"Stand down, Chace," Ty whispered.

A muscle jumped in Keaton's jaw and he pushed off, stepping back one step as the man lifted both his handcuffed hands to wrap around his throat and choked in air.

"Let's go outside," Ty muttered and Keaton, eyes still locked to the kidnapper whose face was battered, bruised and swollen, kept still for a long moment before his body jerked around and he prowled to the door.

Ty gave Sterling a look and slid his eyes through the officers before he followed Keaton. He found him standing at his truck, both hands to its hood, weight leaning into his hands, head bent.

Ty stopped close.

Keaton didn't delay, asking his question to Ty but the words were aimed at his gut. "How do you live with it?"

He knew what Keaton was asking. How did he live with his woman, the woman he needed in order to breathe, getting kidnapped but more, coming that close to losing her.

"Held my baby girl in my arms yesterday, last night and this morning," Ty answered. Keaton pushed away from his truck and turned to him.

"That easy?" he whispered.

"No. Every day it burns in me. Every fuckin' day. And every night she falls asleep beside me. So it's not easy but I trip over one of her heels on the floor, she brings me a shake, I grab my workout bag in the morning and she's sorted it, I get a different kind of burn. A better kind of burn. A burn that means I can live with the other. No problem."

"And her?" Keaton asked.

"Far's I can tell, she don't feel it," Ty answered, and Keaton's brows went up.

"You never see it? Sense it?" he pushed, and Ty shook his head.

"Never. Not now. Not after you pulled her through dealin'

with putting holes in Fuller. She's livin' in the sunshine, new baby, big house she can fill with shit, me. She's got all she ever wanted. Lotta people don't get even a little of what they want. She understands that, appreciates it and doesn't waste time on shit in the past. Her luck changed when she met me, mine when I met her. She understands that too, doesn't question it, just looks forward and keeps guiding me to the light."

Keaton held his eyes.

Then he whispered, "Ella Alexi."

Ty grinned and whispered back, "Ella Alexi."

"She beautiful?"

"Only one thing more beautiful I've ever seen in my life and that's her momma standing beside a Charger outside a prison. But I'll tell you, man, love my wife but I've never felt anything more beautiful than the weight of my baby girl in my arms. So fuckin' heavy, so fuckin' light, so fuckin' tiny, so fuckin' huge. She's everything. Everything that's Lex and me. So she's fuckin' everything."

Keaton brought them full circle, murmuring, "Then it's that easy."

Ty held his eyes.

Then he replied, "Yeah."

Keaton nodded before muttering, "I gotta go get Faye from her folks', bring her in so she can make her statement."

"Go," Ty invited.

"After that, she'll wanna meet Ella."

Ty grinned again. "You do, get the bug."

"Faye?" Keaton asked, his lips twitching.

"No, brother, *you*," Ty answered, and Keaton shook his head.

"Got it already," he told Ty, and Ty felt his brows go up.

Then he asked, "How many?"

"Three."

"Faye on board with that?"

"Yep."

"Lexie wants four."

Keaton's lip twitch turned into a grin. "Now I'm thinkin' I want four."

"Better get to work, man," Ty advised.

Keaton's grin faded before he said quietly, "We got time."

Ty locked his gaze on Keaton and replied just as quietly, "Yeah, Chace, you got time."

Keaton lifted his hand Ty's way, Ty took it but they didn't shake. Their fingers curled tight and they held on a moment, eyes locked, grip firm and strong.

Then they broke and Chace moved to his truck.

Ty moved into the station to tell Sterling he was going back to his wife and baby girl at the hospital.

* * *

Faye

One week later

"Girl time!" Lauren shouted, moving from the fridge with a bottle of champagne toward me sitting at the island in her kitchen in her house. "You guys were supposed to be gone half an hour ago!"

When I sensed movement, I shifted in my chair and watched Tate sauntering down the hall, all tall, dark, bearded badass. I did this thinking that if Chace had never come to town, I'd still have a major crush on Tate Jackson.

Lucky for me, Chace came to town since Chace was *awesome* and since Tate was *taken*.

Tate grinned at me and this solidified the knowledge that if I didn't have Chace, I'd still have a major crush on him. I smiled back as he rounded me and went directly to the cake on the tall stand on the island in front of me. I watched as he shoved his finger into the creamy white frosting, scored it through taking a long finger full with it then he lifted his finger to his mouth and sucked it off.

Oh frak.

Yeah, if I didn't have Chace, I'd *totally* have a crush on Tate Jackson.

"Are you serious?" Laurie asked, and, with effort, I tore my eyes off Tate sucking frosting off his finger to look at Laurie who was, shockingly, unaffected by this and instead of looking like she wanted to jump him, she looked pissed.

"Baby, you girls are not gonna eat this entire cake," Tate replied, and I looked back at him to see he was grinning.

"Who says?" Laurie asked.

"I do," Tate answered.

"Right, that's a challenge we're accepting. We're eating this entire cake," Laurie shot back, I felt my eyes get big and I looked down at the enormous cake.

It looked delicious.

Okay, maybe we could pull it off though I wished I hadn't had lunch.

"You manage that, I'll buy you a piece of Jenna's jewelry," Tate muttered.

"He'll buy one for me anyway," Laurie told me. "I have so much silver I could open my own store."

Tate's brows drew together over narrowed eyes and it was such a scary look, I fought the urge to lean away from him. "You bitchin' about my silver?"

"No," Laurie retorted. "I'm just saying you're generous."

"Sounded like bitchin'," Tate returned.

"Well, it wasn't," Lauren fired back.

"Yeesh, only these two could fight about Dad buyin' Laurie gifts," Jonas, Tate's teenage son, muttered, wandering in, looking like mini-Tate, giving me the understanding that in a few years, me and every woman over twenty-five years of age in Carnal would be moved to become a cougar.

Then *he* went directly to the cake, shoved his finger in, swiped off a load of frosting then shoved his finger in his mouth.

"Jonas!" Lauren snapped.

"What?" he asked, eyes big, mouth full of frosting.

Lauren looked to the ceiling before she aimed her eyes at her boys.

"Get out before I throw the cake at you," she threatened.

"Waste of cake," Jonas muttered.

"Out!" Lauren semi-shouted, her arm coming up, out straight, finger pointed to the back hall.

Tate grinned at Lauren then at Jonas who was grinning at Lauren then his grin went to his dad.

"We better go before her head explodes," Jonas muttered to his dad.

"Right," Tate muttered back and they made a move, saying their good-byes to me. But I watched as they left, Tate hooking Lauren around her belly, he leaned down, kissed her neck and said low but loud enough for me to hear, "Cool it, Ace. I like your head where it is."

She rolled her eyes but I didn't catch the full roll because Tate moved his mouth from her ear to hers and he gave her a short kiss.

When he was done, I heard her say softly, "Later, Captain," which got her another short kiss though I looked away because I noted this one, albeit short, included tongue.

I looked back when I sensed him moving, he gave me a hot-guy, bearded, badass finger flick and he was gone.

I was still watching where he disappeared into the hall and therefore jumped when a champagne cork popped.

I looked to Laurie and grinned a happy, champagne-cork-popping grin.

Lauren grinned back, poured the champagne and brought the glasses to me.

She handed me one then lifted hers whereupon she toasted, "To you and Chace and the time when you'll bicker over stupid shit and love every second of it."

Call me weird but that was the best toast I'd ever heard *in my life*.

I lifted my glass. "To me, Chace and bickering."

We grinned at each other like idiots before we downed half the glass.

Laurie cut the cake.

As we gabbed, we managed to get through a third of it.

So her boys got a treat when they got home.

Which, I suspected, was her intention all along.

*   *   *

Three days later

I idled in my Cherokee as Chace's garage door went up.

No, strike that, *our* garage door went up, since I was now living there.

I loved my apartment. I made every inch of it mine and I thought it was awesome. Further, my stuff didn't really fit with Chace's décor.

When we moved me in and I fretfully shared this with him, he pulled me loosely in his arms, dipped his face close and told me, "This décor isn't mine either. It's Ma's. Do what you want. Anything you want. I don't give a fuck. Just as long as you're happy here."

I'd be happy on a deserted island that had nothing but a palm tree and a lifetime supply of sunscreen as long as Chace was there. And it was because of statements just like that I would.

I didn't tell him that.

I just whispered, "Okay."

The door went up, I drove in, parked, hit the garage door opener to set the door closing and hauled my booty out kind of hoping that Chace felt like pizza since I didn't want to cook. It had been a taxing day at the library. In fact, it had been taxing since the Town Council had its meeting, thus reminding folks they had a library, and it got more taxing after I'd been buried alive, thus making me an object of interest.

I knew it would die down and I was happily anticipating that day.

I moved through the back hall into the kitchen and as I was planting my purse on the island, I called, "Chace! I'm home."

"Just out of the shower!" he called back. "Be right out!"

Hmm. Chace just out of the shower.

Why was I suddenly not tired anymore?

I started to move through the hall, my mind on Chace and his shower when my eyes hit a big box sitting on the sectional.

Then I stopped dead when the box moved.

What the frak?

"Chace!" I called. "There's a box on the couch!"

"Yeah!" he shouted back.

It moved again and I took a step back.

"It's moving!" I yelled.

"Yeah!" he yelled back, and I blinked because he didn't sound surprised.

My head tilted to the side and I moved to the box cautiously.

Then I heard the noise coming from the box and I moved to it swiftly, threw open the loose flaps and stared down at two scrunch-faced, fluffy-haired, tiny Persian kitties, one chocolate point, one lilac.

"Holy frak," I whispered.

"Mew," the lilac point mewed up at me.

"Holy frak!" I shouted, reached in and nabbed the lilac point.

"You opened it," Chace said from behind me, and I whirled to see him standing several feet away in a t-shirt that was tight across his chest and loose running shorts.

"Kitties," I whispered, pressing the squirming Persian to my face.

"You said you wanted a cat," he reminded me of something I didn't think he remembered then went on to inform me, "Pets are like kids. One is not enough. So you got two."

God, he was fraking *awesome*.

I didn't have it in me to say this.

Instead, I repeated in a whisper, "Kitties."

Chace grinned then asked, "You like 'em?"

"They're fluffy." Yep, still whispering.

"Yeah," he replied, still grinning and now moving toward me. "But do you like them?"

"Their faces are all scrunchy."

You got it, I was still whispering.

He stopped toe to toe with me. "I'll take that as an indication you like them."

I nodded as I swallowed down happy tears.

Chace leaned into me but around me. He came back with the chocolate point and lifted it up close so they were kitty face to hot guy face.

My heart melted.

"You got no choice but to be friendly," he told it, being Chace bossy but the heretofore-unknown cute kind.

My heart melted more.

The kitty lifted a paw and pressed it to Chace's nose.

Chace grinned at him.

The rest of me melted.

Chace pulled him down, tucked him feet up in the crook of his arm, other hand scratching his belly and his eyes came to me.

"Both boys. They need names."

"Luke and Han," I stated immediately, and Chace smiled huge.

Then he said, "Fuck no."

I cuddled my kitty to my chest and suggested, "Spock and Kirk?"

"Again, fuck no," Chace repeated.

"Sam and Dean?" I tried.

He shook his head, still smiling.

My eyes narrowed then I suggested, "Starbuck and Apollo?"

"I thought Starbuck was a girl."

Jeez, his television experience was seriously narrow. Everyone knew there were two Starbucks.

"She is, in the new version. She's Dirk Benedict in the old one."

He lifted his kitty to his face and asked, "What do you think? Starbuck and Apollo?"

The kitty just stared at him.

"Starbuck?" he asked.

The kitty stretched his legs straight down.

"Apollo?" he went on, and the kitty put his paw to Chace's nose.

Chace curled him to his chest and looked at me. "This one's Apollo. That one's Starbuck."

"Works for me," I whispered.

Chace studied my face.

Then he muttered, "Cats and bubblemint."

"What?" I asked.

"That does it for you. Cats and bubblemint. You don't know what to do with pearl earrings but you look so happy you're about to burst 'cause of a coupla cats. It doesn't take much for you."

"Yes it does," I contradicted him quietly, he got even closer to me and our kitties started batting at each other with their fluffy paws but I didn't notice because Chace was all I could see.

"What does it take?" he whispered.

"All that's you," I whispered back and suddenly found myself without a cat, Chace didn't have one either and I knew this because I was over his shoulder and he was prowling down the hall.

"Chace! We need to go to the store, get cat food, litter boxes, litter—"

"Done."

God, I loved this man.

But I kept trying.

I mean, I had two scrunch-faced, fluffy kitties. Sex was awesome but *I had kitties*!

"We need to let them out so they can explore."

What I meant was so I could play with them.

I flew through the air, landed on my back in our bed and Chace landed on me.

"They can wait."

"They'll get bored in there."

"Then hurry and show your gratitude."

Oo, that sounded fun.

So I rounded him in my arms but planted a foot in the bed and rolled him to his back so I was on top.

Then, with my hair hanging down both sides of our faces, I whispered, "I can do that."

He grinned up at me, his hands pulling my hair gently away and he whispered back, "So do it."

I smiled down at him.

Then I did it.

*   *   *

One and a half months later

I hit the button on the television remote and looked down at Chace.

"Admit it, you liked it," I ordered.

We'd just watched the pilot episode of the new *Battlestar Galactica*.

"Baby, you sucked me off, rode me, forced my assent to watch the fuckin' thing right before I came then we watched it with you on me in my tee, no panties and my hand on your bare ass. Of course I liked it but I didn't *see* it."

How could a man be annoying and hot at the same time?

"You think Admiral Adama is the bomb," I pushed.

"*Da* bomb," he corrected my street lingo.

"Whatever," I muttered, then, "Admit you think he's awesome."

"Which one was he?"

I slapped his arm and snapped, "Chace!"

He rolled so I was on my back in the couch and he was on me. Then he gave in. A little.

"It didn't suck."

"You liked it," I decided.

"Let's just say, you want me to watch more, you gotta use your mouth on me."

"I do that all the time anyway," I reminded him, and he grinned.

Then he murmured, "Yeah."

"So, every time we, uh...you know, you have to watch one of my programs."

"Deal," he agreed immediately and surprisingly then I would understand why when he added his part of the deal, "You go down on me, you get geek TV. I go down on you, you watch one of my programs."

My eyes narrowed. "You know *Southland* freaks me out."

"That's because you get too involved with the characters."

"Sammy is sweet!" I defended myself.

"But he's not real," Chace replied. "He got in that car accident, you stopped breathing."

"I was surprised."

"Honey, they were in a high-speed chase with a pimp shooting at them. How could this be a surprise?"

This was true.

"Do we have a deal?" he pressed.

"So, breaking this down," I started breaking it down, "essentially, we both watch each other's shows because we both regularly go down on each other."

Chace grinned again. "Essentially."

My hands slid up his tee at the back and my legs moved restlessly as my eyes dropped to his mouth and I whispered, "Right then, time to earn an episode of *Southland.*"

I watched his grin turn into his smile.

Then his head dipped and he kissed me.

Then he set about earning another episode of *Southland.*

When he was done, I didn't tell him, but he earned two.

*   *   *

Deck

Two months later

"Is it done?"

Deck stared at Trane Keaton standing at his office window, staring out at Aspen.

"Dominoes will fall," Deck told him, arms crossed on his chest.

"How long?" Trane asked, not looking at him, the dick.

"Wheels in motion, my guess, the first one'll go down in a week. The rest not long after. It'll take, at most, three months."

"And Bonar is neutralized?" Trane kept at it.

"Bonar has confirmed he's received the message. No blow-back on Chace or me. Before you ask, the kidnapper has too. Sterling is clear. They got enough to worry about without havin' to worry about me. Kidnapper is facing attempted murder charges on top of kidnapping and Bonar and the two boys in your posse conspiracy. Evidence is solid. Case is tight. They'll all go down. They don't need me makin' a hard fall harder."

Trane turned and finally his eyes came to Deck for the first time since Deck entered the room.

"This can't be traced back to you or me?"

He meant him.

Deck didn't call him on it mostly because that would take time and he wanted to get out of there.

"Nope," he answered.

"I have your assurances on that," Trane pushed.

"I answered the question once. I did not lie. I won't answer it again," Deck replied.

Trane held his gaze and nodded.

Then he moved to his desk, lifted his hand and rested it on the top of his high-backed leather desk chair.

"You did it as we agreed," he stated softly.

"Yep," Deck confirmed.

"Painful," Trane went on.

"They'll lose everything."

Trane nodded.

Then he declared, "Chace can't know."

Deck's back went straight at his surprising words.

"What?" he asked.

"You will not tell Chace."

"That wasn't part of the deal," Deck growled.

"You won't tell him."

Deck uncrossed his arms from his chest and planted his hands on his hips. "Man, you just paid me to arrange for every man who had anything to do with his woman gettin' buried alive to lose everything they hold precious. It's the only fuckin' thing you've ever done that even hints at bein' for Chace. They're plannin' a wedding. You did this, he knows, you can get in there and you don't want him to know?"

"I lost my son years ago. I'll not *get in there*, as you put it, no matter what I do."

"You're wrong. This'll help," Deck told him.

"Was what you did legal?" Trane asked.

"Not by a long fuckin' shot but these men colluded in a scheme to *bury his woman alive*. I'm not thinkin' my boy's gonna quibble."

Trane shook his head. "He won't know. You won't tell him."

"Don't keep shit from my boy," Deck growled.

"I'll add an additional one hundred thousand dollars to your final pay," Trane told him.

"Again, I do not keep shit from my boy."

Trane's head shifted to the side. "Do you want him to know so you can receive his gratitude for doing what he cannot to make those men pay?"

"Fuck no."

"Then why would you need to tell him?"

Deck leaned into him and said quietly, "So he can believe, even if it's for a second, one second his whole goddamned life, that his dad has his back. I got a dad who loves me. I got a dad who's proud of me. I got a dad who'd bleed and die for me. I know how it feels. Chace has never had that. So if I could give him that for even one second, I'd give it to him. You doin' this shit for him, for Faye, will give him that. So that's why I need to tell him."

Trane held his gaze.

Then he flipped his hand out, moved to sit in his chair and muttered, "Do what you must."

"Would do that anyway," Deck muttered back, making his own move and this was to get the fuck out of there.

"Jacob," Trane called, Deck sucked air in through his nose and turned back. "I'm proud of him," he whispered.

"Tell him, not me." Deck did not whisper.

"I love him," Trane went on.

"Man, you're talkin' to the wrong guy."

"He thinks I'm filth. If he knows I paid you to engage in illegal activities—"

"Keaton, fuck, man, he dug her out with his bare hands. Trust me on this, he . . . will not . . . *quibble*."

He'd caught Trane's flinch at his "dug her out with his bare hands" even though the man quickly wiped it from his face.

Fuck, was there a heart under all that dick?

Trane looked to his desk and repeated, "Do what you must."

Deck stared at him a second.

Then he got the fuck out of there.

* * *

Chace

Four hours later

He listened to the phone ringing in his ear.

Then he heard, "Chace."

"Make a reservation at Reynaldo's. This weekend. Sunday night. For four."

"Chace," his father whispered, and fuck him, he heard that whisper tremble.

Chace's gut got tight.

"We'll meet you there at seven."

There was nothing then, "Right. Seven."

"Tell Ma I said hi."

"I'll pass that along."

"I'm almost home," Chace told him, seeing the white picket fence up ahead. "I gotta go."

"Of course."

"Later."

"Chace?"

Shit.

Chace gave him something, he was going for more.

"Dad, how 'bout we take this slow," he suggested.

"I like her."

Shit, fuck, *shit*.

"Good."

"She suits you."

Chace sucked in breath.

His father went on. "A good woman for a good man."

Shit, *fuck, shit*!

"Right."

Unfortunately, he wasn't fucking done.

"I heard what you did for that boy and his sister. I'm proud of you."

Shit, fuck, shit!

"Dad—"

"I just wanted you to know."

Chace turned into his drive then hit the garage door opener and into the phone he said, "All right, you wanted me to know. I know."

"All right," Trane replied quietly. "Your mother and I'll look forward to Sunday."

"Great. Later."

"Have a good evening, Chace."

"You too," he returned then disconnected.

He drove into his garage and parked. He was in his new blue Yukon. His old one was parked next to him. When he'd bought the new one, he'd given the old one to Faye and her Cherokee was gracing someone else's garage. She accepted this without much discussion, much like he suspected Sondra did when her ride was phased out and Silas's new one phased in. Faye didn't really care what she drove and since he did and his old Yukon was better than her Cherokee, she went with it without giving him any lip.

When the garage door was going down, he leaned forward and rested his forehead on the steering wheel.

"Shit, fuck, shit," he whispered.

Then he pulled in a breath, got out of his truck, walked through the garage, opened the door, moved into the back hall and was immediately accosted by Apollo.

He bent and scooped up the cat, walked down the hall while avoiding Starbuck who was chasing his feet and saw Faye at the stove, stirring something.

She turned to him and smiled. "Hey honey, how was swimming?"

He stared at her, her gleaming hair, her crystal blue eyes, her cute outfit, her smiling bubblegum lips and felt his gut release.

Then he smiled back and said, "It was good. What's for dinner?"

*   *   *

Faye

Two weeks later

I swam up from the fog of sleep and I did this because I heard Chace whispering in my ear, "Wake up, baby."

I blinked, looked at the alarm clock and saw it was early.

It was Sunday.

I didn't need to get up early anyway, though these days I did to get up with Chace. But Sundays, we *both* could sleep in.

So I was wondering why he wasn't doing that.

I shifted and the pile of cats draped over my feet and ankles shifted, Starbuck, with his usual attitude, doing it on an annoyed mew.

"What?" I asked Chace.

"It snowed last night."

I stared at him.

Then I asked, "So?"

"Come on, baby, get up, wrap up, let's go drink coffee outside."

Coffee outside?

Was he fraking nuts?

I didn't get the chance to ask and had no choice in the matter since he yanked the covers back, grabbed my hand and pulled me out of bed.

I saw he was already wrapped up and he also was sauntering out the door. I considered climbing back into bed but curiosity got the better of me. So I went about brushing my teeth and doing the same, pulling up some leggings under my nightie, one of Chace's sweatshirts over it and some thick socks on my feet.

I met Chace at the end of the hall and he had two steaming mugs. He gave me one and we wandered out the front door. Chace pulled the rockers up to the railing and we settled into them, both immediately lifting our feet to the railing like we had countless times when we sat out there that summer.

Our breath came out in puffs.

The steam from the hot coffee got steamier.

Mine tasted of hazelnut and went down warm.

The plain was startlingly different with a blanket of snow.

Beautiful.

Peaceful.

Chace didn't speak.

Still slightly sleepy, I didn't either. I just sipped my coffee and stared at the snow, the plain, the white-covered hills and mountains beyond with their stark breaks of green pine.

"Common miracle," he muttered, and I looked at him.

"Pardon, honey?"

His eyes didn't leave the plain when he answered, "This. Common miracle. Even common, still miraculous."

I looked at the plain and the instant I did it settled in me he was right.

It was.

Miraculous.

Not only snowfall on the Rockies but him finding me, me finding him, both of us sitting on our porch, drinking coffee, quiet, content, beauty as far as the eye could see.

Absolutely miraculous.

I pulled in breath and turned my head to look back at Chace, noting his unruly curls resting on the scarf wrapped around his neck.

So of course I had to reach out, grab one and tug.

Then I watched as he grinned into his coffee mug.

Yes.

Absolutely.

Miraculous.

*   *   *

Two and a half months later

"Jesus, Faye, only so much Spam a man can eat."

We were in the grocery store and we were bickering.

I looked from the cans in my hands to Chace, "It's nearly Christmas."

"Yeah. So?" he asked.

"Even Outlaw Al needs something special for Christmas," I informed him, then threw the two cans of Spam to join the four cans already in our cart which were jockeying for position with a variety of other canned meat, beans and cat food that wouldn't go to Starbuck and Apollo.

"I should have never told you about him," Chace muttered, hooking a finger in the end of the cart and firmly pulling it down the aisle.

I made no reply since he was wrong and he'd only disagree with me, put my hands to the handle and followed.

"By the way," he said over his shoulder, "saw the bags."

My heart clenched.

"What bags?" I asked, hoping he hadn't found my present stash for him because that would suck fraking *huge*.

He stopped and thus stopped the cart and me.

"She's not even a year old."

I felt my brows draw together and asked, "Who?"

"Ella. You got her, like, seven outfits."

Well, that was good. He found Ella's presents. Not his. Also good, since I hadn't hidden Ella's presents so this meant he wasn't snooping (I hoped).

It was my turn to say, "Yeah. So?"

"Darlin', Lexie already outfits her like she's an American Princess. You do not need to assist in her endeavors."

"It's her first Christmas!" I snapped.

"She's not gonna remember it."

"So? I like baby clothes and she's the only baby I know."

"Jesus," he muttered, beginning to move us along.

I followed him noting he was going at a good clip through the canned food section.

Oh well, Outlaw Al was going to eat well all the way into the new year with what I'd already nabbed.

Chace turned the corner and guided us up the aisle, my hand darting out whenever we passed something we needed and tossing it into our cart. Since I was actually paying attention to shopping and my man wasn't, I ran into the cart when he stopped it and I didn't notice.

He was staring ahead and I looked around him to see a few people in the aisle, no familiar faces so I looked at the back of his head.

"Chace?"

He turned to me.

"You were standing right where you are now. I was at the end of the aisle."

I quit breathing.

Oh God. Oh *God*.

Chace kept talking.

"Near on eight years and I'm finally in this aisle, shoppin' with you."

Well, actually, we'd been in this aisle together dozens of times over the past months.

Still.

"Honey," I whispered.

"Don't know why folks need diamonds and pearls, fur coats, first-class tickets, island adventures when simple shit like this is the best thing you could ever do."

He was absolutely right.

Kind of.

I licked my lips.

Then I asked, "Is it bad that I wouldn't mind an island adventure with you?"

He studied me, warmth in his face before he said, "No."

"And it's not outlandish to think that perhaps your mother will buy me a fur coat for Christmas," I noted. "So, um, you've given me a diamond, she's given me pearls *and* diamonds so that just leaves first-class tickets and I'm okay with coach."

His lips twitched but I wasn't joking. Valerie bought me expensive stuff all the time. It was sweet. It was over the top. But she started to get upset when I demurred so I stopped doing that and it was now tradition.

He moved from his end of the cart to my end of the cart, stopped in front of me, lifted a hand to slide the hair off my shoulder and curled his fingers around my neck.

Then he dipped his face close and muttered, "Only my girl says the word 'outlandish.'"

"It *is* in the English language, Chace. I didn't make it up. I'm sure others say it too," I told him, going for tartly but it came out breathily because he was close, his face was still warm but his gaze was intense.

"How embarrassed are you gonna be after I make out with you in the spot where I first saw you?"

Oh my.

"Um...you say that like it's a given you're going to do that," I remarked.

"It is," he replied.

"Chace—" I started but his hand at my neck pulled me to him and up. His other arm curled around my waist then his mouth was on mine and I had no choice (though I wouldn't pick another one) but to neck in the grocery store aisle with Chace where he first saw me.

When he was done, he turned me toward the handle of our cart, moved in behind me and put his arms around me, his hands beside mine on the handle. He started us forward and I wasn't embarrassed even though other patrons were grinning at me.

No, all I could process was thinking grocery shopping was simple. It was every day.

But it was one of the best things you could ever do.

*   *   *

Chace

Five hours later

In his sleep, Chace sensed the light going out.

Faye was done reading.

Before he could hook her around the waist, he felt her shift into him.

He knew what that meant.

Her hand glided up his hip to his waist.

He knew what that meant too.

He grinned, curled his arms around her and rolled to his back, taking her with him.

Her mouth went to his neck.

"Done?" he whispered into her ear.

"Kind of," she muttered against his neck, her lips gliding down.

His hands slid over the satin of her nightie at her back. "You wanna use me, honey, you gotta do all the work. I'm wiped."

Her lips slid up as her hand stopped playing with his chest hair and moved up his chest, his neck and her thumb came out to stroke his jaw.

"That's too bad," she whispered in his ear. "Because, see, the hero in my book just did all this stuff to the heroine while she was naked and on her knees then—"

She shut up because Chace's arms closed tight around her, he sat up and cats scattered.

The instant he was up, he growled, "On your knees."

"You sure?" she asked, her musical voice lilting and playful, cute and fucking hot. "If you're tired we can sleep."

He lifted her off him and planted her in the bed on her knees.

Then he shifted to his knees behind her, his hands moved to the hem of her nightie, he yanked it up and off and felt her soft, sweet gasp in his dick.

Then his hands glided from her waist to her belly, one going up, one going down.

"You wanna act it out or wing it?" he asked the skin of her neck.

"Wing it," she breathed when his hands hit two particular spots.

He grinned then muttered, "Right, baby."

Then he winged it.

Half an hour later, they came simultaneously, Faye impaled on his cock, her head twisted, forehead pressed into his neck, one of his arms wrapped around her belly, his other hand at her breast, his eyes aimed over her shoulder and down, watching her touch herself while he fucked her.

It was sensational.

Then again, with Faye, from the very beginning, it always was.

* * *

Months later, the night before Chace and Faye's wedding

"Told you you'd make it legal," Deck said.

Deck was sitting beside him in a rocker on his front porch, his feet, like Chace's, up on the railing, legs straight, ankles crossed.

They were both staring at the dark plain, the hazy lights of Carnal the only thing that lit it. He hadn't even turned the porch light on.

Chace didn't reply.

"You didn't waste any time, brother," Deck continued.

Chace disagreed. After pulling his girl out of that box, he wanted to marry her the next day. A year and six weeks' wait was way too fucking long. Faye agreed, they'd talked about a Christmas wedding and were both all for that until Liza stuck her nose in. Then their small, intimate Christmas wedding somehow became a huge summer wedding and that somehow, Chace reckoned, was because his Faye actually wanted that and more, she liked planning her wedding with her sister. They were having a blast. So he let it go.

He also let it go because Liza could be pushy and nosy but she also loved her sister and Faye had an idea of exactly what she wanted. Which was exactly what she was going to get, Liza was making sure of that.

Therefore, at that moment, in his backyard there was a floating deck with an arch sitting on the spot where Faye had been buried and tomorrow they'd stand on it and get married.

Faye's idea, her way of getting rid of that memory.

It was a good way.

Also tomorrow, tables, chairs, tents, a dance floor, another floating deck that would hold DJ equipment and a shitload of flowers and bunting would be delivered.

Luckily, Silas Goodknight was a smart man who loved his daughters deeply. Therefore, he'd been saving for a good long time to give them the weddings they wanted. Not to mention, Chace's mom had horned in and demanded to pay for the cake, catering and booze. After a word from Faye, Silas had given in. So the hit Chace's trust fund took to take care of Miah and Becky didn't mean his girl wouldn't have exactly what she wanted on her day and they'd have to worry about their kids' educations.

She would have what she wanted.

Exactly.

Everything she wanted.

And their kids were covered.

Now she was at her parents' house and he and Deck had come back from Bubba's where they spent a number of hours with the boys having drinks. Not a bachelor party. That shit was shit and he'd made it clear to Deck he didn't need any of it and furthermore did not intend to be hungover when he made Faye his legally, in the eyes of God, standing in front of a reverend, surrounded by friends, family and God's country. So it was just that at Bubba's. Drinks with the boys.

"You aren't gettin' any younger, man," Chace pointed out, his meaning not veiled.

"Not a lotta girls like Faye," Deck muttered and, surprised, Chace looked at him.

"You want a girl like Faye?"

"Nope," Deck replied, took a drag off his beer bottle and kept his eyes on the plain. When he dropped his hand, he went on, "And yep. What she's got inside, that sweet, that strong, can't be beat." Deck looked at him and Chace saw the white flash of his smile. "Though, bigger tits, shorter skirts, tighter tops and high heels on more than just special occasions wouldn't go unappreciated. Just as long as all that comes with class."

Chace got him but he couldn't miss it. Deck made an art of playing the field and it wasn't regular, it was frequent. But Chace didn't miss the fact that the few who had even a modicum of staying power were high maintenance and beyond ballsy. Deck, like Chace, enjoyed the simple life. But Deck, like Boyd Newman, liked the challenge of a woman who brought high class and not a small amount of drama into his life. Unfortunately, he had yet to find one who could do her own thing and find a compromise so they could fit together in their way like Liza and Boyd had.

Or he had. But then he lost her.

"Think your hunting ground should be Denver, bud," Chace murmured his advice, his eyes moving back to the plain.

"Then it's good I've taken a job there," Deck murmured back.

"Gone long?" Chace asked.

"Leave tomorrow and gone as long as it takes," Deck answered.

"Try not to get arrested," Chace muttered, and Deck chuckled.

"Like anyone could catch me," Deck muttered back.

This, fortunately, was true. This also, unfortunately, gave indication of the kind of "job" Deck had taken.

Chace let that go as he always did and moved on to more important matters.

"You know, the heads-up you gave Faye about Ma set her up to deal with that. You at my side when that shit went down with Faye and what you did with Dad—"

"Brother, we don't discuss that shit."

"We don't. Also don't care. In those instances, you gotta know you got my gratitude."

"I already know it, Chace."

"Well, give me somethin', man, and accept it anyway."

"You've had my back a lot of times," Deck reminded him.

"Not one where someone you loved was buried alive."

"This is true," Deck muttered.

"So just give me this and accept my gratitude."

Deck was silent.

Then he whispered, "Do anything for you, man."

"I know," Chace whispered back.

"You know why."

"I do."

"Losin' her was the worst thing to happen to me."

Chace pulled in breath. Deck didn't bring her up. Ever. She wasn't a ghost. She wasn't a memory. As far as Deck was concerned, she didn't exist.

Then, still whispering, he said, "I know."

"Your ending was a fuckuva lot better than mine."

"I know, Deck."

"You kept me from flyin' apart."

Chace didn't reply.

"Do anything for you," Deck whispered.

"Then give me this," Chace pushed. "Move past her. She's gone. Quit dickin' around. Find what I got, Deck. You know how it feels. Find it again."

Deck was silent.

Then he muttered, "We'll see what Denver brings."

Chace knew that was as good as it was going to get so he let it alone.

Chace took a drag from his beer and Deck did the same.

They stared at the plain in silence.

Deck broke it. "Happy for you, brother."

"Not as happy as me."

"No," Deck agreed. "And that's precisely why I'm happy."

Chace grinned at his beer bottle before he took another drag.

Then he sat with his best friend in silence, contemplating what the next day would bring and beyond that, the island adventure that his soon-to-be wife didn't know she was getting for her honeymoon.

Which meant he sat beside his best friend in silence and he did it still grinning.

*   *   *

Faye

The next afternoon, Chace and Faye's wedding reception

It was a moment alone.

A moment after dinner, my first dance with Chace, dancing to (of course) Ella Mae singing "Holding Out for a Hero." A moment after my dance with my dad and Chace's with Valerie. A moment after we cut the enormous, ornate but awesome cake, that moment not being one where we shoved it in each other's faces but we did lick the frosting off each other's fingers to hoots and catcalls we barely heard. After that moment Chace kissed me and he'd done it deeply. And after *that* moment he'd whispered, "Cake. Better than bubblemint." Which made me all melty as well as slightly turned on.

I was sitting by myself and watching Ty and Lexie dancing, Ty having one arm around his again-pregnant wife, his other arm holding his daughter and they were close, grinning at each other and whispering while sweet, pretty Ella pulled at her mom's hair.

My eyes moved to Bubba dancing close with Krystal. Then they moved to Tate doing the same with Laurie, then they moved to my sister doing the same with Boyd and Max doing the same with Nina. And then they moved to Twyla doing the same with her partner, Cindy. Not done, my eyes glided through Mom and Dad, Valerie and Trane, Sunny and Shambles, Wood and Maggie and Sam Sterling and his woman Jada all doing the same thing.

Last, they moved to Chace, who was holding both of Becky's hands and her feet were on top of his feet, she was arched back, grinning up at him, and he had his neck bent and he was grinning down at her in her little bridesmaid gown.

Yeah, Chace needed a princess.

Or, another one.

My gaze shifted from my husband...

My *husband*.

At that thought, I smiled a small smile to myself as my eyes took in friends and family including my brother Jude chatting up Amber, one of the waitresses at Bubba's and

Deck, laughing with Jim-Billy, Stoney and Wings. Finally, they lighted on Miah looking like he was getting into trouble with Robbie and Jarot. Robbie was crawling under a table, Miah stooping to do the same while Jarot appeared to be playing lookout.

All was well in my world.

Very well.

Fraking brilliant.

My body started when two chairs were dragged up to either side of me. I looked up and to my right to see Ally moving in to sit on that side then I looked to the left to see the short man with narrow shoulders, a big belly, thinning light brown hair and a sweet smile taking the seat there.

Benji.

The second he settled, my body drooped to the side, hit his and his arm slid around me.

"So glad you came," I muttered and looked to Ally. "Both of you."

"Wouldn't miss it," Ally muttered.

"Me either," Benji also muttered.

My eyes went to Benji. "It was a long way for you."

His eyes caught mine. "Better than a TV show. Better than a book. Because it's real. Once in a lifetime. So no way I'd miss it. I'd beam to the moon to see you this happy."

"Totally," Ally muttered, and I felt her hand find mine, wrap around and squeeze.

I squeezed back.

Then my gaze went to the dance floor again and I sighed.

"Coming back for Comic-Con. Now that the seal has been broken and we all know each other as in *know each other*, expect you and Chace to meet me there," Benji told me, and my mind filled with thoughts of Chace at a Comic-Con.

Because it did, I burst out laughing.

Chace's eyes came right to me and seeing the look on his face, openly happy, I sighed again but this time on the inside.

I grinned at him but murmured, "I'm not sure that'll ever happen."

"I am," Ally replied and I tore my eyes away from my husband...

My husband.

I looked to her. "No way."

Ally looked to me. "That man would do anything for you. Even commune with a bunch of geeks."

Well, I figured she would know. Since she had one like mine.

I grinned at her.

The song changed to Norah Jones's "Come Away with Me" and I watched Dad claim Becky and Chace's gaze come to me.

Then he lifted a hand and crooked a finger.

"Hot," Ally muttered then, "Righteous."

"I'm being summoned," I told them something they couldn't miss.

"Go, darling," Benji encouraged, his arm giving me a squeeze.

I tossed them both a smile, got up and walked across the grass to the dance floor. I was two feet away when Chace leaned down, grabbed my hand, guided me up and pulled me immediately into his arms. Close. Tight. My arms wrapped around his shoulders and he started us swaying.

I didn't even hear the song. I just felt Chace.

My husband.

"Havin' a good day?" he murmured into the hair on the side of my head where his jaw was resting.

"The best. You?"

His arms gave me a squeeze. "Yeah, baby."

He meant that.

He meant it deeply.

I pressed closer.

"Have I told you I love you today?" I asked.

"Fifteen times," he answered, and my head went slightly back so his tipped down so he could look at me.

"You counted?"

"Never miss you sayin' those words, Faye."

My heart melted.

Then I whispered, "Here's sixteen. I love you, Detective Keaton."

He grinned and his grinning lips came to mine before he whispered back, "Love you too, Mrs. Keaton."

I smiled against his mouth but didn't finish that action since my husband...my *husband*...kissed me.

*   *   *

Six years later

"I'm supposed to talk about my class's future. I'm supposed to reminisce about our past. I'm not going to do either. I know no one is going to remember this speech except me. So I'm going to use it as the opportunity to say what I've needed to say for a long time."

My shoulder in Chace's armpit, his arm around me, our eldest son in his seat at my side, our second eldest boy fidgeting in his seat at Chace's, our toddler daughter sleeping curled up in her daddy's lap, my eyes were trained across the auditorium to Miah giving his valedictorian speech.

"Most everyone here knows what happened to me and my sister. A lot of you even know a number of good people in a town called Carnal that's a state away looked out for us. What you don't know is that when I was alone and scared and hungry and cold, two of those people went out of their way to save me."

Chace's back went straight at the same time as mine.

Miah kept talking.

"They didn't know a thing about me. They didn't know what happened to me or just how bad it was. They didn't know what happened to my sister. But they didn't care. They just knew something was wrong so they did something about it. They bought me food and a sleeping bag and books to read and wrote me notes, telling me about them, the only human connection I had for three years that was good and pure and right. After they started doing that, for the first time in three years, even though I was sleeping in a shed in the forest in the winter cold, I went to sleep not scared. I went to sleep knowing someone was looking out for me. I went to sleep for the first time in a long time knowing that there was good in the world. Weeks later, after I'd again tried to save my sister, I was injured and alone, I lay in that shed in that sleeping bag, but even as the days passed, I knew they wouldn't give up. I knew they would find me. And they did."

My lips started trembling as tears welled up quickly and slid out of my eyes.

"My mother was murdered," Miah continued, and a deep hush stole through the already silent crowd. "My sister and I kidnapped and confined. But even with that, when they came into my life, I learned a lesson that was different than the one I'd been learning for three years. That this world was infested with dark and it can drag you in, hold you down and make you believe that's all there is. But they taught me with the dark comes light and light is stronger and more powerful because it never gives up. That there were good people in this world who sense wrong being done and set about making it right. They didn't talk about it. They didn't think about it. They did it. It cost them time and money and emotion. All of this for a kid they did not know. But they still did it. So if there's anything I want my fellow graduates to take away from today, from this speech, as they move on in their lives, learning to be adults, learning to fit into this world, no matter what they decide to do, who they decide to be, they should endeavor to be good and pure and right. They should be the kind of people who sense wrong being done and set about making it right. Not talk about it or think about it but *do* it. Because the wrong being done can be *very* wrong. It can destroy lives. It can eat away happiness in a way that it will never come back. But if it's stopped and light shines through the dark, it could end in a kid who lost everything but his sister, had no power, was terrified but, years later, stands in front of a room full of people making a valedictorian speech."

Miah's red, wet gaze came to Chace and me.

"I stand here because of you, my Aslan, my Faye, my protectors, and I make the promise that what you gave me, what you taught me, I will live those lessons. I cannot repay you for what you gave me. That's all I can do. All I can do is learn the lesson you taught me and go forward in my life good and pure and right." His voice dipped to a whisper in the microphone and he finished, "Thank you."

Through watery eyes, I watched Miah duck his head and move away from the podium.

I was quietly blubbering.

The auditorium was on their feet.

Chace's arm tightened around my shoulders, I heard him clear his throat but I felt a little arm slide around my belly so I looked down at my son, Jacob.

"Mommy, who's Miah talkin' about?"

I lifted my hand to his cheek, looked into my husband's beautiful eyes in my son's beloved face and whispered, "Your daddy and me."

Jake looked to his dad then the podium and back at me.

"Are you okay?"

"I'm fine, baby," I was still whispering. "Absolutely fine."

And I absolutely was.

Because I knew, without a doubt, finally, that Miah was.

*   *   *

Chace

One day later

"You can show me," Miah said softly, and Chace turned his head and looked at him.

They were sitting on top of a picnic table by the creek just down from his grandparents' home, feet on the seat, eyes, until Chace looked at him, on the rushing water.

He'd grown up healthy and strong. Not tall, none of his kin were tall, he was five eleven. But he had a lean, straight body, long legs, growing broad near to a man's shoulders and he was a good-looking kid, that mop of thick blond hair, those unusual light brown eyes.

He was popular at school. Ran track and cross-country. Class president. Captain of the debate team. Editor of the school newspaper. National Honor Society.

It didn't surprise Chace that he chose sports where he competed individually, on a team but his performance was based on his personal endeavors, but still, he found other activities where he could be a leader and each one he found he *was* the leader.

What did surprise Chace was that he was popular regardless of his intellect, his continued voracious reading, the fact that he was quiet, not shy, not introverted, but an observer, soft-spoken and he didn't speak unless what he had to say meant something.

"Had a chat with Ezra," Chace told him.

"I know," Miah replied.

"Ezra said you're ready."

"That's because I am."

Chace pressed his lips together because he was uncertain he agreed and he looked back at the creek.

"Chace, I talked about it to the counselors a long time ago. To Granddad. To *you* that time you and Faye were up here last year. I'm cool with it," Miah assured him, and Chace sucked in breath.

He looked back at him. "Yesterday was your graduation and your party. In a few months you're off to Columbia. Don't wanna bring up bad shit when all you got is good happening and the same to look forward to."

"I want to do it," Miah stated.

"Miah—"

"Chace," he straightened but kept Chace's eyes, "I *want* to do it. Show me."

Chace sucked in another breath then turned to the folder sitting on the table beside him, flipped it open, pulled out the mug shot and handed it to Miah. Miah bent his head and studied it.

It was the mug shot of the man they suspected murdered Misty and Darren Newcomb.

"He screwed up," Chace told him. "Got him in Oregon. He took an assignment, took to the woods again and some hunters, both ex-military, were up there. Heard them comin', they were experienced, got quiet, watched, didn't like the look of things and hunkered down. Saw it start to go down and they moved in. Incapacitated him. Saved his target. He's freelance, not connected to any organization and there's the possibility that he's responsible for at least a dozen hits in eight states including two in Carnal."

"That's him," Miah said firmly and handed the mug shot back to Chace.

Chace's gut got tight.

Shit, this was it. This was finally fucking *it*.

"You're sure?" he asked quietly.

"Yeah," Miah answered.

"Was a long time ago, bud," Chace reminded him, turning to return the photo to the folder and when he turned back, Miah again locked eyes with him.

"You don't forget that kind of thing. You know it. I told you about it. *All* of it. That's him and I'll testify."

Years ago, Miah's grandparents had been informed that Miah was holding on to this knowledge and thus they'd informed his counselors. So years ago, his therapists helped him deal with what he saw, which was not only Misty's face getting raped but her subsequent murder. Jeremiah had seen the whole thing.

"I'll testify," Miah repeated when Chace didn't speak.

"That'll be tough," Chace replied. "You were young, in a serious situation, if he's extradited to Colorado to stand trial, the defense attorney will go hard."

"A kid, no matter what he's going through, can't make that stuff up," Miah returned.

"This is true," Chace muttered. "But I don't like that for you, that bein' part of your future, the possibility of testifying."

"A wrong has been done," Miah whispered, his gaze unwavering on Chace. "When that happens you set about making it right. *You* taught me that."

Chace closed his eyes and dropped his head.

"I can do it." Miah was still whispering. "I *want* to do it."

Chace opened his eyes and looked at the creek. "I hate this for you."

"I don't," Miah replied. "She was your wife. If I can do that, make him pay, then I can do something for you. So I *want* to do it."

Serious as shit, this kid was a good fucking kid.

Chace lifted his hand, wrapped it around the back of Miah's neck and gave him a squeeze while finding his eyes.

"You're a good kid," he whispered and Miah grinned.

"Not a kid anymore."

Chace shook his head and gave his neck another squeeze while rocking him gently before letting him go. "Nope, you're still a kid."

"Amelia and I did it last night."

Chace blinked and his throat sounded clogged when he asked, "What?"

Miah grinned again. "Went all the way."

Holy fuck.

"Jeremiah—"

"We used...you know, and we're both eighteen. We've been seeing each other since we were sophomores and we'd always planned for graduation being the, um...main event."

Jesus Christ. Where did he go with this?

Miah looked at the creek, still grinning and now muttering, "It was good."

"Was it good for her?"

Miah looked back at him and his grin faded. "Well..." he trailed off and Chace shook his head.

"Gotta make it good for her, bud," he said gently.

"I have with the stuff we've done, uh...*before* but last night it kinda went," his face flushed and he finished on a whisper, "*fast*."

Chace fought back a grin and held his eyes as he advised, "You get that but you only get it once. You two carry on with this shit you do two things, you use protection, *always* and you see to her first, *always*. With her and, should things end with her and you find someone else, with them too. That protection is for her but it's also for you. Don't mess up your or her future by bein' stupid and don't take a woman, ever, without takin' care of her."

Miah pressed his lips together, leaned forward, elbows to his knees and looked to the creek.

Chace's eyes followed his, he leaned forward on his elbows too and kept talking.

"I get where you are, your age, you two bein' together for a while, you think this is a natural progression. I know you and Amelia are tight. But I wish you'd talked to me before you went ahead with this. I'll just say, I know you feel like a man, I know you're lookin' forward to independence but I'll tell you you're still young. You should be young and this shit is adult shit, Miah. The seal is broken and maybe there's no goin' back. But you're a smart guy, always have been, I'm just sayin' you should keep bein' smart, think about this before you do it again with Amelia or any girl. It feels good, I know that. You'll want it, I know that too. It's probably pretty much all you're thinkin' about, I know that too. But it isn't ever just about doing it and it is never just you doin' it. Two people are involved. Always let her know where you're at. It's a connection, a closeness, an intimacy you two share and feelings can get caught up in that. You're not feelin' it outside of doin' it, you let her know where you're at so she doesn't get lost in you. You with me?"

"Yeah," Miah whispered.

Chace wasn't done.

"Amelia is going to the University of Wyoming, buddy. In a few months, you two will be separated. That could stay strong while you two are in different states or you or she might find someone else. Have a mind to that this summer with her and where you guys went last night. You leave, you find some-one else in New York, she's lost in you, you could hurt her. Think about how you feel about her right now, what that might do to her and handle her with care. You still with me?"

"Yeah," Miah repeated on a whisper.

Chace fell silent and Miah didn't speak.

Then Miah spoke.

"How did you know it was Faye?"

Chace felt his lips tip up as his eyes watched the waters run. "Just knew."

"How?"

He turned his head to Miah to see Miah's eyes on him. "You see her, bud, the one that's meant for you, you'll know too."

Miah held his eyes. Then he nodded and looked back at the creek.

Chace did too and they again lapsed into silence until Chace broke it this time.

"Been years, Miah, lookin' for that man. Wantin' to put Misty to rest in my mind. Now she is. Thank you."

He heard Miah take in a breath before he said softly, "You're welcome, Aslan."

Fuck, that socked him in the gut. Every time.

Without taking his gaze from the creek he again lifted his hand, curled it around the back of Miah's neck and gave it a squeeze. Once he was done, he removed his hand, returned his elbow to his knee and sat silently with his boy, no, his boy who was becoming a man and watched the waters flow.

*   *   *

One week later

Chace stood outside the bedroom door, ass and back to the wall, feet out in front of him, ankles crossed, a grin playing on his lips.

He did this listening to his wife reading to her sons, Jake and Silas.

It wasn't the first time. It wouldn't be the last.

As usual, listening to her melodic voice adding nuance and drama to the story, he enjoyed it for a good long while.

Then he moved away from the wall to check on his sleeping baby girl, Twyla.

*   *   *

Three hours later

Faye underneath him, his cock still hard inside her, Chace ran his tongue along her lower lip.

The instant he was done, she ran hers along his.

When she was done, he lifted his lips, kissed her nose then dipped his chin and caught her eyes.

"You gonna read, baby?" he asked but he knew her answer.

Still, she gave it to him.

"Yeah."

He grinned, bent his neck, kissed the indent in her collarbone and slid out.

She slid out of bed and he watched her silk nightie fall over her heart-shaped ass as she walked to the bathroom to clean up.

Chace rolled to his side of the bed, turned out his light and settled in. Then he watched his wife walk back into the room and climb into their bed.

He threw the covers over her.

She grabbed her book.

Chace closed his eyes and fell asleep.

*   *   *

An hour and a half later

Chace sensed the light going out and the bed moved as Faye settled into it.

Sleepily, he reached out an arm, hauled her into him, tucking her under him and he curled into her body.

"Done?" he muttered.

Her hand glided down his arm until her fingers found and laced through his.

"Yeah," she whispered.

"'Night, baby."

"'Night, honey."

He felt his wife's body relax under him as he felt Apollo and Starbuck adjust and settle on and around their feet.

And Chace drifted to sleep knowing that everything was right in the world.

Absolutely everything.

And he knew this because their kids were asleep in their beds under a roof he provided for them doing something he was proud of.

But he knew this more because like the night before, and the one before that, and all of them, every single one since she gave him the gift of her virginity, Chace Keaton and his Faye fell asleep, tucked tight, holding on, together in their bed.

Zara Cinders always knew Ham Reece was
the one—but he wasn't interested
in settling down. Can she get
her traveling man to stay for good?

Please turn this page for an excerpt from

JAGGED.

PROLOGUE

No Promises. No Expectations.

MY EYES OPENED and I saw dark.

I was wide awake and I knew it was early.

This was weird. It might take some time for me to get to sleep but once I found it, I didn't wake up until morning. I usually woke up groggy, though, more willing to turn around, curl up, and fall back to sleep than get up and face the day.

But I was awake in a way that I could easily get up, make coffee, do laundry, and clean my apartment. In a way that I knew I'd never get back to sleep.

Which was totally weird.

On that thought, my phone rang.

I blinked at the clock on my nightstand and saw it was almost four in the morning. Warmth rushed through me and, following close on its heels, dread.

Only one person called at this time. The calls didn't come frequently enough for me, but they came.

Ham.

Shit.

I knew this would happen one day. I'd hoped for a different ending but deep in my heart I always knew this would be how we'd end.

I wanted to delay, let the phone go to voice mail, do what I had to do another time, but I knew I shouldn't. He'd worry.

I always picked up. The only time I didn't was when I'd

fallen off the ladder in the stockroom at my shop. I broke my wrist, conked my head real good, and they'd kept me in the hospital overnight for observation. When Ham got ahold of me after that and found out what happened, he drove right to Gnaw Bone and stayed for a week to take care of me. It was just a broken wrist and I was banged up a bit, but for that week I didn't cook, clean, or do anything but work at my shop.

Ham did all the rest for me.

One of the many reasons why I wished this would end differently.

I also couldn't delay because this needed to be done. No time would be a good time, not for me. I didn't know how Ham would feel about my ending things, which was a problem, and explained why I knew deep in my heart this would be our ending.

So I might as well get it over with.

I grabbed my phone and put it to my ear.

"Hey, darlin'," I greeted, my voice quiet and slightly sleepy.

"Hey, babe," he replied and that warmth washed through me again.

Graham Reece, Ham to me, didn't have an unusual voice. Though, it was attractive. Deep and masculine. But there were times it could go jagged. For instance, when I did something Ham thought was cute or sexy. Or when we were in bed and I was taking him there.

I loved it when his voice went jagged. So much so that even hearing his voice when it was normal reminded me of those times.

Good times.

The best.

I forced my mind from those times.

"You off shift?" I asked.

"Yep, just got home," Ham answered.

Graham Reece worked in bars and, as often as the life he led meant he was looking for a new gig, he never had a problem landing a job. He had a reputation that extended from Bonners Ferry, Idaho, to Tucson, Arizona; Galveston, Texas, to Rapid City, South Dakota.

This was mostly because although he might move around a lot, when you had him, he was as steady as a rock. Not to mention, he poured a mean drink and was so sharp he could take and fill three drink orders at the same time as well as make change in a blink of an eye. Further, he had so much experience he could spot trouble the instant it walked through the door and he had no aversion to handling it. He knew how to do that with little muss and fuss if the threat became real. And, last, he had a certain manner that I knew all bar owners would want in their bar.

This was because there was an edge of mean to his look. If you knew him, you knew that menace was saved only for times it was needed. But if you didn't know him, one look at his forbidding but handsome face, the bulk of his frame, the breadth of his shoulders, his rough, calloused hands, his shrewd eyes, you'd think twice about acting like an asshole.

For men, I would guess this would be off-putting and I knew from experience it stopped many of them from being assholes before they might even start. Though, some men found it a challenge, poked the sleeping bear, and ended up mauled. I knew this from experience, too, seeing as I'd witnessed it more than once.

For women, the look and feel of Graham Reece had one of two results. They were either scared shitless of him, but still thought he was smokin' hot, or they just thought he was downright smokin' hot.

I was the latter.

But I had to quit thinking about this stuff. Thinking

about this stuff made it harder. Thinking about this stuff made me want to rethink ending things.

More, it made me think I should consider why I was rethinking ending things.

I had to suck it up, get this done, even though I didn't want to.

Therefore, I hesitated.

It was a mistake.

"Listen, darlin'," he went on, "tonight's my last night. Got a gig to get to in Flag."

This wasn't a surprise. Ham was in Billings. He'd been there awhile. It was time to move on. New horizons. New pastures. Trading Montana for Arizona. From beautiful to a different kind of beautiful.

Ham's way.

Ham started his life out in Nebraska, but from what he told me, through his adulthood, he was a travelin' man. As far as I knew, the longest he stayed in one place was a year. Usually it was six to eight months.

Ham was not a man who laid down roots. He moved from place to place, rented furnished apartments, and everything he owned could fit easily in the back of his truck.

"Takin' a coupla days to pack and load up," he continued. "Thought I'd swing your way, drag my shit in your place, unload the bike, and we could take off for a few days."

The dread moved through me again as I tossed off the covers and threw my legs over the side of the bed.

"Ham—"

He cut me off. "You can't close the shop. I'll find somethin' to do during the day and we'll go out, do night rides."

Night rides.

The best.

Oh God, I wanted to do that.

But I couldn't do that.

"Darlin'—" I started.

"Or, you can swing it, I'll hang with you for a few days, then you close up and take a vacation, ride with me down to Flag, hang with me for a while."

He was talking time and lots of it.

And he wanted me to be with him for that time.

And, man, oh *freaking* man, I wanted to be with him for that while.

Not to mention, I'd heard Flagstaff was amazing. I lived in the mountains of Colorado so I knew amazing but that didn't mean I didn't want to check out Flag.

I pushed to my feet, moved through the dark to the window, and did this while talking.

"Honey, I have something to tell you."

"Yeah?" he prompted when I said no more.

I pulled my curtains aside and looked at my not-so-spectacular view of the parking lot. They broke ground on my new house in one of Gnaw Bone's land magnate, Curtis Dodd's, developments only four days ago. In the meantime I was living in an apartment facing away from the mountains, with a view of nothing but cars, asphalt, and storage units.

In my new three-bedroom, two-and-half-bath house, I would have panoramas of the Colorado Rockies all around in a development that the HOA decreed would be appropriately, and attractively, xeriscaped.

I couldn't wait.

Though I *could* wait for having a mortgage payment, but everyone had to grow up sometime.

This was my time.

"Zara, you there, babe?" Ham asked when I still didn't speak.

"I'm seein' someone."

It came out in a rush and was met with nothing.

I held my breath and got more nothing.

"Ham?" I called when he didn't speak.

"It exclusive?" he asked and I nearly smiled at the same time I nearly cried.

Again, pure Ham. No promises. No expectations. He called when he called. I called when I called. We hooked up if it worked and we enjoyed ourselves tremendously when we did. If it didn't work, both of us were disappointed (me probably more, but I never let on) but we kept on keeping on, waiting for the next call. The next hookup. The next two days or two weeks when we'd hang out, have fun, laugh, eat, drink, and make love.

Ham understood the concept of exclusive; he just didn't utilize it. He'd respect it, if necessary. But, if he could, he'd also find ways to work around it.

So Ham had no hold on me like I had no hold on him. He had other women, I knew. He didn't hide it nor did he shove it in my face.

He asked no questions about other men.

He wanted it that way.

I did not, but I never said a word because I suspected, if I did, I'd lose him.

Now, he'd lost me.

I just wondered how he'd feel about that.

"We've been seein' each other for almost four months. We haven't had that discussion but exclusive is implied," I answered quietly.

"You into him?" Ham asked.

There was a smile in my voice when I reminded him, "We've been seein' each other for almost four months, darlin'."

But the smile hid my uncertainty.

My boyfriend, Greg, was a great guy. He was steady. He was sweet. He was quiet and there was no drama. He was better than average looking. And there was no doubt he was into me and also no doubt that I liked knowing that.

There *was* doubt, though. All on my side and all of it had to do with if I was into him.

But I wasn't getting any younger. I wanted kids. I wanted to build a family. I wanted to do it in a way that it would take, no fighting, cheating, drama, heartbreak, all this ending in divorce. I wanted to be settled. I wanted to come home at night knowing what my evening would bring. I wanted to wake up the next morning next to someone, knowing what my day would bring. I wanted to give my kids, when I had them, stability and safety.

I also wanted that for myself. I'd never had it, not in my life.

And I wanted it.

And, after being friends with benefits with Graham Reece for five years, I knew that was not going to happen with him. No matter how much I wanted it to.

"So you're into him," I heard him mutter.

"Yeah," I replied and tried to make that one word sound firm.

"Right, then, will he have a problem, I swing by and take you to lunch?" Ham asked.

No, Greg wouldn't have a problem with that. Greg didn't get riled up about much and I knew he wouldn't even get riled up about an ex-lover swinging by to take me to lunch.

Thus me having doubts. Part of me felt I should be cool with a man who trusted me not to fuck him over. Part of me wanted a man who detested the idea of his woman spending time with an ex-lover. Possessiveness was hot. A man who staked his claim, marked his territory.

It wasn't about lack of trust. It was about belonging to someone. It was about them having pride in that and wanting everyone to know it, especially you.

Ham *looked* like a man who would be that way. Knowing I wasn't the only friend he enjoyed benefits with and his ask-no-questions, tell-no-lies approach to relationships proved he just wasn't.

"No, Greg'll be cool with that," I told him and I shouldn't have. With nothing holding him back, that meant Ham would go out of his way to hit Gnaw Bone, take me to lunch. I'd have to see him, want him, and, as ever, not have him. But this time, it would be worse. I wouldn't have him *at all*, including in some of the really good ways I liked to have him.

"Okay, babe, I'll call when I'm close," he said.

"Right," I murmured.

"Now you get to bed, go back to sleep," he ordered.

That was not going to happen.

"Okay, Ham."

"See you soon, darlin'."

"Look forward to it, honey."

"'Night, darlin'."

"'Night, Ham."

He disconnected and I stared out at the parking lot.

That was it. He wanted lunch. He wanted to continue the connection even if the connection had changed.

That was good.

But he wasn't devastated or even slightly miffed that I was moving on, changing our connection.

That was very bad.

I bent my neck until my head hit the cool glass of the window and I stared at the cars in the lot without seeing them.

I did this for a long time.

Then I pulled myself together, moved from the window, made coffee, did laundry, and cleaned my apartment.

*   *   *

Five days later...

I sat in a booth at the side of The Mark, a restaurant in town. I had a ginger ale bubbling on the table in front of me. I was in the side of the booth where I could see the front windows and door.

I knew Ham was about to show because, ten minutes ago, I saw his big, silver Ford F-350 with the trailer hitched to the back holding his vintage Harley slide by. With that massive truck and the addition of a trailer, it would take him a while to find a good parking spot.

But he could walk in any second now.

I was nervous. I was excited.

I was sad.

And I knew I should never have agreed to this.

More sunlight poured through the restaurant and I looked from my ginger ale to the door to see it was open and Ham was moving through. I watched as he smiled at Trudy, a waitress at The Mark who was standing at the hostess station. He gave a head jerk my way. Trudy turned to look at me, smiled, and turned back to Ham, nodding.

Then I watched Ham walk to me.

Ham Reece was not graceful. He was too big to be graceful. He didn't walk. He trudged.

But he was built. He was a bear of a man, tall and big. His mass of thick, dark hair was always a mess. He constantly looked like he'd either just gotten off the back of a bike he'd been riding wild and fast for hours or like he'd just gotten out of bed after he'd been riding a woman wild and fast for hours.

Now was no different, even though he'd just spent hours in the cab of his truck.

It looked good on him.

It always did.

Although big, he was fit and he worked at it. It was not lost on him with the years he'd put in in bars that he needed to be on the top of his game so, although not quick, he was in shape. He ran a lot. He also lifted. Every time I'd been with him, he'd found time to do what he needed to do, even if he was doing crunches on the floor of a hotel with his arms wrapped around something heavy held to his chest.

This meant he had great abs. Great lats. Great thighs. A great ass.

Just great all around.

Yes, I should never have agreed to this.

He got close. His eyes that started out a tawny brown at the irises and radiated out to a richer, darker brown at the edge of his pupils were lit with his smile as his lips grinned at me while he approached.

I slid out of the booth.

Two seconds later, Ham slid his arms around me.

"Hey, cookie," he greeted, his voice jagged. My lungs deflated. He was happy to see me.

"Hey, darlin'." I gave him a squeeze.

He returned the squeeze and let me go but didn't step away.

His eyes caught mine and he stated, "Pretty as ever."

"Hot as could be," I returned, and his grin got bigger as he lifted a hand toward my face.

I braced, waiting for it. No, anticipating it with sheer delight.

But I didn't get it. His grin faded, his hand dropped away, and then he took a half step back and gestured to the booth.

That was when I felt it, all I'd lost with Ham. One could say it wasn't much but when you had him for the brief periods you had him, *you had him*. His attention, his affection, his easy, sweet touches, his deep voice that could go jagged with tenderness or desire. I knew that others might look at what we had and think I hadn't lost much, but they would be wrong. And I knew in that instant exactly how much I was losing.

It hurt like hell.

"Slide your ass in, darlin'," he ordered but didn't wait until I did. He moved to the other side.

I slid in, Ham slid in across from me, and Trudy arrived at our table.

"Drink?" she asked.

"Beer," Ham answered.

"Got a preference?" Trudy went on.

"Cold," Ham told her.

She smiled at him then at me and took herself off.

Ham didn't touch the menu sitting in front of him. He'd been to The Mark more than once. Anyone who had knew what they wanted.

His eyes came to me.

"How much time you got?" he asked.

"Couldn't find anyone to look after the shop so I had to close it down," I said by way of answer.

"In other words, not long," he surmised and he was right.

I owned a shop in Gnaw Bone called Karma. Ham had been there. Ham knew how much work it was. Ham also knew all about my dream of having my own place, being my own boss, answering to no one, and surrounding myself with cool stuff made by cool people. He also knew it was hard work and that I put in that hard work. There were things we didn't discuss but that didn't mean we didn't talk and do it deep. Not only when we were together but when one or the other of us got the itch to call. We could talk on the phone for hours and we did.

So I knew Ham, too.

I nodded. "I did try to find someone but—"

"Don't worry about it, darlin'," he muttered.

"Are you stayin' in town?" I asked. "Maybe, tomorrow—"

"Headed out after this, babe."

I nodded again, trying not to feel as devastated as I felt, an effort that was doomed to fail so it did.

"Thought you'd look different," Ham noted and I focused on his handsome face, taking in the exquisite shape of his full lips, his dark-stubbled strong jaw, the tanned, tight skin stretching across his cheekbones, the heavy brow over those intelligent eyes that was the source of him looking not-so-vaguely threatening.

"What?" I asked.

"Got a man, you're into him, you two got some time in, thought you'd look different."

I forced a smile. "And how would I look different, babe?"

"Happy."

My smile died.

Ham didn't miss it.

His intelligent eyes grew sharp on my face. "This a good guy?"

"Yeah," I answered. It was quick, firm, and honest.

Ham noted that, too, but that didn't change the look in his eyes. "Gotta find a guy who makes you happy," he told me.

I did. You, I thought.

"Greg's sweet. He's mellow, Ham, which I like. He's really nice. He also really likes me and lets it show, and I like that, too. Things are going great," I assured him.

Ham's reply was gentle but honest, as Ham always was.

"Things might be goin' good, Zara, but I can see it on your face, babe, they're not goin' great."

"He's a good guy," I stressed.

"I believe you," Ham returned. "And he's givin' you somethin' you want. I'm all for that, darlin'. But you can't settle for what you want. You gotta find what you need."

I did. You, I thought again and found this conversation was making me slightly pissed and not-so-slightly uncomfortable.

I knew this man. I'd tasted nearly every inch of him. He'd returned the favor. I had five years with him in my life. Four months of that solid and, for me *and* Ham, exclusive back in the day when I was waitressing at The Dog and Ham was bartending. Four months solid of me waking up in his bed every morning from our first date to the day he left town.

Now he was advising me on what kind of man I should settle for.

I didn't like this.

"Maybe we shouldn't talk about Greg," I suggested.

"Might be a good idea," Ham replied, his attention shifting to Trudy, who set his beer on the table.

"You two ready to order?" she asked.

"Turkey and Swiss melt and chips," I ordered.

"Buffalo burger, jack cheese, rings," Ham said after me.

"Gotcha," Trudy replied, snatching up the menus and then she was again off, which meant I again had Ham's attention.

"Last thing I wanna do is piss you off, cookie," he told me quietly.

"You didn't piss me off," I assured him.

"Good, 'cause, your man can handle it, I wanna find a way where I don't lose you."

The instant he was done speaking, I felt my throat tingle.

Oh God, we were already here. I suspected our lunch would lead us here, just not this soon.

We were at the place where I had to make a decision.

Greg wouldn't care if Ham and I worked out a way to stay in each other's lives. Maybe somewhere deep inside

Greg would mind that I kept an ongoing friendship with an ex-lover but I'd be surprised if he'd let that show. Even so, I wouldn't want to do something like that to him.

So that was a consideration.

But also, I had to decide if I could live with even less from Ham than I had before.

No decision, really.

I couldn't. I knew it. I'd known it for ages because I couldn't even live with the little bits of him that he already gave me. I just told myself I could so I wouldn't lose even those little bits.

And, knowing this, finally admitting it, killed me.

"I don't think I could do that to Greg, darlin'," I told him carefully and watched his eyes flare.

"So this is it," he stated.

That was all he gave me. An eye flare and confirmation that he got that this was it. I swallowed past the lump in my throat.

"This is it," I confirmed.

"Do me a favor," he said, then kept talking before I could get a word in. "Don't lose my number."

That knife pushed deeper.

"Ham—" I started.

He shook his head. "You change yours, you call me. I change mine, I'll call you. We don't gotta talk. But don't break that connection, cookie."

"I don't think—"

"Five years, babe, through that shit your parents pulled on you. You breakin' your wrist. Your girl gettin' cancer. We've seen a lot. Don't break that connection."

We had seen a lot. He might not always have been there in person but he was always just a phone call away, even if he was hundreds of miles away.

I closed my eyes and looked down at the table.

"Zara, baby, look at me," he urged and I opened my eyes and turned to him. "Don't break our connection."

"It was always you," I found myself whispering, needing to get it out, give it to him so I could let it go.

I watched his chin jerk back, his face go soft, and then he closed his eyes.

He wasn't expecting that, which also killed. He had to know. I'd given him more than one indication over five freaking years.

Maybe he was in denial. Maybe he didn't care. Maybe he just didn't want that responsibility.

Now, it didn't matter.

"Ham, baby, look at me," I urged. He opened his eyes and there was sadness there. "I won't break our connection," I promised.

The last thing I had to give, I'd give it.

For Graham Reece, I'd give anything.

Unfortunately, he didn't want it.

"Not that man," he said gently.

"I know," I told him.

"Not just you, cookie, know that. I'm just not that man."

"I know, honey."

"Also not the man who wants to walk away from this table not knowin' his girl is gonna be happy."

He needed to stop.

"I'll be happy," I replied.

"You're not being very convincing," Ham returned.

"Broke ground on my house last week, Ham. It's sweet," I told him and watched surprise move over his features. "Great views," I went on. "Roomy. Got a good guy who thinks the world of me." I leaned toward him. "I need to move on, honey." I swallowed again and felt my eyes sting before I finished. "I need to be free to find my happy."

After I was done delivering that, Ham studied me with

intense eyes for long moments that made my splintering heart start to fall apart.

Finally, he stated, "I could never give that to you, baby."

You're wrong. For four months, you gave me everything. Then you left and took it away, I thought.

"I know," I said.

"Want with everything for you to find it," he told me.

"I will, Ham."

"Don't settle, cookie."

"I won't."

I saw his jaw clench but his eyes didn't let mine go.

"I'm sorry," I said. "I should have said this over the phone. I wasn't ready then. I hadn't…well…" I lifted my hands, flipped them out, and then rested them on the table. "Whatever. I shouldn't have made you come out of your way—"

Ham interrupted me. "You gave me the brush-off without me seein' your pretty face, that would piss me off, Zara. I'd come out of my way for you any time you needed it. You know that."

I did. It always confused me but I knew it.

"Yeah, I know that, Ham."

"Him in your life, he fucks you over, it goes bad, it doesn't and you still need me, you'll have my number and that always holds true."

Really, he had to stop.

"Okay, Ham."

"It'll suck, walkin' away from you."

I looked at the table.

"But, one thing I always wanted is for you to be happy," he continued.

I looked at him.

"You mean the world to me, cookie," he finished.

So why? my thoughts screamed.

"You, too, darlin'," I replied.

He reached a hand across the table and wrapped it around mine.

We held on tight as we held each other's eyes.

Then we let go when Trudy came with a refill of my drink.

*   *   *

Half an hour later…

"Go," Ham ordered.

We were standing on the boardwalk outside The Mark. My shop was a ways down the boardwalk, same side.

Now was the time.

This was truly it.

And I didn't want to go.

Tears flooded my eyes.

"Ham, I—"

"Zara, go," he demanded.

I pressed my lips together.

Suddenly, his hand shot up and curled around the side of my neck. His head came down and his lips were crushing mine.

I opened them.

His tongue darted inside.

I lifted a hand to curl it around his wrist at my neck, arched into him and melted into his kiss, committing the smell, feel, and taste of him to memory.

And Ham let me, kissing me hard, wet, and long. A great kiss. A sad kiss. A kiss not filled with promise of good things to come, a kiss filled with the bitter knowledge of good-bye.

We took from each other until we both tasted my tears.

Just as suddenly, his hand and mouth were gone and he'd taken half a step away.

It felt like miles.

"Go." His voice was jagged.

He didn't want to lose me.

Why? my thoughts screamed.

"'Bye, Ham," I whispered.

He jerked up his chin.

I turned away, concentrating on walking down the board-walk to my shop, ignoring anyone who might be around, and trying to ignore the feel of Ham's eyes burning holes into my back.

I didn't get relief until I turned to my shop, unlocked the door and pushed inside.

No. The truth was, I didn't get relief at all, not that day, that week, that year, or ever.

Because I'd walked away from the love of my life.

And he let me.

THE DISH

Where Authors Give You the Inside Scoop

From the desk of Marilyn Pappano

Dear Reader,

The first time Jessy Lawrence, the heroine of my newest novel, A LOVE TO CALL HER OWN, opened her mouth, I knew she was going to be one of my favorite Tallgrass characters. She's mouthy, brassy, and bold, but underneath the sass, she's keeping a secret or two that threatens her tenuous hold on herself. She loves her friends fiercely with the kind of loyalty I value. Oh, and she's a redhead, too. I can always relate to another "ginger," lol.

I love characters with faults—like me. Characters who do stupid things, good things, bad things, unforgivable things. Characters whose lives haven't been the easiest, but they still show up; they still do their best. They know too well it might not be good enough, but they try, and that's what matters, right?

Jessy is one of those characters in spades—estranged from her family, alone in the world except for the margarita girls, dealing with widowhood, guilt, low self-esteem, and addiction—but she meets her match in Dalton Smith.

I was plotting the first book in the series, *A Hero to Come Home To*, when it occurred to me that there's a lot of talk about the men who die in war and the wives they leave behind, but people seem not to notice that some of our casualties are women, who also leave behind spouses, fiancés, family whose lives are drastically altered. Seconds behind that thought, an image popped into my head of the margarita club gathered around their table at The Three Amigos, talking their girl talk, when a broad-shouldered, six-foot-plus, smokin' handsome cowboy walked up, Stetson in hand, and quietly announced that his wife had died in the war.

Now, when I started writing the first scene from Dalton's point of view, I knew immediately that scene was never going to happen. Dalton has more grief than just the loss of a wife. He's angry, bitter, has isolated himself, and damn sure isn't going to ask anyone for help. He's not just wounded but broken—my favorite kind of hero.

It's easy to write love stories for perfect characters, or for one who's tortured when the other's not. I tend to gravitate to the challenge of finding the happily-ever-after for two seriously broken people. They deserve love and happiness, but they have to work so hard for it. There are no simple solutions for these people. Jessy finds it hard to get out of bed in the morning; Dalton has reached rock bottom with no one in his life but his horses and cattle. It says a lot about them that they're willing to work, to risk their hearts, to take those scary steps out of their grief and sorrow and guilt and back into their lives.

Oh yeah, and I can't forget to mention my other two favorite characters in A LOVE TO CALL HER OWN: Oz, the handsome Australian shepherd on the cover; and Oliver, a mistreated, distrusting dog of unknown breed.

I love my puppers, both real and fictional, and hope you like them, too.

Happy reading!

Marilyn Pappano

MarilynPappano.net
Twitter @MarilynPappano
Facebook.com/MarilynPappanoFanPage

From the desk of Kristen Ashley

Dear Reader,

In starting to write *Lady Luck*, the book where Chace Keaton was introduced, I was certain Chace was a bad guy. A dirty cop who was complicit in sending a man to jail for a crime he didn't commit.

Color me stunned when Chace showed up at Ty and Lexie's in *Lady Luck* and a totally different character introduced himself to me.

Now, I am often not the white hat–wearing guy type of girl. My boys have to have at least a bit of an edge (and usually way more than a bit).

That's not to say that I don't get drawn in by the boy next door (quite literally, for instance, with Mitch Lawson of *Law Man*). It just always surprises me when I do.

Therefore, it surprised me when Chace drew me in while he was in Lexie and Ty's closet in *Lady Luck*. I knew in that instant that he had to have his own happily-ever-after. And when Faye Goodknight was introduced later in that book, I knew the path to that was going to be a doozy!

Mentally rubbing my hands together with excitement, when I got down to writing BREATHE, I was certain that it was Chace who would sweep me away.

And he did.

But I *adored* writing Faye.

I love writing about complex, flawed characters, watching them build strength from adversity. Or lean on the strength from adversity they've already built in their lives so they can get through dealing with falling in love with a badass, bossy alpha. The exploration of that is always a thing of beauty for me to be involved in.

Faye, however, knew who she was and what she wanted from life. She had a good family. She lived where she wanted to be. She was shy, but that was her nature. She was no pushover. She had a backbone. But that didn't mean she wasn't thoughtful, sensitive, and loving. She had no issues, no hang-ups, or at least nothing major.

And she was a geek girl.

The inspiration for her came from my nieces, both incredibly intelligent, funny, caring and, beautiful—and both total geek girls. I loved the idea of diving into that (being a bit of a geek girl myself), this concept that is considered stereotypically "on the fringe" but is actually an enormous sect of society that is quite proud of their geekdom. And when I published BREATHE, the geek girls came out of the woodwork, loving seeing one of their own land her hot guy.

But also, it was a pleasure seeing Chace, the one who had major issues and hang-ups, find himself sorted out by his geek girl. I loved watching Faye surprise him, hold up the mirror so he could truly see himself, and take the lead into guiding them both into the happily-ever-after they deserved.

This was one of those books of mine where I could have kept writing forever. Just the antics of the kitties Chace gives to his Faye would be worth a chapter!

But alas, I had to let them go.

Luckily, I get to revisit them whenever I want and let fly the warm thoughts I have of the simple, yet extraordinary lives led by a small-town cop and the librarian wife he adores.

♥ ♥ ♥ ♥ ♥ ♥ ♥ ♥ ♥ ♥ ♥ ♥ ♥ ♥ ♥

From the desk of Sandra Hill

Dear Reader,

Many of you have been begging for a new Tante Lulu story.

When I first started writing my Cajun contemporary books back in 2003, I never expected Tante Lulu would touch so many people's hearts and funny bones. Over the years, readers have fallen in love with the wacky old lady (I like to say, Grandma Moses with cleavage). So many of you have said you have a family member just like her; still more have said they wish they did.

Family…that's what my Cajun/Tante Lulu books are all about. And community…the generosity and unconditional love of friends and neighbors. In these turbulent times, isn't that just what we all want?

You should know that SNOW ON THE BAYOU is the ninth book in my Cajun series, which includes: *The Love Potion*; *Tall, Dark, and Cajun*; *The Cajun Cowboy*; *The Red Hot Cajun*; *Pink Jinx*; *Pearl Jinx*; *Wild Jinx*; and *So Into You*. And there are still more Cajun tales to come, I think. Daniel and Aaron LeDeux, and the newly introduced Simone LeDeux. What do you think?

For more information on these and others of my books, visit my website at www.sandrahill.net or my Facebook page at Sandra Hill Author.

As always, I wish you smiles in your reading.

Sandra Hill

♥ ♥ ♥ ♥ ♥ ♥ ♥ ♥ ♥ ♥ ♥ ♥ ♥ ♥

From the desk of Mimi Jean Pamfiloff

Dearest Humans,

It's the end of the world. You're an invisible, seventy-thousand-year-old virgin. The Universe wants to snub out the one person you'd like to hook up with. Discuss.

And while you do so, I'd like to take a moment to thank each of you for taking this Accidental journey with me and my insane deities. We've been to Mayan cenotes, pirate ships, jungle battles, cursed pyramids, vampire showdowns, a snappy leather-daddy bar in San Antonio, New York City, Santa Cruz, Giza, Sedona, and we've even been to a beautiful Spanish vineyard with an incubus. Ah. So many fun places with so many fascinating, misunderstood, wacky gods and other immortals. And let's not forget Minky the unicorn, too!

It has truly been a pleasure putting you through the twisty curves, and I hope you enjoy this final piece of the puzzle as Máax, our invisible, bad-boy deity extraordinaire, is taught one final lesson by one very resilient woman who refuses to allow the Universe to dictate her fate.

Because ultimately we make our own way in this world, Hungry Hungry Hippos playoffs included.

Happy reading!

Mimi

P.S.: Hope you like the surprise ending.

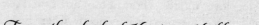

From the desk of Karina Halle

Dear Reader,

Morally ambiguous. Duplicitous. Dangerous.

Those words describe not only the cast of characters in my romantic suspense novel SINS & NEEDLES, book one in the Artists Trilogy, but especially the heroine, Ms. Ellie Watt. Though sinfully sexy and utterly suspenseful, it is Ellie's devious nature and con artist profession that makes SINS & NEEDLES one unique and wild ride.

When I first came up with the idea for SINS & NEEDLES, I wanted to write a book that not only touched on some personal issues of mine (physical scarring, bullying, justification), but dealt with a character little seen in modern literature—the antiheroine. Everywhere you look in books these days you see the bad boy, the criminal, the tattooed heartbreaker and ruthless killer. There are always men in these arguably more interesting roles. Where were all the bad girls? Sure, you could read about women in dubious professions, femme fatales, and cold-hearted killers. But when were they ever the main character? When were they ever a heroine you could also sympathize with?

Ellie Watt is definitely one of the most complex and interesting characters I have ever written, particularly as a heroine. On one hand she has all these terrible qualities; on the other she's just a vulnerable, damaged person trying to survive the only way she knows how. You despise Ellie and yet you can't help but root for her at the same time.

Her love interest, hot tattoo artist and ex-friend Camden McQueen, says it perfectly when he tells her this: "That is what I thought of you, Ellie. Heartless, reckless, selfish, and cruel...Beautiful, sad, wounded, and lost. A freak, a work of art, a liar, and a lover."

Ellie is all those things, making her a walking contradiction but oh, so human. I think Ellie's humanity is what makes her relatable and brings a sense of realism to a novel that's got plenty of hot sex, car chases, gunplay, murder, and cons. No matter what's going on in the story, through all the many twists and turns, you understand her motives and her actions, no matter how skewed they may be.

Of course, it wouldn't be a romance novel without a love interest. What makes SINS & NEEDLES different is that the love interest isn't her foil—Camden McQueen isn't necessarily a "good" man making a clean living. In fact, he may be as damaged as she is—but he does believe that Ellie can change, let go of her past, and find redemption.

That's easier said than done, of course, for a criminal who has never known any better. And it's hard to escape your past when it's literally chasing you, as is the case with Javier Bernal, Ellie's ex-lover whom she conned six years prior. Now a dangerous drug lord, Javier has been hunting Ellie down, wanting to exact revenge for her misdoings. But sometimes revenge comes in a vice and Javier's appearance in the novel reminds Ellie that she can never escape who she really is, that she may not be redeemable.

For a book that's set in the dry, brown desert of southern California, SINS & NEEDLES is painted in shades of gray. There is no real right and wrong in the novel, and the characters, including Ellie, aren't just good or bad. They're just human, just real, just trying to come to terms with their true selves while living in a world that just wants to screw them over.

I hope you enjoy the ride!

♥ ♥ ♥ ♥ ♥ ♥ ♥ ♥ ♥ ♥ ♥ ♥ ♥ ♥ ♥ ♥ ♥

From the desk of Kristen Callihan

Dear Reader,

The first novels I read belonged to my parents. I was a latchkey kid, so while they were at work, I'd poach their paperbacks. Robert Ludlum, Danielle Steel, Jean M. Auel. I read these authors because my parents did. And it was quite the varied education. I developed a taste for action, adventure, sexy love stories, and historical settings.

But it wasn't until I spent a summer at the beach during high school that I began to pick out books for myself. Of course, being completely ignorant of what I might actually want to read on my own, I helped myself to the beach house's library. The first two books I chose were Mario Puzo's *The Godfather* (yes, I actually read the book before seeing the movie) and Anne Rice's *Interview with the Vampire*.

Those two books taught me about the antihero, that a character could do bad things, make the wrong decisions, and still be compelling. We might still want them to succeed. But why? Maybe because we share in their pain. Or maybe it's because they care, passionately, whether it's the desire for discovering the deeper meaning of life or saving the family business.

In EVERNIGHT, Will Thorne is a bit of an antihero. We meet him attempting to murder the heroine. And he makes no apologies for it, at least not at first. He is also a blood drinker, sensual, wicked, and in love with life and beauty.

Thinking on it now, I realize that the books I've read have, in some shape or form, made me into the author

I am today. So perhaps, instead of the old adage "You are what you eat," it really ought to be: "You are what you read."

♥ ♥ ♥ ♥ ♥ ♥ ♥ ♥ ♥ ♥ ♥ ♥ ♥ ♥

From the desk of Laura Drake

Dear Reader,

Hard to believe that SWEET ON YOU is the third book in my Sweet on a Cowboy series set in the world of professional bull riding. The first two, *The Sweet Spot* and *Nothing Sweeter*, involved the life and loves of stock contractors—the ranchers who supply bucking bulls to the circuit. But I couldn't go without writing the story of a bull rider, one of the crazy men who pit themselves against an animal many times stronger and with a much worse attitude.

To introduce you to Katya Smith, the heroine of SWEET ON YOU, I thought I'd share with you her list of life lessons:

1. Remember what your Gypsy grandmother said: Gifts sometimes come in strange wrappings.
2. The good-looking ones aren't *always* assholes.
3. Cowboys aren't the only ones who need a massage. Sometimes bulls do, too.

4. Don't ever forget: You're a soldier. And no one messes with the U.S. military.
5. A goat rodeo has nothing to do with men riding goats.
6. "Courage is being scared to death—and saddling up anyway." —John Wayne
7. Cowgirl hats fit more than just cowgirls.
8. The decision of living in the present or going back to the past is easy once you decide which one you're willing to die for.

I hope you enjoy Katya and Cam's story as much as I enjoyed writing it. And watch for the cameos by JB Denny and Bree and Max Jameson from the first two books!

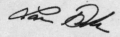

♥ ♥ ♥ ♥ ♥ ♥ ♥ ♥ ♥ ♥ ♥ ♥ ♥ ♥ ♥

From the desk of Anna Campbell

Dear Reader,

I love books about Mr. Cool, Calm, and Collected finding himself all at sea once he falls in love. Which means I've been champing at the bit to write Camden Rothermere's story in WHAT A DUKE DARES.

The Duke of Sedgemoor is a man who is always in control. He never lets messy emotion get in the way of a rational decision. He's the voice of wisdom. He's the one who sorts things out. He's the one with his finger on the pulse.

And that's just the way he likes it.

Sadly for Cam, once his own pulse starts racing under wayward Penelope Thorne's influence, all traces of composure and detachment evaporate under a blast of sensual heat. Which *isn't* just the way he likes it!

Pen Thorne was such fun to write, too. She's loved Cam since she was a girl, but she's smart enough to know it's hopeless. So what happens when scandal forces them to marry? It's the classic immovable object and irresistible force scenario. Pen is such a vibrant, passionate, headstrong presence that Cam hasn't got a chance. Although he puts up a pretty good fight!

Another part of WHAT A DUKE DARES that I really enjoyed writing was the secondary romance involving Pen's rakish brother Harry and innocent Sophie Fairbrother. There's a real touch of Romeo and Juliet about this couple. I hadn't written two love stories in one book before and the contrasting trajectories throw each relationship into high relief. As a reader, I always like to get two romances for the price of one.

If you'd like to know more about WHAT A DUKE DARES and the other books in the Sons of Sin series— *Seven Nights in a Rogue's Bed*, *Days of Rakes and Roses*, and *A Rake's Midnight Kiss*—please check out my website: http://annacampbell.info/books.html.

Happy reading—and may all your dukes be daring!

Best wishes,

Anna Campbell